S0-AKA-091

The Stress of War

The Pressure of War

All of the Danger of War

But No Chance of Victory

Captain Finlander had been a hater and hunter of submarines for decades. But his command of an atomic-powered super destroyer during the height of the Cold War leads him into a situation of almost unbearable frustration—fighting an undeclared half-war where no one can win. And at every moment looms the horrendous possibility which Finlander desperately seeks to avoid but has the power to bring about . . . nuclear holocaust.

ABOUT THE AUTHOR

Born in San Francisco, California, Mark Rascovich lived in Europe from the time he was two years old until he was twenty-one. He attended schools in Germany, England, Sweden and Paris, and was graduated from the Sorbonne. His World War II service included three years as a reconnaisance pilot in the Alaskan and African theaters and concluded with transport duty on the North Atlantic. Since the war, he has engaged in ocean towing, salvage work, marine research and writing. Mr. Rascovich has traveled throughout Europe and the Americas, the Near East and Africa. He holds pilot licenses for land and sea aircraft and for watercraft.

THE BEDFORD INCIDENT

MARK RASCOVICH

CHARTER
NEW YORK

A DIVISION OF CHARTER COMMUNICATIONS INC.
A GROSSET & DUNLAP COMPANY

THE BEDFORD INCIDENT

Copyright © 1963 by Mark Rascovich
Published by arrangement with Atheneum Publishers

Charter Books
A Division of Charter Communications Inc.
A Grosset & Dunlap Company
360 Park Avenue South
New York, New York 10010

This book is affectionately dedicated to
GWEN and ED RIGG
whose kind understanding and warm friendship
have gone far beyond the call of duty
of ordinary inlaws!

2 4 6 8 0 9 7 5 3 1
Manufactured in the United States of America

AUTHOR'S NOTE

Some of the anti-submarine warfare techniques and equipment described in this work have been deliberately obscured. This has been done because the author has had access to certain confidential naval information imparted to him in his capacity of marine researcher and has no wish to betray such trust or embarrass his associates. This in no way impairs the validity of the story, which in essence and spirit remains a potentially true one for as long as we live under the present circumstances.

MARK R. RASCOVICH

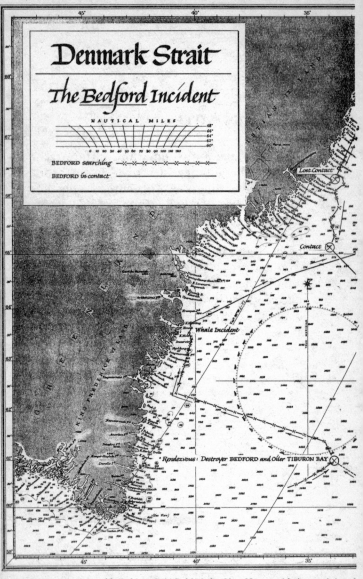

Denmark Strait

The Bedford Incident

NAUTICAL MILES

0 10 20 30 40 50 60 70 80 90 100 110 120

BEDFORD *searching* ✕✕✕✕✕✕✕✕✕✕✕

BEDFORD *in contact* ——————

Lost Contact ⊗

Contact ⊗

Whale Incident

* Rendezvous: Destroyer BEDFORD and Oiler TIBURON BAY ⊗

Adapted from British Admiralty Chart No. 246 with the permission of

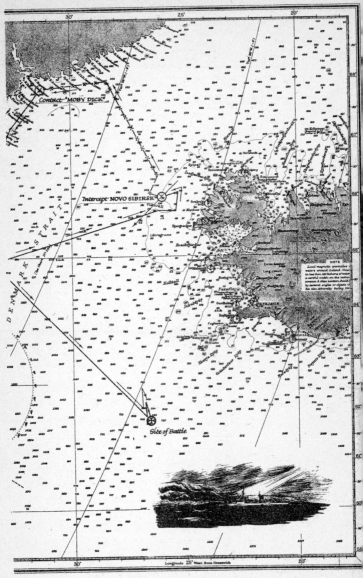

Contact "MOBY DICK"

Intercept NOVO SIBIRSK

Site of Battle

DENMARK STRAIT

Contents

PART ONE   THE WAR   13

PART TWO   THE CHASE   163

PART THREE   THE BATTLE   241

PART ONE

THE WAR

1.

The loudspeaker outside the stateroom door squealed with a discordant facsimile of a bosun's pipe, a sound which was immediately followed by an incongruous hacking and wheezing. It alerted all hands of the U.S.S. *Tiburon Bay* to the fact that their second officer was trying to clear his infected sinuses before delivering an important message over the ship's PA system.

"Now hear this—now hear this! The smoking lamp is out—the smoking lamp is out." It was very like him to put this emphasis on a routine regulation before anything else. If he had to call out "Abandon ship!" he would precede it with "The smoking lamp is out!" The unhappy second officer was not only addicted to colds, but suffered from a phobia about fire, both qualities making him singularly unsuited for service aboard a fleet tanker on cold war duty in arctic waters. "The smoking lamp is out," his voice repeated. "Pumping crews, man your stations for refueling DDL 113 approaching our starboard side. Line handlers and riggers to wear immersion suits. Personnel scheduled for transfer report to highline station on forward main deck. That is all."

Lieutenant Commander Chester Porter listened with his bulky body braced against a sluggish roll of the ship, then zipped up the flap of his blue Valpack bag. "That means we've got less than twenty minutes," he said to Ben Munceford, who was lying in the top bunk of their steel cubicle. "Captain Finlander is awfully sensitive about the *Bedford*'s record for the fastest re-fueling at sea of any destroyer in the navy."

Munceford was nursing a shot of bourbon in a soggy paper cup and continued to drag on a cigarette in spite of the second officer's insistent announcement; he showed very little concern over Porter's implied suggestion that he immediately prepare himself for the impending transfer to the *Bedford*. He had not even dressed and was lying there in a suit of thermal underwear which was unzipped to his navel, the toes of his naked feet playing with the electrical conduits which snaked across the ceiling above his bunk. Munceford had been napping away the forenoon to make up for a late session of cards in the PO mess during the previous night. "I'll wait till you're clear, Doc," he drawled. "No use getting in each other's way."

"I thought you wanted some pictures of this operation," Porter said as he squirmed into a heavy sweater.

Munceford glanced toward the gray opaque eye which was the single porthole of their cabin. "Not enough light out there."

"About as much as you'll get in these high latitudes. In November there's only six hours of daylight here—less when we get farther north."

"That's okay, Doc. I'm more of a reporter than a cameraman anyway. How about one for the road before we head into the great unknown?"

Porter finished pulling on a hooded windbreaker and eyed the bottle which Munceford had produced from under his pillow. "No, thanks, Ben," he answered with a stiff smile. "By the way, I should warn you that the *Bedford* is not run as informally as the *Tiburon Bay*. Even as a guest of the navy, you'll be expected to only drink liquor when it is prescribed by me against shock or snakebite."

Munceford was a rawboned southerner with an incredibly boyish face for his thirty-six years, and when he was piqued, it could take on a childishly petulant expression—as it now did for an instant. "I can take it or leave it," he said, scowling from the surgeon to the bottle.

"The *Bedford* is a go-go ship operated by a bunch of trade-school boys," Porter told him. "Captain Finlander is a cinch to make admiral on the next list."

"Okay, Doc. I'm not going to hold him back," Munceford exclaimed with a laugh. He swung his legs over the edge of the bunk, jumped down, flipped the clamps of the porthole, opened it and tossed the half-full bottle of bourbon into the sea. Then he turned and jokingly saluted the lieutenant commander. "Sir, I beg to report that the U.S.S. *Tiburon Bay* is now bone dry, according to regulations, and that all danger of contaminating the U.S.S. *Bedford* has been removed."

Porter's round red face rippled through a series of expressions of surprise, amusement and anger. "Jesus, Munceford! Don't you even know the rules about dumping floating garbage overboard?" he asked, half laughing, half snarling.

The injured childish look flashed back. "Are we at war, for Christ sakes, Doc?"

"Out here we play it that way. Especially when Finlander is in command."

"This Finlander must be some jonah! You've got me hating him already."

"Oh? I was hoping you'd be an objective sort of correspondent," the surgeon said acidly, then reacted to the sound of bells from deep in the ship's engine room. The vibration of the turning screws dropped to a lower register. "You'd better snap it up. We'll be transferred right after the mail and fresh milk." He picked up his Valpack, opened the door and squeezed himself into the passageway.

After the lieutenant commander had gone, Munce-

ford was left with a frustrated and uneasy feeling. He
was suddenly quite certain that he would not get along
well with the *Bedford* and her captain, that this whole
assignment was jinxed from its start. For a moment he
toyed with the idea of aborting it and returning to port
on the *Tiburon Bay* with a couple of hundred feet of
film and tape describing life on a navy tanker. But, of
course, that would put him in a bad light with the PRO
he had badgered into accrediting him an official navy
correspondent. And then there was Nancy's lawyer
waiting for him on the Stateside docks. Jinxed or not,
he had to go on. With a shrug he opened up the porthole again to toss out his cigarette.

A waft of raw, damp air struck his face, ice cold
compared to the stuffy warmth of the cabin. But he
held the glass open and continued to peer out because
something had caught his attention on the misty
periphery of the lazy swells. There were wisps of sea
smoke drifting off their undulating surfaces and, far out
there, a low bank of fog lay like a translucent gray wall
between the gray sea and gray sky. Out of that fog,
Munceford suddenly noticed the shadow of a vessel's
superstructure materializing like a ghost ship. For an
awesome minute she appeared to be floating on air, her
hull only slowly solidifying, hesitating to touch the sea.
That tall foremast with its lacework of halyards and
aerials remained for a long time the only part crisply
etched against the diffused horizon, a rotating antenna
of a search radar making a strange pulsating effect as it
turned. Gradually the shadowy shape transformed itself
into the classical lines of a destroyer slicing along at
flank speed, plunging and rolling with a weird kind of
slow motion as she thrust ahead, a pale grin of a bow
wave curling from her stem. Crystals glinted with baleful winks out of the ice which sheathed her foredecks
and turrets. But even as she merged into sharp focus,
she retained a mysterious aura of mist which clung to

her as if she had torn loose some shreds out of the fog and wrapped herself in them. On the curve of her bow, between the rise and fall of flying spume, the white number 113 became clearly visible—DDL 113, the U.S.S. *Bedford.*

Ben Munceford stared wide-eyed, shuddering from the cold which was stabbing at his bare chest, and from the sight of the *Bedford.* He suddenly crossed himself as if he were beholding some kind of evil specter. It was a peculiarly senseless thing to do and it made him angrily slam shut the porthole, turning the destroyer into a shapeless blur behind the film of moisture on the glass. Why had he crossed himself like that? He was neither superstitious nor Catholic. Why did the uneasy feeling which had been gnawing at his insides ever since leaving Portsmouth suddenly turn into outright foreboding? He, who prided himself on being a cheerfully cynical person, should not suffer such notions! He looked at himself in the mirror above the tiny washbowl and wondered what was getting under that skin he fancied to be so thick. "Is it Porter turning stuffed shirt all of a sudden?" he asked his reflection. "Or that character Finlander everybody's bowing to the east over? Or maybe Nancy's still bugging me!"

The thought of Nancy aggravated his irritation as he began to dress. If anything wrong was to happen on this trip, it would really be her fault, because he had undertaken it to escape her silken whining in that coffin of a studio apartment in Greenwich Village. Like the other Nancys before her, she had first seduced him with a voluptuous body, then repulsed him with a barren, selfish mind which was nothing but a ganglion of short-circuited female nerves. Like some kind of bull animal, his life with women seemed fated to follow a pattern of courtship, rutting and desertion. "Why can't you get a regular job at home?" they would all eventually scream at him. "Because then I'd be stuck with

both you and the job," he would answer. "At least give
me money for a divorce!" "With your legs and tits,
you'll always find yourself another pigeon if you don't
wait too long." "A wife's got some rights! *I'm going to
see a lawyer!*" "That's why I'm leaving. By-by, honey!"
Well, the other Nancys had got their divorces without
his having to spend a nickel. This one would too, he
hopefully told himself as he stamped his feet into a pair
of old fleece-lined air-force boots. But just to make
sure, he would leave the *Bedford* in Reykjavik, beg a
ride on a MATS plane to London, peddle his story to
one of the American television outfits there, get paid
and be off on some other interesting overseas assignment. No Nancy would ever catch up with *him!* Never!

There was a knock on the cabin door and a young
seaman who bulked monstrously large in his arcrtics
looked in. "The second officer's steaming because you
ain't at the highline station, Mr. Munceford. The *Bedford*'s bearing down on us right now, you know."

Munceford grinned and patted him on the shoulder
with the familiarity he liked to show enlisted men. "It's
okay, sailor. Tell Mr. Boomer to keep his shirt on. I'll
be there in a couple of minutes."

"But you ain't even got your gear together," the boy
exclaimed with a certain admiration. "Can I help you
with any of it?"

"I travel light," Munceford told him and yanked his
duffel bag out of a locker. It had hardly been unpacked
during the four days since they had left Portsmouth,
and all he had to do was to shove in his toilet kit and
some dirty socks.

"What about your camera 'n' stuff?" the seaman
asked, helping him to knot the bag and nodding toward
the large aluminum case under the desk. "Want me to
deliver it to the cargo sling?"

"I'll carry that myself, thanks. Might want to run
off a few feet of film on the way over."

"Mr. Boomer won't allow it, sir," the boy told him. "All baggage gotta go across in a sling on account of we once lost an ensign who went in the drink and was dragged under by some personal gear he'd strapped to himself."

Munceford swung out the case by its leather shoulder strap and plonked it on the lower bunk. He opened it up and the sailor stared with fascination at the jumble of equipment which was jammed into it. At first glance it gave an impression of the wealth of film, tape, cameras and recording gear which a professional TV feature reporter would be expected to carry with him on a navy assignment, but this was an illusion created by the disorder. The single movie camera was an old sixteen-millimeter Bell and Howell, the miniature battery-operated recorder a cheap Japanese make; many boxes of film and tape were pushed down among the filter cases, lens shades and a tangle of microphone cords, yet really not enough to satisfy any professional doing the kind of job Munceford was.

"Gee!" the sailor exclaimed, genuinely impressed. "You sure got some fancy stuff there, sir."

"I only bring old equipment on a story like this," Munceford answered with studied indifference. "Salt air raises hell with cameras and recorders. All this will be written off and thrown away after the job's over."

The sailor's eyes popped. "Christ! I'd like to be around when you start throwing it. Must be a thousand bucks' worth."

Munceford smiled and left the exclamation answered by an effective silence. He had actually bought everything in the case from a New York discount store for a little over two hundred dollars—having borrowed half the cash from a friend who was a technical director for NBC and charged the rest to something which the salesman called Instant-Credit. When he yanked out the camera, there was a general collapse of knicknacks within the case and its contents suddenly did not look at all impressive. He quickly shut the lid, locked it, then looped the strap over the sailor's shoulder. "I'm much obliged to you," he told him. "Tell Mr. Boomer that I'll be along shortly."

The boy left with the duffel bag and camera case, gingerly wiggling through the narrow door as if he were carrying a load of fresh eggs.

Munceford heard the engine-room bells' muffled clang and felt the beat of the *Tiburon Bay*'s engines increase from their idling rumble. The *Bedford*'s siren let out a blast which reached his ears as a distant wail. He looked around the bare cabin with his lips pressed together and a frown on his face as if hesitating to leave it. But then he began to move with some urgency, pulling on the quasimilitary fleece-lined windbreaker which had become the envy of every young sailor aboard. It was made of brown, green, yellow and pink camouflage twill. On the shoulder of the left sleeve blazed the patch of the Strategic Air Command, on the right a patch of the 82nd Airborne Division; on the left breast a submarine insignia was pinned above a combat infantryman's badge; on the right was stitched a leather strip with the word CORRESPONDENT embossed in gold letters upon it. The cap which he carefully adjusted at a rakish angle on his head was of the type worn by soldiers in arctic climates, with a fur lining and large earflaps that neatly snapped together across the crown. Pinned to it was the silver insignia of a paratrooper.

After taking a last look at himself in the mirror, Ben Munceford picked up his camera and hurriedly left the cabin.

2.

Captain Larsen of the U.S.S. *Tiburon Bay* was a Commander, U.S.N.R., who had been recalled to duty from his highly paid civilian job as skipper of a tanker belonging to Standard Oil. Because that company had generously continued paying him half of his regular salary, he was actually making as much as he had become accustomed to and was therefore not as disgruntled as most of the reservists under his command. Mr. Boomer, for instance, he suspected of deliberately nurturing one cold after another in order to be returned for medical reasons to inactive status and thence go back to his fancy marina in Fort Lauderdale. And Mr. Carmichael, the assistant engineering officer, did nothing but worry about a plumbing business in plush Westchester County of New York, from which he had been cruelly torn during a construction boom which flourished regardless of the cold war. Well, only out here did the cold war take on any real meaning. The thermometer attached to the wheelhouse registered eleven degrees below freezing.

As the *Bedford* emerged out of the fog which reduced the surrounding vastness of this frigid ocean to a couple of square miles of visible bleakness, Captain Larsen drew a sigh of envy. There was the real professional navy! The destroyer itself he did not care about so much—even modern ones like the *Bedford* were terrible riding and Larsen had reached the age where he preferred comfort to excitement. What he envied was Captain Finlander's staff of officers, who were one-hundred-per-cent Annapolis graduates, probably *all* with a rating of superior (or better); his enlisted crew were all career men, many of the chiefs being on their third six-year hitch. Even a bucket like the *Tiburon Bay* could be efficiently run with a gang like that! He watched the *Bedford* through his binoculars for a moment, then called toward the wheelhouse: "Log visual contact with DDL 113 at 1350 hours. Captain will take the conn at this time."

The executive officer was standing next to him, his eyes glued to his binoculars, watching the destroyer intently. Lieutenant (J.G.) Laurin Wilburforce also envied the *Bedford,* but for purely romantic reasons. "Jesus! She's gorgeous!" he muttered, as if he were speaking about a beautiful woman who was far above the class of a plain clod like himself. He was indeed an undistinguished-looking young man, but at least he was an Annapolis graduate, the only one aboard the *Tiburon Bay,* and, because of this, was exec in spite of holding a lower rank than several officers under him. Captain Larsen suspected that Wilburforce either had been the lowest in his graduating class (1957) or had somehow managed to sully his record subsequently. He was a dully efficient young officer, but why else would he be exiled to an old fleet oiler manned by reservists, children and exiled thirty-year men? "Will somebody back there acknowledge the captain's orders?" Wilburforce irritably called to the wheelhouse.

Barnwell, the quartermaster, appeared briefly in the door. "Visual contact at 1350 hours and captain taking over conn, both logged, sir." He quickly vanished back into the warm inside.

Wilburforce had not taken his eyes away from the binoculars which he kept trained on the *Bedford.* "Jesus! She must be doing forty knots!" he gasped in admiration.

Captain Larsen grunted and pulled his head deeper

into his parka. "Come to zero-four-zero degrees," he called to the helmsman, then strode to the shelter of the starboard wing, from where he continued to watch the *Bedford*. A blinker light was winking from the destroyer's bridge and he was able to read the challenge: COLDSNAP.

The light on the *Tiburon Bay*'s signal bridge clattered out the countersign, slowly and with some hesitation (another reservist going through halfhearted motions): H-O-A—R——F-R-R-R—O-S-T. Larsen glanced up at the signal bridge with patient suffering, then back at the *Bedford* just in time to see her rap out:

WILL EXECUTE HIGHSPEED BUNKERING AND TRANSFER. HEAD 070 AND MAKE 15 KNOTS.

The *Tiburon Bay*'s signalman hesitated and, instead of acknowledging, asked for a repeat. The *Bedford* expressed her irritation over this inefficiency by repeating the message even faster. Captain Larsen left the shelter and headed for the wheelhouse; before entering it, he looked up to the signal bridge and called with an even voice: "I got the message even if you didn't. Simply acknowledge!"

Two boyish faces peered down at him, glowing with crimson embarrassment in the hoods of their parkas.

Stepping into the wheelhouse, he ordered the helmsman to change course to 070, rang up full ahead on the telegraph, then called the engine room on the telephone: "Give me exactly two-forty revolutions on both screws if that won't shake your engines loose from their beds," he said with a flat inflection.

Mr. Carmichael was at the other end of the line, some four hundred feet aft and a hundred feet below. "Aye, aye, two-forty revs, Captain," he answered. "Request permission to blow my tubes."

"Are you mad?"

"No, sir."

"Request denied."

Captain Larsen shook his head and hung up the instrument. He gave the seaman second-class at the helm a searching glance, trying to remember whether or not he too was an incompetent reservist. High-speed refueling at sea required a sure hand at the wheel, as the 18,000-ton tanker could severely damage the 3,400-ton destroyer if the two came together. Both the helmsman and his relief looked like children—neither of them could be much over twenty, too young to be reservists. Too young for solid experience. But the boy at the wheel had a confident look in his blue eyes, which he kept glued to the gyro-repeater, and Larsen decided to take his chances on him. "Are your kidneys and bowels cleared for a long session, son?"

The blue eyes flicked up for a second and there was laughter in them. "Sure thing, Captain."

"Okay. When 113 pulls alongside, I don't want to see you as much as blink in her direction. Let us fall away one degree and you'll get fed to Finlander in small pieces." He softened the terrible threat with a flash of a grin, then said to the relief: "You stand exactly two feet behind and one foot to the right of the wheel, ready to instantly take over in case your buddy has a seizure—understand?"

"Yes, sir," the other man answered with a nervous smile.

Captain Larsen returned to the starboard wing of the bridge, stopping next to the executive officer, who was bawling out the signalman. Three decks below he could hear half-choked nasal noises which were those of Mr. Boomer bawling out the pumping crew. From somewhere around the port side of the bridge superstructure he heard the curdling profanity of CPO Grisling, who was bawling out men preparing the high-line gear (Grisling was an old pro who would be aboard a carrier if it were not for his unfortunate drinking habits in port). A half-mile astern, the *Bed-*

ford cut through the *Tiburon Bay*'s wake, made a blast on her siren and heeled over in a turn to bring her alongside. She still had a bone in her teeth and it was obvious that Finlander was going to make a hot approach. "I hope the bastard overshoots us," Larsen muttered. He noticed a bulky figure coming up the companionway from the boat deck, and the gold-braided visor peeking out from beneath the hood identified Lieutenant Commander Porter.

"Request permission to come on the bridge, sir," the surgeon said with a snappy salute.

Captain Larsen returned it in a more casual fashion. "No use trying to hide up here, Commander," he told him. "Finlander has come to get you and I've got to hoist you over to him, dead or alive."

Porter laughed politely. "I've come to thank you for a very nice trip, sir, and to pick up the dispatches for DDL 113."

Larsen interrupted his executive officer's lecture to the unhappy signalman. "Mr. Wilburforce, will you go and fetch Finlander's secrets out of our safe, turn them over to Commander Porter and obtain a receipt from him for same. Thank you." While waiting for the documents to be fetched from the chartroom, the captain kept a wary eye on the *Bedford* while engaging in gruff small talk with the surgeon. "I'm glad you enjoyed your days on this dear old oiler, Commander. I'd hoped you would take care of some of our sniffles and piles while you were aboard, but then I realize you've been steeling yourself for your forthcoming ordeal." Noticing a small wiggle in the wake of his ship, he raised his voice to shout. "Steady up, helmsman! You're outmaneuvering that destroyer!" Lowering his voice back to Porter: "How's your shipmate, the glamorous war correspondent, getting on? Hiding in the lazaret, maybe?"

"He's playing it cool, sir." The surgeon laughed with

a doubtful headshake. "I left him in his underwear, still sacked out. He spent half the night playing cards in the enlisted mess, you know."

"Oh. He's a champion of the common man, eh? I suppose he will expose the snobbery which exists between fo'c'sle and quarterdeck aboard the *Bedford*. Finlander will appreciate that." Even as he spoke, he spotted Ben Munceford's jarring camouflage jacket and fur cap coming down the catwalk which bridged the long main deck between the superstructures of the tanker. The captain's normally crinkled eyes narrowed to pained slits. "Yes, Finlander is going to *love* that character," he added, more to himself that to the other officer.

Wilburforce came out of the wheelhouse and handed Porter a large plastic envelope, sealed and with conspicuous lead weights attached to its corners. The surgeon signed the receipt, shook hands with both the exec and the captain, saluted them and left the bridge.

"Have the B flag hoisted, Mr. Wilburforce," Larsen quietly ordered, noting that the *Bedford* was now only a hundred yards astern and still closing fast. The destroyer sheered off a few points to port and white foam erupted around her fantails as her eighty thousand horsepower kicked into reverse to break her speed.

"Jesus! He handles her like a god-damned Chris-Craft!" the executive officer exclaimed with breathless admiration.

Larsen grunted. He estimated that Finlander was not going to overshoot after all and crossed through the wheelhouse to take up his position in the shelter of the port wing.

The tanker plodded ahead, her bow rising and falling with an easy, solid motion through the long, low swells which she was now meeting head on. Mr. Boomer was still shouting at his pumping detail, which cursed with impersonal passion as it struggled with ice-crusted valves, hoses and lines. Grisling's more seasoned profanities blistered the cold air around the highline station. As the booms swung outboard with the whips supporting the hoses, they dropped showers of icicles on the crew below. More cursing. On the shelter deck of the after superstructure, one of the cooks braved the cold in his bare whites, leaned over the rail and pointed a camera at the *Bedford*.

The destroyer had spilled most of her excess speed and was inching up alongside, some hundred feet off the *Tiburon Bay*. Her rolling and pitching were quicker and more nervous than those of the tanker, but her conning was exact and sure. From close quarters, much of the graceful effect of the *Bedford's* lines was lost. Her hull was marred in several places where the undercoating had bled through to form ugly red sores on the gray plates; ice had scarred a lot of the superstructure, which was made of aluminum and shone a dull burnished color where the pain had worn off. She showed all the attrition of hard service in the arctic, yet still gave an impression of enormous power and efficiency. There was an eager rumble from her engine rooms and blowers, almost a living animal-like sound. A few hooded faces peered over the windscreen of the bridge, but otherwise she seemed strangely deserted. Only six men huddled together on the weather deck, grotesque shapes in their arctics and life jackets.

"Ship ready in every respect for bunkering DDL 113," Mr. Wilburforce informed his captain.

Larsen glanced over the bridge to make a quick check that everybody was occupying his assigned station—the exec standing by the annunciator, a talker next to him with his telephone plugged into the jack, the chief quartermaster now in charge of signals, the chief boatswain's mate keeping his eyes peeled over the windscreen and Ensign Fisher, the JOOD, standing in the wheelhouse with a jaundiced eye on the gyro-compass. All was in order, but the captain suddenly bristled as a lanky figure in a fur cap and an outlandish camouflage jacket popped up the companionway.

"Hi, Skipper! Mind if I get a few shots from up here?" Munceford cheerfully asked, brandishing his camera.

"Yes, I do, Mr. Munceford. I'd hate to have you miss your appointment with Captain Finlander, so please report immediately to Chief Grisling at the highline station. Good-by and good luck. . . . Mr. Wilburforce! Hoist the red flag and let's get going."

Ben Munceford stood there for a moment with a pouting smile frozen on his face and an unspoken objection on his lips, but everybody had turned away from him and there was nothing he could do but retreat from the bridge.

The *Bedford* had drawn slightly ahead of the *Tiburon Bay* and was hanging there, still a hundred feet off, jockeying slightly until her speed exactly matched the tanker's fifteen knots. The wash of the two vessels met between them and chopped into irregular patterns. The blinker on the destroyer flashed: EXECUTE.

"Acknowledge affirmative!"

The lamp on the tanker's bridge clattered briefly— this time without hesitation.

The *Bedford* veered inward and dropped back slightly. Suddenly the oily sea between them turned into a churning millrace as the two hulls closed together, eighty . . . seventy . . . sixty . . . fifty . . . and finally only forty feet apart. The destroyer took a roll, and for an instant the revolving radar antenna on her mainmast threatened to hit the tanker's bridge; then she steadied and began maintaining exact station. Messenger lines snaked across from the *Tiburon Bay*'s main deck. The seamen on the *Bedford* moved with precision to pick them up and start hauling over the fuel and highline gear.

"Log commencement of refueling operations as of now."

Two minutes later the talker reported to Captain Larsen that telephone connections were established with the *Bedford*'s bridge. There were no greetings or small talk exchanged between commanders, only a brief, routine discussion between the respective executive officers. "They wish to immediately send over the officer Commander Porter is replacing, sir," Wilburforce informed his captain.

"Must be damned eager to get rid of him. Tell them okay."

The exec spoke a single affirmative into the mouthpiece, then listened for thirty seconds with a frown. "They want us to know, sir," he told Larsen, "that a half-full bottle of whisky was spotted in our wake about three miles back."

The captain did not take his eyes off the men on the *Bedford*'s main deck who were just completing the connection of the fuel hoses. "Apologize," he said, "and compliment them on their very sharp lookout."

3.

On the main deck Lieutenant Commander Porter sat down on a ventilator and waited in acute discomfort for his transfer. He had been helped into the cumbersome rubberized immersion suit which enclosed him from his head to the soles of his feet in its stiff folds, only his face protruding through the opening of the hood and pinched by the tight drawstring. A few feet away a couple of young seamen were making a hilarious game out of prying Ben Munceford into a similar outfit. The surgeon deliberately ignored the clowning and followed with his eyes four sacks of mail wobbling across the highline toward the plunging destroyer-leader.

"Christ! This thing's cutting my balls off!" Munceford squealed with mock agony as one of the men heaved on the zipper.

The sailors brayed in ribald delight. "Better than freezing them off in case you get dunked," one of them explained.

Chief Grisling increased his steady flow of profanity to a torrent which included instructions to the man on the outhaul of the highline to keep an even strain. Farther down the deck, Mr. Boomer's haranguing of the pumping crew was temporarily curtailed by a fit of sneezing. The supply officer, an overage Lieutenant J.G. who looked frozen blue in spite of his enormously thick clothing, nagged at the commissary detail as they stacked stores according to the order of transfer. The pumps clattered. Winches ground their gears. The sea between the two ships hissed and beat against the steel plates of their hulls.

Although he kept his eyes on the *Bedford,* the noise of men and machinery penetrated through the thick rubber hood covering Lieutenant Commander Porter's ears and he became impatient to leave the bedlam of this fleet oiler which Captain Larsen ran like a slovenly tramp steamer. Well, Larsen was nothing but a merchant skipper, really, so what could one expect? You could tell he was used to insolent union crews from the way he handled his men; in fact, he seemed to run the *Tiburon Bay* as un-navylike as possible. The surgeon looked forward to escaping across that trench of rushing water to the smooth discipline and secure service traditions of the *Bedford,* but he regretted that Ben Munceford would be joining him. There was another tramp, an immature and unstable one at that, who made light of discipline and tradition, who made sport of breaking regulations. How could the Navy Department grant such a man the privileges of a correspondent? How could any reputable broadcasting company trust such a judgment? Either he had some special talents which had not shown themselves as yet, or the man was a skilled bluffer and finagler—in any case, a very unpleasant character.

The surgeon sighed heavily and wiggled against the oppressive weight of the immersion suit. He noticed that the mail sacks had reached their destination and were being efficiently manhandled aboard the destroyer. His turn would come soon now and he wondered what awaited him over there. Even though he looked forward to service aboard one of the navy's latest crack ships, there had been several unsettling things which presaged developments of possibly unpleasant nature for him. The cold war had intensified lately and for the first time since the Korean truce Porter sensed that it had a good chance of becoming a hot one. He knew from bitter experience that nothing upset the comfortable routine of his navy life more than real *war*. When the Korean one came along, for instance, he had had to give up his research in forensic medicine at Bethesda to sew up mangled marines on a hospital ship plying between Pusan and Nagasaki. If war came again, it could trap him for the duration on this destroyer—a far different matter from a two- or three-month temporary assignment.

Chief Grisling was suddenly directing his obscenities at the seamen forty feet away on the opposite end of the highline. The *Bedford* should, according to established procedure, send over their own outgoing mail sacks, then receive perishable stores. But now there was a delay. Grisling hung on a stanchion and leaned far out over the side, his leathery face screwed into a gargoyle expression as he tried to make out what was happening. His outrage became nearly apoplectic when he saw that they were switching the rig for personnel transfer instead of mail and stores. His talker, who was connected by telephone to both his own and the *Bedford*'s bridges, confirmed the change of arrangement. Grisling hurled his clipboard with the schedule of transfer across the deck, then bawled at a seaman to retrieve it for him.

Porter knew that the man about to come across would be Lieutenant Barney Hirschfeld, another reason for his vague uneasiness about this cruise. He was replacing Hirschfeld, who had been the *Bedford*'s surgeon since her commissioning ten months ago. This sudden relieving of a medical officer in mid-ocean was very unusual in peacetime operations and had caused Porter some inconvenience when he was ordered to replace him on a couple of days' notice. The whole affair had strange and mysterious overtones. If Hirschfeld had become ill, Porter would have heard about it, so it had to be something else. Something else which Estelle

Hirschfeld obviously knew about—otherwise why had she actually *cursed* the *Bedford* in a painful scene in the Officers' Club? Of course, Estelle tended to be emotional and high-strung, not at all a good steady navy wife like his own Martha. But to curse her husband's ship in public . . . Horrible!

Watching Lieutenant Hirschfeld start his journey to the *Tiburon Bay,* Porter decided he certainly was not sick. He was sitting perfectly upright in the bosun's chair, balancing himself with ease as it swung out over the millrace between the ships and twisting his head around to keep staring back at the *Bedford*'s bridge.

"Hell! That looks too dangerous for me!" Munceford clowned and pretended to take flight. A pair of laughing seamen grabbed him. He broke away from them, suddenly remembered the camera in his hand and began shooting some pictures of the transfer.

Porter got up off the ventilator and shuffled over to where Hirschfeld would touch the deck.

"Stand clear, goddammit . . . *sir,*" Grisling bellowed.

Porter gritted his teeth and shuffled two steps backward.

The destroyer took a long, lazy roll to starboard, slackening the highline so that Hirschfeld was momentarily almost touching the waves and enveloped in spray. Thirty seconds later he was standing on the *Tiburon Bay*'s deck with salt water running in streams off his immersion suit.

"Hello, Barney," Porter greeted him.

Hirschfeld peeled back the rubber hood covering his head and stared at the surgeon with tired eyes which did not seem to recognize him at first. Then he said: "Oh . . . hello, Chester."

They were both in the way of a sudden frenzy of activity, so Porter took Hirschfeld's arm, trying to lead him aside for a few words. But Chief Grisling yelled:

"All right, Commander, as long as the schedule's all screwed up, we'll take you next."

"Take Mr. Munceford ahead of me, Chief," the surgeon snapped.

But Munceford had suddenly decided that he needed some forgotten accessory out of his camera case so he could take pictures on the way over. The case was in a cargo sling far down the deck. Grisling had a fit over this new delay.

"How are you, Barney?" Porter asked the younger officer, trying to ignore the fracas around them.

"Fine, thanks," Hirschfeld replied, starting to peel himself out of his immersion suit.

"Your wife has been worrying about you and . . . so have I."

"How is Estelle?" Hirschfeld asked, evading the implied question.

"Like I say, worried. Maybe something you wrote upset her."

Hirschfeld's dark, troubled face became furrowed by a frown. "What are you pumping me for, Chester? You've obviously gone over everything with Estelle."

"Listen, I only ran into her at the club last week. Mentioned I had orders to replace you. She began laughing hysterically, then called your ship some pretty bad names for a lady. After I calmed her down, she shut up like a clam and finally ran off. That's all I know, so help me, Barney."

Hirschfeld stared at him, not with the shock which Porter had expected, but thoughtfully and perhaps even with a trace of a smile. His mouth opened to speak, but before any words could come out, the bullhorn on the *Bedford*'s bridge rattled across with a loud commanding voice, urgent, impatient and with a steely quality, as though it belonged to the ship itself:

"Belay the socializing, please! Commander Porter

will come over to me immediately. Also do not send our guest until stores are transferred."

Grisling had just dragged Ben Munceford away from a packed cargo sling, where he had failed to get at his camera case, and was about to buckle him into the bosun's chair. Upon hearing the order from the *Bedford,* the old chief boatswain's mate became so overwrought that he could only make a supplicant gesture toward the *Tiburon Bay*'s bridge, then roughly yanked Munceford clear of the highline gear.

Hirschfeld reacted to the vice from the *Bedford* with a fearful start and glanced uneasily toward the bridge of the destroyer. "Finlander is watching us," he whispered hoarsely.

Porter noticed that one of the faces showing above the windscreen was partially obscured by the lenses of a pair of large binoculars aimed right at them. Instinctively lowering his voice, he hurriedly exclaimed: "For God's sake, Barney! What's been happening to you on that ship?"

Hirschfeld refused a direct answer, but quickly and ominously injected: "Just keep your eye on Finlander, that's all."

Chief Grisling was calling Porter's name, but the surgeon had been rooted to the spot by the inflection of Hirschfeld's words. "What do you mean, keep an eye on Finlander?" he demanded, suddenly severe and formal. "You say that as if you were suggesting he has been acting irrationally."

The young medical officer shook his head and laughed bitterly. "Oh, no! You're not going to pin that one on me! He's no Captain Queeg of the *Caine* who's about to have a mutiny. No, sir. If anything, he's the only sane one on that blighted can. Him and the German. He's driving everybody else ..." Hirschfeld stopped abruptly as Chief Grisling stepped up and saluted with a seething politeness.

"Pardon me, sirs, but DDL 113 is most anxiously awaiting the commander's transfer!" His lips continued moving after the audible part of his request was completed, silently mouthing through some of his favorite epithets.

Lieutenant Barney Hirschfeld kicked his feet clear of the soaking immersion suit, said: "Good luck, Chester," in a low voice and hurriedly retreated down the cluttered deck. Shaken and confused, Lieutenant Commander Porter allowed himself to be led by Chief Grisling to the bosun's chair. The straps closed tightly over his thighs and a moment later he swung clear of the *Tiburon Bay*. As the block creaked on the wire overhead and the tanker fell away, his eyes sought to pick out a last glimpse of the surgeon-lieutenant among the crowd of men lining the rail, but the only one he could clearly recognize was Munceford squinting horribly at him through the viewfinder of his camera. Twenty feet beneath him, black water raged, and spume stung his face with icy needles.

4.

Larsen followed with his eyes the progress of the awkward shape dangling like a weird marionette from the highline. He knew it was Lieutenant Commander Porter and found himself sadistically wishing that the two ships would roll together, dunking the starchy surgeon in the freezing Atlantic. The wish startled him a little because Porter was a good officer and a gentleman of adequate intelligence and humor; probably a dedicated doctor too. Perhaps it was that he took the gentleman part somewhat too seriously; or the dedication to it all. But this was no reason to wish him the victim of a cruel prank, so perhaps the real truth was that he resented the professional navy which this man represented. Resented it and envied it, both. It seemed like a hundred years since he had applied for a regular commission, when the last war was over, and been turned down because he had gone to sea instead of to college. That still rankled in the back of his mind, even though he earned as much as an admiral in his job with Standard Oil and commanded far bigger and better tankers than this one. Being a Commander, U.S.N.R., was not really bad in itself. Still ... if he had made it back in 1946, he would certainly have been Captain, U.S.N., by now ... like Finlander.

Larsen's eyes flicked from the highline to the destroyer's bridge, which was so much lower than his own that he could look down into it. The figure in a pure white duffel coat, hunched over the bulwark and watching the operation with a casual sort of alertness, had to be Captain Finlander. The profile was hidden by the upturned collar and when he glanced up at the *Tiburon Bay*'s bridge, the face was shadowed by what appeared to be a long-billed fisherman's cap. Only Finlander would be permitted such eccentricity of dress. In fact, there was something eccentric about such a high-ranking officer being captain of a mere destroyer instead of a missile cruiser or super-carrier—as Larsen would have preferred for himself. But they said that Finlander badgered his superiors into keeping him at sea on the cans, that he loved them with a passion, that he was a superlative seaman who became intransigent and morose on routine shoreside assignments. No doubt a fine seaman was necessary to command a ship in these arctic waters, and perhaps a full captain was necessary because it was such a critical area in the cold war—but a man like that had to be somewhat mad, or childishly romantic, to deliberately seek such an assignment. College or no college, Larsen would have made a less flamboyant, more flexible Captain, U.S.N.

Lieutenant Commander Porter made it over to the *Bedford* without being dunked and was received by a crew fewer and far more silent in their work than those aboard the *Tiburon Bay*. With smooth efficiency they had the outgoing mail sacks on their way within a minute. Captain Larsen cocked his hooded head away from the biting breeze, watched them for a moment, then checked the fuel hoses swaying from their whips and saddles—"the teats of your fat sea cow," Munceford had cracked about them yesterday when they refueled the *Fritjof Nansen* off Cape Farewell. Well—the *Tiburon Bay was* a plodding sea cow, maybe, but the glamorous destroyers could not operate so long and so far from their bases without her. If she failed to show up and nurse them on schedule, they would have to limp home on two boilers, leaving the northeast approaches to the American continent open to probes by Soviet submarines and spy trawlers. So it actually all depended as much on a lowly sea cow and her Commander, U.S.N.R., as it did on ships like the *Bedford* and her Captain, U.S.N. Finlander might make admiral in due time, while Larsen never could surmount his reserve rank. But he did stand in line to become Vice-President in Charge of Marine Operations for Standard Oil eventually . . . and *that* job paid $25,000 per annum, plus bonuses, which in turn would put *both* his sons through M.I.T. with plenty to spare. Then the navy would beg him to have them accept regular commissions—something he would be most cagey about!

"Sir—Lieutenant Hirschfeld is logged aboard and wishes to speak to the captain."

Larsen turned from watching the refueling operation to glance over his shoulder at his executive officer and a man standing next to him wearing nothing but a thin windbreaker and an ordinary cap as protection against the raw cold of the bridge. He was a dark, brooding-looking young man with a hooked nose and heavy black eyebrows arched over it. Handsome in a Jewish way, but the lines around his eyes and mouth suggested a permanently troubled personality.

"You some kind of fresh-air fiend, Lieutenant?" Larsen asked him, then turned his head away from a salute, not out of rudeness, but because he had to keep his eyes on the fueling of the *Bedford.*

"My heavy gear will be over shortly, sir," Hirschfeld answered. "Can't wear too much padding under an immersion suit."

Larsen grunted.

"Sir, I am sorry to disturb you at this time," Hirschfeld continued, "but Captain Finlander ordered me to report to you immediately."

Larsen looked toward the *Bedford*'s bridge and noticed that the figure in the white duffel had a pair of binoculars aimed right at them; at that short distance he could no doubt almost read their lips. "Why, Lieutenant?" he asked.

Hirschfeld spoke as if it were an entirely routine matter, without urgency or emotion. "I am to report, sir, that for the past five days I have been relieved of my duties as surgeon of the U.S.S. *Bedford* and confined to quarters. Captain Finlander requests that this status be continued for me aboard the *Tiburon Bay* and that I have nothing but necessary offical contacts with officers and men under your command until I am put ashore at Portsmouth."

Larsen turned around and stared at him. "You are under arrest?"

"Confined to quarters pending a board of inquiry, sir."

"Inquiry into what, Mr. Hirschfeld?"

"Captain Finlander has ordered me not to discuss the case, which he has placed under maximum security, sir."

Captain Larsen looked back at the *Bedford*'s bridge and saw the glint of binocular lenses still trained on them. "Take the conn, Mr. Wilburforce!" he snapped to his executive officer, then pushed his way past the two men to go over to the telephone talker. "Get me the captain of the *Bedford*, please."

The young quartermaster spoke into his instrument and after a moment informed Larsen: "Sir, the executive officer says that Captain Finlander is busy and unable to talk to you at this time."

Larsen's customary grunt became an angry snarl. "Give me that phone, son!" He pulled the headset off the man's head and stuffed one cup inside his hood to press it against his ear. "This is Captain Larsen speaking," he said into the microphone. "I am also extremely busy at the moment and, I do believe, engaged in the same mission as Captain Finlander. But I trust my exec enough so I can speak on the phone for a minute or two without expecting to founder. I hope Captain Finlander has matters well enough in hand to do likewise."

The voice on the other end of the line was not in the least fazed by this cutting sarcasm. It remained evenly courteous. "Good afternoon, Captain Larsen. This is Commander Allison, executive officer, speaking. If you wait one moment, I will check again with Captain Finlander."

Larsen could still see the *Bedford*'s bridge by standing on tiptoe and could pick out her exec as he poked his head out of the wheelhouse and evidently called to the shape in the white duffel. There was no visible reaction from the latter. A few seconds later the courteous voice came back: "I am sorry, Captain Larsen, but Captain Finlander regrets he is unable to speak to you unless it is an urgent tactical or navigational matter. However, *I* suppose you are actually calling about Lieutenant Hirschfeld, sir?"

Even to an easygoing reserve officer, this was a gross breach of naval etiquette, and if it had not been for his long indoctrination in rudeness aboard unionized merchant ships, Larsen would probably have lost his temper completely. But sardonic humor was his principal and most deadly weapon. "Well, yes, Commander," he answered in a chatty tone. "I am given to understand that the man has committed a crime. Of course, the *Tiburon Bay* is perfectly accustomed to acting as a convict ship for the destroyer fleet, but our chief executioner's mate becomes confused if he is not given a bill of particulars to govern the treatment of individual criminals in his custody."

The voice from the *Bedford* remained unfazed. "I see your point, Captain Larsen. The case is really not as sinister as Lieutenant Hirschfeld's attitude might indicate. You may still treat him as an officer and gentleman, sir."

"Ah! Then he's only committed a misdemeanor. Perhaps a little mischief our medical officers are likely to get into, like supplementing their income by engaging in illegal operations, or pushing narcotics in the ward room, or watering the skipper's supply of medicinal brandy?"

"Well—it's not exactly a joking matter either, Captain," the commander told him, a certain annoyance creeping into his tone.

"I'm only an unsubtle tanker captain, Commander. If it is neither a sinister nor a joking matter, you leave me dangling in confusion."

Commander Allison's voice was suddenly coldly official. "The matter involves medical practice rather than naval discipline, Captain Larsen. As such, it is beyond the concern of officers of the line and therefore should not be a matter of discussion between us. I believe Lieutenant Hirschfeld himself agrees with this. Certainly it is the wish of Captain Finlander that it be treated in that way, and I respectfully submit that you comply with his judgment in the case."

"O-oh! I see! That clears it all up for me," Larsen exclaimed, making a wry grimace. "My compliments to Captain Finlander and my thanks to you, Commander. Out." He pulled the earphone out from under his hood and thrust the instrument back to the talker. Turning around, he found himself facing the young surgeon, who had evidently been standing directly behind him throughout the conversation. The captain looked searchingly into the tense face, then smiled. "As far as I'm concerned, you are welcome aboard this ship, Mr. Hirschfeld. If you choose to confine yourself to your cabin and not socialize with my officers, that's your business and we'll presume you have good reasons. Either way, we'll give you the benefit of doubt. In the meanwhile, there's coffee in the chartroom, so why don't you go in there and thaw out?

A trace of a grateful smile passed over Hirschfeld's lips. "Thank you, sir." He started to move toward the wheelhouse, but hesitated momentarily and said: "It is only fair for me to warn you, Captain, that I'm going to resign from the navy as soon as I get back Stateside."

Wilburforce heard him and stared at him as if he were mad, but Captain Larsen only nodded and took the conn back from his executive officer.

The *Tiburon Bay* and the *Bedford* plowed on at a steady fifteen knots, the big ship heaving with a cumbersome motion as she rose and fell with the swells, the smaller one stamping her forefoot with a nervous, coltish action. The breeze ruffling the surface of those swells was less than Force 1, a mere zephyr wafting down from the north which made the slightly warmer ocean steam with patches of sea smoke. Low banks of fog still compressed the horizon, which had lost its shimmering pearl-gray color and become darker as the short arctic day faded into a gloomy twilight. A ragged patch in the overcast glowed a mysterious amber color for a few moments as it caught the devious rays of a sun setting beyond the pall of scud to the southwest.

Oil flowed from the *Tiburon Bay*'s vast tanks into the bunkers of the *Bedford*, throbbing through the hoses at a rate of better than two tons per minute. The highline swung containers of fresh dairy produce across to the destroyer in hundred-gallon and hundred-pound lots—milk, eggs, butter and ice cream, all less than a week away from Rhode Island farms. Back and forth over the wild trench of water hurtling between the two ships the sling traveled, conveying forty twelve-pound rib roasts, seventy crates of vegetables, twenty-eight hams, a hundred pounds of pork sausage, two hundred and eight pounds of coffee, a bundle of magazines, fifteen full-length feature movies, a case full of fragile transistors and radio tubes, the replacement armature for a burned-out auxiliary generator, seventeen cases of toilet paper, two hundred and forty pounds of soap, two ten-gallon cans of cola syrup, a case of chewing gum, Lieutenant Commander Porter's Valpack, Munceford's duffel bag and camera case. . . . Finally, there was Munceford himself, jerking across with his camera stiffly pressed to his face as he registered a wildly swaying scene of his transfer through spray-splattered optics.

It was at this moment that Captain Larsen was jolted by the muffled clanging of the *Bedford*'s General Quarters alarm, the sound suddenly penetrating the intervening forty feet of hissing sea. Even as the significance of it was penetrating his brain, the bullhorn on the destroyer's bridge blared at him:

"Now hear this, *Tiburon Bay!* We have detected a high-frequency radar emission upon us. Break off operation at once! Break off operation at once!"

Larsen tensed, called back over his shoulder to the talker: "Notify all stations to stand by for break-off!" He glanced at the *Bedford*'s bridge and saw that the white duffel coat had vanished from its position in the wing, then he focused his attention on Ben Munceford, who was dangling from the highline midway between the two ships. The bosun's chair hesitated and stopped; the figure in it looked up from the viewfinder of the camera, the face glowing a startling pink in the hood of the immersion suit as it twisted sideways and upward, staring back questioningly at the tanker's bridge. The line suddenly slackened, and for a second or two Munceford's feet cut a foaming wake in the water rushing beneath him; then the line cracked tight again, catapulting him into violent gyrations which came within a hair of looping the whole rig and jamming it midway. A small object detached itself from the struggling black figure, arcing gracefully through the air before splashing into the sea; it was Munceford's camera on its way to oblivion, a hundred fathoms down. Some howls rose from the *Tiburon Bay*'s main deck, topped by Chief Grisling's profane invocations to the devil.

"Steady up, helmsman!" Captain Larsen roared at the wheelhouse. "Steady up or you'll break the highline and put a man in the screws!"

Mr. Wilburforce screamed "Jesus!" and rushed into the wheelhouse.

By some miracle the highline held, the bosun's chair settled down from its wild swaying and suddenly began moving again toward the *Bedford*. It seemed that the sagging shape encased in black rubber had hardly touched the destroyer's deck before the end of the rig was cast off and allowed to fall clear. Almost simultaneously the fuel hoses were knocked out of the quick-release fittings, their ends splashing into the waves, where they writhed like serpents. The destroyer was clear, pulling ahead and veering away with a rising whine of her turbines, all within a little over a minute since the GQ alarm.

"Tell all stations to retrieve and secure gear as quickly as possible," Captain Larsen told the talker. "I want an immediate report from Mr. Boomer on the amount of bunkers transferred as of break-off." He went into the wheelhouse and interrupted his executive officer's lecture to the helmsman on steering techniques. "You may take the conn, Mr. Wilburforce. Continue on zero-seven-zero for the time being. Might as well slow down until we get the hoses and lines back aboard."

"The *Bedford* is calling on the TBS, sir," the chief quartermaster announced.

Larsen unzipped his parka and flipped back the hood as he walked into the navigation office. When he took off his cap and threw it on top of the chart table, pure white locks of hair fell over his forehead and they made his face suddenly look much older. The TBS radio was attached to the bulkhead next to the LORAN and the chief quartermaster handed him the mike. As he took it, he noticed Lieutenant Hirschfeld slumped in a chair, nursing a mug of coffee.

"Hoarfrost to Coldsnap. Captain speaking."

The voice which came back to him had a strange crackling quality caused by the scrambler which protected the TBS circuit from enemy ears, but he immediately recognized it as belonging to the *Bedford's* executive officer. "Coldsnap to Hoarfrost. We are proceeding to investigate emission. You will leave area immediately and execute maneuver Able Fox before resuming mission to rendezvous and feed Polarbear. Maintain radio silence. Acknowledge and repeat."

Captain Larsen confirmed the order, hung up the receiver and switched the set to stand-by. After calling the new course to Lieutenant Wilburforce, he went to the big thermos and poured himself a cup of coffee, which he wolfed down scalding hot. Hirschfeld had watched him silently while he talked to the *Bedford* and now their eyes met and locked in what became such a long stare that something had to be said.

"Well, Mr. Hirschfeld . . . looks like your Captain Finlander is tearing off on another of his wild war games."

"They are not games, Captain."

"Takes them pretty seriously, eh?"

"Very."

"I've never met him personally. Refueled him twice before, but never met him. But I hear he's a remarkable officer. A real genius at anti-submarine warfare."

"Are you asking me to tell you about Finlander, Captain?" Hirschfeld asked him, cocking one of his sensitive black eyebrows.

Larsen shrugged. "Everybody's curious about Finlander, aren't they?"

"Yes, he's a remarkable officer," the young surgeon

told him in his flat, unemotional voice. "Yes, he's a genius at anti-submarine warfare. And because the cold war is not a real war, he's like Captain Ahab sailing his *Pequod* through a closed season on whales." He contemplated the dregs in his empty cup, dropped his tone to a whisper and added: "But Ahab finally met up with his Moby Dick, didn't he?"

Captain Larsen looked perplexed for a moment, grunted and walked out of the navigation office, thoughtfully crossing the darkening wheelhouse to one of the windows. The *Bedford* was a blur dissolving into the distant murk, leaving only a ghostly white furrow to linger on the swells.

5.

Two seamen had grabbed Ben Munceford as he swung aboard the *Bedford*, roughly manhandled him off the highline and steered him out of the way, leaving him clinging to a stanchion while staring in shock toward the spot, already far astern, where his camera had fallen from his hands. Now there would be nothing to show for his trip, no film for any TV news directors to buy and no pay to alleviate the relentless creeping deficit in his finances—not even fare back to the United States! He felt like screaming at these men that they were a bunch of incompetent asses, but only one paid brief attention to him.

"Welcome aboard, Mr. Munceford," a huge young officer greeted him in passing. "I'm Ensign Ralston, JOOD." His gloved paw shot out and gave Munceford's hand a hearty pump. "Sorry you got roughed up. Couldn't be helped. We've got a GQ on and you'll have to be shunted below for a while. Steward's Mate Collins will take you to your cabin." Without awaiting any reaction, he rushed off to supervise the hurried stowing of stores which were still piled on the destroyer's deck.

"I'll be a son of a bitch!" Munceford spat out between clenched teeth, staring accusingly at the enormous steel flanks of the *Tiburon Bay*, falling away from the *Bedford* with the disconnected hoses and highline dragging in her wash. He could still hear Chief Grisling's fading curses and see Captain Larsen casually leaning over the port wing of his bridge. "God-damned clumsy bastards!" Unheeding his fury, the tanker majestically steamed on while he felt the deck beneath him heave and tilt as the destroyer pulled ahead and sheered away.

"Excuse me, sir, but we've got to clear the deck fast," a man said to him, gripping his arm. The face framed by the hood was that of a handsome Negro. "If you'll step this way, I'll get you out of your suit, then show you to your quarters."

"I'd like to speak to the captain," Munceford fumed, resisting the tug.

The steward's mate merely shook his head and began applying firmer pressure. Munceford had a last glimpse of the crew working in swift silence as they grappled with the tangle of gear and piles of containers, then was shunted over the high combing of a door and plunged into the darkness of the *Bedford*'s interior. His eyes adjusted themselves to the dim red glow of blackout lights in a passageway. The hand gripping his arm shoved him under one of them and began unfastening his immersion suit.

"You know they lost me my camera," Munceford exclaimed bitterly.

"That's rough, sir," the Negro seward sympathized, "but they shouldn't have sent you across with anything loose in your hands. Against regulations." With a firm, quick skill he peeled the rubber folds downward and, for a second, stared in surprise at the gaudy camouflage jacket beneath them.

"That *Tiburon Bay*'s a screwed-up bucket," Munceford told him, angrily kicking his feet clear of the immersion suit. The steward's mate picked it up without answering, threw it on top of another one which was lying in a puddle on the deck, then said: "Follow me, please."

On amazingly silent feet the Negro ran down the passageway, turned a corner, stopped and pressed

Munceford against a bulkhead to allow a group of shadowy figures to run past them. There followed the sound of watertight doors clanging shut from somewhere below, but he plunged down a hatch and companionway, padded along another long corridor, turned another corner, opened a door and pulled aside a curtain to reveal an even smaller cabin than the one Munceford had occupied on the tanker. "This is it, sir," he said. "Top bunk. Starboard locker. Your gear will be brought down after GQ. Now I must go to my battle station." Without any further formalities the steward's mate vanished down the passageway. A few seconds later another watertight door was heard to close with a solid metallic thump.

At first Munceford thought that there would be nobody else occupying the cubicle, it was so sterile and neat. But he noticed a toothbrush stuck in the bracket above the washbowl, and a pipe lay in the ashtray on the tiny desk. He looked around the bulkheads for a porthole, but there was none; a hissing airduct provided the only ventilation. The cabin swayed and pitched with a strangely detached motion, making him feel that he was imprisoned in a sealed tin box which had been cast upon the sea. With a sudden sense of claustrophobia and loneliness, he sat down on the immaculate lower bunk, listening to the urgent whine of the turbines, the only sound to break the oppressive silence. The foreboding which had come over him when he first saw the *Bedford* appear out of the fog returned and changed his anger over the lost camera to a gnawing depression. Where was his cabin mate? Where was *anybody* in this empty, throbbing ship?

Munceford considered leaving the cabin, but decided he would become hopelessly lost in the labyrinth of dark passages and only run up against closed watertight doors, so he lay back on the bunk to rest his muscles wrenched by the wild ride across the highline.

Feeling something hard pressing through the thin pillow, he reached under it and pulled out a small photographic portfolio made of luxurious morocco leather. Flipping it open, he found himself looking into the face of a gaunt, elderly woman with a benign smile; across the tweedy slope of her bosom was a stiffly penned inscription: *To Peter, with Love from Mumsy.*

"Christ! *A Mumsy's boy,* yet!" Munceford exclaimed aloud.

But the frame was the kind with four panels folded accordion fashion and while the two middle sections were empty, the last one contained a photograph of a girl. Such a beautiful girl that she instantly aroused Munceford's old animal instincts and made him forget all his troubles of the moment as he stared at her in fascination. She could have been a natural blond or a redhead, her glossy soft hair very stylish, yet with just the right touch of casualness. The eyebrows were delicate without being weak and the widely separated eyes beneath them had to be either blue or green—there was a wonderfully humorous twinkle in them. Her nose was very fine and ever so slightly turned up. Her full, sensuous lips were drawn into a wistful little smile which created a delicious dimple on her left cheek. The long, aristocratic neck blended into a magnificent pair of bare shoulders and there was a slight suggestion of freckles on her chest where it met the curves of her breasts. These had to be enormously exciting . . . but the photographer had left them to the imagination. In the white space where they should have been, there was scrawled in a boldly impudent hand: *All of me for Pete's sake—Adoring, Shebeona!*

Shebeona! What a name! Ben Munceford pursed his lips to let out a soft whistle, but no sound crossed them. Here was a woman to take your breath away! Those eyes held wisdom, mischief, understanding and fun. But, above all, here was real beauty, earthy and divine all at once. Not of the crude shallow kind of his discarded Nancys! Her voice had to be vibrantly soft, not wheedling or whining or shrill. Yes—here indeed was a woman! If he ever met her, he knew he would be lost. Perhaps even now, while only holding her picture in his hands, he had become lost to her spell. What kind of man was it who possessed her? Did he really possess her? What sort of chap was this Pete to whom she had so humorously and ardently inscribed this photograph? Was she his wife? Fiancée? Or just a girl friend? How intimate was their relationship?

Munceford suddenly became conscious of the fact that he had no right to stare at Shebeona like this, or to lie with her in this bunk. Reluctantly he closed the folds of the portfolio and tucked it back under the pillow. Then he abruptly got up and guiltily brushed aside the curtain to peer into the passageway outside the cabin. It was dark and empty and smelled faintly of fresh paint. He could hear no sound beyond the moaning from the engine rooms. Directly opposite, there was a closed door marked with the numeral 5 and he impulsively stepped over and knocked on it. There was no answer.

"This is a hell of a way to see life on a destroyer," he mumbled bitterly to himself and returned inside his own cabin. The ship heeled and shuddered as she sliced through a big swell. He lost his balance and clumsily flopped back into the lower bunk, but did not bother to get up again. Penetrating through the steel of many bulkheads, the sound of rushing water faintly reached Munceford's ears as the *Bedford* rose up and shook off the spray enveloping her. He lay back on the pillow, feeling the hardness of the frame under it; presently he sneaked another look at Shebeona.

6.

When the GQ alarm sounded, Lieutenant Commander Chester Porter had only been aboard the *Bedford* for some forty minutes. He had just completed a telephone conversation with Commander Allison, the executive officer, in which it was decided to postpone a courtesy call to the bridge until after his gear and some replacement medical stores had arrived and he could report himself ready in every respect to assume his duties as ship's surgeon. The call to battle stations had precipitated matters and startled him a bit, but he was an experienced officer who did not allow small confusions to get the better of him; even though not familiar with this particular vessel, he had served on destroyers before and knew their ways in general. While aboard the *Tiburon Bay,* he had conscientiously plowed through the Qualification Course for this latest class of DDL, something not actually required of a medical officer. However, Lieutenant Commander Porter was a meticulous and precise man who prided himself in always doing a little more for the navy than it required of him. Thus, when the call to General Quarters was so unexpectedly thrust upon him, he promptly sought his post in surgery, where he was gratified to find that a chief pharmacist's mate and two corpsmen had the situation well under control. Whatever had been Lieutenant Hirschfeld's transgressions, they obviously did not include failure to train his medical staff properly.

Porter made certain that the compact surgery was ready to receive casualties, checked sick bay, whose six bunks were fortunately empty, then stepped into the small receiving office and sat down at the desk. The chief pharmacist's mate, who looked more like a bright intern than a sailor, followed him in and reported: "We have two corpsmen stationed on the boat deck and two in the engine room, all ready with first-aid kits. Pharmacist's Mate Engstrom with a party of litter carriers are in the seamen's mess. Chief Steward's Mate Lang and Smythe are organizing an auxiliary dressing station in the wardroom. All according to SOP, sir."

"Good. Looks like you have this department running smoothly. What is your name?"

"McKinley, sir. You will find the complete roster and watch schedule on that clipboard there. The medical log is in the top drawer of the desk. Here is the key to the narcotics locker. It is unlocked during GQ."

The surgeon took the key and carefully clipped it into the ring attached to his belt. "Are morphine ampoules included in the first-aid kits even during practice GQ, McKinley?"

"Yes, sir. You will find that almost all our GQ's are *actual* GQ's."

"Oh? How often does Captain Finlander pull them?"

"Whenever there is a contact, sir. They happen three or four times a week."

"Real intensive training, eh? I suppose we bring in simulated casualties too?"

The pharmacist's mate's high forehead wrinkled in momentary perplexity, as if he were having trouble making the new surgeon understand the situation. Then he smiled. "There's darn little *simulated* stuff aboard the *Bedford*, sir. Everything's for real—except actual bloodletting."

"Well, I am surprised Mr. Hirschfeld hasn't ordered litter-carrying drills. I'll take that up with the captain."

"Yes, sir. In the meanwhile, may I suggest you report to the medical department ready at battle stations.

I had not had time to do that when you came in, Commander."

"Oh, God! And here we are gabbing away!"

McKinley pushed a telephone in front of the surgeon and depressed a button marked BRIDGE. A talker identified himself with a businesslike tone and accepted the report. When Porter hung up, hoping that Finlander would be impressed that he had taken hold so quickly, the chief pharmacist's mate had left and could be seen checking the sterilizers in the surgery. Porter began to get up to join him, but a long roll of the ship pressed him into his chair and he decided that it would be best if he stayed out of the way for the time being. Until he had familiarized himself with things, procedural matters of the department could be run by McKinley, who seemed very competent. So he remained at the desk and engaged himself in the safe activity of examining some of the paperwork which it contained.

The medical log showed that the *Bedford*'s crew were unusually healthy. In leafing through it, the surgeon found very few entries during the twenty-one days the ship had been on patrol. A cook had been treated for grease burns. A seaman first-class had had his throat swabbed for laryngitis. A radar operator had suffered from a stye. A machinist's mate had spent one day in sick bay with suspected appendicitis, which had turned out to be acute indigestion. All of these cases were certified returned to duty in Lieutenant Hirschfeld's precise handwriting. The only thing which caught Porter's eye and struck him as being slightly strange was the fact that a page had been neatly cut out of the log, leaving a blank strip of paper between November 28—six days ago—and November 29. There were actually no missing entries, but as logs are not supposed to be in any way altered or defaced, the surgeon wondered about it briefly. Then he decided that it might have been a matter of accidental damage of spilling of some staining liquid. He leafed through to the present date and signed himself in as medical officer in charge, relieving Lieutenant Hirschfeld.

He next flipped through the hospital inventory forms which were neatly stapled together in a folder, then glanced through the NAVPUBMED file, which appeared complete and very up to date. Finally he opened the deep file drawers which contained the individual medical records of every man aboard the *Bedford*. They were inside 324 indexed folders and he leafed through a couple of them at random before, on a sudden whim, he deliberately picked out Captain Finlander's. It was empty.

"Chief McKinley!"

McKinley came to the door of the office and braced himself against the roll of the ship. "Yes, Commander."

"Where is Captain Finlander's Form 28?"

The pharmacist's mate appeared to flinch slightly and he hesitated a moment before answering. "Two or three days ago Mr. Hirschfeld took it up to the captain's cabin, sir. He did not bring it back."

"Any reason?"

"Well . . . not that I know of, sir."

"Any reason why I shouldn't ask to have it back?"

McKinley's forehead wrinkled. "No, sir . . . not unless it has something to do with the troubles between Mr. Hirschfeld and the captain. . . . That's just a guess on my part," he quickly added.

Porter thought for a moment, staring down at the empty folder. It was not customary to discuss such things with enlisted men, but the medical department was somewhat privileged, so he decided to ask the question preying on his mind. "What was the nature of those troubles, McKinley?"

"I don't know, sir."

"Not even any scuttlebutt?"

McKinley hesitated a fraction before saying: "Everybody likes Captain Finlander. Everybody liked Lieutenant Hirschfeld too, but . . ."

"But what?"

"But he sometimes had some queer medical ideas, sir."

This shocked the surgeon, who was perhaps more jealous of the sanctity of the medical than of the naval profession. "That's not exactly for a pharmacist's mate to judge," he snapped.

"Sorry, sir. You asked me my opinion."

"Well, yes, and you're entitled to it. But I'm saying I don't think it's a *qualified* opinion, that's all." He paused to let the man's very evident discomfiture sink in, then asked: "How long have you been in the navy, McKinley?"

"Ever since I flunked out of pre-med at Duke, three years ago last June."

Porter could not tell whether there was a genuine meekness or subtle arrogance in that answer. Was he confirming his incompetence or rubbing in the fact that he had, at least for a time, attended one of the finest medical colleges in the U.S.A.? Certainly it was evident that this was no ordinary enlisted man who had barely made it through high school in the lower third of his class. Even to qualify for Duke pre-med, a B+ average was necessary. Porter suddenly felt himself on the defensive with this subordinate, and before he could stop himself from saying anything so revealing, he exclaimed: "You should know better than to make irresponsible statements about a medical officer."

The wrinkles on McKinley's forehead rippled and vanished into an expression of blank resignation. "I am sorry, sir," he said, leaving no doubt that he certainly was very unhappy about the whole discussion. However, it did not have to be continued, because at this moment the *Bedford*'s engines suddenly dropped their high whining song to a throbbing whisper. The deceleration which followed was so pronounced that the pharmacist had to grip the bulkhead to stay on his feet and the surgeon, who was seated facing aft, almost fell over backward. Without bothering with the customary bosun's whistle, the PA system came to life with a crackling voice:

"Now hear this! Rig for silent ship! Rig for silent ship!"

Porter suspected the tactical purpose of what was going on, but, jumping at a good reason to break the tension between himself and McKinley, exclaimed with cheerful annoyance: "Now what the hell is happening?"

"Nothing to worry about, sir," the chief pharmacist told him. "We're going to try a maximum-effect sonar sweep of the area. When under way at high speed, the ambient noises tend to blanket our own sound gear."

"Ah! Of course. Well, go ahead and carry on with your duties. I'll handle Captain Finlander's Form 28 myself."

As the *Bedford* wallowed in the swells with bare steerage way and only a murmur from her turbines, the surgeon spent his time memorizing the roster of the medical department, checking through the narcotics locker and inspecting the instruments in the surgery. Finally the engines picked up their normal tone and the *Bedford* modified her sloppy rolling as she steadied on a course at standard cruising speed. A few minutes later the PA announced securing from General Quarters but with the retaining of all battle stations on stand-by— exactly as on a vessel patrolling under real wartime conditions. The telephone in the receiving office rang and Lieutenant Commander Porter was invited to come up on the bridge. Before leaving, he opened the file drawer of the desk, considering whether or not to bring the empty folder with him. But he decided to take up *that* matter later.

7.

Ben Munceford heard the recall from GQ and sat
up on the lower bunk, where he had been lying for the
past hour. He smoothed out some of the wrinkles and
made sure the pillow was in place over Shebeona, then
sat there, disgruntled and impatient, listening for any
sounds which might indicate human activity. He heard
the thumping of running feet, but from the deck above,
and they quickly faded. The lonely isolation persisted.
Then suddenly the curtain was thrust aside and he
found himself looking up at a tall young man in a
navy-blue duffel coat of unfamiliar cut. The insignia on
his cap was also strange to Munceford, who did not
recognize it until he heard the British accent.

"Hello—you must be the reporter! Or should I say
correspondent?" The handsomely serious face broke
into a quick smile.

Munceford half rose to his feet and accepted the
handshake. "I'm Ben Munceford."

"Glad to meet you." His eyes took in the camouflage
jacket carelessly draped over the chair, but he registered no special reaction. "I'm Peter Packer."

The funny named startled Munceford. "I guess
you're with the British navy. How come?"

"Oh, this is a regular Noah's Ark with all sorts of
breeds of animals aboard." He laughed and looked
over his bunk, which had not been returned to its
former state of perfection. "Would you prefer the
lower berth, Munceford? All the same to me."

"No, thanks. I'm okay in the upper. But I'd sure as hell like to get out of this cell and look around."

Packer shook himself out of his duffel. He was wearing a white turtleneck sweater under it. "You've been stuck here all through GQ, I gather. What a bore!"

"That's not the half of it. Lost my camera from the highline."

"Oh, dear! Bad day all around, eh?"

Munceford winced at the "oh, dear."

Packer smiled pleasantly and opened his locker to hang up his coat. Everything in it was stowed with neat precision. "The ECM lads sniffed the emission of a strange radar while we were refueling," he explained. "The Russians watch us even as we watch them, you know. Only it isn't fair, because this is *our* part of the playing field. Not that *we* don't sneak over into theirs occasionally, of course." He moved to the washbowl and began to lather his hands vigorously. "But that doesn't mean we don't react with proper indignation when we catch them over here. So we get lots of jolly GQ's and chase each other all over the ocean. A nuisance, but keeps us on our toes."

"I'm surprised I wasn't just cut loose and dropped in the drink, like my camera," Munceford observed sourly.

The British officer finished splashing water on his face and answered through the folds of a towel: "Oh, Captain Finlander was watching you, all right. I distinctly heard him say: 'Let's get that man across if we can. He may give us some good publicity.' He's got a marvelous dry wit, old Finlander!" Packer laughed at the recollection.

Munceford's churlish expression did not change as he contemplated the English officer. "So what did all this eager-beaver stuff accomplish?" he asked. "Did you find one of those Red trawlers lurking around making like it was fishing?"

"No. The emission was most likely from a sub which submerged long before we got within range." He was back at his locker, taking from it a jacket with one and a half gold stripes on its sleeves and crowns embossed on the gold buttons. There was not a wrinkle in it. "We're over a deep trench here with some currents which cause temperature layering. Makes sonar unreliable. A sub can hang deep, undetected. The Russians haven't got any nuclear units that we know about, but they can go down a thousand feet or better, which is pretty safe in these waters."

"In other words, they screw us."

Packer turned and his face was deadly earnest. "Never fear, Munceford. You can tell your readers that in naval matters we're giving the Russians a bad inferiority complex."

"I haven't got readers. I'm in television and radio."

"Ah. Sounds more exciting. I like the telly."

"What exactly is your reason for being here?"

"Communication liaison with NATO. And, of course, spying for the Admiralty on your latest type of destroyer."

The curtain whipped aside and the door was suddenly filled by the hulking shape of Ensign Ralston, the officer who had briefly greeted, then deserted Munceford when he was first dumped aboard the *Bedford.* "Damn right he's a spy!" he loudly exclaimed. "But we're perfectly safe because the Limey navy can't afford expensive toys like this any more. . . . You all squared away, Mr. Munceford?"

Munceford looked hopefully at this magnificent American animal who must have been a tackle on the Annapolis football team as well as in the top third of his class—which could hardly have graduated more than a year ago. He was scowling with ferocious affection at the English officer and, before Munceford could answer his question, said:

"I gather you've become acquainted with *Left'nant* Peter Packer of Her Majesty's Royal Navy." He pronounced the name *Peterpacker*, all run together with emphasis on the *p*'s. "He's not only a very funny chap, but has a very funny name too. The ship's company gets knocked out every time it's called over the PA."

Lieutenant Packer was calmly looking himself over in the tiny mirror. "That's all right, chaps," he said. "I have a couple of middle initials in reserve for the day when I make flag rank. Admiral Sir P. L. M. Packer sounds dignified enough."

"The day you make admiral, Pete, your navy will be down to one ceremonial barge."

"Rowed by Yankee ensigns!" Packer quickly injected.

The two officers laughed at each other and Munceford emerged out of his grouch to join in the mirth. "I've got to remember to tape some of you guys' dialouge," he told them.

"Any time," the ensign agreed. "But I want you to understand that I write all of Peterpacker's funny lines for him. . . . Keee-rist! What's *this?*" He stepped into the cabin and picked up Munceford's camouflage jacket off the chair, holding it between thumb and forefinger as if it were not entirely sanitary, and eyeing the profusion of badges and patches with amazement. Spotting the fur cap, he picked it up too, examined it and, removing his own, put it on his close-cropped blond head. "Keee-rist!" he exclaimed again, staring at himself in the mirror. "What is it?"

Packer shrugged. "Anybody can see it's the official uniform of an American war correspondent."

Munceford was used to taking some kidding about his dress and really enjoyed the attention he derived from it. He had even once worn it up to the production offices of CBS News, a very conforming and dignified place of business. But he seldom had received the hilarious reaction which Ensign Ralston now gave him.

"It's pure crazy!" he boomed in delight, draping the jacket across his own enormous chest. "Crazy as hell! Gee, welcome aboard, Mr. Munceford, and join the club. We're *all* crazy aboard the *Bedford,* you know. So certified by our former medical officer. So you'll fit in perfectly. Here! Put this outfit on, please! I've got to see you in it."

Munceford laughed and obliged him, creating a terrible jam in the tiny cabin as he stood up in it together with the giant ensign and tall lieutenant. When he had the jacket on, Ralston transferred the cap to his head, then stepped back and examined him with more curiosity than hilarity.

"You cruise on a pigboat?" he asked, indicating the submariner's insignia.

"Only for a week out of Key West," Munceford admitted. "Just an ordinary diesel rig. I'm bucking for an assignment on a nuke, though."

"And you've jumped with the paratroops too?" Ralston asked, pointing at the patch of the 82nd Airborne Division.

"Yes—I followed a pair of recruits through jump school and took the course myself to get the feel of what they went through."

Ralston's rugged face showed genuine admiration. "You really believe in living your stories, don't you."

The conversation was interrupted by the arrival of Steward's Mate Collins, who was bringing in Munceford's camera case and duffel bag. The squeeze in the cabin became intolerable and Ralston took Munceford by the arm, dragging him out into the passageway. "I actually came down to escort you to the bridge and meet our skipper. He'll love that outfit of yours. Come on, Mr. Munceford."

"Call me Ben," Munceford told him, now feeling almost completely cheered up. Maybe he could scrounge a camera from somebody aboard. This ensign was all right and the Englishman was not really too bad. But, remembering Lieutenant Commander Porter's ominous hints about the captain, he asked: "What is this Finlander like?" as he followed Ralston down the narrow passageway.

The ensign made a circle with his thumb and forefinger, but did not answer. They went through a watertight door and up a companionway to the next deck. Then another long, cramped passage lit only by the red blackout lights. The low ceiling was crammed with pipes and conduits, the gray metal walls sporadically broken by closed doors. They had not met a single man anywhere, so far.

"Where the heck are the three-hundred-odd people who are supposed to be on this ship?" Munceford asked.

Ralston's rolling gait, which balanced perfectly with the motions of the destroyer, did not falter in its steady progress. "On stand-by battle stations," he answered softly over his shoulder. "Or at work. Or sacked out." His former boyishly boisterous manner seemed to have turned completely businesslike.

The ensign turned a corner and suddenly vanished upward. Munceford blinked, then noticed a ladder leading vertically up a shaft containing the same red glow as the passageways; Ralston's silhouette was springing catlike up the steel rungs. Moving slower and more cautiously, he followed. The ladder passed a small recess, or landing, containing a closed metal door on which was stenciled the word RESTRICTED in large red letters; above it a small blue bulb burned with a faint light. "What's in there?" Munceford asked.

"CIC," Ralston's answer came down, barely audible as he continued climbing up the shaft. They were obviously going to some place on a higher level, but

Munceford had lost all sense of direction and was completely confused. The shaft ended in an open hatch and he shot past the last rungs without touching them as the ensign reached down and boosted him up with an iron grip on his arm.

He found himself deposited in a large area which was not even lit by the red blackout lights. It was almost totally dark, much colder, and he immediately sensed that it was occupied by a number of men. As his eyes adjusted themselves, he made out their shadowy shapes and noticed the silhouette of one which stood out more clearly against a pale green glow emanating from what he recognized to be a binnacle and gyro-compass. So this had to be the wheelhouse and although it was only a few minutes past four, it was already shrouded by a black night. Except for a faint pinging sound which Munceford identified as sonar, and the soft moaning of the wind sweeping the bridge outside, a complete silence prevailed. The effect was eery and tense.

Munceford took a couple of cautious steps, then stopped because the grip on his arm was gone and he lost Ensign Ralston among the other shadowy figures. As he stood there, the door to the port wing of the bridge opened and for a brief moment the wheelhouse was filled with the sound of sea and the ice-cold draft of salt air; then the door rolled shut on silent runners. A low voice said: "Cover is ten-ten again, sir. No sight possible." There followed a subdued conversation in which Munceford could not catch a single word. Somebody passed very close to him and as he turned his head to follow their movement, he noticed a radar scanner, its sweeper revolving with a cold phosphorescent fire. Behind him there were the green and red and amber pinpricks of some kind of control panel.

Beyond the helmsman, the glass of windows glistened faintly and Munceford was talking a tentative step in their direction when the strong grip on his arm returned and he found himself led off in the opposite direction. A curtain was swept aside and he suddenly found himself in the same soft red light which seemed to prevail throughout most of the ship. Ensign Ralston had him in tow again and was introducing him to an officer bent over a chart.

"Sir, this is our guest, Mr. Ben Munceford."

"How are you, Captain?"

The officer shook his head. "I'm not the captain. I'm the exec, Commander Allison. Captain Finlander apologizes for delaying in meeting you, but he and Commander Porter went down to his cabin on some business. He will see you a little later. In the meanwhile, I hope to make you feel at home."

Munceford felt a stab of guilty uneasiness over the fact that Porter was getting to Finlander before him. He fumbled the handshake with Commander Allison, who was a short, robust man with a big nose. "Have you ever been out with the navy before, Mr. Munceford?" the executive officer asked him.

Munceford hesitated before answering, hoping that Ralston would inject something to the effect that he was an experienced military correspondent who had dived in submarines, jumped with paratroops and flown with the Strategic Air Command. But now that he was on the bridge, the ensign's transformation was complete. His demeanor and silence were rock-like and Munceford's hesitation became a suspicion of uncertainty. "Yes," he finally said. "Submarines, and also on a short DE cruise with a reserve unit. DE's are kind of like destroyers, so I'm not completely lost here."

"I see," Commander Allison said. His eyes were suddenly glued to the camouflage jacket and Munceford became aware that it glowed with a hideous hodge-podge effect in the red light. For the first time he felt embarrassed over it. "Well, DE's are somewhat similar, of course," the exec agreed, as if he actually resented the comparison. "But this DDL is damned near as big as a cruiser. However, the main thing to remember is that we are not on a reservists' cruise, Mr. Munceford. We are an active part of NATO defenses and operate our ship virtually under wartime conditions. And *that* reminds me—may I see your credentials, please?"

The abrupt request took Munceford completely by surprise. He fumbled inside his jacket and brought out the creased envelope which contained the orders from the Navy Department attaching "Munceford, Benjamin, J., Civilian Correspondent," to DDL 113 for a period of two weeks, handing it to the commander. Then he fished his wallet out of his back pocket, picked about among the few bills and many dog-eared membership cards for his War Department correspondent's ID. Finding the plastic square, he gave it to the exec with the same resentful feeling he had often felt when handing his driver's license to a tough cop.

"Thank you." Commander Allison briefly checked the orders and the ID, then gave the latter to the ensign. "Mr. Ralston, will you please note in the log that Mr. Munceford's credentials have been checked and enter the serial number of this ID." He flashed a thin smile at Munceford. "Like I say, we operate under virtual wartime conditions. There's a lot of highly classified equipment on this ship."

"And what would you have done if my credentials hadn't been in order? Thrown me overboard, Commander?"

The smile remained, but the executive officer obviously did not think this question funny. "We would confine you to quarters while the matter was being checked through with COMFLANT," he answered dryly and turned his attention to the chart from which he had been diverted when Munceford was brought before him. "Maybe you are interested in the *Bedford*'s current position and our projected patrol for the next week. This is where we are." He pointed with a stubby finger to an X penciled over a course line. "Approximately at the southwest entrance to the Denmark Strait. From here we will patrol through it toward the general vicinity of Jan Mayen Island—here." The stubby finger jabbed a tiny speck in the vastness of the arctic ocean to the northeast of Iceland. "The course line shown here is nice and straight, but it probably won't work out that way in practice. Radar and sonar contacts have to be investigated. Ice conditions and weather can get awfully bad, pushing us off course. How are your sea legs, by the way?" He stole another doubtful glance at Munceford's jacket when he asked the question.

"I can make out, Commander. Do you expect we will run into Russian subs?"

"Some."

"How about their trawlers?"

"Some of those too."

"I'm getting the impression that they are far more active than has been let on at home. Is that so, Commander?"

Allison's answer came clipped and definite. "I will let Captain Finlander brief you on the tactical situation, Mr. Munceford. He will have to decide what to tell you and what not to tell you. Frankly, I am surprised that you are here at all. This area is far too critical to make a TV show out of it." He pronounced TV as if it were a dirty word.

"You mean you want to fight yourselves a sort of private cold war out here?" Munceford acidly asked. From this moment on, he knew they would dislike each other. The commander did not answer him. Ensign Ralston returned to the chart table and handed the ID card back to the executive officer, who in turn passed it on to Munceford. For a moment there was a painful silence while the camouflage jacket received another strongly disapproving scrutiny.

"It gets pretty cold in these latitudes," Allison finally said. "Mr. Ralston, will you see that Mr. Munceford is issued some regulation arctics out of our slop chest, please."

"Oh, don't trouble yourselves," Munceford protested. "This is my regular working outfit and it keeps me plenty warm enough." But as he said this, Ralston snapped out: "Yes, sir," to the commander.

"Now, if you'll excuse me, I've got some duties to perform," Allison politely but firmly announced.

Munceford found himself started on the long return journey through the *Bedford*'s intricate interior maze of passages, once again following behind the ensign's broad back. On the way down the shaft from the bridge, he ventured to observe: "The commander is an abrupt cuss, isn't he?"

"He's okay by us," Ralston answered shortly.

They went the rest of the way in silence. When they reached the cabin they found Lieutenant Packer seated at the desk, writing in a black notebook. Pipe-tobacco smoke hung in a blue mist around his head.

"All right, Pete!" Ralston boomed out with a startling return of his former hearty manner, which he evidently reserved entirely for this area. "Quit scribbling complaints about us to your Admiralty and take charge of entertaining our guest. I think he needs a drink."

"A drink?" Munceford exclaimed with hopeful surprise.

Packer put down his pen. "Don't expect too much," he drawled. "This navy isn't trusted with the real stuff. You have a choice of a whisky sour without whisky or a Bloody Mary without blood. What did you think of our old man?"

"Didn't meet him," Munceford answered, then

added with a wry grimace: "But I met a Commander Allison. He could charm the balls off a brass monkey." He immediately sensed a frosting of the two officers' demeanor, but did not care. His ugly mood had returned and his boyish face showed it.

"And what do you think of the ship as a whole?" Packer asked evenly. "Any interesting snap judgments there too?"

Ralston snickered.

"The corridors are clean and all the doors neatly closed, as far as I could see—which wasn't much, on account of the peculiar indirect lighting."

"That's so our eyes can quickly become adjusted to total darkness if we have to go on deck," Packer explained. "Kind of gloomy at first, but you'll get used to it. Let me take you to the wardroom and I'll show you some of the gayer side of life on the *Bedford*." He knocked the ashes out of his pipe and got up from the desk.

"The wardroom is warm and cozy," Ralston pointedly told Munceford. "You won't need your jacket in there." Before hurriedly leaving ahead of them, he gave it a last amused glance. "It's sensational, Ben! It knocked out Commander Allison! . . . See you later."

As Munceford took it off, he swore to himself he would wear his jacket as much as he damned well liked and to hell with Allison.

8.

The *Bedford*'s wardroom was not exactly gay, but it turned out to be at least cheerful in décor and almost spacious. One bulkhead was covered by blue drapes with green and gold palm trees which created an incongruously frivolous departure from the austere warship's atmosphere and the cold, dark sea she was traversing. The opposite bulkhead gave the impression of having been paneled with walnut, but it was actually a very clever kind of plastic coating which created this illusion. The proper naval touch was provided by a framed reproduction of the *Bonhomme Richard* engaging the *Serapis*. There were two long tables, one of which was being set for the evening meal by a steward in a spotless white jacket; he was dropping stainless steel cutlery into the individual compartments of a mahogany rolling-guard fitted over the tablecloth. The surrounding charis were functionally comfortable and padded with a blue vinyl which matched the drapes; a small settee was covered with the same material and next to it was a stand full of very battered magazines. A sideboard held a steaming silver thermos of coffee and two jugs, one containing a red, the other a yellow liquid.

Two lieutenants (J.G.) were seated at the empty table, poring over a large sheet of paper filled with complex electrical diagrams and were so immersed in a deep discussion when Munceford and Packer entered that they did not even look up. But the Englishman went right over to them and started the introductions.

"Gentlemen, I want you to meet Mr. Munceford, the TV reporter who is going to be with us for a week or so. Ben, this is Lieutenants Krindlemeyer and Spitzer, the electronic wizards of the old *Bedford*."

The two officers bobbed to their feet with vacantly surprised expressions. Although one was dark and the other light-complected, they somehow looked identical and both stared myopically at Munceford through identical spectacles. "Where did you come from?" Spitzer asked as he shook hands.

"Do you only know what goes on in the sky and under the sea?" Lieutenant Packer asked. "Aren't you aware there was an eighteen-thousand-ton tanker alongside of us this afternoon?"

"Oh, that! Sure. We picked up the *Tiburon Bay* on the QB-two-R when she was fifty-eight miles off."

"Yes," Krindlemeyer confirmed. "And detected her emissions at over eighty. Do you know at what range she picked *us* up on her radar, Mr. Munceford?"

"No. I was sacked out."

"These ECM chaps live on a pink cloud all of their own," Packer explained, steering Munceford away from them and toward the sideboard. There he introduced him to the steward, whose name was Martin and who regarded him with considerable curiosity.

"Are you going to put us on TV, Mr. Munceford?" he asked.

"Sure am," he answered, not really knowing *how* without a camera.

"Us ordinary guys too?" the steward asked with a sly glance at the officers.

Packer screwed his face into a grimace which was supposed to express a lampoon of British stuffiness. "Well, of course, Martin. This is the democratic American navy, isn't it? Absolutely anything goes."

"I wasn't knocking the system, sir," Martin answered softly and with a twinkle of amusement. He glanced toward Krindlemeyer and Spitzer, who had resumed droning at each other over the diagrams. "It's all the fancy education around here that gets an ordinary mortal down. There was a time when you'd pick up some good dirty jokes in a destroyer's wardroom."

Both Packer and Munceford chuckled.

"By the way, sir, you got some letters," the steward announced in a normal voice and handed Packer four of them from a tray on the sideboard which was stacked with mail.

"Oh, thanks, Martin!" the Englishman casually exclaimed and shoved them into his coat pocket, but not so quickly that he did not take time for a hasty glance over the handwriting on the envelopes. Three of them were in Mumsy's precise penmanship; only one was addressed with Shebeona's bold scrawl. This gave Munceford a peculiar sense of gratification when he noticed it. He did not want that beautiful creature to be a puritanically faithful navy wife or sweetheart whose letters caught up with her sailor boy in carload lots. The near indifference of the recipient was also encouraging. "What's your poison, Ben?" Packer was asking. "The whisky sours are spiked with lemon extract. The Bloody Mary's with tabasco sauce and the stuff Martin puts in his hair."

The steward chucked as he left through the pantry door.

"I'm a whisky drinker, myself," Munceford answered without much enthusiasm over the prospects of an ersatz. "Are you a married man, Pete?"

"Not bloody likely on my salary. Are you?"

"Just getting rid of my third."

"Gad! You must have something to do with the population explosion we hear so much about."

"Hell, no! I'm a pillar to the birth-control industry." This changed his companion's grin to a frown of mild shock.

Lieutenant Packer mixed the drinks by simply dropping an ice cube in each glass and pouring the juices over them, but he did it with a flare and conviction which indicated a determination to kid himself as well as Munceford. Even when he sipped the concoction, Munceford was not entirely sure that it was *nothing* but fruit juice. "Almost fools you," he admitted as they sat down at the opposite end of the table from the oblivious Krindlemeyer and Spitzer.

"What do you mean *almost*?" the Englishman laughed. "Twenty or thirty of these and you'd be in sick bay."

Munceford noticed that he was subconsciously fondling the pocket containing the letters. He wanted to ask whether he was engaged, but instead inquired: "Is it a fact that there isn't a drop of hard stuff aboard? Not even up here in the arctic ocean?"

"Surgeon has some. If it were old Hirschfeld, I'd say you might stand a chance, but I don't know about the new chap. I may throw a fit in a day or two and try him."

"I bunked with Commander Porter on the *Tiburon Bay*. He's pretty straight-laced. If Hirschfeld was so cooperative, why did you get rid of him?"

Packer reacted with a sudden frown and an icy: "What do you mean by that?"

"Well . . . nothing in particular. I only thought—"

"Lieutenant Hirschfeld is a closed subject," the Englishman interrupted with surprising vehemence. "Forget it."

Munceford blinked, sighed, stared down into his glass and wished to God in Heaven it would miraculously change into one-hundred-proof bourbon. If ever he had needed a real drink, it was now. He thought of the bottle he had tossed out of the porthole of the *Tiburon Bay* just to needle Porter, now lost forever on a dark, empty sea a hundred miles astern. Perhaps it would drift ashore on the Greenland coast where some Eskimo would pick it up and get roaring drunk. He wished he were that Eskimo right now. He wished he were anywhere but on this destroyer.

Lieutenant Packer sensed that he might have inadvertently betrayed a secret which was not suspected, that he had unfairly been rude to Munceford, and suddenly became very flustered about it. He glanced up the table toward Krindlemeyer and Spitzer, who remained preoccupied with their own electronic problems, then toward the pantry door, which was swinging silently back and forth on its hinges as the *Bedford* breasted the swells. "I'm sorry, Ben," he said with an earnest whisper. "I know it was accidental, but don't ask any questions about Hirschfeld on this ship. He's a devil of a sore subject. Had a big row with the skipper."

"Is Finlander so hard to get along with?" Munceford asked without bothering to lower his voice.

Captain Finlander is one of the finest officers I have ever known," Packer answered, also raising his voice to a normal level and with a certain defiance in it. "And that includes my own Royal Navy, which is going some, believe me."

"Well, okay."

There had been no reaction from Krindlemeyer and Spitzer, who could have heard the last remarks. Martin came in, distributed some ketchup bottles in slots of the dinner table's rolling-guard and left. Munceford sipped his fruit juice and noticed that Packer's right hand was still nervously resting on the pocket containing the letters. "Look, Pete," he said. "You don't have to entertain me. Go ahead and read your letters."

"Oh, they can wait."

"Hell, go ahead! You haven't heard from Shebeona for weeks!"

Packer's jaw dropped open. "How do you know her name?" he stammered.

Munceford felt himself flushing a bright scarlet. He bit his lips, rocked back in his chair, then pounded his fist on the table and exclaimed: "Oh, damn!"

Spitzer looked up from his electronic diagrams, but from the expression on his face it was hard to tell whether he had been startled by the profanity or was staring into space at some imaginary blackboard filled with phantom equations.

"How do you know her name?" the Englishman demanded again, this time with a sharp insistence.

"Pete . . . I lay down on your bunk this afternoon. I felt the frame under the pillow. So I looked. So shoot me. So I'm sorry!"

"I'd damned well think you would be. That sort of thing isn't done, really. Very bad manners." His voice was very low, very even and very angry.

"I said I'm sorry, Pete. Now go ahead and read your letters."

"Thanks. I think I will." Lieutenant Packer got up from his seat opposite Munceford, moved to another chair at the center of the table, twisted his back to him and in a moment was a thousand miles away as he opened the first letter with restrained agitation and began to read. It was from Shebeona and only filled half the page.

Munceford drained his insipid drink and, after finally tearing his eyes away from the letter, stared smugly at the palm trees on the drapes, which swayed with a peculiar realism as the roll of the *Bedford* rippled the material. The steward padded in on silent feet, deposited some butter dishes on the dinner table and left. The turbines hummed softly and their vibration set up a momentary resonance in a cup full of coffee spoons on the sideboard, making them buzz with a thin metallic sound. The murmur of Krindlemeyer's and Spitzer's whispered conversation suddenly seemed almost loud and Munceford could not help overhearing it.

"You've got to remember that when you interrupt an inductive circuit, switches will create arcs," one of them was saying, his nose almost touching the sheet of diagrams. "That would give you peaks and craters in the contacts."

"Right, but I think this is a matter of contact bounce," the other answered. "There's a sequential repeater on that circuit with a rate of ten milliseconds. The operating time is considerably longer than the bounce, and that's what produces the noise in the system."

"And, Jesus, we can't allow any noise on this ship," Munceford muttered between clenched teeth. He got up and took his empty glass to the sideboard, where he debated with himself whether to switch over to the pitcher containing the red juice. The yellow had left an unpleasant sour-sweet taste in his mouth. He was standing there contemplating the problem with a morose indifference when Lieutenant Commander Porter entered the wardroom and saw him.

"Hello, Ben. Having withdrawal pains?" he quipped with a sadistic smirk.

"You tell me, Doc," Munceford shot back. "I've been seeing blondes and palm trees, and it hurts right *here.*" He patted his rump.

"I prescribe a bland diet and plenty of fresh ocean air," Porter answered, reaching for the red jug. "The captain has asked me to tell you he will see you in his cabin now."

"God! And here I am reeking of fruit juice! Oh, well—I might as well have *everybody* aboard on my tail. Where do I go?"

"Turn left outside this door, stagger twenty feet along the passageway and knock on the door marked

CAPTAIN," the surgeon directed him dryly, then turned toward the other officers and loudly introduced himself: "Hello, gentlemen. I am Commander Porter, your new medical officer."

Lieutenant Peter Packer looked up with a start and jumped to his feet, quickly shoving his letters into a pocket. As Munceford left the wardroom, he saw Krindlemeyer and Spitzer rise and briefly come out of their technical trance with the same vaguely amazed expression they had shown when they met him.

9.

Captain Erik J. Finlander was a man of medium build but with an unusually large head—or perhaps it was the very heavy jaw and pronounced brows which made it appear that way. Or maybe the thin neck with the very prominent arteries, one of which was crossed by the scar of what must once have been a nearly fatal wound. His hair was cropped short and the color and texture of a steel brush; the eyebrows were the same and joined together over the bridge of a nose which had been broken a long time ago. His eyes were the greenish-gray of the North Atlantic, set deep under heavy lids and among many little wrinkles etched by a combination of humor, temper and driving winds. He was ugly. He was also handsome. And when he smiled, all the hardness in his face vanished—except in the eyes, which merely mellowed from a cold gleam to a mischievous twinkle.

"Very glad to meet you at last, Mr. Munceford," he exclaimed in a voice which had a quiet, husky quality. "I wanted us to get together much sooner, but this has been kind of a busy day."

"That's okay, Captain. Quite okay." Munceford answered, wondering whether or not this was the sort of looking man he had expected.

"I also want to apologize for the shaking up you got on the highline," Finlander told him, still keeping a strong grip on his hand. "Was that an expensive camera you lost?"

"About five hundred, new," Munceford lied, managing to sound casual.

Captain Finlander winced and transferred his grip to Munceford's elbow, steering him into the middle of his cabin. It was not as large as Munceford had expected, but a luxurious touch was provided by the same plastic "paneling" used in the wardroom, and by a bulkhead-to-bulkhead carpet of deep red color. Munceford was surprised to find another man standing at the desk and his first impression was that he was a civilian. He wore a black leather jacket without any insignia, and his trousers were tucked into a pair of non-regulation black rubber boots. When he looked up from the papers he was examining, the face was either that of a young sixty- or old forty-year-old; it was heavily lined, hard and somewhat melancholy.

"I'd like you to meet Commodore Wolfgang Schrepke of the DBM," Finlander said. When he saw Munceford's blank expression, he smiled and added: "That's the Deutches Bundes Marine—West German Navy to you."

"How do you do?" Schrepke said, giving him a quick, hard handshake. He spoke with a harsh German accent.

"The commodore and I have a matter to discuss for a minute or two," Finlander apologized pleasantly. "In the meanwhile, have yourself a drink and sit down." He pointed toward a chest on which stood a tray with two pitchers—one containing red, the other gold-colored fluid.

This time Munceford picked the Bloody Mary and sat down in a chair to wait. He felt himself hopefully impressed by Finlander, but confused by the presence of the German. The rank of commodore he associated with yacht clubs and had a vague recollection that it had been discontinued in the American navy since World War II. But he remembered it was just below admiral—more rank than Finlander! Yet the man looked like a chief bosun of a freighter. After his low conversation with the captain was ended—it was about something they called low-frequency returns—he put on a battered naval officer's cap with gold on the visor, excused himself with a polite military formality and stalked out of the cabin.

Finlander put the papers away in a drawer of his desk and came over to pour himself a drink. He seemed to be closely appraising Munceford and also reading his puzzled thoughts. "Commodore Schrepke is an anti-submarine warfare expert with NATO naval forces," he explained after the door had shut behind the German. "You have heard of him, of course? No? Well, during the war he was one of Dönitz's ace U-boat commanders. Sank over two hundred thousand tons of Allied shipping. It's funny how things turn out, but we find it's probable that I depth-charged him while escorting a convoy to Murmansk. Now here we are sixteen years later, serving together *against* the Russians."

"That *is* a story," Munceford said, really impressed.

"Yes, but I don't know that it should be publicized. A lot of our Congressmen and their constituents are sensitive about foreigners serving on our ships, especially Germans. Sometimes I don't think we are at all ready for the NATO concept. Yet we've *got* to make it work. Frankly, I myself still have an ingrained dislike of all U-boat crews, a hangover from my younger days when I fought them with more passion than science. But now I control my feelings, get along with men like Schrepke and try to do a strictly professional job." He raised his drink of tomato juice, his eyes boring into Munceford over the rim of the glass. "Cheers! ... Well, now ... back to the matter of the lost camera. I suppose, like all press people, you've got cases full of assorted replacements, so you'll be able to carry on."

"As a matter of fact, no," Munceford answered, then found himself lying to Finlander in spite of an uneasy feeling that the man could see right through him. "I accidentally smashed my spare aboard the *Tiburon Bay*. Didn't even bother to bring it with me to the *Bedford*."

"Then to put it exactly, you are in a fix," Finlander exclaimed, his bristling eyebrows curving into a Mephisto expression.

"Can't shoot any movies. But I have a tape recorder, which means I can produce something for radio, at least."

Captain Finlander had been about to sit down, but now he went back to the desk, dialed a number on the telephone and ordered whoever answered: "Send Yeoman Pinelli to the captain's quarters at once, please." Almost the instant he hung up, the ship's PA system could be heard paging that individual. As Finlander came back to sit down, he said: "The destroyer service is nothing if not versatile, so we'll probably be able to put you back in business, Munceford. In the meanwhile, give me your first impressions of my ship."

Munceford remembered what Commander Allison had said about the *Bedford* and assumed it would be pleasing to her captain. "She's damn near as big as a cruiser. Much more impressive than the little DE I once did a story on."

"My first command was a DE during World War II," Finlander informed him. "I built a reputation as a U-boat killer, you know, and did it with that type of ship, one of the best classes ever designed. So don't be overly impressed by size, which in itself means little. For instance, not far from where we are steaming right now lies the sunken remains of the largest battle cruiser ever built, the H.M.S. *Hood*. A single hit from the

Bismarck blew her to pieces in 1942 during the first minute of the hour she and her two-thousand-man crew were supposed to justify their existence. Incidentally, and to speak of strange coincidences which seem to devil the *Bedford*, a son of one of the *Hood*'s officers is aboard this ship—Lieutenant P. L. M. Packer of the Royal Navy."

"I'll be damned!" Munceford exclaimed. "Why, I'm sharing a cabin with him. Seems like a—"

"Yes, yes . . . he's a good boy," Finlander interrupted him with a certain impatience. "The Packers have been in the British navy since they stopped the Armada. Between then and the *Bismarck* action, not a single one has ever found a dry grave for himself—something which would worry me if I were superstitious. Well, anyway, the point I was trying to make before getting sidetracked was that the most impressive thing about the *Bedford* is not her size, but the sophistication of her weaponry, which gives her the contradictory characteristics of specialization and flexibility. She's an engineering marvel and a scientific miracle; she is also a cranky and complex bitch at times, which means she can still make an old destroyerman feel at home. All right—what's your impression of the crew?"

Munceford decided to try to be candid. "The few I've met are kind of puzzling characters. I'm mostly impressed by their absence and silence."

Captain Finlander laughed softly. "Well, for one thing, we have automation to eliminate much of the manpower which used to be necessary to operate a ship of this size. For another, we are hunters—*stalking* kind of hunters—who track by ear a foe who is also intently listening for *us*. To be quiet and stealthy becomes second nature under the circumstances; I deliberately instill this in my men. The fact that we are fighting a nebulous cold war without decisively obtainable tactical objectives has a lot to do with creating some puzzling characters among us. Take myself, for instance. . . ." He leaned forward in his chair, thrusting his face toward Munceford, who found himself staring back almost as though hypnotized.

"As captain, I must key all my men to an intense fighting pitch and keep them keyed that way through hundreds of boring sweeps through an ocean most of them can't even see, only feel through bruised and wretched muscles. Then, if we get a contact, I must key them to an even finer pitch so they hang on, close up and drive in for a kill they know will end in nothing but the dull mockery of an anti-climax. The same man who extracted every last measure of their skills, who numbed their minds to the fact that this is nothing but a sadistic game, must belay all their efforts with a few bellicose words over the ship's PA. 'Well done, men! You've given those Commies down there an inkling of what it is like to die in a submarine. Now stand down from General Quarters. The movie in enlisted mess tonight will be Liz Taylor in *Butterfield 8.*' . . . The truth really is that the Commie submariners have learned more from the operation than we have and will be twice as hard to pin down next time. But we've got to oblige them with this training, and that's the sort of thing which strains the minds of officers and thinking men on destroyers in this cold-war zone—understand?"

Munceford was not sure that he did, although Finlander was eloquent to the point of being spellbinding. "I get the idea that there's a lot more Russian submarine activity here than is generally realized."

"It's a free ocean," the captain answered with a bitter chuckle. "Technically, they can come and go as they please, cold war or no cold war. So can we. Contrary to certain scuttlebutt, we aren't out to spy on each other's missile ranges or atomic tests. That kind of work can be done cheaper and easier by one man in a U-2 type of aircraft. It is DEW-line and NORAD emissions Soviet subs are recording and checking out to help them penetrate our defenses when the time comes. I also suspect scouting and ranging of submarine missile-firing positions. These are objectives worth tremendous risks. They are worth killing over."

"You *actually* attack them?"

Those wiry eyebrows arranged themselves into a sly expression. "Do you mean officially?"

"I mean . . . does anybody get hurt, Captain Finlander?"

"Fear hurts. Unrelenting tension becomes a physical pain. Uncertainty and frustration can turn into a crippling agony. But I suppose that to you, actual killing is the ultimate hurt, so I can truthfully answer: *no*, nobody has been hurt—so far." His eyes left Munceford's face for a moment, flicking to the gyro-repeater and clock attached to the bulkhead above his desk. "Where is Pinelli?" he asked with sudden irritation. "It's been four minutes since I called him."

Munceford was trying to correlate in his mind the implications of what Finlander had told him. "Jesus! I may be on to a real hot story for a change!" he exclaimed. "What's going on out here will come as a hell of a shock to a lot of people."

Finlander's eyes snapped into him. "I'm giving you background material, *not* a story, Munceford. This is not a piece of political taffy to be pulled and fingered by pundits and politicians, like they are doing with Berlin and Laos. Those items have at least a certain sticky elasticity. *This* is the hard-core, *war* part of the cold war. Here we clash in the privacy of a black, empty ocean with no audience but our own conscience; both parties want to keep it that way because the stakes are such that no compromise is possible. If you doubt me, then ask yourself what the United States has left if its DEW-line and NORAD systems are cracked. What have the Soviets got if they never crack them? So both parties need secrecy to protect their freedom of maneuvering against each other. So don't expect to run wild with your story."

Munceford hunched down in his chair. "You feel, like Commander Allison, that I shouldn't be here, Captain?" he countered defensively.

Finlander laughed, but with a cold light in his eyes. "Did Buck hurt your feelings already?" he asked. "Well, you've got to understand that an exec who is privy to too many of his captain's darkest secrets becomes tense and cautious with strangers. His responsibilities make him more conscious of simple, tactical requirements than subtleties of strategy. And, believe it or not, Munceford, your being aboard is a matter of strategy."

Munceford blinked. "What?"

"Take my word for it and leave it at that. Go anywhere you like on my ship except in the CIC, where I'd want you escorted. Please be careful on deck and only move out there when the crew are around. You'll find that we've got a lot in common with the subs in that we travel buttoned up most of the time. Too cold outside, for one thing; too rough, for another." He reacted to a knock on the door, glanced at the clock and shouted: "Enter!"

A yeoman came in, saluted and remained stiffly at attention as he announced himself: "Yeoman Pinelli reporting to the captain as ordered, sir." He was much out of breath.

"Good evening, Pinelli," the captain greeted him with a pleasant gruffness. "What took you so long? Were you up in the crow's-nest?"

"In the shower, sir."

"In that case, you did well," Finlander told him, bringing relief to his worried face. "I'm sorry to break into your off-watch period, Pinelli, but it seems Mr.

Munceford has already managed to lose or break all his movie cameras. Do you have any we can spare?"

"We have three, sir. Two Model Seventy-H's and an Arri."

Finlander turned to Munceford. "Seems you have a choice. Which would you like?"

"The Seventy-H is fine," Munceford told him. He would have preferred an Arri, which was a two-thousand-dollar camera, but he was afraid he would show his ignorance by being unable to operate it.

"All right, Pinelli, let him have one of those. And I want to you to assist Mr. Munceford in every way you can. Maybe you will learn something from him." With a very subtle gleam of malice, he informed Munceford: "Yeoman Pinelli is the *Bedford*'s official photographer, but he only gets pictures of ASROC launchings, the inside of boilers, hedgehog patterns and dull things like that. I hope you'll be patient with him."

Munceford instantly knew that this ordinary-looking sailor was probably a very skilled professional photographer. This put him on his guard because he was a rather sloppy one himself and sensitive about it. But he said: "I'm sure we'll get along fine and I'll be glad to show him any tricks I know." The yeoman gave him a somewhat baleful look, and after the captain had dismissed him, Munceford observed: "You certainly have a variety of talents aboard."

Finlander nodded his big head. "Time was when a destroyer could be run by nothing but a gang of ham-fisted sailors with their guts in gimbals. Today, men like that would be about as effective as a crew of Vikings plucked out of the tenth century."

"Still takes guts, I bet," Munceford injected.

"Sure, sure! Listen to me. I can't give you much more time." Captain Finlander seemed bent upon delivering a monologue, speaking with a quiet intensity which discouraged the conversational form. "Something less than forty per cent of my complement are seamen in the strict sense of the term. The rest could staff the science department of a medium-sized college. Take your pick of subjects! Thermodynamics, microwave analysis, submarine ultrasonics, computer circuitry, guidance systems, dielectric telemetry, doppler and inertial navigation systems, meteorology, physical oceanography—I have specialists in all these fields." His face darkened and he added beneath his breath, more to himself than to Munceford: "I even had a psychiatrist to muddle in all that brainpower."

Munceford almost asked him if he were referring to Lieutenant Hirschfeld, but remember Packer's warning in the nick of time and said nothing. Finlander continued:

"We carry a million dollars' worth of education on a ship like this, and have to fight for every nickel of it. For the first time in history, the navy has to contend with presss gangs from colleges and industry who are out to pick off our people for their own classrooms and labs. Instead of plying them with booze in waterfront dives, they lure them into fancy hotel suites and cajole them with promises of wealth, status and fringe benefits. They get Annapolis men to resign their commissions after the navy has put them through M.I.T. post-graduate courses; they secretly sign up enlisted technicians with a year still to go on their hitches. We can't afford to lose these men, especially since they are three times as hard to train for the navy as for any civilian job, where all they've got to do is to sit on their rumps with a slide rule or computer. *We've* got to make halfway decent seamen and fighters out of them, too. It's very hard to find men with all three qualifications: fighter, seaman and scientist. For instance, after our last patrol I had to ship home a genius on sonar gear, simply because he could not stop vomiting all over the Combat Information Center when the going got rough—which it inevitably does up here. Then I had a guidance-systems man with an IQ of one-sixty-three who got to brooding about warheads and started infecting his division with pacifistic ideas. He had to go too. If I can't keep a fighting spirit in this ship, or keep her scientific gear operating at peak efficiency, or keep her steaming through anything this ocean can throw at me—then, for any one of those reasons, I might as well open her seacocks and scuttle her. Are you beginning to grasp some of the problems, Munceford?"

Munceford wagged his head in a noncommittal motion. "Sort of—but how do you keep going with all those troubles, Captain?"

"The book recommends to instill pride of service and a strong sense of duty," Finlander answered him with a wrinkling of his nose. "It also says to give the men frequent current-affairs talks so they know what it's all about. That sort of thing doesn't even stem the tears of a reservist crying to return to his junior vice-presidency. A professional needs something far more concrete to dedicate him. The brutal truth is that nothing will do it as well as a *real* enemy challenging him to fight. And that's where I hold an advantage over commanders in other cold-war areas. We're not here to make faces at Commies over a wall; we're not in a base area indoctrinating simpleminded natives into the complex savagery of modern guerrilla tactics; we're not sitting in an air-conditioned Florida blockhouse trying to shoot a bigger hole in the moon, weather permitting. Here we *hunt* Russians. Here we have our enemy and, more than accepting his challenge, go after him without any inhibitions of containment policies or technical inferiorities. We miss the kill, but have become addicted to the chase, and I admit that I shamelessly use its exhilaration to inspire my crew." He stopped and stared thoughtfully at Munceford through half-closed eyes which seemed to smolder beneath the heavy lids. "Are you shocked?" he asked.

"Well, surprised, sir," Munceford answered and winced a little over finding himself "sirring" Finlander. He had always made it a point to address *all* officers on an equal basis. "And I wonder if this won't provoke a real attack one day; if somebody won't lose their temper and pull a trigger."

"Oh, you mean that old saw about somebody accidentally starting a war?" the captain countered with a contemptuous flick of his head. "We're not amateurs on either side, acting impetuously or subject to fits of temper. Nor do we have any red telephone or a bunch of keys which serially unlock the firing switches. But the whole business is so inherently calculated and technical that it is naturally kept under control at all times."

"And really only a game, after all," Munceford said with an unconvinced laugh. "Maybe the Commies get a kick out of bitching you too." He immediately sensed that he had said the wrong thing.

Finlander's eyes narrowed and the scar on his throat began to pulse visibly, betraying an inner pressure. But his voice remained even. "Bitching me?" he repeated. "I don't know what has been whispered to you about that. I make no secret over being concerned over *one* Russian sub. But bitching implies unrequited frustration." He paused with lips pressed together into a thin, hard line, and Munceford waited breathlessly, suspecting he had inadvertently touched a sore point which was about to be revealed. He was not expecting what came next.

"Have you read *Moby Dick?*" the captain asked.

"Uh . . . well, I saw the movie. All about whaling and . . ." He received such a coldly contemptuous look that it stopped him in mid-sentence.

"It's not *all* about whaling. Well, never mind." He

twisted impatiently in his chair and suddenly seemed quite uninterested in continuing the discussion. When a knock on the cabin door broke the painful silence between them, it was with relief that he shouted: "Enter!"

It was Commodore Schrepke, and behind him a steward was carrying a tray full of food. Finlander got up and exclaimed: "Dinnertime already? Good. I'm starved. But first have yourself a quick drink, Commodore."

Munceford thought that he was about to be invited to have dinner in the captain's cabin, but as the steward passed him to put the tray down on the desk, he saw it only contained service for two. Finlander quickly dispelled any remaining notions that he had been accepted on such intimate terms. "If you'll forgive me, Munceford," he told him, "the commodore and I will dine alone together in order to go over the day's operations. I'm sure you'll find some interesting company in the wardroom."

Munceford got up. "Yeah-okay. Thanks for your time, Captain."

"Quite all right. We will talk some more after you get settled." He turned to Schrepke, who was pouring himself some juice. "You should tell Mr. Munceford some of your U-boat experiences, Commodore. It would help him understand the over-all picture of ASW operations."

Schrepke glanced at Munceford and it was as if he decided then and there that he wanted no part of him. "There are several books on the subject," he said with a forbidding politeness. "My own experiences are of no interest to the American press, thank you." As he spoke, he took a small silver hip flask from his pocket and blatantly proceeded to spike his drink with its contents. Munceford stared in amazement at this flagrant violation of American navy regulations, then shifted his eyes to Captain Finlander, expecting a blistering reaction from him. The heavy eyebrows were drawn together in an ominous line and the scar on the throat pulsed a dull red; but he said nothing.

Schrepke raised his glass, exclaimed *"Prosit,"* drained the drink with a grimace indicating a pleasurable pain, looked right through Munceford and caught the expression on Finlander's face. "I presume, Captain, that Lieutenant Hirschfeld's medical prescriptions are still valid even though he himself has been removed from his practice aboard your ship." There was an unmistakable note of irony in his voice.

The steward fumbled a plate, barely managing a noisy retrieve against the edge of the desk.

Captain Finlander glared at the German, then wheeled away from him without answering. He grasped Munceford by the arm and ushered him toward the door. "You will find that submariners who've been overly hunted develop permanent instabilities in their nervous systems," he said so loudly that it was obviously intended as a direct jab at Schrepke. "So killing them isn't always necessary. . . . I will see you tomorrow. Good night."

The cabin door slammed shut and Munceford found himself alone in the dim red glow of the passageway. He stood there for a moment, listening, half expecting to hear an explosion inside the captain's cabin. None came. So he shuffled off in the direction of the wardroom, bracing himself against the bulkheads as he tried to balance his movements with those of the destroyer.

Munceford found eight officers in the wardroom who were already halfway through their supper. Lieutenant Peter Packer was the only familiar face and he made the introductions so quickly that the names hardly impressed themselves on his memory: "Ensign Lissholm . . . Commander Franklin . . . Lieutenants Har-

well . . . Petersen . . . Goodfellow . . . Brubeck . . .
Samuels . . ."

None did more than nod or mumble a barely com-
prehensible word of welcome through a mouthful of
roast beef and mashed potatoes. There was a minor
confusion on one side of the table as everybody had to
squeeze down in order to make room for him. Nobody
tried to engage him in conversation, but neither did
they talk among themselves; most of them were occupied with reading mail delivered by the *Tiburon Bay*
while eating at the same time. Steward Martin put
down a plate in front of Munceford which was heaped
with meat and vegetables, all washed in a miniature
surf of gravy activated by the roll of the *Bedford*. The
lieutenant next to him automatically passed salt, pepper and a sticky bottle of Worcestershire. The commander giggled softly over something amusing in his
letter. The ensign squeezed up the last of his gravy
with a piece of bread, then sat back and began picking
his teeth, one hand shielding the other according to
best Annapolis etiquette. He watched as Munceford
tried to separate a piece of fat from a piece of lean,
and finally asked with offhand interest: "Was the chow
any good on the *Tiburon Bay?*"

"What? . . . Oh, sure. Pretty fair."

"113 serves steak or roast beef three times a week."

"Fine. I was on a sub for a while and they served all
the steak we could eat."

The ensign said: "They need it," and terminated
that conversation by turning his attention upon a dish
of chocolate ice cream which the steward put before
him. Nobody asked Munceford about his experiences
on a sub, and for a moment he was tempted to announce loudly that when they did not eat steak, submariners lived on prairie oysters. But instead he filled
his mouth with food, masticating as silently as the rest,
his thoughts going back to his session with Captain

Finlander. He had not really made up his mind whether he liked the captain or not; he was a strange, yet compelling personality. But at least he *talked*. At least he seemed to care about Munceford being present on the *Bedford*. What was it he had said? ". . . *believe it or not, Munceford, your being aboard is a matter of strategy*." What had he meant by that? Some sinister implication behind it, as there was behind some other things he had said?

After a while Lieutenant Packer announced to nobody in particular that he had to attend to some decoding and left without having given his cabin mate a glance or a word since the cursory introductions; he was evidently still sore over the incident with Shebeona's photograph. One by one, the other officers finished their meals, folded up their letters and departed too. The commander was the last one to leave, and before passing out the door, he stopped a moment and looked back at Munceford. "Which broadcasting company did you say you work for?" he asked.

"I'm free-lance."

The commander frowned. "But you're on a definite assignment, aren't you?"

"Well . . . NBC has expressed a lot of interest."

"Uh-huh. Good night."

Munceford found himself alone in the wardroom with a dish of melting ice cream and a cup of tepid coffee, the commander's question having channeled his thoughts into fresh worries. An assistant director of NBC's news department *had* expressed interest, but with certain reservations. The story had to show some fresh action scenes from a destroyer on arctic patrol, it had to give a clear insight into the operational problems, it had to contain human interest and drama. Otherwise, the best he could hope for was the sale of stock footage at the going rate of $1.25 per foot—perhaps $250 as against $5,000 for a feature. How could he meet those requirements if Captain Finlander insisted upon the secrecy of the operation? How could he get human interest and drama if men like Commodore Schrepke were evasive and uncooperative? How Nancy would laugh if she could see him in this predicament! Yet Finlander obviously wanted *some* kind of story. What? Well, he'd have to stay on the good side of that man, no matter how difficult and strange he turned out to be.

Munceford drained his cup and left the wardroom to pick his way through the empty passageways toward his cabin, which he found only after making several wrong turns. Packer was not there and the cubicle was as lonely and oppressive as ever. Neatly laid out on his bunk were a regulation navy arctic parka and, on top of it, a shiny new Model 70-H camera, complete with three lenses in its turret. Munceford stared for a moment at this evidence of the *Bedford*'s enormous efficiency, but without any particular admiration or gratitude. He listened tensely to the silence beyond the whine of the turbines and hiss of the ventilator, then turned his attention to Packer's bunk, which was once again immaculate in taut perfection. Leaning down, he surreptitiously slipped his hand beneath the pillow, cautiously probing under it with his fingers. There was nothing there. Shebeona had been removed to safety by her jealous lover and Munceford found himself thwarted in this innocent game of cuckoldry. He had hoped to go to bed with her exquisite beauty refreshed in his mind's eye, but instead there would only be Finlander, whose face remained indelibly burned into it.

10.

The heavy overcast cleared during the night, and by 0500, when the cooks sleepily manned their galley, the *Bedford* was steaming over a glass-calm ocean which mirrored a fantastic dome of starlit space. There was no moon, but northern lights rippled across the heavens with curtains of cold blue fire which cast their luminescence over the ship, sharply etching her on a silent course twixt abyss and infinity. Her tall mast described lazy circles around the constellation of Corona Borealis; the stars also touched the sea around her and broke into sprays of dancing diamonds in her wake. On the bridge the quartermaster of the watch came out of the wheelhouse to check the thermometer for his hourly weather entry in the log; it stood at two degrees above zero. He also checked from a respectful distance the figure crouching by the windscreen, the same figure which had been there the hour before, in exactly the same position, not facing up and outward like a man entranced by the arctic night, but staring downward at the black waters sweeping by the hull beneath him. Black leather glistened with a faint sheen where it was stretched tight over broad, hunched shoulders. In these dark hours before dawn Commodore Wolfgang Schrepke could always be found here, unless the bridge was so swept by freezing spume as to become untenable even for him. No duty called him here; no officer of his rank stood a regular watch. He came only for his own troubled reasons to find a brooding solitude with the sea, to stare into it like an insomniac contemplating a cemetery which holds too many of his departed kin.

At 0600 reveille was piped through the ship's PA and men began stirring inside her. Deep down in her lower vitals, where the biting cold of the arctic ocean was replaced by a humid heat radiating from roaring boilers, Fireman Second Class Bert Meggs checked dials and made a minor adjustment to the steam manifolds to compensate for the hot-water requirements of shipmates taking their morning showers. In the galley the first couple of hundred pancakes were coming off the griddles to be stacked by messmen in the steam tables; fumes containing the tingling aroma of frying bacon were sucked into the ventilators and wafted into the freezing outside air, where they rose on a following breeze and stimulated the nostrils of Seaman Willy Kolinsky, crowded high up in the crow's nest. He shifted his cramped position and pressed himself harder against the heater coil which kept the *Bedford*'s masthead lookout from freezing to death in his lonely perch. Above him the radar antenna whirred softly as it turned, sweeping the night with its sensory microwaves. The northern lights had faded, but no trace of dawn had as yet replaced their glow, and the night enveloped the ship, darker than ever. Ensign Ralston emerged from the wheelhouse with a sextant and unerringly sought out Regulus among the sparkling myriads above; Commodore Schrepke finally moved away from his isolation in the wing and stepped up behind the young officer, watching him for a moment as he took his three-star sight. Then the German retreated to his cabin and Ralston went into the navigation office to calculate his position and check it against the observation made a half-hour earlier by Lieutenant Harwell.

The watch changed at 0745 and only then was there a faint lightening on the eastern horizon which began washing out the stars hanging low in that quadrant of the sky. The thermometer on the bridge now registered exactly zero degrees, and because of this extreme cold there was no muster or inspection on deck this morning. Only a detail of gunners showed up to traverse the turrets and launchers in order to make certain they had not become frozen in their tracks during the night. In the chartroom Commander Allison sipped coffee with the OOD while listening on the monitoring circuit of the communicator system as the weapons-control officer checked all his stations from the CIC. Captain Finlander finished a spartan breakfast in the isolation of his cabin, put on his white duffel coat and the long-billed fisherman's cap with its tiny silver eagle and went up on the bridge to watch the dawning. From there he descended into the tense twilight world of the CIC and silently joined Lieutenant Spitzer's vigil behind the sonar operators, listening with them to the hollow pings and watching the sterile green glow of PPI scopes in their consoles. After a while he shifted his position to the main search-radar scanner and saw the sweeper activate incadescent rows of blobs to the west—the return from mountain ranges on the Greenland coast thirty miles away. Up in the crow's-nest a new lookout, Seaman First Class Robert W. Jones, also spotted those mountains, but as a jagged white line appearing with startling suddenness on the horizon where snowy peaks were kindled by the first streak of dawn and reflected back its light. Jones picked up the phone and dutifully reported his sighting to the bridge, seventy feet below him. In the Communications Center three radio operators sat at their sets listening to a cacophony of jumbled Morse signals, their trained ears separating the vital from the trivial; near them Lieutenant Peter Packer, R.N., tuned a receiver to the commercial ship-to-shore RT frequency and suddenly found himself listening to a voice speaking English with a thick north-country accent. He listened with a wistful sentimentality as the man talked about a poor catch of codfish he was bringing back to Grimsby. In his cabin Ben Munceford woke up, found himself as alone as ever, rolled out of his bunk and wondered if he were too late for breakfast.

At 0921 the sun at last cracked the rim of the sea to the east and reluctantly rose out of it, a pale burnished disk without the slightest trace of warming red. For a long time some of the larger stars successfully defied it to extinguish their light. In the crow's-nest Seaman Jones adjusted his binoculars and carefully studied the horizon ahead of the *Bedford*. He had caught some flashes out there, something like weak blinker signals, but he quickly identified the source and telephoned the bridge to report drifting ice ahead. It gave him great satisfaction to do this because he knew that neither radar nor sonar had been able to detect this hazard in spite of all their intricate technological gobbledygook—a good pair of eyes was still needed. In the wheelhouse Captain Finlander discussed the report with the OOD, Lieutenant Harwell.

"That will be floe ice drifting down from north of us," the captain said. "With this light wind, it's certain to be scattered."

"Shall I change course four or five degrees right, sir?"

Finlander frowned. "If our mission was merely to steam along with a passenger liner, that would be an excellent idea." He waited for some reaction which did not come quick enough to suit him. "What *is* our mission, Mr. Harwell?"

"To patrol for Russian submarine activity, sir."

"And if you were a Russian submarine commander operating under these sea conditions, what would you do, Mr. Harwell?"

"I would use the ice to screen my movements, sir."

"Correct. As a matter of fact, don't you think you

might move closer to the Greenland coast so as to confuse any tracking destroyer's radar and sonar sweeps?"

"Yes, sir."

"Then act accordingly, Mr. Harwell."

"You mean move closer to the coast, sir?"

"I suggest at least ten miles closer. I also suggest a series of maximum-effect sonar sweeps."

"Every fifteen minutes, sir?"

Finlander sighed like a teacher priming a difficult student. "Why every fifteen minutes? To help the Russian set his schedule accordingly for silent running? Come on, Mr. Harwell! Try being a little unpredictable about it." Finlander flashed him a condescending grin, pulled up the collar of his white duffel coat and went out on the bridge. Lieutenant Harwell ordered the helmsman to bring the *Bedford* to a new heading which put the distant line of snow-capped mountains right over her bow. Ten minutes later he alerted the ship for a maximum-effect sonar sweep and signaled the engine room to stop engines. While the destroyer coasted silently over the lightly ruffled swells, Lieutenant Spitzer and his sonarmen intently listened and watched their PPI screens. But the surrounding deep remained as silent as it is legendarily supposed to be.

Inside the crow's-nest a twenty-year-old seaman second-class nicknamed Squarehead (John Thorbjornsen was his improbable real name) had relieved Jones, who climbed halfway down the tube-like inside of the mainmast, there to steal a quick smoke. (This was the only safe place on the *Bedford* to steal a smoke on watch.) Squarehead felt the faint vibration of the engines fade out and took the opportunity to rest the objectives of his binoculars against the glass of the windshield, thus steadying them for a minute examination of the horizon. As he peered, his body remained relaxed, his jaws masticating rhythmically on a wad of gum. His sharp young eyes, made tenfold more efficient by the powerful lenses, picked out crevasses and faults in the glaciers of the Greenland mountains and noticed the shimmering line of ice beneath them; the ice looked as though it hugged the coast, but he knew it stretched out several miles beyond. Shifting the binoculars slightly, he picked another piece of the horizon for careful scrutiny. Then another. Then the jaws suddenly stopped and went slack. His body did not visibly tense, but he held his breath for about ten seconds, took his eyes from the binoculars and blinked them a couple of times before looking again. His pupils contracted to black pinpoints against the brilliant glare of the morning sunlight on the sea. He was watching a pair of skua gulls persistently circling a spot nearly two miles away But his interest was not that of a birdwatcher. Rather he was trying to make out what interested *them*. Finally he communicated his suspicions to Seaman Jones, perched in the shaft below him.

"I think I got something."

"What?"

"Garbage."

Jones quickly tamped out his cigarette in the palm of his gloved hand and slipped the butt into a pocket of his parka so as to leave no evidence of his misdemeanor. Then he sprang up the rungs and squeezed himself into the crow's-nest with Squarehead. "Where away?" he asked.

Space was so cramped that there was no longer room to wield the binoculars. "Zero-two-zero—about two miles. Not sure, though."

"Well, okay. Report any sighting even if you're not sure. Besides, you know how the skipper loves garbage."

Squarehead nodded and reached for the telephone.

11.

In sick bay Lieutenant Commander Chester Porter had attended his first full-fledged muster of his department—which consisted of only *two* permanently assigned men, Chief Pharmacist's Mate McKinley and Pharmacist Engstom, a lanky boy with rimless glasses. However, under battle conditions eight stewards and commissary men were assigned as corpsmen and litter carriers, and it was up to him to have them trained in these, their secondary duties. This morning they all squeezed into the empty sick bay, and when Porter looked them over, he felt this was not much of a command for an officer of his rank; but he blamed his pride with the thought that, technically at least, he was chief medical officer of the 1st Destroyer Division, NATONAV 1—which meant that the medical departments of two other destroyers, patrolling somewhere within the fifteen-thousand-square-mile area, came under his nominal control.

McKinley introduced each man to the surgeon, who then made a short speech in which he omitted the customary flattering references to his predecessor. He expressed satisfaction over the condition of the department, but stated his intentions of running some litter-carrying drills in the immediate future. After the men were dismissed from muster, one of them requested a word with him. It was Collins, the Negro steward. Porter asked him to step inside the receiving office.

"Sir, after my hitch is up, I intend to qualify for medical school," Collins told him with a respectful but firm directness. "Lieutenant Hirschfeld has been tutor-, ing me in pre-med subjects during off-duty time. I am wondering if the commander would kindly do the same."

The surgeon was taken by surprise. "Well, now ... ah, that's very commendable," he fumbled and shot a questioning glance at McKinley, who was standing in the door. He expected his chief pharmacist to correct the word "tutoring," which implied an unusual personal attention from an officer. But McKinley did not intervene. "Ah ... how old are you, Collins?"

"Twenty-four, sir." He looked much older.

"You realize it takes eight years of college and medical school to make a doctor?" Collins obviously knew this, so he went on to ask: "How much education have you had?"

"I graduated from high school with an A average, sir," Collins answered without a trace of cockiness or even pride in his voice.

"Well, now ... that's fine. Very fine. But pre-med studies in addition to your other duties?"

"I intend to return to the navy after I obtain my degree, sir," Collins told him, then added: "I would very much appreciate the commander's help."

Lieutenant Commander Porter felt a twinge of old prejudices welling up inside of him as he pictured this handsome Negro as a medical officer in the navy. He knew it was a terrible fault, but deep down he firmly believed that Negroes should be stewards and nothing more. That was what he had been brought up to believe; that was what had been accepted in the navy during nearly half of his career in it. He was ashamed of this attitude, but his only way of reacting to it was to be scrupulously, painfully, insincerely fair. "Naturally, I will try to help you every way I can, Collins," he said, looking down at the steel top of his desk. "But you must give me time to settle into my new job.

Then I'd like to go over the work you did with Lieutenant Hirschfeld and see what can be done."

Collins said: "Thank you very much, Commander," saluted and left to clean up the officers' toilets.

After he was gone, McKinley added to the surgeon's discomfiture. "That man has a superior rating throughout, sir. I hope you can find time to work with him."

"I didn't say I wouldn't," the surgeon snapped defensively; then a look of malice came into his eyes. "How much do *you* help him, McKinley? Didn't you tell me you've had pre-med at Duke? Wouldn't that qualify *you* to tutor him?"

McKinley smiled and shook his head. "He's far beyond where I left off, sir. On neurocellular structures right now, I believe." He excused himself to attend to some duties in the surgery.

Porter decided he would talk to Captain Finlander about Collins—which would naturally lead to a discussion of Lieutenant Hirschfeld and thence to the matter of the captain's missing Form 28. He and Finlander had had a pleasant meeting yesterday afternoon during which he had been much impressed by that officer's lucid description of the *Bedford*'s operational problems, but there had been no opportunity to deal specifically with those of the medical department. As captains should be, Finlander was only concerned with the over-all picture, not details. However, the surgeon had analyzed him as a man who missed nothing, a man one could talk to and be understood by. Whatever Hirschfeld had implied about him—he was wrong.

The surgeon was about to reach for the telephone and call Finlander to ask for an appointment at his convenience when Pharmacist Engstrom came to the door and announced: "Commodore Schrepke requests to see the commander, sir." The German officer was behind him and politely waited for Porter to invite him into the office—which he instantly did while respect-fully standing up.

Schrepke said, "Good morning, Commander. I will only take a few minutes of your time," then shot a look at the pharmacist which made him close the door to give them complete privacy.

"I hope you are not feeling sick, sir," the surgeon said, trying to avoid looking too pointedly at the German's strangely un-naval dress. The black leather jacket would be more in keeping for a motorcyclist, but he vaguely remembered that U-boat crews used to wear something like that during the last war.

"I feel very good, thank you," Schrepke told him. "I am here because your captain informs me a prescription given by the former medical officer should be renewed by yourself."

"Oh? Just one moment, sir." Porter opened the file drawer and the German patiently waited while he searched for his Form 28. But there was none in the folder, only a plain sheet on which were typed the man's name, serial number, blood type and a notation: *foreign officer-Form 28 waived*. In the lower left corner, in Lieutenant Hirschfeld's handwriting, was written: *Medication provided by subject officer may be taken at his own discretion*. This brought a perplexed frown to the surgeon's face. Here was another strange irregularity in the *Bedford*'s medical records! "I am afraid Lieutenant Hirschfeld neglected to either note the prescription or the nature of the condition it is sup-posed to treat," he said to Schrepke.

"That is all right, Commander. The doctor and I had an understanding."

He said it as if this were the most natural thing, yet there was something in his guttural tone which put Porter on his guard. "What was the medicine?" he asked.

"Schnapps."

"Schnapps, sir!"

"Yes—schnapps." Commodore Schrepke suddenly produced his little silver hip flask and put it down on the desk in front of the astounded surgeon.

Lieutenant Commander Porter stared at the flask, then slowly picked it up and turned it over in his hands. It was quite old, had several buckles in it and some engraving which had almost been worn off. Beneath a crest, which he recognized as that of the Nazi navy, he made out an inscription in German script, but of this he could only read: U-797. Opening the cap, he sniffed a strong whiff of what smelled like pure alcohol. "B-but, sir . . . this isn't really medicine."

"It is the only kind I have ever taken in my life."

"Yes, but—"

"You carry brandy in your medical supplies, do you not, Commander?"

"Yes, of course, but you see—"

"Well, I carry schnapps in mine," Schrepke snapped, beginning to show signs of irritation.

As the surgeon tried to collect his thoughts to decide whether to overlook the whole thing or act according to strict navy regulations, he heard the PA announce a maximum-effect sonar sweep and felt the turbines slow down to a murmur. "I don't know, Commodore," he said. "Perhaps I had better check this out with Captain Finlander. B-but you say *he* suggested you see me about it?"

Schrepke reached out and retrieved the flask, putting it back in his pocket. "It really makes no difference to me what you do, Commander," he said. "I have nothing to hide, only prefer everything on record and in order so as to cause no embarrassments. But it does not really matter. I am sorry I troubled you."

He started to leave and Porter jumped up out of his chair, very flustered. "Please, Commodore. You must

understand my position in this. If only you could explain . . . well, I mean, why do you *have* to have
schnapps?"

Schrepke's face wrinkled in deliberately exaggerated
thought, an expression which made his hard features
almost comical for a moment. "I don't really know,
Commander." He shrugged. "I have had three schnapps
a day since I joined the navy in 1931. One in the
morning, one at noon and one at night. I have had
them that way ashore, on the ocean, under the ocean,
and your English allies were even so kind as to let me
have them when I was their prisoner of war. *Why* I
must have schnapps, I can't really explain. But if you
are worried that I am an alcoholic . . ."

"Good God, *no*, sir!"

"Then perhaps you and your navy will indulge an
old sailor, yes?" He did not await any answer and excused himself with a quick explanation that he was due
to join the captain on the bridge.

After he had gone, Lieutenant Commander Porter
sat staring at the folder until he became aware that
McKinley was standing in the door, looking in at him.
"What do you know about *this* lack of records, Chief?"
the surgeon asked, holding up the sheet of paper.

McKinley evidently knew enough about it so he did
not have to study it. "Commodore Schrepke is kind of
a special case, sir."

"Damn right! No proper forms. Motorcyclist jacket.
Carries his booze on his hip. I'll say he's special! A full
admiral couldn't get away with that in our navy. Why
the hell should he? But I suppose Lieutenant Hirschfeld concocted some obscure justification."

McKinley shrugged. "Only that the commodore is
very senior and has never been able to get over his experiences in the war. If a few shots a day make him
feel better, well, that's legitimate medication."

"Hell, McKinley! Our submarine boys had some shaking experiences too, you know."

"Yes, sir. But Commodore Schrepke was sunk twice and is the only commander in history who ever got all his men out of a wrecked sub lying over a hundred feet deep. Some of them burst their lungs on the way up, but he kept the survivors together until they were rescued ten hours later. The second time he was sunk, a British can blew him to the surface the day before the war was over. Only he and one sailor got clear, but when the Limeys tried to pick him up, he fought them off and attempted to swim away and drown himself. They caught him and put him in a POW camp, where he stayed for a year while they tried to decide whether or not he was a war criminal. He had too many Nazi medals, besides having sent down nearly one hundred of our ships. But once he towed survivors in lifeboats for a couple of hundred miles just to make sure they had a fighting chance, and not even our boys ever took risks like that. So they let him go, and he went home to Germany to try and find his wife and kids. His home was in the Russian zone, and he was there just long enough to find out his family had all been killed. Then the Russians picked him up. They had captured a number of the latest U-boats in half-finished condition and needed experts to help put them together and operate them. So he spent the next two years at forced labor in Russian yards until he managed to escape. He and another German officer *sailed* across the Baltic in an open boat during the dead of winter; the other man froze to death within sight of the Swedish coast, but he made it. The Russians claimed he had not only sabotaged some of their submarines, but also killed a guard while escaping, so they raised so much hell that the Swedes were about to agree to extradite him. He escaped again, perhaps while the Swedes looked the other way, and finally reached West Germany. When the German navy was reactivated, they gave him back his commission and, because he knows all about Russian subs, he was put in charge of ASW work. The sonar boys tell me Commodore Schrepke is so sharp he can listen to a signal or analyze its trace and tell you what type of sub it is, what kind of engines it has and whether it's been out long enough to have barnacles growing on its hull." The chief pharmacist grinned at his own exaggeration, then added very seriously: "He is a strange duck, but, kraut or no kraut, he's also one hell of a fine naval officer."

The surgeon said nothing for a moment, looking down at that nearly blank piece of paper which was all the official record he had of this man Schrepke. "How do you know all this?" he finally asked.

"Captain Finlander spread the word just before the commodore joined us last month, sir. He himself never talks about his past that I know of. . . . Do you want me to enter his visit this morning in the medical log, sir?"

"Hell, no! Not until I talk to Finlander about him," Porter answered testily. "But I'll tell you one thing, Chief. I'm going to go through *all* these records with a fine-tooth comb. I don't want any more surprises." He opened the file drawer all the way and lifted out a fistful of Form 28's.

McKinley laughed. "You've already stumbled on the only two cases that aren't kosher, Commander," he said and withdrew.

Undeterred, the surgeon plunged into his self-imposed paperwork. But he had difficulty in concentrating, not only because his mind kept slipping back to dwell on Commodore Schrepke, the captain's missing Form 28, Hirschfeld's mysterious dismissal and the strange lingering of his presence aboard, but also because the *Bedford* seemed to be going through some strange maneuvers. The maximum sweep had been ter-

minated and her engines were all ahead standard, yet
he could feel her weave on a constantly changing
course. The sea was still flat calm with only a slight
trace of oily swells, but as she turned, she would heel
slightly and the motion would change in a disconcerting
manner. He wished the receiving office had a porthole
so he could see the ocean. He wished he had some patients from other departments so he could pick up
some scuttlebutt from them. And as he thought this, it
struck him that it was also peculiar that so few of the
Bedford's crew ever reported for sick call. All the other
ships he had served on which had over three hundred
crew would produce at least a half-dozen minor cases a
day, including the inevitable hypochondriacs and
malingerers. But not on the *Bedford*. As he checked
the forms, he hoped he would find somebody who was
overdue for a regular physical examination. By the
time he had gone through five or six and found nothing
out of order or unusual, he gave up the project and decided to write a letter to his wife. Lieutenant Commander Chester Porter wrote at least one page a day to
his wife when he was at sea, posting off a ten- to fif-
teen-page epistle whenever he reached port or connected with a supply ship.

Dearest Martha:—Well, I made it to the Bedford
*and am just settling down aboard her . . . or trying my
best to. During the transfer I met Barney Hirschfeld
for a moment and think he's in a real mess of some
kind, although I'm not quite sure what. Better not say
anything to Estelle about it for the time being. Had a
long talk with Captain Finlander and think he is*

He was sitting there, tapping his front teeth with the
pen while wondering whether he *really* wanted to write
that Finlander was "a fine officer who will be a
pleasure to serve under" when he heard the noise of

some men entering the surgery. Patients? He decided he did not want to write Martha any definite opinions quite yet, tore up the sheet of paper and threw it in the wastebasket. Then he got up and went to find out what was happening.

Two seamen had come into the surgery and Porter could tell at a glance that they were perfectly healthy. But he was astounded to find them emptying the contents of a bucket into the sink while Chief Pharmacist McKinley was watching with eager anticipation. The contents of the bucket were unmistakably garbage.

"What in hell are you doing?" Porter exploded.

The two seamen came to attention. McKinley smiled. "Seems we've picked up some goodies, Commander," he said pleasantly.

"What's this garbage doing in my surgery?" the surgeon bellowed, certain he was being made the butt of some kind of insubordinate prank. This belief was heightened by the smugly amused expressions on the faces of the seamen.

"It's all part of our total AWS program, sir," McKinley told him. As Porter glowered into the sink at what appeared to be some moldy cheese rinds, potato peelings, vegetable scraps and half-dissolved bread crusts, the chief pharmacists went to a cabinet and brought out a microscope case. "Captain Finlander says hunting submarines is sometimes like hunting animals," he explained while setting up the instrument. "You can tell a lot by their droppings. For instance, from this garbage we might be able to tell the nationality of the ship it came from, how long since they threw it overboard and, from that, whether it was a Russian sub still within our immediate area."

The surgeon was now almost speechless. "You mean to tell me I'm expected to do some kind of pathological work on this vile stuff?" he stammered.

"Oh, no, sir," McKinley shot back. "That's a smelly

job only for enlisted men." The two seamen laughed quite openly, then shrank back and hurriedly left the surgery with their bucket as Porter wheeled on them. The chief pharmacist sobered and worriedly looked at his superior. "I'm sorry, sir. I guess I should have forewarned you about this. But, no kidding, it's SOP for us to pick up any floating refuse and go over it pretty thoroughly. Two weeks ago we tracked a sub—the one we call Moby Dick because he bugs hell out of the skipper—and lost all sonar contact. But then we picked up two loads of his garbage and knew he was still in the area. Red cabbage with lots of black pepper is a dead giveaway of Russian ships. If it's got traces of hydrogenated fats—butter, you know, sir—it's pretty certain it comes from submariners because, like our own, they get the fanciest rations. Trawlers cook in vegetable oils mostly; the Norwegian ones in fish oils. The state of decomposition of the cells tells us how long it's been soaking in salt water. Really pretty simple and sometimes effective."

"I'll be a son of a bitch!" the surgeon exclaimed, again starting at the filthy mess in the gleaming sink.

"Don't worry about it, sir. I'll take care of the whole thing. Excuse me." McKinley respectfully pushed the lieutenant commander away from the sink and, with a pair of forceps, gingerly transferred some soggy potato peelings to an enamel tray. "Potatoes are real dandy for determining how fresh the droppings are," he explained and began preparing the specimen for microscopic study and doing it with all the starry-eyed eagerness of a young scientist on the track of a cure for cancer.

12.

Ben Munceford had been too late for breakfast.
The wardroom was deserted when he arrived there a
little after eight thirty, the officers having scattered to
their respective duties and the stewards having reported
to meet the new surgeon. But there were a thermos full
of coffee and a plate of very good doughnuts on the
sideboard, so he was able to stem his hunger, although
the lingering smell of bacon and eggs left him with a
frustrated yearning. When he finished ten minutes later,
he found himself still alone and set out in search of
some activity, having in mind to find the shaft which
led to the wheelhouse and bridge. He quickly became
lost in the passageways and wound up going through a
door which opened upon the main deck. Starlight still
shone through a pale dawn and the cold bit savagely at
his ears. He quickly retreated inside and eventually
found his way back to his cabin, withdrawing into it in
a very disgruntled state of mind. The next twenty
minutes he spent examining and loading the movie
camera which had been loaned to him. Then he tried
on the regulation arctic parka; it fitted him well, but
he decided to wear his own camouflage jacket this morning just to flaunt his independence at the surly executive officer. He was putting it on, preparing himself for
another lone reconnaissance through the *Bedford,*
when there was a knock and Yeoman Pinelli came
through the curtain.

"Good morning, sir. I'm sorry I'm late, sir," he said,

addressing Munceford with the same formality he would show toward an officer.

"Late for what, sailor?" Munceford asked.

"The captain asked me to assist you, sir," Pinelli reminded him. He spotted the camera lying on the desk and picked it up, handling it with the familiar ease of a professional photographer. "Is this satisfactory, sir? Are the lenses what you want?"

"They'll do, thanks."

Pinelli noticed the empty film box. "You've loaded it with *that,* sir?" he asked with a frown. "I'd advise a faster emulsion. The light is very poor and the few daylight hours are usually socked in anyway. We use a Tri-X type of film and push its ASA rating to four hundred at least. Have you got plenty of that kind, sir?"

"No."

"I'll let you have some. How about a Solarpack for night and interior shots?"

"Didn't think I'd need one. Besides, I was told to travel as light as possible." He saw the shocked expression on the yeoman's dark Italian face as he stared down at the jumble of photographic knickknacks in the case which was open at the side of the desk. Reaching out with his foot, he kicked the lid closed. "Look, sailor. I don't want to put you to a lot of trouble over gear and stuff. All I need is to have somebody show me around the ship so I won't keep getting lost. That's all."

"The captain told me to assist you, sir," Pinelli doggedly insisted. He was now looking at Munceford's jacket, and the strain of keeping control of his facial muscles made them do strange things. "If you will follow me, I'll take you to the darkroom and get you straightened out . . . ah, I mean fixed up, sir. By the way, it's thirty-two degrees below freezing outside."

"I've got thermal long-johns and a sweater on under this," Munceford snapped. "So let's get going, okay?"

Another long trek through the *Bedford*'s gently heaving, red-lit, deserted passageways. Then Pinelli opened a door and motioned Munceford inside a darkroom which immediately impressed him as a marvel of technical and organizational efficiency. Developing tanks and contact printers; a sixteen-millimeter automatic motion-picture film processor; a sink with thermostat and circulator; compartmented shelves holding trays, chemicals, print papers and a better assortment of film than most camera stores ashore could offer; a filing cabinet and a desk; a felt-lined, glass-topped case full of lenses, each neatly snapped into a holder and with its optics protected by rubber caps; another case held graphics, miniature and movie cameras. All of this was compressed into an air-conditioned space measuring no more than eight by twelve feet; every inch had been carefully designed for maximum utility. As the yeoman reloaded his camera for him with more suitable film, Munceford looked around and realized that nobody on this ship would be impressed with his own skills and equipment. "How much has all this set back the poor taxpayers?" he ungraciously asked.

"I don't know, sir. I didn't buy it myself." Pinelli matched Munceford's tone with a snidely polite one of his own.

"From the looks of it, you'd think that getting pictures of the enemy was the main business of the *Bedford*."

"Well, we do that too, sir," Pinelli told him. "There's a teloptic Mark VII mounted on a turret topside which can get a recognizable shot of the officers on the bridge of a ship two miles away. It can be tracked automatically by radar, just like the guns and rocket launchers. But mostly we shoot for technical records, like the captain told you, sir." He handed him back the camera, which he had loaded three times as fast as Munceford could have done it. "There! Figure ASA four hundred on this emulsion if you are shooting for TV negative. Now I'll rig you a Solarpack light." He went to one of the equipment cases and unlocked it with a key out of a large bunch he carried on a brass ring.

Munceford's jealous resentment of this sailor's obvious technical superiority was overcome by a curiosity over his background. "Listen, stop sirring me. I'm no officer, you know. What's your first name?"

"Vincente, sir."

"Mine's Ben."

No answer.

"All right, be formal if you like. How come you know so much about photography? Is that part of navy training these days?"

"The navy has had an official photographic section since March of 1922, sir," Pinelli dryly informed him as he checked the battery of the Solarpack. "I was an apprentice in the photo labs of Time Inc., but decided the navy could give me the all-round experience I need in the profession, so I signed up for a four-year hitch. When I muster out, I'll have my old job back with a promotion."

"Doing it the long, hard way, eh?"

"Is there any other worth a damn, sir?" the yeoman asked, then hung the Solarpack by its strap over Munceford's shoulder. "Where do you want to start shooting?"

Munceford made a wry grin. "So let's do it that long, hard way you admire so much, Vincente. Bottom up, from the engine room?"

Yeoman Pinelli shook his head and shrugged. "Okay, but it looks like one of those rare days when we will have some sun. You won't have too many opportunities to work on deck, and if you want my advice, I suggest you take advantage of them."

"All right—on deck, then."

Pinelli wiggled into his parka and selected a camera of his own to take with him. "The captain wants some pictures of you working, sir," he explained. "I guess it's for the PRO at COMFLANT. Hope it's all right with you."

Munceford would normally have welcomed his picture being taken for a Fleet Headquarters, but somehow he had a feeling that Pinelli considered himself to have been assigned to cover the activities of a freak. "What the captain wants, the captain gets." He shrugged with resentful indifference and followed the yeoman out of the darkroom. They emerged into the cold morning sunlight of the foredeck just in time to witness the garbage operation.

Munceford blinked and squinted his eyes to get them adjusted to the sudden brilliant light shimmering from sea and sky. To his surprise, he found that the *Bedford* had almost stopped. A couple of hundred yards away, slabs of drifting pan ice were bobbing on the glassy swells, their polished surfaces catching the sun rays and throwing them back at the ship in blinding flashes. A pair of skua gulls circled the bow with plaintive calls, protesting the *Bedford*'s stealthy approach to the raft of garbage which had, until a few minutes ago, been their rightful treasure trove. Some hooded heads were peering over the windscreen of the bridge, watching a pair of seamen wielding a dip net at the end of a twenty-foot aluminum pole. They swung it over the side and leaned far across the lifelines, moving carefully and goblin-like in their heavy arctic clothing.

"What in hell's going on here?" Munceford asked.

"We call it the cherry-picking detail," Yeoman Pinelli answered. "Actually collecting refuse to check if it originates from a Russian sub." When Munceford eagerly began to move toward the scene of action, simultaneously trying to yank his exposure meter out of a pocket, he followed him, calling out: "Shoot it at F-twenty-two, sir. It's awfully bright."

"You and your damned fast emulsions!" Munceford grumbled, then shouted at the two seamen with the dip net: "Hey, you guys! Hold it a second! I want to line up a shot of this!"

The two men turned their heads and stared with startled surprise at the approaching figure in the garish camouflage jacket, then were jolted back to their job by a bellow from the bridge: "Wake up, down there! If I have to make another approach, it'll be your hides!"

Munceford had still not quite grasped what was happening, but sensed it was something unusual and should be recorded on film. As he frantically wound up the camera, he began to run to reach a position close enough for a good shot. He was still running while bending into an awkward crouch and raising the viewfinder to his eye when he sailed out over a sheet of pure ice sheathing part of the foredeck. Suddenly he was entirely horizontal and suspended in mid-air for a flailing instant before landing flat on his back with a dull thump; the camera hit with a more brittle sound and went skidding off in the opposite direction, shedding several bright little component parts as it did so. As the wind was knocked out of him, it blasted across his lips in the form of a single coarse four-letter epithet which rang loudly over the still arctic sea and was clearly heard by the masthead lookouts leaning out of their crow's-nest, one hundred and ten feet above. It was also heard on the bridge, of course, where more heads popped over the windscreen, including one in a long-billed fisherman's cap. The only two men who could not afford to look at the strange sight were the seamen manipulating the dip net; they had just plunged it into the raft of unsavory flotsam now heaved upward on the long pole and swung it back in over the deck with its meshed sack bulging with dripping garbage. Munceford sat up and was splattered by an ice-cold sobering little shower as it passed over his head. He heard a sharp *che-click* of a camera shutter, then Yeoman Pinelli reached him and yanked him to his feet, exclaiming:

"Jesus, sir! Be careful! There's lots of ice on deck!" He did not linger to waste any sympathy on the correspondent, but turned his attention to the far more important movie camera. Retrieving it and its dislodged pieces out of the scupper, he tenderly began to examine them.

Munceford clamped his mouth down over more bitter profanity which was starting to well up out of him and felt his face burn in spite of the freezing cold. Somehow he managed to make a sound which was like a laugh. "That was a damned fool thing to do! I hope the camera isn't busted."

"I'll have to check it out," Pinelli sourly answered. He aimed it at the two seamen who were busy emptying the contents of the net into a bucket and shot a few feet of film. "Sounds all right, but . . ." He shook his head doubtfully, then reacted to the captain's voice calling down to him from the bridge:

"Pinelli! Will you take a secure grip on Mr. Munceford and escort him up here, please!"

13.

"What kind of clumsy loudmouths are being issued War Department press cards these days?" Commander Allison asked the captain with disgust. They
were on the bridge, looking down on the foredeck.

Finlander smiled. "Munceford's no Ernie Pyle, but I
think he's just what we want. What they call a hack in
his profession. He won't come up with anything much,
yet our records will show a card-holding correspondent
has covered the operation, proving everything has to be
above board and run as safely as any friendly little cold
war should. Right?" He gave his executive officer a sly
wink and turned to the OOD, who was standing behind
them. "All right, Mr. Harwell, resume your base
course, but try to stay clear of the ice."

They all went into the wheelhouse, where Lieutenant
Harwell rang up ALL AHEAD STANDARD on the annunciator and gave the helmsman a heading which would
continue taking the *Bedford* northward along the
Greenland coast. Ensign Bascomb, a lanky meteorological officer on loan from the Naval Air Service, came
in from his morning observations and took personal
credit for the fine weather. Chief Quartermaster Rickmers, a leathery veteran of eighteen years of destroyer
duty, cynically predicted snow by afternoon. The
talker, a redheaded seaman attached by a headset and
cord to the master communication panel, announced:
"Masthead lookout reports a whale spouting; bearing
zero-five-zero, estimate one mile range."

Captain Finlander glanced through a window in that

direction and was able to catch a vanishing puff of vapor rising above a swirl on a distant swell. His wiry eyebrows cocked themselves in a mischievous line and he nudged Commander Allison with his elbow. "Ask the CIC if they have anything to report. Ask it sort of casual-like without tipping them off about the whale."

The executive officer went to the communication panel and picked up the phone; after a minute's conversation he hung up and informed the captain: "Mr. Spitzer reports all readouts negative ... except one whale which they picked up twenty minutes ago, now bearing zero-five-eight at two-zero-five-zero yards, making six knots on a northeasterly heading, sir. By the way, Queffle is on the MTS."

Finlander made a gesture of mock anger over having been deprived of catching the *Bedford's* underwater-detection experts flatfooted, then he laughed. "Very good! Nothing much gets by our boy Queffle. . . . Mr. Harwell! Compliment the masthead lookouts on their alertness and accurate range estimation. *No!* Belay that! I'll do it myself and make those boys' day for them. Who are they?"

"Jones and Thorbjornsen, seamen second, sir."

The captain telephoned the crow's-nest and expressed his pleasure to the lookouts in a few tersely complimentary words. When he hung up and turned around, he found himself facing Yeoman Pinelli and Ben Munceford. He did not react at all to the camouflage jacket with its odd collection of insignia and only made an oblique hint at having seen the pratfall on the foredeck. "Good morning, Mr. Munceford. Good morning, Pinelli. Have we suffered another camera casualty this morning?"

Pinelli was still carrying the instrument and gave it a quick, confirming examination. "No, sir—only a bent sunshade and chipped paint."

"Anything chipped or bent on *you*, Munceford?" Finlander inquired.

"I've got a pretty hard ass, Captain," Munceford answered, managing a laugh to cover his embarrassment. The bravado did not go over at all, bringing a wrinkling of Commander Allison's nose and a hardening glint in Finlander's crinkly eyes.

"All right, Pinelli, you are relieved of your escort duties for the time being. I will take Mr. Munceford in town myself." He waited while the yeoman reluctantly returned the camera to the correspondent, acknowledged his salute, then took Munceford by the arm and steered him into a corner of the wheelhouse. When he spoke, he dropped his voice somewhat, but not so low that he could not be heard by the half-dozen men in there. "Are you really a naturally coarse man," he asked, "or do you pretend to be because you think it makes you fit in with what you fancy to be a rough bunch of sailors?"

Munceford's face arranged itself into a defensive pout. "I hadn't given it any thought, Captain. I—"

"Don't be offended, Munceford, and don't think I am a prude," Finlander told him, speaking like a stern but just father. "A normal amount of mild swearing is all right, but I do not permit within my hearing the kind of profane words which are vulgar vernaculars of copulation and certain bodily excretions. It's not because they shock my sensitive nature. I have forgotten more hard language than most men on this bridge will ever learn. But the kind of expletive which came off the foredeck a few minutes ago is offensive to me because it indicates a loss of self-control—and *that* is something I cannot tolerate on my ship. If it takes thought and concentration to keep from senselessly cursing through a trying situation, so much the better. Thought and concentration are the crux of this operation. Self-control is essential to it."

An unwilling apology began curling off Munceford's lips. "I'm sorry I offended you, but—"

Finlander's severity switched back to a gruff good humor with a bewildering suddenness, the bristling brows relaxing from their rigid line, the scar on his throat fading from an ugly red. "Very good, Munceford! This is, after all, part of the necessary background material for your story about us, so don't take it too personally. Have you found any good picture material yet?"

"Well, I was going to shoot some of the garbage collecting, but . . ."

The captain waved a hand to indicate that he disapproved of that subject matter. He looked around for his executive officer and called him over. "Buck! It's such an unusually fine day that I think we should organize a ball game on the fantail later this morning when the light is best for photography. Would you speak to Mr. Ralston about it, please." Turning back to Munceford, he said: "Now, *that* should interest the TV viewers, don't you agree? A volleyball game on a destroyer cruising near the arctic circle in the dead of winter! The kind of thing which shows the high morale of our forces, right? If the boys can play ball, they've got the situation well in hand, right?"

If Munceford had not been so angry over the lecture on profanity, he might have detected a subtly ironic overtone in the captain's voice and noticed a sly glint in the deep-set eyes. But now he became even angrier because Finlander was turning out to fancy himself an amateur movie director—one of his pet hates. "I guess there must be a couple of million feet of film of servicemen playing volleyball all over the world, Captain," he told him.

"Precisely!" Finlander exclaimed, seemingly too pleased with himself to take notice of the disgusted tone. "And we'll show the *Bedford* has one of the best teams. Now, let me see. What else can we line up for you, Munceford? . . . Ah, yes! *Whales!* Of course! Whales and volleyball. Don't you think that would make a terrific combination for television?" This time he did not wait for an answer. He hurried over to the communications panel, pushed a button and spoke into the microphone: "CIC, this is the captain speaking. Do you still have a readout on that whale?" An affirmative answer came out of the speaker, including the range and bearing of the animal. "Very good, Mr. Spitzer. Lock on and close. Mr. Munceford would like some pictures of it and you can show him how good you are at sonar tracking at the same time. The bridge will yield the conn to CIC now." He turned from the intercom and looked toward Lieutenant Harwell. "Did you get that, OOD?"

"Yes, sir. I'm yielding the conn to CIC for sonar tracking exercise. Steering now on automatic remote control."

Munceford thought that he detected suppressed laughter in Harwell's voice and suddenly became aware that everybody in the wheelhouse seemed to be holding himself in check with some difficulty. Chief Quartermaster Rickmers had turned his back on him and his shoulders appeared to be shaking convulsively; the helmsman made a weird coughing noise. All the others were deliberately averting their faces from him. Was Finlander making him the butt of a joke after having dressed him down a few moments ago? "Look here," he loudly protested. "I like to shoot film off the cuff and candid-like, getting things the way they happen naturally. There's no need to trouble with a lot of setups on my account, see."

Finlander came over and took him by the arm, leading him toward the door to the open bridge. "I believe in *making* things happen," he retorted. "Besides, it is no trouble at all. We certainly must uphold the navy's tradition of being cooperative with the press!" As they moved out of the wheelhouse, Munceford came within a fraction of digging his heels in and resisting the captain's pull, but something warned him to be careful and he reluctantly allowed himself to be guided to the forward windscreen. "The whale will soon appear close ahead of us," Finlander told him, selecting a position and pointing him in the right direction. "All you've got to do is to have your camera ready, keep alert and wait." With that he hurried back into the wheelhouse, leaving Munceford alone there, staring at the empty sea.

He did not really believe that any whale would appear at all and strongly suspected that he was being made the victim of an elaborate practical joke—like sending a "boot" on a mission to procure feathers for a crow's-nest. But it was not the prospect of such a joke which disturbed him so much; in spite of his self-esteem, he had steeled himself to take a certain amount of ribbing. It was being publicly dressed down for his language and then told *how* to shoot his story which rankled; the icy breeze sweeping over the bridge could not cool his burning resentment over this. To make matters worse, for the first time in his stormy career he felt that he was at the mercy of an absolute authority without any possibility of telling him to go to hell and then quitting forthwith—his preferred technique for coping with such a situation.

Whales and volleyball! Did Finlander really think he would be pleased with such material for his story? Was he going to interfere like this throughout the assignment? Murceford had experienced self-appointed movie directors before, the kind who wanted to produce the whole show as well as star in it. He had had some rough dealings with such people, including some important ones like a U.S. Senator, a Mormon bishop and a captain of industry who considered himself as unassailable as any captain of the navy. A distorted camera angle, a quote edited out of context—these were formidable weapons in the hands of a disgruntled television correspondent. Of course, the aggrieved subjects could and did retaliate, which had something to do with why Ben Munceford only found himself on assignments which were too inconvenient or risky for the more established reporters to cover. Like crawling out on a fortieth-floor ledge to interview a prospective suicide, or making a delayed-drop parachute jump with the paramedics for the sake of a few feet of spectacular film. News directors could occasionally use such a man to liven up the routine work of the precociously dignified, status-conscious "commentator-analysts" who had lately taken over the field. Not too often and always on speculation with no prior committment, of course—all of which suited Ben Munceford fine. No boss, no strings, no pussy-footing home office, everything strictly on a take-it-or-leave-it and go-to-hell basis. But could he make it work here on the *Bedford?*

His eyes caught a fleeting glimpse of a swirl ahead of the ship. He left the spot Finlander had assigned him and walked out to the wing of the bridge where the lookout was stationed. "Say, sailor!" Munceford said to him. "Is there really a whale somewhere out there?"

The seaman neither turned nor took his eyes off the quadrant of ocean he had been assigned to watch. "Excuse me, sir," he answered. "Lookouts are only permitted to speak to the OOD while on duty."

"Oops! My mistake!" Munceford snapped. He was about to needle the man with a sarcastic remark about the dedication of the *Bedford*'s crew when he heard a loud whooshing sound. He turned toward it just in time to see a large whale broach and spout no more than fifty yards ahead of the bow. The animal was badly frightened by this ship which was suddenly pursuing it and filling the protecting deep with an uproar of electronic signals; its huge fluke rose high with a cascade of spray, then vanished through the vortex of a creamy whirlpool. Munceford was jolted out of his paralyzed surprise when the lookout softly, and mockingly, exclaimed: "Thar' she blows!"

"I'll be damned!" Munceford yelled and belatedly raised his camera to shoot useless footage of the fading ripples left by the sounding whale. He became aware that Captain Finlander and Commander Allison had come to the door of the wheelhouse and were watching him.

"You've got to be quicker than that!" the captain disparagingly shouted.

Fuming, Munceford returned to his original position at the windscreen, propped his camera over the edge of it and waited for another opportunity with his finger on the trigger. All right! If this ship spent the taxpayers' money chasing after whales, then, by God, he would see to it that they at least got a movie out of it! Volleyball and whales! Finlander's cold war! But would they believe it?

14.

On this morning there was another young man aboard the *Bedford* suffering from a disturbed state of mind, the same kind of disturbance occasioned by a vacillation between anger and the peculiar kind of fear generated by injured pride; but, unlike Ben Munceford, there was no question of any lack of discipline or self-control, these qualities having been indelibly impressed upon his character throughout a spartan boyhood spent in English public school and naval college. Lieutenant P. L. M. Packer, R.N., knew how to submerge his personal troubles and at least give the outward appearance of the classically jaunty and efficient British naval officer. The human nervous system can stand only so much suppression for a given amount of time before it starts to cripple itself, but Packer's training helped him to contain or delay this effect; he was also helped by the motto on his family crest—not one of those inscribed in the dead foreign language of Latin, but consisting of a single succinct English word: *Endure.* Simple, forthright and sometimes tremendously difficult to live up to. So difficult, in fact, that all male Packers seemed destined to die in the attempt. It was this family curse which was preying upon his mind this morning, not because of his own physical fear of it, but because of Shebeona's evident decision that she was not prepared to accept the motto as her own, especially if it meant to *Endure* a widow's weeds.

Lieutenant Packer had completed the coding and decoding of routine signals which constituted the *Bed-*

ford's daily contact with NATONAV 1, of transmitting the weather report, of monitoring the traffic to other scattered units of their flotilla spread so thinly over this vast ocean, of estimating the schedule of even skimpier air patrols by intercepting and deciphering position reports on the NATOAVIAN frequency. All business to do with NATO signals was his responsibility, but since this was only a small part of the Communications Center work, it took only a couple of hours of his time each day. Everything else was handled by Lieutenant Andrew S. Beeker and his smoothly efficient staff of radio specialists, which meant that Packer had much time left over in which to brood about the navy he loved and his beloved who hated it.

"Anything exciting I can help you with?" Packer asked Beeker, poking his head inside the EDA room, which housed the high-frequency direction finder (HUFF-DUFF) and multiplex emission sensors (MESS-PLEX).

"No, thanks, Peter. Take five." Lieutenant Beeker almost always declined any help from Packer, who suspected he carried a latent germ of anglophobia in his pragmatic heart. In spite of his youth and low rank, Lieutenant Andrew S. Beeker was one of the foremost radio-communications experts in the United States Navy, the author of an official text with the formidable title: *Theory and Practice of Emmissions Detection and Analyses in Naval Tactics*. He had been born twenty-eight years ago in a slum section of Chicago, escaping by only one day from having been foreign-born, a status which would have made his Annapolis appointment virtually unattainable in spite of his extraordinary aptitudes. His parents were refugees from the Russian Revolution who had taken nearly ten years to make it from Kiev to Chicago, via Istanbul, Marseille, Lisbon, Havana and Toronto. They had baptized him Andrei Simeonovitch Beikerman—a name which was

changed in the nick of time so that he was able to enter the Naval Academy as Midshipman Andrew S.
Beeker. A few friends called him Andy, but mostly he
was known as The Beek—in spite of the fact that he
had a rather thick, blunt Slavic nose. The Beek could
receive seventy words per minute of Russian Morse
and that was one of the principal reasons for his
presence aboard the *Bedford*; that, and the fact that
he could instantly recognize a Russian transmission,
often identify the ship (or submarine) it originated from
and pinpoint its location within a square mile with his
HUFF-DUFF. The Beek would undoubtedly be a full
commander within the next ten years, but that would
be as far as he would go; he was, after all, nothing but
a technically brilliant Russian Jew and the navy had
already had its unnerving experience with one of those
who reached flag rank. To Lieutenant Packer, however,
Beeker was simply an American midwesterner reared a
thousand miles from blue water and in a city whose
mayor had once threatened to punch King George V
in the nose.

"I'd be glad to pick through the red frequencies for
you," the Englishman offered with a kind of defeated
enthusiasm. He knew The Beek would only say again:

"No, thanks, Pete. Take five."

So Packer went back to his desk in the main radio
room, sat down and listened absently to the twittering
Morse signals which came off the monitoring circuits,
stared dully at the backs of the operators guarding
their sets and finally, reluctantly, took Shebeona's letter
out of his pocket and read it for the fifteenth time since
it had arrived yesterday.

*Peter, darling! It was wonderful to get your letters at
last, but again I had to wait too long for them. Of
course it isn't your fault—I know there are no post
boxes in that beastly ocean of yours. It's simply that*

*the waiting and the worrying becomes too unbearable
for me and the fulfillments too elusively fleeting. I have
felt the same lines eating into my face which I have
seen in your mother's and know their roots are deep in
a lonely heart, far beyond the aid of cold creams and
pancake makeups. Alas, my poor Peter, my love is not
turning out as unselfish as hers and therefore is not
worthy of you.*

*Alan Sternway has asked me to marry him and I have
accepted. I am awfully fond of Alan—that's all. But he
will always be there and, anyway, I am told that one's
first love is only good for tender memories. These I will
have of you for as long as I live. Devotedly—Shebeona.*

Packer had to smooth out many wrinkles in the
faintly scented pink stationery in order to read those
words; last night he had angrily crumpled up the letter
and almost ruined it. Now those wrinkles made him
think of the lines in his mother's face which Shebeona
spoke about. It was unthinkable to him that her beauty
would ever be marred by such things, yet his mother
must once have been almost as beautiful. There was
that wedding picture he had found in the attic to prove
it; in spite of the ghastly fashions of the mid-thirties, it
showed a lovely girl all aglow next to a young naval officer who looked extraordinarily like himself. Seven
years remained before widowhood. Seven years which
for her contained only thirty days each of fulfilled love,
all the rest being the long wait while her husband's
ship cruised from one distant station to the next, moving inexorably toward that fatal rendezvous with the
long rifles of the *Bismarck*. When the Battle of the
Denmark Strait took place, Peter was less than five
years old; the only man he could remember from early
childhood was the one who came to tell of his father's
death. He had never really known his father, and now

he wondered how well his mother had known him. And his grandmother, who had lost her husband in the Battle of Jutland—how well had she known *him*? Even in the long period of peace which followed the Napoleonic Wars the naval Packers had managed to get themselves killed at sea: Sir John had survived Trafalgar only to be killed in a skirmish with an American slaver, and Sir Winston had foundered in the ice of the Antarctica he had been sent to explore. . . . Could he really blame Shebeona?

His gloomy thoughts were interrupted by The Beek, who came out of the EDA room and called an order to his chief radio technician: "Benton! Patch in a tape and record the transmission on three-point-nine megacycles while I take a HUFF-DUFF on it!"

Lieutenant Packer quickly put away Shebeona's letter and jumped up to reach the bank of recorders ahead of Chief Benton. "You got something hot?" he called to Beeker.

"I think it's a bogey—that so-called research ship *Novo Sibirsk* which always seems to indicate the presence of Moby Dick. The transmission is about three hundred miles off." He quickly vanished back inside the EDA room.

"I'll take care of the recording, sir," Chief Benton told the English officer, respectfully but firmly nudging him aside.

Packer watcned him for a moment, then slumped back into his chair and began to shuffle absently through the file copies of the morning's dispatches. He did not bring out the letter again, but his mind could not tear itself away from it. What would his mother say about the broken engagement? She always looked forward so much to the weekends when Shebeona would drive out to the old house in Surrey and keep her company for a few hours—the two waiting women, the old widowed one and the young engaged one who had so much of that kind of waiting ahead of her. There would be no more visits now, because Shebeona would, of course, be with Alan Sternway.

Peter's anger boiled up as he thought of Alan Sternway and it almost broke the blank surface expression on his face. The Sternways had once been a distinguished service family too, but Alan believed that the dissolution of the British Empire had relieved him from any obligation to conform to tradition. Instead of going into the navy, he had joined the merchant marine, and instead of going to sea, he sold tickets in block lots to other Englishmen who were also serving their ties with history and emigrating out of the country. Alan's ships did not even fly the Red Duster, but were refurbished tubs under Panamanian registry, owned by Italians who fronted for Greek-American financiers. Old Admiral Sir Percival Sternway would be tossing restlessly in his grave over his son's doings, but all Alan tossed was money. Enough money for a flat in Mayfair, an American Thunderbird, vacations on Capri—*and Shebeona!* Damn her! If there were lines eating into her beautiful face, they were those of dissolution of character, of failure to *Endure*, not the attrition of abiding with her heart's true love. To reject him and marry a man like Alan Sternway was as bad as ... as bad as marrying a man like Ben Munceford! Well—*he* had been attracted to her, hadn't he! Maybe that was her type, after all!

"Sir, I have an action signal from Narwhale!" one of the radiomen announced, yanking a sheet out of his typewriter and sailing it over onto Packer's desk. Narwhale was the code name of the Norwegian destroyer *Fritiof Nansen*, and when the NATO communicator ran her message through the decoder, he found that she too had picked up the Russian transmission on 3.9 megacycles and was drawing the *Bedford*'s attention to it.

"Do they think we are asleep?" Lieutenant Beeker dryly asked when he read the signal.

"Rather trying to show us *they* aren't," Packer answered. "Shall we call the bridge about this, Beek?"

"No. Let's wait a moment and give Captain Finlander a nice complete package of information." During the next couple of minutes Beeker listened to the tape recording which Chief Benton had made of the transmission, then checked it against a master recording of sample transmissions he had compiled of all the known Russian vessels frequenting the area. Only his trained ear could pick up subtle differences and likenesses, and finally he announced with absolute certainty: "It's the *Novo Sibirsk,* all right. Now we had better keep our ears glued to their submarine frequencies for Moby Dick." He sat down and quickly typed out the information on a message sheet, including the exact position as determined by his HUFF-DUFF bearing, clipped the signal from Narwhale to it and called for a messenger.

"Wait—let me take it to the bridge, Beek," Packer pleaded, then impulsively explained: "I want to ask to speak to the captain, anyway."

The Beek looked a little suspicious. "You do? Why?"

"It's a personal matter. I need his permission to send a telegram to . . . er, ah, home." He suddenly felt himself blushing as the American officer scrutinized him with a puzzled curiosity.

"That's only permitted in emergencies, you know, Pete. Did you have bad news in the mail yesterday?"

"You might say so," Packer answered, making a desperate attempt to sound casual about it.

"Nobody's died, have they?"

"Yes—I suppose *I* have a little." He said it with a shrug and a bitter little laugh. Then, with a sudden switch to complete indifference, he reversed himself and exclaimed: "Never mind. I'll catch the skipper this evening if I still feel like getting in touch with home."

He started to return to his desk, but Beeker stopped him, shoved the papers into his hand and swung him around toward the door as if suddenly anxious to get rid of any kind of problem which was beyond the scope of radio technology. As Packer left, he settled down to make a translation of the intercepted Russian transmission.

Outside the Communications Center the sun had climbed higher into the clear sky and begun to counter the terrible cold left by the long winter night; given more time, its rays might have driven the temperature upward to somewhere close to mere freezing, but another night was due only three hours past high noon and the thermometer would soon start another downward plunge. In the meanwhile the arctic ocean had lost the dazzling shimmer of dawn and taken on the spectacular deep blue color it wears on its rare fine days. The slick parts where a flat calm prevailed were like undulating sheets of polished steel; other parts ruffled by cat's-paws of icy zephyrs changed their hue to a gunmetal patina which spread, contracted, vanished and reappeared on the slopes of the restlessly quiescent swells. On the eastern horizon, sea and sky met in a sharp unbroken line, but to the west the frosted pinnacles and crags of Greenland's mountains stood out with a startling clarity which made them seem much closer than they actually were. Between them and the ship, remnants of an icefield drifted in strangely orderly columns, like flattened snowmen floating down an invisible stream within the sea. The *Bedford*'s wake curved away from their course, cutting a softer emerald swath through the hard blue of the surface.

Lieutenant Packer stopped on his mission to the bridge to allow his eyes to take all this in and his mind to savor the remoteness of it from the troubles assailing him from faraway England. It made Shebeona and Alan Sternway and their trite little love triangle seem utterly unreal and unimportant. This ship and this bleak but protecting sea were all that mattered and all that was real for him, as it had been for all the Packers before him. No! He would send no pleading message. Certainly not! Let *them* have each other and let *him* have this. But, God, it was so cold! And lonely!

A quickening of the pulse from the engine room, together with a slight heeling of the deck as the *Bedford* tightened her turn, brought Packer out of his brooding. The ship was being put through some kind of seemingly erratic maneuver, but undoubtedly it had a calculated purpose which had to do with the frequent ASW exercises which Captain Finlander devised to keep the CIC in a constant state of alertness. Remembering the papers fluttering in his gloved hand, Packer hurried to the bridge, where he reported to Commander Allison inside the wheelhouse:

"Sir, I have a radio-intelligence report for the captain."

Finlander was only ten feet away, but with his ear close to the sonar monitor's speaker, listening intently as CIC kept relentlessly on top of the hapless whale. Packer was hoping he would notice him and step over to circumvent the through-channel procedure, but his attention was completely absorbed in the persistent *ping-ying . . . ping-ying*. Allison took the report and checked through it to determine whether it warranted immediately disturbing the captain—which he decided it did. Holding it up in front of Finlander's face, he silently put one finger against the significant words: "*Novo Sibirsk*"—and had the report snatched out of his hand. When the captain finished reading it, there was the fire of excitement smoldering in his eyes. "Excellent! This may mean the hunt is on. Let's start a tactical plot and do some figuring, Buck." Beckoning his executive officer to follow him into the chartroom, he hurried off without ever noticing Packer—who felt a pang of frustration. Well, the captain would be too busy for a while to bother about anybody's personal problems. And, anyway, hadn't he decided not to send a message to Shebeona . . . not immediately, at least?

"What's the big deal, Pete?" Lieutenant Harwell had sidled up alongside him to find out what was so important it had been brought up by the NATO liaison officer instead of by ordinary messenger.

"The Beek sniffed out Moby Dick's mother—that's all."

"That's all!" Harwell let out a meaningful whistle, then slapped his hands together. "That's all, he says! So let's cut out this horsing around and get going! What's holding the skipper back?"

"Maybe the fact that the emission originated from somewhere three hundred miles northeast. It's my guess H.M.S. *Obdurate* is in a better position to do something about it." Even as he spoke, he heard the scuttlebutt start its whispering course through the wheelhouse and knew that in a matter of minutes it would permeate the entire ship.

Harwell made a disparaging snort which was only part joking. "We'll never give up Moby Dick to any Limey can, boy!" he exclaimed. "Not as long as the *Bedford* is in the same ocean."

Packer flashed a grin and needled him back. "Yes—and maybe that's why nobody ever catches him."

Harwell recoiled with a horrified expression. "Jesus, Peterpacker!" he whispered with an uneasy glance toward the curtained entrance to the chartroom. "What's happened to make you no longer want to go on living? Only a desperate character would say anything like that on this bridge!"

He was joking, of course, but the Englishman nodded seriously. "You don't know *how* desperate, Dick." With a wry grimace he turned and went out onto the open bridge. He had decided to take his time about returning to the Communications Center. Maybe Captain Finlander would quickly break off whatever exercise was taking place, lay a course toward the *Novo Sibirsk*, then come out here to restlessly join the lookouts in watching the sea. Maybe engage him in conversation. A conversation which could lead up to the subject of home. A casual request for permission to send a personal telegram. But supposing he wanted to know the *nature* of the telegram—that would be perfectly within a commanding officer's right, of course. Could he think up something innocuous which would still convey his anguish to Shebeona? He noticed that, besides the lookout, the only other person on this side of the bridge was Ben Munceford, who was leaning over the windscreen, clutching his camera and staring at the sea beyond the bow.

"Hello, Ben," he greeted him, placing himself next to him. "You look like you expected a chorus line of mermaids to pop out of the sea."

Munceford looked up with a start. "Well, well!" he exclaimed with a pouting smile. "It's the jealous English lover boy. How're you today? Still mad at me?"

"All right, Ben—I guess I deserve that," Packer answered after gritting his teeth together for an instant. "I'm sorry I acted so badly last night."

"Well, okay, Pete! Like I told you, I had no business with your girl's photograph."

For a moment they both silently watched the sea. Then the English officer asked: "You found her very attractive, didn't you?"

"Damned handsome broad. I'm not going to stick my neck out with you by saying any more than that.

Say, where is that silly whale? It's been fifteen or twenty minutes since it was up last."

"Oh, is that what we're doing? The old Ahab stuff. If it's a humpback whale, which it probably is, it's good for about a thirty-minute dive. Much less if badly scared. . . . She's about to be married, you know."

"Yeah, I got that message. To you."

"No. Not to me. To somebody else." Packer horrified himself as much over actually putting the calamity into words as over *whom* he was saying them to. He made it much worse by adding: "So, you see, it doesn't really matter to me whether you are interested in her or not."

Ben Munceford looked at him sharply, his freckled face wrenching itself into sardonic surprise. "Say! Don't tell me that was a Dear John letter you got yesterday. The old kiss-off?" He spoke so loudly that the lookout in the wing might have heard it. The Englishman's face remained inscrutable, his eyes still on the coldly sunlit sea, so it was not his reaction which made Munceford abruptly switch his manner to one of genuine concern. It was the fact that he suddenly realized this was the only person aboard the *Bedford* who was trying to act like an ordinary mortal human being with him. "Listen, Pete!" he said in a much lower and more sympathetic voice. "Don't let them get you down! All women are emotionally unstable opportunists. I ought to know—I'm just shedding my third wife, so I've learned in the school of hard knocks, believe you me. Like if you love cats, you're going to get yourself clawed from time to time. It hurts, but it heals. So don't let it get you down."

Packer nodded, but toward the sea. "There is your whale," he said.

"Damn! Skunked again!" Munceford exclaimed and fumbled with his camera. However, this time the whale did not immediately sound. The long frantic chase had so exhausted it that it wallowed on the surface, painfully spouting vapor through its blowhole, a weirdly scalloped flipper waving listlessly in the air as it half rolled, showing a pale, fluted belly. There was something pathetic about its floundering effort to get out of the way of the *Bedford*'s sharp prow, and only in the nick of time did the fluke make a churning stroke to propel its hulk clear of the slicing column of steel bearing down upon it. With his camera still grinding away and his eye glued to the viewfinder, Munceford raced to the edge of the bridge, photographing an unsteady but dramatic sequence as the huge, half-submerged blimp of a beast was buffeted by the wash of the passing ship. He did not stop shooting until it had fallen astern and floundered in the foaming wake which stretched in a pale blue, crazily looping serpentine track across the sea behind them. Then he looked up with a grin of satisfaction which almost immediately changed into a frown. "Say!" he said to Packer, who had followed him across the bridge, "couldn't you call this cruelty to a dumb animal? I don't know if I like it being done on my account."

Before the Englishman could answer him, Lieutenants Spitzer and Krindlemeyer came out of the wheelhouse and stared astern through binoculars at a swirl where the whale was attempting to sound. They both looked very pleased and Spitzer gleefully exclaimed: "Boy! Human and system control were all go on that run! We got a perfect trace too. Those hypersonic pulses drove him crazy!"

Munceford heard him quite clearly and although he did not fully understand what he was talking about, it somehow further offended one of his few sensitivities—an almost maudlin love of animals. "How would *you* like to be chased with hypersonic whatnots anyway—eh?" He lifted the movie camera, pointed it at the two officers and shot a quick sequence of their faces as they gaped at him in confused amazement. It must have been a very unflattering shot.

Lieutenant Peter Packer was suddenly amused by the incident and became full of suppressed laughter. "Look here, Ben, old boy," he said after Krindlemeyer and Spitzer had slunk back into the wheelhouse, "if you think they were chasing that whale for *your* benefit, forget it. Destroyermen and submariners hate whales because they bugger up their sonar systems with false echoes. I dare say more depth charges have been wasted on whales than on real targets, and it's still damned hard to tell the difference, even with our latest models. So, you see, partly out of spite and partly for necessary practice, Finlander frequently allows the CIC to make runs on them like this."

"Are you saying they can't tell the difference between a whale and a submarine even with all the high-priced brains and equipment on this ship?" Munceford asked with a sneer. "That's great! And I think maybe it's news."

Packer's amusement turned to alarm. "I didn't say that, so don't quote me on it," he answered, keeping his eyes on the wheelhouse door. "What I do say is that it is sometimes difficult. Every creature in the sea, from whale to plankton, makes a noise of some kind and can give a return echo on sonar. It is a matter of gaining experience in making proper identification, of learning thousands of separate sounds and characteristic echoes, often picking them out of the confusion. The deep isn't always silent and still. It can be as uproarious as an Italian street riot. And, speaking of underwater sounds, here's the *Bedford*'s special magician at sorting them out!"

Munceford followed his gaze and saw what appeared to be an ordinary seaman come out of the wheelhouse and step to the after bulwark of the bridge to scan the sea astern of the ship, evidently searching for a sign of the whale which had finally managed to dive out of sight. He was a very young, very skinny boy, bare-headed except for a pair of earphones clamped to his head, the oversized cups bulging out, but above his ears, and with the connecting cord dangling around his knees. He was wearing an unzipped windbreaker which bore no insignia of his rating, and, instead of the usual heavy boots worn in this climate, he had a pair of ordinary navy oxfords on his feet. In one hand he clutched a black notebook, in the other a ballpoint pen. After squinting at the empty sea for a moment, he made an almost effeminate gesture of annoyance, looked about the bridge and, spotting Lieutenant Packer, trotted toward him with a peculiar skipping gait.

"Mr. Packer!" He hailed the officer without any formality at all and with a voice which still contained a strident note of puberty. "Did you make out what kind of whale that was?"

"A humpback, I believe."

"Are you sure, sir? Did you get a good look?"

"Quite sure, Queffle," Parker insisted with a kind of patient indulgence.

"Darn it!" the boy exclaimed with the petulance of an innocent child. "I wish they'd assign a marine biologist to this ship. I suggested one, you know—but no! I get an oceanographer instead. Now, what earthly help is an oceanographer in cataloguing ambient noises of animal origin, I ask you?"

"I am sure Lieutenant Burger is doing his very best," Packer told him acidly.

"Oh, yes, sir. I didn't mean anything personal, of course. And, actually, I am quite sure it *was* a humpback. My own readout on the MTS indicated it, you see. So let's record it as such." He began scribbling in the notebook, his long, bony fingers, already an unhealthy purplish crimson from the cold, curling around the pen in a painful, double-jointed grip.

When he had completed his notes, Packer got around to introducing Munceford to him: "Ben, this is Sonarman Second Class Merlin Queffle, our ace sonar operator. It is rumored that Captain Finlander ran roughshod over a dozen destroyer and submarine skippers in order to obtain the services of this lad. Unfortunately, he is perfectly aware of his own importance and treats his ordinary mortal shipmates in a most cavalier fashion . . . up to and including the executive officer."

Queefle took the sacrasm with a guileless smile which revealed his front teeth to be very large and very crooked. "Oh, get off it, sir," he exclaimed with a high-pitched giggle, then turned to Munceford and extended a slender hand toward him. "You must be the television man who joined us yesterday. Glad to meet you. Gee, that's a sharp jacket you're wearing. I like it!"

Ben Munceford had been staring at and listening to this strange young sailor with an openly amazed disbelief. Now he was a little slow in grasping the offered handshake, and when he did, it felt somewhat like grasping a bunch of wilted asparagus. "How are you, Kwivvle?"

"*Queffle*, sir," the sonarman corrected him. "Merlin P. Queffle. It's French . . . Breton, really. A lot of my friends call me the Breton Kid."

"And some call him Merlin the Magician," Packer injected.

"Oh, get off it, sir. . . ."

"Because he has ESP," the English officer persisted in explaining to Munceford. "A formidable secret weapon in submarine tracking."

"ESP? What the hell is that?"

"Extrasensory perception," Queffle brightly told him, with neither humility nor bombast. "The idea is that I'm supposed to be able to *sense* whether or not a subsurface sound is of man-made origin. Well, the long fancy name is all right, I suppose, and I do kind of enjoy the ring of it. But I prefer to think I'm simply in tune with the sea and what goes on down there. I'm from a long line of Grand Bank fishermen and captains, although you'd never guess it to look at me." He jokingly sucked in his cheeks to exaggerate their gauntness, then flashed a buck-toothed smile. "My mother played violin with the Boston Symphony before she married my father, and I suppose I inherited my sensitive ears from her. Anyway, the combination seems to make me pretty hot on the sonar and—" He would have rambled on about himself in an unabated torrent had he not been rudely interrupted by an angry voice calling his name from the wheelhouse door.

"Queffle! What the devil are you doing out there without cap and gloves?" It was the OOD, Lieutenant Harwell, and he came rushing toward them with a belligerent annoyance which at first boded ill for the sonarman, but then somehow quickly and mysteriously abated. The dressing down which followed was not only mild but almost pleading. "Do you realize what the temperature is out here, Queffle? Twelve degrees! For God's sake, boy! What do you think the captain would do to me if you caught a cold in your ears during my watch? Besides, it's against regulations to enter the bridge without proper dress, you know. Please go back inside at once. *Please!*"

Queffle had watched the OOD's approach and listened to his words without any special alarm; now he looked around and sniffed the brisk slipstream sweeping the bridge, his nostrils and lips parting slightly and giving him an extraordinary rabbit-like appearance. "It really is quite cold, isn't it?" he agreed, then excused himself and ambled off toward the wheelhouse door.

"Damn it, Pete! You should know better than to let him stand out here like that," Harwell rebuked Lieutenant Packer. "Don't you remember there was hell to pay when Queffle got infected sinuses last month?"

The Englishman laughed, but somewhat cautiously. Sorry, but, frankly, I'm awfully inhibited about how to handle your precious Merlin. Delicate, precocious children always have thrown me, actually."

"Now, don't give me that, Pete," Harwell angrily retorted. "Merlin Queffle is an enlisted sailor in the United States Navy and should be treated like one."

"Then why don't you?" Packer instantly countered, the humor gone from his eyes, leaving them coldly serious.

Lieutenant Harwell became terribly flustered as well as angry. "B-because ... uh ... because, you know damn well why! Although I see no reason for him to come up here in the first place. I'm going to speak to Spitzer about that. With two million dollars' worth of sonar gear aboard this ship, I can't understand why we've got to pamper a primad—" He abruptly stopped himself in midsentence as Commander Allison stepped out on the bridge and came toward them.

"I hate to break up your gossiping in the sun," he dryly announced to Harwell, "but we seem to have a tactical situation shaping up and there are a few details to be taken care of by the OOD—which is you, is it not, Mr. Harwell? Fine! First bring the ship to sixty-five degrees and increase her speed to eighteen knots. Then please send your JOOD to find Commodore Schrepke, present the captain's compliments and ask him to come to the bridge. Also notify Lieutenants Spitzer, Beeker and Burger to report to the captain's day cabin in exactly five minutes. That will do to start with."

Harwell said: "Aye, aye, sir," then could not contain himself from asking: "Are we on to Moby Dick, sir?"

"Maybe—maybe not. But you know the skipper. So get cracking and play it like we are!" He waited until

Harwell had rushed back into the wheelhouse and called the new course to the helmsman, then he turned to Ben Munceford, gave his camouflage jacket an icy look and said: "Ensign Ralston is organizing a volleyball game on the fantail. I suggest you lay aft with your camera, Mr. Munceford."

"But I'd rather stick around here if there's going to be some kind of action, and—"

"The captain wants pictures of the volleyball." Allison cut off his protest with a slight, yet very threatening rise in his tone. "You must not keep the men waiting on deck in this temperature." Again he waited, this time while Munceford sulkily left the bridge. The executive officer's body was racked by a distasteful shudder inside his bulky parka and he said to Lieutenant Packer: "It must be rough on you, sharing a cabin with that man."

"He's not really so bad when you get to know him, sir," the Englishman answered with a certain hesitation. "I really suspect the brashness is a front."

"I hope you don't judge our American press by him," Allison growled. "I thought that type of reporter went out years ago, but evidently it has been reinstated by television."

"Don't worry, sir—we have that kind in England too." He coughed and cleared his throat, then blurted out: "I suppose the captain's awfully busy right now."

"Yes. . . . Something which I could help you with?"

Packer met the probing look in the commander's green eyes, and the indecision over whether to send a message to Shebeona became a jab of physical pain in his chest. He hoped it did not show in his face. "Oh, nothing important, sir. It can wait." He forced a smile, then covered his embarrassment with a sudden urgent exclamation: "Goodness! If Lieutenant Beeker is to report to the bridge, I must relieve him immediately at the Communications Center. Excuse me, sir."

He rushed off, leaving Commander Allison thoughtfully staring after him before turning his eyes to comtemplate the distant, snow-crusted ramparts of Greenland's coast. The *Bedford* was picking up speed, and although the arctic ocean was still lying placid around her, she began to generate her own wind, which chilled the meager warmth of the sun. It gnawed with cold little fangs on his exposed face and he turned his back to it, looking aft toward the wake which had straightened out, unraveling itself from the twisting track of the whale hunt. He saw six men emerge onto the main deck, dressed in heavy sweatshirts and pants, and hurry toward the fantail, the last one in line hefting a ball as he ran.

15.

Standing alone on his bridge in a blackening, brooding mood, Erik Finlander watched this lovely day on the arctic ocean end with a breathtaking sunset. Even with his mind troubled by a tangled skein of plots and travails, he remained aware of every detail of it.

Some high cirrus clouds had come drifting across the clear sky, fashioned by stratospheric winds into delicate brush strokes of pearl white. In the land-bound west, fingers of mist had crept out of the fiords and closed around the coast, hiding in a silvery shroud all but the glacier crowns of the mountains and the glittering seaward edge of the icepack. Now, as the sun dipped, swelling into a red ball of fire, her shimmering disk hesitating and slightly flattening to the touch of the sawtooth escarpment of Greenland's frozen highlands, all things in the firmament, ocean and land became briefly kindled by the splendor of her departing glory. The clouds burst into flames. The soft surging swells were splattered by a froth of rubies. Even the austere warship, slicing along her hunter's course, shed for these moments her steely quality and turned into a ship of fire trailing a comet's tail of illuminated foam. Then the sun slipped behind the mountains with a startling suddenness, and from the darkening east the onrushing winter night cast its mantle to extinguish the afterglow. Red turned a dull gold, gradually tarnishing into a uniform bluish mauve which soon draped everything in a melancholy veil of deepening twilight. Only one thin thread of brilliance remained, a long, arrow-straight vapor trail stretching across the sky, headed by a tiny silver cross which was an aircraft flying so high it was still a speck in the eye of the sun.

Finlander was aware of the presence of the plane, but did not seem to pay it any particular attention. Through the small monitoring speaker which was attached to the bulwark beneath his elbow, he had been subconsciously listening to the reaction of the *Bedford* when her radar picked up the faint *pip* while it was still one hundred and forty miles away. The air-defense officer had immediately pulled an alert, the CIC starting to feed target information into the computers, which in turn digested and analyzed in a flash, then fed the results into the battery of TERRIER missiles poised in their launcher. Communications had issued a challenge which was quickly answered by the correct countersign, identifying the jet as an RB-47 on reconnaissance patrol out of Thule AFB. As a final precaution, Yeoman Pinelli had aimed his turreted Mark VII camera at the minute silver cross as it unraveled its wispy line to a point directly overhead, the huge lens gobbling up the intervening forty thousand feet, and in ten seconds producing a close-up on Polaroid film. The captain had heard those section commanders concerned report these procedures to the bridge and knew they were handling the matter properly without any necessity for his intervention. After a cursory glance upward, he dismissed the aircraft from his mind and turned his eyes from the sky to the sea which contained somewhere in its darkening vastness the real enemy occupying his thoughts.

Time was standing still for Finlander now, for the twilight periods before dawn and after sunset were ever the time of reconning for submariner and sub-hunter alike. The time to contest with each other for the ambush, to maneuver and countermaneuver for the weather gauge of darkness and light. Time to attack.

Time to kill. Time to die. Time for captains to isolate themselves in taut watchfulness in conning tower or bridge. And that was where Erik Finlander would always be found during his every dawn and every sunset at sea since taking command of his first ship back in 1943. That was why time stood still, even retraced itself for him during these moments. Nothing had changed. It was always the same, whether on old four-stack cans or modern super-destroyers like the *Bedford*, whether in actual conflict or supposedly bloodless cold war where the intent to kill could not—or *should* not—be implemented. The sham of it only served to tense a captain like Finlander who had once tasted blood, his own as well as the enemy's.

The deep scar on his throat, now tingling with an accustomed pain as the icy wind probed the collar of his duffel, had been inflicted upon him in these same Greenland-Icelandic waters during that other peculiar cold war, the one which existed between Germany and the United States in the months before open warfare inevitably erupted. He had been exec on a recommissioned old four-piper, the U.S.S. *Benjamin Crocker*, engaged in what Washington called a "neutrality patrol"—a convenient subterfuge for aiding the hard-pressed British navy. The torpedo which came streaking out of the twilight (a twilight exactly like this one), ripping the old destroyer in two and sinking her in sixty seconds, had brought formal apologies from the Nazi government which in no way inhibited their informal gloating. It had also brought a Navy Cross to a young machinist's mate second class, Lauchlan S. MacKay, who supported in the freezing water a lieutenant (J.G.) and at the same time pinched closed the terrible wound in his throat, doing this for the better part of an hour before they were rescued. Ever since that awful sunset of eighteen years ago Erik Finlander had held on to a seething hatred of submarines through peace and war; he had likewise held on to that man Lauchlan S. MacKay, keeping him with him through a formidable roster of illustrious destroyers, including the *Bedford*, in whose engine room he was now the reigning chief.

Revenge had come to Captain Finlander, but too far away from the scene of treachery and defeat. He had sunk the U-784, the U-866 and the U-1020, but all in the Central Atlantic or Azores. His luck had not been as good on the Murmansk convoy routes, although he had participated in kills where the final fatal stick of depth charges was delivered by Canadian frigates; while given official credit for "assists," he did not count these himself. Thus he scoured this arctic sea today as if it still concealed the U-boat which had blooded him in the realities of submarine warfare, as if the same enemy commander lurked down there, ready to shrug off a "mistake" and pass on the responsibility for apologies to a cynical government, one still subject to the caprice of an absolute tyrant. Finlander's good sense told him, of course, that the chances were overwhelming that the U-boat which had sunk the *Benjamin Crocker* and killed one hundred and four of her crew, including two of his Annapolis classmates, had itself been eventually sunk during the course of that war—in the final tally, only one out of four German submarines had survived to be scrapped or impressed into the Soviet navy. Only a few U-boat commanders remained alive today, only one of these on active service, and that one relegated to an advisory capacity on Finlander's own ship. Commodore Schrepke, he was sure, would be ensconced in the opposite side of the *Bedford*'s bridge, driven by similar compulsions to the same lonely twilight vigil—the same, yet so different, his mind not only plagued by memories of terror and defeat in these waters, but by trepidation over his unnatural purpose aboard a former enemy's ship. A strange and subtly cruel fate, one which held an almost morbid fascination for Captain Finlander.

Being a man who could command a strong grip on reality, he also permitted himself certain flights of fancy, a kind of masochistic nurturing of old hurts and hatreds, of mulling over superstitions and omens, of deliberately playing these against his obsession. He believed, for instance, that the Denmark Strait had it in for him, that the presence here of the Russian submarine his men called Moby Dick boded old scores to be settled through a fated encounter threatened by an ill-starred past. Already they had twice met, and each time the submarine had mysteriously vanished, leaving his frustrated specialists helpless at the consoles of their miraculous electronic detection apparatus, but himself more stubbornly determined than ever. Like its legendary namesake, *this* Moby Dick only drove the pursuing captain to further tempt the very fate he suspected to be deviling his wake. Foolish superstition to occupy the mind of an intelligent naval officer? Perhaps for some, but Erik Finlander could afford such broodings and even turn them to his own advantage since they had made him more flexible and more alert. They instilled in him a healthy skepticism about the complex scientific accouterments of his ship and their hold upon their technological servitors, making him depend at least equally upon the basic instincts of a human animal who had been both the hunter and the hunted. Never again would he stand and hesitate as he spied the split-second flash of sunset on the objective lens of a periscope, wondering because sonar was giving no return echo whether it was only the glint of a drifting bottle, glass fisherman's float or piece of ice, then realizing too late the fallibility of man-made instruments as torpedo wakes blossomed out of the dark waters a couple of seconds before the shattering explosion. One hundred and four shipmates had died because of too much trust in scientific gadgetry and too little in human instincts, his own blood barely stemmed from flowing out of his body by the convulsive grip of Chief MacKay's grimy thumb and forefinger. A far-off glinting little flash like . . .

"Lookout! Didn't you spot that reflection out there off the starboard bow?" Finlander shouted at the seaman huddled in the wing.

The boy gave a start and his head seemed to rise up out of the folds of his parka as if activated by a spring. "Y-yes, sir. I think . . . I might have seen a couple of winking sort of flashes, like . . . like off a bottle, or ice, or something like that, Captain, sir. . . ."

Finlander's gloved fist swung down beneath the combing of the bulwark and hit the red lever next to the speaker. The silence which had lulled the *Bedford* was torn apart by the raucous clang of her GQ alarm. Almost instantly the wheelhouse door thrust open and the OOD stuck his head out, eyes wide and questioning. "Possible visual contact, bearing three-zero-zero relative, one thousand yards," the captain called to him with a controlled urgency. "Execute Maneuver Able immediately, Mr. Collins . . . then relieve your starboard lookout!"

As the *Bedford* picked up speed and heeled in a turn toward the suspected enemy, the captain remained where he was, once again listening with a kind of alert detachment to his section commanders as their voices came through the speaker, reporting their respective battle stations closed up. He did not react to the somewhat irritated tone of Lieutenant Krindlemeyer as he announced from the CIC that all readouts on the detecting gear were negative; the ECM officers were never less than patronizing about "eyeball" contacts, often taking them as a direct affront to their instruments. Nor did he give more than a curt, perfunctory explanation of the GQ alarm to Commander Allison when he joined him and began sweeping the empty gloom ahead with his binoculars. But as the unfortunate seaman who had been lookout shuffled past him, Finlander's hand shot out and stopped him with a hard grip on his shoulder. "Do you know why I'm busting you off my bridge, sailor?" he asked in a voice which was both gentle and implacable.

It was too dark now to see the face inside the hood, but the answer told of the misery which was there. "Captain, sir . . . one *thinks* one sees all sorts of things out there that just ain't so," he protested, trying to express the suffering his responsibility entailed rather than make excuses for himself. "One don't like to sing out against the sonar and radar reading without being sure. One got to think it over. One—"

"All right, son!" his captain interrupted him. "If you had not seen those flames, you would not be blamed. Our eyes can't catch everything in this kind of light. But you admitted to me you *did* see them, yet did nothing about it. It's not your duty to evaluate a sighting, only to report it. I don't want to see you up here again until you have so thoroughly familiarized yourself with the duties of a lookout that you instinctively react correctly. Now go below."

The sailor saluted stiffly, then sagged as he moved away, crushed by his failure. Finlander turned back to lean over the bridge bulwark and scan the sea. "I want you to ream out that kid's section commander, Buck," he gruffly told Allison. "He is a good boy and we owe him the proper indoctrination before making him responsible for the lives of his shipmates. I want it explained to him—and to *all* our lookouts—that sonar and radar also sometimes see things that are not there. Sometimes fail to see things that *are*. I want it understood by all hands that this ship depends first of all on her men, not her machines, which must always remain subservient to us. Even to an ordinary seaman. Understood?"

Out of the speaker came Krindlemeyer's plaintive voice reporting all readouts still negative. Allison said: "Yes, Captain," without taking his binoculars from his eyes.

The GQ turned out to be abortive. Within ten minutes the *Bedford* was secured from battle stations and once again returned to her northward base course, skirting the now invisible edge of the Greenland icepack. Commander Allison returned to the navigation office. A new lookout, doubly on his guard because of the calamity which had befallen his mate, took up his position in the starboard wing and probed the black emptiness of his assigned quadrant of ocean with fearfully alert young eyes. Commodore Schrepke came over from his isolation on the opposite side of the bridge and stood for a moment next to Captain Finlander, who was waiting out the last fading shimmer of afterglow staining the western horizon. "All Soviet periscopes are hooded to prevent reflections," he quietly said in his fluently precise German-English. It was a statement of fact, not a reproach. Finlander barely nodded and remained silent. He owed explanations of his actions to nobody on this ship, not even to this, his technical superior in rank. Nor did he say anything when the commodore added before withdrawing in the dark: "But you did the right thing. Those hoods sometimes get knocked off."

The quartermaster of the watch came out to record the hourly temperature reading and exclaimed loudly over the thermometer's accelerating plunge since sunset, then quickly retreated into the warmth of the wheelhouse. But the captain remained where he was, now alone on the bridge with the lookout, watching the first faint flare of northern lights darting among the stars, wondering if the commander of Moby Dick was watching them too and praying they would illuminate a safe passage into some secret fiord where he would plot a submarine missile launch against Thule ... or Montreal ... or New York. Inside the icepack he would be safe, safe until he sooner or later must come out and rendezvous with the *Novo Sibirsk*; then the chances would be good for a solid contact! Especially if this fine weather held without snow to hash up the radar and storm-scattered icefloes to bedevil sonar with false echoes. But fine weather never held for long in these waters, and the cirrus clouds, so beautiful with their filigree tracery aglow from the cold fires of the night sky, were precursors of another dismal blizzard. Finlander sighed, straightened up from his hunched position, stretched the freezing stiffness out of his arms, then went down to his cabin. There he found, patiently waiting, Lieutenant P. L. M. Packer, R.N.

"Sir, I would appreciate a word with you regarding a private matter—if it is convenient, of course."

The bristly eyebrows gave a quick flicker of surprise, then settled back into a severe black line. The captain nodded and motioned the young English officer to follow him into his cabin. As he shook himself out of his white duffel coat, he said: "Sit down. I will be with you in a minute," and vanished inside his bathroom, where he proceeded to thaw out the numbing cold in his face by splashing it with hot water.

Packer perched himself uneasily on the edge of a chair and thought that he had picked a bad time to speak to the captain. He appeared in a forbidding mood. But when Finlander came back through the louvered door, he seemed also to have thawed his frosty manner somewhat. "Now, then, what can I do for the Royal Navy?" he inquired.

Packer suppressed his nervousness and smiled. "It's really something for plain Peter Packer, sir. Well ... you see, I hear that you are permitting normal wireless traffic even though we are on a sweep after Moby Dick. In that case, I would very much like to get off a 'personal.' The truth is, I'm having some bother at home."

"Nothing serious, I hope?"

"I want to stop somebody close to me from doing something awfully foolish, sir."

The young officer sounded so coolly casual that Finlander had to peer intently into his eyes to see the trouble behind them. "I don't mean to pry, Mr. Packer," he told him, "but you will have to tell me more than that. Although we are officially operating under peacetime conditions which permit a certain number of 'personals' to be transmitted, war conditions are in fact imposed upon us." Having spoken as a captain, he dropped into a chair and tried to bridge the wide gap of age and rank with a softer tone. "Our friends and relations are constantly doing foolish things while we are at sea," he sighed. "That is one of the hazards of our profession."

"I realize that, sir. But this particular foolishness rather vitally affects me."

"A girl?"

"Yes, sir."

Finlander shook his head as if this was turning into an altogether too frivolous problem. "At your age the foolishness of girls assumes a major importance—I know that. But when you reach mine and look back on it, you'll realize it was all froth on the waves which rolled on regardless."

Packer's voice was suddenly not a bit casual. "I respectfully submit, Captain, that I am not your age, and to me, right at this moment, this is the most important thing in my life."

"More so than your navy career?" Finlander shot back.

"It is completely tied up with it, Captain."

"I see. Then I gather this is a matter of a broken engagement—right?"

"Yes, sir," Packer answered in a lowered voice.

"And another man?"

The Englishman's hesitation betrayed that this was so, even when he finally blurted out: "Shebeona is worried by my absence on long patrols and about ... well, the rather uncertain future of it all."

Finlander nodded. "Absence and uncertainty must be faced by our womenfolk. Good navy wives are very hard to find. Yes, harder today in our indulgent soft society than in my own courting days. I never did find one myself, you know." His face twisted into a strange sort of pained grimace as he paused for a moment. "I cannot pretend to be an expert on women, Mr. Packer, but it seems to me that if this girl is so troubled by the prospects even now when she should be at her most ardent, you should pass her up as a bad risk."

"Captain, sir, I appreciate your advice on the matter," Packer answered with a chilly respect, "but I only wanted to trouble you for permission to transmit a personal message home. That is all."

Finlander silently contemplated him for a moment, then said: "Permission granted. You may inform Lieutenant Beeker I am allowing you to transmit ten words."

"*Ten* words, sir?"

"Ten words, Mr. Packer. Under the circumstances, I do not believe excessive loquaciousness on the subject would be fitting for either yourself or my ship."

With that the discussion ended, the English officer rising out of his chair, thanking the captain for his time and quickly taking his leave. Finlander remained seated for several minutes after he had gone, hands clasped under his chin, his brow furrowed by thought. Then he got up and moved to his desk, picked up the telephone and dialed the Communications Center. When Lieu-

tenant Beeker answered, he told him: "Mr. Packer will
shortly submit a 'personal' with my permission for its
transmittal. Before you sent it, I want you to phone me
its contents for my personal clearance. This is a confidential matter and Lieutenant Packer is not to be embarrassed in any way whatsoever. . . . Thank you."

It was almost an hour later when The Beek called
back and read to Captain Finlander a telegram containing exactly ten words over which Lieutenant P. L.
M. Packer had agonized in the solitude of his cabin.
With Shebeona's photograph before him, he had written and rewritten, racking his mind for the exactly
right ten words, trying out dramatic ones, dryly witty
ones, mildly sarcastic ones, even ones which were
outright pleading. Then Ben Munceford had come
bursting in and hoisted himself into the upper bunk,
from where he launched a steady flow of griping about
his assignment on the *Bedford*, at the same time surreptitiously eying Shebeona and the growing column of
scratched-out ten-word lines with which his companion
was filling the pad. Growing more and more agitated
and self-conscious, Packer finally capitulated to forthright simplicity and hastily wrote on a fresh sheet:

I BEG YOU RECONSIDER AND AWAIT MY RETURN—
LOVE, PETER.

After crumpling the others and stuffing them into his
pocket, he hurriedly left for the Communications Center. As soon as he signed the transmittal order and departed, Lieutenant Beeker telephoned the captain.

Finlander listened to the message with his eyes
closed, then left the line tense with a long painful
silence as he thought back to long, long ago when *he*
had begged a beautiful bitch whom he passionately,
blindly loved. But she had married a wealthy stock-
broker instead, then a banker, then an oil tycoon. If
she had acceded to his begging, he would have wound
up like them, a flaccid, shorebound source of alimony,

fighting cholesterol and surtaxes. He had not thought about her for years, but now her face came back to him in a brief flash of remembrance, hazy in detail except for that selfish, sensuous half-smile her lips had always worn. An angry, impulsive and negative reaction almost expressed itself in words, but he managed to choke them back. "All right, Mr. Beeker," he said at last with something approaching sadness. "Let it go. Let it go if there's no priority traffic."

PART TWO

THE CHASE

1.

With a caprice typical of the arctic's weather system, the thermometer began climbing during the night and when a leaden dawn seeped through the thick overcast, it was twenty degrees warmer than it had been during the previous sunny day. But it did not *feel* at all warmer. Flurries of fine snow rode squalls of raw wind just strong enough to foam the top of steep swells being funneled through the narrows separating Iceland and Greenland. The *Bedford* was angling across the seas with long, cork-screwing rolls, occasionally throwing burst of spray over her long foredeck and adding to the weird surrealistic sculptures the freezing slush was creating on exposed parts of her superstructure. The gunners who came out to clear the traversing and elevation mechanisms cursed this savage thing which the meteorological officer euphemistically called a "warm front."

The glass-eyed aluminum capsule which was the crow's-nest on the mainmast flew through the air in lurching captive arcs which failed to disrupt the digestive processes of Squarehead Thorbjornsen's stomach. He had filled himself with fried eggs, ham and hash-brown potatoes before going on watch, washing it all down with two glasses of milk and a mug of double-sweetened coffee. His belly made sloshing sounds like a barrel full of fermenting pickles, but this did not bother him at all. What bothered him was the visibility beyond the rocking wiper blades. In the squalls it was less than a half-mile and when the scudding clouds dragged their dirty gray skirts to mast level, the bow itself vanished in a misty blur. The OOD had telephoned a warning about keeping a sharp lookout for drifting ice, but this was becoming extremely difficult, and that worried Squarehead, who had recently seen a movie about the sinking of the *Titanic*. Big icebergs were not common in the Denmark Strait during this time of the year, yet sometimes huge floes would be wrenched off the icepack and set adrift; they could be big enough to chew through the *Bedford*'s lightly built hull. "I sure hope radar is getting through this muck," he shouted down to Seaman Jones, resting in the shaft below him. "My own eyes sure as hell ain't!"

The OOD, Lieutenant Petersen, was also very much concerned with the possibility of heavy floes suddenly appearing ahead of his ship. But having alerted the "eyeball watch" to this, he himself had taken up station at the navigational radar in the wheelhouse, switched it to its most sensitive one-mile range and proceeded to follow the sweeper as though hypnotized. As it spun round and round the glowing tube, myriads of tiny sparks were kindled by the snow flurries to confuse the more solid echoes of ice. He would have liked to slow the *Bedford* down, but they were still some distance from the estimated position of the *Novo Sibirsk* and Finlander wanted to get a look at the Russian in daylight—for what that was worth in this dismal gloom.

The captain had stood his customary dawn watch in the starboard wing of the bridge, then, as if something of significance had been mysteriously communicated to him out there in the swirl of spume and snow, had ordered a change of course before retiring to his day cabin. A change of course which would take the *Bedford* across to the Icelandic side of the strait. He gave no reason, and, of course, nobody asked for one. Not even Commander Allison. Commodore Schrepke had come in from his solitary communion in the port wing a few minutes later, his black leather jacket a-shimmer with caked snow. He checked the gyro-compass, grunted and silently departed. The relief lookouts peeled back their hoods and steamed themselves on the heater coils in the back of the wheelhouse.

In the insulated twilight world of the CIC, Lieutenant Spitzer noticed that his tactical radar was becoming obscured by hash created by snow and the sharpness of the signal was turning fuzzy as freezing slush began coating the antenna revolving on the mainmast. He got up from his console at Master Control and adjusted the rheostat which shot more current into the heater elements in the antenna. Next he checked the echo-ranging signal, to which a sonarman was listening with a relaxed concentration as his body swayed with the roll of the ship. At eighteen knots the system was bothered by ambient sounds which made it crackle like a pocket radio being played in a thunderstorm, but this was an inherent limitation and the operators had been carefully trained to pick out a hard contact through the static. *One* might miss it, but there were three of them continuously on duty. And standing by there was Merlin Queffle, who had once, during a special demonstration for a Senate Naval Affairs Appropriations Subcommittee, homed in the *Bedford* on the bubbles from a frogman's breathing apparatus. To the delight of Captain Finlander and his grateful admiral, these political gentlemen had rushed back to Washington and restored to the budget thirty millions of dollars which had been lopped off by an economy-minded soldier-President. Ever since that occasion Merlin Queffle had been a privileged character aboard this ship. But Lieutenant Spitzer loathed the skinny, bucktoothed little enlisted technician who in blithe and brash ignorance could work miracles with fantastically complicated submarine-detection devices of which engineering principles he only had the haziest understanding. Yet Spitzer could never implement his loathing because Queffle not only was the key to Finlander's very circumspect confidence in the department, but never gave any really concrete cause for a rebuke. He simply was a naturally abrasive, dedicated little bore.

"I feel like raising a hot contact today, sir," he cackled at Spitzer, his rodent tusks glowing a sickly green in the reflection of the PPI scope. "We're going to dish up Moby Dick on toast for the skipper real soon. I just feel it in my earbones, sir!" Queffle was constantly referring to his "earbones," being fully conscious of their enormous importance.

"Take care they don't swell up so they clog your whole head," Spitzer sourly answered him and, with Queffle's high-pitched laughter ringing in his own ears, fled through the hatch leading down to the CSP room, where Lieutenant Krindlemeyer presided alone over his robot faculty of mathematical wizards—the *Bedford*'s awesome battery of electronic computers. Down here all the intricate calculations relative to navigation, target analyses, even meteorological and oceanographic data of strategic nature were solved in a fraction of a second by a fabulous interlocking system of artificial brain cells which had a memory as well as a certain fundamental power of reasoning. There was also a perfectly ordinary electric coffee percolator which provided Krindlemeyer and Spitzer their only counter-regulationary vice, a potent brew of special java which they imbibed in the inviolate privacy of this inner scientific sanctum, like priests nipping sacramental wine in a sacristy. This they did now to the soothing accompaniment of the insect-like sounds of computer circuitry and the rustle of whirling spools of data tape. Even when their masters relaxed, these robot genies never did. But perhaps the privacy was not so complete after all, because sooner or later that damned intercom would inevitably break in with something like:

"Bridge to CSP! Stand by to process RAOB data. Balloon launch minus sixty seconds and holding."

On the narrow deck in the inadequate lee of the after stack, Ben Munceford was aiming his camera at Ensign Bascomb and two seamen who were struggling with the meteorological balloon, which was threatening to destroy itself as it whipped about in the wind. In a recklessly caustic mood, he had come up to the pilothouse after breakfast and, after making sure Finlander was not within earshot, loudly asked: "Volleyball, anyone?" The wisecrack brought no laughter, but Commander Allison had come out of the chartroom to inform him the captain wanted film of the meteorological officer at work to show TV viewers that "we also perform a vital peacetime service." Another dull subject! And one which would have to be shot in inadequate light with snow flying around to fog up the lenses. Why the hell couldn't Finlander and Allison let him handle this story in his own way? Yet, when Munceford found out that Ensign Bascomb was actually going to try to launch an instrument-carrying balloon in this weather, he became interested and did his best to line up some usable pictures of the operation.

The seamen clawed at the wildly buffeted gasbag, trying to hold it down while the met officer struggled to clear the coils of nylon cord which supported the radiosonde and radar target. Hands were made clumsy by thick, sopping gloves on which ice had formed in stiffly articulated globs. Eyes winced half-shut from the sting of flying brine. The slick deck canted dangerously with the ship's steep rolls. As the collar of his camouflage jacket beat against his frozen cheeks, Munceford braced himself with one arm hooked around a stanchion and squinted at the scene through his camera's viewfinder. Behind him, the ubiquitous Pinelli clung to a lifeline and wearily shouted into his ear: "F-one-point-five, sir!"

Suddenly a wild thrust of wind tore the balloon from the grip of the two seamen, shooting it off horizontally along the deck. The nylon cord snaked out of Bascomb's fumbling hands and snapped tight with a bowstring *twang* as the instrument package and target were yanked aloft. "Keep it from fouling!" the met officer bawled and in the next instant slipped and fell. "Munceford! Fend it off!" he screamed from his sprawled position.

Munceford was directly in the path of the box dangling from the cord and could easily have shoved it clear of the obstructions, but he kept grinding away with his camera instead. It was Pinelli who leaped forward in the nick of time and kept it from tangling. The big orange ball was momentarily sucked downward in the turbulence to leeward of the speeding destroyer, its cargo skipping the wave tops and making a series of white splashes in the gray walls of water. Then it shot upward and remained a bright blob astern for only a few seconds before fading into the scud. Munceford swung his camera around and shot a few additional feet of Bascomb as he lay on the deck, staring after the balloon with an expression of relieved misery. "Say! That was a good bit!" the correspondent exclaimed gleefully. "Let's do some more of that!"

Bascomb gave him a disgusted look. "You're a gusty son of a bitch, Munceford, for a TV reporter . . . but mostly son of a bitch!" Then he gratefully said to Yeoman Pinelli: "Thanks for the hand, sailor! You saved that instrument package from smashing to hell."

In the Communications Center, Lieutenant Beeker briefly checked the telemetry signals coming from the balloon as it soared up unseen through the icy muck covering the ocean, then assigned Lieutenant Packer to monitoring the tape and feeding the data down to the CSP room. The Beek was anxious to keep the Englishman busy. He wanted no emotional upsets in his department, especially since he had been made the key figure in the hunt for Moby Dick. Using this vital job as an excuse to leave Packer abruptly to the routine RAOB duty, he quickly retreated to the EDA room, where the direction finders and emission sensors had been on stand-by since 2300 hours of yesterday.

Twice during the night Beeker had been routed out of his cabin to monitor intercepted transmissions from the *Novo Sibirsk,* each time having to report to Finlander with a rough translation of what appeared to him to be pseudo-scientific oceanographic jibberish. At 0328 a fragmentary signal, too brief for either taping or a HUFF-DUFF bearing, had been picked up on a frequency often used by Soviet submarines, and this had ended all chance for sleep. Ever since then he had been on continuous duty in the EDA room, waiting and listening in vain and fending off Finlander's frequent impatient calls. Evidently the captain too was spending a sleepless night, his mind uneasy and enervated by the suspected proximity of his enemy. An hour ago he had sent Lieutenant Burger, the *Bedford*'s oceanographic expert, to go over the translations of the *Novo Sibirsk* intercepts, and that officer was still seated next to The Beek, painstakingly plowing through the text, questioning this and that word or sentence for possible Russian double meaning, slang or colloquialism. Burger did not have a quick mind or much imagination and was redundantly thorough—a plodder, The Beek thought as he was diverted from concentrating on the sounds in his earphones to explain to him for the third time that he would be responsible for nothing but *literal* translations. And at that moment the same mysterious signal which they had heard during the night came crackling through in a short, staccato burst of Morse.

Chief Benton lunged for the HUFF-DUFF and Lieutenant Beeker jumped to pinpoint the frequency on the MESS-PLEX, but the signal lasted for less than five seconds. They waited for over five minutes, tensely poised to plot it if it was repeated. But it was not. Benton let fly the kind of four-letter expletive which Finlander had prohibited on the *Bedford*. The Beek slumped back into his chair, thought for a moment while rubbing the swarthy stubble on his jaw, then picked up the phone and called the captain. "We just intercepted another one, sir. Stronger than the last, but still too quick for a bearing."

"Well, could you read the signal?" Finlander's edgy voice demanded.

"No, sir. They put something like two five-letter groups through a scrambler." The Beek had thought he recognized two of those letters, but he was the kind of officer who hated to commit himself without being absolutely sure. Especially not with Finlander.

There followed a short, disappointed silence on the line, then: "I want you and Mr. Burger to report to my day cabin at once, please."

Captain Finlander was seated at his desk, the scar on his throat pulsing a stark red over the collar of a non-regulation sweater, his eyes cold glints beneath the heavy lids. The lines in his face were rigidly set like those of an angry, inanimate mask, but his voice had that soft, dispassionate quality which made his sarcasm all the more biting. "Our Soviet adversaries must know this ship carries one of the navy's top radio-intelligence officers aboard and are deliberately setting out to make a fool of him," he observed when Lieutenants Beeker and Burger presented themselves in the day cabin.

The Beek's face remained expressionless. "You may certainly count on them knowing we are in the area, sir," he answered. "And they must realize we are well equipped to intercept their signals."

"Are we?" Finlander countered.

"Neither of those intercepts lasted over five seconds," his communications officer patiently explained. "We need twenty seconds for the sensors to register a frequency and twelve seconds for the HUFF-DUFF to take a bearing with any kind of reliability factor, and—"

"I have acquainted myself with the technical capabilities of my ship's detection gear," Finlander interrupted him. "They are fascinating gadgets on the whole, Mr. Beeker. But they can't play a hunch. I have asked you up here to find out if you can excel them in this respect."

"I know you want me to suggest those signals came from Moby Dick, Captain, and indicate he is somewhere near us," The Beek answered, then adamantly added: "I regret I have no way of supporting such a premise."

Finlander gave a disgusted snort. "Can your mind only react to a given, measurable set of impulses, like your machines? Couldn't you just plain guess occasionally, Mr. Beeker? On whether or not this last signal was of Russian origin, for instance?"

The Beek's face flushed slightly, but he still resisted being drawn out. "Even that would be rash with only a couple of scrambled five-letter groups to go on, sir. I have ordered the suspected frequency continuously guarded by recorder, so if they come on again, perhaps . . ." He stopped, wavering under the piercing gaze, and after a painful hesitation suddenly blurted out: "Well . . . as a ball-park guess, Captain . . . I'd say they *were* Russian."

Finlander's black eyebrows cocked upward as he pounced. "Aha! Assuming so, it is also reasonable to assume they were intended for the *Novo Sibirsk*— right? Then why did she not acknowledge?"

Lieutenant Beeker feel into the trap. "It could be that the *Novo Sibirsk* would only query Moby Dick if she did *not* receive the signal. In other words, sir, silence constitutes an acknowledgment that the message was received according to a predetermined schedule."

The captain's face became animated by a quick, caustic grin of triumph. "My goodness, Mr. Beeker! You are given to playing purely human hunches after all! So don't look so sheepish about it, boy! That casts aspersions on my own judgment, because I happen to agree with your hunch." He turned from the discomfited communications officer and sharply scrutinized his oceanographic expert. "Well, Mr. Burger. Have you been able to make anything interesting out of the translations of the *Novo Sibirsk* intercepts?"

Lieutenant (J.G.) Kurt Burger cleared his throat with a series of hacking little coughs. "I have it all here, sir," he answered, holding out a neat file folder.

Finlander made no move to accept it. "Please don't shove paperwork in my face, Mr. Burger. Simply give me as short-winded a verbal rundown as you can."

Another series of coughs rattled out of Burger's throat, betraying his nervousness. But he had decided to act in contrast to Lieutenant Beeker and come out with an opinion without being coaxed. "It seems quite clear that these transmissions are coded tactical intelligence reports disguised as oceanographic observations."

"How do you arrive at that conclusion?" the captain inquired with a frown.

"They contain data supposedly gathered by Nansen bottle and bathythermograph, sir," Burger explained. "This is quite normal stuff for a research vessel, but it isn't normal to send back the information by radio to home base. It would simply be logged and held for evaluation at the end of the cruise. Then there is another, far more important discrepancy, sir." He paused for an exaggerated dramatic effect which merely made Finlander impatient. "The data contained in the transmissions is just enough at variance with the conditions up here to be highly suspect. Assuming the Soviets would not man a research vessel with incompetent oceanographers, it is a reasonable conclusion that their reports actually convey information of a completely different kind." His round face took on a self-satisfied expression which quickly returned to one of nervousness when the captain tartly asked:

"Such as what?"

"Well, sir ... that is difficult to determine without thoroughly analyzing a whole series of such reports. It could be, ah ... well, regarding submarine operations in this area, or possibly airborne telemetric analyses of our radar emissions, or even tactical hydrographic information." No longer sure of himself, Burger became fidgety and his eyes flicked from the captain to The Beek, who had been listening with a detached interest. "I'm not a cryptographer, you know, gentlemen," he added defensively.

"I am aware of your limitations, Mr. Burger," Finlander told him. "What I am wondering is whether the Commies would be stupid enough to send out obviously faked scientific data over the air."

"Yes, but ... they would hardly expect to have their transmission closely monitored by a fully qualified oceanographer," Burger answered with a timidly smug tone.

The captain looked into the lieutenant's blue eyes, which were permanently bloodshot from too much reading, and wondered about the effectiveness of this strange new type of naval officer. Burger had graduated near the top of his class at Annapolis, been detached for post-graduate work at M.I.T., detached again to serve on the scientific staff of a Woods Hole Oceanographic Institution research ship, then assigned to the Office of Naval Research, from where he had been sent to the *Bedford* for the purpose of "determining the efficacy and practical usefulness of including an oceanographic specialist on the manning table of an ASW vessel under operational conditions"—or so the orders had read. Maybe Bureau of Personnel simply didn't know what the hell to do with this overeducated genius! Finlander would personally have preferred to be given another all-round young line officer like Ensign Ralston, or if it had to be a narrowly specialized type, then another Merlin Queffle, who seemed to get more results out of the scientific apparatus aboard the ship than the scientists who were actually responsible for them. But Queffle had barely managed to graduate from high school, while this Burger had his Master's degree, so the captain had to be cautious about allowing himself to be influenced by his natural prejudices. "Thank you," he said to the oceanographer. "I'll think over your ideas, Mr. Burger."

After dismissing the two officers, Finlander went out into the navigation office, where he thoughtfully leaned over the chart table, his face darkly inscrutable. Commander Allison came up behind him, waited to be noticed and, when he was not, spoke up: "Anything new for the tactical plot, sir?"

"Yes," Finlander answered loudly and with a firm conviction. "Moby Dick is *here!*" He slammed his hand down on the chart with fingers spread wide, sweeping it along the Greenland coast from Scoresby Sound to Cape Hildebrandt.

Allison looked surprised. "You mean The Beek stuck his neck out on those signals?"

The hand on the chart rose in a contemptuous flourish. "The sticking out of necks remains the exclusive privilege of commanding officers, Buck. No hemming 'n' hawing. No equivocations. No academic procrastinations. One just weighs all the evidence, the solid and the nebulous, the educated guess and the pure hunch, then turns all the ifs, buts and maybes into a definite tactical proposition. *Moby Dick is here!*" The hand slammed down again. "Let's go nail him . . . after we intimidate his illegitimate mother, the *Novo Sibirsk*."

Wheeling away from the chart table, Finlander swept through the blackout curtain into the wheelhouse, stalked up to a snow-flecked window and peered out at the javelin-shaped bow as it streamed a plume of white spray. Beyond it, the massive slopes of the swells turned milky and blended into the leaden clouds which had dropped lower and became more turbulent as they were whipped along by the freshening nor'easter. Neither sea nor sky had a drop of color to relieve the oppressive, all-pervading sullen drabness which seeped through the clouded windows to fill the wheelhouse with gloom. It was eleven o'clock in the morning, yet as dark as if day were failing to shake off the grip of winter night. Finlander turned away from the depressing view, brushed past the OOD and moved over to the communications panel. "Quartermaster! I want to address ship's company, please."

After the piercing notes of the taped bosun's pipe faded on a melancholy minor key, Finlander's voice permeated every part of the *Bedford*.

"This is the captain speaking. I have every reason to believe that within the next twenty-four hours we shall close with our enemy. I am referring to the Russian submarine we call Moby Dick and I openly call him our enemy because he is intruding upon this part of the ocean with the objective of softening our defenses against the avowed Soviet purpose of burying us. While we are aware of our responsibility as part of NATO forces, we must primarily act as American sailors faced with a threat against our home shores. If any of you doubt this threat and are tempted to give the Russian leaders' protestations of peaceful intentions the benefit of doubt, then ask yourselves why his submarines prowl submerged through these waters attended by naval auxiliaries masquerading as innocent research vessels. Make no mistake about this! Their presence here is by nature of a clandestine operation preparatory to an eventual attack against our country. Any other interpretation is nothing but wishful thinking. But I am not going to deliver an orientation lecture on the evils of the Communist conspiracy, gentlemen. Suffice it to reaffirm that we are the professional complement of a United States warship—the *only* ship standing between our country's safety and that particular phase of Soviet aggression represented by the operation of Moby Dick and its charlatan consort, the *Novo Sibirsk*. I intend to show them that we are as ruthlessly determined upon thwarting their purpose as they are in committing it. I intend to hunt down Moby Dick, lock him in our sonar beams and hang on to him until he has no choice but to surface in our full view, then sneak home with no other truth to report than the certain prospects of defeat."

The captain paused to allow his words to sink home. When he resumed his speech, a slight—very slight—note of irony had crept into his tone.

"It was written about a hundred years ago that a certain Captain Ahab hunted a demon whale called Mocha Dick—or Moby Dick—and that he nailed a gold coin to the mizzenmast of his ship, promising this reward to the man who first spotted that whale and brought about a final reckoning with it. If I dealt in gold coin, or if you yourselves sought such, then none of us would be here, so I will make no such offer to the man who puts me on to our Moby Dick. All I will promise him is some slight favor over his shipmates when Christmas leaves are being allotted ... and an emphatic 'well done' which I will put down in his record with my own hand. To ensure equal opportunity for all hands in gaining this sailor's reward, I am ordering my departmental commanders, including Engineering and Commissary, to rotate their men into stand-by tactical assignments with the regular sonar, radar and eyeball watches. I am convinced that this will be all the incentive you need to excel the already high standards of duty aboard this ship during the critical week ahead. Thank you."

Down in the receiving office of the ship's hospital, Lieutenant Commander Chester Porter listened to the captain's speech as it came through the speaker above his desk, a look of perplexed wonder on his face. When it was finished, he gave out a low whistle and said to Ensign Ralston: "My gosh! The skipper is a real tiger, isn't he! I suppose every man will jump at the chance for some extra leave and a commendation in his jacket."

Ralston had continued to stare at the speaker after it fell silent, a kind of luminous eagerness lingering in his eyes; now he came to with a start and shrugged his broad shoulders. "We all jump for Captain Finlander, regardless of any rewards, sir. And mark my words, the Commie commander of Moby Dick will rue the day he put to sea to cross this ship's course! ... Now, sir, to get back to the matter of your litter-carrying drill. My objection can be overruled, of course, by Lieutenant Aherne or the exec. But I think you'll find them opposed to saddling the men with any work not directly connected with the operation at hand."

The surgeon frowned uncertainly at the ensign and experienced a resurgence of his frustrating feeling of being merely tolerated as a required item on the *Bedford*'s manning table. After breakfast he had dutifully presented himself in sick bay to await patients who never came. After sitting around uselessly for an hour, he had decided to pull a sanitation inspection of the galley. The cooks had appeared quite shocked, but were respectfully cooperative while showing him food lockers and refrigeration rooms which considerably exceeded regulations in their spotless cleanliness; that had turned out to be another hour wasted. Then, remembering that Lieutenant Hirschfeld had failed to carry out litter-carrying drills during GQ's, he had seized upon the idea of rectifying this situation at the very next alarm. For effective drills it would be necessary to arrange with other department commanders for simulated casualties, so he had optimistically set about organizing this. Picking Engineering as his first choice, he had descended into the engine room, where Commander Franklin had flatly refused his request. "Sorry, Doc! Can't spare any of my men just to play dead!" This had punctured his ardor somewhat, but he had stubbornly persisted and next accosted a more junior officer, Ensign Ralston, asking him, as assistant fire control, to allot him a couple of men out of relief crews. They should, after all, not be very busy during a GQ. But, to his surprise, Ralston had vigorously objected, even implying that the whole idea of litter-carrying drills was nonsensical. "Lieutenant Hirschfeld never went in for stuff like that, sir!" he had informed Porter and now was suggesting that his stand would be supported all along the chain of command—including the executive officer, who, of course, spoke for the captain.

"Seems to me Captain Finlander runs a real taut ship and would want all prescribed drill schedules complied with, Mr. Ralston," Porter protested in a plaintive voice.

The ensign smiled condescendingly. "You don't quite get the picture, Commander Porter. The captain is damned quick to throw away the book when it makes no sense to go by it. He's a stickler for operational performance, not for conformity with piddling sub-paragraphs appended to NAVREGs. He allows plenty of leeway in how you do a job, as long as you get it done *effectively*. Oh, sure ... maybe some stuffed-shirt fleet inspector could pick on him for this minor infraction or that petty non-compliance, but you can bet your life we'd all make it our personal business to make any criticism of the *Bedford* sound utterly ridiculous."

Lieutenant Commander Porter was by no means accustomed to being talked down to in this way by an ensign, but he was only able to say: "My gosh! He certainly inspires a tremendous loyalty."

"And *performance*, sir," Ralston added, getting up from his chair and preparing to leave. "And don't worry! If litter drills were really necessary, he would be right on your tail, Commander—if you'll excuse me for being so blunt." He spoke pleasantly and continued in a lighthearted tone as he moved to the door. "Between you and me, there won't be any more old-fashioned battle casualties. If the *Bedford* were to take a hit, it would most likely be from a missile or torpedo containing at least a half-ton of amatol, if not actually a nuclear warhead. Our own supply of high explosives, rocket propellant and superheated steam would certainly go off regardless of all our automatic damage-control systems. The ship would blow to pieces. Maybe two or three freak survivors would find themselves in the water, but they'd be quickly incinerated by burning oil. Everything over in a matter of seconds. Total obliteration or total survival, that's the prospect, sir." Noticing the expression on the surgeon's face, he began to laugh outright—without actually meaning to be cruel, yet that was the effect. "Don't feel too bad about it, Commander. The odds are overwhelmingly in favor of total survival—*because of Captain Erik J. Finlander.* Now, if you'll pardon me, sir, I must prepare to go on watch." He left with a salute which was more a cheery wave.

Lieutenant Commander Porter sat there seething, but he was the kind of man whose temper never seemed to erupt at the right moment and therefore was always quite ineffective. When he finally shot out of his chair, rushed through surgery past a startled McKinley and burst into the passageway, Ensign Ralston was long since gone. He had intended to dress him down for not only being presumptuous and somewhat insolent but also quite illogical for a supposedly professionally trained navy man. Certainly warships had a tendency to blow up—but, on the other hand, plenty of them had remained afloat while being battered into hulks, then made it to port. "And the crew were damned grateful for a good medical department too!" he exclaimed aloud. "A medical department properly drilled in litter carrying!"

Ben Munceford came around a corner, stared at him and then up and down the deserted passageway. "What's up, Chester?" he asked with a puzzled expression on his freckled face. "Who are you talking to?"

The surgeon felt himself turning scarlet. "Nobody. . . . I mean . . . I was asking if you'd be interested in acting as a simulated casualty in a litter-carrying drill?"

"Hell, no!" Munceford answered, then reacted as if Porter should be humored. "But I tell you what, Chester. Let me know when you get it organized and I'll take some pictures. It ought to go good with whales, volleyball, balloon flying and all the other shipboard activities of this cruise. Okay?"

"You go to the devil!" Porter snarled at him and stalked off in the direction of his cabin.

"A bunch of nuts!" Munceford muttered to himself after Porter was beyond hearing, then shrugged and headed for his own quarters.

When the surgeon stalked into his cabin he was surprised to find Steward's Mate Collins there, ostensibly to collect laundry, but actually rummaging through the small collection of medical volumes on the bookshelf above the bunk. "What are you doing with those?" Porter sharply asked the Negro.

Collins showed no trace of embarrassment. "I'm gathering up some books Lieutenant Hirschfeld left behind, sir," he explained. "He asked me to ship them to him together with some which he let me keep for my studies."

"I thought they all belonged to the ship's medical library," the surgeon told him irritably. "In any case, I'd like to check them against the department inventory."

Collins took this with better grace than the implication would warrant. "Yes, sir," he quietly agreed. He should have left the cabin with his laundry bag, but lingered and asked: "Has the commander settled down enough to consider my request of yesterday?"

"What request? ... Oh, yes! You are the one who wants to become a doctor." Lieutenant Commander Porter barely checked himself from shouting "You don't know when you're well off!" Instead he dropped into the chair and, after gnawing on his knuckles for a moment, fixed Collins with a jaundiced eye and said: "Yes—I might help you with your studies when I have time. But I would expect you to do me an occasional favor in return. For instance, during the next GQ I've got something right up the alley for a man with your keen medical interests. ..."

2.

The *Bedford* caught up with the *Novo Sibirsk* during the early afternoon when dusk was extinguishing the feeble daylight which had permeated the clouded Denmark Strait. Snow squalls had continued to follow one upon the other and the Russian suddenly materialized out of one of them, blossoming from a nebulous dark blotch into a solid, chunky little ship snorting along with spray bursting around her raked bow like vapor from a bucking workhorse. Thin smudges of diesel exhaust puffed out of her short stack, whose bright red band with the gold hammer-and-sickle insignia made a startling splash of color in the sullenly monotone seascape. There was less than a mile between the two vessels when the American destroyer sighted the Russian, who doggedly held his course as the warship bore down on him.

All of the "eyeball watch" on the *Bedford* sang out within seconds of one another, but without creating any surprise, as the officers on the bridge and in the CIC had been plotting the *Novo Sibirsk* position during the past two and a half hours. The Beek had picked up the emissions of the Russian's radar and, by computing their strength and bearing, had enabled Finlander to circle the perimeter of maximum-return echo and make his approach behind the shielding effects of the snow squalls and Iceland's mountainous coast. At least, that had been the tactical concept. Chances were, of course, that the Russians' detection equipment was as good as the Americans'. Yet, if they had known of the *Bed-*

ford's approach, they did not betray this fact by taking evasive actions. When the two ships were within three miles of each other, the CIC had reported a hard sonar contact which they plotted very close to the *Novo Sibirsk* and Captain Finlander had come near ordering battle stations in the brief hope of actually catching Moby Dick being serviced by its supply vessel. But Merlin Queffle's miraculous ears had quickly identified the contact as something much smaller than a submarine, and shortly thereafter Lieutenant Spitzer had obtained a trace of the echo which clearly indicated that the Russian was towing some kind of underwater object at the end of a long steel cable—probably a hydrographic device or biological trawl. Now, as the bridge watch focused their binoculars on the *Novo Sibirsk*, they could make out the cable streaming from a gallows frame on the forward welldock.

"So chalk up another one for our boy Queffle," Captain Finlander exclaimed with a mirthless chuckle. "The Commies are putting on their usual innocent act!"

"Probably heard us coming and decided to try and look scientific," Commander Allison growled through the closed face flap of his arctic hood; his big nose stuck out beyond it and glowed with almost the same red as the Russian's stack.

The captain looked around his snow-swept bridge for his oceanographic expert and spotted him trying to crouch out of the way of the icy spume whipping over the windscreen. "Say, Mr. Burger! What kind of gear are they working? Anything you recognize as legitimate?"

Lieutenant Burger reluctantly exposed himself to the elements and poked his face over the side, his eyes squinting painfully through his binoculars, which quickly fogged up. "Can't tell, sir," he answered. "Not without knowing what's at the other end of that tow cable."

"Lot of use you are to me!" Finlander shouted back at him, but more jokingly than with real rancor. He suddenly seemed strangely elated and full of caustic good humor. When the CIC called up and warned of the rapidly closing range on a collision course, he said to the OOD: "I suppose it won't do to run her down, Mr. Petersen. Just intimidate her, that's all. And make sure Pinelli gets some good snapshots."

As Petersen rushed back to the pilothouse, he brushed past Commodore Schrepke, who was just stepping out on the bridge. The German officer unhurriedly strode up alongside Finlander and raised his huge Zeiss glasses for a long, careful scrutiny of the Russian.

"Can you pick out anything compromising about her, Commodore?" the captain asked.

Schrepke took his time before answering, then spoke in clipped sentences without taking the binoculars from his eyes. "She has much depth and beam for extra bunkers. There are large-capacity fuel valves on deck. Booms and winches are unusually heavy. The bow is reinforced against ice. Radar and wireless antennas indicate extensive communication and detection equipment. Her lines suggest East German construction, probably in the yards of Stettin."

"Ah! We are faced with proof of German enterprise wherever we go!" Finlander exclaimed dryly.

Schrepke gave him a quick, hard look, retorted: "We are what our friends and enemies have made us, Captain," and removed himself to an unoccupied part of the bridge, from where he continued to study the *Novo Sibirsk* apart from the other officers.

As the *Bedford* closed with the Russian and details of the other ship began emerging more clearly out of the diffusing snow flurries, Yeoman Pinelli crouched in the turret of his Mark VII camera, his right eye pressed hard against the rubber cup of its viewfinder.

The cross-hairs were lined up on the *Novo Sibirsk*'s bridge and he found himself looking into the faces of a group of men who appeared to be staring right back at him; one of them aimed a Leica-type camera and they snapped each other's picture almost simultaneously. Pinelli smiled and activated the traversing mechanism of the gyro-stabilized turret, sweeping the howitzer-sized lens over the alleged research vessel and shooting close-ups of her superstructure and fittings. The red warning light was flashing on his control panel, indicating that it was too dark for good exposures, but he continued to press the trigger because he knew that even bad pictures could be immensely valuable to Naval Intelligence. Down on the *Bedford*'s main deck some other, far less sophisticated cameras were also being aimed at the Russian by a few sailors who had ventured out into the snow and spray to obtain proof that they had met the enemy. These would be far worse pictures, but still good enough to strike awe among family and barroom acquaintances.

By the time the two ships were some three hundred yards apart, with the *Bedford* slowing down to cross close astern of the *Novo Sibirsk*, a number of Russian crewmen had swarmed out on deck to line the railings and stare at the big American destroyer. Their faces were pink blobs framed by the darker hoods of their arctics—the same clumsy, heavy arctics used by anybody forced to work in this bitter climate. But, of course, there was also the inevitable sprinkling of rugged individualists who came out bareheaded and wearing nothing but their working fatigues—as in the American or English navies, these seemed to be engine-room or galley personnel with an obsessive need to show themselves off as fresh-air fiends. In fact, these Russian sailors looked remarkably like their American counterparts, clean, neat, well-fed, rosy-cheeked youths. Lieutenant Burger remarked that there were no women among them, pointing out this was unusual for a Soviet research vessel, an observation which Captain Finlander took note of and complimented him for. With a rare flash of humor, Commander Allison added that they also lacked that shaggy, piratical appearance affected by the bona-fide working oceanographic fraternity, hinting that this in itself was highly suspicious! That brought a sly smile to Finlander's lips, then a startled exclamation when he spotted two Russian sailors hurrying toward the stern of their ship, where the ensign of the U.S.S.R. was snapping its red folds in the wind. "Good Lord! Don't tell me they are going so far as to dip their colors to us!"

The executive officer watched them intently through his binoculars, and when they aligned themselves in a formal position by the jackstaff looking back toward their own bridge for a signal, he said: "I suppose we better play along and prepare to acknowledge their salute." He was about to order Ensign Ralston to rush a detail to stand by the colors when the captain intervened, his lighthearted manner completely gone.

"I exchange no courtesies with ships operating under false colors, Buck!" he snapped. "Have you forgotten this is a Soviet wolf in sheep's clothing?"

Allison shrugged. "All right, sir. But if we add insult to injury, that captain is a cinch to lodge a formal protest through diplomatic channels, accusing us of 'buzzing' his ship. . . . We're passing him pretty close," he added with a slight note of reproach.

"Dear me!" Finlander retorted with a sarcastic grimace. "While I don't give a damn about embarrassing our State Department, I certainly don't want to rattle my exec!" While everybody on the bridge but Allison cringed, he bellowed over his shoulder toward the pilothouse: "Pass at legal distance, Mr. Petersen! No more! No less!"

All the binoculars on the *Bedford*'s bridge were

trained again on the *Novo Sibirsk* as the faint shrill of a bosun's pipe came drifting across the intervening waves. It was presumably the signal from the Russian OOD to dip their colors to the American warship as age-old naval custom required, and Chief Quartermaster Rickmers anticipated the ceremony by gleefully growling between clenched teeth: "Come on, you Red cruds! Tip your hat to Uncle Sam!"

The two Russian sailors bent down out of sight, but not to untie the halyard of their ensign. When they straightened up they were hefting a garbage can between them which had been hidden behind the railing. Tipping it over the edge, they deliberately dumped the contents into the path of the American ship. A moment later the *Bedford* was forced to churn through the degrading mess staining the white foam of the Russian's wake and one of those sailors swept an imaginary hat off his head and gave her a ceremonious bow. Carried and chilled by the arctic wind, some deep Slavic laughter wafted across the bare hundred yards between ships. On the destroyer's bridge there was a stunned silence, but from one of her amateur photographers somewhere amidships of the main deck there came a defiant, salty bellow:

"Shit on you too, Ivan!"

The silence on the brdige lasted for a few seconds more before Ensign Ralston came out of his shock, gave a fearful glance toward Captain Finlander and wheeled on the chief quartermaster. "Rickmers! Put whoever yelled that obscenity on report!"

The captain had remained hunched over the railing, watching the Russian's slop defile the hull of his ship, without betraying his fury; the upturned collar of his white duffel hid the scar on his throat. But when he heard Ralston's order, he looked up and quietly told him: "Belay that! Let's make allowances for extreme provocation when it's warranted." Then he asked Allison in an equally quiet tone: "Do you still feel like exchanging courtesies with the Commies, Buck?" When his executive officer shook his head and maintained a tight-lipped silence, he gave him a forgiving slap on the shoulder. "All right, then! If it's any consolation to you, I came within a hair of falling for it too. Friendly-enemies deal! Dip the colors regardless, as an expression of the universal brotherhood of all men who pursue their duty on the cruel sea! ... Well, at least we don't have to analyze that load of garbage to know its significance!"

Ensign Ralston seethed beyond the point of containing himself. "Why don't we steam upwind and give them a good long dose of our dirtiest smoke, sir?" he blurted out.

Finlander gave him a balefully crushing stare from beneath his snow-flecked brows. "I prefer to leave the dirty little act of defiance to the more amateurish elements among our enemies, Mr. Ralston," he answered coldly, then addressed himself to Allison and the OOD: "Very good. I think we have intimidated this customer in spite of his show of insolence. At least he will suspect we know what he is up to and—*remember*—nothing is more demoralizing than to have the secrecy stripped from one's secret mission. So let's leave him stew about it while we go after his pet pigboat, Moby Dick."

As the *Bedford* pulled away and the *Novo Sibirsk* began to dissolve into the gloomy shroud of another squall, most of the bridge watch retreated into the pilothouse, there to thaw out their numbed faces and ice-crusted clothing. The lookouts remained, once again straining their eyes over a darkening, empty sea; and Captain Finlander remained because this fading gray oblivion was another sunless sunset. Wolfgang Schrepke, also compelled by old habits, moved toward his solitary vigil in the opposite wing of the bridge, but first paused by the captain to say: "I noticed one more thing about that Russian."

"Yes, sir?"

"Those large discharge valves. I recall them to be of the type used for transfer of concentrated hydrogen peroxide."

"Yes?"

"That was the fuel used by our Walther-type U-boat propulsion plants. As a Russian prisoner I was assigned to work on their copy of such a unit. You can look for Moby Dick to be a Chelnikoff class with a submerged maximum speed of twenty-five knots and a duration of thirty hours without schnorkeling."

"Thank you, Commodore."

Down below deck there were two men who were totally oblivious of what had taken place beyond their cabins during the past forty minutes. One was Lieutenant Commander Chester Porter, who had stretched out on his bunk with one of the books he had found in Lieutenant Hirschfeld's collection, Montcalm's *War Psychology in Primitive and Modern Man.* For over two hours he had been absorbed in it, being frequently sidetracked by the profuse marginal notes and the more detailed loose-leaf ones stuck in between pertinent pages. It was these writings by Lieutenant Hirschfeld which he had studied with an increasingly disturbed fascination. Finally he had got up off the bunk and began to pace back and forth over the narrow confines of his cabin, still reading and muttering disconnected excerpts to himself in agitated whispers: "... stresses far exceeding those of any normal peacetime patrol ... producing hate syndromes ... war's only natural release, *killing*, is denied ... aggravating latent aberrations without recourse to normal checks and balances. ..."

And one deck lower, Ben Munceford had escaped into his even more isolated cabin (it was actually located below the waterline), determined to avoid any of Finlander's cornball production ideas for the balance of the afternoon. After dark he would venture forth and try to tape some interviews of the crew—*enlisted* crew. In the meanwhile he planned to digest his lunch in peace and maybe doze off a bit. The only thing which prevented this was his shameless desire to refresh the vision of Shebeona in his mind, and that caused him to poke about Lieutenant Packer's locker and drawers. He stopped short of a full scale shakedown search and, when he failed to find her, disgustedly heaved himself up into his bunk, where he lay thinking about Nancy III just to discourage himself on the subject of women. Still Shebeona's picture haunted him. But he soon went to sleep anyway.

3.

When the watch changed at 0400 of the following morning, it was pouring with rain. The thermometer indicated a fraction under twenty-nine degrees Fahrenheit, yet it rained a thick, penetrating, all-soaking rain which fell out of a windless, opaque blackness, washing off all the snow which had accumulated on the *Bedford* during the previous day and substituting a sheathing of glass-slick ice. Every raindrop which touched the ship seemed to freeze solid instantly. The decks were like newly surfaced skating rinks, and ice covered even the lifelines, the handholds, the vertical surfaces and the antennas, from where it would break loose at intervals, falling and clattering against the superstructure like showers of pebbles. The seas had flattened out as the ship came under the lee of the Greenland coast and her motions were reduced to an occasional easy roll as she drove silently through the night; the wind had completely died out and the only movement in the bitterly saturated air was created by the eighteen-knot forward velocity of the destroyer herself. Both bridge lookouts slipped and fell before they had been on watch for more than a few minutes.

One of the lookouts who promptly fell as soon as he stepped out on the bridge was Fireman Second Class Bertrand W. Meggs, and he would not have been there at all had it not been for Captain Finlander's order to give all of the *Bedford*'s crew a crack at spotting Moby Dick. Meggs had been pleased when Chief MacKay picked him to represent Engineering on the bridge for an hour, but his pleasure had turned into trepidation when he was so rudely acquainted with the appalling topside conditions. It was not so much the fall, although it had been hard enough to leave a throbbing ache in his back and shoulder, but when he finally worked himself out to his post in the port wing by a series of uncertain shuffles and slides, he had blinked his eyes to make sure they were open, then held a hand out in front of his face and been absolutely unable to see it. It was then that the futility of his assignment struck him, the uselessness of his exchanging a warm, bright post at No. 1 boiler for this sodden, freezing, black agony. Moby Dick could have surfaced right alongside without being spotted! Meggs had never in his life seen such a black night, or such a cold, wet one! The quartermaster had made him put on a sou'wester and a slicker over his regular arctics, but a chill was creeping up his bruised backside and an icy little stream of water working its way down his neck, seeping through the collar past two sweaters, shirt and thermal long-johns, to dampen his chest. The rain splattered on the sou'wester pulled down over the closed hood of his parka, making a patter like rain on a tarpaper roof; it was so loud that all other sounds were blotted out, even the hissing of the destroyer's wash.

It crossed Meggs's mind that he was being allowed to take this "eyeball" lookout assignment simply because the sharpest, best-trained eyes on the ship could not see a god-damned thing through this muck anyway—so let some poor nearsighted son of a bitch out of the boiler rooms waste his time trying for a captain's prize! The quartermaster and his regular "eyeballs" were probably sitting on the heaters in the pilothouse, laughing at him. Well—to hell with them! He would try anyway. Maybe a miracle would happen and the god-damned Russian sub would come steaming along the surface with his navigation lights ablaze. Or trailing a bright patch of phosphorescence. Yes! There was sometimes an amazing phosphorescence in these black waters!

Fireman Meggs cautiously felt his way along the railing of the bridge, leaning far out and trying to see if there was any glow in the wash, fifty feet below. But he could see nothing. It was as if the ship were mysteriously flying through the night, supported by nothing but the trillions of raindrops. Then he suddenly bumped up against something like wet leather, soft, yet with a hardness underneath which briefly rippled with a living action. "Jesus! Who's that? Somebody else out here?" he gasped.

"Yes, obviously, sailor."

Meggs's shock subsided and he was happy to find some human company in this stygian blackness, but also irritated because he was not being trusted with the lookout job by himself. "You mean they're wasting *two* of us out here! That's a bunch of crap, by God! Even if they gave us a seeing-eye dog apiece, we wouldn't be worth a fart in the wind!"

The other man took his time before answering, then rather curtly agreed: "It is quite thick."

"Thicker than the inside of an undertaker's drawers, brother! I can't even tell who the hell you are. One of the regular 'eyeballs' around here?"

Again the other man hesitated before answering, but this time he spoke with a somewhat lighter tone. "Yes, I suppose you might call me that."

Fireman Second Class Bert Meggs finally caught the Germanic accent in the voice speaking to him out of the dark and a shock of outright fear shot through his chest. "Christ almighty! You sound like ... I mean, are you? ... Yes, Jesus! You are the commodore!" He almost slipped and fell again as he backed off across the icy deck. "Excuse me, sir! It's just so horrible damned black out here I can't see my hand in front of my f . . . face, sir."

"It's all right, sailor," Schrepke told him, sternly, yet somehow also reassuring. "You must not worry about speaking to me or about this very dark night. A good lookout does more than just look. He must *listen*, no? Have you listened yet, sailor?"

"Listened, sir?"

"Yes. Try it now."

Meggs listened and heard only the hard patter of rain against his sou'wester.

"Do you not hear something?" the Germanic voice patiently prodded him out of the black vacuum.

Meggs yanked off the sou'wester and tore open the snaps of his thick woolen hood. When he had bared his head and felt the sting of raindrops on his scalp, he leaned far out over the railing and stared into the void, but straining his ears rather than his eyes. And now he heard it! A weird deep rumbling which seemed to surge faintly above the soft noise of rain falling into the sea. It had an eery, menacing quality which raised the hackles in the back of his neck and set his heart to wildly beating. "Oh, God, sir! What is it?"

"Ah! You hear it too, then. Ice in breakers."

"Ice in breakers?"

"It won't get you your captain's prize, sailor, but I believe he would be grateful if you reported it," Schrepke quietly suggested.

"Ice and breakers! Jesus Christ!" Meggs exclaimed and, wheeling for the pilothouse, began a frantic shuffling, sliding rush for its door. Yanking it open, he electrified the shadowy figures inside by yelling at the top of his voice:

"Ice and breakers ahead!"

Three minutes later Captain Finlander came out on the port wing, bareheaded and wearing only his white duffel over white pajamas. He became an almost ghostly figure, shimmering with a pale luminescence as he stood there in the pitch-black night, intently listening. His ship was more silent than ever since her engines had been stopped and she wallowed sluggishly over the oily swells. But the ominous rumbling was so pronounced now that it filled the blackness all around with a tangible threat which could be felt as well as heard. The captain absorbed its vibrations for a moment, then unerringly addressed himself to the invisible Meggs. "Did you sound off about this, lad?"

"Yessir . . . sort of, but . . ." He hesitated, gingerly groped around for Schrepke and was thrown into speechless confusion when he found the German had mysteriously vanished from his side.

The captain had little time to waste and so gave him none to recover and explain what had happened. "Well done, Meggs!" Returning inside the wheelhouse, he joined a badly rattled OOD, Lieutenant Petersen, who was staring at the radar scope with something closely akin to hatred. "All right, Mr. Petersen," Finlander mildly admonished him. "There's no use in venting your frustrations on that inanimate object. It has simply been overwhelmed by conditions which—*please note*—can only be coped with by ordinary frail human beings. Well, perhaps I am being unfair. Fireman Meggs seems neither ordinary or frail, God bless him!"

Behind them a voice crackled out of a speaker on the communications panel:

"CIC to bridge! The MTS is picking up strong ice echoes now, bearing three-one-zero, range two-four-zero-zero."

"Oh, Lord, that's close!" Petersen exclaimed and moved to acknowledge, but Finlander beat him to it.

"Congratulations, CIC!" the captain acidly purred into the microphone. "The eyeball watch appreciates having their reports confirmed by your scientists—even belatedly. Now could we trouble you to keep track of that ice, please? We don't want it closer than a thousand yards or so, if it can be helped. Thank you." Although he was needling them, he spoke without anger and there was something reassuring in the mere fact that he was being flippant about it. Obviously he did not consider the situation dangerous even though they had come close to smashing into the icefields hugging the Greenland coast. He even grinned at Petersen and managed to draw a nervous smile in response. "I suggest you forget radar for the time being and use the master fathometer to help you hold us hove to while I go backstage and cast the navigational bones with Commander Allison."

"Yes, sir. And I'm sorry I messed things up."

"Messed what up? Are we in trouble? No! Just had another close shave which is part of the hazards of arctic operations, that's all. Go to it, boy!"

Commander Allison had also been urgently routed out of his cabin. He was the kind of man who always yanked on his trousers under such circumstances, then rushed for a bridge while still wearing the top of his pajamas. He and the captain made an odd, un-naval-looking pair as they bent over the chart, carefully studying it in the glow of the red blackout light, each still wearing part of his sleeping garb and part uniform. "The Inertial Navigator and our last reliable radar bearing don't check out, sir," the exec told Finlander. "We should be *here*—about sixty miles southwest of Cape Tupinier and still well off the hundred-fathom curve. But I'm afraid we are in fact badly off our reckoning if surf noises can be heard."

"Not necessarily, Buck. I don't see any reason to question our pampered Inertial Navigational System as long as the CSP room doesn't flood or freeze up. Furthermore, I even doubt if those are shoreside breakers we hear out there. Could very well be a grounded berg left over from last season with a raft of growlers in its backwash to create the uproar. In any case, I'm more concerned about Moby Dick's position than our own—which can't be off more than a mile or two at the very worst. . . . Good Lord, Buck! When will you give up those screaming striped pajamas?"

"I'll buy a nice conservative set of white silks when I make captain. . . . I take it you want to go by the INS position, sir?"

"I see no alternative, do you? With radar haywire and the overcast too thick for any old-fashioned celestial help, that's when we've got to go along with Krindlemeyer and Spitzer's bag of scientific tricks, right?" Finlander's eyebrows cocked suddenly into their most sardonic expression. "And by the way, Buck! You never will make captain if I write in your fitness report that you barge around my bridge in that barber-pole outfit casting aspersions on the navy's pet navigational whizbang. Shocking reactionary attitude, I'd say. Like going around plumping for battlewagons and gunboats." He shook his head and made some disapproving clucking sounds. "Well, I'm going back to bed, but don't hesitate to call me if there's anything I can do."

"Sweet dreams!" Allison threw after him with a stiff, one-sided grin, noticing that the captain was not taking the situation so lightly as to return to the luxury of the double-sized bunk in his stateroom, but retired to the spartan day cabin behind the navigation office. The executive officer still felt worried, but the gnawing apprehension which had flooded his mind when the OOD's panicked call first brought him rushing to the bridge had subsided. Stepping into the wheelhouse, he took his foulweather gear off its hook on the bulkhead and slipped it on over his pajama tops. He asked the JOOD to send a messenger below for the captain's and his own clothing, then went out into the freezing sleet to check for himself the grim sounds which filled the surrounding night.

During the next hour the *Bedford* remained in the same spot, rolling and heaving lazily while her position was maintained in the absolute darkness by using the fathometer to pick a reference point off the bottom, one hundred and ninety fathoms down. The distant rumble rose and fell without increasing its threat on the average. The downpour slowly moderated and by two bells it was more of a thick, penetrating mist than actual rain. But when the quartermaster of the watch recorded the hourly temperature reading, it had dropped two degrees to twenty-seven Fahrenheit—which meant that the destroyer's unbalancing coating of ice would be freezing more solidly than ever to her superstructure. In thickness it built up only inch by inch, but in aggregate weight, ton by ton. This was why she was getting more sluggish and slower in recovering herself after the low swells passed beneath her keel.

The unnatural cadence of his ship's motions was one of the things which kept Captain Finlander from dozing off as he lay on the bunk in the day cabin, wrapped in the folds of a regulation navy blanket over which he had pulled his white duffel. Raw drafts wafted past the blackout curtains every time somebody opened the wheelhouse doors to the open bridge—which was often as Petersen or Allison stepped out to look and listen, or the lookouts relieved one another at twenty-minute intervals. Ice falling off the halyards and shrouds occasionally rattled against the roof of the pilothouse; the gyro-repeater on the bulkhead went *click-click-click* every time the ship changed heading. Of these things Finlander was conscious as he lay there, and in the back of his mind the old horror of all destroyermen operating in the arctic, capsizing by sheer weight of ice, began haunting him. Back at BUSHIPS, all kinds of geniuses were figuring out how to decontaminate a ship which had been subjected to radiation, but not even the civil service deadheads in the bureau were given the assignment of figuring out how to decontaminate what this filthy night was depositing on the *Bedford*. Well, none too many ships had gone down under the press of ice lately, had they? . . . There was only that Danish corvette two years ago. And a supply ship the year before that. Surely the *Bedford* could never be overwhelmed by such an ignominious fate! Not *his* ship! . . . Maybe the Commie commander of Moby Dick was counting on him nurturing exactly these fears. Counting on it while he himself took advantage of his own craft's natural superiority under such conditions, exposing nothing but the conning tower, periscopes, radar and sensory antennas to the horrible smothering, congealing sleet. If it got too bad, all a submarine had to do was to submerge into the warming bosom of the deep, thaw out for a while, then try again. . . . Finlander pressed his eyes tightly closed, feigning sleep to himself and dreaming of sticking it out until his ship became a nightmare glob of ice. . . .

"Sir! Sir! The Beek just picked up another of those fragmentary signals. Much stronger this time!"

Finlander sat up and found himself staring into the dim faces of Commander Allison and Lieutenant Petersen. "Very good!" he exclaimed with a transparently forced casualness in his voice. "Very good! I'm glad he's so much on the ball. Any bearing?"

"No, sir. But he estimates it's no farther than seventy miles. It pretty well *has* to be seventy miles north or south."

The captain blinked, rubbed his face very hard, driving his knuckles deep into his eyes, then shook his head. "As simple as that, eh? Seventy miles north or seventy miles south. Well, let's see. The ice is probably nearly on the bottom in Scoresby Sound and awfully thick around the entrance. Dangerous stuff for a pigboat of the old type. So let's say seventy miles south. Anything from the *Novo Sibirsk* which might indicate reporting our position?"

"Nothing since last evening's long-winded complaint about us to SOVFLOT, sir. Moby Dick probably monitored that."

Finlander managed a smile. "Very good. Obviously they quickly lost radar contact with us in the sleet and now we are being screened by the Greenland coast. That's perfect. Get under way and start creeping to the southward along the edge of the pack. Keep radar and sonar on low scales. And keep me informed of developments, gentlemen." He lowered himself back into a horizontal position and pulled the blanket over his face, once again closing his eyes. As Lieutenant Petersen tiptoed out of the day cabin behind the executive officer, he whispered: "How the hell does the skipper wake out of a sound sleep and instantly give a sound evaluation of a tactical situation?"

Allison only grunted.

Finlander's mind was not only awake, but racing as he lay beneath the prickly warmth of the blanket. Seventy miles between him and the detested Moby Dick! The Beek had to be pretty sure of himself to voluntarily make such an optimistic estimate. A pity he could not also have provided a bearing! Seventy miles north or south along this coast could—if he had picked the wrong direction—mean a two-hundred-and-ten-mile error, which meant eleven hours' lost steaming, which meant most certainly a total abort. Stick out your neck, Commanding Officer, and decide! Yes, the ice was very thick to the north and in Scoresby Sound a sub could get itself trapped, yet some submarines were specially built to poke up through the floes, some skippers like Moby Dick's and the *Bedford*'s were unorthodox daredevils. Finlander smiled with his eyes closed, then quickly squelched any glimmer of kinship with his Soviet counterpart. He'd give him coldly professional credit, but that was all. And he was betting he would be operating below Cape Brewster, where the icepack would remain comparatively loose for another two weeks. *Click-click-click-click* chattered the gyro-repeater as the ship turned south; a faint tremor shook the cabin as the turbines picked up revolutions. Three bells were struck and as the melodious sound pene-trated through the folds of the blanket it brought him a comforting thought about being able to doze for an-other hour—maybe really sleep. Instead he found him-self standing before Admiral Sorensen, the grizzled little Dane who commanded NATONAV 1 and took sadistic pleasure in dressing down American officers. "You ekted unwisely in turning sou'd, Kep'n," he said with a pronunciation which was exactly like that of a countryman of his own who was a famous comedian in the United States; but Sorensen was a man devoid of even the slightest sense of comedy. "You should heff turn nor'd, ja? You should heff antizipate de unlikely, ja? Very unwise, Kep'n . . . very unwise. . . ." His an-gry red face dissolved away with the rising clamor of a GQ alarm.

Captain Finlander shot out of his bunk, kicked him-self free of the tangling blanket and, sweeping the duf-fel over his shoulders, ran for the wheelhouse. But Commander Allison was already coming for him and they met in the navigation office.

"It's really only an air alert, sir," the exec told the captain with a weary irritation.

"Then why the GQ, Buck? I'd like to save our en-ergy for sub-hunting, you know."

"The CIC has been pretty jumpy during the last hour. Spitzer claims he has a UFO on the sky sweeper. Thinks it may be a balloon, but isn't absolutely sure. Range is sixty-two miles, altitude twelve thousand, bearing zero-one-five. I think it's a stray RAOBs from Thule. Shall we secure battle stations, sir?"

Finlander had moved to the chart and stood looking down at it with his brows knitted together in a concentrated bristle. "Not yet, no. Sixty-two miles almost due south of us, is it? And fifteen minutes ago we picked up that mysterious signal. Maybe we are finding some pieces that will fit together, and maybe just a few more will give us a pretty clear picture." He reached for the telephone, dialed Communications Center and asked for Lieutenant Beeker. "Any way you can check out possible Soviet airborne telemetrics?" he inquired.

"If they are close enough, *maybe*, sir," The Beek's tired voice hedged.

"Will sixty-two miles do, Mr. Beeker?"

The Beek's voice lost its weariness. "If that's all, Captain, there's a fair chance. Give me five minutes."

"I'll give you three, then two more to get up here!" Hanging up, he turned to Allison. "I want the meteorological officer to report to me on the double with all his latest synoptics."

Lieutenant Petersen stuck his head through the blackout curtain of the wheelhouse. "The CIC reports the UFO definitely identified as a balloon moving slowly northeast and gaining altitude. Sorry about the false alarm, sir. Shall I secure?"

"Not unless you can satisfactorily explain its presence," Finlander retorted.

Petersen's expression became confused, then startled. "You mean it might have been launched by Moby Dick, sir? Should I order the ADO to stand by to shoot it down?"

"Let's not reveal our position by getting trigger happy, Mr. Petersen. Simply ask CIC to keep accurate track of it." The telephone diverted him with an urgent buzzing. It was The Beek, reporting a little over two minutes after receiving his assignment, to inform the captain that they were recording strong telemetric signals whose range and bearing checked with the CIC's contact. Finlander ordered him to hurry to the bridge, then told Allison: "Piece number one just fell in place, Buck. Now I need another from the met officer. Where is he?"

Even as he asked, Ensign Bascomb came bursting through the blackout curtain and breathlessly announced himself. His clothes looked as if he had dived into them on the fly and he was still fumbling with one hand to hitch up his pants properly; with the other he clutched a roll of weather maps. Finlander reached out and yanked him over to the chart table.

"I've got a fascinating little problem for you, weatherman! Using all available meteorological and target-analyses data, I want you to backtrack a balloon to give me an accurate estimate of the position from where it was launched and when. I'm going into the day cabin to get dressed and when I come back I'll need that information ready."

When he returned four minutes later fully clothed, Lieutenants Beeker and Krindlemeyer had joined the other officers and in a dark corner of the navigation office Finlander glimpsed a shadowy figure with the glint of black leather. The others were clustered around Ensign Bascomb, who was hunched over the chart table, his whole demeanor an agony of concentration, telephone wedged between shoulder and ear, a slide rule in his left hand, the right scribbling figures on the weather chart which he had superimposed over the navigational one.

The captain elbowed his way through the crowd and placed himself next to him. "Well, Bascomb?"

The met officer hung up the phone, made a few quick additional calculations on the margin of his chart, then said: "Assuming it is an average-sized instrument carrier filled with hydrogen, and assuming a rate of ascent of six hundred feet per minute, and assuming wind patterns have been fairly constant, and

temperatures *there* are about what they are here, then
. . . the launch should have taken place twenty-four
minutes ago from *this* position." He laid the parallel
ruler along a course drawn from the balloon's known
position and drew a rather faint, uncertain circle off a
nameless promontory of the Greenland coast. "Of
course, sir, this is assuming a hell of a lot of things
and, of course, I am aware that this places the
launching site in thick ice."

Finlander pulled him away from the chart, took a
pair of dividers and pricked off the distance. "Seventy-
four miles! It checks! Very good, Mr. Bascomb!" With
a pencil he made the circle firmly black. "I have one
more question to ask Mr. Beeker. Would you classify
those telemetrics as standard RAOB's stuff for weather
forecasting?"

The Beek shook his head. "No, sir. More likely microwave analyses."

Finlander nodded. "Then here's the picture as I see
it. The Commie pigboat is lying off this point with its
conning tower stuck up through the ice as a launching
platform for airborne microwave detectors intended to
gather information on emissions from our DEW-line
system. The fragmentary intercepts we've been picking
up are most likely his command to the *Novo Sibirsk* to
start monitoring the telemetric data, which they in turn
relay on to Moscow disguised as oceanographic observations." He looked around him at their faces and
paused to give anybody the chance to add or detract
from his evaluation. None spoke. He smiled and suddenly slammed a fist into the palm of his other hand.
"Moby Dick has spouted for us, gentlemen! Let's go
after him! His radar is probably as fouled as ours, so
here is a fine chance to sneak up on him undetected
under cover of darkness. We move in blacked out, all
high-frequency stuff turned off and under absolute radio silence. This is it! From here on we go all out!"

4.

While the *Bedford* drove purposefully but blindly through a morning as black and cold as winter midnight, her bridge lookouts doubled to compensate for the muzzling of her electronic detection gear, a clash took place in the wardroom brought about by tensions beyond those generated by the perilous action at hand. Perhaps heeding the dangers of speeding in complete darkness along the iceclogged, uncertainly charted Greenland coast, or perhaps only wanting to keep his crew keyed to the chase he had begun, Captain Finlander did not secure his ship from battle stations. Only a few men at a time were permitted to stand down in turns for hot breakfast, and it was because of this that none but Commander Allison and Ensign Ralston were in the wardroom when Ben Munceford came up from his cabin, still rubbing sleep from his eyes. It was natural for him to ask: "What's up? Where is everybody?" It was maybe as natural for the executive officer to contemptuously counter: "You mean you slept all through a GQ? That's what I call being a live-wire reporter!"

"I turned out when the alarm sounded at five thirty," Munceford replied with a scowl. "But the scuttlebutt had it to be nothing but some balloon, so I went back to bed." When Ralston glanced at the exec with a loud snicker, Munceford's tone became sharp. "So? What's it all about?"

Allison filled his mouth with eggs and concentrated on smearing a heap of jam on a piece of tast. Ralston savored a scalding draft of coffee, gulped it down and casually answered: "Oh, nothing much, Ben. We damned near piled into an icefield at eighteen knots, which isn't too unusual in this kind of operation, of course. And, oh, yes—we're on to Moby Dick and kind of getting set to pounce on him right now. That's all, isn't it, Commander?"

"Yes, Mr. Ralston," Allison agreed, biting off a large chunk of toast and continuing through the mouthful. "I suppose we've been amiss in not providing Mr. Munceford with a printed program. It slipped my mind that these TV correspondents have to work off official handouts."

Ben Munceford's face turned a mottled red beneath the freckles. Yesterday afternoon they had left him oblivious in his cabin while they passed within a hundred yards of a Russian spy ship; now this! He furiously threw his jacket down on a chair and stalked over to the coffee urn on the sideboard. "You guys make a stranger feel right at home, don't you! Christ! If I'd been on deck when we passed that Commie yesterday, I might have jumped over the side just to join the other outcasts." He instantly realized the enormity of what he had said and regretted it, but the hurt kept seething inside him.

Ralston gave him a look of incredulous disgust which became a leer when the executive officer exclaimed: "If we had known that, we certainly would have taken the trouble to notify you, Mr. Munceford."

Munceford burned his lips on the coffee and spluttered. "Damn it, I'm sorry! So I've goofed! But I'm still trying to do a job on this ship."

"Sure you are, Ben." Ralston shrugged with indifference.

Two other ensigns from Engineering came into the wardroom and threw everybody cheery greetings before attacking the platters of food, so Munceford clamped down on his temper and seated himself next to them. Ralston gulped the last of his breakfast, excused himself to Commander Allison and headed for the door; as he passed the chair, he deftly lifted the camouflage jacket off it and took it with him. If the executive officer noticed the action he paid no attention to it and Munceford was sulkily staring into his cup of coffee while dunking a doughnut. He had lost his appetite and it was not until he abruptly got up to escape topside and think things out that he missed his jacket. He stared at the empty chair for a moment, then spun around and faced Allison, who had also risen to leave. "All right! Who took it?" he demanded, his fury now out of control.

"Who took what?" the exec coldly inquired.

"It was your snotty ensign playing smart, right?"

The two engineering ensigns stopped eating and gaped.

"Oh, you're talking about that infantryman's sport coat of yours," Allison said without a glimmer of humor.

"You know god-damned well what I'm talking about!" Munceford shouted. "I want my jacket back. If I don't get it back, I'm going to raise hell with the captain about this childish crap!"

Commander Allison's voice dropped to a snarling whisper. "Complaints to the captain are channeled through the executive officer. Unfortunately he is too busy right now to be worried about a missing item of your wardrobe. Is that clear, Mr. Munceford?"

"Yeah, so I guess I can settle that one for myself with Ralston! But don't think I'm not on to the crazy way this operation is being carried on. That's what I'm going to get to the bottom of, with or without your almighty Captain Finlander. I may be a screwball kind of correspondent, but I'm god-damned curious and don't get scared off from prying in dark corners."

Even before he finished his outburst, Allison was roughly shoving his way past him. But he also had to push past Lieutenant Commander Chester Porter, who was on his way in to breakfast. The surgeon had heard the last exchange and wore an appalled look on his face which turned into consternation when the executive officer whipped back and asked him: "Say, Doc! Where was Steward's Mate Collins this morning when the captain wanted some foot shot up to his day cabin?"

"Ah ... er ... uh ... Collins? Oh, well, you see, I'd organized a little litter-carrying drill during the GQ and Collins was the simulated casualty and——"

"What?" Allison exploded. "Do both of you characters foisted on us by the *Tiburon Bay* figure you've joined some kind of picnic? Some company outing? Some seascout cruise? Damn it all to hell, get with it!!" With a gesture of utter disgust he turned away and vanished down the passageway.

The surgeon recoiled against the bulkhead and appeared close to slumping to the deck. Uncomprehendingly he blinked at Munceford, who was suddenly strangely sobered by the executive officer's violent outburst. "Yeah, Doc!" he sighed with a low, bitter drawl. "Let's you and me get with it and find out what these cats put in their needles."

A flash of sheer horror came over Lieutenant Commander Porter's expression, but the two engineering ensigns somehow triggered nervous chuckles out of each other and one of them said: "Gosh! I guess these TV types actually do talk like that, don't they!"

By 0940 hours the total darkness had given way to a cold, clammy twilight and the tension on the bridge slackened somewhat as a flat colorless ocean began to gain definition in a widening ring of visibility around the speeding destroyer. Close above her, the overcast pressed down like a sagging ceiling which threatened to collapse at any moment, but the space between clouds and sea was free of sleet and only partially obscured by random patches of fog. Vapor wafted from the faces of the lookouts as they drew sighs of relief and Lieutenant Harwell's tensely alert position in the open doorway of the pilothouse relaxed slightly. But Captain Finlander did not relax or move from his position in the exposed wing; indeed, he quickly brought his men back to their former state of nerves by ordering more speed as the curtain of night drew away; it was as if he were trying to keep up with it and use it as a shield in his approach to Moby Dick. Twenty-one . . . twenty-three . . . then twenty-six knots made the ship tremble from the power of her turbines, and the wake roared as it shot out from beneath the stern in a thrashing maelstrom of foam. Down in the CIC they had to shut down the low-power echo-ranging which had been their dubious insurance against smashing into heavy ice and now, deprived of all their electronic sight and hearing, the men sat idly in the dark, suffering the agonies of the deaf and the blind.

Little by little the twilight lifted and presently the coastal icepack became visible two miles off the starboard beam as a pale white line paralleling their course. Again there were sighs of relief on the bridge, but also gasps of dismay when the improving light revealed their own ship to them. All the familiar lines were subtly distorted by the frozen sheathing deposited by last night's sleet, all the solid battleship gray turned into a translucent and sickly pallor beneath the skin of ice. It covered every part of the *Bedford* above her waterline and had formed clusters of soot-stained icicles snaking like congealed tentacles from the rims of her stacks. Gnarled stalactites hung from the muzzles of the DP guns while others had fused lifelines and shrouds to the deck plates. Most startling of all were the coxcomb shapes curling off the masthead and crow's-nest, and the spiked clusters which had been created by the centrifugal effect on the rims of the radar antennas. As Captain Finlander glanced up at these, the nightmare which had haunted his half-sleep during the night briefly came back and stung him with its reality, but then something else caught his attention. "Buck! What's that flying from our main signal halyard?"

Commander Allison wiped some freezing moisture the wind had stung out of his eyes, peered upward and caught sight of a crazy pennant flashing a mottled conglomeration of colors against the gloomy cloud ceiling. He instantly became filled with rage and embarrassment. "Sir, that is Mr. Munceford's jacket!" he shouted back at the captain in a deeply offended tone.

There came a very fleeting twist of amusement on Finlander's lips before he sternly ordered: "Haul it down!" then dismissed the matter and returned his attention to scanning the seas ahead.

Allison angrily ordered Chief Rickmers to lower the offensive garment from its lofty position above the *Bedford*'s bridge. What bothered him the most was that he would have to discipline Ensign Ralston, humiliating that splendid young officer instead of the horrible Munceford! Then he sickened more when Munceford suddenly appeared on the scene.

The correspondent peered around the ice-crusted bridge, then raised his eyes skyward. Inevitably he spied his jacket and followed it downward until its wild flapping was belayed by Rickmers' gloved fists. Gritting his teeth, Allison placed himself between him and the captain.

But Munceford made no motion until Rickmers came alongside him, gingerly holding the jacket between thumb and forefinger; then he reached out and stopped him. Quickly removing the regulation navy parka he had worn to the bridge, Munceford retrieved his own and squirmed into its shreds, which hung on him with its bright, torn patches of divisional insignia like part of a clown's costume. There was something clownish too about the way the freckles stood out on his livid face, but there was none of that quality in his voice. "Thank you, Chief," he said, handing over the parka. "I won't be needing this one now."

Rickmers mumbled something entirely unintelligible, glanced unhappily toward the fuming executive officer, then fled inside the pilothouse.

"Awful raw morning!" Munceford exclaimed casually to Allison and ambled off to another part of the bridge. Tears burned against his cheek, then froze as he hunched down and fiddled with his camera.

By 1015 hours it was full daylight, although still a depressing and foreboding facsimile of the term. Visibility improved until the barren escarpments of Greenland could be seen as a hazy black wall looming beyond the wide barrier of pack ice, its top blending into the clouds and distance giving it a weird marbled effect caused by snow-clogged crevasses. The overcast clung from the wall, seemed to sag low over the *Bedford*'s masthead, then stretch out over the open wastes of the Denmark Strait, where it grew thin in patches, allowing ghostly halos of sunlight to illuminate parts of the horizon.

After checking their position with the INS, Allison approached Captain Finlander and announced: "We will be abeam Moby Dick's estimated position in eighteen minutes, sir."

"Very good, Buck. Hold this speed and heading for ten more minutes, then stop engines and coast in toward the edge of the pack. Alert CIC to have all detection gear warmed up and ready for instant use. Ask them to put Queffle on the QBH hydrophones. No echo-ranging or radar without orders." He squinted uneasily toward the ragged sun patches bleeding through the gray of the eastern sky. "Pray our nice neutral background doesn't break up on us!"

Ten minutes later the *Bedford's* speed abruptly slackened, the white water rushing from her stem and stern fell away and gradually abated into a soft murmur. A complete, tense silence enveloped the entire ship as she turned toward the icepack, stealthily approaching it on momentum only. The JOOD took a visual bearing on the coast through the pelorus and confirmed their position with a low voice. Nobody else on the bridge spoke as all eyes strained through binoculars, sweeping the vast expanse of ice which stretched from the black edge of the sea for four miles to the coast. The individual floes began to stand out as they drew nearer and they could be heard grinding against one another although the sea was so flat that no motion could be seen in the pack. It gave an overwhelming impression of total immobility, desolation and frozen emptiness. Ensign Bascomb could make out the promontory he had picked to mark the Russian sub's probable location, a grim headland looming darker against the dark escarpment and looking as if no living thing had been near it since the beginning of time. Finding himself standing close to the captain, he began to edge away uncomfortably, but stopped when Finlander said either to him or all of them: "Be patient! ... Keep looking and be patient!"

Even Ben Munceford looked hard after shooting a few feet of film of the bleak panorama, and as he looked, a childishly romantic notion crossed his mind of being the one who actually spotted Moby Dick. Wouldn't that fracture these Annapolis snobs! They would have to give him a prize, of course—but what! Maybe a new camouflage jacket!

"All QBH readouts negative!" the CIC reported over the intercom.

Up in the icicled crow's-nest, Squarehead loosed a stream of profanity at the windows, which were streaked by distorting frozen ripples. He pounded on the switch controlling the wipers, which were still solidly stuck. Then he threw all his weight upward against the hatch in the roof of the aluminum box, and, to his surprise, it finally flew open, throwing a shower of frozen particles to the decks below. With a satisfied grunt he heaved himself through the narrow opening and perched his buttocks on the ten-inch rim, which was pure, slick ice. Seaman Jones sprang up off the top rung in the shaft, clamped his arms around Squarehead's legs and fearfully shouted: "For God's sake, be careful!"

Squarehead did not even glance down at the long freefall to certain death which could be the result of a slip. He only looked up at the frame of the tactical radar antenna, gauging whether it would clear his head in case it started rotating. Then he said: "Pass me up them ten-by-fifties, Jonesy, and quit ruining the press of my pants!" The binoculars were handed up to him, but even as he reached for them, he suddenly exclaimed: "Jesus! We're on fire!"

The *Bedford* was indeed on fire! The cold fires of billions of ice crystals suddenly energized in a long slanting ray of sunlight which had found an infinitesimal rip in the protecting overcast, shot through it and scored a bull's-eye. For an agonized eternity of five seconds the drab warship blazed and sparkled like a diamond caught in the beam of a burglar's flashlight, exploding out of the hiding gloom with a clarion burst of glory. No marine artist could have captured her fantastic beauty at this moment, nor could any living eye within fifteen miles around have failed to notice her! The clouds quickly swirled in and smothered the sunbeam, but the damage had been done and a chorus of groans rose from the bridge.

"We might as well shoot off some flares and do a good job of announcing ourselves," Commander Allison bitterly exclaimed. "But I suppose turning on the radar will do for a starter."

"No—hold it a few moments more!" Finlander ordered.

Tense silence fell over the bridge again while everybody scanned the ice, but now with less hope than before. The ship had almost stopped and was within a hundred yards of the edge of the icepack, which appeared much looser from close quarters—and the floes bigger and more individually solid. The first little growlers hit the hull with disturbingly loud clangs. It was an unpleasant noise, but had nowhere near the effect of the howl which suddenly came from high up the mast:

"Masthead to bridge! . . . I see something like a big chunk of ice out there that's moving by itself!"

All faces on the bridge, including the captain's, turned upward and stared in various degrees of shock at the figure far up the mast, precariously perched on the rim of the crow's-nest while excitedly waving one arm toward some objective in the icepack.

Commander Allison gasped, then cupped his gloved hands around his mouth and cut loose his most powerful quarterdeck bellow. "Don't you know how to report a sighting properly, you damned fool? Get back inside there and use the telephone!"

The figure waved and screamed again in wild, oblivious excitement. "Like a piece of moving ice! . . . It's him! . . . Going down! Going down—" He came within a fraction of falling, then suddenly vanished as if somebody had yanked him out of sight from below.

Allison was grabbing for the telephone in the external communication box, but Captain Finlander needed no clarification of the garbled sighting report. "A moving icefloe!" he exclaimed to himself. "Of course! He's got his conning tower painted white!" Rising his binoculars and training them in the general direction indicated by the frantic lookout, he forced every last ounce of effort out of his optic nerves, trying to catch every detail of every pan, chunk and boulder-sized piece of ice among the thousands which came into his view. He tensed for a second when he thought he caught a motion in the congealed conglomeration of shapes out there, then sagged when it seemed only an illusion ... then jumped a foot into the air when the speaker sang out:

"Bridge from CIC! We have a hard contact on the QBH! Request permission to start echo-ranging!"

"Granted!" Finlander yelled in a spontaneous flash of wild elation which electrified the men around him far more than had the lookout's performance a moment ago. "Boys, we've got him! Got him cold two miles inside Greenland waters!" He shoved his fisherman's cap to the back of his head and laughed. And suddenly all the others were laughing too. Even Allison laughed. Ensign Bascomb swelled up and let out a hoot. The OOD began to jig. The enlisted lookouts, talkers and signalmen grinned and thumped one another on the back. Ben Munceford smiled, but thinly, as he stared out over the icepack in the direction everybody else was pointing—and saw absolutely nothing. He accepted as fact that *something* was out there, evidently Moby Dick, and that it was somehow trapped by the *Bedford*, but he still could not fully understand all the uproar.

"So you've got him!" he exclaimed. "So what are you going to do about it?"

The captain heard the question and took fleeting notice of Munceford's presence on the bridge for the first time this morning; both the question and the sight of the tattered camouflage jacket may have helped sober him, yet he proceeded to ignore the correspondent. The smile was still there, but turned grim, and his voice became fully businesslike as he started issuing orders. "Buck! Tell CIC to lock on the track! Have Fire Control put their ASROCs on stand-by and start feeding target data to the systems! OOD! Keep out of the ice and conn the ship to intercept any attempt to break for open sea! Yeoman! Take down this message for immediate transmission!" He began dictating it within the hearing of Ben Munceford, perhaps purposefully so as to answer his question: "Code Double-A, Most Urgent and Immediate Action to COMAD, NATONAV 1: Have flushed Soviet Russian submarine conducting military reconnaissance inside, *repeat inside,* Greenland-Danish territorial waters, position sixteen miles north Helvigstadt Bay, stop. Request immediate authority to challenge and interdict, stop. Signed Commanding Officer, Coldsnap."

5.

In the Communications Center, Lieutenant P. L.
M. Packer, R.N., finally snapped out of the brooding
lethargy which he had been fighting all morning since
being deprived of his normal duties. Radio silence left
him with nothing to do and the continued GQ nowhere
to go but remain at his battle station—a desk. Yes, he
had ambled into the EDA room while Lieutenant
Beeker sat in silent communion with his HUFF-DUFF
and MESS-PLEX, patiently trying to divine any scraps
of radio intelligence out of the ether. He had listened
to the low chatter of the idle operators speculating
about their chances of catching Moby Dick, but without himself becoming exhilarated by the chase. To the
contrary, his depression had deepened and at the bottom of it there was the throbbing hurt of Shebeona.
But now, when Finlander's message was given to him
for transmittal to NATONAV 1, he at last began to be
caught up in the excitement which permeated the ship.
It was only a matter of a few minutes to run it through
the encoder and have one of the operators flash it on
its way. His spirits lifted even more when a familiar
voice came in over the PA circuit:

"This is the captain speaking! We sighted Moby
Dick a short while ago as he submerged through the
icepack and now have him securely locked in our sonar
beam. He has no sounding for deep dives, no clear
water for high-speed runs under the ice, and we stand
between him and the open sea. I have dispatched a
message to our Fleet Headquarters with this good news

and asking for permission to deal with him. Shortly we shall fire a charge close enough to him that he will fully realize the fatal consequences of not meekly surfacing under our guns! This has been a long, trying stretch at battle stations, but please bear with me for a little longer. The payoff is at hand! Thank you."

"By Jove!" Packer exclaimed. "Looks like we might get cracking, doesn't it!" The Beek gave him a somewhat condescending smile and replaced the one cup of his earphones which he had lifted off an ear in order to hear the captain's short speech; he casually called to Chief Benton:

"Keep tabs on the long-wave frequencies in case that sub starts attempting any underwater transmissions!"

The English officer stepped out on deck for the next few moments, took some invigorating lungfuls of cold air and noticed with satisfaction that the ASROC launcher had been elevated into firing position and trained to starboard, the yellow-green snout of the missile's warhead pointing menacingly toward the icepack. Then Benton called out to him that a NATONAV message was coming in and he rushed back to his decoding machine. When he read the strip it fed into his hands, he gave a quite un-English whoop. The message said:

NATONAV 1 TO COMMANDING OFFICER COLDSNAP—RE YOUR TACREP 11–23–1305Z ACT AT YOUR OWN DISCRETION ACCORDING IMMEDIATE TACTICAL REQUIREMENTS OF SITUATION STOP—SIGNED SORENSON, COMAD.

Lieutenant Packer had barely put down the telephone after enjoying a delighted "Very good!" from Captain Finlander when Chief Benton shouted to him: "Hold it! Here comes one from home plate, sir!" A few minutes later all of his enthusiasm was dampened as he drew the following message out of the decoder.

COMFLANT TO COMMANDING OFFICER COLDSNAP—
HAVE INTERCEPTED YOUR TACREP 11–23–1305Z TO
COLDSNAP STOP COMMEND EXCELLENT WORK BUT RE-
GRET MUST FORBID ANY ACTION WITHOUT CONFIRMA-
TION THIS HEADQUARTERS DUE CRITICAL RUSSAMERI-
CAN CRISIS BERLIN AND ELSEWHERE STOP SUGGEST
PASSIVE SHADOW TACTICS UNTIL FURTHER ORDERS
STOP—SIGNED BALDWIN, CINCLANT.

"What a bloody shame!" Packer sighed, reaching the
phone again. "It's going to turn out just another
bitched-up inter-Allied raspberry!"

Captain Erik Finlander turned livid and began pacing the navigation office like a caged tiger. His eyes
blazed with fury, the scar on his throat pulsed crimson
and looked as if it might rupture and start hemor-
rhaging at any moment. The messenger who had
brought him copies of the conflicting messages from
NATONAV 1 and COMFLANT cringed as he hurriedly fled. Allison, his face set in a less animated expression of anger, pressed himself against the chart
table and braced for what he felt certain would be a
blast which would demolish the captain's own standing
orders against vile language. Yet when Finlander finally found his speech, it was still controlled beneath
the trembling of rage and totally devoid of profanity. It
was the vehemence of the delivery which made it so
chilling.

"For once we have a chance to act decisively against
creeping Soviet aggression! For once we are able to
nail a Russian redhanded inside NATO allies' territorial waters and with virtual proof of his subversive intentions! Nice neutral little Sweden with her toy navy
has the guts to depth-charge Commie pigboats they
catch violating her shores. Even Admiral Sorensen of
pipsqueak Denmark is prepared to act decisively in the
interest of NATO obligations. But big, tough, armed-

to-the-teeth United States of America, winner of every war it ever fought, champion of liberty and rule of law, must hesitate and talk it over! Talk, talk, talk, concede and back up and pussyfoot and procrastinate! That's what they are doing, you know, Buck! My tacrep sent cold chills down the atrophied spines fused to the upholstery of COMFLANT and they got on the hotline to the State Department fags, who have no spines at all! So now they're talk-talk-talking while we sit up here in the arctic on top of that Bolshevik submarine commander who's recovering more of his wits with each second!" He stemmed the torrent for a moment to listen to a voice from the CIC, which had been reporting over the open intercom every other minute since their contact with Moby Dick:

"Positive target echo ... bearing zero-three-one, steady ... range two-two-five-zero, steady ... depth zero-seven-five, steady ..."

For an instant Finlander looked as though he was about to drive his fist through the speaker. Commander Allison made a half-hearted effort to sooth him: "Maybe the staff at COMFLANT only want a little time to evaluate the situation for themselves, sir."

As he stalked past the chart table, the captain slammed the flat of his hand against it, making pencils, dividers and rulers jump high in the air. "That's what *I* am here for!" he shouted. "Because I *am* here, I know the situation. I'm not asking them to allow me to commit a warlike act. I'm asking they permit me to expose the warlike intentions of a nation who has mesmerized half the world with its eternal blathering about peaceful coexistence! And, above all, I'm asking for this chance to show that the American navy is able and determined to put a stop to this kind of intimidation of our own country!" He slammed the table once more, paced several more turns around the navigation office, then came to an abrupt halt when he found him-

self face to face with Commodore Wolfgang Schrepke
as he stepped in from the wheelhouse.

"Is there anything amiss, Captain?" the German inquired, unzipping his leather jacket and removing his
brine-stained cap.

Without a word Finlander thrust the two crumpled
messages at him. Schrepke took them, stepped over to
the chart table, spread them out under the light,
smoothed out their wrinkles and carefully read each in
turn. Then he straightened up and said: "I would say
your Fleet Headquarters have relieved you of a terrible
responsibility which Admiral Sorenson was so quick to
conveniently place upon your shoulders."

This stopped Finlander short with a glint of surprise.
Another fragment of last night's nightmares flashed
through his mind, the part where the sly Admiral
Sorensen was dressing him down, snarling: *"You ekted
unwisely. Kep'n!"*—but he quickly smothered this vision
in his current anger. "Indeed, Commodore Schrepke?
Well, unlike some of my European colleagues, I do not
shrink from responsibility for my actions!" He buttoned up his white duffel and slapped the long oilled
cap on his head, the moved to leave.

"Do we secure from battle stations, sir?" Allison
called after him.

"No!" Finlander shouted back and swept out
through the blackout curtain.

6.

The *Bedford* doggedly weaved along the ragged edge of the icepack at a slow six knots to keep prodding the submarine with relentless echo-ranging signals. Moby Dick was moving southward beneath the protective shield of ice, staying between one and two miles offshore and about the same distance from his pursuer, keeping as deep as the shallow, reef-strewn coastal waters would allow, which meant somewhat less than forty fathoms. In the destroyer's CIC they could occasionally hear his sonar pinging in short bursts, obviously ranging ahead to detect rocks and skerries which might fatally block his course through the black deep. "That devil either has better charts than we, or he is a madman!" Lieutenant Spitzer observed with a certain gruding admiration as he checked the submarine's progress on the combat plot.

From time to time Moby Dick would stop to listen on his passive sonar system, in which case the *Bedford* would do the same. Perhaps the Soviet commander was hoping to draw his opponent into the icepack as a rabbit draws a fox into an impenetrable thicket of brambles from where it would be lucky to extricate itself with a whole skin, let alone make a kill! But the sullen Finlander would not allow his turbulent feelings to trick him into any rash action. So the creeping, stalking game resumed after each one of these tense pauses.

An hour dragged by, then another. The overcast which had shown signs of breaking up earlier during the day solidified and turned a bluish leaden color, and presently a fine snow began falling. The harsh rock faces of the distant mountains became softly hazy in the thickening weather and began a play of hide-and-seek with the shifting flurries. As the destroyer moved farther south and came out of the lee of the great northeast bight of Greenland, deep ocean swells regained their powers, slowly at first, with gently heaving widely separated crests, then steeper and closer. The icepack came alive in their surge and began to grind and fill the air with a horrible gnashing rumble. This sound filled the deep too and the CIC reported that echo-ranging was becoming disturbed, triggering Captain Finlander to send off another urgent, top-secret plea to both NATONAV 1 and COMFLANT:

... TACTICAL SITUATION DETERIORATING IN FAVOR TRANSGRESSOR STOP AGAIN URGENTLY REQUEST PERMISSION CHALLENGE AND INTERDICT BEFORE OPPORTUNITY LOST. ...

After an interminable delay which actually only lasted for fifteen minutes, NATONAV 1 came through with an uncomforting answer:

... AM AMPLIFYING YOUR SITUATION TO COMFLANT WITH POSITIVE RECOMMENDATIONS STOP IF YOU NEED ASSISTANCE WILL ORDER POLARBEAR TO YOUR POSITION WHICH CAN MAKE IN EIGHT HOURS STOP—SIGNED SORENSEN, COMAD.

... ONLY ASSISTANCE REQUIRED IS AUTHORITY TO TAKE ACTION. ...

To this came a peremptory one-word signal from COMFLANT:

WAIT

And as they waited, the early afternoon became a melancholy, snow-filled dusk, then suddenly winter night.

After his brief flurry of activity in the Communications Center occasioned by the captain's exchanges with admirals thousands of miles removed from this dismal scene of action, Lieutenant P. L. M. Packer gradually sank back into the depression which had gripped his spirits last night and this morning. Again he was let down by an idleness which aggravated the attrition of his deep personal troubles. Leaning listlessly over his immaculate desk, he stared at the radio-telephone unit attached to the bulkhead a few feet away. As he stared, the wistful thought came to his mind that all he had to do was flip a switch, punch a channel selector, call the Marine Operator at Kirkeness, ask for London——GErrard 2075——and forthwith bridge the horrible void between himself and Shebeona. *"Hello darling! . . . Didn't you get my telegram?"*

"Here comes a deferred personal over Code C circuit, sir!" one of the radio operators announced and started clacking away on his machine.

Packer came out of his chair and had to check himself from making an undignified rush for the decoder. The Beek was standing in the doorway to the EDA room, munching on a huge sandwich, the wires trailing from his inevitable earphones and connecting him to the MESS-PLEX like an umbilical cord. He was watching the Englishman with a kind of uncomfortable concern as he drew the printed strip through his hands.

PERSONAL SEAMAN 1 THORBJORNSEN, JOHN B., COLDSNAP VIA NATONAV MACKAY——A NEW BOOT REPORTED FOR DUTY THIS DOGWATCH WEIGHING 6 POUNDS 4 OUNCES SOAKING WET AND HOLLERING A LUSTY ALLS WELL STOP CONGRATULATIONS DAD STOP ——SIGNED GRANDPOP.

Because he sensed The Beek's eyes on him, Lieutenant Packer hid his bitter disappointment, forced a grin, read the message aloud and filled the austere Communications Center with a bright moment of cheerful laughter.

At 1620 hours Lieutenant Commander Chester Porter finally came to enter a patient in the ship's medical log. A gunner's mate was virtually dragged into the surgery by his section chief with both hands badly frostbitten from clearing ice off an ASROC launcher. The surgeon treated him and noticed how the hands shook from something more than pain, but there was defiance in the man's redrimmed eyes when he firmly declined being relieved from duty. Porter reluctantly discharged him and returned to the receiving office, where he resumed perusing through the now well-thumbed *War Psychology in Primitive and Modern Man.* All day long he had had little to do but sit there absorbing the text and Lieutenant Hirschfeld's marginal notes. However, after a short while he now closed it and locked it away in his desk, then pulled on his arctics. Leaving Chief Pharmacist McKinley in charge of the sterile inactivity of sick bay, he resolutely set off for the bridge. But on the way up there his resolution wavered slightly and he digressed on a visit into the armored cavern of the CIC. "How are things going? Pretty rough?" he asked Lieutenant Krindlemeyer, who had taken over Central Control while Spitzer was wolfing down an early dinner in the wardroom.

Krindlemeyer peered at the surgeon through his rimless glasses with a blankly owlish expression and answered: "Why, hello, Doc! All systems are go here!"

The surgeon listened to the raucous jumble of sound which was coming in over the sonar audio monitors, winced at the frantic splatters of light in the PPI scopes and watched the chief plotter record the latest tactical data on the big board, then call it up to the bridge in a low, hoarse voice. He noticed the forcibly relaxed attitudes of Lieutenant Aherne and Ensign Ralston at the glowing Fire Control console, the endlessly masticating jaws of the sonar and radar operators, and especially noticed the nervous jiggling on Merlin Queffle's right knee as he sat at the MTS, eyes tightly shut, forehead wrinkled as he pressed the earphones to his ears. Porter took all this in for a minute or two, gained fresh resolve from what he saw, then quietly slipped out through the steel door.

Captain Finlander was seated on the edge of the bunk in his day cabin, his duffel open, cap shoved back, in his hands a bowl of steaming bean soup which he was stirring without much enthusiasm when the surgeon timidly pushed aside the blackout curtain and peered in. "How are things going, sir? Pretty rough?"

Finlander looked up with a scowl which lasted long enough for Lieutenant Commander Porter to take warning, but the following forced grin betrayed him into stepping inside the cabin.

"Hello, Doc!" the captain greeted him with a kind of bitter cordiality. "Somebody once said something about being able to take care of his enemies, but God preserve him from his friends. In this case, *my* friends at Fleet Headquarters!"

Porter laughed politely and dared to perch himself casually on the edge on the desk. "Oh, well—I suppose they've got a lot of things to consider in a situation like this. Things fraught with dangerous consequences if the wrong decisions are made, right?"

Finlander gave him a baleful stare which should have been the final warning, then took a mouthful of soup instead of answering.

The surgeon looked up at the clock on the bulkhead. "Gosh, Captain! We certainly have been at battle stations for an awful long stretch, haven't we?"

"Eleven hours and fourteen minutes," Finlander snapped without looking at the clock. "What about it, Commander Porter? Have there been any intolerable hardships worked on the medical department?"

"Oh, no, sir. I've only had one case of frostbite, but ..." He stopped himself, suddenly fearfully aware of the captain's dangerous mood.

"But what?" Finlander demanded and in his agitation slopped some of the soup out of the bowl. He glowered down at the greasy red stain spreading over pure white wool, then his eyes snapped back to the surgeon, blazing with a terrible light beneath the black brows.

"B-but I, ah ... noticed an increasing strain showing in the men, sir, and ..."

"You think this is news to me?" Finlander shouted, now playing his temper as though it were a discordant percussion instrument. "They know I will never secure from battle stations while we are closed with the enemy. *Never!* But, all right, Doc? So they are strained by this filthy, freezing, frustrating job. Are you giving me a medical opinion that they can't take it any more?"

"Maybe it's more like they're ready to take on too much, sir."

"What the devil do you mean by that, Commander?"

"Well, like ... this Moby Dick business is all very well—just as long as *you* don't take the part of Ahab too seriously, sir." He gave a nervous laugh, then froze rigid.

The bowl of soup had splattered on the deck as Captain Finlander shot to his feet. He was actually shorter and slighter of build than the bulky surgeon, but he suddenly towered over him and caused him to begin to pitifully shrivel. His voice came forth a full octave lower than before, and with twice the vehemence. "Ahab? Ahab? My name is Erik J. Finlander! I am a captain of the United States Navy and commanding officer of the U.S.S. *Bedford!* That's *who* and *what* I am, sir! Nobody else! Nothing else! And you, sir, will instantly remove yourself from my presence and return to your battle station. Dismissed!!"

Lieutenant Commander Chester Porter quivered before this blast like a jelly suddenly exposed to a violent wind. He slid off the edge of the desk and with a trembling "Y-yes, sir!" slunk out through the curtain. A wet stain was left on a fold where his face had brushed against it.

7.

Moby Dick made his successful break for the open sea sometime between 0150 and 0230 hours of the following morning. The exact minute remained undetermined because the CIC had been thrown into a state of confusion by a very large gam of whales which had run headlong into the scene of creeping battle. They radiated an impossible cacophony of submarine noises, aggravating the already difficult tracking conditions brought about by a now thoroughly activated icepack pounding in breaking seas. To make matters worse, the *Bedford*'s sonar genius, Merlin the Magician, had had to be relieved during the late evening after being on duty for sixteen hours with only a few short breaks. Lieutenant Spitzer had sent him below, secretly happy to be rid of him and wanting to trust the relieving sonarman, who, for over ten fatal minutes, even disputed the fact that it was whales obscuring the tenuous signal they were intermittently receiving off the submarine. Then one of the animals surfaced in the turbulent blackness, unseen but so close to the ship that is vaporous spout swept over the bridge, enveloping Captain Finlander where he stood in swirling snow with an unmistakable fishy halitosis. "Get Queffle back on that MTS immediately!" he yelled over the intercom.

It only took four minutes to return Queffle to the CIC and only a minute more of concentrated, aggrieved listening over the earphone and peering into the PPI scope before he came up with his cocksure diagnosis of the trouble: "Right whales! Fifty or sixty of them! They blanked our hard contact!"

Seething with impotent rage and frustration, Lieutenant Spitzer had no alternative but call to the bridge: "Contact lost! Readouts obscured and blanked by biological and hydrographic interference!"

Finlander heard the baleful voice squawking out of the speaker in the wing and immediately rushed for the wheelhouse. "Don't they understand he's broken out of the pack astern of us? Reverse your course! Make flank speed for ten minutes, then start a maximum-effect sweep!"

The *Bedford* heeled over in a sharp turn and began to pound through the huge swells. Clouds of spray mingled with the snow, and the jarring which shook her from keel to masthead broke loose the remains of yesterday's ice, shedding it in rattling cascades along her flanks. The destroyer drove through the night and ice-clogged black ocean at a perilous thirty-two knots, and when she finally stopped at the end of this wild retracing run to listen for her lost quarry, a final ironic blow was struck at her captain. It came in the form of a message from COMFLANT:

... PERMISSION GRANTED TO CHALLENGE AND INTERDICT STOP EXPECT YOU TO ACT PROMPTLY WITH PRUDENT FORCE AGAINST ANY TRESPASS IN NATO TERRITORIAL WATERS. ...

Finlander held the scrap of yellow paper which had been delivered to him from the Communications Center at this bitter moment, studying it in the sickly green glow from the navigational radar. Commander Allison read it over his shoulder and shrank away from him, expecting a blast—which did not come. The captain only sucked in his breath and held it for an interminable period before letting go with a prolonged wheeze.

Then he stepped over to the intercom and called Spitzer: "What have you got down there now besides interesting wildlife, CIC?" he inquired with fathomless suffering in his voice.

"All readouts negative, sir."

"All right. I'm coming down." He turned to his executive officer. "You take the conn, Buck. I'm going to personally take over the CIC and keep them going until they fall out of their upholstered chairs and have to be carried into sick bay. I'm going to hunt that Commie pigboat until the barnacles grow so thick on this hull we can no longer move. I'm going to catch him, Buck! I'm going to catch him!"

They did catch Moby Dick nine hours later where the blizzard had free reign over mountainous swells running a good twenty miles off the territorial limits of Greenland. But perhaps to use the word *catch* would not be entirely correct—because all that really happened was that the protagonists caught sight of each other through the thick snow and spume for about thirty seconds.

When the watch had changed at 0800 and the *Bedford* was still vainly searching the empty deep, Captain Finlander reluctantly secured the ship from battle stations, yet himself keeping the CIC on full combat alert. He came to regret this action when Moby Dick suddenly materialized with hardly a warning on any of the detection devices. This shocking thing happened simply because the Russian submarine was cautiously poking her snorkel up through the wild seas in order to breathe after the long submerged action and was too close to the heaving surface for the sonar beams to register a return echo. One of those seas almost broached him and for something like thirty seconds the big conning tower thrust clear out of water. A half-smothered "eyeball" lookout in the port wing of the bridge and a bleary-eyed radar operator in the CIC both sang out together. Commodore Schrepke also saw him and was able to get a quick look through his binoculars which confirmed to him it was a Chelnikoff-class submarine.

The GQ alarm went off, propelling two thirds of the crew out of their bunks almost before they had had time to settle into them.

"Go after him, Buck! Force him down!" Finlander bellowed into the intercom, then started to rush for the bridge. But he quickly realized he would never make it in time and dropped back into his seat at Central Control. Moby Dick was crash-diving—but at least Queffle had a solid contact on the MTS. The hunt was on again!

The Russian submarine had plenty of sounding now that he was well out in the Denmark Strait and he used it well. Pressing down to seven hundred feet, where no trace of the surface turbulence could reach him, he cracked on close to twenty-five knots, taking violent evasive actions along a generally southeasterly course. This made it hard for the *Bedford* to track him accurately, having to fight the huge moving walls of water contesting her pursuit, as well as maintain a speed which made her sonar gear crackle and splatter with ambient noises. Yet she held the contact, mainly because of Merlin Queffle's phenomenal sensitivity and Finlander's skillful tactics of rush-stop-listen-rush. Stubbornly he hung on while more interminable hours dragged by, the horrible bone-wrenching rolls of the destroyer adding a physical pain to the mental agony.

At 1123 hours Lieutenant Packer telephoned Finlander to give him an urgent message from NATONAV 1, asking for amplification of the situation. The captain crisply ordered him to transmit the single cipher which would indicate to both NATONAV 1 and COMFLANT that a critical tactical operation was in progress necessitating radio silence.

Noon passed, cold, gray and engulfed in the swirling

folds of a full-fledged blizzard. The watch changed with the ship on battle stations. Commander Allison, showing himself more and more the quiet man of iron determination and endurance, plotted their position in the navigation office and noted that they were close to where the *Tiburon Bay* had refueled them only four days ago. He ignored Ben Munceford, who likewise had not left the bridge since the previous morning and was still wearing his frightful shredded camouflage jacket. "I'm not going to be caught in the sack again with something going on!" he overheard him say to Lieutenant Harwell when the latter told him he was crazy to take the grind with the rest of them.

1530 hours and the grim dusk slipped into an impenetrable darkness. In the log the weather was tersely described: "Heavy snow ... Temperature 21 F. ... Wind N. Force 4 ... Seastate 5 with NNE swells." The plot in CIC sent up the target information every other minute: "... Hard contact ... bearing zero-zero-five, steady ... range five-five-zero, steady ... depth one hundred fifty fathoms, steady ... target making twenty-four knots, two-four knots ..." The captain did not make his sunset watch this afternoon; Commodore Schrepke stood it more alone than ever.

When all track of time had ceased to be something sensed by the human mind, 2215 hours came and with it a sudden fading to complete silence on all the sonar receivers in the CIC. Moby Dick had been executing some strangely erratic maneuvers during the past twenty minutes, zigzagging and nearly reversing his course in such a way that Finlander would have suspected he was about to launch a torpedo attack if he had not at the same time pressed down closer to the bottom—*which suddenly seemed to swallow him up!*

The *Bedford* coasted to a stop, heaved to and rolled sickeningly broadside to the seas while making a maximum-effect sonar sweep. Silence! Next she cut a slow, outward spiraling circle, still listening. Silence!

Merlin Queffle looked up from his MTS console with an almost comical perplexity on his pinched, haggard face. "Jeez! It's like he went down a hole or something!" he exclaimed in an outraged falsetto.

His dismay spread through the gloomy CIC like a contagious virus. But Finlander spoke up from the Central Control in a firm, confident voice. "He's got to be there! We're not dealing with the Flying Dutchman, but living men working a rather old type of submarine. They've got only two ways to go: up or down. . . . Cut to a passive sweep on the QBH!"

The listened for five . . . ten . . . fifteen endless minutes. Silence. Then Lieutenant Krindlemeyer's spectacles suddenly flashed over the rim of the hatch to the CSP room and his nasal voice blandly announced: "I'm getting an awfully strong magnetic disturbance down here which suggests there may be a much bigger hunk of iron below us than a submarine."

Lieutenant Spitzer gave a funny squeal and reached across the captain to switch on the magnetometer. It's needle jumped across the scale. Finlander seemed to have caught the implication instantly, although he did nothing but casually call the bridge over the intercom: "Buck! Check our *exact* position, please! Give us any pertinent information on what's on the bottom."

A few minutes later Allison gave their exact position; then he added with a tinge of surprise: "Sir, we happen to be right over the wreck of the H.M.S. *Hood,* the old British battle cruiser!"

For the first time in nearly two days Finlander's face broke into a genuinely spontaneous grin. He leaned back in his chair, stretched his arms over his head, then replied: "Very good! Very good! That's what I thought! . . . All right. Let's thrash around the area a bit, like we were horribly confused. Then rig silent and let's wait for him to get short of breath! . . . I think I ought to let everybody in on this development, Buck. Will you patch in this circuit through ship's PA, please!"

In the Communications Center, Lieutenant P. L. M. Packer was at his desk, guarding this, his useless battle station on the U.S.S. *Bedford*. He only gradually came out of his slumped position as the captain's cheerful voice came over the PA speaker.

"Moby Dick has given us a long, hard chase, gentlemen, but now I think I can safely tell you that he has outsmarted himself. We have lost contact, true! But we know exactly where he is hiding. Fate has it that we are directly above the wreck of a huge English warship— the H.M.S. *Hood*—which was sunk in battle during the last war. Apparently our Commie enemy knew of its location pretty accurately and has probably used it often to shield himself with over forty thousand tons of steel to fox our detection devices. Very smart! But now we are on to that and will be waiting when he has to come up—which should be fairly soon. So hang on, men! The end of our trial is in sight! . . . Thank you."

Packer was rigidly standing up directly under the speaker when the captain finished. He kept on staring at it for over a minute before turning away and dazedly walking past The Beek, who had at last fallen asleep, seated upright in his chair. He passed the row of idle operators, who stared curiously after him, then only shrugged because his behavior had been a bit peculiar lately. Funny ducks, these Limeys!

Lieutenant Packer went through the door leading out on deck without bothering to put on his parka and gantlets. Moving out into the night, he lifted his bare hands to shield his face from the cruel sting of the blizzard, shuffled to the railing and peered over it as if seeking something in the angry black void of the sea. He stood there until a wave bigger than the others rose up and hurled an icy blow at him, and only then did he shy back as if recoiling from the cold grip of death reaching out for him from the deep.

He was drenched to the skin, but he did not hurry down to his cabin to change. He walked slowly, and when he got there and pushed aside the curtain, he found Ben Munceford at the desk, loading tape into his portable recorder.

The correspondent looked at the Englishman with surprise. "My God, Pete, what's happened to you? Did Communications spring a leak?"

Packer merely shook his head and absently began to peel off his sopping clothes.

Munceford resumed loading the recorder while idly drawling away. "Well, it all beats me, anyway. Now that you think you've got that sub pinned down under a wreck or something, what exactly is going to happen next? As far as I can see, all that Russki has to do is come up and tell us to leave him the hell alone now, or he'll file a nasty complaint at the U.N. . . . Say, Pete! What *is* the matter? You not only look wet, but sick too."

"I'm all right, thanks," Packer said, stripping off his shirt.

"Are you still moping over your love life? Still, after two whole days? Is that what's eating you, man?" He laughed, not cruelly but trying to kid him and with an encouraging slap on the shoulder.

"I couldn't care less about love at this moment," the Englishman told him with a flat, unemotional voice.

"Then show me you don't care, Pete! And, most important of all, show *yourself!*" Munceford was still trying to joss him and did not at all expect the reaction he got.

"All right—I will!" Packer retorted. He stepped over to his bunk, bent down and reached up for the under part of the one above it. There was a tearing of tape. Then he was suddenly handing Shebeona's photograph to Munceford, even forcing him to take it. "There you are, Ben! A nice pin-up for you, old man!" His body was racked by a sudden shudder and he whipped a towel around himself to run out to the hot shower.

PART THREE

THE BATTLE

1.

The time was 0400, the forty-second hour of the chase, the sixty hour since the *Bedford* had started circling over the wreck of the *Hood* like a wolf circling the lair of its trapped prey. The wind had dropped to a bare Force 2, but the snow kept falling and the sea heaved to the cadence of swells which continued marching through the night in endless columns of giants. As she alternately lay hove to or jogging against the drift, the destroyer rolled, pitched and corkscrewed with violent, unpredictable motions which added wrenching aches to the numbing cold plaguing her lookouts and gunners.

Every ten minutes Chief Gunner's Mate Cantrell had to punch the STANDBY-HOLD switch on the panel and crawl out of his armored cubicle to climb precariously up the icy sides of the RAT launcher, clear the missile of snow and freezing slush, then back to his station and return the switch to READY-LAUNCH. In the crow's-nest, where every wild roll of the *Bedford* was multiplied tenfold, Seaman Jones was whipping about through a nightmarish world of absolute darkness; he could not even see the snowflakes brushing against the windshield a few inches beyond his nose. But he kept straining his eyes, trying to judge his relative position to the sea, watching, watching for any telltale swirl of phosphorescence which might betray the fact that Moby Dick was surfacing. He still believed implicitly in his eyes, all the more so since he knew sonar contact had failed. Yet sometimes he could not help losing all sense of direction and, especially during some of the worst rolls, felt as if he was about to be hurled free of the ship. It had happened once—on the *Brinkley*—that the crow's-nest had been completely wrenched from its fastenings to the mast and become the coffin of the drowning lookout. But he did not think about that horrible accident. As his captain had told him to do, he thought about the enemy and kept a smoldering anger going inside him. He thought about those Russian submariners hiding in the placid, motionless deep while he was being slowly beaten to death up here. "I hope you suffocate, you dirty Red bastards!" he snarled.

In the CIC nobody had spoken a word for nearly half an hour. The armor and insulation shut out all sounds of the sea and there was none in here beyond the endlessly repetitive minor-key *ping* of the sonar—which came through crisp and clear, without any fuzz and crackle of a return echo. Captain Finlander was still occupying the chair at Central Control, hunched forward with his arms folded across his chest, his body so rigidly conforming to the *Bedford*'s gyrations that it seemed a part of her. His eyes still watched the PPI scopes, but now they were flicking more often to the men at the consoles. He had become aware of the weariness which was slowly dulling their tense alertness, noticing the fitful contrapuntal actions of their muscles as they failed to synchronize with the rolls and pitches of the ship, perceiving a subtle bloodshot haze glazing their eyes. He studied Queffle with special concentration. The boy's face was damp and shone with a greenish pallor as he hunched over the primary tactical sonar, his eyes too close to the scope to focus effectively, the bony fingers pressing the earphones too hard against his ears to allow perceptive hearing. Suddenly he looked back over his shoulder toward Central Control, a desperate frustrated action in violation of regulations, then visibly flinched when he met his captain's gaze and instantly returned his attention to the fruitless vigil at his instrument. Finlander tried to flash him a reassuring nod, but Queffle had turned away too quickly. Yet not so quickly that the captain had not caught that look of despair. The extraordinary powers of the Breton Kid were failing him. In fact, all the finely tuned fighting pitch of the CIC was draining away, its subdued twilight of glowing tubes and dials turning into a deepening gloom full of frustration and foreboding.

"Number-two ASROC reports iced up and on STANDBY-HOLD," the talker droned with a tired monotone. Ensign Ralston let out a groan.

Finlander knew it was becoming urgent that something happen to bolster the sagging spirits of his men. Nothing he could say would do it. It had to be something more stimulating than a few encouraging words—or taunting ones—from their captain. If only he could flush out Moby Dick with a stick of hedgehogs! What god-damn good was a war without something to go *bang* and jar one out of the deadly rote of it all? How futile this stalking, waiting game! Yet how vital that it be won by refusing to capitulate to its very futility! The *Bedford* or Moby Dick, one or the other, *had* to sneak away or come gasping to the surface with all offensive spirit so thoroughly demolished that they would be henceforth useless as a ship's complement. It *had* to be the Russian. Yet it was the *Bedford*'s men who were wavering now.

Finlander wanted to yell "Get with it or that obsolete submarine will lick us!" but instead he leaned back in the chair, stretched his arms over his head, let out a noisy yawn and exclaimed: "The Commies must have figured out a new secret weapon, men. They're trying to bore us to death."

There was no reaction—not even a chuckle from Ensign Ralston.

"By God!" Finlander loudly exploded. "Under any other conditions I'd dock everybody in here two days' shore leave for failing to react to commanding officer's wisecracks."

"I bet those fucking Russians are splitting their sides . . . *sir*."

Finlander shot to his feet and wheeled, his body propelled by an electrifying combination of shock and anger. It was Lieutenant Spitzer who had spoken up from the dark corner where he had wedged himself in between a bulkhead and an amplifier rack. His voice had not only a strange high pitch but a belligerent tone which was entirely foreign to him. His balding pate glistened with a sickly pallor beneath the wilting blond strands of hair; his eyes showed the same beady green luminescence as the lights on the control boards. His colorless lips were parted by a leer which appeared entirely toothless in the harsh reflected half-light. As the captain glared at him, sucking in his breath for a withering rebuke, the *Bedford* rolled, steeply canting the deck and causing the usually self-effacing ECM officer to rise up and loom menacingly above him. The blast never came, as Finlander caught his breath in surprise. But there must have been something in his own demeanor which sobered Spitzer because he was as suddenly transformed back to his more normal personality.

"I'm sorry, Captain," he gulped with a miserable whine. "It just slipped out of me, sir. I mean . . . well, I just wonder if the Russians are down there at all, sir."

It took Finlander a few seconds before he got enough of a grip on himself to be nothing but sarcastic. "You confuse us, Lieutenant. Are they there or aren't they? Please make up your mind."

Spitzer looked as though he were trying to push himself through the bulkhead. "Well, sir . . . there's no readout on any of the gear to suggest they are. But maybe Queffle can *feel* them." There was a touch of sarcasm here too.

Out of the corner of his eye, the captain noticed Queffle cringe. He heard the talker by the plot drone out: "Number-one ASROC reports iced up and on STANDBY-HOLD." He looked away from Spitzer to the Weapons Status Board and saw the light of No. 1 AS-ROC switch from green to amber. No. 2 was likewise amber, which meant that both launchers were inoperative and the *Bedford* was deprived of her most vital anti-submarine weaponry at this critical time. "We certainly must have BUWEAPS develop effective de-icing gear," Finlander growled. "If we had to make a kill we'd be in a horrible jam right now." He turned back to Spitzer, trying to steady the man with a casual tone. "But all your detecting systems are go, aren't they, Jeff?"

"As far as I can tell, sir."

"So sit down at Central Control and make sure, boy!' Finlander motioned him into the chair he had vacated, then stepped over to check the recording graph of the master fathometer. The needle was just tracing another distinctive hump over the flat bottom as, from the bridge above, Commander Allison accurately conned the *Bedford* to pass over the *Hood* for the sixth time in the last hour. Above the contour of the wreck there was not the slightest shadow to suggest that anything as large as Moby Dick was hanging above it. As improbable as it was that the submarine could have sneaked away without being picked up by any of the detecting gear, the situation certainly had become doubtful. On top of all this uncertainty which Finlander knew was permeating the mind of everybody in the CIC, there had been evidence of conflict between their captain and departmental commander. Morale and efficiency were now held together by a very thin thread. Something had to be done—immediately.

Finlander moved along the row of ECM operators and stopped behind Queffle, who kept his eyes staring at his PPI scope and his hands convulsively pressing the earphones to his head. He was aware of the close presence of his captain, and Finlander felt his muscles knotting tight as he touched the boy's shoulder, making him shy away slightly. "All right, Queffle. You're relieved for a while." There was no reaction, and Finlander suddenly pried the fingers open and pulled the earphones from Queffle's head. "Come on, son! Relax!"

Queffle twisted around in his seat and looked up at Finlander with a desperate expression. "I can pick him up, sir. I know I can pick him up. It's just a matter of concentrating on it awhile longer. Don't yank me off now, sir. Please! Please!" He was pleading like a boy begging his coach to give him a last chance to salvage the impending defeat of his team.

"Ease up, Queffle," Finlander said with surprising gentleness. "You're not even sure he's still down there."

"I d-don't know for sure he *isn't,*" Queffle stammered. "I think he might be. He must be. If only I could concentrate enough."

Ensign Ralston suddenly spoke up loudly from his position at Fire Control and there was something of the same pleading in his voice. "Captain, sir, couldn't we drop a shallow charge? If he thought we weren't kidding, he might be bluffed into making a run for it."

One of the stand-by sonar operators let out an approving growl. Finlander realized with a wave of relief that the morale was not as bad as he had suspected. "That's a good idea. Mr. Ralston," he answered, "but I don't think it would work with this character. He's as smart and tough as they come. We've got to face up to that."

"And give up, sir?" Ralston exclaimed, appalled.

"You know me better than that!" Finlander retorted and suddenly found himself addressing everybody in the CIC. "Moby Dick is as smart and tough as they come among submariners. But we are as smart and tough as they come among submarine hunters. So it's going to be a close call like . . ." He paused for a moment, thinking back. "Like a game I once played with another smart submariner—Stoltz of the U-1020. It took me fifty-two hours to pin him down and kill him. . . . *Fifty-two hours!*" He paused again and his face seemed to harden with the inspiration of fresh determination as he recalled the action. "I didn't win that one by giving up. I won it by making Stoltz *think* I had given up. All right! I'll show you how it happened!" He was suddenly full of a tense suppressed excitement which he sensed was being communicated to his men. He also sensed that he was irrevocably putting at stake their confidence in him by demanding from them a last ounce of perseverance in this nebulous battle. He was betting against all the evidence of the *Bedford*'s electronic gear, against the wavering extrasensory perception of his own pet magician, Merlin Queffle. He was betting that Moby Dick *was* down there, still hiding in the protective shadow of the hulk of the *Hood,* and that he could fox him. Turning to Spitzer, he ordered: "Secure the maximum-effect sweep! Put your department on stand-by GQ. *Relax!* Have the galley send up sandwiches and coffee for all hands. I'm going up on the bridge to brief Commander Allison on the trap we're going to spring." He hooked his hand under Queffle's arm and pulled him out of the chair.

The Breton Kid resisted with a nearly subordinate violence: "You're not yanking me off, sir!" he protested. "You've got to let me see this through!"

Finlander laughed. "Certainly, Queffle! But I'm not going to throw you into the final play with your senses

befuddled by fatigue and tension. Come with me."
Steadying the skinny little sonarman against a violent
gyration of the *Bedford*, the captain led him to the
door. After it clanged shut behind them, Lieutenant
Spitzer leaned back in his seat at Central Control and
announced:

"Okay—so it's all systems guarded for stand-by GQ.
Reliefs, take over your stations. All others relax like
the skipper said."

The order was obeyed, but with an atmosphere of
tense expectancy.

2.

In the darkness of the wheelhouse Commander Allison was perched on the captain's chair, which had been moved in front of the recorder of the fathometer. Like a blind man probing his way along with an invisible stick, he was navigating back and forth, back and forth, over the wreck of the *Hood* by watching the trace of the bottom contour of the graph while calling out changes of course to the helmsman. Lieutenant Petersen, the OOD, was standing next to the gyro-compass, checking every move of the wheel. Ensign Whitaker, the JOOD, leaned heavily on the annunciator, listening with unflagging concentration for the frequent engine-room orders. Next to the quartermaster and talker, two bridge lookouts huddled by the heater, thawing themselves out after being relieved from an agonizing twenty-minute watch on the snow-lashed bridge. Only Commander Allison's and the helmsman's faces stood out clearly in the gloom, illuminated by the instruments before them; all others were only vaguely visible as blacker shapes in the surrounding blackness.

Merlin Queffle came up through the shaft, being pushed along by Captain Finlander and securely held by his possessive grip. They stopped by Commander Allison, and the captain exclaimed: "You are doing a terrific job of navigating off the bottom, Buck."

Allison flipped his head away from the fathometer as though he had been awakened out of a trance. "Hello, Captain. Well, sir . . . it's pretty flat down there and the *Hood* stands out like a sore thumb. We've got our drift down pat, so it's only a matter of establishing a fixed pattern of maneuvers." His eyes moved to Queffle, noticing the sonarman's hangdog look. "What's the score in CIC? Still lost contact?"

"He's down there, all right," Finlander answered, sounding absolutely confident. "But we're going to change our tactics. Turn over the conn to your OOD and come into the navigation office, Buck. I'll tell you what we're about to pull."

Finlander had not released his grip on Queffle and he now guided him into the navigation office and through it into his day cabin. There he found Ben Munceford curled up on the bunk, fast asleep. Unceremoniously he shook him awake. "Heave out, Munceford! If you're going to sack out through this action, do it in your own cabin!" As the bunk was vacated by the sleepily startled correspondent, the captain gently shoved the Breton Kid down on it. "Now you lie down and relax your nerves, son," he said. "Just let your mind go blank for a while. I'm going to send to the galley for your favorite drink and sandwich. What would you like?"

"Gee—nothing, I guess, sir," Queffle mumbled. "I think I feel kind of sick."

"Okay. I'll fix you up." Pushing Munceford out of the way, he went to the bulkhead and dialed the ship's hospital. Lieutenant Commander Porter's weary voice answered the call. "Doc! I want some brandy to the bridge on the double. Bring it yourself and whatever is necessary to put an exhausted man back in shape for another couple of hours." Before the surgeon could ask him for any details, Finlander hung up on him and dialed the galley. "This is the captain speaking. Send a messman up to my day cabin with a peanut-butter-and-jelly sandwich and a thick chocolate malted. On the double." When he turned from the phone, he saw Munceford standing over the bunk, staring down at

Queffle, who was lying there with his hands over his face. "Get out of here, Munceford. From now on, make yourself as scarce as possible."

Munceford shrugged and almost fell out of the cabin, propelled by a deep pitch of the destroyer. Finlander sat down on the edge of the bunk and put his hand on Queffle's chest, trying to belay its heaving. "Listen to me, boy," he said in a tone which was gruffly soothing. "I know how you feel. I know you think you've failed us. But that is not true at all. Talents like yours don't just suddenly evaporate. They may become dulled by tension and fatigue, but never simply vanish into nothing. So I want you to know I'm still convinced you're the best sonarman in the whole navy. I'm going to give you a chance to prove it in a little while and have no doubts that you'll come through. Okay, Merlin? Are you with me?"

The hands fell away from the gaunt face and there was a look of wonderment in those bloodshot eyes. "You're the best captain in the navy, sir," the Breton Kid whispered.

Finlander's forehead wrinkled into lines of embarrassment above the thistly brows. "I can be no better than my boys," he answered, gave him a reassuring pat on the shoulder, then quickly left the cabin.

Commander Allison was waiting by the chart table in the navigation office, his eyes watching the gyro-repeater above it, his fingers absently twirling a pair of dividers. When the captain joined him, he turned and looked at him with a calm expectancy. "Something wrong with Queffle, sir?"

"The boy's worn out. But we've got to have him back in shape within an hour. Porter is coming up to nurse him for a while. Here's what I want done. . . ." The captain leaned on the table and began to subconsciously sketch out the maneuver with a pencil as he spoke. "Belay jogging over the *Hood*. Turn into the seas and leave the area at flank speed. Pick a course so that when we eventually turn around, we will be able to drift back to this exact spot with a minimum of engine maneuvers or noise. I want Moby Dick to think we've picked up a false contact and rushed off to investigate it. Or, better still, that we have given up. Let's get at least ten miles away before we sneak back on him. To confuse his sonar even more, have the engine room gradually reduce the revolutions as we draw away. I have ordered CIC to guard on passive so they won't hear our pings. . . . Any comments, Buck?"

Allison looked thoughtfully at the sketch which Finlander had traced on the chart. "Do you think the Russian commander will fall for such a simple old trick, sir?" he asked.

"The simple old tricks sometimes are the undoing of men who have grown too complex in their thinking. I also am sure he's been under terrific pressure for these past forty-two hours. That, combined with oxygen starvation, may well be clouding his judgment."

Allison nodded and said: "Possibly, sir."

"But the main thing I'm counting on is that you'll be able to make our return run so quietly that he won't pick us up. The sea is still pretty rough, so chances are his sonar is bothered by a lot of surface hash. That will screen us to some extent. Yet if we take a real bad sea ourselves, it could give us away. It's up to you and Engineering to make the sneakiest approach ever pulled. Can you do it?"

Commander Allison nodded again, but there was a tinge of doubt in his demeanor which made Finlander ask: "So what's bothering you about the plan, Buck?"

"It's sound as such, sir," the executive officer answered. "But I am wondering whether we should check it with Commodore Schrepke. A mere formality, but—"

"Where is he?" Finlander impatiently interrupted.

"In his usual place on the starboard wing, sir."

Finlander made a face. "Even in this tactical situation? Well, that cinches it as far as I'm concerned. The man is too brooding and withdrawn to be entirely normal. And I know what's eating away at his insides. He's still a U-boatman—a *defeated* U-boatman who knows he should be among the thirty thousand of his colleagues whose bones litter the floor of this ocean. He feels himself a traitor to them, not because he is working with Americans, but because he's working with destroyermen, the mortal enemy of all submariners. Well, I grant you, traitors can be useful, but not when their professional detachment becomes inhibited by remorse and guilt. I have nothing against Schrepke personally, nor do I not respect his rank, but I say let's leave him out there in his own purgatory and go about our business. . . . Do you agree?"

"We can do without him, sir, especially since he hasn't bothered to make any suggestions," Allison answered.

"Very well. So let's pull out of her, Buck."

Both men were startled by a voice behind them which loudly asked: "Do we stand down from General Quarters, Captain?" It was Lieutenant Commander Porter, who had entered the navigation office unnoticed and was standing there with a first-aid kit slung over one shoulder.

Finlander looked sharply at him. "No, Doc. I don't want the whole ship's complement to feel the fight is over. I want them to stay keyed up."

"They're far *too* keyed up, sir," the surgeon warned with an accusing tone. "Sooner or later, some of them are going to start caving in."

The captain's eyes became smoldering slits beneath the shadowing brows. "Then I'll let you patch them up *after* this action is over, Commander Porter. In the meantime you will go into my day cabin and work on Queffle. *Medically*—not with any mollycoddling psychiatric mish-mash, sir. I suggest a shot of brandy to begin with."

The surgeon's haggard pallor flushed into a deep shade of mortification. "Has the captain any other medical advice for me?" he asked.

"I advise you to proceed with extreme care, Commander," came the seething retort.

"Thank you, Captain." Porter sullenly turned away and headed for the day cabin.

Commander Allison watched him go with a troubled expression on his face. "Don't misunderstand my mentioning this, sir," he said to Finlander, "but it's going to look bad for us to have serious trouble with *two* surgeons in a row."

"Our only worry is to accomplish our tactical mission, Buck," Finlander answered, "then everything else will take care of itself. Go ahead and execute the maneuver immediately."

Allison said "Aye, aye, sir," and hurried out of the navigation office.

Finlander remained at the table, looking down on the chart with all the lines of his face compressed into a dark scowl. His eyes were on the penciled outline of his plan, but his mind was momentarily festering on the sore subject of surgeons. If it were not for the fact that his executive officer was absolutely right in his fears, he would signal a request to COMFLANT to have Porter relieved. But that would, of course, bring a fleet inspector along with the replacement. The only answer was to either bend the surgeon into the *Bedford* mold or break him so thoroughly that he would come to doubt his own judgment. At least Porter was nothing more dangerous than a confused naval conformist, not a zealot in the cause of humanity, like Hirschfeld. It was definitely not worth the risk of triggering an upheaval at COMFLANT by requesting his replacement. But the man had to be watched. . . .

Finlander was just turning to go into the day cabin when he was alerted by the sound of a familiar *click* which stopped him in his tracks. Looking in the direction of the crisp little noise, he spotted the lanky shape of Ben Munceford in the dark corner by the chart locker.

"Didn't I make it clear you are to make yourself scarce around here, Munceford?" the captain challenged.

"And I did too," Munceford replied with an insolent grin. "At least I thought I was being as unobtrusive as a mouse caught in an alley cats' convention." As he stepped out of his dark corner and up to the chart table, its light revealed the flash of chrome and plastic in his hands.

"As usual, your humor is shallow and out of place," Finlander said, looking down at the tape recorder and fighting back an intense urge to smash it to the deck. "And to tape a discussion between myself and my officers without our permission is a flagrant breach of trust and ethics."

Munceford managed to keep smiling. "Well, Captain, you know I like to get spontaneous off-the-cuff stuff. It has so much more authenticity than faked setups. Besides, why get in an uproar when everything's going to be checked by the PRO at COMFLANT before it's released?"

"It's also going to be checked by the commanding officer of this ship before it gets that far," the captain told him icily. "I think you've gotten all the authenticity you need from my bridge. From now on concentrate your efforts on other parts of the *Bedford*."

"Like maybe CIC?"

"You stay out of CIC!" Finlander shouted with such violence that Munceford shied away from him, his face momentarily flustered with the old childish petulance. The captain instantly recovered control of himself. "I want no diversions down there whatever. Besides, *everything* in CIC is classified, so it's of no pertinence to your assignment. Understand? Good. Now get out." He kept his eyes fixed on the correspondent until he passed through the blackout curtain to the wheelhouse, then turned and went into the day cabin, there to check up on the surgeon's treatment of his prized sonarman.

3.

In the *Bedford*'s engine-room flats there was neither gloom nor raw chill. Lights illuminating the huge control panel were bright, glinting off polished steel, enamel and jewel-like splashes of bronze. The air sang with the melodious monotone of the turbines and was warm with a faintly pungent odor of dry steam and lube oil. There was a certain weariness here too, but not of the tense kind prevailing on the bridge or in CIC. Engineers are a special breed whose nervous systems are so finely tuned to the machinery in their charge that nothing on or under the wild ocean outside seems to upset their equilibrium, unless it be combined with an erratic flicker of a needle or a strident ambient noise out of a reduction-gear casing. Like Chief Machinist's Mate Lauchlan S. MacKay, who had been almost continuously on duty since the previous morning, as long as Captain Finlander, the Breton Kid, Commander Allison, Chief Quartermaster Rickmers or Lieutenants Spitzer and Krindlemeyer. He was both as fatigued and as enervated as any of them, but the reaction was a capriciousness strange in such an old hand, manifested by his starting to mix a Scottish burr into his Boston flat *a*'s. He was seated at the throttles, leaning back in his chair while fondling a cup of boiler-room coffee, his feet propped upon the control pedestal, his eyes critically appraising a minute nervous twitch in No. 3 boiler's pressure gauge. Into the account of his and Finlander's action against U-1020, he injected a non-sequitur observation that "these auto-

matic fur'rnaces with their thermostatic controls still
don't match a detail of flesh-'n'-blood firemen for keeping an even strrrain on the manifolds."

Lieutenant Commander Sanford Franklin jerked
himself upright in the chair next to MacKay and
pounced on this opportunity to stem the flow of remi-
niscences from the chief's engagements with U-1020
... 784 ... 866 ... and other sanguinary but insignifi-
cant naval battles of a bygone war, all of which he
knew by heart and did not need to sustain him in this
prolonged current contest with Moby Dick. "So why
don't you have the thermostats calibrated instead of
just sitting there bitching about them, Mac?" he demanded.

MacKay lolled his head to port against the roll of
the ship and carefully scratched around the naval of his
exposed belly. "That I will after things calm doon. But
since it takes physicists to nur'rse the pettyfoggin' ail-
ments of this engine room, one must beware of exposing such lubbers to falling into the machinery, causing
worse damage than an anemic transistor.'

Commander Franklin winced. "Jesus, Mac. You
must be flipping, putting on that phony Scottish accent.
I'd better have you relieved and sent up to sick bay to
get your psychosis reamed out."

MacKay guffawed, blowing a fine black spray of
coffee over his chin. "Hoot, mon, Command'rr! If
Lieutenant Hirschfeld was there, I'd willingly go, but
..." He brought himself up short as the telephone suddenly interrupted him with a ring which loudly jarred
above the sound of the turbines. With a flippantly insubordinate gesture, he picked up the receiver and
tossed it at the engineering officer, who barely managed
to catch it in mid-air.

"Engine-room Control. Commander Franklin."

The executive officer was on the other end of the
line, and in a few clipped sentences he outlined Fin-

lander's coming maneuver to outwit Moby Dick and the part Engineering was expected to play in it. "Steam out of here like a locomotive," Allison finished by saying, "and come back as silent as driftwood."

"Aye, aye! And it may work at that!" Commander Franklin swiveled around in his chair and threw the phone back at MacKay. "We're about to pull a fake play, Chief. Stand by for flank speed. And you've got about ten minutes to blow tubes and do any other noisy chores needed."

"Chr-rist! It's going to be U-1020 all over!" MacKay exclaimed. Pulling his feet off the console, he threw his cup of coffee into the trash bin, quickly slipped his upper plate out of his mouth and into his shirt pocket and had his hands on the throttles just as the annunciator clanged and switched to ALL AHEAD FLANK. "Hang on, lad! It will be a wild ride!" He shoved the levers smoothly ahead until they touched the emergency gates. From below them the sound of the turbines surged until they reached a frenzied pitch of full power. Franklin looked down there and saw a machinist grab a handhold to keep himself from falling as the propellers bit savagely into the sea and sucked down the stern before thrusting the *Bedford* ahead. Her bow butted solidly into a huge swell which sent a shudder through the ship as she began heeling hard over in a turn. The machinist hung there for dear life, momentarily completely off balance, his face peering up in alarm at the engineering officer. Then he grinned, shook his head and recovered himself.

In the galley the chief cook also grabbed for a handhold, this one on the stove, where he had taken a chance on frying thirty pounds of pork sausage for breakfast. The turbines were three decks down and beyond nine watertight compartments, but he could feel their sudden surge of power through the soles of his shoes. Even as he glanced over his shoulder toward the

VIOLENT MANEUVER light, it flashed from amber to red. As the destroyer leaped ahead, smashed through the big swell and heeled steeply, he helplessly watched the hot grease flow off the griddle into the trap, then slosh over it and run onto the tile deck. A hundred sausages rolled and butted against one another like a stampeding herd of little fat pigs; a half-dozen jumped the guard rail and splashed into the spreading puddle of grease. The chief cook swore and yelled: "Belay hot breakfast!" The assistant cook echoed his curse and began pulling himself hand over hand along the steam table to help scoop the sausages into a pan. But as he jumped across to the stove, he slipped in the grease and hit the deck hard.

The chief cook waited for ten seconds until the *Bedford* began straightening up on her keel, then let go of the stove handhold and crouched down by his assistant, who was looking foolishly at his arm. It was broken.

"Lie down flat, Andy, and press it to your chest so it don't hit nothing else," he said, all his anger changed to sympathetic concern. Then he clawed his way over to the opposite bulkhead, reached for the telephone and dialed sick bay. "A coreman to the galley! We got a casualty!"

In the Communications Center, Lieutenant Peter Packer had just taken a routine HUFF-DUFF bearing on transmission from the *Tiburon Bay* when he felt the quickening pulse of the *Bedford*'s engines. His hasty calculation plotted the tanker's position as somewhat less than two hundred miles south-southwest of their own, and it was perhaps natural for him to think that Finlander had decided to break off the preposterous cat-and-mouse game with Moby Dick to speed toward a rendezvous. He looked up at the PA speaker, expecting an announcement to stand down from GQ, but no sound came out of it. Instead there came a base-drum boom as the destroyer hit a heavy sea, followed by the whoosh of spray flying over her entire superstructure. Packer had to brace himself against the plotting table as the *Bedford* lay over in a violently contested accelerating turn. A glance at the gyro-repeater would have told him that she was *not* turning toward the *Tiburon Bay,* rather away from her, pointing her plunging bow northeast toward the desolate blackness of the Denmark Strait. But once he sensed that the endless jogging over the wreck of the *Hood* had definitely come to an end, he suddenly could think of nothing except that the only brief closeness to his father which he had known in his whole life was likewise ending. With each turn of the thundering screws, they were torn farther and farther apart, the schism of death's oblivion once again widening between them—most likely, this time forever!

Lieutenant Packer tore off the earphones and rushed into the radio room, where he grabbed the dozing Lieutenant Beeker and shook him awake. "Look here, Beek! Cover for me a few minutes. I absolutely have to go out on deck."

Beeker blinked at him. "What's the matter, Peterpacker? You going to puke after standing everything this long?"

"No, damn it! I've got to go out for a while, that's all. Do you mind?" He yelled it out with such vehemence that all three radio operators turned from their sets and stared at him.

Beeker shot himself erect in his chair with a startled expression. "Well, okay, Packer. Go ahead!" the communicator exclaimed. But his permission was entirely superfluous, as the British officer was already halfway to the door. He yanked his parka off its hook and, while still struggling into it, vanished through an icy blast and a slam.

A solid wall of snow-filled wind swept down the deck, thrust into Packer's crouched body and propelled it along the heaving, slush-coated plates. Blotches of spume rushed past the *Bedford*'s flanks, flaring a ghostly white before fading back into the absolute night; the diffused blue halos of the battle lights on the main yard performed wild gyrations against the black void of the sky. Particles of ice were wrenched loose from the mast and came clattering down, an occasional larger icicle hitting the deck with a resounding clang. The blower intakes roared angrily as they gulped huge quantities of air for the *Bedford*'s throbbing boiler rooms, and in an eery falsetto accompaniment the halyards and radar antennas began to wail in the slipstream. But Lieutenant Packer noticed none of these things. For a wild moment he was skidding along without moving his feet, miraculously missing the cleats and hose connections which cluttered the deck. Somehow he hooked an arm around a davit of the whaleboat and pivoted around it, changing his course to right angles. A stanchion on the edge of the deck burned his gloveless hands with a searing cold, but kept him from pitching over the side. He hung there, leaning far out, staring into the thirty-knot wash, and beyond it through the calming blackness of the deep into two hundred and ten fathoms of eternity. While the snow lashed his face with squalls of stinging ice needles, he felt a wordless prayer for his unknown father, the *Hood* and all the lost souls calling to him from her algid hulk.

In the starboard wing of the bridge, another man was staring down into the black rushing sea. Commodore Schrepke had been there since leaving the CIC a little after 0300, occasionally fighting the terrible cold by pacing a few steps while slapping his arms across his chest and cracking off the snow freezing to his leather jacket, but mostly crouched by the windscreen and following the battle between the *Bedford* and the Russian submarine without any benefit of fathometers or sonar. In his mind there was a built-in sensory system which not only kept track of the destroyer's seemingly aimless jogging over the black surface, but was also in almost tangible communication with the craft hiding in the blacker deep beneath it. He had done so many times what those submariners were doing now that he could live and feel every moment of every man, bridging the years since he had experienced the same thing as if they had never existed. Perhaps there was a German among the Russians down there. An old U-boatman like himself, and like himself serving in a foreign naval vessel, but a Soviet one because fate had presented no choice and he had finally thrown over any scruples and capitulated to a pitiless destiny. Perhaps it even was one of his own boys, like Raschnau or Manteufel, both of whom had vanished into the faceless maw of Soviet forced labor. Perhaps. Only one thing he knew for certain, and that was that there were no Communists or Nazis or Democrats, Easterners or Westerners or international agnostics hiding down there in the sepulchral sanctuary of the dead British battle cruiser. Only humanoids reduced to the ultimate equality of stark terror, each fighting his own loneliness and desperately binding up his own bowels and backbone with a last thin thread of discipline while listening to the sounds of the hated destroyer's relentless stalking overhead.

When Schrepke felt the *Bedford*'s engines surge with a burst of power and a sudden squall of stinging cold spray whipped over the bridge as she leaped ahead, his heart jumped with relief in his chest, probably in unison with the heart of the Russian commander of Moby Dick. Just as *he* would, he found himself muttering a fervent prayer that the destroyer was breaking off the action and steaming away. But he quickly sensed that there was another, more sinister purpose in the maneuver. The *Bedford* was accelerating and turning, moving on through the range of speed of a normal withdrawal in these sea conditions, failing to pick up the southerly heading which the commodore knew to be her base course, instead coming around until her bow pointed directly into the swells and starting to hurdle them like a greyhound in a steeplechase. Finlander was turning north, and there could be no reason for this except *one*. Schrepke remained where he was for several minutes, staring over the side while enduring the freezing, brine-filled wind, trying to divine whether or not the Russian commander was suspecting the trap being laid for him. Then he turned and rocked toward the wheelhouse.

Lieutenant Commander Porter was genuinely shocked when Commodore Schrepke suddenly appeared in the door of the day cabin, looking in at him, Finlander and Queffle, who was eagerly draining the last of his malted milk. The German was almost solidly caked with frozen slush, his face blotched, his eyes swollen. "My God, sir!" the surgeon exclaimed. "You're badly frostbitten!"

Schrepke stuck the fingers of his right hand in his mouth and pulled off the glove with his teeth, then forced open the stiff folds of his leather jacket. Bits of ice fell from his muffler and made brittle sounds as they hit the deck. "I am all right, Doctor," he said with a smile which looked as though it too should break loose crusts of ice. "But perhaps you will prescribe something warming, no?"

Finlander stared at him with a tinge of shock. "Give him one on the house, Commander," he ordered the surgeon.

"Thank you," Schrepke said. "I will take it in a hot cup of coffee." He remained in the door, bracing himself there against the now bone-rattling pitches of the racing destroyer. His eyes were on the sonarman seated on the bunk, and a look of doubt came to his face, as if seeing Queffle there might make a difference in his evaluation of the situation. "Is your young magician being rewarded for a completed performance, or is he being primed for a grand finale of his black art?" If there was sarcasm in the question, it was not directed at the boy who stared back at him, uncomprehending.

"Queffle is resting," Finlander answered guardedly, "and recuperating after over twenty-four hours of intermittent duty."

"And while he is resting, you are utilizing that time to give the submarine the impression you are departing. Right, Captain?"

"Right, Commodore."

Schrepke nodded, all doubt gone from his face. "Will you please step into the chartroom with me, Captain," he said and abruptly turned from the door, going in there himself without waiting for an answer. He had spoken to Finlander as a superior officer to a subordinate.

Lieutenant Commander Porter was leaning over the small desk, trying to aim a splash of brandy into the sloshing cup of coffee he had poured out of the thermos jug. He immediately sensed an electrifying tension after the German had spoken, most of it emanating from Captain Finlander, who hesitated for a long moment before following him out of the cabin. Merlin Queffle must have felt it too, because he exclaimed in a nervous whisper: "Geez, Commander! Is he going to chew the skipper over *me?*"

"No, Queffle. Of course not."

"Then what, sir?"

"Nothing that's your business."

For a moment the surgeon wondered whether it was *his* business either, but he was itching to hear the exchange between the captain and the commodore, and, after all, he had an excuse since Schrepke had requested the spiked coffee. So he steeled himself and went after them.

The two men were standing in the pool of red light by the chart table. "... and I would appreciate to know exactly what your tactical objective is in continuing the action, Captain," Commodore Schrepke was saying, his guttural English containing a steely Prussian edge.

"I believe you know it perfectly well, sir," Finlander answered him. "To force the Russian to the surface."

"You had him surfaced yesterday, Captain, but forced him down again."

Finlander smiled. "He was not ripe then, Commodore. I am not playing games. My purpose is to so exhaust him and shatter his morale that he will be unable to accomplish the purpose of his trespass on this side of the ocean."

Schrepke noticed the surgeon and reached out for the cup of coffee in his hand, waited a couple of seconds for the *Bedford* to shake herself free of a huge sea, then took a deep gulp of the brew. "In my judgment, these harassment tactics have gone too far and should be terminated immediately," he bluntly told Finlander after recovering from the invigorating pain of the drink.

Finlander shook his head adamantly. "I will break off when it is firmly established in the minds of both my own and the Russian's crew that I'm doing so only on my terms."

Schrepke rolled the cup in his hands, warming his numb fingers with its heat. "How do you know what is in the minds of the Russian crew, Captain? By the electronic phantasmagorias in CIC? Surely not, when they so often short-circuit themselves on their own complexity or are so oversensitive as to become alarmed over a bed of shrimp. Or do you count on the mystic powers of young Queffle? Of course not! You know as well as I do that his only true talent is an accidentally high acuity of hearing. Between those ears there is nothing more formidable than a quite ordinary brain belonging to a confused boy. But if you want to believe in any kind of extrasensory perception, then believe in *mine*. Yes, Captain—*I* have been in that submarine ever since you started chasing it two days ago. I can tell you her captain and crew are now reduced to such a state of desperation that they may no longer act in any way except as animals fighting for survival. I can tell you this because it has happened to me in submarines, so you see there is nothing really mystical about my powers either. I merely remember and put myself in their place."

Finlander had listened with his huge head cocked to one side, his eyes burning behind their network of tired wrinkles, the scar on his throat throbbing. Lieutenant Commander Porter could feel the tremendous pressure building up in the man and wondered whether he was about to finally lose his temper with the one person aboard who was immune to his powers. But the explosion was delayed and something like a smile came to Finlander's lips as he asked: "Is that what you do when you seclude yourself in the wing of my bridge, Commodore? Commune with your old U-boat comrades?"

"In a way, that is my purpose here, Captain, is it not? And I am now giving you the benefit of my findings. Stop this madness before one or the other is driven to precipitate a fatal tragedy."

Finlander appeared to flinch slightly at the word "madness," but his head rocked in one firm negative motion. "I am sorry, sir. I can't break off yet. And for your information, it isn't a question of one or *the other*. Everything is firmly in control aboard *my* ship."

Lieutenant Commander Porter shocked himself by suddenly blurting out: "I respectfully disagree, Captain, sir" and brought upon himself the explosion he had expected to be directed against the German officer.

"Damn you, Porter!" Finlander shouted, his face a livid mask as he wheeled on the surgeon. "Who invited you to partake in this discussion? Get out!"

As if she were echoing her commander's fury, the *Bedford* slammed into a wave and leaped through a hurricane of spray before wildly pitching into the next trough. Porter collided heavily with Schrepke, who had to steady him and then kept a surprisingly hard grip on his arm after the destroyer recovered herself. The surgeon wanted to flee the bridge and Finlander's wrath, but found himself held back by the German.

"Please stay," Schrepke said with a commanding insistence. "I do believe a medical opinion may be in order here."

"What are you insinuating, sir?" Finlander yelled, his voice ringing above the roar of the destroyer's thrusting through the sea. His eyes were no longer slits, but wide and bulging; the wiry eyebrows no longer formed a solid bristle across the bridge of his nose, but had broken adrift among the anguished furrows of his forehead. Lieutenant Commander Porter yanked himself free of Schrepke's grip and recoiled backward. This, then, was the explosion he had feared, but far more horrible than he had ever dreamed. "What sort of medical opinion?" the captain screamed, completely beside himself. "Out with it! You want to throw a bunch of catch-all psychiatric accusations at me you've picked up from Hirschfeld? All right! But spit them out right here and now. Say I've brainwashed my crew and turned them into a bunch of schizos. Then tell *them* and let them laugh you off my ship."

Commodore Schrepke bent away from the blast slightly, but countered in a coolly controlled voice: "I was going to say nothing more than that they are, in their own way, as overwrought as the crew of the submarine, and as liable to make fatal mistakes in this dangerous game." He turned to the stunned surgeon and calmly asked: "Do you not agree with me, Doctor?"

"Go ahead—*Doctor!*" Finlander viciously shouted. "I *dare* you to agree with him!"

Lieutenant Commander Chester Porter suddenly found himself the focal point of the stares of both men, the captain's eyes wild and fearfully threatening, the commodore's gimlets of blue ice which seemed to be penetrating to his soul. He felt a confusion of fear, indecision and bitter frustration welling up inside him, but of the three, fear was predominant. And when he noticed that a fourth man, Commander Allison, had come into the navigation office and was also watching him intently, fear submerged all other feeling. His mouth opened and closed fitfully without a sound coming out of it, the ineffectual silence lasting for a mortifying eternity until the executive officer bailed him out of it.

"Sick bay has just reported a casualty, Commander," he announced. "A broken bone needing your immediate attention."

While the surgeon hesitated a moment longer, Finlander's hand shot out and seized Allison's arm. "I will at least get a straight answer out of you, Buck!" he shouted. "Tell me if this operation has been conducted in an irresponsible, overzealous—in fact, *mad*—fashion."

Allison looked into the face of his captain, then turned his head toward Commodore Schrepke. There came a suggestion of a wrinkling of his beaked nose. There also came one of his rare smiles, but it seemed only to creep up one side of his face, leaving it with an expression of half amused contempt, half sullen truculence. "Maybe so, Captain," he slowly answered, "but only to a frightened submariner."

Finlander let out a single, gleeful "Ha!"

Schrepke shook his head and blinked his eyes as if he disbelieved what he had heard. "I asked a question of Commander Porter," he persisted, "and expect an answer from him."

But the surgeon had been edging away from the chart table and now seized his chance to escape. "Begging your pardon, Commodore," he hastily pleaded, "it seems I'm urgently needed in sick bay." He lunged toward the door, staggering like a whipped drunkard as the *Bedford* violently heaved and shuddered under his feet. His arms flailed at the blackout curtain and in a moment he had clawed his way through it and was gone.

With the surgeon's retreat, all the fury drained out of Captain Finlander and he regained control of himself as suddenly as he had lost it. There was even a gleam of triumph in his eyes as he stared toward the still swirling folds of the curtain. He knew now that he would not have to request the relief of his medical officer. He knew that Bucky Allison was firmly standing by him. Changing his hard grip on his exec's arm to a slap on the shoulder, he told him: "She seems to be working pretty hard, Buck. Have Engineering start easing off the revs before we get any more broken bones aboard. I doubt if our doctor is in shape for a lot of surgery this morning." When he found himself alone with the German officer, he managed a thin smile and said: "I am sorry I lost my temper, sir. It was foolish of me and really quite unnecessary to prove my point."

The malice in the apology did not go unnoticed by Commodore Schrepke, but he was still looking down at the empty spot on the deck where Lieutenant Commander Porter had stood swaying uncertainly a few moments before. He sighed deeply and a shadow of bitter irony briefly animated the inscrutable hardness of his face. "I have at least found out," he said, "that we

Germans are not the only ones guilty of breeding submissive militarists."

Having demolished Porter, Finlander had enough resurgence of confidence to press home his advantage over the German officer. "With all due respect, Commodore, I suggest your guilt is rather one of having survived defeat," he answered, deliberately twisting the knife.

Schrepke stiffened almost imperceptibly, then shook his head as if all this had been an unpleasant but irrelevant deviation from the main issue. The unfamiliar commanding tone returned to his voice as he spoke, looking directly into Finlander's eyes. "I must act in this situation according to my responsibilities as senior NATO officer aboard—"

"And I will act upon it according to the prerogatives of the commanding officer of a United States naval vessel," Finlander loudly injected. "In my judgment, it would prejudice the interests of my service to break off the action at this time. That is final, sir!"

"In that case I wish to officially go on record as being opposed to that judgment, Captain."

"That is your privilege, sir. Anything else?"

"Yes—I want you to understand I intend to communicate my opposition to Admiral Sorensen at NATO-NAV 1."

"That too is your privilege, Commodore," Finlander answered dryly, "but I strongly advise you to await the outcome before putting yourself on record in one way or the other. It would make you look foolish to have tried to stop an action which resulted in thwarting the Soviet navy's most notorious intruder operation."

"Regardless of the outcome, Captain, you have run the most appalling risks for very dubious objectives," Schrepke retorted. He drained his now cold cup of coffee, then began zipping up his leather jacket. "However, since I am unable to make you understand that, let's terminate a useless argument."

As the German moved to leave, Finlander blocked his way, suddenly switching to a manner of patronizing familiarity.

"Look here, Wolfgang. Our relationship has been good on this patrol. Believe me, I do respect you as a man and naval officer. It is very painful to me that this respect is not mutual."

"But it is, Erik," Schrepke replied without a trace of geniality. "You have my respect. But it is the respect of fear. Frankly, your executive officer was right ... you *frighten* me." He touched the visor of his cap, side-stepped Finlander and walked out of the chart-room.

The captain followed him with a frown containing both satisfaction and perplexity. He stopped a few steps inside the blacked-out wheelhouse, listening to the door of the bridge open and close, feeling the chilling blast of wind which Schrepke had let in from the night as he left. Then he cautiously moved across the heaving deck, checked the compass over the helmsman's rocking shoulders and joined Commander Allison, who was intently studying the dimly illuminated face of the automatic course recorder.

"I see you've sent our frightened U-boat veteran back to his hermit ledge," the exec said without taking his eyes from the instrument.

"Don't kid yourself, Buck," Finlander answered him testily. "Wolfgang Schrepke isn't frightened of anything in this world."

4.

The *Bedford*'s captain and executive officer both assumed that the German had returned to his secluded spot on the bridge, there to brood in loneliness over his ineffectual attempt to divert the course of events. But this was a mistaken assumption. He was actually on his way to the Communications Center. Heading there via an exterior companionway and the narrow deck below the bridge, pulling himself along, stanchion to stanchion, through the turbulent blackness. When he had said that he intended to protest the operation to NATONAV 1 and Admiral Sorensen, he had not meant it would be done only in due course after the patrol was completed, although there was some malice aforethought in leaving that impression. He intended to do it *immediately* and in spite of the radio silence imposed by Finlander during the action against Moby Dick. To accomplish this he was counting on two factors: finding Lieutenant Packer, NATO liaison officer for communications, on duty, and by convincing the Englishman of the urgency of transmitting the signal forthwith. Finlander had a right to impose radio silence on his ship, but not at the expense of severing the senior naval officer aboard from contact with his Fleet Headquarters. So there certainly was justification in attempting to circumvent the captain's authority in this matter. And as he pressed on against the lashing wind, Schrepke also thought that he must break Finlander's hegemony over the minds of his crew. He had to find at least one officer—and one with more backbone than the surgeon—to back him up in his attempt to forestall what might become a tragedy; at least find one to give him some moral support so he would not be so damnably much the despised lone German. Of all the men aboard this blighted ship, Lieutenant Peter Packer was his only hope.

Schrepke found the starboard entrance to the Communications Center to be securely dogged, so he had to continue where the deck bent around the forward funnel and turned into nothing more than a catwalk which crossed thwartship to the port side. Whirlwinds whipped around the tall moaning stack and had built a drift of snow which tripped his boots in its cold softness; as the destroyer lurched, he fell and almost rolled between the icicled lifelines to the main deck, invisible in the blackness far below him. But as he lay there for a moment, trying to catch his breath and clear his nostrils of the flying snowflakes, his eyes made out the ominous shape of the ASROC missile poised in its launcher, its dark shadow rising from the void, its green-painted warhead strangely luminous, like a cyclops' eye staring out of a cavern. Dimly he made out a figure clambering on the launcher itself, flailing with what appeared to be an ordinary broom at the frozen spume clogging the steel tracks.

"Das is doch wahnsinn!" Schrepke yelled in a sudden outburst of pure anguish. But although the man could not have been more than ten feet below and beyond the catwalk, he did not hear the cry, which was torn away by the wind and drowned in the roar of the sea.

Schrepke staggered to his feet, half slid along the grating where it changed from snow to ice, reached the port deck and turned to fight his way back toward the Communications Center. But as he passed the whaleboat davit, a huge wall of spray erupted out of the wash, and in the instant before it blew away he saw silhouetted against it a man slumped over the wire lifeline. It was only a fleeting glimpse, but it stopped him because he had recognized Lieutenant Packer.

"What in God's name are you doing out here?" the commodore shouted with genuine shock as he pulled himself alongside the Englishman. "Are you sick?"

Packer straightened up with a start, peered into Schrepke's face, then hunched back onto the lifeline. "Yes, I'm sick, Commodore Schrepke," he answered bitterly. "Sick at heart." His eyes returned to the black rush of sea hissing against the hull.

Schrepke felt a sudden surge of hope. Was this young lieutenant suffering from the same forebodings as himself? "Then you should do something about it," he shouted over the wind and put a hand on his shoulder. "Maybe we should *both* do something about it, eh?"

Packer twisted away from his touch and faced him again. Although it was too dark to see the expression on his face, the vehemence in his voice told Schrepke it would not be a friendly one. "I only want one thing from you, sir. Just one thing, that's all. Tell me if you had anything to do with sinking the *Hood*. Did you?"

Schrepke was completely taken aback by the question. "The *Hood?* . . . She was sunk by the *Bismarck*, a battleship. I served in U-boats. What do you—"

"Did your U-boat have any part of the action, sir?" Packer interrupted him with a nearly savage insistence.

Schrepke edged in closer, trying to get an impression of his eyes. "My boat was at sea under orders to intercept British units but . . . I was several hundred miles away when the *Hood* blew up." His tone sharpened as he recovered from his surprise. "Why do you ask me this, Lieutenant? You were nothing but a boy when that happened."

"Nothing but a boy," Packer echoed his words. "An orphan boy. My father died in the *Hood.*"

Schrepke suddenly understood why the young officer was out here alone with the sea and raised his gloved hand to touch his shoulder again, but Packer recoiled from him and he was left with his arm raised as if to strike a blow rather than make a gesture of sympathy. He felt the return of the empty loneliness inside him and it seemed to freeze and harden his whole being. "I am sorry," was all he managed to blurt out and he knew how callous it sounded with his harsh German accent. "It does no good to grieve about it now. Not even when we pass over the grave of your father's ship, it does no good."

"It does good to know whom to hate," Packer shouted at him. "I was thinking that maybe I should hate you, sir. Like I hate that god-damned bloody submarine down there, defiling the *Hood* with her filthy presence. I wish Captain Finlander would sink it and to hell with this play-acting. We're all going to try to kill each other soon anyway, so why not now? Why not get down to some serious hating and killing right now?" He turned away and stared off into the night, expecting and getting no answer. But as the silence between them became prolonged, the lieutenant's turbulent feelings slowly abated and deeply ingrained discipline began regaining control. He suddenly became aware of how rudely he had addressed an officer who would have been an admiral in his own navy. With a frantic apology on his lips he wheeled around and was startled to find himself alone. Commodore Schrepke was gone. Even when he lunged away from the lifeline, peering hard through the flying snow, he could see no trace of him. "Oh, God!" he muttered miserably to himself. "I've made a damned fool of myself! I'll have to apologize tomorrow."

5.

Ben Munceford had left the bridge and gone out on the main deck to chill his burning anger after the clash with Captain Finlander. He had stood alone in the dark, sheltered from the snow and spume by an ice-coated life raft, hooking one arm through its lashing and hanging on, hating the *Bedford* and her captain. But he had not been there more than a few minutes when the destroyer's wild burst of speed through the swells brought floods of freezing water rushing down the deck. Over the roar of the wake he heard the metallic clang of doors being closed and dogged. He barely managed to splash through a torrent and escape back inside. A seaman slammed the door on his heels without as much as a glance at him, then vanished. Moving with a kind of listless uncertainty, bouncing from bulkhead to bulkhead as the ship pounded from crest to trough, he struggled along the passageway, gravitating toward the wardroom because hunger was gnawing among the other unpleasant feelings in his insides. The wardroom had been converted into an emergency first-aid station during the GQ, but the coremen had been returned to mess duties in an effort to get out a hot meal for the rest of the crew. Nobody was there.

Munceford found only some cold dregs in the coffee thermos, but in a tray there were sandwiches left over from last night's dry chow. Ham and cheese on unbuttered bread, curling and turning stale around the edges. He took one, pushed aside the stacked litters, slumped down at a table and began eating, making a grimace over the crumbly sour taste. On the second bite he gagged and gave up, concentrating his thoughts on the events which were confusing and upsetting his mind so much. Shoving the sandwich aside, he took the tape recorder out of its case, placed it in front of him, switched it on and rewound the tape. Then he pressed the playback button and put his ear down against the tiny speaker.

Out of the plastic box came the voices of Finlander and Allison, thin and weirdly hollow, and sometimes nearly smothered by the rumble of distorted background noises of the *Bedford*'s rolling and heaving. It was a terrible recording, one which no technical director of a broadcasting station would pass as airworthy, yet it was intelligible and to Munceford contained an elusive importance which he could sense but not fully understand. He listened with his eyes closed to the discussion of the plan to lure Moby Dick to the surface, to Finlander's judgment against Commodore Schrepke, to his cutting interchange with Lieutenant Commander Porter. When it was over, he rolled it back and played it through again. This time he found himself no longer thinking of it as show material, but as part of a case to be presented in a court-martial. *As evidence.*

Evidence of what? Were matters aboard the *Bedford* really building toward a court-martial? Was the hounding of Moby Dick finally transgressing the accepted conduct of a cold war? Was the mounting irritation between Finlander and the surgeon building toward a serious clash—like the one he had had with Hirschfeld? There were intimations of these possibilities on the tape, but still nothing concrete or outright damning. It was the tone rather than the words. Somehow all the tense feeling of foredoomed predatory purpose which permeated this ship seeped between the lines transcribed on the acetate ribbon—or was that feeling entirely in his own mind? And if it was, was it an accurate one? While listening to the tape for the third time, he began to toy with the idea of preventing Finlander from confiscating it, of somehow smuggling it off the *Bedford*. He suddenly realized that he needed *more* material like this, either sneaked recordings or comments from somebody aboard whom he could get to really speak out.

Munceford stopped the recorder and sat there staring down at it, his thoughts vacillating from conviction to doubt, from moral principle to crass indifference. Why meddle? Was he supposed to be one of those egghead correspondents who "report in depth"? Finlander himself had made it perfectly clear that he was here because he was nothing but a hack who would not probe too deeply, yet give the illusion that everything was aboveboard in the *Bedford*'s private cold war. All right! Why not play ball? Maybe Finlander would finally and dramatically force Moby Dick to surface in broad daylight and he would be able to get some good shots of the Russian submarine. That would undoubtedly be worth a thousand-dollar bonus from any TV network. No questions would be asked about the circumstances. If the whole story was presented from the point of view of the brave, dedicated American naval officer maintaining a vigil in the cruel arctic, inspiring his valiant crew to endure all the hardships of the patrol, then Captain Finlander would come out of it all smelling like a budding vice-admiral. Ben Munceford would become a bona-fide, star-spangled, ass-kissing naval correspondent. His hands fondled the ERASE button on the recorder . . . but he did not press it. For no other clear reason than perhaps sheer contrariness or the fascination of toying with a potentially dangerous course, he pushed the one marked RECORD, palmed the microphone and softly spoke into it:

"As you have heard from the talk on the *Bedford*'s

bridge, strange things are going on aboard this ship. Even as the captain and the executive officer lay their plans to trap the Russian submarine they call Moby Dick, there are cross-currents of guilt and conflict. It is a detached world of its own, this world of the *Bedford*. A little lost world at war, detached from the rest of the world at peace."

Munceford stopped the tape, rolled it back and listened to himself. What he said sounded trite and melodramatic, but still he did not erase it. Instead he thought to add to his commentary, but the words would not flow and he found himself sitting there with his mouth open, the tape rolling and nothing but the throb of the turbines being recorded. But in spite of his ineptness, this accidentally became a dramatic pause to emphasize the sudden shrill sound of the bosun's pipe as it blasted through the PA speaker on the bulkhead; instinctively he turned the mike toward it.

"This is the captain speaking!" Finlander's voice crackled through, its tone well modulated, yet with just the right touch of intensity. "I know all hands are weary and disgusted right now, and thinking that the efforts of the last two days have been in vain. Maybe some of you even believe that Moby Dick has been deliberately making fools of us and those Commies are laughing as they hear us retreat with nothing but another petty humiliation to heap on the many endured by our country in this cold war. Personally, I doubt it. They have too little clean air left for a good laugh. But if they believe we're running with our tails between our legs, so much the better because it will make them careless. And if *you* believe it, that's all right too, because then it will make you mad enough to stick this out till hell freezes over—which it looks to me like it's about to do outside right now! In any case, I'm turning this ship around in a few minutes and am going to close in on Moby Dick like a cat stalking a dark alley.

When our rat decides it's safe to come out of its hole, we'll be there to pounce. Sounds simple enough, but you all know it will mean more hours of silent stalking, of patient waiting, of uncertainty, of doubt. Well, sit tight and, above all, sit silent. I want every man, whether he is guarding a sonar receiver or watching a steam guage or sweeping snow off a launcher, to listen, concentrate and keep his whole being alert that this ship will tingle like a living animal of prey about to attack. If the Russians down there suspect our presence at all, let it be because they sense this, and then let's see if they come up laughing!"

The PA circuit clicked off and Munceford kept staring up at the speaker for a long moment while his recorder ran on. Then he turned the microphone in his palm toward his own mouth and said into it: "Yes . . . a lost little world at war, complete with its own God of War who speaks to us from his Olympian tower of gray steel. Must we believe in him?"

"Do *you* believe in him?" a voice broke in with a jarring sneer.

Munceford jumped around in his chair and felt himself flushing scarlet as he saw Commodore Schrepke standing in the doorway, icy brine running off his skin and black leather. He had obviously been there throughout the captain's speech, perhaps longer, watching and listening. Now he stepped into the wardroom, checked the empty thermos, then turned on Munceford with a look of contempt tinged with sardonic amusement. "Do you believe in him?" he asked again.

"I . . . I don't know," Munceford stammered.

Schrepke moved in on him and stood swaying with the roll of the ship, pawing at the folds of his jacket to reach the flask in his hip pocket. "You don't know?" he repeated, mimicking his uncertain tone. "Then why do you blather such unmitigated nonsense into your machine? You think it something inspirational to go with your pictures of brave sailors and their sturdy man-of-war, no doubt. Something to fertilize the seeds of patriotism among your grubbing burghers at home, eh? So they pay their taxes more willingly and cheer the parades more loudly and listen more devoutly to the bellicose speeches of their politicians, eh? Ah, yes! Otherwise they might forget our cold war out here and become too preoccupied with the hot business of buying for less and selling for more.... But if you don't know whether you believe in it, how can you do a proper job?"

"It's just a story, that's all."

"Oh, just a story, eh?" Schrepke retorted and took a quick pull from his flask. After the alcohol had seared his throat, his voice took on a frightening rasping quality. "I have often noticed how you correspondents treat everything just as a story. Stories to be peopled by your own pet goblins, giants, dwarfs, and frogs who are princes, and rich old kings who trade in fairy princesses. Yes, indeed, these are your stories!" He took another drink, then stuffed the flask back into his pocket. "You terrify or inspire or delude your people with these stories, yet you yourself don't know whether you believe in them or not. Does this not strike you as stupid?"

"Well, all right, Commodore! Now that you've finally decided to talk to me, go ahead and give your version of the truth," Munceford urged, edging the microphone toward him. "I represent a free press, you know. All opinions are welcome."

Schrepke suddenly became aware that the recorder was still running and had taken down everything he had just said. His face twitched with a shock of fury, his fist came up, then swung down, crashing into the table as if it were encased in mail instead of leather. But as quickly as he had reacted, Munceford had been quicker, yanking **his** precious tape recorder out of the way of the smashing blow. "Thank you, sir!" he exclaimed, pressing the instrument protectively against his chest. "Thank you! That was a very eloquent—and a very *German*—expression of opinion."

Schrepke's fist cocked again, but this time he hesitated, although he could doubtless have knocked the correspondent senseless. Then a violent roll, indicating that the *Bedford* was turning, threw him off balance and he suddenly needed both hands to brace himself against the table. As the ship recovered her equilibrium, so did he his temper. "What do you know of German opinion?" he coldly demanded. "Is your knowledge based on the horror stories fed you in the kindergarten of your trade? Concentration camps, U-boats and goose-stepping legions—these are the things which mean Germany to you, not so?"

Munceford had twisted himself out of the chair and sprung toward the door, where he stopped now, poised to escape if the German officer gave any further signs of violence. "Those things seem more on your own mind than anybody else's," he taunted him.

"Indeed they are!" Schrepke answered with a bitter laugh. "And many more like them. Such as trapped men dying in crushed submarines, cities being incinerated in fire storms and defeated armies herded into the victor's barracoons. I could add many details to your horror stories, my poor little unblooded sanguinary war correspondent! All kinds of personally experienced horrors except one—the ultimate nuclear horror which has become the exclusive province of my former enemies and judges! The irony of this escapes you, I'm sure, but it is nevertheless there. Here am I, a German officer born under Kaiser Wilhelm and weaned by Adolf Hitler, yet so inhibited in a game which you Americans and Russians indulge in with all the cruel juvenile relish of children playing at war. . . . Is your machine still recording all this nicely for you? The sounds of a German pouring ashes on his head sells very well, after all!"

Munceford frowned as he fumbled with his tape recorder, his violent evasive action of a few moments ago having temporarily indisposed it. "If the way things are handled on the *Bedford* has you so upset, Commodore, why don't you do something about it?" he asked testily.

Wolfgang Schrepke snatched a sandwich and slumped into the chair vacated by Munceford. There was suddenly a weary resignation in his demeanor as he shrugged off the question. "If you can't make up your mind whether or not you believe in Captain Finlander, then I suggest you interview Commander Porter instead of me. That should confuse your addled brain even more, my friend!" He chuckled and shook his head. "Finlander and Porter! There is a fascinating study in opposing archetypes of your peculiar American military! ... One the vainglorious, benevolent martinet who despises weakness, yet feeds his own strength upon it, consuming his subordinates like an inspired cannibal; the other, the plodding officer-intellectual who charts his course by rectitude and platitude, horrified by a colleague as ruthless as Finlander, yet attaching himself to him with the loyalty of a barnacle. Another irony over your head, eh? Ah, well ... *das macht nichts aus!*" He took a bite out of the sandwich and, abruptly dismissing Munceford's presence from his consciousness, sank into a brooding contemplation.

Not even by Finlander himself had Munceford's intelligence been so insulted, yet the old defensive belligerence did not boil up, which indicated that his mind had also been stimulated. In spite of himself, the taciturn commodore had just bared his breast to him, allowing a revealing glimpse of the seething beneath the disciplined exterior. Munceford at least understood that Schrepke would not have done this had he not been in a state of extreme alarm over something. Over his cloistered isolation on this ship? Not likely, since it was largely self-imposed; anyway, that hard character was sufficient unto itself. Then it had to be over this action against Moby Dick! His mind groped with urgent questions he wanted to ask the German, sincere questions, yet he was defeated by the barrier between them. But there could be no sop for his curiosity now. If this man would not satisfy it, then somebody else! *Commander Porter!* Yes, that had been a good suggestion, perhaps more deliberate than facetious. Because they both knew that Porter was the weakest link in Finlander's chain of command.

It was with a quickening realization that time was running out that Munceford shoved his recorder into its case and left the wardroom. The vibrations of the turbines had dropped to a bare tremor and the motion of the *Bedford* eased with a distinct change of rhythm which indicated she had turned her stern to the seas. The final run on Moby Dick had started! He knew he could not change the course of events, but he ran down the passageway as if he could.

The surgeon had finished setting the cook's broken arm and curtly ordered him into sick bay in spite of his eager protestations about being fit for duty. Chief McKinley escorted the disgruntled man out of surgery as he angrily brandished his splinted arm to show it did not bother him at all. Pharmacist Engstrom laughed and said something about "crazy seacooks" as he started cleaning up the debris of plaster and bandages around the operating table; he looked up with surprise when Ben Munceford came bursting through the blackout curtain. "You're too late if you've come to cover our only casualty in this battle," he greeted him.

"Yeah? Well, it doesn't look like it's over yet," Munceford answered. "Maybe more people will get hurt before we're through."

"It'll be those Commie pigboatmen, in that case," Engstrom scoffed.

Lieutenant Commander Porter gave Munceford a hostile look and retreated into the receiving office, there to escape in the paperwork which the navy appended even to simple operations like the one he had just performed. When he saw that Munceford insisted on following him, he snapped: "So what do you want?"

"Listen, Chester. I know we never hit it off, but I'd like to talk to you."

"About what?" the surgeon asked with complete disinterest.

"Well . . . *things*. The *Bedford*. The way this Moby Dick affair is working out. Frankly, I'm confused as hell and need your help."

"What's the matter, Ben?" Porter asked acidly. "Is the hot-shot TV reporter losing his grip?"

"I'm not so hot. I've found that out on this trip."

The surgeon gave him a curious, surprised look, then sighed. "So don't let it get you. Finlander cuts us all down to size sooner or later."

"Yeah. I heard him cut you to yours awhile ago."

Porter stiffened and glared stonily down at the top of his desk, but he said nothing.

"All right, don't get sore," Munceford continued. "He polished me off too. And I'm sure he must have raked Commodore Schrepke worse than either of us, because he just blew his top to me a few minutes ago. Became about as human as his iron-assed kind ever can. The point is, Schrepke not only outranks Finlander, but he's got enough experience in this business to be able to tell whether it's being run right or wrong; you've got to hand him that much, no matter what you think of him. It all adds up to something lousing up this well-oiled war machine. *What?*"

The surgeon continued to stare down at the desk.

"The captain and commodore did have a disagreement over whether or not to break off this action," he cautiously admitted.

"You heard it?"

"Yes. I was present." A shudder at the recollection loosened his reserve and he added with feeling: "It was the worst blow-up I've ever been involved in on a navy bridge."

"So you were involved. And I get the idea Schrepke expected you to back him up. But you didn't."

Porter tried to cover a flinch by looking up sharply. "I am an *American* naval officer, damn it!"

Munceford slipped the tape recorder out of its case. "Would you like to hear what Schrepke says you are?" he asked. When he received no answer, he put the recorder on the desk, switched it on, rewound the tape a few feet, then played it back. Porter listened silently, the muscles of his jaws twitching beneath the pale skin as the Germanic English rasped at him out of the plastic box.

"*. . . the plodding officer-intellectual who charts his course by rectitude and platitude . . .*"

When Schrepke's voice faded out, Munceford held out the microphone and switched over to RECORD. "Do you have any comment, Commander?" he pointedly asked.

The surgeon stared at the microphone as if it were the head of a cobra. His lips pressed together and his head shook angrily, but there was something like desperation in his eyes.

"Come on!" Munceford wheedled. "Isn't it the opinion of at least two of the better brains aboard that things are being pushed beyond a very dangerous point? That a hell of a lot more is at stake than the pride of an American and a Commie captain? Aren't you one of the *Bedford*'s officers who believe this?"

Porter's lips remained tightly sealed, but his head

was suddenly nodding instead of shaking. His body was beginning to sag, as if caving in under the weight of the truth. Munceford pressed in on him, brandishing the microphone in his face. "You *do* believe it! Then say so, for God's sake! I believe it too, so it won't be only you and the German against everybody else on this crazy ship. But we've got to get together on it. We've got to get it on record—okay?" He was about to grab the surgeon by the shoulder and shake him when he was diverted by a sharp voice behind him.

"Shall I heave this character out, sir?" It was Engstrom, standing in the doorway of the receiving office with an angry, perplexed expression on his face.

Ben Munceford straightened up and felt a cold pang of frustration, but he swung the microphone toward him and announced with a sarcastic tone: "Ah, here is Pharmacist's Mate Engstrom, a man who is not so shy about expressing himself. So what is your opinion about this action, Mr. Pharmacist's Mate? Go ahead and tell us!"

"Sure!" Engstrom hissed belligerently, then cut loose a torrent. "I say it's a tough enough deal out here without having some mealy-mouthed civilian trying to put doubts in our minds about it all and making us think it's wrong what we're doing. We're chasing a god-damned Red spy sub on our side of the ocean, and that's good enough for me and ought to be good enough for you besides being god-damned grateful somebody's doing the job for you so you're free to run around and shoot your mouth off—okay, smart guy?"

Munceford's freckles rippled under a grin which was almost genuine. "Now, there's a loud and simple opinion if I've ever heard one," he exclaimed and turned back to Porter. "It should inspire the commander to put in his own two cents' worth."

"Shall I heave this character out, sir?" Engstrom again asked his CO, this time stepping into the office with his arms flexing for action. There was something pathetically frightening about the skinny, bespectacled boy's ferociousness, and it seemed to jolt the surgeon out of his daze. He reached out and put his hand over the microphone Munceford was pointing at him and said:

"Never mind, Engstrom. I can handle it. You go back to your station." He waited until the pharmacist's mate had reluctantly backed out of the door, then took his hand off the microphone. His haggard face wrinkled into a pained frown of concentration as his lips soundlessly rehearsed the words he was groping for.

Munceford tensed as he waited for him to speak, wondering whether the man was at last ready to muster the courage of his convictions and openly condemn Finlander's vendetta against Moby Dick. It would come too late to influence the immediate events, but at least it would give some real substance to this story. He would no longer be just a hack. "So come on, Commander. You almost got it off your chest a moment ago. So do it now!"

Lieutenant Commander Porter tore his eyes away from the microphone and looked directly into Munceford's face.

"As a doctor," he began, articulating his words carefully, "my doubts and fears over this action are medical. Psychosomatic, really. The crew of this ship are torn by conflicting emotional stresses which far exceed those of any ordinary peacetime patrol. The necessity to savagely and relentlessly exert their power as fighters creates a hate syndrome; their natural revulsion over having to act contrary to deeply ingrained American permissive instincts creates a guilt complex. This is nothing new for Americans at war, of course, only we are *not* at war. The natural release of war's tremendous pressures—*killing*—is denied. Frustration builds and compounds the pressure until it begins to make men unpredictably aggressive, withdrawn, volatile, lethargic ... in psychiatric terms, they are aggravating latent aberrations without recourse to normal checks and balances. ...

"And perfectly capable of losing control of themselves," Munceford eagerly coaxed.

The surgeon shook his head, but only to protest the interruption. "That is my simple diagnosis of this action as an ordinary medical man," he persisted, "but I am also a *navy* doctor and must accept the risks of any given naval situation. Certain degrees of schizophrenia may be among them, and unfortunately the opportunities for group therapy are extremely limited out here. So instead of therapy, we use a man like Finlander to keep things from falling apart."

Munceford frowned and protested: "But surely the four stripes on his sleeve don't make *him* immune to cracking up!"

Porter squirmed in his chair. "I agreed there are risks," he answered with a rising pitch. "I agreed we are under a severe strain. I will even agree that Captain Finlander is taking terrible chances. But then so is the Russian commander; furthermore, he is still down there continuing to take them. And *that* is the whole point and justification of what we are doing. As a naval officer, I refuse to challenge the judgment of my captain. I actually suspect he is made of the same stuff as John Paul Jones and a lot of other patriotic heroes we have been taught to revere in our history. To doubt him would be the same as to doubt them, to reject all the benefits Americans have derived from the aggressive spirit of men like him." His lips pressed together, cutting off the flow of words, and he leaned back with a somewhat melancholy look of smugness.

Ben Munceford blinked and shook his head, then switched off the recorder. "Well," he sighed, "that was a beautiful speech and I suppose Finlander will be delighted to hear it if he gets his hands on this tape. But I still wonder whether you believe it deep down. You certainly haven't been acting so god-damned inspired lately."

The surgeon squirmed uncomfortably. "I've been scared and ... I'm still scared. But when the chips are down, Commodore Schrepke cannot make me disloyal to my ship and my captain. Nor can you. Now, if you will excuse me, I've got to fill out a casualty report."

"Okay, Commander. Thanks a bunch. I'm sorry I disturbed you."

After Ben Munceford left him, Lieutenant Commander Porter sat there staring for a long time at the assistant cook's Form 28 without touching his pen to it. For a moment tears brimmed his eyes, but they quickly dried, leaving a stinging little hurt outside and an emptiness inside, as if everything in him had finally dried up.

Munceford stood in the passageway outside the ship's hospital, hesitating as he realized that he really had nowhere to go now. Nowhere that really mattered. He did not want to return to the wardroom in case Schrepke was still there, so he headed in the opposite direction and found himself at the hatch leading down to Engineering Control. He lifted it open and felt a waft of oily warmth strike his face and squinted against the bright lights reflecting off polished metal gratings. The noises from the engine room were now no more than a tensely suppressed humming. He eased himself through the hatch and went down the ladder.

Lieutenant Commander Franklin and Lieutenant Brubeck were standing at the main panel, looking like scientists in their spotless white coveralls as they checked the multitude of dials and recorders, making notes on complex charts attached to clipboards. They merely accorded Munceford a quick glance when he stepped off the ladder and walked up to them. "So how's the war going down here?" he asked with his old flippant manner returning.

"All systems are go," Brubeck answered shortly. He did not take his eyes from an oscilloscope whose fiery green line was dancing nervously. "The cycling of number-two WP generator has a flutter, sir," he said to Franklin.

The lieutenant commander watched it for a few seconds. "It's within functional limits, but keep checking it."

Munceford moved over to the master control console and sat down in an empty chair next to Chief MacKay, who was crouched over the throttles as if he expected an order from the bridge at any moment. His leathery face was screwed up into a grimace of intense concentration, his eyes glued to the revolution indicators.

"You bearing up under the strain, Chief?" Munceford asked him.

MacKay's head jerked around. "What? Oh, it's you, Mr. Munceford!" The grimace became a grin. "Sure! No sweat at all."

"What are you feeling right now, Mac? A hate syndrome? A guilt complex? Or both mixed together?"

The chief's face went as blank as a piece of rock. "Uh? What was that?"

"I mean, how do you feel about it all? Good or bad?"

"I feel I'm doing my job, and that's good, ain't it?" He looked at Munceford as if he had asked a very foolish question, then remembered his duty and turned back to the rev counters. But he added with a scowl: "I only wish we could take this son-of-a-bitch all the way—like Finlander and I did on U-1020. But we can't, and that's bad. Too god-damned bad!"

Lieutenant Commander Franklin came up behind Munceford. "Please don't take Chief MacKay's mind off his work, Mr. Munceford. The bridge has asked for hair-trigger reactions on the throttles. . . . May I trouble you for my seat? Thank you."

Munceford quickly got up and moved to the railing which separated Engineering Control from the engine room below. His eyes followed the white shape of Lieutenant Brubeck as he noiselessly scrambled down the series of ladders and scurried along the gratings between the huge turbine casings, then crouched down to nurse some small part of a generator. A machinist joined him and they both knelt before the machinery, their hands waving and motioning as if they were making incantations before an altar.

Munceford hooked one leg around a stanchion of the railing to brace himself against the long, corkscrewing pitches of the *Bedford*, took out his tape recorder and erased everything on the tape.

6.

After addressing the crew over the ship's PA, Captain Finlander seated himself in his chair by the wheelhouse window and stared blankly through the glass at the blackness beyond it. He remained there, isolating himself with his own thoughts, until Commander Allison brought the *Bedford* around and set her on a return course for the wreck of the *Hood,* her power reduced so that she was partly surfing down the swells rolling up on her stern, partly loping along under the slow paddling revolutions of her screws. Then he got up and joined his executive officer to watch with him the difficult work of the helmsman.

"Steer like you've never steered in your life," Allison told the seaman at the wheel. "If you feel her getting away from you, don't wait for orders. Catch her before she makes a noisy splash." He knew it was the trickiest kind of conning any helmsman could take on, this blind running before the seas with bare steerage way. A big wave could broach the ship, its rush of water negating the bite of both rudder and propellers unless the counter-measures were instantaneously accurate. So he had Ensign Whitaker keep an open circuit to the engine room, ready to call for immediate backing on one or the other propeller in case the rudder lost control. There was as much strain on Ensign Whitaker as on the helmsman because a wrong order to Chief MacKay would fatally aggravate an impending broach.

But Finlander knew that the greatest strain of all was falling on Bucky Allison. His calculations and minute corrections had to bring the ship back over an infinitesimal, invisible reference point lying two hundred and ten fathoms below a black void of heaving ocean. The forty-one thousand tons of twisted metal which had been the *Hood* were nothing but a needle in a liquid haystack. Closer to the Iceland coast it might have been possible to take some radar bearings to help him, but it was too far and the hash created by the heavy snowfall too heavy. "How are you going to make it, Buck?" Finlander asked the exec as he checked his stop-watch in the reflected glow of the automatic course recorder.

"By pilotage and—I hope—by some sort of ESP of my own," Allison answered.

"If anybody has a sixth sense for this sort of thing, you do." They both held their breath for a moment as they felt the *Bedford*'s stern begin to slew around under the thrust of a steep sea. The boy at the wheel let out an agonized little grunt, his reflexes reacting with explosive speed as he spun the steel disk. The ship steadied and the sea slid under her, coasting her along on her stealthy way. The captain let out a soundless gasp of relief, then said: "All right. I leave the bridge to you, Buck. I'm going back to sweat it out in the CIC."

On the way there, Finlander stopped in his day cabin and found Merlin Queffle lying on the bunk, staring up at the ceiling. He sat up when the captain came in and exclaimed with a nervous eagerness: "I'm ready, sir!"

The captain studied him for a moment. "You didn't really rest, did you, Queffle?"

"Sure, sir. I'm all right now."

"Now you listen to me, son! If you can't pick up anything on the sound gear, I don't want you to blame yourself. It will simply mean that the Russian has evaded us, that he just isn't around any more. And that is *my* responsibility, not yours. So don't go flying to pieces over it. Understand?"

"He's there, sir," Queffle answered and bared his rabbit teeth in what was supposed to be a confident smile. "I can feel him in my earbones already."

Finlander remembered what Commodore Schrepke had said about this sonarman's talents and shoved him back on the bunk somewhat roughly. "Maybe what you feel is your own blood pounding in your ears," he said. "You can't detect Moby Dick without sonar. So don't try to kid me by saying you hear things you think I want you to hear. We're not playing around with some kind of supernatural séance here, but conducting a tough ASW operation. Stick to factual readouts of our detection systems—okay? All right, so let's get going!" He yanked Queffle to his feet and gave him a shove toward the door.

Lieutenant Spitzer had put the CIC back on full GQ immediately upon the *Bedford*'s turnaround. Krindle-meyer, his alter ego, had come up from the CSP room and was leaning over his shoulder at Central Control, myopically peering at the scopes and dials through his bifocals. Lieutenant Aherne had relieved Ensign Ralston at Fire Control, but the latter hovered close to the console, watching its rows of winking lights with as much eagerness as if he were still in charge. The radar and sonar operators were in silent concentration at their posts and the CPO on the plotting board was poised to process any contact they managed to pick up. There was still weariness in everybody's face, but it was an undercurrent submerged by the nervous tension which hung in the air like a physically gaseous thing. If anything, it increased when Captain Finlander came through the steel door with Merlin Queffle in tow.

"You stand by as relief on MTS for the time being," he told the Breton Kid. "I don't want you in harness until we close the range some more."

Queffle started to protest, but sulkily obeyed and placed himself behind the operator at the Master Tactical Sonar console. Captain Finlander walked over to Krindlemeyer and Spitzer. "What's the status, gentlemen?" he asked.

"All systems go, sir," Spitzer reported.

"Sensitivity should be eighty per cent according to input efficiency from CSP, sir," Krindlemeyer reported, peering balefully at his captain over the edges of his spectacles. "Layering zero. Sea-return four-point-five, sir."

"Very good," Finlander said. "We should be able to hear a porpoise fart at six miles' range with that kind of saturation." As Krindlemeyer and Spitzer chuckled dutifully, he stepped over to Fire Control. "I see our weapons all seem accidentally in a state of readiness," he said as he checked the status board.

Lieutenant Aherne nodded. "Yes, sir. With the seas behind us and this slow speed, there's not much problem of spray slushing up the launchers."

"Just so those gunners keep on the ball," Ensign Ralston injected irritably, "and aren't lulled to sleep by the easy going."

"Simmer down, Mr. Ralston," the captain shot at him over his shoulder. "Or I'll send you topside on an inspection just to see how easy the going is out there."

"I'd be glad to go, sir."

"I said simmer down! ... Lieutenant Aherne, have you been clearing your auxiliary firing circuits periodically?"

"Yes, sir. And local control is standing by on the hedgehog."

"Very good. It seems there's nothing I can criticize here except possibly a bit of overanxiousness on the part of your junior fire-control officer." He wheeled on Ensign Ralston, who was leaning over the board and fiddling with a perfectly adjusted rheostat. "If you're so darn eager to keep busy during your relief period, Ensign Ralston, how about calling the galley and asking my steward to shoot me up some breakfast?"

"Certainly, sir. Bacon and eggs?"

"My guess is everybody's getting another lot of dry rations this morning. That will have to do for me too."

Ralston hurried to the telephone talker by the plotting board while the captain moved in behind the sonar operators and inspected their blank PPI scopes. Because they were listening on passive systems, there were no pings coming in over the speakers—only a faint hissing sound. The tactical radar scope, however, was cluttered with hash caused by the snow, and unless Moby Dick suddenly snorted within a few hundred yards of the *Bedford,* it could not possibly pick up any contact. But that did not keep the radarman from studying the blur of pulsating blobs with an intense red-eyed concentration.

When he completed his round of the CIC's complex interlocking functions and found them operating to his complete satisfaction, Finlander returned to the Central Control station and seated himself next to Spitzer. "All right," he exclaimed as he hunched down in his seat and crossed his arms over his chest, "nothing to do now but wait while we close in."

7.

A half-hour dragged by. Not a glimmer of a signal penetrated the silence of the deep. Commander Allison reported from the bridge that he estimated the *Bedford* had returned to within six miles of the *Hood,* a range clearly sufficient to pick up Moby Dick's echo-ranging if he started probing toward the surface. But there was not even the *clickety-click* of a single shrimp. It was as if all the myriad beings which inhabit a cubic mile of ocean were holding their breath in suspense along with the protagonists of this stalking conflict. Merlin Queffle stared at the PPI screen from over the shoulder of his relief and strained his ears toward the muted speaker. His hands were entwined over his left knee, which danced an agonized, unceasing beat; at increasingly frequent intervals he shot a pleading glance toward his captain, whose eyes appeared only half open as he sat swaying in his chair at Central Control.

But Finlander's half-open eyes did not mean he was only half awake, although the *Bedford*'s long steep yawing, strangely dampened compared with earlier, was having a nightmarish lullaby effect on her crew. He was aware not only of Queffle's suffering, but of the states of mind of all the men in the CIC, while at the same time his own kept analyzing and evaluating the situation minute by tense, endless minute. Would Moby Dick move out of hiding without an echo-ranging sweep? Possibly. But most probably that sly Russian was doing exactly the same thing he was, listening on passive sonar and refusing to be drawn into a rash action even though he might suspect the destroyer had long since retired out of range. But could he already have pulled out while the *Bedford* was at the apogee of her deception maneuver? *Was* that possible? Should he have kept Queffle on sonar to guard against such a move? Should he put him in *now?* The temptation was tremendous to order Spitzer to start a maximum-effect sweep and fill the surrounding ocean with its tactile electronic fingers—which, of course, could pick up Moby Dick if he had started to rise and move, but would also send him scurrying back into hiding and return the battle to its previous deadlock. This patient, silent waiting was better, no matter how trying on the nerves.

Steward's Mate Collins came into the CIC with the captain's breakfast tray, which contained some pork sausages and a half-scrambled, half-fried egg, rendered unrecognizable by the pitching griddle of the galley. Finlander was pleased and relieved his tensions in some casual banter with the Negro steward. "Well, well! Hot chow! I feel like a pampered character, Collins. My compliments to the cook! Stay awhile and watch, so you can tell him we too are on the job!" Collins nodded politely, then looked around him, taking in the many luminous scopes and dials, and the men making their trance-like obeisance to them. His face remained inscrutable, an expression which the captain mistook for awe. "All these instruments and technicians are pretty impressive, aren't they, Collins?" he said through a mouthful of egg. "Maybe impressive enough to inspire a bright boy like you to switch his ambitions from medicine to electronics?"

"No, sir," the Negro answered politely but firmly.

Finlander looked at him more carefully and more accurately appraised his demeanor. "Oh? Commander Porter has been brainwashing you, I suppose."

"No, sir, only tutoring me in my studies."

"Yes—all shrouded in the hokus-pokus of medicine's mystical mission to succor suffering humanity," Finlander said with outright derision. "That's old witch-doctor stuff, Collins! Today the electronic scientist has taken over the navy, the world and outer space. You should get out of the dark ages, boy."

"It's still dark enough in here for witchcraft, sir," Collins answered quietly. This brought a peculiar look from Lieutenant Spitzer, who swiveled around in his chair and stared at him for a moment. Finlander frowned too, but then was gracious enough to laugh.

"All right, Collins. I give in! When we get back to Newport, I'm going to recommend you be sent to Pharmacist School. That may help you get into college and pre-med after your hitch is over. The rest is up to you." He turned away from the genuinely grateful "Thank you, Captain!" and redirected his full attention to the tactical situation at hand. He called the bridge and asked Commander Allison for another estimate of the ship's position. Five miles from the *Hood*—closing at the rate of a mile every eight minutes. His eyes swept along the rows of empty PPI scopes, then fixed themselves upon Merlin Queffle's dancing knee. "Queffle! Get in there and see if you can pick up anything!"

The Breton Kid shot to his feet and yanked his relief away from the console. In a moment he was hunched at the set, his hands pressing the earphones over his head, his eyes bulging toward the scope. The knee no longer danced.

Ensign Ralston's nervousness was also abated when, a few minutes later, he relieved Lieutenant Aherne at Fire Control. But there was nothing for him to do there except wait, as everybody else was doing, and as the hands of the clock crept on, his tension began building up again.

Spitzer and Krindlemeyer exchanged positions, the latter vanishing down the hatch to check on things in the CSP room below. The ready light of No. 1 ASROC flashed to amber and the telephone talker reported it was being cleared of slush, but the trouble could not have been serious as the light went back to red within two minutes.

Eight more minutes of empty, inactive, gut-sucking silence. Another mile slipped by. Then one of those freak swells, much bigger than the others, caught up with the *Bedford* and began skidding her sideways down its slope. A tremor vibrated the deck and bulkheads of the CIC as the starboard engine reversed to brake the impending broach, but she heeled over steeper and steeper, and the tremor became a shuddering with a muffled rumble which jarred and shook everybody to the marrow. The ship did not broach completely, but perilously hung on the brink while burying herself in a thundering rush of white water. The sonar speakers and scopes crackled and sparkled with the hash of her own turbulence. Merlin Queffle cringed in his seat, pried up the cups of his earphones as if they were blasting a physical pain into his head and shot a horrified look at his captain. Finlander's knuckles turned white as he gripped the arms of his chair and his eyes bored through the network of conduits and steel plating overhead, penetrating to the struggling helmsman up there. Slowly the *Bedford* recovered herself and stopped laboring, but Lieutenant Krindelmeyer spoke up with an ominous tone.

"That could have been picked up on enemy's passive system."

"For how far?" the captain demanded.

"The needle hit twenty-six. Two miles at least, sir."

Commander Allison's voice came down through the bridge intercom, speaking with a controlled chagrin. "Sorry, gentlemen! She got away from us for a moment there. A very big sea."

Finlander looked as if he were about to shout a furious criticism into the microphone, but instead he calmly said: "All right, Buck! Keep on your toes. They usually come in three's." He was right. Two more big waves caught the *Bedford,* but smaller than the first, and with the helm thoroughly alerted. The splash was not as bad, yet enough to agitate the scopes and needles.

Had they been heard? Was there no reaction only because there was *nothing* down there? The questions tore at Finlander's brain, but he did not yield to impulse as Ensign Ralston did.

"Mightn't we as well shoot the works and start echo-ranging, sir?" the young officer exclaimed in anguish.

"No!" Finlander retorted. "But maybe Moby Dick will be that foolish if he thought he heard us. Queffle! Turn those earbones of yours on to maximum. Krindlemeyer! Patch him into the QBH hydrophone and stream it out. Bridge! Reduce revs and hold her for a QBH sweep."

Lieutenant Krindlemeyer's fingers flew over the switches. Queffle hunched down, knotting himself into an agonized ball of concentration. For two ... three ... four minutes everybody in the CIC breathed only enough to keep himself from exploding. The tense silence was broken only when the door opened and Commodore Schrepke stepped inside, allowing it to slam shut with a raucous metallic clang which made everybody jump.

Captain Finlander twisted around and glared at the German. Schrepke glanced about him with a cold glint in his eyes, then retreated into a corner, there to wait and watch with the rest of them.

8.

At 0645 Commander Allison estimated that he had brought the *Bedford* within a half-mile of the *Hood*. It was only a guess, but an educated one backed up by his considerable seaman's instinct for the effects of wind and waves. Twenty minutes earlier he had shut down the master fathometer, depriving himself of his "blind man's stick" in retracing his steps by the bottom contour. That instrument transmitted a strong submarine signal, and although it went straight down in a narrow cone, he was taking no chances that the Russian would hear it. The near broach had shaken him enough. But if he had to navigate the last few miles by guess and by God, then he needed to do it closer to the elements and outside the stifling confines of the blacked-out wheelhouse. The helmsman who so nearly lost control had vomited immediately after saving the situation, permeating the darkness around him with a horrible rancid smell; the relief lookouts, thawing out by the heater during their twenty-minute rests, cooked in their soaking clothes and added a peculiar pungent odor of their own. The executive officer squirmed into his parka and went out on the bridge.

It was even darker out there, of course, but the wind and snow were crisply clean, and he could hear and feel the sea surging along the hull of his ship. It was not blowing hard, less than Force 2 from the northeast; the swells were rolling along as big as ever, but without breaking and with longer periods between them. Snowflakes swirled and danced around his face, invisible, but stinging when they brushed against his skin. As he moved along the edge of the windscreen, he bumped into the port lookout, who jumped as if he had been awakened from being asleep on his feet.

"Watch it, son! Keep moving and keep looking."

A frightened apology came stuttering from the dim shape. Allison moved on to the wing and noticed that Commodore Schrepke was no longer in his usual place, but he did not give that much thought. For two or three minutes he concentrated on sensing the unseen forces of the arctic night which were affecting his ship. He only considered the navigational problem at hand and did not speculate about where Moby Dick was out there, lurking just beneath the black waves or in the blacker deep—or not there at all. That was CIC's problem, Finlander's and that poor skinny kid Merlin Queffle, who was tearing his nerves to shreds over his MTS. All Allison had to worry about was putting the *Bedford* back over the *Hood*—although he realized that only blind luck would put him *exactly* over it without using the fathometer. But they were close, very close now. He crossed the bridge and stepped back inside the wheelhouse, picked up the telephone and called the CIC.

"We are plus or minus a thousand yards."

"Are you sure, Buck?" Finlander's voice asked.

"As sure as I possibly can be, sir."

"Right. Stop engines and let's listen awhile."

Commander Allison passed the order on to Ensign Whitaker and went back out onto the bridge. As she lost steerage way, the *Bedford* slowly swung broadside to the swells and began rolling heavily as she lay dead in the water.

Up in the masthead lookout, Seaman Jones had just spelled Squarehead and he muttered furiously as he felt the motion begin to accelerate from the relatively mild one when the ship was loping along a following sea.

"Here we go again, like a god-damned yo-yo!" he shouted down to his partner. Suddenly he smelled the smoke of a cheap cigar come wafting up the shaft, trapping itself in the pitching crow's-nest. "Jesus, Squarehead! If you don't put that thing out, I'm going to puke on your head, so help me!"

Squarehead laughed, tamped out the precious cigar in his glove and tenderly put it back inside his jacket pocket. It was the last one, reserved for himself, of the twenty he had distributed in honor of the birth of his son. Wedging himself into the tube of the mast with one leg hooked through a rung of the ladder, he closed his eyes and thought about the remote joys of buying toys for Christmas.

Down in the CIC, Lieutenant Spitzer confirmed the accuracy of Commander Allison's conning. Switching on the magnetometer, he detected a definite reaction from the needle. "We are in a fairly strong magnetic field, Captain. The wreck of the *Hood,* most likely."

"Or possibly a big fat Russian pigboat?" Finlander asked.

Spitzer shrugged. "Possibly, sir. But at least we know the *Hood* can't go anywhere. *It's* there."

"What do I have to do to give you some faith in your own skills, Spitzer?" the captain wondered wryly. "Very good. Let's remain on passive while we pull a QBH on him. He's got to make a move sometime, even if it's just to ride his tanks up for a snort. He's been going for forty-three hours and forty minutes." In the back of his mind he was wondering how he would de-brief these men if it turned out that Moby Dick had managed to sneak away and was long since departed. He forced that dismal problem out of his mind, leaned back in his chair and congealed his body into an atti-tude of patience. But the strain was beginning to tell on him as it was doing on everybody else. The abysmal silence was getting on his own nerves. He noticed that

Queffle's knee was dancing again and he had to suppress an urge to yell at him to control that abominable muscular twitching. However, it was Ralston who gave him a chance to vent his mounting pressures. The ensign swore when it came time for him to give up his position at the firing switches to Lieutenant Aherne.

"Just my damned luck to have to sit on my hands when things may get hot! Hell!"

"If you don't keep yourself under better control, Mr. Ralston," the captain shouted at him, "I'll send you below!" Then he wheeled on his hapless ECM officer. "It's also your job to maintain discipline in this department, Mr. Spitzer. Look up from your instruments just once in a while and see what's going on in here!"

Spitzer peered around with something which passed for severity. "All right! Everybody ease up. It's only an exercise."

Captain Finlander erupted violently for the second time that morning. "It is *not* only an exercise!" he bellowed at Spitzer. "There's a real, live Commie submarine down there and you're letting everybody get sloppy careless about it. Wake them up!"

Spitzer cringed in his chair. "B-but, sir. I thought you were reprimanding Mr. Ralston for being overanxious."

"Are you arguing with me, Mr. Spitzer?"

"N-no, sir . . . no." He turned from the livid Finlander and this time pressed forth a genuine snarling kind of anger. "Get on the ball in here, damn it!" he shouted at everybody in general, then singled out Ensign Ralston in particular. "You, Mr. Ralston! Try to alternate with Mr. Aherne without any hysterical demonstrations, okay? Go into the head and stick your face in cold water or something."

"I'm sorry, sir," Ralston gulped, speaking to the captain, not Spitzer. "I admit I'm overexcited and must control myself. I am sorry." He slumped down unhappily in the chair behind Aherne and stared into the sweating palms of his hands.

Normally Captain Finlander would have accepted the apology and even soothed Ralston with a few encouraging words; the young ensign was one of his favorites. But now he chose to ignore him and instead began to worry about whether he had unduly shaken his vital ECM officer, a man whom he did not understand at all and subconsciously distrusted. As proud as he was of this technological marvel of a ship, the scientific types necessary to run her sometimes baffled and irritated him. There was too much science and too little navy in them and he wondered how they would react when the chips were down, in a real naval battle. But then it struck him that this time it was Ralston, the epitome of the young Annapolis line officer, who was at fault. Later he would have to at least soften his rebuke to Spitzer. But for the time being he continued to seethe, his eyes fixing themselves on Queffle's dancing knee.

"Queffle! You're going to wear a hole through the deck with your jiggling!"

The Breton Kid did not react in the least, being lost in his own world of divining the deep, everything beyond the earphones and PPI scope totally shut out. His relief, sitting behind him, heard the captain and reached out, putting a restraining hand on the offending knee. Queffle's hand left its tense position on the left earphone, swung down and viciously parried the gentle touch. The relief jumped back and stared helplessly toward Captain Finlander.

"Oh, hell! Let him alone!"

For several minutes the captain sat back, watching and listening to the completely inert readouts. As the *Bedford* wallowed in the troughs and topped the crests broadside too, the rolls became extreme and the aches and pains in tired bodies became aggravated by the motion. Through the open hatch to the CSP room came the sound of Krindlemeyer's slide rule falling off the desk and clattering noisily against the deck.

"Can't you keep things properly secured down there?" Finlander shouted.

Spitzer almost simultaneously hit the appropriate intercom button on his communications panel and yelped into the microphone: "For Christ sake's, Krindle! We're supposed to be rigged silent!"

A long, uneasy and sterile silence followed during which Finlander gradually became aware of a prickly feeling in the back of his neck. When he finally turned around and looked behind him, he found himself staring into the impassive face of Commodore Schrepke. The German had not moved from his position against the bulkhead since entering the CIC nearly an hour earlier. The two men locked eyes for a long moment.

"Well, Commodore," Finlander finally exclaimed, managing a nearly pleasant tone, "how do you estimate the situation? Don't you think our Commie friends are nearing the end of their endurance?"

Schrepke nodded. "They are only men just like your own crew. And you can see how near the end of theirs *they* are."

Finlander's face blackened, but he managed to maintain an even tone by a tremendous effort at controlling himself. "Don't let a little family squabbling fool you, Commodore," he answered. "We're a long way from the end of our rope. Anyway, longer than the Russian is from his, I bet."

The black leather rippled under a shrug of the massive shoulders. "The strain is worse in a submarine, no doubt about that."

Finlander nodded and thought for a moment. Then he asked the German officer: "What would you do if you were in the Russian's place right now?"

"I would not lie down there and suffocate," Schrepke retorted.

Finlander nodded again, this time with evident satisfaction. "Then it's only a matter of time," he exclaimed loudly enough for everybody in CIC to hear him.

But time passed and nothing happened. The terrible rolling continued to inflict a ceaseless torture of perpetual motion. Spitzer noticed that the needle of the magnetometer was registering a fading magnetic radiation from the *Hood,* which clearly indicated they were drifting away from it. One dubious encouragement came when the radarman reported his scope was clearing of hash, indicating the snowfall was easing up, and providing at least four miles of effective radar scanning; but no blip was activated by the sweeper.

Up on the bridge, Commander Allison took notice of the lightening snow; it was still pitch black, so he could only feel the lessening sting of the flakes against his numbed face. The wind was freshening and veering uneasily around the compass, upsetting his estimation of their drift. However, there was little doubt in his mind that they had now passed to the southwest of the wreck. Stepping into the wheelhouse, he reported this to the CIC.

In the Communications Center, Lieutenant Packer had cleared his troubled mind and stood behind one of the radio operators as he recieved a priority signal from NATONAV 1, requesting immediate acknowledgment and a tacrep. When the operator looked at him questioningly, he shook his head, picked up the phone and called Captain Finlander about it.

"Maintain radio silence as ordered!" he was told curtly.

A few minutes later they intercepted an exchange between NATONAV 1 and the *Fritiof Nansen.* When he decoded it, Packer found that the destroyer was being ordered to their position to investigate the *Bed-*

ford's silence. They were obviously becoming alarmed at NATONAV 1 and he began to wonder if he might not be partially blamed for not keeping them informed. Perhaps they would expect him to protest to Captain Finlander and Commodore Schrepke. As he mulled this over, Lieutenant Beeker came in from the EDA room and announced: "We're picking up some weak radar emissions."

"The *Tiburon Bay?*" Packer asked.

"Negative. Probably the *Novo Sibirsk.*"

"Ouch! The Russian mother ship is coming to look for her lost chick!" Packer exclaimed. "Of course! They have been out of touch too for over forty-three hours!" He grabbed the phone and called the captain again.

After receiving the second report from Communications Center, Finlander's mind became a turmoil of thoughts, all unpleasant. With no signs of a contact, NATONAV 1 getting excited, the *Fritiof Nansen* on the way and the *Novo Sibirsk* probably approaching their position, he was coming to realize that his tactical situation was rapidly deteriorating. It would be at least four hours before the Russian "research ship" could reach the area, but it would be compromising to allow her to find the *Bedford* here. The *Nansen* should be stopped from a useless digression; NATONAV would have to be answered very soon, or his own COM-FLANT would start screaming too. It had finally become urgent to consider breaking off this action, of admitting that Moby Dick had outmaneuvered him again, that even an old-fashioned Russian snort boat could evade a super-destroyer like the *Bedford.* What chance would there then be against the atomic units the Russian navy was readying? Finlander fought down a surging feeling of wild frustration and tried to keep his mind professionally objective. For a moment he stared at Queffle's dancing knee, then swiveled around in his seat to face Commodore Schrepke.

"Could you have made a mistake in identity?" he asked the German. "Could Moby Dick be a later class with some advanced kind of oxygen regenerators aboard?"

"I do not think so, Captain."

"Then he *has* to come up?"

"Yes—he has to come up."

Finlander turned away and glanced at the battle clock. Forty-five hours and three minutes. Time was running out, but maybe he could squeeze out just a little more. Perhaps those Russians were gasping out their last minutes of endurance down there right now, the diving officer poised to blow all tanks. Or perhaps they were a hundred miles away, laughing as they approached their rendezvous with the *Novo Sibirsk*. But then why was the *Novo Sibirsk* heading this way with her powerful search radar probing the night? He *had* to still be down there.

"We are completely out of the magnetic field, Captain," Lieutenant Spitzer informed him.

Finlander got up from his chair and staggered against the rolling to place himself behind Merlin Queffle and stare at the empty luminous disk of the PPI scope. It did not contain the faintest spark of activity. Well . . . as a last-ditch resort, they might as well start a maximum-effect active sonar sweep. "Mr. Spitzer! Belay the QBH and—"

His words were cut off by a piercing yell from Merlin Queffle which froze him and everybody else in the CIC: *"Wait! . . . Wait!"*

A couple of seconds passed in an agonized, stunned silence.

Then Queffle screamed again: "I hear him! . . . I hear him! . . . I have a *contact!*"

Finlander spun around and bounded back to Central

Control, jumping into the chair and simultaneously yanking the talker set over his head. "Bridge! We have a contact! We will conn from CIC." Then he was momentarily diverted by the shocking sight of Lieutenant Aherne suddenly turning away from his switches and attempting to direct a stream of vomit into a paper cup. Ensign Ralston was staring stupidly at the fire-control officer, apparently paralyzed by the strange sight.

"God damn it to hell, Ralston!" Finlander screamed. "Don't just sit there! Relieve that man!"

Ralston let out a shocked yelp, yanked Aherne out of the chair and took his place. "All weapons arm-safe!" he called out with a trembling voice. "All systems go!"

Queffle had hunched back over his console after his initial outburst and seemed knotted into an attitude of prayer, his eyes closed as he ignored the PPI scope and pressed every last ounce of his nervous energy into the rubber cups of the phones. All eyes were upon him, all minds questioning him.

"Are you *sure*, Queffle?"

The Breton Kid gradually relaxed as if he were coming out of a trance and Finlander had a horrible feeling that he was about to admit to hallucinations. But the sonarman grinned and said: "Definite audio contact growing stronger." As he said it, a faint blob blossomed on the PPI scope, and he added: "Contact now bearing zero-four-zero, range three-two-double-zero closing, depth one-eight-zero."

Captain Finlander let out a long wheezing sigh, shedding all of his agonizing doubts and fears, and cheerfully exclaimed: "Very good! Let him come! Let him come! Stand by for the payoff! . . . Talker! Alert the engine room for maneuvering. Silence throughout ship." He swung around to shoot a triumphant grin at Commodore Schrepke, but it froze on his lips when he saw that Ben Munceford had entered the CIC and was standing next to the German. The correspondent's face wore a churlishly defiant half-smile as he turned his hands palm out toward the captain to show that he was armed with neither camera or tape recorder. Commodore Schrepke was distastefully edging away from him while otherwise ignoring his presence and locking his gaze on the plotting board. For a second Finlander thought of ordering somebody to throw Munceford out, but there had been enough disruptions in the CIC, so he shrugged indifferently and turned his full attention to the board—where Moby Dick was at long last appearing again as a white X edged in black.

9.

After the initial excitement of regaining contact with the Russian submarine, there followed another period of tense waiting while they tracked his creeping movement up from the deep and along a northeasterly course which gradually put the silently drifting *Bedford* between it and the sheltering wreck of the *Hood*. Moby Dick was rigged for silent running with his screws barely turning, but he created just enough disturbance to energize the destroyer's listening gear, which in turn registered the vibrations upon Queffle's sensitive ears and kindled a pip on the PPI, pinpointing his position. The tension in the CIC remained highly charged, but the overtones of hysteria had gone with the corroding elements of doubt and uncertainty. It was now a cold, calculating, even businesslike tension in which all outward functions were performed with exaggerated calm.

"Contact . . . bearing zero-five-six . . . range two-nine-five-zero, closing . . . depth, one-four-zero, rising. . . . Contact . . ."

This droned calling of target information was not really necessary because it was being automatically fed from Queffle's MTS into the computer circuitry of the CSP room, there to be masticated and digested in a millionth-second gulp by Krindlemeyer's and Spitzer's martian robot, thence flashed back through a network of conduits, finally animating the cells of a deadly sort of senseless intelligence in the warheads of the poised ASROC's. If ordered to go by a flick of Ensign Ral-

315

ston's finger, they knew *where* even before the plotter had finished calling out the target information.

Terrifyingly marvelous, Ben Munceford thought, without really understanding how any of it worked.

Lieutenant Spitzer was more concerned with how *well* the systems were working. A weak transistor, a collapsed diode, a micro-soldered filament vibrated loose—any one could throw the whole thing into a meaningless confusion. There were built-in monitors, auxiliary circuits and fail-safe devices, of course—electronic ganglions watching over electronic ganglions—but he kept a visual check on it all through the rows of winking lights and flicking needles spread out on the console before him. And then, as a final double-check, Ensign Ralston was manually feeding the target information into the weapons by punching matching numbers on a keyboard with his right hand. The left one rested on the firing switches—as yet locked by the red safety bar.

Suddenly the glowing blob on the MTS scope began to fade out. Finlander leaned forward, eyebrows arching, jaw jutting.

"Contact fading on bearing zero-six-four ... range two-nine-three-zero, steady ... depth one-double-zero, steady. Target has stopped. Target has stopped."

"He's listening for us," Finlander whispered.

"I have audio contact," Queffle reported. "Target engines are stopped, but I hear his auxiliaries. Sounds like a hot bearing."

Finlander smiled thinly. "Let's hope Commander Franklin keeps ours cool! Do you think he can hear us, Mr. Spitzer?" he asked the ECM officer.

"If they've got a man like Queffle, they might hear our hull break the wave patterns, sir. Otherwise we are a pretty inert target."

"All right. Let him sweat. We'll surprise him at the right moment. ... Mr. Ralston! Contact Yeoman

Pinelli in hedgehog local control and tell him to man his camera. Stand by the magnesium flares for a flash shot. When Moby Dick surfaces we'll make him say cheese and I think I'll send the chief of the Soviet Naval Staff a copy of the picture—compliments of the U.S.S. *Bedford!*"

Ralston grinned, called hedgehog control and transmitted the order.

But Finlander's plan was not to be. As the next swell lifted the *Bedford,* passed under her hull, then sucked her into the following trough, the attendant wrenching motion broke loose a huge chunk of ice which had formed around the housing of the radar antenna motor on the mainmast. Squarehead saw it flash by within inches of his face as he peered through the windshield of the crow's-nest, making him gasp: "Christ! What was that!" It hurtled downward through the blackness, broke into smaller pieces as it glanced off the forward stack, then crashed onto the main deck like an avalanche of rocks. A single hundred-pound piece hit the tarpaulin cover of the whale-boat, was hurled back into the air by the trampoline effect and made a huge splash in the sea, fifty yards away. The bridge lookout gave a yell: "Man or heavy object overboard!" He had been unable to tell which and was thoroughly alarmed. Commander Allison rushed across the bridge and stared out into the darkness.

In the CIC the ice was heard hitting the deck as a muffled rumble, but the chunk which fell in the sea made all the sound gear crackle. The PPI scopes flared like frightened green eyes. Merlin Queffle jumped in his seat and yelled: "Jeeze! Something big fell off the ship!"

"That tears it!" Spitzer exclaimed. "A deaf old woman could hear that without her ear trumpet."

"Shut up!" Finlander snarled, staring intently at the scopes, hoping they would get away with the calamity, but his ECM officer had been right. In the next instant the submarine's active sonar waves rippled against the *Bedford*'s hull and set her sensors to wildly reacting. The captain ground his fist into his palm. "Switch to active echo-ranging!" he ordered Spitzer, then called through the conning circuit: "All ahead standard! Come left to one-two-five degrees!"

A shudder rippled through the hull as the engines burst into life and the propellers bit into the water. The speakers vibrated with a strong return echo and the sonar PPI's registered such a brilliant blip of Moby Dick that it was like having a picture of him poised there, two thousand yards away and one hundred fathoms down.

Commander Allison's voice came over the bridge intercom: "We just shed five hundred pounds of ice off the foretop. Sorry."

"Never mind, Buck!" Finlander snapped back. "We're still giving him one hell of a surprise. Contact is positive."

It was so positive that even Ben Munceford could clearly make out what was happening. The Russian submarine was turning away while still pressing toward the surface and Finlander was conning the *Bedford* so as to catch up and place himself on top of him. If this had been real war, Moby Dick would clearly be finished—*but it wasn't real war.* Munceford glanced at Commodore Schrepke, edged up to him and asked: "So we've got him cold! So what do we do with him now?"

Schrepke's face was an unfathomable mask, but one drained of all color. He shook off Munceford and stepped up behind Finlander, leaning over him. "Let him surface, Captain," he rasped with as much pleading as he was capable of using.

"He's still acting too smart. I'm going to push that

red devil's nose into his own bilges. Helm, come five degrees left!"

"He's more desperate than smart at this point, Captain," Schrepke pressed him. "You are going to force him to fight. This is a careful, responsible commander you're dealing with, but he has reached his limits. Let him surface and let him go, or he is going to fight."

If Spitzer heard the ominous prediction, he pretended not to. Finlander looked up at the German for a moment. "You think he's going to shoot at us, do you, Commodore?"

"I know I would in his place," Schrepke answered. "So would you."

Finlander turned and leaned toward Ensign Ralston. "Fire Control! Arm number-one ASROC!"

Ralston looked up from his dials with a startled expression which immediately switched to one of intense anticipation. His hand shook as it flipped the red safety bar and the warning horn cut through the CIC with its short, sibilant blast. "Number-one ASROC armed and ready, sir!"

Finlander looked back into Schrepke's face, his expression challenging, yet icy calm. "All right, Commodore. Let him try anything he wants to."

"Captain, you are a fool!" Schrepke hissed at him, throwing every bit of the fear and anger which he felt into the words. This time Lieutenant Spitzer glanced up from his panel with an incredulous expression.

The scar on Finlander's throat pulsed angrily as he glowered at the German. "I'm not going to shoot first, Commodore. But if he fires a torpedo at me, then . . ." His voice rose up above the pinging of the sonar and the range-calling of the plotter. ". . . then I'll fire one!"

"Fire one!" Ensign Ralston's voice echoed in a high pitch of excitement.

Captain Finlander wheeled in his seat and his body

was suddenly racked by a spasm which came together with a passing faint tremor through the *Bedford*.

The stunned silence which ensued was broken by the talker at the plotting board. "Number-one ASROC launched and clear," he announced in a matter-of-fact voice which almost instantly turned into a weird squeal of amazement. "Jesus Christ aw'mighty! *It really is!*"

His anguished exclamation was immediately followed by Commander Allison's voice through the bridge intercom, and for once it sounded as if he were thoroughly shaken. "CIC! ... CIC! Number-one AS-ROC has fired!"

"For God's sake, Ralston!" Finlander gulped hoarsely, rising to his feet in shocked horror and tearing off his headset.

The ensign's taut muscles began turning to jelly and he suddenly sagged down in his seat, trembling violently as he stared at the hand still gripping the firing switch. He yanked it away as if it had burned him. "B-but, sir ... you said *fire one* ... didn't you?"

"It is done now," Schrepke exclaimed with a clipped finality. "It is all over and done now."

All eyes watched the PPI scope of the Master Tactical Sonar with hypnotic fascination. A second, smaller blip suddenly blossomed on it, close to the bigger one which was Moby Dick. "ASROC has separated from rocket booster and has entered the sea ... on target ... all systems go!" the plotter announced with a quavering voice. The small blob wavered around the bigger one, hovered around it for what became an agonized eternity ...

"Oh God! Miss him! Miss him!"

... but then seemed to join it and cause a single bright flare which quickly died and faded out to nothing. Queffle pried up his earphones just as the speaker erupted in a horrible cacophony of grating, tearing, ripping sounds. It gradually diminished to a crackling patter, but then the shock wave of a tremendous underwater explosion hit the *Bedford*'s steel hull, making her tremble and ring with a ghostly boom, like the tolling of a huge bell. Then silence.

"I heard her break up!" Merlin Queffle screamed. "I heard them dying down there!" He tore off his earphones and collapsed over the console, his body racked by sobs.

All eyes remained on the sonarman for only a moment before slowly turning upon the captain. Everybody knew what had happened now and the shattering reality of it was beginning to penetrate home. Forty-five hours, eighteen minutes since it started, and now it had ended in forty fatal seconds. The Russian submarine they had wistfully called Moby Dick had been blown to pieces and the hundred-odd men aboard her scattered to the deep. They all knew it—except possibly Ben Munceford, who could not immediately bring himself to believe this had actually happened before his eyes and stupidly mumbled: "What's the matter? . . . What's going on?" until his words were choked off by the awful realization.

10.

Lieutenant Spitzer secured the CIC, giving his orders in a steady voice, but with a peculiar trance-like expression on his face. One by one the men trooped out, some staring with curious awe at the brooding figure of their captain slumped at Central Control, others clumsily avoiding a look at him as they passed. The CPO of plot helped Lieutenant Aherne, who was too sick to fully understand what had happened; two sonarmen supported Merlin Queffle between them, dragging him through the door still blubbering about hearing men die in the black deep. Finally only Commodore Schrepke and Ensign Ralston were left with Finlander in the silent room, now darker than ever since all the dials and ·scopes had been extinguished. The assistant fire-control officer had remained paralyzed at his console, looking down at the fatal switch with glazed, red-rimmed eyes. But now he got up and stepped over to the captain, braced himself and exclaimed with a pathetic fortitude: "Sir, it was all my fault. I am prepared to take full responsibility for what happened."

Finlander did not appear to hear him.

"Sir, please . . ."

Commodore Schrepke reached out and took Ralston by the arm, gently pulling him away and guiding him toward the door. "Your captain cannot talk to you now," he said. "And no matter what you tell him, he knows where the responsibility lies. He certainly knows that your blame is but an incidental one. So do not waste his time with self-reproaches." He did not say it harshly, perhaps even with a tinge of sympathy, but the ensign suddenly began to shake uncontrollably and tears began streaming down his cheeks. Schrepke steadied him and, reaching under his leather jacket, brought out his tarnished silver flask. "Here, my boy. You need a little medicine."

The tears did not stop as Ralston stared at the flask, but he suddenly struck it away as if it contained poison. "You are going to crucify him for this, aren't you?" he yelled at the German.

"I am neither Judas nor Pontius Pilate," Schrepke answered him evenly, "but a sailor who will give up only to death many secrets as terrible as this."

Ralston fended off his helping hand, straightened himself up and through a tremendous effort suppressed his trembling. But he could not stop crying. Fumbling for the iron door, he yanked it open and fled.

Schrepke went back to Central Control and sat down in the chair next to Findlander. He felt the engines stop and knew that the *Bedford* was coasting in over the spot where Moby Dick had died. Finlander seemed completely oblivious of it and sunk in deep thought, but suddenly he spoke up and asked: "What did you mean, Wolfgang, when you said you would only give up secrets like this to death?"

The German did not answer him immediately and when he did, it was to say: "I was talking to a hysterical boy."

Finlander looked Schrepke straight in the eyes. "Were you suggesting that what I have done can be covered up in some way? Kept a deep, dark secret?"

Schrepke hesitated a moment with a faint nodding of his head. "What would happen if it became general knowledge that we sank a Soviet submarine on the high seas after deliberately tracking him for forty-eight hours?" he asked.

"All hell would break loose," the captain quietly replied.

"A nuclear hell, Erik?"

Finlander's long silence betrayed the fact that he feared such a possibility, but he said: "That would be sheer insanity, to precipitate nuclear war over an incident such as this."

"The incident itself proves how rampant insanity is."

A half-hour ago this reply would have triggered Finlander's temper, but now he took it with an unflinching calm which was, perhaps, far more frightening. He said simply: "Yes."

They were both diverted by the sounds of annunciator signals being transmitted from the bridge to the engine room and looked at the gyro-repeater and rudder indicator above the Control Center. Commander Allison was maneuvering the *Bedford* in a slow, tight circle. "I must go up on the bridge," the captain muttered without making the move. "I must see this thing through to the end and carry the responsibility all the way. I will, of course, log your protests agains the action, Wolfgang. You attempted to stop it and you must be absolved."

Schrepke shook his head. "I am not looking for absolution, nor could I ever find it. What do you think the Russian government will do when they find out that a senior officer of the West German navy was aboard the ship which sank their submarine? Would they accept his protestations that he acceded to the orders of the captain? Some of my colleagues were hanged not so long ago with the same kind of excuse on their lips. And they deserved their fate. For my own part, I must accept my responsibility. I cannot do it with pride or honor, but at least I can try for courage."

Finlander leaned forward and tried to see Schrepke's face, which was only a blur in the faint glow of the red blackout lights. He opened his mouth to speak when the bridge intercom crackled to life and Commander Allison's voice interrupted him: "Could the captain please come to the bridge? This is urgent."

"In a few minutes, Buck! You carry on."

Allison became insistent and it was evident that he was still badly rattled. "Captain Finlander! We are circling the area of the sinking. There is oil and wreckage, but no signs of survivors. EDA reports an increasingly strong radar emission on the Soviet frequency. Estimate eighty miles away. Communications has intercepted repeated calls for Moby Dick originating from the same range and bearing as the radar emissions. Communications also reports repeated calls to us from NATONAV 1 and Polarbear. I recommend immediate action, sir."

Before Finlander could answer him, he felt an iron grip clamp down on his arm. Schrepke's other hand shot out and locked the microphone button in the off position so that Allison could not hear what he was going to say.

"Tell him to reopen communications with NATO-NAV 1 and report contact lost and action broken off—*no more.*"

"You still think there is a way of covering up this thing?" Finlander asked him with both doubt and hope.

"We cannot risk having the Soviets break the code of an action report. I most emphatically suggest you keep any mention of it off the air, Captain. I speak officially, but also as your friend. Do not make any action report."

A tremendous load seemed to fall suddenly from Finlander's shoulders. "Yes, sir," he agreed, his hands waving before him as if grasping at a solution he had glimpsed in the darkness. "You are right. We will keep the secrecy of this and pass it on as such to our Fleet Headquarters, who then will have no choice but do the same . . . will they? Of course not! Obviously the Commies know nothing about it as yet! They haven't heard from their precious pigboat for over forty-five hours—and now they *never will*. So it can be done!" He pushed Schrepke's hand away from the intercom lever and spoke into the microphone with much of his old vigor and confidence. "Buck! Reopen standard Code C communication channels with NATONAV 1 and report to them contact is lost, action broken off and we are resuming base course."

"No action report, sir?"

"Negative. Negative. The lid is down tight on that. Search the area for five more minutes, then retire away from radar emissions for thirty minutes before resuming base course. Announce a special briefing of all offwatch officers in the wardroom at 0700. I'll be right up . . . so keep an even strain, Buck!" When he switched off and rose up out of the chair, there was a fatalistic kind of cheerfulness about him. "Well, I'm going to leave this electronic chamber of horrors and cleanse myself in the wind and spray of a good, old-fashioned open bridge. It's my guess that I won't be permitted that privilege much longer. . . . Are you coming?"

Commodore Schrepke began to lift himself from his seat, but froze halfway up as Commander Allison's voice came through the intercom again:

"Captain! We have picked up human remains!"

Schrepke slumped back into the chair. "If you don't mind, I will stay here until we are under way again," he rasped.

"I understand, sir," Finlander whispered. "The flotsam of a smashed submarine must bring back terrible memories for you. I understand."

"But we must still be practical about such things. Especially in this case. Remove all the evidence you can. And about the slick of oil—I suggest you pump some of your own into it so that if the *Novo Sibirsk* finds it, it will not be so easily identifiable."

"That is a very good idea," Finlander agreed. He put his hand on Schrepke's shoulder in a hesitant gesture of friendship. "You are a very fine officer, Wolfgang. We may have had our quarrels and old enmities have stood between us, but, no matter what happens to me now, I will tell them you are a fine officer and that I consider you a good friend. Please believe I mean it."

Commodore Schrepke answered with a wistful irony: "What you feel for me now is the kinship of the damned, my poor captain." The hand pulled away from his shoulder, but the dark figure remained by his side for a moment. "Go clean up matters on your bridge, Erik," the German urged him. "You have only little time left."

"All right. Lock the door when you leave."

After Finlander had gone, Schrepke remained in his seat for a couple of minutes to give him plenty of time to climb the shaft to the bridge. Then he got up and went over to Fire Control, leaned down over the console and carefully read the labels along the rows of switches. Finding the one he wanted, he gingerly grasped it between thumb and forefinger, slowly, very slowly pushing it forward. Two red lights winked on. On the Weapons Status Board a sign lighted up, reading NO. 2 ASROC—LOCAL CONTROL. He stood there for a moment, listening and tensely waiting, as if he expected some kind of drastic reaction to what he had done. But the intercoms remained silent; no alarm sounded, nobody came bursting in. With a deep sigh he left, rammed home the automatic locking bar of the CIC door, climbed down the shaft to the main deck, then on through silent passageways to his own cabin. There he brought out his small leather suitcase, opened it and from beneath the neat packing of socks and underwear brought forth his service pistol. He methodically examined its magazine and chamber, then put it down on the desk. From a drawer he took a shabby wallet, and from it a fading, dog-eared photograph of a smiling woman with a solemn-faced blond young boy. This too he put down on the desk. Before seating himself for a last communion with his dead family, he carefully checked his watch as if to predetermine how much time he could allot to them.

11.

Outside of her gloomy interior, the *Bedford* had suddenly erupted in a blaze of lights. From her armored honeycombs of compartments and stations, men had poured out on deck and swarmed to the railing and lifelines, from where they silently stared into the sea. Scattered snowflakes still danced in the brilliant periphery created by the floodlights and they sparkled like floating diamonds when caught in the more powerful beam of the probing searchlight. On the heaving dark swells, a darker blotch of oil, perhaps an acre wide, stained the sea like a pool of black blood, viscous and shimmering weirdly with dull flashes of iridescence; here and there it was coagulating around bobbing lumps of shapeless debris. Two seamen on the foredeck were wielding the same long-handled dip nets they used to pick up garbage for the surgeon's analysis, trying to snare these lumps as Commander Allison slowly maneuvered the ship through the slick. One of them had been put in a bucket, which was being passed from man to man in a fitful journey toward the bridge; some stopped its progress momentarily to look at the contents with morbid shock, others closed their eyes and practically threw it on to the next link in the human chain. One seaman fainted as soon as it left his hands. Chief Quartermaster Rickmers, the last to receive it, put it down under the light by the wheelhouse door, where it arrived just as Captain Finlander was stepping out on the bridge in his white duffel.

A stunned, awe-struck circle formed around the

bucket and among the men as Ben Munceford, paralyzed with his camera in his hands as he gaped at what had been a full-grown, living man only an hour ago—now a mangled, oil-soaked glob of gore contained in a two-gallon bucket with plenty of room to spare.

"Th-that ... that ain't human, in Christ's name?" Munceford gulped.

"No, not any more," a seaman answered and turned away.

Captain Finlander said: "It is the pressure of the deep which did it, not the explosion." It was almost as if he were denying his complicity, but actually this last incontrovertible piece of evidence of what he had done was searing itself upon his mind. He had seen such remains before when nearly twenty years ago he had blown to pieces the ill-starred U-1020. For that action he had received the Navy Cross; for this one he would receive excoriation and infamy. No matter how well the navy would be able to protect the terrible secret, there was no protection possible for him, and, in some small measure, this grisly butcher's scrap which had once been a man would be avenged.

Commander Allison waited for his captain to order that something be done with the remains, but when he continued to stare at them along with the others, Allison took the initiative upon himself. "Mr. Whitaker! Throw something over that and carry it down to Commander Porter for dispositon."

This seemed to snap Ben Munceford out of his paralysis. "Wait!" he exclaimed and, raising his camera, snapped on its brilliant Solarpack light.

Without a word Captain Finlander struck out with his gloved fist and exploded the light with a single blow. Everybody jumped back, cringing from the shower of hot glass. Munceford yelped and dropped the camera. When he started to bend down to retrieve it, the captain kicked it beyond his reach. Munceford straightened up and glared at him, white-faced and shaking, but there was no childish petulance in his manner. "That will do you no good," he said. "You can bust up all the cameras you like, tear up all the tapes and do your damnedest to muzzle me, Captain. But it will do you no good. I finally have this story straight in every detail. I'm going to see to it the truth is told."

"The matter will shortly be out of my hands, Mr. Munceford," the captain answered with an icy calm. "In the meanwhile I am having you confined to your cabin. You will remain there until we dock in Reykjavik. If you attempt to move about this ship— even to the wardroom—you will be locked in the brig. Mr. Whitaker! Escort Mr. Munceford below."

Ensign Whitaker picked up the bucket with one hand and took Munceford's arm with the other. The circle of men opened up, allowed them to pass, then scattered to line the windscreen and peer down at the brilliantly illuminated oil slick lapping at the *Bedford*'s hull.

Captain Finlander slowly walked to the part of the bridge where Commodore Schrepke used to spend his lonely vigils and, like him, stared down into the fouled sea. Commander Allison stood silently behind him for a moment, then joined him shoulder to shoulder. "How in God's name did this happen, Erik?" he asked.

"A misunderstood order, I think," Finlander quietly answered. "The details are all a mixed-up nightmare in my own mind, but they don't matter for the moment. There were eleven men in the CIC when it happened and the Investigation Board will pick the pieces out of their brains and fit them together for my court-martial. Right now I must do better what I have been trying to do all along, so help me God, and that is to protect my country. The *Bedford* must be made a more silent ship than she has ever been before."

Allison looked down at the men swarming along the foredeck below the bridge, leaning over lifelines or clambering on the turrets in groups of ten and twenty. There must have been a hundred in view down there, peering and pointing at the stain of Moby Dick's killing, letting it saturate permanently into their consciences. "This is going to be an awfully rough one, Erik," the executive officer whispered. "Awfully rough. I admit I'm badly scared."

"So am I, Buck," the captain replied, then added a bitterly suppressed outburst: "The cold war! How can governments expect their military to guide their actions by such a blatantly sordid euphemism? Is there really such a thing possible as a half-war? Can one half-fight with these deadly weapons? Did those Russian submariners half-threaten us? Are they now only half-dead down there? Should I only have half-feared them when the crews of so many American ships and planes are totally dead as a result of Russian actions? Does it not all naturally culminate in a totality of death and destruction? The answer lies in that bucket they passed up to this bridge a few minutes ago. I'd like to pass it on around among the world's cabinets and make every last politician take a good long look. Look and see what this cold war really is. The same as any war. Death." Finlander shook himself and checked the luminous dial of his watch. "All right, Buck. Let's get out of here before those Soviet radar emissions get strong enough to give them a return echo. I'm going to run home to Uncle Sam, tell him what a terrible thing I have done, accept my beating and hope that he can protect himself and the rest of his children from the consequences."

Without a word Commander Allison turned and walked off toward the wheelhouse. Captain Finlander remained where he was, looking down at the men below him. Then he leaned far over the windscreen, cupped a hand to his mouth and shouted to them: "Take a last look, men! Let the sight and feel of it sink in. Let it burn into your hearts and minds so well that you will never have to ask or speak about it among yourselves in order to recall it. Then, when the lights go out, clear the decks and seal it all up inside of you. From this moment on, learn to live with this secret, because if you become in the least bit careless with it, then an infinitely more terrible thing may strike far beyond this ship. There could be a millionfold more dead than those wretches who have perished here—God rest their souls!" For a moment longer he stared down at the hundred white faces looking up at him, watching that whiteness ripple away as they turned back for a last glance at the oil slick, then he nodded at Rickmers, who was standing by the wheelhouse door. The chief nodded back, vanished inside, and an instant later all the floods and exterior lights went out on the *Bedford* as he pulled the main blackout switch. The ship's decks emptied of life, once again became deserted and lashed by cold spray as she gained speed and retreated into the dark folds of the arctic night.

As the *Bedford* got under way, Lieutenant Beeker drew a sigh of relief and left the EDA room, where he had been anxiously monitoring the Russian radar emissions. "I was wondering if the skipper was going to hang around and let the *Novo Sibirsk* pick us up," he said to Lieutenant Packer. "Their microwaves are getting pretty solid now. Not more than sixty miles away."

Packer had just completed supervising the reopening of communications with NATONAV 1, had coded and transmitted the captain's messages to them and was now standing by the radio operators who were receiving and acknowledging some routine FOX Scheds—a kind of calm before the storm of amplification requests he suspected would soon be crackling out of the ether. His duty here had prevented him from going out on deck to witness the brief salvage operation, but one of the stand-by operators had brought back a crudely lucid eyewitness account. He had been one of the men who had helped pass the bucket up to the bridge. Somewhere in the back of the English officer's weary mind the idea began to crystallize that they were *actually* at war. They *had* to be, since there had been a killing. Sometime during this awful long arctic night it must have started, although they had intercepted no messages about it from NATONAV 1 or any other fleet headquarters or task force. Well, these days war would start in secrecy, of course. Just sudden actions with sudden deaths, as there had just been out here. "Moby Dick tried to slip us a fish!" the relief radio operator had passed on the scuttlebutt, "but the skipper was on his toes and beat the bastard to it!"

And here came the quick promotions which always went hand in hand with war. The operator on Channel 5 received some personals and Lieutenant Packer quickly unscrambled them on the decoding machine:

ERIK J. FINLANDER, CAPTAIN, USN, COLDSNAP VIA NATONAV GENAVRAD—YOU HAVE MADE ADMIRALS LIST STOP A CINCH FOR CONFORMATION IF YOU KEEP UP SPLENDID WORK STOP WELCOME TO THE CLUB AND CONGRATULATIONS—SIGNED RIERSEN, BENTLEY, MC-LAURIN.

"A cracking day for the skipper," Packer muttered to himself, then stiffened as he ran the next one through the decoder. The printed strip it fed into his hand read:

P. L. M. PACKER, LIEUTENANT RN, COLDSNAP VIA NA-
TONAV MACKAY——FIND I WOULD RATHER HAVE YOU AND
LOSE YOU THAN NEVER HAVE YOU AT ALL STOP SO
COME BACK AND LET US LOVE WELL IF NOT WISELY
FOR WHATEVER TIME YOUR NAVY ALLOWS US——SIGNED
SHEBEONA.

Packer read it through a second, a third and a fourth
time. He passed a trembling hand over his face, his
palm rasping against the stubble sprouting over his
jaws, then read it a fifth time. His mind was a complete
confusion now, a numbed mixture of thoughts of war,
death and love. Shebeona wanted him back! But wasn't
the very thing she feared happening already? Would
she stick if there was war? Would she quickly become
another forgotten Packer widow?

Lieutenant Beeker came up behind him. "Was one
of those personals for you, Pete?" he asked, glancing
over his shoulder at the strips of paper in his hand.
"Bad news?"

Packer quickly whipped Shebeona's cablegram out
of sight. "One was for me. Nothing serious, really. The
other seems to indicate your navy has a brand-new admiral." He handed him the one about Finlander.

Beeker glanced through it and exclaimed: "God! I
wonder if this will hold good after we dock. Well, better let him enjoy it while he can. Messenger!" He
stuffed it into a yellow envelope and dispatched it to
the bridge, then noticed that the Englishman was still
leaning over the decoder with a drawn, blank expression on his face. "Are you all right, Pete?"

"I don't know," Packer answered. "Everything
seems all so god-awfully mixed up. What is happening?
Are we at war? Has the whole world been plunged into
darkness or is it only *us*, Beek?"

Beeker peered carefully into his face for a moment
and frowned as if he wondered about this himself. He

turned to the rows of radio operators and called out: "Hey, Swanson! You're guarding GB circuits. Anything unusual happening on the outside?"

Swanson shrugged. "No, Mr. Beeker. Nothing much. The President has agreed to meet with Khrushchev sometime soon. There's some kind of scandal in New York City about rats in the schools. The Green Bay Packers got taken seventeen-nothing. The big news from both sides of the pond seems to be about Jack Paar lousing up the deal in Berlin."

Beeker sighed with relief, then turned back to Packer and smiled. "You see, everything's absolutely normal. . . . Look, I'll run the store for a while if you want to take a break, Pete. You seem pretty beat, boy."

Packer was suddenly both eager to accept this offer and strangely exhilarated by a fresh flood of nervous energy. "Thanks a lot, Beek!" he exclaimed. "I'll be back very soon and you can call me immediately if there's an avalanche of top-secret squawks out of NA-TONAV 1. But I do need to get down to my cabin right away. As a matter of fact . . . I absolutely *have* to!"

He left the Communications Center and as he progressed on his downward journey through the *Bedford*'s pitching decks and passageways, his pace quickened with the full realization that Shebeona wanted him and no war had come between them as yet. At the same time, something near panic gripped him as he remembered that *Munceford* had her picture now. What madness could have driven him to give away Shebeona's photograph to that man! Allowing him to possess even a paper likeness of her suddenly rankled Packer as if Munceford possessed her physically. He began to run. Run with a wild, fearful, elated recklessness. And as he whipped around the corner of the passageway leading to his cabin, he violently collided with Commodore Schrepke.

The two men almost fell over and had to claw at each other to keep their balance. Lieutenant Packer's hand slipped against cold leather and when it clamped down on the man's waist, it was over something hard and butt-shaped beneath the folds. The impression flashed through his brain that it felt like a gun, but, realizing who it was, he knew it had to be Schrepke's famous schnapps flask. With a frantic apology, he disengaged himself from the German officer.

Schrepke kept a grip on his arm and pinned him against the bulkhead beneath the red blackout light. "Ah, it's you, *Lieutenant* Packer! Still in a state of agitation, I see. What has happened to the cool, level-headed British navy?"

"I'm awfully sorry, sir," Packer gasped, out of breath, and more befuddled than ever. "It's just been a bad night all round for me." He was shocked to find this made Schrepke laugh. He had never before seen the German even smile.

"A bad one for all of us, so never mind," the commodore answered and gave him a comforting pat on the shoulder.

Packer peered into his face and saw that the laughter was not in his eyes, which had a peculiarly restive look of sadness in them. "I have been meaning to also apologize for the way I behaved earlier this morning, Commodore. There was no excuse for it. Especially since I have a feeling you needed me for something. . . . You did, didn't you, sir?"

"Yes, I did. I thought you and I could do something about all this."

"All *what*, sir?"

"It does not matter any more. Fate was against us and it is too late."

The sadness had seeped into his voice now and it

sounded so uncharacteristic of him that Packer was completely baffled. "Is there something wrong? Can I help you, sir?"

"No, my boy. The wrong which has been done can only be helped by totally obliterating it. This task I must face alone." The gloved hand crept up Packer's arm, crossed his shoulder and momentarily brushed against his cheek in a gesture which was clumsily tender. "You know, I would have had a son of your age. I never got to know or understand him either. But I love him just the same." He pulled away his hand, turned and quickly vanished down the passageway.

Lieutenant Packer remained pressed against the bulkhead for almost a minute, then he shook himself back to reality and slowly walked the remaining twenty steps to his cabin. When he pulled aside the curtain, he found Ben Munceford sitting on his bunk.

"Well, well, good old Peterpacker!" the American exclaimed with a caustic imitation of an Englishman's English. "Have you come to gloat like Schrepke? To rub my nose in the dirt and tell me what a stupid bastard I am?"

Packer had been glancing back down the passageway, but now he faced Munceford and coldly answered: "No, Ben. I only want you to return Shebeona's picture."

Munceford's head snapped back with a wince. "What? Here we've illegally sunk a Russian sub, brought the world to the brink of atomic war and all you can think of is a pin-up of some broad! Jesus! And they call *me* superficial!"

Packer advanced on him and clenched both fists. "Give her back to me, Munceford. Right now."

Munceford snickered and squirmed away along the edge of the bunk. "Well, okay, okay! Let me see . . . what the hell did I do with her?"

Packer's hands lashed out, grabbed him by his shirt

and yanked him to his feet. "Give her back!" he shouted and began to shake him violently. But something clattered to the deck as he did it, and when he caught the flash of tarnished silver, it had an instant sobering effect upon him. It was Commodore Schrepke's flask.

Munceford pulled himself free of the Englishman's grip and dropped all of his sarcastic manner. "All right, Pete! I'll get your picture for you. Just spare me any more fits on this ship. I've just about had a bellyful of them." He went to his locker, opened it up and started rummaging in the tangle of dirty clothes. He found the photograph lying in the bottom corner, picked it up and, without a glance at the beautiful girl on it, held it out toward Packer.

But the lieutenant did not reach for it. He was holding the flask in his hand, staring at it with a perplexed frown. "How did you get this?" he asked.

Munceford snapped it out of his hand and shoved the photograph into it instead. "Here! You keep your girl and I'll keep the booze. Each to his own, okay?"

Packer held the picture as if it no longer mattered in the least. Something like fear was in his eyes as he asked again: "How did you get that flask? It belongs to Commodore Schrepke."

Munceford flopped back down on the bunk and started to unscrew the stopper. "Sure it does. That Dutchman dropped in on me awhile ago. I suppose I disturbed his sulking next door when Finlander's strong-arm boy brought me down here after I got kicked off the bridge. I'm kind of under arrest, you know. Anyway, he came in to see why I was cursing a blue streak and, by God, I told him. Like I'm going to tell everybody who comes within shouting distance of me from here on out." He took a deep draft out of the flask and made a terrible grimace. "Christ! What I'd give for a decent shot of real American bourbon whisky! This German rot-gut gags you more with each drink!"

All of Packer's anger had drained out of him, and he leaned over Munceford with a deadly earnest expression on his tired face. "For God's sake, Ben! Have you somehow got yourself raving drunk? If you have, say so. If you haven't, tell me what you know about Schrepke. Why did he give you the flask?"

"He said he gave it to me so I'd anesthetize myself," Munceford answered heatedly, "because, he said, he couldn't stand the screams of cowards. Well, hell! I'm not a coward, I'm only a fool. I wasn't screaming, I was cursing. When I scream, it will only be to make this story heard in spite of anything he thinks he can do to stop it. He can blow up this ship, he can . . . Hey! Where are you going?"

Lieutenant Peter Packer had suddenly straightened up as if a spring had been released in his backbone, whirled around and hurled himself through the curtain into the passageway outside the cabin. Munceford stared at the rippling blue folds of material as they closed behind him, frowned over the fading sound of his running, then shrugged. "He can ply me with all the anesthetic he wants to. All the Schrepkes and Finlanders of the whole damned world combined won't shut me up. Besides, I'm a changed man. I'm getting smart. And . . . I've kicked the habit!" He turned the flask upside down and let the remaining schnapps splatter on the deck. There were only a few drops left.

12.

Lieutenant Packer shot up the shaft, stumbled into the wheelhouse and was so winded by his long frantic run up from the cabin deck that he fell across the radar pedestal and hung there, gasping for breath. There was a startled shuffling among the relief lookouts and Chief Quartermaster Rickmers squinted through the dark and rasped: "Who is that?" When nothing but agonized panting answered the challenge, Ensign Whitaker switched on his hooded flashlight and directed its beam toward the sound. "Peterpacker! What's the matter with you, for God's sake?"

"Is . . . is Commodore Schrepke on the bridge?" the Englishman managed to blurt out.

"No—he's not in his usual perch, but—"

"I've got to see the captain immediately!" The tone of his voice caused another uneasy stirring among the men in the wheelhouse. The helmsman dared a quick, startled glance over his shoulder.

Whitaker moved up to the radar pedestal, thrusting the beam of his flashlight into Packer's white face. "The captain is in his day cabin with the exec. But I don't think—"

"I've got to see him!" Packer yelled and pushed the flashlight away. He spun around, almost bowled over Rickmers, ran through the blackout curtain of the navigation office and burst into the day cabin, where he half collapsed against the deck.

Captain Finlander was stretched out on the bunk, talking in a low voice to Commander Allison, who was

341

leaning against the bulkhead next to it. Both men stared in amazement at the intruder.

"Captain, sir! . . . I think Commodore Schrepke has gone mad! He's prowling about the ship with a pistol!"

Allison stared at Packer as if *he* were the one who had gone mad. It took Finlander a moment to react, then he wearily raised himself and swung his legs over the edge of the bunk. The crumpled radiogram announcing his impending promotion to flag rank fell to the deck and he stiffly bent down to pick it up before saying: "Carrying a pistol does not necessarily indicate insanity, Mr. Packer."

Allison shot in: "But to break in unannounced on your commanding officer could, and . . ." What he saw in the young officer's face suddenly made him stop and sharply ask: "Are you sure there is something wrong with him?"

"Sir, I ran into him . . . only a few minutes ago," Packer insisted, pressing forth his words in painful spurts. "He had . . . an unholstered pistol in his belt . . . and said very queer things . . . about totally obliterating a wrong . . . and acted strange with Munceford, and . . ."

"That one's likely to drive anybody nuts!" the exec snorted. "Pull yourself together, man, and make sense!"

But Lieutenant Packer would not be put off. "Spoke of anesthetizing him . . . said something to me about it . . . being too late . . . was on his way up and . . . he *laughed!*" Gulping down a very deep breath, he held it for a second in a tremendous effort to get hold of himself. When he let go, his voice rose to a near scream: "Sir! I'm absolutely positive he's planning to do something awful and it will happen any minute now!"

"Well, son," the captain said as if he were trying to soothe a hysterical child, "he can't very well sink this ship with a pistol."

"Can't he, sir? A pistol . . . and all the live warheads aboard?"

Allison and Finlander exchanged incredulous looks which contained the first glimmers of alarm. Ensign Whitaker had come to the door and was staring at Packer with a stunned expression; behind him, Chief Rickmers strained to see inside the cabin. The captain passed a hand over his eyes and it noticeably shook. "All right. But before we lose control in another uproar, let's make sure the commodore isn't in his usual place out on the bridge."

"He is not, sir," Whitaker positively injected.

Now Finlander got up off the bunk, strode over to the desk, pushed aside the sagging Packer and picked up the telephone. "This is the captain speaking. Immediately page Commodore Schrepke and ask him to come to the bridge. This is urgent. Request him to confirm to me by nearest phone that he is on his way." After hanging up, he checked his watch and looked into the Englishman's face. "If he does not report in exactly one minute, I'll have the JOOD take a detail and search the ship. Does that make you feel any better?"

Lieutenant Packer shook his head and whispered so low that only Finlander could barely hear him: "Fate was against us . . . it is too late. . . ." He was looking down at the crumpled photograph of Shebeona, which he still clutched in his hand.

Commodore Schrepke heard his name called over the PA system speaker inside the control turret of No. 2 ASROC launcher. He had been standing in the lee of it, pressing himself close to its steel side, staring out into the black void of the ocean, feeling the bite of the wind and sting of the snowflakes which were once again racing through the arctic night, allowing himself a few weirdly incongruous thoughts for a man about to die. Why had he spent so much of his life on this cursed sea which seemed eternally shrouded by the icy darkness of death? The same sea which had caressed the lovely shores of Marienstrand with gentle sun-dancing waves when a boy first heard her siren call and launched his toy ship upon her. Now she would get him at last, yet much too late. She had long since bared her heart to him and revealed its cold black abyss, which contained nothing but the ghosts of men who had perished as they fought her and one another. She had turned bright devotion into sullen obsession and pride into ignominious oblivion. This cold, cold sea and her cold, cold war!

Schrepke was brought back to his task when the bosun's pipe shrilled above the sound of wind and his name was called again. He glanced up at the dim mass of the bridge, then peered in through the slit in the control turret's door. He could see the red light burning bright on the panel and knew that nobody had been into the CIC to close the switches he had opened. Taking off his leather jacket, he let it drop to the deck. Then he pushed the pistol more securely into his belt and started climbing up the steel framework of the launcher.

When he reached the rocket booster and felt the smooth curve of it, he pulled off his gloves and fumbled blindly in the dark for the disconnected power cable. His fingers closed on its coils and pulled. With his other hand he reached for the contact to receive it. For what seemed an eternity his fingers searched along the slick, icy metal. Suddenly the ship's bullhorn on the base of the mainmast blared out:

"Commodore Schrepke! Are you on deck? You are urgently needed by the captain." The voice boomed through the darkness with a fearful, detached kind of desperation, and a second later floodlights flared on, one after another. The gray steel ramparts of the *Bedford*'s superstructure emerged out of the gloom into sharply etched lines of brilliant illumination and deep shadow, all a-swirl in whirlwinds of flying snow.

At the same instant Commodore Schrepke found the connector and drove home the fangs of the power cable. The warhead was armed. With methodical haste he resumed his grim climb toward the end where waited eleven hundred pounds of high explosives.

A small searchlight on the signal bridge burst on, probed about the decks, then suddenly caught the black figure crawling out on the launcher and fixed it in a glaring halo. A voice yelled: "There he is! There he is! Oh, God—stop him! Stop him, somebody!" But the *Bedford* dipped and rolled through a wave and seemed to nudge him along his way.

On the bridge Captain Finlander stood hatless in the biting wind, staring with a fatally entranced fascination. "He must have armed the system when I left him," he exclaimed softly to himself.

The entire bridge watch, excepting the helmsman abandoned to his unyielding duty in the empty wheel-house, were lining the railing alongside their captain, but only Commander Allison heard his words and was stuck by their terrible portent. "Fly down to the CIC!" he screamed at Ensign Whitaker. "Run for our lives and kill the firing circuits! Run! *Run!*"

Whitaker tore himself away with a yell of terror, but Captain Finlander knew that he would never make it in time. Schrepke had almost reached the deadly tip of the missile where the ice-crusted percussion pin wait-ed with a cold gleam in the glare of the searchlight. Out of the corner of his eye he saw Allison lift the mi-crophone of the bullhorn to his mouth and draw in his breath to scream at the German, but he reached out and yanked it away, then brought it to his own mouth instead:

"Why are you doing this, Wolfgang? Why?" His voice rang out from the gray muzzle on the mast, not frantic with pleading, but with a fatalistic resignation which told that he knew the answer to be foregone and was willing to accept it.

Every man on the bridge could clearly see Commodore Schrepke draw the pistol from his belt as he straddled the part of the missile which protruded beyond the structure of the launcher. He turned his face toward them when he heard the captain's question and as he did that, his hat blew off and crazily fluttered away to vanish in the dark beyond the rushing wake. Then his voice came back to them, answering loudly and clearly without benefit of electronic amplification:

"Only when Captain Ahab vanishes from the face of the seas along with his Moby Dick, and not a single trace of either is left to inflame the vengeance of their kin . . . only then can there follow peace!"

Somewhere along the forward part of the superstructure of the *Bedford* there came the sound of iron doors bursting open and the confused clatter of running feet. But they were too far away. The decks below the bridge were still empty as Commander Allison leaned over the railing and yelled: "Shoot him! Shoot him down!" He straightened up and shouted again to the helpless men around him: "Shoot him! . . . My God! Among all the fantastic weaponry of this ship, is there nothing with which to shoot a lone madman?" Then he saw Schrepke aim his pistol at the warhead and, together with all the other men on the bridge, recoiled and threw himself down behind the thin metal shield of the combing. Only Captain Finlander remained upright, facing the end unflinching.

A fiery red rose blossomed out from the *Bedford's* waist, appeared to hang suspended in a convulsed ball of flaming petals, then burst into an obliterating explosion outward and upward. In the foretop Seamen Thorbjornsen and Jones saw its searing glow rising toward them as they pressed their faces against the glass windshield of the crow's-nest; it protected them from being instantly incinerated as it enveloped the foretop, but they felt the mainmast buckle and start to fall and knew they would be dead in a few seconds. The explosion acted downward too, ripping through decks and bulkheads which bulged and flew apart into splatters of molten metal. Warheads in No. 2 magazine ignited themselves spontaneously from the searing heat and concussion, adding their energy to the holocaust. No. 1 boiler blew up with a deafening roar which Fireman Bert Meggs never heard because he was scalded to death in one thousandth of a second; the other three boilers went in quick succession, bursting their casings and releasing all of the *Bedford*'s eighty thousand horsepower in a cataclysmal storm of fire and superheated steam. It tore through the open watertight doors to the engine room, then collapsed the entire bulkhead. Ruptured fuel lines spewed black oil into the inferno where scorched flesh mingled with molten metal. Up at the Master Control, Lieutenant Commander Franklin's and Chief MacKay's last living sight was of the turbines rising up off their beds and the steel hull breaking apart like cardboard to allow a wall of green water to fall in upon them; they died only a fraction of a second later than Fireman Meggs, only two seconds after Commodore Schrepke had pulled the trigger of his pistol. By the third second the *Bedford*'s amidships was enveloped in a cascade of explosions which broke her in two between the crumbling funnels. The Beek fell screaming through a fiery crevasse which engulfed him and his beloved HUFF-DUFF. The severed after section slewed off sideways and was almost instantly driven under by the still turning screws; nearly one hundred enlisted men lying in their bunks were taken from living to eternal sleep with but the briefest nightmare transition. . . . Only one man among them, Collins, the Negro steward, suffered a little longer. He was awake, having faithfully resumed his medical studies instead of seeking sleep when the action was over, and now looked up from the delicate sketch he was making of the human heart, meeting death in full consciousness as he was probing the mysteries of life.

But even in her death throes the *Bedford*'s intricate automation systems were attempting to function and save her. In the forward part, which remained afloat and still slicing through the waves at nearly twenty knots, fire alarms were clanging with a feeble din compared to the uproar of explosions. Automatic watertight doors were activated by their miraculous mechanisms and started to close, but mostly too late and well behind the columns of fire which were racing through the passageways. In sick bay Merlin Queffle's hypersensitive eardrums were blown in by the shock wave racing ahead of the flames which cremated him an instant later, as they did Ensign Ralston in the next bunk. Lieutenant Commander Chester Porter died in the receiving office with his pen poised over the ensign's Form 28 in which he had just recorded the young officer's nervous breakdown with a certain smug satisfaction. No. 9 fuel-oil tank, only half full of oil and choked with fumes by a clogged vent, ignited and exploded, breaking through the bulkhead to the wardroom, where Lieutenants Krindlemeyer and Spitzer were holding an oblivious and weary post-mortem of the action against Moby Dick; they died trying to think of ways of making their miraculous electronic weaponry safe from human errors. The next explosion, still less than five seconds after the first, took place in a rocket-propellant storage compartment, which in turn burst the armored walls of No. 1 magazine containing two hundred hedgehog depth charges. With a final roar the *Bedford* now broke apart once more, the third piece spewing writhing serpentines of fire after the flaming ball which had shot into the night and turned the snowflakes for miles around into floating rubies. In his cabin Ben Munceford had been gripping the edge of his bunk, his body knotting tighter as each blast which racked through the ship came one upon the other with the sound of an approaching thunderbolt, and now he screamed as he saw the walls buckle around him, then peel away. Ice-cold water rushed in, turned the flickering lights green before extinguishing them, then engulfed everything in a sinking maelstrom of absolute darkness. But Ben Munceford flailed and fought against it as if he could keep up the sinking ship with his own furious will to live.

It so chanced that as the *Bedford* was sucked down into the deep, a part of her disintegrating hull broke loose and driven by the upward force of trapped air shot back to the surface of the roiled sea. Within this wreckage was carried one single man, Ben Munceford, hurled clear before he could burst his lungs in his wild struggle. His ship was gone, but she had left the sea on fire, and for another perilous moment burning oil threatened to break his gasping hold on life. Then the big swells intervened, scattering the flames, extinguishing them and plunging all into merciful darkness. A charred life raft, blown from its lashings but still buoyant, found the floundering man and allowed him to use the last of his strength to claw himself over its still steaming sides. With his body annointed by an insulating slime of oil, he lay upon the raft, his blood fighting the bitter cold with the fortifying effect of the alcohol it had absorbed only a short time before, but with his mind slipping into a limbo as black as the deep which had taken all his shipmates. Thus he floated on a dirge-like main, one hour passing, then another, until a gray dawn finally overtook the night. The unharming Greenland sharks glided by as if with padlocks on their mouths; the savage skua gulls sailed with sheathed beaks. On the fourth hour a ship drew near, nearer, and picked him up at last. It was the devious cruising *Novo Sibirsk,* who, in her retracing search after her missing children, found only another orphan.

CHARTER BOOKS—The best in mystery and suspense!
JOHN CREASEY

"Consistently the most satisfying of mystery novelists."
—The New York Post

☐ **A SPLINTER OF GLASS**   77800-3 $1.50
A tiny clue was all Superintendent West had to solve a huge gold theft—and a murder.

☐ **THEFT OF MAGNA CARTA**   80554-X $1.50
Scotland Yard searches for international thieves before a priceless treasure vanishes.

CHARTER BOOKS—The best in guides for healthier living!

☐ **INSTANT HEALTH THE NATURE WAY**   37079-9 $1.50
Put natural foods to work to fortify your body against disease.   Carlson Wade

☐ **HERBAL REMEDIES**   32761-3 $1.95
The classic book of herbal medications, with centuries-old, proven remedies you can make.   Simmonite/Culpeper

☐ **INFANT CARE**   37058-6 $1.95
by U.S. Dept. of Health, Education and Welfare.
The most famous book in America on pregnancy and child care, revised and updated.

CHARTER BOOKS, Book Mailing Service
P.O. Box 690, Rockville Centre, N.Y. 11570

Please send me the titles checked above.

I enclose $_____ . Add 50¢ handling fee per book.

Name_____

Address _____

City_____ State _____ Zip_____

                                                    Cb

NICK CARTER

"Nick Carter out-Bonds James Bond."
—<u>Buffalo Evening News</u>

Exciting, international espionage adventure with Nick Carter, Killmaster N3 of AXE, the super-secret agency!

☐ THE ULTIMATE CODE   84308-5 $1.50
Nick Carter delivers a decoding machine to Athens—and finds himself in a CIA trap.

☐ BEIRUT INCIDENT   05378-5 $1.50
Killmaster infiltrates the Mafia to stop a new breed of underworld killer.

☐ THE NIGHT OF THE AVENGER   57496-3 $1.50
From Calcutta, to Peking, to Moscow, to Washington, AXE must prevent total war.

☐ THE SIGN OF THE COBRA   76346-4 $1.50
A bizarre religious cult plus a terrifying discovery join forces against N3.

☐ THE GREEN WOLF CONNECTION   30328-5 $1.50
Middle-eastern oil is the name of the game, and the sheiks were masters of terror.

Available wherever paperbacks are sold or use this coupon.

CHARTER BOOKS, Book Mailing Service
P.O. Box 690, Rockville Centre, N.Y. 11570

Please send me the titles checked above.

I enclose $_____. Add 50¢ handling fee per book.

Name_____

Address _____

City_____ State _____ Zip_____
                                        Db

S0-AVZ-238

After leaving the Army Paul Geddes practised for a time
as a lawyer. He later rejoined government service, working in London and abroad. He now lives in East Sussex.

Hazel

By the same author

The High Game
A November Wind
The Ottawa Allegation
Hangman
A State of Corruption

PAUL GEDDES

Goliath

GRAFTON BOOKS

A Division of the Collins Publishing Group

LONDON GLASGOW
TORONTO SYDNEY AUCKLAND

Grafton Books
A Division of the Collins Publishing Group
8 Grafton Street, London W1X 3LA

Published by Grafton Books 1988

First published in Great Britain by
The Bodley Head Ltd 1986

Copyright © Paul Geddes 1986

ISBN 0-586-07367-1

Printed and bound in Great Britain by
Collins, Glasgow

Set in Times

All rights reserved. No part of this publication may
be reproduced, stored in a retrieval system, or
transmitted, in any form, or by any means, electronic,
mechanical, photocopying, recording or otherwise,
without the prior permission of the publishers.

This book is sold subject to the condition that it
shall not, by way of trade or otherwise, be lent,
re-sold, hired out or otherwise circulated
without the publisher's prior consent in any
form of binding or cover other than that in
which it is published and without a similar
condition including this condition being imposed
on the subsequent purchaser.

1

To understand all the events of that autumn, one must go back to something at the beginning of the year.

As the first real snow of winter fell, there was a killing in Wimpole Street. At six-thirty in the evening, Max Bevelmann, a medical practitioner with a variety of exotic qualifications, director of the Enriched Consciousness Institute and similar ventures, left his consulting rooms. He entered his Rolls which stood at the kerb, divinely immune from the harassments of wardens, the ignominy of the clamp. Lowering the window beside him, Bevelmann craned his head out into a whitening world to monitor the traffic behind. Then he eased forward through the vacant space left by a car that had driven off moments before.

The explosion caused by the bomb beneath the front wheels of the Rolls astonishingly left his head intact. Deposited with macabre neatness on the area steps of a house on the opposite side of Wimpole Street, it lay upright, to enrich the consciousness of the caretaker there and anyone else who happened to look. The remainder of the body disintegrated, became a miscellany of items for men with plastic bags to tease from the crevices of twisted metal. For this task they had to wait some time. The force of the explosion had lifted the shell of the car on to the railings of a clinic a few doors away from Bevelmann's rooms; it was morning before the crane brought in by the police finally winched it free.

The investigation into the origin of the bomb moved

uncertainly at first. Bevelmann had plenty of ill-wishers. But none, it seemed, stood to profit from his death, while any who might have been tempted to repay past injuries were able to establish their innocence. Only when the police began to take account of faint indications that the bomb might not have been intended for Bevelmann at all, might instead have fallen off another car to which it had been insecurely fitted and become lodged under the Rolls, was progress made.

From a list of visitors to the clinic and other consulting rooms near Bevelmann's who might at the critical time have used the parking space in front of the Rolls, emerged the name of Señor Felipe Baroja, a Basque politician. The Foreign Office was consulted: it replied that Baroja was a former leader of ETA's military wing who had decided the struggle for complete independence of the Basque provinces of Spain was no longer justified and had spoken out against continuing a terrorist campaign. In doing so, Baroja had earned the bitter enmity of colleagues in ETA who suspected him of collusion with the central government in Madrid.

In-fighting between Basques became the preferred theory for the explosion that had killed Bevelmann. The Ambassador in Madrid was asked to consult the Spanish government. His report left no room for further doubt. Baroja, whose visit to London had been for a consultation about a serious heart condition, was certainly a marked man: one attempt on his life by extremist Basques had already been made in Spain and others were feared. He was expected to return to London in October for an operation. Because of his central role in secret negotiations with others in ETA considering the abandonment of armed struggle, the Spanish government had expressed the hope that maximum security protection would be given during his second visit.

Appropriate noises were therefore made by the Foreign Office to the Home Office and the Commissioner for the Metropolitan Police was directed to make sure his Special Branch had its finger entirely out during the coming months.

An uneasy calm descended. After a colourful exploration of Bevelmann's professional and private life, the newspapers, like the public at large, ignorant of the Baroja angle, lost interest in the killing. Memories faded. Even the caretaker of the house opposite Bevelmann's empty consulting rooms finally ceased to avert her eyes when, climbing the area steps she reached the point where Bevelmann's head had lain, reddening the snow.

It was Fender who, one night in October, first caught the echo of that earlier killing. Gazing at another twisted shell of a car, precariously at rest on the portico of a house, he had a sudden sense of re-enactment. The image of Bevelmann's Rolls, caught by the television news camera before it was lifted from the clinic railings, flickered in his mind. The temptation to play with the idea of some connection, unlikely though that seemed, was momentarily strong.

Then the person by his side spoke. Turning to listen, Fender let the other image go. The idea was, after all absurd . . .

2

Twice Antrim had made discreet reconnaissance among the others. He had already been introduced to the majority of those in the age group that mattered; it was the remainder he had needed to study. When he returned to the drawing room, to sit watching Rylance exercise easy charm on the wife of the local Chief Constable, his earlier impression had been confirmed. In this gathering he was unique.

Not that he could be confident of recognizing every senior official who swam in Whitehall's shifting waters. Permanent Secretaries he knew well enough and most of the Deputy Secretaries too; he had met them when he had done the rounds of Departments to introduce himself after his appointment as Director of the Central Crimes Bureau. But his memory for faces was no longer infallible. Moreover, in Rylance's sprawling empire, the Ministry of Defence, there were certainly some he had never seen.

But if they had been lurking amongst the assorted dinner jackets and evening dresses of this weekend junket of Rylance's, he would have known. Coming from a different world, first the Army, then Intelligence, had given him a nose for them. On occasions such as this, officials gave off an *odour*. It arose from a compound of unease and austere watchfulness, from an inability to surrender themselves to uninhibited luxury when the source of it all was a Minister. The eyes were alert for others of their kind whose presence required evaluation, the smiles transitory as vague thoughts of the Public

Accounts Committee floated through their minds. And there was always the danger that spouses, plucked from suburban frugality for a night of splendour, were losing their heads in the pink champagne.

He had needed to give only the briefest of glances at those in the ballroom which Rylance had built on to the rear of the house. They represented a separate segment of the party, imported from the square mile round Harrods for the birthday of Camilla, Rylance's nineteen-year-old daughter by his previous marriage. No senior official would be at play amongst *them*. The others in the house, leaving aside Rylance's Parliamentary Secretary, the Lord Lieutenant of the county and the Chief Constable with their respective wives, divided into three groups – the local hunt, members of Rylance's constituency association and businessmen he had known in the days of building his fortune out of computer software. Only one struck Antrim as difficult to place, a man with a Zapata moustache and disenchanted eyes; the front of his dress shirt was frilled. He could surely be ruled out as well, Antrim had decided. So that was that. He really was the only official present.

A movement was beginning in the direction of the adjoining room. Beyond a buffet, a uniformed platoon of the Rylances' inside staff could be seen. Antrim drained his glass and followed others in. The question that awaited answer was *why* he was unique. Rylance's invitation for him to join a party to the races and then to stay overnight had hardly been justified by the extent of past acquaintance. There had been no corruption cases in Defence of sufficient importance for Antrim to need to brief him personally, nor did any threaten as far as he knew. Apart from a conversation about the Bureau's functions at the wedding of a niece of Antrim's who had turned out to be

Rylance's goddaughter, they had had no dealings. And the wedding had been too long ago for there to be a plausible connection.

He could think of only one explanation: Rylance's move from Defence to the Home Office was imminent and he was starting to acquaint himself with those he would be controlling. When Pagett, the Secretary to the Cabinet, delicately easing one leg across another and raising the trouser crease with thumb and forefinger in his customary signal of an intimacy to come, had spoken of it, Antrim had gained the impression that nothing would happen before Christmas. But perhaps the plan had been advanced.

The Chief Constable's wife was making polite noises about the appearance of the buffet. A surfeit of flowers had been strewn round the dishes. Elaborate things had been done with the salads. He supposed the dazzle, the tendency to overkill, to be something Evelyn Rylance had brought with her from the parties of her earlier life in Beverly Hills. Not that he had sensed vulgarity when she had received him for lunch in the morning, or later, watching her organize the departure for the races. Slim enough to be a model, well but not over-dressed, with hair massed in auburn curls that were carefully untidy, speaking to everyone with the same brisk intensity laced with laconic smiles, she had played the part of the ideal hostess, a formidable contender in the stakes to be champion of Whitehall's American wives.

Rylance himself had not arrived until halfway through the races. He had been kept in the Ministry by some crisis in the Middle East necessitating the mobilization of a contingency force. After talking to the Service Chiefs, he had stayed to record as many television and radio interviews as sweating Information Officers could drum up for

10

a Saturday lunchtime. To Antrim his greeting had been an enquiry about the state of the betting. But as he had moved away to speak to others, he had said, as though of an agenda already agreed, 'We'll have our private talk tonight.'

With loaded plate, Antrim paused at the entrance to the picture gallery in which tables had been laid. All of them seemed to be occupied by members of the ballroom gang. Gazing about for another harbour, he found at his elbow the man with the Zapata moustache. He was nodding towards the conservatory at the end of the gallery.

It was almost empty. They seated themselves among languorous flowers and humid greenery; a fountain played into a stone-lined pool. When their wine had been brought, the man said, 'I don't believe we've met. My name's Warrilow, Hector Warrilow.'

The name was faintly familiar: the political editor of some monthly that had folded, an occasional writer in the Sundays. But there was something else too. A casual remark made once by Pagett was fretting at his mind but he couldn't quite recall it. He was saved by Warrilow speaking again. 'I write Jeffrey's speeches.'

Of course, he remembered now: Rylance's auto-cue, Pagett had said, does it quite well.

'And you?' Warrilow asked.

'Antrim. I'm Director of the Central Crimes Bureau.'

'Ah, master of that mysterious outfit in Somerset Square!'

'Not mysterious at all. There's a plate at the entrance. Our names and pittances are all in the Civil Service list. What do you find mysterious?'

'I suppose one can never quite credit that, even in today's world, corruption in the public service is really big

11

enough to take up all your time. One imagines you're Up to Something Else.' Warrilow detached skin from a chicken wing. 'And then, there's your status: civil servants dealing with crime. That must make for problems with the police, surely?' His gaze lifted: for a few seconds those dead eyes were animated. A typical ploy of a journalist encountered on a social occasion, Antrim thought sourly – putting a question to which he knew the answer perfectly well, in the hope it would provoke a scrap of copy for the future.

'Read the Horsley Report which recommended the setting up of the Bureau. You'll see why there had to be something independent of the police.'

'But although you investigate you don't prosecute.'

'That's for the police to do. The Bureau tell them where to look for evidence. We each understand what the other's job is.'

Warrilow shook his head, simulating bafflement. The trick was not to be provoked, instead to serve into Warrilow's court without delay. 'Tell me about writing speeches for politicians. Do you find it rewarding?'

'I only write for Jeffrey of course – he asked me to help when he heard he was getting Defence on which he didn't have too many thoughts of his own when he began. The answer is, in his case, yes, I do,' He was already sounding a little defensive. 'Having one's lines immortalized in that chocolatey voice is curiously satisfying. You begin to think you're hearing yourself as you *ought* to be.'

'I once met a man who wrote gags for Bob Hope,' Antrim said. 'But I suppose that's a little different.'

Warrilow took it well, even smiled. But they sat in silence for a while. Since they had blazed the trail to the conservatory, it had been filling up, mostly with members of the local hunt. A foursome appeared in the doorway.

12

They were from the birthday party. Camilla Rylance was leading. In a bare-shouldered dress, her blonde hair drawn back at the neck, she looked more attractive than at the races. Notwithstanding traces of puppy fat and a careless walk, she was undoubtedly beddable.

Bringing up the rear of the foursome was a youth in an ancient dinner jacket and a stiff-fronted shirt. His razor-edge collar had left weals on the sides of his throat. The youth's eyes were very bright and his shoulders see-sawed to some private music as he walked. Occasionally he bowed to tables on his route.

'A little chemical help I think,' Warrilow said.

'Perhaps.'

'I went into the lavatory by the ballroom half an hour ago. There were two of them standing by the washbasin. One said, "Sorry, do you want to come here?" They moved to one side and went on snorting as though that was the most normal thing to go to a lavatory for. I washed my hands and went out.' He shrugged. 'I suppose it was cocaine. You have to warm heroin, don't you?'

He nodded neutrally. He suspected that Warrilow was once more fishing for a reaction. The foursome was making a lot of noise at the table it had chosen at the end of the conservatory. They seemed extraordinarily callow. Yet, as he gazed at the sheen of Camilla's skin, thought how his fingers would begin by delicately tracing the shoulder line, he felt a twinge of envy.

'It doesn't trouble your official conscience . . .?' Warrilow said.

'Fortunately, it's paid to concern itself with other things.' He looked again at the youth and wondered how the Chief Constable would have handled it, had he been in the lavatory instead of Warrilow. Judiciously no doubt, not judicially.

13

Warrilow had reached out to pluck a petal from the hydrangea beside their table. He held it up to the light. He had obviously been drinking a good deal before they sat down. 'Of course, it's hardly the most desirable thing to be going on under the roof of a Home Secretary.'

He was not trying out a speculation, he plainly knew what was planned. So Rylance had even let his speech-writer in on the move. So much for the aura of secrecy Pagett had created. 'You see that as his next post, do you?' Antrim said.

Warrilow's smile implied that he was not to be fooled by such disingenuousness. 'Jeffrey has to decide which way to jump over this new GOLIATH weapon first. In the spring he seemed convinced we had to have it. Then he set up this enquiry which has produced these bloody leakages to the press. However, once he *has* decided and it's gone through Cabinet, he'll be into the Home Office like a shot. The PM can't wait to get your present master out to grass. But you must know all this of course.'

Clearly Warrilow was well-informed. Boorish and need-ling though he might be, if he was on the inside track to this extent, it might pay to cultivate him in days to come. 'Do you think he's changing his mind about buying GOLIATH from the Americans?' Antrim asked.

'Could be. He's certainly less enthusiastic than he was. The enquiry committee will go whichever way he wants to push them. But I expect Evelyn will decide in the end.'

He didn't seem to be joking. 'You mean she's influen-tial in a thing like this?'

'Definitely. Jeffrey's political career is *her* career. She makes the decisions with him whenever she can. Over GOLIATH she's seen the amount of opposition that's been building up in the country, and not just from CND. It scares people. I think Evelyn's worried that going on with buying it could damage him politically for a long time. In which case, you may take it she'll be against. Never underestimate Evelyn's influence.'

It sounded a useful piece of intelligence. 'Will you stay with him when he moves from Defence?'

'He wants me to. I think I shall find home affairs more attractive – less technology to mug up. And law and order are very reliable for getting the pulses skipping, especially at Party Conferences.' Warrilow flicked the hydrangea petal away and sat back with a satisfied gesture. 'The move will be good in more than one way. Jeffrey needs to widen his appeal, acquire a little more of the common touch. The Home Office needn't be a bed of nails if you give the punters what they want.'

Camilla's party were already on their feet again, returning to the buffet for seconds. The hyperactive youth had acquired a pair of serving tongs from somewhere. He was making elaborate efforts to draw down the zip of Camilla's dress as she walked ahead of him. Warrilow said, 'She's going to be quite something in a year or two.'

'Did her mother and Rylance divorce?'

'No, Diana Rylance died of leukaemia. Nice, gentle creature – much too withdrawn for a politician's wife. From the point of view of Jeffrey's career, Evelyn is streets ahead. She works at it. When Jeffrey joined the Cabinet her own car was a Porsche. It went the next day. In its place is a white Jaguar XJS with Union Jack transfers on the door panels. Flashy, you may say; but effective. It gets her noticed. Evelyn intends to be the first ex-air hostess to rule the roost at No. 10.' When Antrim raised his eyebrows, Warrilow went on, 'You know that's how she began in the States, don't you?' There was amused malice in his voice.

'A lot of things could go wrong on the way.'

15

'Agreed. But Jeffrey's the right age. He's able. He hasn't made a mess of anything he's been given. He may get jeered at by my fellow hacks on the Sundays as a *Novus Homo* but that isn't going to matter when the crunch comes. It may even do him some good. Just because he likes scarlet linings in his suits and wears the odd gold chain doesn't mean he can't run things better than the old gang. I would say that for the younger generation and a lot of others too Jeffrey is the acceptable face of commercial success. Now that Ropner has thrown in his hand and gone off to that curious United Nations job, my money's on Jeffrey for No. 10 within five years. He wants to get there very much. And if he ever shows signs of resting on his oars Evelyn will apply the goad.'

Antrim drained his glass and thought about Evelyn Rylance. One could envy Rylance possession of that elegant driving force. Her ambition and energy apart, he wondered what she was really like. Sexually adept, no doubt, in a cold-blooded way. If the risk were not too great, it would be interesting to discover if he could sample her. But he suspected that he might then become aware of a core more steel-like than his own. Vulnerability, an openness to pain, was what he looked for increasingly as the years went by. Clearly she had lost that a long time ago.

'Presumably she stopped being an air hostess when she married her first husband.'

'Yes, that was Sam Giordano, the film producer. They had a couple of daughters and then she opened a boutique in Beverly Hills. It became *the* place for Hollywood people to buy imported fashion jewellery. She also moved into Giordano's production company. Before they divorced I gather she'd established herself as an almost equal partner.'

16

'Then Rylance came along . . .'

'He'd known them both quite a while. He told me that he used to stay with them on his trips to the States when he was still in software. Giordano had some interest in that area. The divorce was an amicable affair as these things go. Perhaps Giordano thought it would be nice to be able to take his own decisions again. And Evelyn, having come to the conclusion that she was never going to get him into the White House, reckoned that an English politician on the way up and with enough money to maintain her lifestyle wasn't too bad an exchange.' It was obvious that Warrilow was not over-fond of Evelyn.

A servant arrived to invite them to return to the buffet. There seemed to be enough puddings and sweets to last a fair-sized hotel a fortnight. A lot of them were of the sculptural kind; the centre piece was a swan in ice. They stayed to eat standing. Rylance was visible in the drawing room beyond. He was seated on the arm of a chair, chatting up two elderly females, probably from his constituency committee. After a few minutes he rose and advanced towards the buffet. His smile contrived to convey, to anyone he passed en route, both extreme approachability and a delicate warning that now was not a convenient moment.

He placed a hand on Antrim's shoulder. 'I hope you'll forgive all this scramble. We'd planned a separate dinner in here, leaving the young to pig it with a buffet next to the ballroom. But Evelyn decided this morning that the staff simply couldn't cope with the double act. Has it been too ghastly?'

He didn't wait for a response before turning to Warrilow. 'I looked through your notes on the way down, Hector. Admirable as ever. I do just wonder about the Agincourt bit. Can I really get away with that?'

17

'I think so.'

'Not too strong a whiff of Laurence Olivier . . .?'

Once more he failed to wait for an answer, turning back to Antrim, the hand still on his shoulder. 'Shall we have our few words? Let's go to the library.'

They sat in blue leather armchairs with a bottle of Remy Martin between them. While a servant poured their coffee, Antrim watched Rylance clipping a cigar. He had rounded his lips ready to receive it; they were heavy, disagreeably moist. Yet, despite the lips, the high colour and the slackness beneath the chin, the effect conveyed by his features was not unattractive. It was the eyes that redeemed them. Framed by lashes that were unusually long, they had a lustre and depth of expression that startled. Compelling was the word the newspaper profile writers preferred. Had Rylance been a woman, they would have said beautiful and been right.

When the door closed behind the servant, Rylance said, 'What I need your help on, Antrim, is a private matter.'

So he was not just wanting to familiarize himself with one of his future dominions against the day when he became Home Secretary. An alarm bell sounded in Antrim's head.

'As you may know, I have two stepdaughters through my present wife. They grew up in America but came over to England later. Jacqueline, the elder, is in the process of getting divorced from a member of the Bar who's gone off with someone else. At the moment she's in Majorca, trying to sort herself out. Lauren who is twenty-two stayed with us for a few months then went to live with a friend who works in television – a woman. Lauren has now disappeared. The man she's gone with is a Basque. I'd have no objection to that in the ordinary way. But he happens to be a terrorist. I want your help in finding her.'

18

'*My help*?'

'That of your department.'

He searched for temporizing words. 'You've considered normal methods . . .'

'Such as?'

'A private detective agency.'

'We've tried one. There are reasons why we prefer not to go further along that road.'

'Perhaps the police – '

'I don't wish them to be involved. Not knowingly.'

Antrim shifted in his chair. 'I should like to help, of course. The difficulty is that it would be rather a long way outside the Bureau's charter. Our responsibility – '

Rylance said smoothly. 'The Home Secretary is aware of course I'm consulting you. Since you and I will be seeing a good deal more of each other I should be grateful if you would find a way of doing this.' He paused, smiling. 'You *had* heard I'm taking over the Home Office . . . ?'

'I understood there was a possibility – '

'As soon as I've been able to resolve a particular problem of weapons policy the move will take place. As you can imagine, I should find my position as Home Secretary intolerable if this business of Lauren and the Spaniard had not also been cleared up. The relationship would get to the press sooner or later. I don't have to spell out what they would make of it.'

He was not bothering to use any finesse in putting the pressure on. What the consultation with the Home Secretary had amounted to was dubious: almost certainly not about actually using the Bureau's resources. This was going to be just between Rylance and Antrim himself. Antrim watched the Remy Martin being poured into his glass and had the sensation he had entered a trap. 'You

19

believe that if you can locate Lauren you'll be able to persuade her to break with the Basque?'

'I have no influence with her. But her mother certainly does. She's confident she will make her see reason.'

''Do you believe they're still in this country?'

'Probably not.' Rylance pursed his lips and looked into his glass for a moment. 'Let me tell you the story from the beginning. My wife and I first heard about the relationship in the early summer. All we knew then was that Lauren had met a Spaniard who was supposed to be studying politics here. We weren't in any way worried. However, Lauren started expressing some very radical views soon after, talking of the Basque separatists and the IRA having ideals in common. I decided to make enquiries about the man whose name is Luis Fernandes. I discovered he was a secret member of ETA's military wing, a terrorist. My wife confronted Lauren with the news and said she ought to break with Fernandes. She refused to accept what my wife told her. The next thing we discovered was that she had left the house of the friend she lived with in Pimlico and gone off with Fernandes.

'The private detective my wife employed to try to locate them got nowhere. It's true we made things difficult for him. He wasn't allowed to reveal to anyone that we were employing him or to give the impression there was concern about Lauren's whereabouts. Nor did I feel we could tell him what I knew about Fernandes' background since I'd got the information through my Department. We've now paid the detective off. I believe we're not going to locate them unless official resources are brought to bear.'

'Surely the police –'

'Naturally I've considered them. But I should not feel confident about the security of any enquiries I asked them

20

to make. At present they're investigating a tiresome series of leakages from my office which relate to the weapons policy issue I mentioned. Although the enquiry was supposed to be conducted with maximum secrecy I found that within forty-eight hours the press had been tipped off about it. However, I have another reason why I prefer one of your officers to carry out the enquiry. If Lauren is to be traced, it's most likely to be through her friends. I can't think she hasn't revealed to at least one of them where she is. From what you once told me about the staffing of your department, the sort of people you employ are more likely than the average police officer to get them to talk freely. Of course, I would expect your man to use some suitable story so that a hue and cry isn't suspected. My name must be kept out of it. I assume he would be able to get help from the police and other official agencies without revealing anything. For example, Fernandes' movements as an alien must have been the subject of some record.'

It was plain that he had thought it through. Enquiries by the Bureau in the official world would not strike anybody as likely to have originated with a request from Rylance; he would be getting access to machinery, at home and abroad, that no private detective could use and, moreover, through a secure cut-out. The fact remained there was no flavour of corruption to provide an excuse for intervention. Rylance had no right to expect help from any government agency in looking for the girl. If it got to the Opposition or the press that official resources were being used, there would be an almighty row. On the other hand, there wasn't any reason why it should get out. The enquiry could be limited to one or two people in the Bureau.

Rylance was watching him through his cigar smoke.

Faintly in the background Antrim could hear the thump of the group playing in the ballroom. He said slowly, 'And you are simply asking that we find Lauren? Nothing more?'

'Nothing more. I would not want your people to approach her or disclose themselves in any way. We just need to know where she is so that my wife can make a further attempt to get her to see reason. She might still refuse I suppose. But Evelyn can be very persuasive. In any case, it has to be tried.'

There was no way of escaping without giving a direct refusal. That would put paid to any hope of reasonable relations with Rylance in the future. He had to take the risk and hitch his waggon to Rylance's star. After all, if Warrilow was right, that was where it ought to be.

'I'll do what I can to help,' he said. 'We may not succeed of couse.'

Rylance smiled, nodding his head slightly. 'I felt sure I could rely on you.' He seemed to be offering congratulations rather than thanks.

'Shall I send an officer round on Monday to get more details?'

'I'd rather he saw my wife – she will be more helpful than I can be.' Rylance took a pad from his pocket and scribbled on it. 'This is her private telephone at our house in Chester Square. Tell him to ring her there – no one else will answer.' He drained his glass and stood up. 'Let's join the others.' It was as though he considered the problem solved already. At the door he began to say something about how they might spend the following morning when a bleeping sound came from his left wrist. He pressed a button at the side of his watch. 'Forgive me, an interview with my Opposition shadow is coming up on the box. I must see it in case there's anything I need to answer in time for the Sundays.' He eased Antrim through the door and turned. His thoughts were already with the television set in the corner of the room.

A corridor door to the garden stood ajar. Antrim stepped outside. The night had turned mild, almost summer-like. On this side of the house the paths were lit by lamps concealed beneath bushes. Ahead of him, a couple from the ballroom party were moving hand in hand towards a summer house. The girl walked with a lazy grace. Her back was bare and he saw her flesh glimmer as she passed one of the hidden lamps. The man's free hand was stroking her cheek. As they disappeared inside the summer house, desire asserted itself once more. He thought of himself approaching to listen, waiting for the crucial moment to burst in and see in the girl's eyes a certain subtle mingling of fear and lust. He was trembling a little. Aside from the Bureau, that precise image and its pursuit sometimes seemed all that mattered now, an obsession driving him forward on to a tightrope that stretched more dangerously with each day. Ahead lay crisis, perhaps humiliation. Yet the prospect only exhilarated.

He tried to push the thoughts away. Turning the corner of the house, he found himself on the main drive. Beneath his shoes the gravel crunched with a satisfying evenness; freshly raked that morning no doubt. The flower beds beyond, seen earlier in the day, had borne witness to the same unremitting attention. When he went to his bedroom he would experience a similar sensation to now, a mixture of melancholy and jealousy, as his gaze moved from bed linen to silk-lined walls, from the spun-crystal lamp beside the bed to the oak-table bearing the bowl of old roses, the bottle of mineral water and the cut-glass tumbler. Rylance's wealth had created something he had once had in his own grasp and then lost. During his marriage to Juliet, with injections from her trust fund, he had fashioned a perfect small country house out of a draughty ruin, had entertained with almost equal style, had even begun to think of abandoning the Bureau to behave like a gentleman farmer. But he had reckoned without Juliet deciding, as she moved into resentful middle age, to take umbrage at his *affaires*. She had divorced him, taken instead an Irishman met at a point-to-point who was more willing to forego adultery in exchange for such comfortable board and keep. So he had lost the house, filched by Juliet's lawyers in a settlement that left him the flat in Harley Street, the Aston Martin and precious little else. From the windows of the flat, watching the consultants step spryly from their limousines to greet the latest batch of punters from Kuwait and Bahrein, he would sometimes wonder if the houses they were creating with all that loot were as his had been.

In the distance he heard voices; someone called out that Charles had fallen down the ha ha. He could see a gleam of shirt fronts moving on the edge of the formal garden. A girl sang a few bars of a song he didn't know. He was beginning to feel old and irrelevant which was surely ridiculous in his mid-forties. Before the shirt fronts could reach him, he went back to the house in search of a drink.

From an armchair in the drawing room, too near to be ignored as he passed, Warrilow called his name. 'Business disposed of?'

It was getting on his nerves, being treated by Warrilow as though they were equals. 'Yes.'

'Not a corruption case in the Ministry to add to the other horrors? Are you putting your ferets in?' He was blatantly fishing.

24

'Nothing like that.'

'Jeffrey hasn't reappeared. I'd hoped for a few humble words myself.'

'He stayed to watch his Opposition spokesman on TV.'

'Ah,' Warrilow settled back in his armchair. He was on his way to getting completely drunk, the outward corners of the eyes more downturned than ever. 'He never stops. That's what gives him the edge over the others. He's going to make No. 10 all right.' He looked up at Antrim lazily. 'I hope you were able to help.'

His expression was sardonic. It occurred to Antrim to wonder if Warrilow had really guessed what Rylance had been talking about. Perhaps he was in the secret. That would be disturbing. He took cover, so far as he could. 'Just advice,' he said. 'Nothing more.'

3

Mansell heard the door of his office swing open, far enough to jar the filing cabinet that stood behind. Without raising his eyes, he knew with absolute certainty who his visitor was. Eighteen months of Antrim as Director of the Bureau left no room for doubt.

Over the extra gin he now prescribed himself before lunch, Mansell sometimes dwelt on the passing of courtesy. Long gone the days of Lorimount, the Bureau's first Director, telephoning to enquire if he would find it convenient to step along for a few words. He had never appreciated at the time the gentle stroking applied by Lorimount when introducing Mansell to visitors: my Head of Personnel . . . vital job in a Department of this kind . . . always like to get his view. Soft soap of course; moreover it had to be acknowledged that in Lorimount's last years, a failing nerve and anxiety to postpone the moment of decision had meant getting a view from virtually everyone, down to the office cleaners. Yet those emollient touches had eased the daily grind. Now, with Antrim's elevation, all that had vanished, along with men raising hats in greeting and women being graceful when offered seats on the Underground.

Stubbornly he went on reading papers until Antrim spoke his name. Then he lifted his head and fashioned a sort of smile. 'Good weekend?'

'Pleasant enough.'

Antrim seated himself and took out a cheroot. In his double-breasted waistcoat and high-collared shirt with its repellent mauve stripes, he seemed to Mansell the antithesis of what an official should look like. Of course, he had come from Intelligence. Perhaps in the grey world, dandyism was the consolation for being faceless.

'Rylance's wife is always written up as very attractive. Is she?'

Antrim flicked at a speck of fluff on his sleeve. 'I wasn't over-impressed. I preferred what I saw of Rylance's daughter from his first marriage. Still very young – but she has something.'

Mansell watched Antrim's eyes following the smoke from his cheroot and knew he was thinking about the Something. At the time his marriage was foundering, it had seemed he could think of nothing else. He had cut a swathe through the secretaries, then lifted his sights to Antonia Strachan who had had the misfortune to be working alongside him on a case. She had just escaped making a mess of her life, but only just. Since his appointment as Director of the Bureau, the goatishness had not been so evident. Perhaps he had external arrangements to satisfy tastes that by some accounts had become both specialized and alarming. But the disagreeable possibility remained that on Mansell's desk one day would appear instructions to transfer to Antrim's private office in some nebulous capacity a tasty morsel glimpsed at a typewriter or in the gold fish bowl of the Registry. Returning home to Twickenham and reaching for the whisky bottle that night, he would have to announce: now I have become Antrim's ponce.

He left his desk and seated himself in the armchair opposite Antrim. 'Who else was there from Whitehall?'

'Just Yates, his Parliamentary Secretary. No officials.' When Mansell raised his eyebrows, Antrim went on, 'Rylance invited me because he wanted to discuss something away from his office, an enquiry he needs carrying out. He felt we would handle it more discreetly than anyone else. It's rather personal.'

'Does that mean it isn't official?'

'In a way. But it could have serious official implications. I've no doubt we have to help. In any case Rylance's goodwill is going to be important to us in the future.'

There was clearly an inner meaning to the reference to Rylance's goodwill but he courted a rebuff if he enquired what it was. Antrim was about to embark, not for the first time, on something that would take him outside the Bureau's charter. He sighed silently.

'I need a good officer to work full-time on it.' Antrim said. 'I've decided to use Egerton. Perhaps you'll arrange to make him available.'

At moments like this, with not even a pretence of consultation by Antrim, he had learned to show no annoyance. 'Any special reason?'

'He seems bright. And he has the sort of social background I want. He should go down all right with Rylance and the other people he'll have to meet.'

Mansell smiled agreeably, searching him mind for ways of making Antrim uneasy. 'I can understand your being tempted to take a risk with him.'

'Risk?'

'I was thinking of his newness. It's less than eighteen months since we recruited him. You'll remember we took him on in rather a hurry. Because his experience matched what we needed on the Beynon case, you decided we wouldn't wait for all the usual enquiries into his background.'

'*I* decided?'

'Yes.'

'When?'

'After the selection board meeting, you said we should rely on the personal referees he'd provided together with the very favourable employer's report. Apart from confirming his academic qualifications we didn't go any further into his background.'

Antrim raised a hand, brushing it all aside. 'He's given no cause for worry since, has he?'

'No.'

'Well, then . . .?'

'It's simply that we still don't know him particularly well – he hasn't been given enough exposure. This is obviously a delicate case. Can we be sure he's right for it?'

'I see no reason why he shouldn't be. After all, when Antonia Strachan went to Rome with Ludo Fender, Egerton took on a good deal of her work. His performance was perfectly adequate.'

'Bryant was keeping an eye on the section.'

'The fact is, he was satisfactory.'

It was time to switch horses. 'The other thing that occurs to me is that the Beynon case is virtually ready to be handed over to the police. It's very intricate financial stuff. No one else has the facts at his finger tips.'

'He can't have been doing the case totally on his own.'

'The detailed work had been almost all his. I gather it's so complicated, it will take the best part of a week briefing the police.'

Antrim was silent. Knees crossed, he had begun to move a foot up and down. He was either accepting the need to think again or working up to his refusal-to-be-thwarted act. Mansell began. 'If I might make a suggestion – Gilmour who's back from sick leave would – ' But Antrim was already speaking again.

'Antonia will have to work up the financial detail herself. If she needs help, put somebody in, Gilmour if

29

you like. It's Egerton I want. Apart from his other qualities, I remember an American connection in his c.v. It could be helpful.'

Mansell rose and went to call up Egerton's record on his VDU screen. He had not really expected to win, had only gone through the motions of arguing in the interests of self respect. Irritatingly he couldn't now remember what the American connection had been.

Antrim crossed to watch the screen with him, grunted with satisfaction when it told its tale. Resigning from the merchant bankers who had been his employers since he had come down from Oxford, Egerton had spent the nine months before joining the Bureau in the United States. Mansell now recalled him describing it at his selection board. There had been a cousin in New York, the younger son of a peer who had made a success in American advertising and settled down there. Egerton had gone out to stay with him. He had thought he might join the cousin's company. But it hadn't worked out.

Antrim said, 'There's an American angle to the enquiry. The experience could give him an edge.'

'It doesn't seem to have amounted to much.'

'That doesn't worry me.'

Mansell switched off the VDU and sat down. 'How long is this enquiry likely to take? For staff planning purposes, I'd like to be given some idea what it amounts to.'

Antrim was already moving towards the door. He said over his shoulder, 'Sorry, Andrew, it's really very delicate. You'll just have to accept Egerton's off strength for as long as Rylance needs him.' He paused by the mirror above the filing cabinet. He was inspecting grey hairs sprouting among the gold. 'I'd better see him over lunch since I've appointments for the rest of the morning. Tell him to contact Baxter to find out what time I want him at the club.' He didn't close the door behind him.

30

Mansell sat and stared silently through the gap. When his secretary appeared and began to shut the door, he said, 'That man . . .'

She nodded, knowing the play backwards by now. Going to the cupboard under the bookcase she took out the bottle of gin. 'Don't take it so personally.'

She was irritatingly sensible of course. 'Get yourself a glass,' he said.

The great silver egg that was the roast meat trolley had arrived at the table. As Antrim turned to examine the joint, Egerton let his eyes wander to the long windows of the dining room. A few leaves from the plane tree in the corner of the courtyard outside had floated down to the white painted tables and chairs. It was still just warm enough to sit outside in comfort. At a table near the fountain in the courtyard's centre, a family party were having drinks before their lunch, parents and two daughters. The father couldn't be anything other than a retired soldier. The daughters were still schoolgirls; they looked about them hopefully for handsome youths and saw none.

The atmosphere was quieter, duller, than Egerton had expected of Antrim's choice of club. The little he had seen and heard of him since arriving in the Bureau suggested a taste for more modish surroundings. But perhaps the choice hadn't reflected inclination but had been part of a game of displaying *gravitas*, reassuring those in Whitehall with whom he dealt that ostentatious clothes and a taste for fast cars didn't mean a basic unreliability.

It would be interesting to know at what point he had decided he should begin sending that signal out. Long before he became Director presumably. Perhaps as early as Egerton's own age he had laid in this membership, like

31

a case of good wine maturing for the future, to be produced at the right time as an emblem of taste and sound judgement. If he wanted to emulate Antrim, he ought to be thinking of doing the same, collecting credentials like this to add to the other cards of identity.

The silver egg moved on. Sipping claret Antrim said, 'So that is what I want you to do. I take it you see no difficulty in handing over your present work straight away.'

He knew enough about Antrim to understand he should see nothing of the kind. 'I'm sure in a couple of days – '

'No, not a couple of days, I want you to start this afternoon.'

'My section head – '

'Antonia Strachan will have been told by Personnel this morning that you're off all other work. She'll have some-one else posted in if necessary.'

'May I talk to her about this?'

'I suppose you may need to take advice occasionally . . . All right, you can talk to her. But to no one else. And you report only to me. Understood?'

Egerton nodded. He was still trying to come to terms with the surprise of having been chosen for this task. Hardly any of his colleagues in the Bureau had as exiguous a track record. In the Beynon case he felt he had performed well enough, albeit with Antonia Strachan always at his elbow. But he had reconciled himself to several years of working for others before being let loose on as delicate an enquiry as this. 'When I ask the police and other departments for help, you say I must conceal I'm interested in the girl. There's to be no exception to that?'

'None. You ask about Fernandes. Never her.'

'He'll seem an unlikely target for the Bureau.'

'If you're challenged, you'll have to think of something that makes him likely, won't you?'

The curtness of response shook him out of his mild euphoria. Antrim went on, 'You'll also need a good cover story for use when you're talking to the girl's friends and other people who might know where she's gone. They mustn't know you work for the Bureau or that there's any search on. Settle the story with Antonia Strachan.'

Someone en route to a round table in the centre of the room, which seemed to be for unaccompanied lunchers, paused and talked to Antrim about some meeting they had attended together. He eavesdropped for a while but gave up trying to understand in the face of jargon so heavily laced with nicknames. Presumably this was how Antrim spent most lunch times, exchanging Whitehall gossip over prime cuts and claret. He had been greeted by the head waiter as someone special; the waitress who served their vegetables had asked tenderly after his health. To be cosseted in this handsome room for an hour or so each day seemed agreeable consolation for whatever the burdens of office might be.

The man who had paused made some wry parting comment and went to his seat. Antrim glanced at his watch and summoned the cheese trolley. Over Stilton his gaze wandered, mostly in the direction of the women in the room. Now that he had delivered his instructions, small talk with Egerton evidently had no appeal. He raised only one topic before their meal ended, asking if Egerton had met anyone from California during his stay in America.

'I don't remember doing so.'

'Mrs Rylance is a Californian. It's important that you get on with her. Some of the girl's friends you'll need to talk to will probably be American as well.' He snapped a

33

cheese biscuit between his fingers. 'Didn't you travel about the States while you were there?'

'No.'

'Why was that?'

'I didn't have the opportunity.'

'In *nine months*?' Antrim's eyebrows were raised.

He felt himself going cold. 'I was unwell for part of the time.'

'So where *did* you go apart from New York?'

'Minnesota.'

For a second or two there seemed a danger that Antrim might go on with the questioning, but then he glanced again at his watch. 'We'll have to miss coffee. I've a meeting.' He rose.

Following in Antrim's wake as they left the room, Egerton fought back the tension. His skin crawled in the old way, though not, thank God, for the same reasons. The probing about the States had been a moment of truth somehow evaded ever since his recruitment. Next time, there might be no escape.

4

'Today?'

Antonia Strachan raised her arms towards the ceiling in a gesture that mingled outrage with imprecation. She lay back in her chair. 'I don't believe it.'

Egerton said, 'I think Personnel were supposed to have told you this morning. He made the point that you'd get someone else posted in, if necessary.'

'Golden Boy's promises have a way of evaporating when put to the test.' She sat forward again, shaking her head. 'Forget what I just said.'

He smiled. 'I didn't know he was called that.'

'I happened to meet a woman last summer who'd known him when he worked in Intelligence. Apparently that was his name there.'

'About the Beynon case. I could stay on in the evenings – '

She was shaking her head again in resignation this time. 'Don't worry, we'll manage. I'm glad he's given you the job. I'm sure you'll do it well. Just be careful though.'

He was uncertain how to interpret the cautionary words. 'It doesn't sound dangerous. Not unless I fall foul of the Basque boyfriend. But I'm under strict orders not to make actual contact anyway.'

'I meant that it's . . . unusual. If it had to be justi-fied . . .' She let the words trail. 'He no doubt had his reasons for taking it on. But don't go out on a limb. You might get sawn off with it.'

'By whom?'

She shrugged. 'Just see that the moves you make always have his approval. Preferably in writing.'

The telephone rang and she turned to answer it. Strands of black hair had fallen across one cheek; she shook them back with a movement familiar to him. She was unquestionably beautiful. Working as her subordinate, he recognized the fact, albeit with a certain detachment. He didn't know her age but noting the faint lines at the corners of the eyes and on the throat he guessed the middle thirties. At first he had come to see that cool, sometimes mocking manner as a way of facing a world that had perhaps been rough. He knew she lived alone because when he had first been posted to her section he had visited her flat in Little Venice for a meal. He had heard that she had been married but the husband had died in an accident years ago. It seemed inconceivable that someone else had not by now passed muster and been invited to know her undefended.

Her eyes had caught him studying her while she talked into the receiver. He glanced away. She was examining him with a faint smile when he looked again as she put the phone down. He had the sensation she had glimpsed his thoughts and had been amused. She said 'Well, that was it – Personnel telling me you're needed for "special duties". I suppose you want to go on using your own office?'

'It would be convenient when I have to consult you. He told me I should do that.'

Her eyebrows rose. 'How flattering. Well, let me have the Beynon file before you get immersed in this other thing. We'll have to go over it together some time. No doubt I'll end up briefing the police myself. Good luck with Rylance's wife. According to the press, she's quite something.' Her look was faintly derisive.

* * *

36

He made three calls before he got an answer from Evelyn Rylance's line. At first he thought a man had answered, the register of the voice was so low. The tones were laconic but pleasant enough. She'd expected his call but had been at some political lunch that had gone on and on. He agreed to present himself at the house in Chester Square at six thirty.

It was nearly five o'clock. If he left the Bureau straightaway, there would be time to buy something for his evening meal, drop it in at his flat and shower before he called on her. Cutting through Soho Square on his way to the Italian grocer in Old Compton Street, he saw the slight figure approaching and knew it was Gail a fraction of a second before she recognized him. She ran the last few yards holding her arms out. They kissed. He held her close, glad and sad at the same time, but mostly glad because at least it meant she was still around.

Two years had not done the things he feared, although she had lost weight and had stopped taking trouble with her hair; now it was an urchin cut that seemed an insult to the romantic qualities of her features.

He best remembered the hair when it had been shoulder-length, although as often as not swept up in a loose golden swirl, from which strands escaped to spill distractingly against one cheek. Then the face – all soft planes and a mouth shaped as though anticipating a smile – had been as vulnerable as now. But the expression had been unhaunted. He had never imagined her then as threatened, only needing to be cherished.

Today her clothing struck him as a grim complement to the urchin cut. Below what looked like a navvy's blue jacket were jeans that ended in thick woollen socks and sneakers. The sneakers were heavily soiled. Perhaps after all she hadn't been dressed so very differently the first time he had seen her, wheeling a bicycle out of college all those aeons ago. But then the effect would have been no more than jokey, lacking real significance.

He looked into her eyes. They were the identical grey of Antrim's, he noticed. But unlike Antrim's, there was still laughter behind them. It was that silent laughter as much as her beauty that had captivated him once. Seeing it again was like having a hand gently squeeze his heart.

She kept her forearms resting on his shoulders. 'When did you get back? I bet you've been back *ages*! Why didn't you write? Only one mingy postcard . . .!'

'I meant to write again.'

'Tell me about New York.'

Some time he would have to admit how long he had been back, find an excuse for not having tried to make contact with her or Julian or any of the others. When he first returned to London, it had seemed the safest thing – postponing the moment of seeing them until he felt sure he couldn't be sucked back into that world. After he had been taken on by the Bureau, there had been another reason for putting it off. He had become someone who had joined The Other Side. He had imagined the expressions on their faces when he told them, sensed the chill that would follow. They would see it as a kind of betrayal.

She wasn't waiting for him to reply to her questions. 'You look marvellous, you must have had a super time. How could you *make* yourself come back? Have you gone into that dreary bank again?'

'No, I'm working for the goverment.' He held up the black briefcase with the official crest on the flap and grinned apologetically.

'You! A civil servant?'

'Yes.'

At least she stopped herself laughing, simply shook her head incredulously.

'And you,' he asked. 'What are you doing?'

'Oh, well,' she said, 'bits and pieces. The last thing was unpacking china at Harrods. But it got rather a bore.'

'How's Julian?'

She stared into his face for a moment, then looked away as though noticing someone across the square. 'You don't know?'

'Know what?'

'He died a year ago.'

He stared back at her, appalled. 'How?'

'Jamie was away for a week or two and Julian bought from somebody he didn't really know, a man he met when he was filming in France. Apparently the stuff had been cut with something lethal. He died trying to get to the phone after he'd injected. I'd gone to buy some food. It all happened inside twenty minutes.' She was being very controlled.

He put his cheek against hers and wished that he could have drawn the pain into himself. 'I am so sorry.'

She compressed her lips and smiled. 'After that I wasn't too good for a while. Ma got to hear about it of course. She and Leo arrived the day I had to get out of the flat Julian had rented and more or less dumped me in the back of his car.'

He managed to remember that Leo was her stepfather; he had married her mother the year Gail had come down from Oxford.

'Leo said I had to go for a cure to a place in Devon. I felt too depressed to argue, so that's where I went. They search your room every day to see if you've smuggled anything in. After a fortnight I just left. Ma had hysterics when she discovered. They stopped my allowance then. I suppose it's not surprising.'

'Where are you living?'

'I've got a room in Notting Hill that Jamie found for me. The house is owned by a very nice Indian from Gujerat. His wife comes up with food sometimes because they think I don't eat enough.'

'I suppose you see Jamie quite a bit. How is he?'

'Getting rich.' She laughed. 'But just the same. We're both just the same.' She took one of his hands and squeezed it between hers. Looking down he winced to see where her nails were bitten back to.

'But *you've* changed,' she said.

He shrugged.

'Have you stopped?'

'Yes.'

'Completely?'

'Yes.'

She was shaking her head slowly. 'How was it?'

'Easier than I expected. Much easier.'

She went on shaking her head. He tried to imagine what she was thinking: he's gone over; soon he won't even understand any more. 'There's a lot to tell you,' he said. 'Come and see my new flat one night.'

'Where is it?'

'Prince of Wales Drive, it looks out over Battersea Park. When I wake up I see ducks on the lake.'

She was impressed. 'All alone?'

'Not quite. I have a neighbour called Gwen. The way the flats have been sub-divided in the past means that we have a common lobby where she stands her pot plants. When her lover from the fire brigade isn't around she keeps her door open to monitor my private life.' He turned her face towards him. 'So will you come?'

He thought for a moment she was going to make some excuse. Eventually she said, 'That would be nice,' but still seemed doubtful. He told himself she was thinking, now

Julian's dead, he's going to be a bore again, just as he was at Oxford.

They fixed on the following night. Looking at his watch he realized there was no time to get the *pasta*; it would be scrambled eggs again for supper. 'I'll have to go, there's somebody I'm supposed to interview tonight.' He chose the words carefully, not wanting her to think he was off enjoying himself in his new world.

She danced a little on her toes as though cold then stood still with hunched shoulders, pulling herself together. 'Right. See you tomorrow.'

As she turned away, he asked, 'Where are you off to?'

She waved vaguely in the direction of Shaftsbury Avenue. 'Meeting one or two people.'

It wasn't like her to be vague. He wondered what that meant. Perhaps she was pushing now. With her allowance cut off and only occasional jobs, that might be the only way she could be sure of scoring. In one of those alleys near Foyles or further down, towards Cambridge Circus, dependent on where the police had last been spotted, he imagined her slipping packets to people who had come up with the cash an hour or so ago.

She looked back at him, lifting a hand briefly. He felt suddenly hopeless, thinking of the risk she might be running in a few moments. If he was right, it meant Jamie was giving her more smack than she needed for herself. Knowing him, that wasn't so unlikely, although he must be aware of the danger to himself if she was caught.

She certainly wouldn't have a shortage of customers. After the first time, they'd know they were on to a good thing. Because, unless he'd changed since Oxford, Jamie would only be supplying the best. Nothing cut, no Chinese. Just pure white Thai.

5

Twilight heavy with autumn dampness was falling when he arrived at Chester Square. He parked the Mini next to a bright red Golf. Climbing out, he caught the smell of woodsmoke from a fire of still-smouldering twigs in the central gardens. A policeman, presumably on protection duty, stolidly watched him mount the steps of the Rylances' house.

His finger had not reached the bell push when the door opened; he was almost pushed backwards by a girl of eighteen or nineteen in a brown leather skirt and shaggy jersey. The ring of car keys she had been holding tinkled on the steps.

He bent and handed them to her.

'Terribly sorry,' she said.

Egerton smiled. 'I've an appointment with Mrs Rylance.'

The girl's eyes had fixed on the official briefcase. It seemed to disconcert her. 'Oh, gosh, Chief Superintendent Clayton? But I thought you were coming tomorrow!'

Being taken for a policeman was a new experience. Perhaps his time in the Bureau had already stamped him with the look of a lackey of law enforcement. He shook his head. 'My name's Egerton, Mark Egerton.'

She wasn't stopping to listen, her agitation was too great. 'You see, I was going to *telephone* beforehand. It's *very* difficult here. Couldn't we – ' She broke off, glancing back into the house.

The accent was unalloyed Sloane. So Rylance's other

42

American stepdaughter could be ruled out. This was presumably Camilla, daughter of his first marriage. She was a pale, almost ash blonde with a pushed forward mouth and freckles disarmingly sprinkled on the cheeks and forehead. She needed to lose a few pounds but there was nothing else wrong at all. He began, 'You misunderstand, I'm not – '

A woman was approaching from the other side of the hall. He recognized her immediately from Antrim's description. Slender, graceful in movement, she had an air of cool purposefulness. Under the light of the hall chandelier her hair was the colour of chestnut leaves about to fall. 'Mr Egerton?'

'Yes.'

'Evelyn Rylance.' She held out a hand. 'Come in.' As on the telephone, he was struck by how deep the voice was. She was in full fig for some evening function, wearing a dark blue sheath dress that left one shoulder bare. Her eyes moved past him to the girl. 'I thought you'd gone out.'

Camilla had reddened. She said, 'I was going just as he arrived.' She glanced up at Egerton. 'Perhaps we'll meet again . . .' Ducking her head in an embarrassed way she hurried down the steps to the red Golf.

Evelyn Rylance closed the door. Turning back to Egerton, she appraised him. 'You're younger than I expected.' She turned on a sudden, brilliant smile. She wanted him to be affected by it and he was. 'But, then, your Director – is that what you call him? He's pretty young, isn't he?'

'Forty-seven, I think.'

'And you?'

'Twenty-six.'

She gave a light nod of the head. It might have meant

43

approval or simply that her own calculations had been confirmed. Diamond drop earrings danced against her throat. The skin was completely taut and smooth; yet she could hardly be younger than Antrim.

She led him to a room with a bar in one corner. He asked for a glass of Perrier. She opened a bottle of vegetable juice for herself and moved towards the door again. 'We'll talk upstairs. In an hour I have to go to a very boring dinner. I need some air to set me up.'

For a moment he thought she meant they were adjourning to a roof terrace. But on the first floor she opened another door. The room was difficult to categorize. In origin plainly a large dressing room, one half of it was still being used as that; the other half was furnished as an office with desk, typewriter and telephone. Beside the desk was a small table on which stood a black box with metal circles on its face. Through another doorway he could see paraphernalia for keeping her face and figure the way they were: exercise bicycle, rowing machine, a bar suspended from the ceiling.

Evelyn seated herself in a chair next to the black box. He sat down opposite her and took his folder out of the briefcase. She had clicked a switch on the box and begun passing a filament embedded in a piece of card in front of the two metal circles. It was clear that he was supposed to stay quiet for a while.

Now that he could study them unobserved, her features seemed as perfect as the skin. Yet there *was* something amiss; after a moment out two, he realized what it was. She had had a nose job and the surgeon had been a little too keen to reverse the effect of what had been there before. A quarter of a centimetre needed to go back before she would look entirely real.

Without turning from the box, she said. 'Understand about ions?'

He had to ask her to repeat it.

'Ions. Active ions get eliminated from the atmosphere in big cities, they're wiped out. Without negative ions your battery's flat. Some people take speed to give them a lift. Ions are the natural way. This is a micro air processor. It filters out pollutants and produces the negative ions.' Apparently satisfied by her check with the filament, she sat back. 'There ought to be one of these in every office. Tell your Mr Antrim to get you fitted up.'

The Californian accent which had been subdued on the telephone was quite strong now, the voice agreeably throaty. Although there was only a table lamp alight she put on a pair of dark glasses. 'What's your first name?'

'Mark.'

'So *you've* been slated to find Lauren.'

'I'll do my best.'

'I hope so. Because I have to be able to talk to her. She's in the process of ruining her own life and maybe my husband's. To say nothing of mine.' Unexpectedly she produced the brief, brittle smile again. 'By that typewriter there, Mark, you'll see an envelope. I've typed out for you a list of names. They're people I know are friends of Lauren. She could have given any of them some hint of where she is. You'll also find I've included the report of the private investigator we used.'

He opened the envelope. The detective's report was five pages long. There was a fair amount of padding, no doubt directed to justifying the size of the bill that had originally been attached to it. The theme delicately woven through the report was that if it hadn't been for the restraints under which he'd laboured at Evelyn Rylance's insistence, he would have brought home the bacon. It was signed 'William Carter Ingalls' in writing that made it plain his ego was surviving the reverse; typed underneath the signature were words which also headed each sheet of the notepaper, 'Certified Private Investigator and Security Consultant'. It wasn't clear who had certified him.

'Was Mr Ingalls recommended to you?'

'He was used by my ex-husband, Sam Giordano, when we suspected a British producer was two-timing us over a deal. He got results for us then. But maybe he's no good any more.'

She had made it sound as though the deal had been as much her business as Giordano's. Although Antrim had spoken of her first husband as having been a film producer, he hadn't suggested she had also been in the business. Perhaps she had counted for something in Hollywood and in the film world generally. He wondered how it compared with being the wife of the Secretary of State for Defence.

He glanced quickly through the list of names and addresses, then at the photograph of Lauren clipped to it. She was a dark-haired, serious-looking girl with heavier features than her mother but a nicer smile; she was holding a spaniel in her arms. Evelyn Rylance said, 'That shot's a year or two old. But she hasn't changed – that's the way she looks.'

'When was the last time you saw her?'

'One day in the middle of July. I talked to her about Fernandes, that he was a terrorist and she'd make a mess of everything if she didn't give him up. She wouldn't listen. She wasn't living with him then, she was staying with her friend, Lisa Husak, the address is in the list I've given you. We had one or two phone conversations after that, I was trying to make her see reason. Then she telephoned me at the end of July. She said she was going

46

away with Fernandes and it would be no good trying to find her because we wouldn't.' She reached for her vegetable juice. 'She was always a rebel. But I never thought she would go this far.'

That somebody of Lauren's age had dug her toes in over the man she had chosen for a lover didn't seem to warrant all that much surprise. But it obviously wasn't politic to say so. 'So you got no hint where they might be planning to go . . .'

'No. It could be Spain I suppose since that's his country.'

His spirits drooped. He could picture himself combing the Basque provinces until the end of time. 'You've no photograph of Fernandes I suppose . . .'

'I never set eyes on the man.'

He looked down at her list again. 'Have you spoken to any of these people yourself?'

'What for?'

'In case they had news.'

'One or two telephoned me early on to ask if I knew where they could contact her. I said that she'd gone on a trip and I didn't know when she'd be back.'

'Perhaps if you had asked Lisa Husak for example – '

She interrupted him. 'Listen, I'm not going round asking people if they can tell me where my daughter is. Certainly not Lisa Husak who works in television and would probably tell somebody there was a story worth following up.'

It was obvious she had a temper that flared easily. But he had to allow for the fact that she must be anxious. 'At the time she went, was she in any sort of employment?'

'She'd been teaching at a school for young kids, Hazlewood School – it's somewhere in Chelsea. The boys wear funny caps and long socks. You'll see from Ingalls' report that he talked to one of the teachers there. She didn't contribute anything.'

'Her father, Mr Giordano, you've checked she hasn't written to him?'

'I called him in Beverly Hills some weeks ago. He'd heard nothing. He came up with the idea of using Ingalls to find her.'

'And your other daughter?'

He saw her compress her lips. 'Jacqueline. She's in Majorca. She had a messy divorce not long ago. There's some sort of artistic community round the place where she's staying – Jacqueline is the cultured member of the family.' The dark glasses made it impossible to see her expression but he was pretty confident it was sardonic.

'Were they close – Lauren and Jacqueline?'

'At one time. But not after Jacqueline married. He's a tax lawyer. Lauren called him a Fascist but she likes to sound progressive.'

'Now the marriage has broken up, they could be on close terms again perhaps?'

'I wrote to Jacqueline. She wrote back saying she had no news. Because Jacqueline can be tricky I got Ingalls to check through a Spanish agency that Lauren and Fernandes weren't there with her.'

He persisted. 'Lauren might have told her where she is but asked her to say nothing.' When he sensed she was thinking about it, he went on, 'Would you like that possibility explored?'

She was silent for a while. Eventually she said, 'Maybe you ought to check the idea out. I'll talk to my husband about it.'

He had chalked up a brownie point. 'That leaves one other member of the family, your stepdaughter.'

Evelyn shook her head. 'You can forget Camilla, they

never got on. Lauren would never have told her where she was going with Fernandes. I don't want Camilla approached or let in on the fact these enquiries are being made. She'd spill everything to those crazy friends of hers.' She took off the dark glasses. 'What was she talking to you about earlier?'

'She'd got the idea I must be a police officer, a Chief Superintendent Clayton.'

'What did you say?'

'Simply that I had an appointment with you. I didn't mention what we were going to discuss.'

She looked pleased. 'If you should see her again let her go on assuming it was something to do with the leakages.'

'I'm afraid I don't understand.'

'That's what Clayton's due to call about. Some papers from my husband's department have been getting to the press – secret papers. The *Globe* have printed the details. Clayton wants to look at the arrangements my husband has for the papers he brings home to work on. Apparently he also wants to talk to me about the study where the papers are kept and whether the servants can get in when we're not around. If he thinks I'm some sort of hophead who doesn't know how to control what goes on in this house, Mr Clayton's going to get his balls chewed off.'

It seemed he was well out of the business of the leakages enquiry. He put the envelope and his own notes in the briefcase. 'I think that's all I need at the moment. I'll go and work out my programme.'

'Telephone me on this number when you have any news. My husband will want to see you himself when he has time. You'd better write your office and private numbers on that pad so that we can get you.'

She smiled pleasantly enough but it was plain she reckoned he was their personal propery now. As he stood up she went on, 'You've got it clear, have you? No one is to know we're employing you or that there's a search on. No one. Don't let's have any mistakes about that.'

'I understand.'

She smiled again as though she realized her manner might be becoming counterproductive. 'I'm sorry. I come on rather strong when I'm worried. I have to get to Lauren somehow and make her see reason.'

He nodded. 'Of course.' She stayed where she was so presumably the ionizing still had a way to go. His fingers were on the door handle when she called out. 'There'll be something good in this for you, Mark. As long as you move fast.'

He had switched on the ignition in the Mini when he became aware that someone was tapping his side window. Lowering it he saw Camilla. She was protecting her hair from rain that had begun to fall by holding a magazine over her head. 'Hullo,' she said.'

He nodded. 'Hullo again.'

'I saw you just as I got back.' It was probaly true; but it crossed his mind that she might have been sitting in the red Golf all the time, waiting to way-lay him.

'I'm awfully sorry to bother you, but could I get in for a sec?'

He could hardly refuse. Leaning across he opened the passenger door for her.

She scrambled in. 'I wanted to talk to you earlier. But since you'd come to see Evelyn . . .' She placed the magazine in her lap as though about to read it and stared down at the cover. 'The fact is I think I've got a clue about how the leakages might have happened. I wanted to tell you, but not when Evelyn was around.'

He began to regret acceptance of Evelyn Rylance's airy dictat that if he met Camilla again he was to let her go on thinking that the leakages were his bag. It hadn't occurred to him that she would once more cross his path, certainly not this evening. 'Wouldn't you like to keep all this for Superintendent Clayton?'

'But Evelyn will be there then. Please let me explain.'

He resigned himself to listening.

'When Pa brings a box of papers home from the department he works on them in his study. It's on the first floor at the back of the house. The door's kept locked when he's not there so that none of the servants can get in and empty wastepaper baskets and things like that. There's also a safe he puts papers in at night.

'My bedroom is above his study. A few evenings ago I was in front of the window changing before going out to a party. When I was practically starkers I looked up and realized that somebody was watching me with a pair of binoculars from one of the flats in the block behind the house. I nipped smartly back and didn't think anything more about it until yesterday when Pa announced that the policeman who's in charge of the leakage enquiries wanted to come and check on the security of papers when they were in the house. Then I remembered Pa's desk is right in the window.'

'You think somebody has been able to get to the window?'

'No that's impossible. But isn't it true that telephoto lenses on cameras can be so fantastic nowadays that papers on Pa's desk could be photographed from the apartment block behind?'

'It's possible. But I haven't looked to see how far away the block is.'

She turned more towards him, encouraged by his response. There was something touching about her enthusiasm for her idea. 'What I thought was that if the papers that got to the *Globe* were amongst any of those Pa

brought home to work on, that could be the answer –
somebody like the man with the binoculars in one of the
upper-floor flats working with a telephoto lens.'

'I see.'

'So you don't think I'm talking nonsense?'

'No. Could you identify the flat in which you saw this
man?'

She shook her head. 'I backed away so quickly I didn't
register it.'

'Tell me why you didn't feel you could talk about this
when your stepmother's around.'

When she grimaced, he went on, 'You could have told
you father, couldn't you?'

'Yes.'

'Why didn't you?'

'I suppose this will sound terribly weedy.' She sighed.
'When Pa took over Defence, a little cove from the
department's security set-up came to the house to look at
the study. He had a safe put in and new locks on the
door. He also decided there had to be net curtains to
prevent overlooking from the flats. So they were put up
and he came round to see them in place. But Evelyn
loathes net curtains, she's all for wide-open living.' She
paused and shrugged. 'At least she says she is. Anyway,
as soon as this security chap had gone she had the curtains
pushed right back. The result is that in the ordinary way,
unless it's getting dark and Pa doesn't for some reason
put his desk lamp on, it must be possible to get a view of
anything on his desk.'

'You're saying that while you don't actually *know*, this
could be the answer to the leakages, but you don't want
your father or your stepmother to be told you suggested
it?'

'Particularly not Evelyn. She's built up this image of

52

being super-efficient, which she is in a way, of being the absolutely perfect wife. She'd *kill* me if she thought I'd ratted on her. On the other hand Pa is very upset about the leakages and it won't do him any good at all if they go on.'

'But if what you've just told me can't be used to explain to your father how they can be stopped in future, what do you suggest is done?'

'I've thought about that. There's a space against the wall by the window where the desk could go and still give plenty of light. Nobody in the flats could see it then. If you told Pa that it had been discovered that net curtains no longer give enough protection and that the desk has to be moved, he'd agree and not suspect anything.'

It was a neat answer to the problem although he was rather sorry to think Evelyn would escape being fingered as less perfect than the image she had cultivated. A way of unloading the story was taking shape in his mind. He would telephone Bellamy in Special Branch, whom he'd met over a case that had involved corruption in the Department of Trade and the export of embargoed equipment, and ask him to pass on a message to Clayton. A source whose information could not be quoted to the Rylances had reported the net curtains were not being used and that long-distance photography of Rylance's desk from the apartment block was possibly taking place. Moving the desk would probably be advisable. If Clayton asked for access to the source, Bellamy would have to tell him the answer was a lemon.

'All right,' he said. 'Leave it to me. I'll make sure your idea's explored and that neither your father nor Mrs Rylance knows that any of this comes from you. Moving the desk is a good idea anyway. Actually I didn't talk to Mrs Rylance about the details of the enquiry today but

I'll see Chief Superintendent Clayton gets the facts. To avoid embarrassment you'd better not mention our talk if you meet him when he calls at the house.'

'Super,' she said. 'Absolutely super.' She showed not the smallest interest in what he and Evelyn had really been discussing. 'I'm so glad I caught you. I couldn't see how I was going to handle it and not land myself in the shit.'

She paused hesitating. 'Would you think it an appalling cheek to ask you to tell me if you decide my idea is probably right – about the photography?'

'I'm not sure I could do that.'

'Won't you try? I wouldn't breathe a word.'

He could hardly tell her he wasn't likely to know himself. And, after all, he needed to do no more than ask Bellamy some time to find out if Clayton had found the report useful. He took the magazine from her and wrote on a corner of the cover. 'That's the telephone number of my flat, you'll get me there in the evenings, usually after seven o'clock. Give me a ring in a few days and I may have some news.'

She studied the number closely as though she feared it might fade away and she had to memorize it without delay. 'Super,' she said again. She was a little gauche, he thought; but there was something touching about her.

As he drove away, she stood on the pavement waving, the magazine once more held over her head. In his driving mirror he saw the policeman salute when she turned to go up the steps of the house and she gave him a wave as well. In her brown leather skirt and white jersey she looked almost edible, a chocolate éclair of a girl.

6

Once only had Egerton visited Antrim's office. It had been on his first day in the Bureau, now no more than a confused series of impressions, like the shifting patterns of a kaleidoscope.

He could recall walking along this corridor with Mansell, the Head of Personnel, entering this ante room. When the double doors had opened, he had gone in and listened to five minutes' pep talk from Antrim on what was expected of him. Hovering outside, like a small fruit fly, had been Baxter, Antrim's Private Secretary. That was all he remembered of the visit.

This morning as he entered, there was Baxter again, a diminutive, all-seeing *concièrge*, just visible behind the piles of papers and files that covered his desk. Do not ignore or underestimate Baxter, people said. Don't let that pinkcheeked appearance, that shy smile, deceive you. Baxter the Minder will drop you in it as soon as look at you. Also, remember Baxter's ambition is limitless. Best to think of him as Antrim writ small; but growing.

'Yes?' said Baxter. He was reading, a faint smile on his face as though some elegance of syntax or inwardness of meaning had charmed him. He hadn't looked up at all. Perhaps he was now so powerful he no longer needed to vary the politeness of his response according to the status of the traffic.

'The Director wanted me to report about a case he asked me to take on yesterday.'

Baxter lifted his head, quite affably. 'Oh, yes, your

lunch at his club . . .' He exuded omniscience, a total confidence that nothing new of any importance could be happening without his knowledge.

'Is he free?' Egerton asked.

'I'm afraid not. The Assistant Directors are in there talking about next year's estimates.' Baxter eyes returned to his reading matter. 'If you'll let me know what you wanted to tell him, I'll see that he hears when he's free.'

Instinct told him that the omniscience was not in fact entire. 'It's all right, I'll wait.'

Baxter allowed him a less affable look. 'Just trying to save you time. He may be quite a while.' He turned a page. 'If you're going to hang on, there's a copy of *The Times* over there.' He was pointing to the far corner of the ante room where visitors were corralled before he let them through the gate.

Twenty minutes passed before the double doors opened. Egerton watched them file out, the Assistant Directors, that body of superior beings of whom he still knew only one or two. They stood exchanging cryptic glances, the occasional joke. He thought he detected a hint of discreet disaffection. Perhaps that was the mood in which most of the meetings in Antrim's room dispersed.

Mansell had seen Egerton and nodded a greeting. He was talking to Kendick, the Legal Adviser: Kendick with the crooked shoulder and pebble glasses and the air of being resigned to catastrophe, if not by lunch time, certainly before another day dawned. Off and on during the early stages of the Beynon enquiry, Kendick had told Egerton disaster was imminent, that by his failure to grasp that what mattered was not discovering the facts but the seemly strands of admissible evidence he courted a terrible retribution – if not from the Attorney General then before the bar of Parliament itself. Somehow Egerton had brought the ship almost into port, fact and evidence stacked neatly side by side on its decks, and even Kendick had relaxed enough to address him by a Christian name, although admittedly not the right one.

The Assistant Directors trickled out into the corridor. Baxter who had been foraging among them for briefs for some meeting Antrim was due to attend next week vanished through the double doors. Further time passed. He had read even the Nature Notes before Baxter nodded to him over the threshold of the sanctum.

Antrim was relaxing after his budget meeting. He lay back in his swivel chair, feet resting in a half-open drawer of the desk. He looked pleased with himself. Perhaps the Assistant Directors had been enjoyably flogged, told to get more work out of less staff and to use fewer paper clips in the process. He waved Egerton to a seat. 'So how did it go?'

'She produced a list of Lauren's friends and the private detective's report. I said I'd let her know as soon as there was any progress.'

'No ideas of her own where they might have gone?'

'None, apart from Spain.'

Antrim raised an eyebrow. 'You got on with her, I hope?'

He avoided a direct answer although on the whole he had. 'I have the impression she won't be very understanding if we can't find the girl.'

'Then you'd better not fail.'

Antrim's tone was flippant, but Egerton registered the shift back of the pronoun. 'If she and Fernandes *are* in Spain, perhaps lying low because he doesn't want to attract the attention of the Spanish police, it could prove impossible.'

'No reason to think that yet. Have you got all your

enquiries out to departments about Fernandes' movements?'

'I've asked the Home Office and the Security Service for anything they have. I'm having air line passenger lists checked for around the time they might have left the country.'

'But you've tied your enquiry to Fernandes alone . . .'

'Yes.'

'What about the Yard?'

'Someone there is ringing me back later this morning.' Egerton watched Antrim lighting one of his small cigars. 'I'd like your approval for the cover story I'll use when I talk to Lauren's friends.'

'What is it?'

'I shall take the line that I deal in antiques. A few months ago Lauren met me at a party and heard what I did. She gave me a couple of Japanese *inros* to sell for her on the basis that since I had good contacts in the oriental art world I'd get her a fair price. I've got the cash in hand and want to pay it over but have discovered she's gone away.'

'Will you use your own name?'

'Yes. If pressed I'll also give my address in Battersea. Then people can look me up in the telephone directory and see that I exist.'

Antrim inspected the tip of the cigar. 'What are *inros*?'

'Small cases that used to be carried at the waist in Japan. At one time they contained a man's personal seal and ink. They're usually lacquered. They can be very beautiful.'

Antrim waved away the aesthetics. 'Do you know anything about them?'

'Enough. My father started to collect them when he

was Military Attaché in Tokyo. I still have one but my mother had to sell the rest when he died.'

'I suppose it's as good a story as any. Let's hope the private detective didn't use anything like it, since he'll have seen most of the same people.' Antrim yawned and glanced at his watch; at almost the same moment Baxter's face appeared round the door in mute enquiry. 'Ring and tell him I'll be ten minutes late,' Antrim said. 'I'm not going to break my neck for some Treasury *babu*.'

Rising to his feet he stretched and sighed. The hang of the jacket from the shoulders told the same expensive story as the silk shirt and crocodile skin shoes. Rumour had it that after being divorced by his wife he had been hard-pressed to maintain his customary living standards. Promotion to be Director of the Bureau had saved the day apparently; but even a salary at that level could hardly be too much for these tastes.

'I understand Rylance wants to see me as well. She said they'd contact me when he was ready.'

Antrim was gathering up papers to put in his briefcase. 'Make sure you talk to me beforehand. You're still working from this office. I don't want that forgotten.' He glanced at himself in the mirror beside the door. Satisfied, he went out through the ante room with Baxter prancing beside him to deliver some last-minute message about his meeting.

Back in Egerton's own room, the phone was ringing. It was Bellamy, calling him back from the yard.

'What's new?' Bellamy asked.

'I've a snippet that may be useful although not to you personally. Do you know a Superintendent Clayton who's concerned with the leakages from the MOD?'

'That would be Detective Chief Superintendent Clayton, may the Lord preserve him,' Bellamy said portentously, 'He's in charge of the Serious Crimes Squad.'

'Do you mean that leakage is a serious crime?'

'Mass murder, piracy on the high seas, leakages – there's nothing between them,' Bellamy said, 'What do you want from Clayton?'

'Nothing. I hoped you'd pass on to him some information I picked up last night. The source, who is well placed to know, says that if the documents that have been leaked to the *Globe* lately were amongst any that Rylance had been taking home to work on, there's a very good chance they were photographed with a telephoto lens while they were sitting on the Minister's desk in his study. The reason is that there's a block of flats that overlooks the house and although there are net curtains in the study they're usually drawn *back*. Furthermore a man has been seen watching the house with binoculars from the flats.'

Bellamy laughed. 'Who's your source – the window cleaner?'

'Never mind. Just tell Clayton my source *knows* it could have happened like that. But when he's talking to Rylance and his wife he mustn't let on he's aware the net curtains aren't being used properly. And he shouldn't be surprised to find them in position if he makes an appointment to visit the house to look for himself.'

Egerton could sense Bellamy working up to another crack about the source; somehow he managed to resist it. 'All right, I've got that. Any more?'

'Should he decide that what my source says could be a true bill, Clayton might like to consider telling the Minister that there are cameras these days against which net curtains are no protection and the desk has got to be moved out of a line of sight from the flats. That'll get over the problem of not being frank with him about what he knows.'

60

'I don't think Clayton enjoys being told how to handle his cases. Are there such cameras.'

'I've no idea. But I'm offering him the thought free of charge.'

'Do you know what he's going to say?' Bellamy said. 'Tell your friend in the Bureau to ante-up with his something-something source and let me get on with the job properly.'

'If he does, you can tell him to forget it because this is all he's getting.'

When Bellamy uttered a resigned grunt, he went on, 'Now that I've made your day, perhaps I can ask you for something. I'm interested in a man called Fernandes, Luis Fernandes, a Basque. I don't have a London address for him but he was here doing some sort of research into British politics until the end of July. I believe he may then have taken off with a girl friend. You presumably have a nice fat file on him because he happens to be a terrorist when he's at home in Spain.'

'What do you want to know about him?'

'Anything you've got. But most of all where he's gone to. If it's thought he's back in Spain and the Spanish police might have a line on him I'd be very grateful for anything you can give me from that quarter.'

Bellamy was silent, presumably making notes. Eventually he said, 'Fred Rivers, the chap who deals with Basques, is off for a couple of days. But I'll make some enquiries.'

'I'd appreciate it if you could do it fairly quickly.'

Before he rang off, Bellamy said, 'About the leakages: don't be surprised if you get a call from Clayton saying he intends to go higher if you won't introduce him to your source.'

Afterwards he wondered for a while how he would

handle it if Clayton *did* act up. But there was no point in getting worried about hypothetical problems. He took out Evelyn Rylance's list. It was very short, even bearing in mind that Lauren hadn't been living in England more than a year or two. Perhaps Evelyn Rylance hadn't had much idea where and with whom Lauren spent most of her time. Seven of the people on the list lived in central London; that left a woman in Cornwall and a married couple who ran a school for handicapped children in Fife. The sensible course was obviously to take the London group first and begin with Lisa Husak since Ingalls' report showed he had not been able to meet her. A call to her home number produced no reply and he rang the switchboards of all the television companies he could trace. Half an hour later, his spirits dampened by denials from every quarter of anybody named Husak being employed, he tried the other London numbers of people on the list and raised not a single reply. One of them, an Angela Montague on a City exchange, seemed perpetually engaged. It began to look as though he would only make progress in the evenings when they returned from work or whatever they got up to in the daytime.

He told himself that physical reconnaissance could hardly be less productive than being mocked by ringing tones that went on and on; Lisa Husak's house might well be split into apartments in which case he stood a chance of learning where she worked from one of the occupants. He put on his coat and took a bus to Pimlico.

Hope began to fade as he gazed at the house from across the street. It was surely too small to be divided, a Victorian clerk's house that gentrification had provided with a colour-washed façade and brass door furniture. But crossing the street he noticed two bells beside the door. He rang the one marked Husak, expecting and getting nothing, then tried the other: Victor Crispin, said the card alongside the bell in a neat italic hand. A voice answered through the door porter almost at once; when he stated his business he was unhesitatingly invited in. At least he'd found somebody to talk to.

Crispin occupied the upper floor of the house. A slight figure in jeans and a skin-tight tee-shirt, he stood beaming at the head of the stairs as though Egerton was the answer to some sort of prayer. '*Hullo*,' he said, 'what do you say to a cup of coffee?'

In the room where he left Egerton while he went to make the coffee was the evidence of what he had so eagerly abandoned, a typewriter surrounded by paper and assorted books standing on a table near a window. A publisher's letter lying open amongst the debris of screwed up notes on the floor offered a clue to the warmth of his reception. Crispin was in gaol with his typewriter: a commissioned book on Trends in the Development of Community Theatre was unspooling at interminable length. No diversion was likely to be too inconvenient, no conversation too inane if they stopped him getting on with it.

Crispin arrived back with the coffee cups and a barrel of muesli biscuits. Making room for the tray, he picked up a bowl of flowers and almost deposited it on a book shelf before abruptly abandoning the idea.

'That would never do for Fred, would it?' he said. He spoke in a way that implied Fred was well known to Egerton and the prohibition must have occurred to him no less forcibly.

He received the cover story about *inros* with a flattering interest and spoke warmly of Lauren; but the extent of his knowledge proved minimal. He had met her twice only. The first time had been when he and Fred had been invited to drinks by Lisa; the second while Fred was visiting his mother in Bexhill and Crispin had joined the two of them and Lauren's friend, Luis, for a restaurant meal one night in July. He had never been told Luis's surname. Lauren had been introduced as Lauren Giordano; it was plain he didn't know of the connection with Rylance.

Luis, it seemed, had powerful shoulders and jet black hair curling tightly into the neck. Crispin mentioned them with a faraway look; Egerton wondered how the absent Fred had reacted to such unbridled admiration when he got back from filial duties in Bexhill. The restaurant where they had eaten had been a Basque-run place in Camden Town. Halfway through their meal they had been joined by someone Crispin gathered was Luis's brother; he had been addressed as Garcia.

Crispin's gossip was entertaining but it wasn't leading anywhere useful. He didn't even have much idea when Lauren had actually left the flat downstairs. He thought it was shortly after Lisa had had her apartment taken apart by burglars.

'When does Lisa usually get back from wherever she works?' Egerton asked. 'I'll try phoning her.'

Crispin folded his arms and looked sympathetic. 'Not much point I'm afraid.' He had a way of pushing his fingers within the sleeves of the tee-shirt and stroking his skin affectionately. 'She's away in Singapore making an epic about World War II with the film company she joined when she left BBC television. They've been at it for weeks. The postcard she sent me the other day said she expected to be away for another fortnight.'

The absence of Husak in any of the television companies was now explained. But that was no comfort.

'Why don't you try the restaurant?' Crispin suggested.

'If you think she's gone away with Luis, it's worth asking there. He obviously knew the owner very well – I'm not sure they weren't related. He might have some news of Luis or the brother.'

The chance seemed slight. But he had nothing better to do for the moment. 'Could you tell me the name?'

'El Portalón. It's off Camden Street. I remember it being a few minutes from the Underground station.'

He was rising to leave when Crispin held up a hand apologetically. He had thought of something else to postpone the moment of getting back to community theatre. He went to a drawer and returned with something wrapped in tissue paper. It was an *inro*. Someone had given it to Fred ages ago. 'I don't imagine it's much good,' Crispin said hopefully.

The decoration on the *inro* showed a fat owl perched on a branch and looked as if it might be eighteenth century. 'Actually it could be rather valuable.' Egerton said. He glanced at Crispin's expression and knew he had to do better for him. 'As a gift, it's perhaps a *bit* ambiguous.'

Crispin was wrapping it up again. 'How do you mean – ambiguous?'

'The owl's the symbol of ingratitude. Perhaps the giver didn't know that.'

'I *see*,' Crispin said. He stretched the vowel a very long way. 'Fancy that.' He stopped wrapping and placed the *inro* on the table, owl side uppermost. From the head of the stairs he called after Egerton as he left. 'Lovely to see you.' He looked braced enough to face even the typewriter.

It was after twelve o'clock. Lunch at El Portalón, together with a little probing, seemed as good an idea as any. He took the Underground to Camden Town.

El Portalón had once been a butcher's shop, the glazed tiles and lettering were still visible each side of its windows. The extent to which it scorned the vanities of most Spanish restaurants outside Spain was at first sight forbidding. The tables were paper-covered, the chairs the metal and plastic kind advertised to stack in piles of fifty. At the back of the main room, a smaller one was visible, past a dusty velvet curtain that didn't meet the floor; apart from a large television set it seemed to be as spartan as the rest of the place. A Relais Routiers sign might have restored a little hope but the only announcement to the curious, apart from the name above the door, was a card in the window advertising a coach that ran to San Sebastian once a fortnight.

Egerton seated himself at a table with a single artificial rose and ordered what proved to be rabbit stew. Most of his fellow lunchers were plainly Spanish. Those arriving after him were greeted with varying mixtures of formality and familiarity by a man who seemed to be the proprietor. He wore a suit that was too large and a white shirt buttoned high above his Adam's apple. There was no tie with the shirt and he was not a careful shaver; yet he had an air, a certain distinction. Moving between the tables to conduct grave conversations, he would occasionally turn to bark in the direction of the kitchen in a language that bore no relation to Spanish or any other tongue Egerton knew. To question him without likelihood of interruption was going to have to wait until business slackened.

Egerton had finished his second cup of coffee before the moment seemed ripe. He raised a hand. Dexterously adjusting chair angles on the way, the man approached and looked solicitous.

'I wonder if you can help me about someone who is well known to you. The name is Fernandes.'

66

The man smiled. 'It is quite a common name.'

'There are two brothers, Luis and Garcia. One of them has a girlfriend who is American. They were eating here in the summer. Have you seen them lately?'

The man paused, considering. 'Not lately.'

'How long ago?'

The man's lips rounded as he drew breath; his expression told of looking down great corridors of time. 'I cannot remember – many many weeks.'

'Do you know where either could be contacted?'

The man shook his head in sorrow. 'Is there some message you might leave perhaps?' Before Egerton could reply, a demand for a bill from a nearby table drew him away. When he returned, he flourished a pen and pad. 'If you would give me your name and telephone number, perhaps one of them will come in. Or perhaps another friend will have news.'

It sounded fairly hopeless but there was nothing to lose. He gave the details then added a five pound note to the amount of his bill. 'Will you look after the waiter, please?'

The man inclined his head as if to say he had known from the start he was dealing with a true gentleman. At the door he called out, 'I shall not forget.'

In a phone booth in the Underground station he took out Evelyn's list again. Two of the London numbers answered this time. On the first, he got no further than Angela Montague's secretary; but when he mentioned Lauren's name there was a pause while she consulted elsewhere. Eventually she gave him an appointment with Ms Montague for four o'clock the next day.

On the other line the voice of a cleaning lady told him that if it was important to talk to Miss Sally Kirkwood before the evening he ought to try her number at the American Embassy. Things were looking up; he checked

Ingalls' report to confirm his impression that, like Lisa Husak, she had also been uncontactable when he carried out his enquiries, then dialled the Embassy.

Ms Kirkwood had a pleasant voice but the going was sticky for a while. She listened to his story of the *inro* cash burning a hole in his pocket in total silence then asked him how he had discovered her name. When he told her it had been as a result of contacting Evelyn Rylance, the answer didn't seem to make things easier. Gradually he thawed her out. She wouldn't say whether she knew where Lauren was but she did agree to meet him for a drink at six o'clock near the Embassy.

He paused in the phone box to review the position. Gail would be coming at seven thirty and so far he had bought no food for their meal. If he picked something up from Harrods he would then be only a few minutes' walk from the school where Lauren had worked. Although Ingalls had already been over the ground there, he ought to make sure he'd missed nothing.

Rain that had been threatening during the morning had become a relentless downpour as he arrived at Hazlewood School. Although it was barely a quarter to four, small figures in coloured socks and blazers were already darting past him into the maws of cars double-parked outside. Fortunately the staff were still there. After two fruitless encounters he found himself in classroom 4, gently dripping on a wooden bench and taking tea with Flora, by common consent the teacher who had been closest to Lauren.

She was in her forties and on the heavy side, with the intimidating qualities of the pure in heart. She accepted his story about the *inro* with an eager concern that pricked his conscience and went on to mention Ingalls' previous canter over the ground as the sort of coincidence that life's rich tapestry innocently provided. Ingalls, she told him, worked in a bank and Lauren had mentioned to him at a party that a flat was coming up that might suit him. He'd lost the bit of paper on which he had noted down the details and her mother hadn't been able to help. Not a bad story, Egerton reflected; less interesting than his own and perhaps on that account better.

'So you've absolutely no idea where she might have gone,' he said.

'Not really. I imagine she's somewhere with her boy-friend, Luis – they'd planned it for ages.'

He tried looking surprised. 'Luis Fernandes? I didn't know they were that close!'

Flora smiled, hugging to herself knowledge unshared, then relented. 'Oh, yes! Twin souls.' She rolled her eyes towards heaven.

'What brought them together?'

'I'm not sure. Lauren had so many interests. Protecting the enviroment, peace – all that.'

'Peace?' he repeated.

'Gosh, yes! To achieve something really big for peace, she said, would be the most satisfying thing in the world.' She sighed. 'I wish I could have seen more of her, she was a tremendous person. We got together when we worked for the Save the Seals campaign. But she was only here for two terms.'

That was all she could tell him. He tried to imagine Lauren and Luis Fernandes together; while she was busy saving the seal, he would presumably be planning ways of blowing up Spanish policemen or whatever his speciality in ETA was. It seemed an odd combination.

He left Flora and launched himself once more into the rain. There were no taxis to be had. He rode the Under-ground, stacked with other steaming bodies, his trousers clinging to his legs. By the time he reached the Audley in

Mount Street where Sally Kirkwood had agreed to meet him, he had had enough of his first day looking for Lauren Giordano.

Sally Kirkwood arrived in a yellow oilskin coat, shaking a flowered umbrella boldly over the occupants of nearby tables as she advanced into the bar. Her large saucer spectacles gave her an intense expression. He thought she might turn out to be another Flora but the attack with which she downed her Vodka Martini pointed to a brisker life style. As on the telephone, she began with a disconcerting degree of reserve. Not until the third Martini did things really improve; his mention of his own visit to New York seemed to be what finally lowered her guard. When she produced a pack of Marlboros and offered him one, he knew she was taking him on board. She snapped her lighter for them both.

'I was afraid you might turn out to be some sort of detective employed by her mother to find her. I wouldn't like to be a part of that.'

He wondered if Ingalls would have passed the test if he had ever managed to meet her.

'You knew Lauren pretty well . . .'

'I didn't see a lot of her but I felt I did. We flew back together on the same plane from New York earlier in the year. She'd been staying with her father, Sam Giordano. You know who I mean?'

'Yes.'

'Apparently she hadn't seen him for a while and decided to make the trip on the spur of the moment. Odd really, because Lauren's interests are definitely not Hollywood.'

'I gather she was keen on ecology and that sort of thing?'

'Non-violence is really what she cares about most. She's

70

gone away with a man who feels the same way. She's a very concerned person.'

He frowned. 'You say she's gone off with somebody who believes in non-violence?'

'Yes, Luis Fernandes.'

'Have you met him?'

'No, but she talked to me about him a lot, about what he wants for his people. He's a Basque, very proud.'

'Basques don't have a particularly non-violent reputation.' he said cautiously.

'Violence would never be acceptable to Lauren. She might be ruthless in other ways if she thought what she was doing was for a good cause. But the means would still matter to her.'

Either Lauren was in for a major shock one day or she had gone to a lot of trouble to fool friends like Flora and Sally Kirkwood about Fernandes' attitude to life. Egerton glanced at the clock over the bar. If he was going to be back in Prince of Wales Drive before Gail showed up he needed to hurry things along. 'Can you think of any way that I can get this money to her?'

She pushed her lips forward playing with her glass which was empty again. 'I know what I'd do.' She half-rose, eyeing his Perrier bottle. 'Are you staying on that stuff?'

He took the glass from between her fingers and made her sit down again. She certainly wasn't another Flora, after three Martinis she didn't look even mildly flushed.

When he came back from the bar, she had taken her spectacles off and was polishing them with the end of the silk scarf she had worn on her head. Her eyes were big and solemn. He guessed that under a brittle manner she was very alone. 'So what *would* you do,' he asked.

'I'd contact her sister, Jacqueline. Lauren told me she'd

gone to stay in a village in Majorca called Deya. I don't know the address but you could probably get that out of their mother. The reason is something Lauren said when we had lunch a few days before she took off. That was when she told me she was going. Something had happened between her mother and herself. She wouldn't say what, but I had the impression that it was the trip to see her father in the States that had triggered it. She talked about having taken the biggest decision in her life.'

'Presumably she meant going away with Fernandes?'

'No, I'm sure she wasn't talking about that. She said it was the sort of decision about which one feels both ashamed and proud. I tried to get her to explain but she wouldn't. She just said with a little smile, "This is between me and David."'

'David? Not Luis?'

'No, David.'

'But who is David?'

'I've no idea.' She lit another cigarette. 'Anyway, what I was going to say is that when I asked how I'd be able to contact her, she said that she'd write but couldn't tell anybody for a while where she'd be. I said, "Do you mean nobody at all's going to know?" And she replied, "Well, maybe Jacqueline might have an idea."'

It was his first real step forward. Moreover it confirmed his feeling from the beginning that the possibility that Jacqueline knew something ought to be checked.

'You mentioned her trip to her father in the States perhaps had a link with her decision to go away with Fernandes. Could it mean they've gone there?'

She was shaking her head. 'No, I bet they're in Spain. She told me Luis was planning to go later this year anyway. By now she's probably become more Spanish than the Spanish.' She burped behind her hand. 'Or Basque than the Basques.'

Her glass was empty again. She looked into its depths as though weighing the thought of yet another refill. Then she seemed to decide that the evening could be faced after all and reached for the umbrella. 'Give me your number, I'll call you if I hear from Lauren or think of anything else.' He wrote it down on a page of her diary. She thrust it into her handbag. 'St John's Wood, here we come,' she said.

When they parted he stood for a moment, watching her move waywardly along Mount Street towards Park Lane. The heels of her shoes were on the high side to be coping with the consequences of four Martinis. He wondered if he ought to have walked her to the bus stop. But then he saw her free arm shoot out. With surprising speed she ran across the street and vanished into the black hole of a taxi.

7

Although it was well after seven o'clock, the snarls in the rush hour traffic which the rain had brought with it had still not unravelled. Egerton's bus ground its way in shuddering spasms down Park Lane and Sloane Street. The whole of central London seemed congealed for the night. By the Guards' barracks he finally abandoned riding and began to foot it to Prince of Wales Drive, sure that Gail would be waiting, soaked and forlorn at the entrance to his apartment block.

But there was no sign of her. He climbed the stairs, wondering if she had forgotten the day or simply given up. In the shared lobby to their two flats, he found Gwen hovering among her pot plants. He recognized the signs at once: she had been lying in wait. 'I heard your bell ring. When I found it was a friend I felt you wouldn't want me to leave her standing in the rain.' It was her hoarse-whisper voice, her stage aside. Confidentiality was not the object, just the appearance of it.

He swallowed irritation. 'Absolutely right.' After all, he ought to be grateful. It was the steady erosion of privacy whenever she took charge of his life that got to him. The mistake, made at the very beginning, had been to leave the spare key with her. But someone had to deal with visitations from the gas and electricity boards, from the builder trying to cure the damp rot in the kitchen and from the only man in England who knew how to fix the Japanese cooker he'd bought with the flat. Gwen, the ever-present, churning out woollies for the boutiques on her knitting machine, was indispensable to his domestic economy.

Gail was on the sofa, her legs drawn up beneath her. She was reading his copy of *Time Out*. He saw with pleasure that the jeans and donkey jacket had been abandoned for a skirt and blouse: she had decided to be feminine for the evening. Even the urchin cut seemed less harsh. Under the lamplight, the pale down along the cheekbone was infinitely tender. When he kissed her, he smelled a scent familiar from long ago, recalling happiness and misery in more or less equal parts.

He poured a drink for her, changed his clothes and went to cook the chops. She followed him into the kitchen and peeled the potatoes. 'I know your secret,' she said.

'Which one?'

'Where you work. When I picked up a magazine from the table there was a pay slip underneath with the name of your department at the top.'

He remembered meaning to put it away before Gwen had a chance to look round.

'The Central Crimes Bureau!' She made it sound the most bizarre thing in the world. 'So you're really a policeman!'

'No, I'm not.'

'Then what?'

'An ordinary official. Mostly the job's investigating corruption in government, looking for snouts in the public money trough, that sort of thing. The police do the prosecuting when it's possible – which it often isn't.'

'Whatever made you join?'

'When I got back from the States I answered an advertisement. It sounded interesting. The man who used to be my boss at the bank wrote me up in a nice way. And apparently it was thought my experience could be useful. So they took me on.'

She was looking into an eye of one of the potatoes, as though imagining it all going on within. 'They didn't mind?'

'Mind what?'

'I thought they were stuffy in the civil service about drugs.'

'I'd stopped long before I joined.'

'They didn't ask if you'd ever been on them?'

'No.'

She dropped the potato into the saucepan with the others and lit a jet on the stove. 'I suppose they wouldn't like it if they knew?'

He shrugged and reached for his Perrier. She was looking at his glass. 'Do you just drink that now?'

'I have wine occasionally. But no spirits. It's part of the new me.'

'*Verboten*?'

'I'm not even supposed to have wine.'

She rolled her eyes.

'It's quite bearable,' he said. 'Honestly.' He turned the grill up on the chops. 'Could you mix vinaigrette for the avocados?'

She sighed, then moved to the cupboard and located ingredients in the intuitive way he associated with her. 'How did you do it?'

'I went to a clinic in New York my cousin knew about. Then to a place in Minnesota.'

'Was that the real reason you went to America?'

'No, I only made up my mind when I was there.'

'And you've never wanted to since . . .?'

'No.'

She was staring, perhaps not quite believing him yet.

'Clever you.'

'It didn't feel clever. Just necessary.'

She picked up the potato peeler and turned it on its point on the draining board as though driving home a screw. 'It didn't work for me when I was in the place in Devon.'

'You have to want to do it.'

She poked him suddenly with the peeler. 'You are so *pi*!' She was laughing in an exasperated way.

When they were eating she reverted to what the Bureau might do if they found out. Her probing was making him jumpy. 'I hope they'd simply accept it isn't relevant now. Anyway they're not likely to know.'

'Somebody might tell them.'

'It would have to be somebody who knew at Oxford. Like you or Jamie.' He just stopped himself adding Julian's name.

She nodded. 'I suppose you don't have to worry really.'

But that wasn't quite true. Increasingly since his conversation with Antrim yesterday, he had reflected how it could seep back to the Bureau through casual gossip. Gail even, although she had loved him before Julian came along, perhaps still did a bit, might be careless just when the ears were flapping of somebody who fed the Drugs Squad at the Yard with information.

As they drank the wine he had bought, his spirits became lighter. She talked about the jobs she had done since Julian's death, made him laugh with imitations of the people she had worked with, and of some of the customers she had served; they didn't get on to the way the jobs had ended.

'Tell me about Jamie,' he said.

It seemed that he was riding high. A grand apartment, a Porsche, a bungalow built for his mother outside Glasgow. Even before Egerton had left for America, the talent developed at Oxford for supplying what people asked for, with the maximum of charm and the minimum of fuss, had been getting him noticed about London. For those in need of his special sort of music, he was the perfect impresario, civilized, discreet, ungreedy. Even, to complicate it all, kind.

He shook his head at the end of her recital. Impossible to identify his exact feelings about Jamie – Jamie who had saved his life one summer's afternoon in their first year at Oxford – who had also helped him begin destroying it . . .

'One day he'll get caught,' he said.

'Not Jamie.'

He started collecting their empty plates. 'Now that you don't get an allowance from home, how are you paying for the stuff?'

'Jamie doesn't seem to mind when I can't. He also lets me have a bit over.'

'You mean you're pushing . . .'

She reddened. 'Occasionally.'

'That's why he gives you the extra . . .?'

'I suppose so.'

'But you're *doing it on the street*?'

'Yes, sometimes.'

'Don't you realize the risks?'

'I'm terribly careful.'

'They're bound to spot you sooner or later. They use cameras in upstairs rooms as well as people on the ground.'

She shrugged. 'If they get me, they get me.' He couldn't make out whether she really was indifferent or was just pretending to be, but the words chilled him.

He fetched the acacia honey ice cream which had been the main reason he had gone to Harrods and watched her

78

taste the first mouthful. Her eyes widened. 'You remembered.' She shook her head and leaned across to link her fingers in his. 'You couldn't know how often I think of that summer. If I'm really low I go back there and imagine it all again.'

He felt a spurt of happiness that she'd said it and a little hope. But perhaps she was simply trying to please him.

The telephone was ringing. He squeezed her hand and went to answer it. A man asked his name and then rang off without even the hint of an apology. He returned to the table. She smiled and went on eating the ice cream. The moment had died. He might never discover if she had meant the words.

Later they sat, chastely gazing at the news on the box. She began to bite at the quick beside a thumb nail. He guessed she was going back over their conversation in the kitchen; the thought that he had escaped the habit both fascinated and nagged at her. She said, as though the earlier conversation hadn't ended, 'Do you know what I couldn't face? Losing the works, not just the fix, the whole works. Never being able to go to the drawer and see them waiting for me, my very own works. Being able to think, in a few hours I'm going to find a spot for you and you'll make the prick and then – whoosh, we're home again.'

He couldn't let her get away with jazzing it up. 'If you're saying it's really the ritual you want, the Japanese tea ceremony's supposed to be very good. And it doesn't actually kill you.'

She didn't smile. He could see she was still thinking about the works, about the impossibility of life without their consolation. Once he had played with the idea of keeping his own works, but for a different reason. They would have been in their cardboard box with a blood-stained handkerchief and a note on which would have been written the exact time and place in Manhattan they had last been used. The box was to be his talisman against the devils of the future, a reminder of that moment when he stood shaking over the bowl while he tried to fill the syringe and people shuffled past to the urinal beyond. That was what he had planned on the way to the clinic, the truth he would preserve to confront the black dogs whenever they came again. Later in Minnesota, he had winced at the theatricality of the notion. And by then the syringe and the blood-stained handkerchief had long since disappeared.

The television news was ending with a report on famine in Central Africa. Gail's attention veered away from her thoughts and became trapped by the pictures. Intrepidly the camera zoomed in on the sunken eyes and shrivelled limbs on the hospital mattresses, waited patiently for the scarecrow cattle to stagger and fall. Great pictures, an editor somewhere had said.

Gail put her head against his shoulder and shut out the screen. A faintly disagreeable odour rose from her skin, breaking through the surface of the scent. He kissed her hair, more in guilt at his awareness and hatred of the odour than anything else. If she wanted to stay the night, he couldn't turn her away. But that meant she would need to fix before they finally parted and the thought of her doing it while she was with him was more than he could bear. Her handbag was open beside her. Unsuccessfully he tried to peer inside to discover if she was carrying a syringe.

Presumably she hadn't had the thought because she suddenly lifted her head and stood up, saying she must go, the nice little Gujerati landlord would have to let her in because she had lost her latch key.

When he dropped her at the house, a gaunt peeling affair in a terrace on the north side of Notting Hill, she said, 'Next time it's going to be a party. We'll go on the town. I don't think you're having fun any more. We've got to stop you getting *old*.'

She kissed him quickly, just away from his mouth, ran up the steps and pressed a bell. When a light appeared behind the transom, she didn't look round again but raised her fists above her head, imitating a boxer's salute to victory. He had a sudden terrible premonition that one day she would be gone like Julian and this gesture of empty triumph would be etched on his mind for ever.

On a chair in the sitting room when he returned to his flat he found a rain-spattered copy of the *Mail*. Presumably Gail had brought it with her. He didn't feel in a mood to wash the dishes. Pouring himself the rest of the wine he settled down with the paper.

On the Show Page a name caught his eye. Sam Giordano, fresh from producing a block-buster in the States, was in London for talks en route to Rome where his new production was about to start. The reporter who had interviewed him in his suite at Claridges had asked if he had any plans to see his former wife, now married to the Secretary of State for Defence. Well, Giordano had said, Evelyn and I have remained very good friends and I'm a great admirer of Jeffrey who used to stay at my house in Beverly Hills in the old days whenever he had business on the West Coast. I expect we'll get together. Of course my daughters are over here in Europe and I expect to see them too. Although we're in different parts of the world now, we all feel very close.

8

Thinking about it afterwards, he wondered how he could have doubted that the man who stepped out of the green Vauxhall as he left his flat the next morning was following him. He had first glimpsed him when turning to watch a line of ducks which had forsaken the lake to stare at wild life in Prince of Wales Drive; the man was locking the car door, a stocky figure in blouson and navy slacks. That he hurried to catch the same bus was unremarkable: commuters, avoiding the expense of inner London parking, often left their cars for the day along the edge of Battersea Park. Only when his figure remained visible in the distance as Egerton was walking the last few hundred yards to the Bureau building in Somerset Square did the coincidence seem interesting. Egerton turned sharply into the mews behind the Square and slipped into the unmarked entrance to the Bureau's garage. From the darkness beside the ramp he watched. The other also turned into the mews. He was walking quickly but showed no signs of being disconcerted by Egerton's disappearance. At the end of the mews, without apparent hesitation, he again turned, right this time, away from the Square. He didn't reappear. It was an odd event; but to conclude that the man had been tailing him seemed excessive. Pressing the button for the security guard to let him in, he forgot the incident.

He sat idle in his office for a while, wondering how best to arrange the day. Apart from Sally Kirkwood's conviction that Jacqueline was more likely than anyone to know

Lauren's whereabouts, the other interesting thing to emerge from their conversation had been her suggestion of a link between Lauren's visit to her father in the States and the disappearance with Fernandes. Since Sam Giordano was in London, it seemed a possible pointer to pursuing the idea with him: Giordano might recall some conversation with her that hadn't seemed significant before. But to tackle him without Evelyn Rylance having given her approval was obviously undesirable. Giordano had told the *Mail* reporter he expected to see her and Rylance during his visit. In that event she might prefer to tell him herself what Sally Kirkwood had said.

Her private number at Chester Square remained unanswered when he rang. It was barely nine forty. She hadn't spoken of going away, had if anything implied the contrary. Perhaps she was out jogging in Chester Square gardens after a breakfast of negative ions and a preliminary work-out on the exercise bicycle. He decided to keep ringing at intervals.

He filled in with trying the remaining numbers on her list of Lauren's friends. More of the London numbers answered this time. They listened to his story with mild interest but expressed themselves as having nothing to contribute on the subject of Lauren's whereabouts. There were references to having already said this to a man who seemed to think Lauren had found a flat for him. None of them offered to take down his name in case they got news.

He moved on to the two numbers he had for people outside the London area. The male member of the couple who ran the school for handicapped children told him that if he wanted to unload a cheque he could find a good home for it. The woman in Cornwall talked about Lauren's sterling character at great length. But she too had nothing useful to suggest.

At midday, having made his fourth unsuccessful call to Evelyn's number, he decided to ring through on the ordinary house line. A servant answered and at least solved one riddle: Evelyn was away in Brussels for two days. Apparently she was a member of a party of Ministers' wives who had gone to learn about the glories of the European Community from the wife of a UK Commissioner there.

Egerton cursed. By the time she returned Giordano might have left for Rome. It seemed foolish to let slip the opportunity of seeing him. Obviously he knew the Rylances had employed an investigator to look for Lauren since he himself had suggested Ingalls for the role. There need be no mention of the Bureau; Egerton could simply say he had taken over from Ingalls.

He looked up Claridges' number, half-dialled, then decided to play safe and take advice from Antonia first. But when he tried her door he found it locked. Her secretary reported she was out until the late afternoon. He went back to his desk and told himself he was paid to use his initiative sometimes.

A female voice with an accent rather like Evelyn's came on the line when he got through to Giordano's suite. Mr Giordano was in conference somewhere and she didn't know when the hell he'd be back. She didn't sound like a secretary, not the conventional kind anyway. She asked him in a bored voice what he was calling about. He told her.

A little interest flickered in her voice. 'What about Lauren?' she said.

'I'm making some enquiries. Mr Giordano knows about them. There's one point on which I'd like to consult him.'

'Are you one of Ingalls' people?'

'No, I'm not. But it *is* the same enquiry.'

She grunted and said he could ring back at five o'clock when Mr Giordano might be available. He looked at his diary: the appointment with Angela Montague was for four o'clock so it seemed to fit reasonably well. Before she rang off she asked him what had happened with Ingalls. He told her nothing had happened, that was why he was on the job. 'That goddamn girl,' she said.

Angela Montague's office was perched high in a block of pigmented concrete off London Wall. Red sandstone was probably what the architect's water-colour sketch had promised, but it had turned out the colour of stale bacon. Egerton waited in a hessian-walled room where girls sat fiddling with VDU's or speaking into telephones. After a while he deducted from the answers they were giving to callers that Angela ran an investment advice service through advertisements in the press; one had appeared the day before which no doubt explained why he had not been able to get through on his first attempt.

When he was finally shown into the presence, he paused uncertainly. With a grey flannel suit, Missoni tie and short beard, Ms Montague seemed to be pushing back the gender frontier pretty far. He allowed himself to be seated in a black leather chair and to be handed a cup of coffee from an espresso machine. Montague said with pencil poised, 'Delighted to meet a friend of Lauren's. Before I ask how much you have in mind to invest, would you care to tell me what holdings you have at present?'

The misunderstanding was laid at the door of the secretary Egerton had spoken to the previous afternoon. Montague tried, not very hard, to conceal his irritation. They were off to an unpromising start. 'I really can't discuss the affairs of a client, as I explained on the telephone to someone else who telephoned about Miss Giordano not long ago.'

It was becoming steadily more unproductive, trailing along in Ingalls' footprints. 'I don't want you to do that. I simply want to be put in a position to pay her some money.'

The magic word softened Montague a little. 'Quite frankly I don't know where she is at present. She promised to provide an address but so far I haven't heard.'

'You knew she was going away . . .'

'Oh, yes, she came and told me.' His gaze ranged over Egerton's suit and shirt. He began to display a faint geniality. Perhaps he was thinking that, after all, Egerton might turn into an investor one day. He said he'd met Lauren at a party soon after she came to England since when he'd handled all her financial affairs. Two months ago she'd told him she was going abroad and wanted an account in a Swiss bank in Geneva to which all her investment income was to be paid in future. He'd arranged it for her.

'So she's in Switzerland?'

'I doubt it. I gathered she was planning to go to Spain eventually but was likely to be somewhere else for a while. The point of the Geneva bank was that she needed the money out of England in a place which could be reached easily from anywhere in Europe.'

'You can't give me the name of the bank?'

'I'm not authorized to do that I'm afraid. If you care to let me have a cheque for the funds you're holding I'll see they're transferred to her account there.'

He clearly wasn't going to be shifted from that. Egerton stood up. 'Thank you. I'll hang on to the cash a bit longer,

86

I think.' At the door he said. 'Do your clients find it a bit confusing when they meet you?'

'Very few do. My service is largely intended for people who can't travel to London.'

'But the name – '

'Many women nowadays prefer to take financial advice from one of their own sex. All my staff are women. They deal with the calls and correspondence.'

It had to be said. 'But *you're* a man.'

Montague opened the door. He had consulted a half-hunter on the way to it as a sign that they were now in extra time. 'I aim to give my clients the best of all worlds,' he said.

Out in London Wall again, Egerton went to look for a call box. When he got through to Claridges, the same woman answered from Giordano's suite. It was obvious that she'd forgotten all about his earlier call. Her voice became remote, she was relaying his words to someone in the background. When she addressed him again it was to say he could come if he was snappy.

Although the air outside was mild, a fire had been lit in the foyer at Claridges. In a reception room beyond, Egerton could see men and women sunk in the *accidie* between afternoon tea and the first drink. On one side, a piano and other musical instruments pointed to a trio having been lately active. A waiter moved silently to and fro, adjusting empty chairs.

The woman who admitted him to Giordano's suite was in her late forties, not unlike Evelyn Rylance to look at except that her colouring was blonde and she lacked the other's tigerish quality. She was dressed in a white towelling robe and wearing high-heeled mules. Leading him into a drawing room she poured him a Perrier from the forest of bottles on a side table. While she fixed a freshener to her own drink she made laconic inquiries about the weather in the streets, the best place for cashmere cardigans and the precise location of Annabel's. By the time that was over it seemed he had passed a test of sorts because she took him by the hand. Leading him to a televison set she said, 'Tell me what the hell this is.'

'It's cricket,' he said, 'being played in Australia.'

'It *is*!?' She shook her head, marvelling, and called over her shoulder in the direction of a door behind them. 'Sam, I'm *watching cricket*!'

There was no audible response. She went on frowning at the set for perhaps ten seconds before her interest evaporated. Switching it off she drained her glass and handed it to Egerton for a refill. It was as though they had known each other for years although not quite as equals.

As he was pouring her whisky she asked, 'Is that suit custom built?'

'No.'

'Sam's ordering six suits tomorrow from some little guy in Savile Row he's known for years. He says it's the hand stitching that makes the difference. What do you *know* about that – something the machines still can't do!' As with the cricket she seemed in the instant to be deeply interested. Then she was away again, walking the room, prospecting for something else that might really grip her this time. Trying a radio beside the television set she located some forties jazz. As she stood back to listen, the door to which she had addressed her announcement about cricket opened and Giordano appeared.

He was naked, a stocky tanned figure going bald on top but with grizzled hair forming a flourishing mat down the thorax and abdomen. He paused, glancing from one to the other with parrot-bright eyes, then allowed his attention to be caught by the jazz. Extending sideways a hand holding a bath towel, he advanced with a little run as though towards a camera, not quite up on his toes, the eyes half-closed. He raised his eyebrows at the woman.

'Don't ask me,' the woman said, turning away.

'Lana Turner.'

'Jesus,' she said.

Giordano winked at Egerton. 'My greatest fan.' He exuded a mixture of geniality and powerful menace. The woman fetched him a drink while he seated himself in an armchair with the towel wrapped tightly round his waist. 'So you've taken over looking for Lauren?'

'Yes.'

'Well, it looks as though you couldn't do worse than that wimp Ingalls.' He looked at the woman. 'When are we going, Joanie?'

'They're sending a car at eight.'

He turned back. 'My social secretary, Egerton.' He winked again.

'Like hell,' Joan said. 'I've had enough of taking your goddam messages. Tell the hotel to do it.' She went back to the television set.

Giordano yawned. 'So what do you want, Egerton? We haven't much time.'

'A friend of Lauren's I spoke to yesterday felt sure there was some sort of connection between Lauren's stay with you and her going off with Fernandes.'

Giordano lifted one of his legs to rest the ankle on the knee of the other. He began to search for hard skin under the foot. 'Is that so?'

'It struck me that perhaps she'd met somebody at your house who could be the key. Or that you might remember

89

putting some idea to her, making a suggestion that she might have acted on.'

Joan called out. 'Lauren wouldn't buy suggestions from Sam, that's for sure.'

'And I'll tell you why,' Giordano said. 'I'm not serious. I don't wear stickers on my tits about the end of civilized life as we know it. I don't bleed for whales.'

'Seals,' Joan said.

'Whales, seals, sharks – they're all in the same bag. Lauren wants nobody to touch nothing. She's making the world safe for Jaws.'

The telephone rang. Giordano looked at Joan. When she didn't stir, he padded across the room to take the call. He stayed standing as he talked, his responses alternating between outraged disbelief and heavy menace. Finally he said, 'Well, you tell him, pussy cat, that if he doesn't come up with the money by the day after I check in at the Excelsior in Rome, I'm going personally to break his goddam hands.'

He returned to his armchair, leaving two damp patches on the carpet beside the telephone, where his feet had been. 'Women lawyers. I have to pull my punches in case they get hysterical. You think I'm too soft?' He scratched his chest, looking enquiringly at Egerton but went on without waiting for an answer. 'This friend of Lauren's – what exactly did she say? Had Lauren talked to her about her stay in my house?'

'I suppose so but she didn't know anything specific about it. It was just a feeling that seeing you, staying with you, had made Lauren's mind up to do something big.'

'Big?'

'Yes.'

'She said that?'

'Yes.'

90

Giordano studied his face for a few moments; he seemed to be trying to make a calculation about Egerton. Then he stood up and drew the towel meditatively between his legs, dealing with a few precious spots still damp. 'But that's all . . .?'

'Except that Lauren mentioned some person named David who may be connected with it. Does that mean anything?'

Giordano was frowning in concentration. Then he shrugged. 'None of this stuff makes sense. She met no Davids in my house. And nothing I said to her gave her a reason for taking off.' He stood up. 'I have to get dressed, Egerton. Did you tell my ex-wife you were coming to see me?'

'No, I tried to contact her this morning but she's away visiting the European Community headquarters in Brussels.'

Joan had looked round at the mention of Evelyn. Her eye caught Giordano's and he winked at her. 'Evelyn sounds like a real politico these days.' He moved towards the door. 'When we were together, Egerton, Washington was the place she always wanted to be, with all those crooks shooting their mouths off. Remember that TV film of Jackie O. showing people the White House? She liked that.' He produced a wolfish grin then threw the towel magisterially over one shoulder. 'You find Lauren, Egerton. Like her mother, I got a few things to say to her. Such as I don't expect a daughter of mine to go off with a goddamn Communist.'

Egerton turned to say goodbye to Joan. She raised her glass to him. 'Come and teach me cricket some time.' It seemed he had made a bigger hit there than he had supposed.

Giordano had the door open. He looked up and down

the corridor in the hope of scandalizing some passing citizen but there was nobody about. 'When I was a kid C. Aubrey Smith once drove his car over my foot. Then he blamed me for scratching his fender. So I don't go for people who play cricket.' After the door closed Egerton could hear Joan's voice raised. She was asking Giordano what that bullshit was about C. Aubrey Smith.

Down in the foyer the scene had changed. Somnolence had lifted. People were moving purposefully, demanding attention at the porter's desk. Evening had brought its urgencies, new challenges for the senses. In the street outside a party of four in evening dress were climbing into a chauffeured Bentley. The doorman turned to glance at Egerton, but only for a second. They both knew there wasn't another Bentley further up the street, riding gently at anchor for him. No glittering challenge waited out there. He was a man who lived in Battersea now, with a mortgage and rates and service charges to pay before he started eating. He was someone who didn't even have a flexible friend in his pocket to take the waiting out of wanting, because there were still too many debts to be paid off from the days of wine and roses and the other thing.

He wondered idly where Giordano and Joan would be spending the evening. Even that vaguely threatening and unpredictable company would have the edge on scrambled eggs back at Prince of Wales Drive. Gail had been right: he wasn't having any fun. When the clinic took away the habit, something else had gone with it, a feeling of expectation, a sense that out there limitless experience was waiting to be tasted. He didn't ask for euphoria, perpetual sunbursts; just a lift to the heart now and then. Since he had joined the Bureau, existence had been like a film shot in black and white. If he didn't pull out of this mood he'd become like all those defeated faces he saw as he rode the 137 each day. Staying late to read files and improve his promotion chances, pounding the track in Battersea Park to keep the flab at bay and making occasional duty visits at weekends to sister and godchild weren't adding up to a life.

He crossed Berkeley Square. The last of the marquees erected in the gardens for a charity function the night before were being removed. According to a poster, it had been something to do with the protection of wildlife. If Lauren Giordano had still been around, perhaps she would have gone, with a reluctant Fernandes in tow: making the world safe for Jaws.

Something about the way Giordano had talked about Lauren and her visit to him had a hollow ring. There was knowledge that he hadn't cared to reveal. Sally Kirkwood had been right in sensing that the visit had changed things for Lauren. But whatever Giordano might be holding back, he could swear he was genuinely ignorant about her whereabouts.

He had arrived at Piccadilly. Standing opposite the Ritz, waiting for the lights to change, he glanced down at a blonde in a coupé that had drawn up beside him. Her head was turned towards the driver as she talked, one arm resting on his shoulders. He was about thirty, lean-featured with thick black hair that needed a trim; if it hadn't been for a certain rattiness he would have qualified as handsome. As the lights changed and the car swung left down Piccadilly, the blonde sat back. In her expression Egerton saw that oddly seductive combination of naïvety and determination already familiar from their meeting at the house in Chester Square. It was Camilla Rylance.

* * *

Walking from the delicatessen with the eggs for supper, Egerton paused briefly by the Mini for the ritual morning and evening check: aerial still intact, no fresh messages scratched on the bonnet, all four wheels in place. Another day when the Indians had stayed up in the hills.

As he felt for his key in front of the entrance to the apartment block, he was vaguely conscious that two figures had disembarked from a car parked a few places in front of the Mini and were approaching. Someone said, 'Mr Egerton?'

Turning, left hand still deep in his trouser pocket, he inclined his head slightly. The alteration of plane made the blow aimed at a point behind his ear less than accurate; so that, although blackness descended, some remnant of stupefied consciousness remained. Hands were reaching under his arms, turning him fully about, carrying him to where other hands reached out to take possession of him. His face was plunged into ribbed material that smelled of cigarette smoke and dust. An engine started and he knew he was in a car.

He felt his limbs begin to stir; it was as though they were conducting their own uncoordinated protest. Dazed as he was, he knew that wasn't wise and tried to control them. Someone became displeased. His hair was gripped, pulled down so that his chin was touching his chest and this time the blow was perfect. Down he went, down it seemed through the seat and floor of the car, through everything, down into total obliteration.

When he returned to consciousness, he at first had no memory of the attack. It was as though he had simply slipped out of time for a while. He became aware by degrees that he was sitting up, his head against wooden palings. Through a mist he saw, beyond a line of parked cars, a familiar sight, the façade of his own apartment

94

block. He had been dumped more or less on his doorstep.

The mist, he was relieved to discover, was not in his own vision; it had drifted across from the lake in Battersea Park to settle on the line of buildings that stretched towards Albert Bridge. A drum beat had started in his head. When he touched the skin behind his right ear, it was puffed and sticky. He held out his wrist until he could glimpse his watch face in the light of the street lamps: twenty past ten. After seeing Camilla, he had caught his bus and gone straight to the delicatessen; he had stayed chatting there for perhaps twenty minutes. That meant he must have spent at least an hour, either with the people who had attacked him or stacked against the palings. Few walked on this side of Prince of Wales Drive at night. Any who had seen him unconscious had presumably decided he was drunk and better left to sleep it off.

Struggling to his feet, he went through his pockets. To his surprise his cheque book was still there; so were his wallet, bank card and keys. Puzzled, he checked again. The envelope containing the list of Lauren's friends supplied by Evelyn Rylance seemed more crumpled than before but that could have happened in his pocket; the list itself remained inside. He could find only one sign that the attackers had searched him. The compartment of the wallet in which he kept his Bureau pass and a few photographs had had its contents taken out and replaced; the snapshot of Gail and himself, taken on Magdalen Bridge the summer of the year they had met, was on top instead of his Bureau pass.

Half an hour later, with the lump behind his ear bathed and most of the filth removed from his clothing, he could think of nothing useful to be done about the attack, at least not at this time of night. Aspirin was already dulling the headache; the idea of calling at a hospital was unattractive. He ought, of course, to telephone the police. But that would bring an even more bored constable round to take a statement. He hadn't got the number of the car into which he had been bundled nor could he even give the sketchiest description of his attackers. Since he was simply going to end up as another mugging statistic in the Incident Book, he might as well leave it until the morning when he could call at the local station on his way to the Bureau.

He was in bed when he remembered how the day had begun, with the man who had followed him on to his bus. Obviously the mugging had a connection. What it was he had no idea. But after all, he had become a part of the evening's urgencies. The challenge had still to reveal itself. But somebody out there was *interested*.

9

He was shaving next morning when he heard the telephone. The time was barely seven thirty. He could think of no one who would call him so early in the ordinary way. Wiping soap from his chin, he prepared for crisis.

The voice was a man's, pleasantly authoritative.

'Jeffrey Rylance here. I believe my wife mentioned I wanted to hear how you were getting on.'

For a second he wondered if somebody was playing a practical joke. He had not imagined Rylance putting through a personal call to him, certainly not at this time of day. Rylance went on, 'I suggest you come to my room at the House of Commons this evening. Make it six forty-five. If I'm not there my secretary will look after you. Can you manage that?'

'Certainly.'

'I prefer you not to say you're an official when you call. I'll tell my secretary to expect someone of your name and that you're a constituent. When you arrive at the House, that's the line to take with the police on the door.'

Delivered in that brown velvet voice, the words did not sound hectoring, merely firm. The assumption conveyed was that clear instructions were all their relationship needed.

Back in the bathroom, he reflected on a suddenly urgent priority: to chase Bellamy at Special Branch for anything he had been able to discover about Luis Fernandes' movements. A report of the results of his own enquiries would sound pretty thin. Apart from the question mark over Lauren's trip to her father in the summer, all he would have to offer was Montague's disclosure of having opened a bank account in Geneva, plus his own conviction, reinforced by what Sally Kirkwood had said, that if anybody knew where Lauren now was, it was her sister Jacqueline.

Bellamy proved elusive. According to his office, he was out for an unspecified period and couldn't be contacted. Several people had gone sick in the Special Protection squad where Bellamy had once served; he'd been taken off his normal duties to nursemaid an Arab Emir round London. The only thing left, it seemed, was to contact whoever was actually running the Basque desk. He went to Antonia's room to borrow her directory for the Branch. She was writing a minute in a file.

'Did you get my note?' he asked.

She nodded. 'You should have waited until Rylance's wife got back. But in your shoes I'd probably have done the same.' She gave him a smile. 'Anyway, how *was* life at Claridges?'

'Very civilized.'

'And Sam Giordano?'

'Not so civilized.'

'Did he have anything worthwhile to offer?'

'Not really. I rather suspect he's holding something back about Lauren's visit to him. But I'm equally certain he doesn't know where she is now.'

He sat down. 'Rylance called me at my flat before breakfast this morning. His staff must have a tough time if that's the way he functions normally. Anyway he wants a report on the state of play. I'm going to his room at the House of Commons tonight.'

'Well, well,' she said. She turned sideways from the

98

desk towards the window. 'And you've told master about this?'

'I called on him as soon as I got to the office.'

'How did he react?'

'He was put out that Rylance hadn't fixed the meeting through him. Also that he'll be away tomorrow and won't know at once what transpires. He's working in the office on Saturday morning and I have to come in and report.'

She was looking through the window, smiling. 'I expect he found it all *very* irritating.'

Nothing in her expression or manner hinted that there had been the *affaire* between her and Antrim that office gossip alleged. Apparently it had happened when Antrim was in the throes of being divorced by his wife. The *affaire* had ended when a Canadian policeman named Muir had appeared on the scene. He had wanted her to marry him and go back to Canada, but she had never gone. No one knew why. Behind that detached, often ironical expression was something mysterious that had defied the probing of admirers and the merely inquisitive alike.

'I need something hard from Special Branch about Fernandes if I'm to convince Rylance I'm really trying. Unfortunately – '

She interrupted him, snapping her fingers. 'I meant to tell you – Bellamy was trying to get you first thing this morning. I took the call since you weren't in. He's on some protection job but hopes to be able to telephone you soon after twelve thirty. I gather you've given them a shock in Special Branch.'

'What sort of shock?'

'He didn't say.' She glanced at her wristwatch and rose, shutting the file. 'Good luck with Rylance. I hope you won't find him in too bad a temper because of the piece in the *Globe*.' Seeing his puzzlement, she went on, 'You'd better read it beforehand. Apparently they've another secret paper from his office.'

He was almost at the door when she exclaimed. 'Your *head* – whatever happened?'

He hadn't thought the lump would be visible through his hair. He told her the story.

'Have you reported it?'

'I called at the local police station on my way in this morning. They were very polite and said there was A Lot of It About.'

'But it doesn't make sense if nothing was taken.'

'I know, I'm still trying to work it out.' He didn't care to admit how barren his thoughts had been. He was about to tell her about the man who had followed him the previous morning, when she looked at her watch again and swore.

'I must go, the man who's lunching me gets very scratchy if he's kept waiting.' She picked up her handbag. 'We ought to think a bit more about the mugging. Could it be backwash from the Beynon case?. We know he hates your guts. You'd better be careful.' She didn't smile as she went out of the door.

In the Press Room he looked up the *Globe*'s story. it was on the front page. There was also a leader, full of high-mindedness about the *Globe*'s Duty to Inform a public panting for its guidance. But the story was a genuinely impressive scoop. It seemed to be based on the summary conclusions of the Committee Rylance had set up to consider alternatives in defence weaponry if GOLIATH were to be dropped. The Committee had said that to achieve a comparable level of protection over the next ten years without GOLIATH would be difficult. It *could* be secured by a further investment in existing weapons but involving much higher cost to the defence budget. On the

100

other hand if that course was adopted British manufacturers would benefit as would the level of unemployment. Some fairly detailed figures were quoted in the story.

Presumably the *Globe* was not among the papers delivered to Rylance at Chester Square otherwise he would surely have sounded tetchier on the telephone. But by evening he would no doubt have been through enough fall-out from the article to be spitting blood. That made it even more vital to have something encouraging to offer on the search for Lauren.

Back in his own office, he wrote up his meetings with Montague and Giordano, reminding himself of Antonia's aversion to purple prose; since he was supposed to refer to her for advice, he could hardly refrain – not that he wanted to – from showing her his file notes. Off and on, his mind turned to her lunch appointment. He felt idly curious about the man who got scratchy if she kept him waiting. Some chalk-striped admirer, impatiently devouring olives in the American bar at the Savoy? Or an aged uncle, grumpily pacing the hall of the Ladies' entrance to his club?

Bellamy came through at a quarter to one. He was speaking from a call box and sounded in a hurry. 'We ought to meet.'

'Fine – as soon as you like.'

'I'm free until one forty-five when I have to be back with my Emir again. Could you join me for a sandwich at St Stephen's Tavern, across the road from Parliament?'

'I hope you've some news for me.'

'I've more than that,' Bellamy said.

Egerton watched him thread his way through the crowd in the bar, a stubby figure in a blue hopsack suit that seemed to fit too snugly to have an automatic tucked away beneath it. He was a determined mover, swift to tap the shoulders of those who didn't shift from his path sharply enough. The word from rugby football fanciers in the Bureau was that the police had never had a better stand-off half.

Egerton handed him his beer. 'How's your Emir?'

'Very civil.'

'Where did you go with him – the Foreign Office?'

'No, this morning was strictly business: Harrods. We bought twenty-five videos.' Bellamy downed slightly under half his pint with no evident movement of the throat. 'I'd forgotten what this lark was like. Let's get something to eat.'

With their sandwiches they beat a path towards the corner of the room. 'Luis Fernandes,' Bellamy said, 'You wanted to know his whereabouts.'

'Yes.'

'The answer is we've no idea and we couldn't have cared less until you asked. All I can tell you is that he flew out of Heathrow on an Air France flight to Paris on the 27th of July.'

'Accompanied?'

'Can't say. In fact there's hardly anything we *can* say about him and for a very good reason. According to our information he's not a terrorist.'

'*Not*?'

'No. When he first came here we asked the Spanish police what his form was. They told us that although he'd been a member of ETA at one time, he'd definitely moved away from involvement in terrorist activity when the present Spanish government won the elections. He now claims to be committed to pursuing Basque aims by peaceful constitutional means. That's what the Spanish told us and appeared to believe themselves.' Bellamy lifted a corner of his sandwich. He wrinkled his nose before deciding it was just fuel after all. 'Luis has a brother however, Garcia, who is a different kettle of fish. Nobody questions that *he's* a terrorist. In the ordinary way he wouldn't be allowed to land in this country. He came in on a false passport earlier this year and although we'd already had warning from the Spanish police, at their request he wasn't stopped. He was going to see Luis while he was here according to their information and they believed there was a fair chance that as a result of the meeting Garcia who is still very close to his brother would be persuaded to join the non-violent Basque movement which Luis supports. If that happened it would have been a major blow to one of the most dangerous ETA terrorist groups. Are you with me so far?'

'Yes.'

'Well, it didn't work. Garcia is still the leader of a murder squad that operates from a base in French Basque country – that's down in the south-west corner of France. So Luis didn't pull off the trick as the Spaniards hoped. But did he really *try* to? According to *you*, Luis is a terrorist himself, after all. Fred Rivers on the Basque desk wants to know why you say that. Did Garcia convert Luis back again? Or have the Spanish had it wrong all the time?'

Egerton hesitated, fumbling for prevarications that would not sound uncooperative. 'I can't tell you the answer, I'm afraid.'

'But what's your source?'

'I can't tell you that either. The information came from somebody reliable, somebody who had the means to discover the facts.'

'Spanish?'

'No, British.'

'This is a human source then?'

'Yes.'

103

'How can you be sure he didn't mix the two brothers up?'

'In his position he isn't likely to have made that mistake. It was definitely Luis he was talking about.'

Bellamy grimaced and turned to elbow his way to the bar with their empty glasses. When he came back, he said, 'I'm told that to date we've been working on the assumption that the Spanish police have good coverage of the situation and also that they've been frank with us. If they haven't, that's worrying.'

'I see that.'

'There's a lot of current aggro about Basques. According to one report Garcia Fernandes is back in this country. It's thought he may be planning some sort of terrorist operation here, God knows what, perhaps he's going to blow up the Spanish Embassy – Fred Rivers seems to have an idea but won't tell me any details. What he *did* tell me was that if you have anything reliable to contribute, he needs to know – now.'

'I'm seeing the person concerned tonight.'

'Good, then I'll tell Fred you'll be ringing him direct.'

Bellamy raised his glass, celebrating the fact that he was out from under; looking about him, he appraised the talent, nodding briefly to someone he recognized, offered scandalous intelligence about a Member of Parliament loudly demanding service at the bar. 'By the way,' he said, 'you've made a friend: Detective Chief Superintendent Clayton, no less.'

It took a second or two before the connection came back to him: the leakages to the *Globe*, Camilla Rylance's story of the man with the binoculars. 'The long distance photography idea was right . . .?'

'It's got a lot going for it. The morning you phoned me, Clayton sent somebody around the block of flats behind the Rylance house to find out what could be seen. It would be possible to get a good camera shot on a desk in Rylance's study window from several of the flats. What's more the net curtains were drawn *back*. However, when Clayton kept an appointment he had with Mrs Rylance that afternoon, they'd been drawn *across*.' Bellamy grinned at the infinite duplicity of man and woman kind.

'What did he do?'

'Had the desk moved away from the window so that it couldn't be overlooked. He didn't say why and it seems she didn't ask either, which is interesting. He's now checking on the occupants of the flats. The porter of the block says that one of them has girls up there to use as photographic models. He gives out that he does it professionally but the porter believes it's just for kicks. Clayton's waiting to be sure his checks on the other people don't throw up any better bets. Then he'll interview this guy, using the visits by the girls as a bit of leverage. Anyway I was to tell you – thanks.'

To be viewed with favour by a Detective Chief Superintendent couldn't be bad. But that wouldn't last if the steer turned out in the end to be wrong. 'When I saw the fresh leakage in today's *Globe* it struck me that the photography theory might not hold water after all. I guessed Clayton would have had the desk moved pretty quickly. But according to the *Globe* the document they've now seen has only just been submitted to Rylance.'

Bellamy shook his head. 'I slipped into the Yard before coming here and happened to meet Clayton. I told him I was seeing you and asked if the new leakage made a difference. It doesn't. What the *Globe* have got isn't the Report that's just been submitted but a draft of the conclusions which the Chairman of the Committee let Rylance have some time ago so that he'd know what was in the wind. One or two discrepancies make this definite. Clayton's satisfied that although the *Globe* has run three stories about GOLIATH, in a sort of historical progression as though they had got each separately, there was almost certainly just *one* leakage.'

He glanced at his watch and then at their glasses. 'One for the road, I think.' He had a rugby man's hollow legs. When he came back with his fresh pint, he went on, 'The stories as I understand it were, first, Rylance's decision to set up a committee to review the proposal to buy GOLIATH and consider if there were feasible alternatives; second, the personal minute from the Chief of the Defence Staff hinting at top brass resignations if GOLIATH was cancelled; and third, today's piece on the committee's conclusions. The papers that formed the basis for all these stories were worked on by Rylance at his house a week or so before the first leakage appeared. All the photographer needed was patience and a bit of luck to get the lot at one time.' Bellamy raised his glass. 'Of course, this assumes they *are* genuine leakages.'

'You've just said they are.'

'The *contents* are genuine. But the question you have to ask is – do the leakages perhaps suit Rylance? The first story will have done him no harm with the public and quite a few in his own Party. It quoted him as saying that no fresh nuclear option like GOLIATH should be pursued if a practicable alternative could be found. In other words, look at me, I don't forget that nuclear weapons are terrible and that the Great British Public don't want any more than are absolutely necessary. Even this latest story could be useful if he's preparing to come down against GOLIATH. Of course he'll stick over breaches of security in his department. But that may be a price he's willing to pay in the interests of softening his image. It's the sort of game these chaps play, isn't it? After all, he's expecting to become Home Secretary soon. Perhaps he doesn't want to go there looking too hawkish.'

The remark about Rylance's imminent move from Defence was a genuine aside, he obviously assumed that the news had reached Egerton. But if it had been whispered in the Bureau, it had not been in his hearing. Antrim's concern to be obliging to Rylance over trying to locate Lauren suddenly became easier to understand.

They came out of the pub into watery sunlight. Bellamy said, 'Don't be too long coming back about this Basque business. Rivers is an awkward bugger when he's roused.'

Turning quickly he crossed over Bridge Street. As he moved along the railings outside the Houses of Parliament, he broke into an easy trot. A ragged column of tourists, bear-led by a guide, was surging along the pavement in the opposite direction, but he didn't pause, brushing them aside like a setter going through bracken.

10

Visitors to the Public Gallery were being herded out when
he arrived for his appointment with Rylance. A man with
a beard and a proprietorial air, presumably an MP, stood
pressing the flesh of each in turn, dispensing farewell
charm. A coach was drawn up waiting to take them back
to the real world.

Negotiating a rabbit warren of corridors with the aid of
an attendant, Egerton reached a small ante room. A
secretary was reading a novel beside a typewriter. She
acknowledged he was expected. Rylance was apparently
with the Prime Minister however; this made the time of
his return a plaything of fate. She sat him down with a
newspaper.

An odd sort of calm prevailed. He sensed he had
reached the end of one run in the rabbit warren; behind
these walls were other runs, other beings, almost certainly
making noise. But here was the stillness of a capsule. Half
an hour passed with a single diversion, a girl who
appeared silently from the corridor. She perched herself
beside the secretary's typewriter for whispered gossip and
swung her legs interestingly.

He had abandoned the newspaper by the time the door
was flung wide and Rylance entered. He tossed a folder
of papers in front of the secretary. 'Forty balls-aching
minutes and I don't know if he agrees even now.'

She gave him the standard secretarial smile of sympathy
which conveyed that it had no doubt been hell but she
knew he'd get over it. Rising, notebook in hand, she said,

'Private Office were on about the *Globe* story. The head of Security wonders if you want to see him again tonight.'

'God forbid.'

Impassively she drew a line through an entry in the notebook then pointed behind him. 'Mr Egerton.'

He wheeled sharply. Although he was carrying too much weight, his movements were very rapid; he took in Egerton's appearance with a single dispassionate glance. 'Right.' Making his way into a room beyond the secretary's table, he sat down on a sofa, reached for a cigar and pointed towards the chair. The secretary shut the door behind them.

'Been with the Bureau long?'

'Just over eighteen months.'

'What were you doing before?'

'I worked in a merchant bank – Hogarths.'

Rylance seemed encouraged. 'Impressive people.' He was beginning to unwind after the frustrating interview with the Prime Minister. 'What made you leave them?'

'I felt banking wasn't for me.'

He raised his eyebrows: the answer had lacked appeal. No doubt a move from merchant banking into public bureaucracy struck him as eccentric if not bizarre. Leaning back with a grunt he rested his head on the edge of the sofa and closed his eyes. The eyelashes were extraordinarily long and thick; they might almost have had mascara on them. Beneath his chin, the flesh swelled like a chicken's breast. 'Well, let's hear how you're getting on.'

Egerton took a deep breath. 'I've no lead so far to where Lauren is living. What I *have* discovered is that a bank account was opened for her in Geneva at the time she went away.'

'Which bank?'

'The person who arranged it won't reveal that.'

'Who is he?'

He told him. Rylance's eyes remained closed. 'Presumably the identity of the bank is on a file in his office?'

'Yes.'

'Well, can't you get at it? I imagine you're equipped in the Bureau to carry out a little operation of that sort, aren't you?'

He cleared his throat. Nothing Antrim had said had prepared him for quite such a buccaneering approach. He said carefully, 'Having regard to Swiss banking practice I doubt if it would do us any good if we *knew* the bank. We'd never persuade them to reveal Lauren's address. And I'm fairly sure Montague doesn't have that in his files. She told him she would write with it later but she hadn't done so at the time I saw him.'

It seemed for a moment as if Rylance might be going to persist with a demand for a quiet little burglary. But then he sighed. 'All right. What have you got on Fernandes' movements?'

'According to the police he left London on the 27th of July on a flight to Paris. They can't say if he had anyone with him.'

'And . . .?'

'That's all.

Rylance opened his eyes. 'All? Surely you've got other channels through which you can discover where Fernandes went from there? Aren't you and the police in touch with *foreign* police services? What about INTERPOL and that sort of thing?'

They had reached the crunch. 'Unfortunately Fernandes doesn't seem to have been viewed as being of criminal or security interest. According to the Special Branch they were told by the Spanish police that he wasn't a terrorist. His brother Garcia is. But not Luis. Could you tell me where you got the information that he's also a terrorist?'

Rylance was looking at the tip of his cigar. 'The security people I expect. I can't really remember.'

'Was it in a written report?'

'No, oral.' He shrugged. 'I suppose that whoever told me was mixing the two brothers up.' He seemed oddly uninterested in what had happened. 'I expect I got my Private Office to make the enquiry and a mistake occurred somewhere along the line. Anyway that's water under the bridge. Whether he's a terrorist or not, it's still important for us to know where he and Lauren are.'

'But if he's *not* a terrorist, surely your principal anxiety is removed?'

'Not really. It doesn't mean it's desirable for the relationship to become permanent. From what Lauren told us, it's clear that Fernandes is, at best, very radical in his views. My wife is extremely anxious. Having to appear unconcerned while getting absolutely no news of Lauren's whereabouts has been a great strain for her. I don't want that to go on for months on end.'

It was difficult to see why appearing unconcerned was going to remain necessary in the future. The only likely explanation seemed to be that her vanity was so great she couldn't bear the thought of the world learning that her daughter had gone away with, in the words of Sam Giordano, a goddamn Communist. And Fernandes probably wasn't even that.

In any case, the basis for himself being involved in looking for Lauren seemed to have been removed. The Rylances ought to go back to William Carter Ingalls, unsatisfactory though they'd found him. But he could scarcely take that line without reference to Antrim who

111

might decide that now he'd started the job he'd better finish it.

Rylance said, 'I hear from my wife you think it would be worthwhile checking with Lauren's sister.'

'Yes. One of Lauren's friends also believes that Jacqueline is the most likely person to know where Lauren is.'

'Which friend was this?'

'Sally Kirkwood. She works at the American Embassy.'

Rylance was chewing his lip. 'Lauren and Jacqueline did seem very close at one time, I've wondered myself if they might have stayed in touch without telling my wife. Not that I know either of them very well.' He threw the cigar into a metal waste bucket as though suddenly bored with it. 'Do you believe you could find a way of exploring this without revealing that you're working under our instructions?' Like Evelyn, he clearly saw Egerton as a hired hand for the duration of the search.

'It's possible.' He groped for a diplomatic form of words to reserve his position. 'Of course it would depend on the view my Director takes about going on with the investigation. In the light of what now seem to be the true facts about Luis Fernandes' security status.'

Rylance was staring at him; he opened his mouth as if to say a great deal then changed his mind. He smiled. 'I fancy your Director will see the logic of your going on. If he's in doubt perhaps you'll ask him to speak to me.' He took out a pocket diary and copied something from it on to a scrap pad. 'That is Jacqueline's address in Deya. There's no telephone apparently. As far as I know she is living alone. You may find her in a . . . rather erratic condition.' He grimaced. 'I should be grateful if you would get off quickly. I have reasons for wanting a result out of this enquiry by the end of the month.'

Rylance rose to his feet. He stared grimly at the Pugin

paper on the walls for a moment, then crossed to his desk and began glancing at the papers on it as though in search of distraction. He was displaying a sudden tension. At last he said, 'Well, is there anything else?'

'Very little, I'm afraid. I called on Mr Giordano last night since I'd noticed he was staying at Claridges. I thought he might possibly be able to help.'

Rylance frowned. 'Did my wife suggest you should see him?'

'No. When I was talking to Sally Kirkwood she told me she felt something happened when Lauren was visiting her father earlier in the year which had a link with her going away with Fernandes. Since Mr Giordano was supposed to be in London for only a day or two I thought it would be sensible to follow it up with him straight away. I tried to reach your wife beforehand but I understand she's in Brussels. I hope that was all right.'

'Did he say anything useful?'

'He could think of nothing that fitted Sally Kirkwood's theory.'

Rylance went on frowning. Then he shrugged and looked at his watch; it was a clear signal that he was closing the interview. Egerton rose. 'Did Lauren ever speak of a person named David?'

Rylance shook his head. 'Not to me. Why?'

'He seems to have played a part in her life during the summer. He doesn't appear on the list of friends your wife gave me. But he could have something to contribute about her whereabouts.'

'I'll ask my wife. If it means anything to her, she'll get in touch with you.' He moved to the door. 'I should like a report on progress in another week's time. Please tell your Director that.' He held out a limp hand.

In the ante room the secretary was reading her novel again. She took Egerton back through the rabbit warren. At the exit on to Millbank he found himself caught up in a cluster of visitors also leaving. Once more somebody was shaking their hands in turn. Before he could escape, his own was grasped. The man grasping it gave him a winning smile. 'So glad you could come. Now you'll know we're not as bad as we sound.'

A girl was standing in the entrance to his apartment block and for a moment he thought it was Gail. But when she turned her head to greet him he realized it was the wife of the lawyer who lived in the flat above. He felt an absurdly sharp stab of disappointment. When they had parted the other evening he had not meant to leave the prospect of their next meeting quite so open-ended; not now Julian was dead. He suddenly wanted to see her, very much.

Turning, he got into the Mini and drove to the house in Notting Hill where he had dropped her. A small, bright-eyed Indian in overalls opened the door; he was holding a paint brush wrapped in a rag to stop it dripping. When Egerton asked for Gail, he shook his head regretfully: she was out.

'You don't have any idea where, I suppose?'

The Indian shook his head again. 'Nice dress. So maybe party.'

There was a pub on the other side of the street. He felt a strong impulse to break the rules and go inside for a scotch. But he gritted his teeth and drove back to Prince of Wales Drive.

The phone was ringing as he opened the door of the flat and for a second his hopes rose. But it was Camilla Rylance. She began with a rush of words as though nervous of his reaction to her call, spoke of trying to get him twice before, apologized for bothering him when he must be very busy. He sensed she was trying to judge his mood all the time she was speaking. Eventually she got to the point. 'I wondered if you'd seen the article in today's *Globe*?'

'Yes.'

'I suppose everybody's running round in circles. I haven't seen my father today but he must be absolutely choked.

Preoccupied though Rylance had seemed once or twice, it hadn't struck Egerton that the leakage was weighing very heavily on his mind. But at Rylance's level there were presumably a dozen things demanding attention at any time. If he allowed himself to be hypnotized by one of them, he'd never get through the work.

Camilla was saying, 'It's really about that I rang. I wonder if I could possibly see you? I've spotted the man with the binoculars again. Of course the desk's been moved. But it shows he's still keeping watch.'

He was getting bored with the leakage saga and even more with maintaining the pretence that he was in some way connected with the people carrying out the investigation. 'I see. Well, thanks for letting me know.'

'Can you tell me anything about how the enquiry's going?'

'It's a bit early to say. But Superintendent Clayton was very glad to get the information you gave me.'

'Oh good,' she said vaguely. She hesitated. 'I expect I'm being an awful bore . . . but I would love to talk to you if you can spare the time. Only for a few minutes. Perhaps we could have a drink somewhere?' Her voice trailed away.

The tentativeness of her appeal was hard to resist. He

was conscious moreover that he quite liked the idea of seeing her again; her remembered image had become touching and a little seductive. 'All right,' he said. 'What about tomorrow?'

Her voice lifted in a surge of relief. 'Super.' They settled on the bar at Trader Vic's.

Just before she ended the call, she said, 'This is terribly sweet of you, Mark. I can call you Mark, can't I?'

11

Waiting for her in Trader Vic's, a pineapple juice at his side, he stared at the whisky bottles behind the bar. If it's only the drink you feel you're missing they'd said – fine, you're lucky. Think about other things to take your mind off it.

He lifted his gaze conscientiously. Suspended from a roof of imitation bamboo and plaited straw was a canoe; more Polynesian artefacts of a miscellaneous character loomed from different corners of the room. He studied them all. Concentrating on other things was painless as long as it didn't include the day so far. That had been a write-off.

It had begun with a call from Rivers in Special Branch, at first reasonably genial but rapidly cooling. 'Bellamy told me that the report about Luis Fernandes being a terrorist came from you.'

'Yes.'

'There's a big push on over Basques at the moment. Could I get something straight about your source? You say he's reliable and in a good position to know facts of this sort.'

'I did say that.'

'So he's into Basque poltitics . . . ?'

'Not really.'

'Then what?'

'I'm afraid I can't say more.' He had hesitated then before deciding to come out with what seemed inescapable. 'As a matter of fact I don't now rate the report as reliable.'

There was silence at the other end. 'I'm sorry,' he said, 'but that's the way it looks now.'

'You mean you were talking about the brother, not Luis – that your source mixed them up?'

'That's one explanation. I'm not sure it's the right one.'

'What else could it be?'

He sensed Rivers' impatience growing. 'The situation's rather complicated. As I said, I'm sorry. I suggest you forget all about it.'

'You're withdrawing the report . . .'

'I didn't put it in the form of a report. But, yes, I am.'

Rivers had said, after another pause, 'I don't think we've met, Egerton. I'm told you're fairly new in the Bureau. In our business we don't call sources reliable unless we've bloody good reasons for doing so. Not if we want to be thought professional.' Then he had put down the phone.

The afternoon had brought an even less agreeable encounter, this time face to face. A superintendent from the Yard had visited Antonia to be briefed on the Beynon case and she had asked Egerton to join them. He had been chilly from the start. Except when he had a question to ask, he had listened to Egerton's account of his investigation with eyes that never left a point above the door. Early in the meeting, he had fastened on an issue of protocol, wanting to know why Egerton had made a direct contact with Pasquier of the Sûreté in Paris, instead of first going through the Yard's liaison channel. When it emerged that Pasquier had pushed the boat out to the extent of making special enquiries for Egerton into Beynon's property investment activities in Paris, the atmosphere had become even more strained. That might not have mattered if the superintendent hadn't been able to go on to pick holes in the investigation. But he had pointed out a line of enquiry that remained with its end hanging loose. He would need to check it out before applying for any of the search warrants. Arguably it was something best done by the Yard anyway. But they all knew that Egerton had missed the trick.

He gazed gloomily into his pineapple juice. Camilla was now twenty minutes late. About him, men and women drank livelier fluids and talked prosperously. He learned about the new season's grouse, the price of Rollers in Brussels and the current temperature range in Acapulco. Someone had left an evening paper on the bar. He opened it. On the front page was a photograph of Rylance in full throat at some public meeting earlier in the year. The eyes flashed, the gaze was lifted towards the horizon, even the jaw was unfleshy shot from beneath. Today he had apparently not looked so good; he had been taking stick in the House of Commons for the latest leakage. Under the headline STORM OVER LEAKED REPORT were the details of the Opposition's attack over the *Globe*'s latest coup garnished with references to general mayhem in the security burrows of Whitehall.

At last he saw Camilla at the entrance to the bar, wearing her distracted look, waving with relief when she recognized him. He listened to a complicated explanation for her lateness that involved a hairdresser and a traffic warden. She had on a short grey jersey dress with hooped black tights that would have been death to legs less slim. He observed that she had inherited the remarkable eye-lashes he had noticed on Rylance the day before; fringing these dark blue eyes they came into their own. Her breasts brushed lightly against his arm as she settled on the next

119

bar stool. He decided that, after all, the day was not a complete write-off.

She asked, without having to look, for the most expensive drink on the card. While it was being mixed, he saw her eyes move to the headline in his newspaper. 'How does it feel, having a father who's always in the public eye?' he asked.

She shrugged and took a cigarette from her bag. 'I'm used to it. Before he went into politics Pa was always being written up as a whizz in the computer world and he loves publicity. Ma didn't enjoy it much.'

'Were you still at school when she died?'

'Yes. Nobody let on to me how ill she was until just before the end. I blamed Pa for ages. When he remarried I wouldn't speak to either of them to begin with. Evelyn eventually persuaded me that all I was doing was cutting off my nose. Evelyn's *very* persuasive.'

'How do you get on with your stepsisters?'

'Jacqueline married soon after she came over from America so I haven't seen much of her. She's a culture bug. Lauren's rather intense in a different way. I imagine she thinks I'm just too frivolous for words. Anyway, I don't see her either these days because she's pushed off with a Spanish boyfriend, God knows where. Evelyn won't talk about it.'

They had drifted into the subject so easily, there didn't seem any reason not to explore further. 'Doesn't she write?' he asked.

'She wouldn't write to me. I don't know whether Evelyn's heard. I shouldn't be surprised if they've gone to America. Her father is a film producer there and Lauren was apparently his pet when she was younger.'

Clearly she had nothing useful to offer on Lauren's

120

movements; she even seemed to be unaware that Giordano had been in London.

When her drink arrived, she said, 'I expect you want to hear about the chap with the binoculars.'

He summoned up an appearance of lively interest while she launched into an account of her second sighting; this time she had remembered to note the flat from which he was watching and also the time. 'It was about nine in the morning. I'd just got up and went to have my bath. Then I nipped back into the bedroom to find some stuff I use to dewhisker my legs. There he was, bang up against his window. Incidentally Pa was in his study making some early morning calls before going off to the Department.'

It could have been the morning when he'd been a recipient of one of them, he thought. He let his eyes drop. She had crossed her legs to show a fair amount of thigh; dewhiskered or not, it appeared exceptionally inviting.

'I hope you can tell me a bit about the investigation,' she said. 'I'm dying to know if you think I'm right.'

'As I told you, I'm not really involved in the actual enquiry.'

'But you must have heard *something*.' Her hand was on his arm. 'What does Superintendent Clayton *say*?'

She wasn't going to give up. He reached for his glass to give himself time to think. There seemed no great harm in telling her what he had learned from Bellamy. She was, after all, the source of the lead. He looked at her solemnly. 'You understand this is very confidential.'

'I promise not to breathe a word.'

He gave her the bare bones. She watched him intently as he spoke, drinking in the words. At the end she said, 'So he thinks I'm right.'

'It's possible.'

She was childishly pleased. A momentary fear gripped

121

him that she might retail the facts to some Hooray Henry like the one he'd seen her with in the car in Piccadilly; then it would turn up in a gossip column. 'Look,' he said, 'I've no authority to tell you any of this. If you pass it to somebody else – '

She was shaking her head earnestly. 'I absolutely won't. You can trust me.'

He had to accept her word; and in fact she seemed perfectly serious about it. She reached across him to stub out her cigarette. 'It's been terribly sweet of you,' she said. Under the light scent she was wearing, there seemed to be the smell of sun about her although there had been no glimmer of it all day. He experienced a sudden sharp hunger such as he had hardly known in recent months, a desire to go on breathing the odour of her skin and to taste the essence of her. He wondered if she would be willing to spend the evening with him. He was in no shape financially to pay for the sort of junket she would probably expect. But he could ring the bank tomorrow before the cheques went through the works; some jacking-up of his overdraft must be possible.

She had finished her drink and was reaching for her handbag so there was no time to be lost. 'Would you let me take you to dinner?'

Her eyes widened. 'Tonight?'

'We could eat here or go on somewhere else. Just as you like.'

She became uneasy as it sunk it. 'That's terribly nice. Really I can't think of anything I'd like better.' She put her hand on his arm again. Vague sentences of disengagement were being assembled. 'The awful thing is – I've actually arranged to meet someone quite soon . . . and then we're going on . . . I'm so sorry . . . terribly sweet of you to suggest it.'

122

The invitation had been a *gaffe*, he realized, never for one moment had she contemplated their relationship moving off the plane on which she had established it during their meeting at Chester Square. That spontaneous manner, that appealing vulnerability, they were not exactly part of an act; but she was conscious enough of their effect to use them for her purposes. He shook his head, smiling. 'Another time perhaps.'

'Yes, of course, I'd love that.' She glanced at her watch. 'Do you mind *terribly* if I *fly*? I seem to have been late for everything today.'

He saw her into a taxi then made his way to the 137 stop opposite the Hilton entrance. A bus was disappearing as he reached it. He might as well accept that this really wasn't his day. All that remained to crown it would be to get himself mugged again. Nobody hostile seemed to be awaiting him at the entrance to his block. Seeing Gwen appear in their lobby as soon as he opened the door to it produced a momentary twinge of apprehension. But her news was mundane: the builders had called again to look at the damp rot in the kitchen; they'd said they'd be back in a week or so. He smiled with relief. Gwen's hair was in rollers which meant either that it was bingo night or her admirer from the London Fire Service was expected for a little spontaneous combustion. Before she could put him in the picture, his telephone began to ring and he made his escape.

It was Gail's voice. He felt a sudden glow. 'What are you doing?' she asked.

'Nothing.'

'Perfect, we're coming to collect you.'

'Who are "we"?'

'It's a secret. There's a new club opening in Beak Street. We're taking you. It's your Coming Out party.'

123

She coughed theatrically. 'Let me read that again. It's your Coming Back to Life party.'

This time the voice had a lift to it which had been absent the evening she had visited him for supper. Some of the gaiety and zest he remembered from the summer they had met seemed to have returned. To be with her in those days had been like walking on a volcano's rim with no time to glance down into the crater. Caution began to pluck at him.

'I'm not sure I can manage it.'

'Why?'

'Cash is very tight at the moment.'

'You don't have to worry – it's a freebie. Eats as well as drinks.'

'I'm also going abroad for my department probably, tomorrow or the next day. There are things I need to do.'

It sounded totally wet. 'Don't be so *old*,' she said. 'They'll get done. What you need is some *fun*.'

His reluctance was only half-hearted. 'All right,' he said, 'I'm on.'

Within seconds of replacing the receiver, he heard Gwen's knock. Cursing under his breath, he went to see what she wanted this time. She was holding his laundry box. 'Going out?' she asked. Obviously she had been listening in the lobby while he talked to Gail. He nodded, fumbling for money to pay her.

'The girl I let in the other evening?'

He went on nodding. There was no point in prevarication. No part of his domestic habits remained unknown to her. She had probably even deduced by now what he did in the Bureau. All that remained to be charted was his sexual bent on which she must feel he had provided disappointingly inadequate data since moving in. Her

124

expression was indulgent. He could imagine her thinking: looks like he's normal after all.

Gail arrived half an hour later than her forecast. With alarm he saw that the other person climbing the stairs behind her was Jamie. Gail was wearing a long satin skirt and a cobwebby top; either her exotic bird phase was over or she had decided that this was not the evening for a Spectacular. Jamie seemed to have become a dandy. That scruffy, thrown-together appearance of his Oxford days had been gradually fading from the time he came down and settled in London. Now it had totally vanished. The suit was a dazzling white with shoes to match. Beneath the suit was a pleated silk shirt the colour of Victoria plums. Odd bits of jewellery were visible here and there. None of it seemed tiresomely affected because his manner was unchanged, a heavy-lidded amiability that declined to accept anything as remotely serious.

He still looked as fit as in his football-playing days. If he had started drugging since he had certainly found the right balance. But it was difficult to imagine he ever would. At Oxford his great success had been in combining the role of universal provider with that of non-participator. All he had ever done was smoke a little hash at times when it would have seemed stuffy to refuse. Floating to Oxford on the wings of charm and quick-wittedness from the Glasgow suburb where his mother taught in the local school, he had decided, early on, that he didn't want a degree or even a Blue, just the reputation for being the indispensable organizer of revels. It had made him money of course but not very much in those days. All he'd had to show for it had been an old Aston Martin. The bonanza hadn't started until he came to London.

While he fixed their drinks, they wandered about the flat. Rude comments were offered on the curtains and the

125

age of the lavatory fittings. When he showed them the outsize bed bought as part of the deal with the previous owner they rolled their eyes and collapsed upon it.

They continued to make mild fun of him but he was aware of affection in their voices. The misgiving he had felt on seeing Jamie faded, to be replaced by a slow surge of elation. He went to the kitchen and poured himself a glass of wine in place of the Perrier he had opened. He had almost forgotten how, when they were both on form, life ceased to be dreary and even the commonplace became incandescent.

Returning to the sitting room, he raised his glass to them and grinned. 'So what's the name of this new club?'

12

Dido's. It came back as the first thing of all when he opened his eyes to morning light: Dido's. His brain locked on it, turned the word into a recurring cry while he lay inert, unwilling to start the hammers inside his skull by moving. Nobody had explained why the club had that name. A negress in a sheath of sequins had been in frequent evidence. She had greeted with a kiss Jamie and others who had been admitted to her magic circle, sometimes giving a great shout of triumphant affection. No doubt she had been Dido. Aeneas had never appeared; somewhere out of sight he had been counting the bottles of champagne as they left the kitchen perhaps.

The night was returning in disconnected frames which towards the end had only the vaguest form. As he entered the club he had been conscious of an old feeling, a kindling of anticipation. Then, as Jamie disappeared into a group in the far corner and Gail became engulfed by faces reaching forward to kiss or whisper, the feeling gave way to a chill. Involuntarily he was becoming distanced from his surroundings. It was not that their predictability now bored him, the strobes and lasers, the metallic paper on the walls, the perspex floor lit from beneath; he could still experience the tug of this night world of scent and sweat, of hectic or calculating eyes. But the figures that eddied about him belonged to a sealed-off section of his life. When a few smiled in recognition, he greeted them self-consciously, spoke about his American visit as though it had ended only yesterday and moved on before the questions could become too probing. The terms on which acquaintance could be renewed had changed irretrievably. Somewhere, in New York or Minnesota, he had lost the sense of belonging here.

He was trying to locate Gail when he saw a face recently familiar although at first he had difficulty in placing it. It belonged to a youngish man in dinner jacket and red bow tie who was holding court at the bar. He had the air of knowing, or expecting to know, all; while he talked his eyes ranged the room as if it were a landscape. It was the driver of the sports car in which Egerton had seen Camilla the evening of his call on Sam Giordano at Claridges. This was perhaps the date she had been hurrying away from Trader Vic's to join. He studied the people clustered round the man but couldn't see her.

When he found Gail, he asked if she recognized him. She glanced across. 'Simon Bowe.'

'Who is he?'

'A gossip writer on one of the give-away magazines.'

'He looks very pleased with himself.'

'Madly ambitious – on the way up according to Jamie. He never misses any of these things.' She glanced across again. 'Is it really him you're interested in, or the blonde?'

When he looked once more in Bowe's direction, he saw that Camilla had materialized by his side. She had changed out of the jersey dress into a little black jacket and what looked like silver jodhpurs.

'Does she turn you on?'

'She's quite attractive.'

Gail was appraising her. 'I imagine you ending up with somebody like that. Cuddly and fertile.' Then she had pulled a face at him and called out to someone who had just arrived.

* * *

He lifted his head gingerly so that he could look at Gail as she slept. She lay neatly in the centre of the bed, one hand beneath the pillow on which they both had their heads. Her lips were parted as though at the prospect of something agreeable. Seeing her like this, he could almost dismiss his fear that she was going downhill. And yet, when he looked closer, there was an underlying pallor, an unevenness to her skin that was wrong. At the club he had thought of her as a tropical fish, darting and shimmering through the crowd, always elusive. When she returned to his side, she was tender as though she had discovered him afresh and only he mattered. Her energy had been breathtaking. But he was sure she had fixed when she went to the powder room.

That must have been about nine hours ago. It wouldn't be long before she needed the next one. If he let her sleep on he wouldn't see the signs of her wanting it before he left for the Bureau.

Gently he raised the sheet away from her body. Her top was bare but she was still wearing briefs. So, presumably, Nothing had Happened when they finally dropped into bed. Recollection of events after they had arrived back from Dido's offered no guidance on that score; but he had drunk so much wine, there and later, that it hardly seemed he would have been in a competent state anyway. Jamie, as ever, had been the most pulled-together at the end of the evening, a little more heavy-lidded perhaps but with all his muscles functioning to order. Almost the last frame on the memory track was of him, fiddling through stations on the radio, the jacket of the white suit folded on the sofa beside him. At what stage he had given that up and joined Gail and himself in the Emperor bed was unknowable. But there he was, beyond Gail, dead to the world yet faintly smiling.

129

It was five minutes to eight: time to pull himself together, preparatory to reporting to Antrim at the Bureau. Slipping out of the bed he went to the bathroom to shower and shave. Torn Alka Seltzer packaging lay on the floor. Neither Jamie nor Gail was likely to have bothered to look for that sort of thing so presumably *he* had taken the tablets. He was in fact steadier in the head than he had expected. He began to see the night as a test from which he had emerged successfully. The past had reached up and fallen back again without him.

Neither Gail nor Jamie had stirred when he returned to the bedroom for his clothes. Jamie lay very neatly, still with the faint smile on his face. It gave him the look of a man who knew he was sleeping and found it good. He was turned away from Gail so that no part of his body would touch hers. That was a characteristic, the avoidance of physical contact, except on those few occasions he would disappear with a boy or girl who had shaken him out of his neutrality. When it was over he would be uncommunicative about what had occurred. The other person would also be silent, bewildered to have become so soon a footnote.

He was back in the kitchen, making toast and waiting for the kettle to boil, when he was aware of a movement behind him. It was Jamie, now completely dressed. Apart from the stubble on his chin he looked unchanged from the previous evening, the suit uncreased, the shoes still close enough to white.

'We seem to have stayed over,' he said.

'How do you feel.'

'Fine.'

'Is Gail still asleep?'

'I think so.'

He reached past Jamie for the tea. 'There's something

I want to say before she wakes up. She's got to finish with smack. Now. I know she's tried once and failed. She's got to try again. I don't want her to end up like Julian.'

Jamie gazed through the window. A rubbish collection truck had double-parked beside his Porsche. 'She'd never get stuff like *that* from me.'

'It's still poisoning her. She says you're giving her more than she needs anyway. You realize she's dealing, I suppose?'

'I knew she needed money. If I'd offered cash she wouldn't have taken it.'

'But the *risk*! She'll be arrested sooner or later. It's a risk for you as well.'

'I'll live with that. Anyway I know she wouldn't talk if it happened.' Jamie turned and smiled, wanting to be rid of dismal speculation. 'You're getting bloody serious in your old age.'

He persisted doggedly. 'If I can persuade her to go somewhere for treatment, will you help?'

'In what way?'

'She *has* to stay with the treatment this time. I'll try to make her. But she might ask you to slip stuff to her without my knowing.'

'What do I do then?'

'You've got to refuse.'

Jamie took out a cigarette. 'You're in love with her still, aren't you?'

'Never mind. Do you promise?'

He was smiling again. 'All right.'

As always, he was being amiably biddable, ready to fit in with whatever seemed broadly reasonable by his own lights. His degree of detachment might have been repellent in another. In Jamie it was a neutral fact that needed to be overcome; when it was, his resource as a friend and ally amounted to no small thing. Never less than when pulling one away from a bloody end in an Oxford river.

Egerton heard Gail's voice calling from the bedroom; she was asking where everybody was. He took her a mug of tea and sat on the bed. She lay, smiling faintly at him.

'I wasn't going to wake you,' he said.

'Why are you dressed already – it's Saturday isn't it?'

'I have to go to the office. But I want to talk some time. Will you still be around this afternoon? Can you wait until I've finished at the Bureau?'

She was chewing her lip. 'No, I can't stay. I've promised to see some people. Tomorrow perhaps?'

He shook his head. 'I'll have left on my trip – assuming my boss doesn't veto it. Are you absolutely sure you can't manage it today?'

'I really can't.' She went on chewing her lip. She wasn't going to tell him any more; but he could guess what she'd be doing.

'What's your trip?' she asked.

'To Majorca. I have to interview somebody in a place called Deyá.'

'Lucky old you.' She sat up, wrapping the sheet tightly over her breasts as though against the cold. He thought he could see tension working at the corners of her mouth but it might have been his imagination searching for tell-tale signs. 'So what are we due to talk about?'

'You.'

She looked at him mockingly. 'Are you planning to take me in hand?'

'Perhaps.'

'The blonde you lusted after last night would be *much* more rewarding.'

'I want you to start to cut down on the smack while I'm away.'

132

She groaned.

'It's getting to you.'

'It isn't.'

'I know it is.'

She lay back and closed her eyes. She wanted to be rid of him, to escape. He told himself that she was thinking he'd turned into a Born Again bore. He said, 'I'm not going to let up on you.'

'You shouldn't try to make people's decisions for them.'

'It's going to be your decision. Eventually.'

'Why should that happen?'

'It's the only way you'll get me off your back.'

She opened her eyes to stare silently at the ceiling. He leaned over and kissed her gently on the lips. At first she made no response. Then her hands reached up and she was holding his head tightly against her.

'I love you,' he said. 'That could be inconvenient. You may as well face the fact because it won't go away.'

Back in the kitchen as he was preparing to leave he said, 'Don't let her fix here, Jamie. If she has to do it, I don't want it to happen here. Ever.'

While Egerton was speaking, Antrim had begun to unwrap the package that stood in the centre of his blotter. A piece of highly coloured marble emerged; it was set on an ebony base to which was attached a metal plate with an inscription. The marble had no form that was immediately recognizable. Antrim studied the inscription impassively. 'You're telling me the Secretary of State simply invented his story of having been told Luis Fernandes was a terrorist?'

'I can't be sure but I think it's likely.'

'Why should he do that?'

'It provides a justification for asking your help in finding

Lauren. He knew you were bound to refuse him otherwise.'

Antrim bent to open a side drawer of his desk. He dropped the marble object inside with a grimace. 'Why do you dismiss his explanation that one of his staff put a query to the security people and in the process Luis Fernandes was mixed up with his brother?'

'Somehow it didn't ring true.'

Antrim was staring at him. There was an uncomfortable silence. Antrim said, 'I hope you're not going to persuade me I made a mistake when I selected you for this enquiry, Egerton.'

He looked down. 'I just felt you ought to know how it looked to me, in case you consider we're no longer justified in going on with the search.'

'You want to abandon it halfway through . . .'

'I'm not saying that. But can we justify – '

'Leave the justifying to me. *I* decide what this department does. And because the Secretary of State for Defence made a mistake – ' Antrim paused ' – for whatever reason, doesn't convince me we should back out of what we've agreed to do.' He was screwing into a tight ball the tissue paper that had been wrapped round the piece of marble. 'Do you want me to take you off the enquiry?'

Egerton gritted his teeth. 'No, sir.'

There was another silence. Eventually Antrim said, 'Very well, perhaps we can get down to what needs to be done now. Since Rylance accepts that the sister may very well be the only person who knows Lauren's whereabouts, you'd better go and see her. It shouldn't take more than forty-eight hours. The cover story you've been using won't be any use of course.'

'I realize that.'

'You're quite confident, are you, that Montague wasn't

134

lying when he said he didn't have an address for Lauren?'

Earlier in their talk he had let Antrim know of Rylance's assumption that a little burglary of Montague's office would be considered part of the package if it was likely to produce results. Antrim had raised his eyebrows and gone to look out of the window, presumably to brood on the implications of that from a future Home Secretary. 'How very interesting,' he had said.

'I'm sure he wasn't lying.'

Antrim sighed and sat back in his swivel chair. 'All right. Telephone me from Deya as soon as you've formed a view on whether the sister knows anything. I'll need to keep Rylance in the picture. Tell Baxter I want him as you go out.'

When Egerton reached the door, he said, 'Just remember, for the future, Egerton, I'm running this department.' He enjoyed showing the whip.

Baxter was stirring sugar into a cup of coffee. Having to come in on a Saturday morning because Antrim had decided to work didn't seem to be irking him. He placed a saucer with several biscuits on it over the cup to keep it warm; but what went on inside the inner room was his real nourishment. 'Did he open that package while you were in there?' he asked.

'Yes.'

'What was in it?'

'A lump of marble.'

Baxter produced his all-knowing smile. 'Parting gift from the Head of the Pakistan Anti-Corruption Office. We'd rather hoped for mangoes.' He picked up pad and pencil. 'Progress on your front?'

'Not much.'

'I gather you're up in the stratosphere, high-wire stuff.

Try not to fall off, won't you?' He disappeared through the double doors.

Antonia had asked to be told the outcome of the talk with Antrim. He telephoned her at her flat. When he had finished, she sighed. 'So you're still on the case.'

'Just.'

'When do you leave for Majorca?'

'Tomorrow. I'd made a provisional booking before I reported.'

'You presumably guessed what he was going to say . . .'

'Not entirely. But I could see he'd find it very uncomfortable to tell Rylance we weren't going to help any more.'

'Are you unhappy about it.'

'No. Having started the thing, I'd like to see if I can find her. As he said, it's his business whether we ought to be doing it.'

She made a non-committal noise. 'Well, Jacqueline may have the answer. I hope you get her talking.'

'I'm taking a tape recorder and a Minox.' He laughed. 'Do you recommend a weapon?'

She didn't laugh back. 'I might,' she said, 'if you could tell me what that mugging meant.'

13

From the balcony outside his bedroom he could see bodies already stretched beside the swimming pool, oiled and motionless. To his right the village of Deya clung to its hillside, half in shadow, half bathed in a sun that seemed undimmed by the onset of autumn. The scent of gardenias rose to his nostrils from the hotel gardens below. This time yesterday he had stepped off a 137 bus into a steady drizzle and the remains of somebody's hamburger. Even if failure lay ahead, there were worse ways of spending an October morning than this; and all on the Queen too. To consolidate the festive feeling, he went down to reception and bought a postcard to send to Gail.

When he had posted it, he strolled in the gardens for a while. Whatever Rylance had meant when he had talked of Jacqueline's condition being erratic, it seemed sensible to give her scope to get a grip on the day. By the time he finally set out for the address Rylance had provided, the perfumed languor of the garden and the gleam of brown flesh gliding through the pool had given him the sensation of embarking on an adventure.

The street proved to be little more than an intermittently paved track. It led steeply downwards from the village in the direction of the sea. On one side, across a small stream, there were groves of lemon trees and small vegetable plots. Village cottages ran along the other side except where, as the track began to peter out, two or three villas had been built.

Jacqueline's house was the last of the cottages. Fresh

paint, a new door, a certain uniformity about the window boxes, set it apart from the rest; it had obviously been done up for letting. Precariously parked on a steep slope of grass beside the front wall was a dusty MG Metro with a cracked side window.

He strolled past, glancing into those windows that were unshuttered for signs of life, but there were none. By the first of the villas he halted and looked back. A small boy seated on a wooden bridge across the stream called to him. 'Señor.' The boy was pointing down the street in the direction of the sea; he grinned. Placing his hands flat on the boards of the bridge, he arched his back in an ecstasy of knowledge. By some mysterious process he had exactly gauged Egerton's purpose.

Egerton hesitated. His vague plan had been to call at the cottage pretending he had heard it was to let, not to appear to be looking for Jacqueline. But the boy was pointing again. 'Señor . . . playa.' Nothing was going to alter the conclusion he had already reached. Egerton gave him a wave and went on down the track.

By the time he reached the beach, the track had given way to a stony path. He had supposed he would find a stretch of sand or shingle with coloured umbrellas and more bodies like those beside the hotel pool. Instead he entered a rocky inlet. Beside fishing boats drawn up in the shade of a cliff men were mending nets. A few children, obviously locals, played on the edge of the sea. Nobody at all lay on the beach.

Turning away he saw to his rear a primitive-looking bar constructed of timber. A verandah ran along its front with two or three tables and empty chairs on it. Seated at the bar with her back to the sea was a woman. Her head was lowered over a glass of wine so that, apart from the sapphire blue beach dress, he could see little more than

138

the hair caught up in a loose *chignon*. It was exactly the colour of Evelyn Rylance's.

He took a bar stool a little distance from her and ordered a drink. As the barman served it the woman turned to look at Egerton over the rim of her sunglasses. With one hand she moved her almost empty glass to and fro along the bar top. 'You wouldn't have a cigarette, would you?' she asked. The voice was lighter than her mother's, the Californian accent less noticeable; a year or two married to the barrister had perhaps clipped the vowels. She was very tanned and wore no make-up.

He bought a packet of cigarettes from the barman. When he had lit one for her she exhaled smoke as though she had waited a very long time for it. 'Perhaps you'll join me in a drink,' he said.

While her glass was being refilled, she said, 'See? A friend.' The barman smiled and made an enigmatic movement with his head. It wasn't clear he had understood her. She twisted abruptly back to Egerton. 'So who *are* you, friend?'

He told him his name and that he was on a short visit to write an article about Deya, a quick job for an airline magazine.

'I'll tell you *all* about Deya,' she said. 'But it won't be any use for the magazine. Deya is the pits, take it from me.'

She drew cigarette smoke down to the lower reaches of her stomach. She was only half-drunk but anxious to get on with the job. He picked up his cue. 'So what exactly is wrong with Deya?'

She talked laconically about the place, leaning towards him in a pretence of making the conversation private from the barman, while occasionally glancing back in the hope she wasn't succeeding. What was wrong seemed to boil

139

down not so much to Deya itself as the expectations that had drawn her there. Some Wordsworthian vision mysteriously acquired years before at Berkeley had filled her imagination. She had rented the cottage unseen for six months through a travel agent in London and had arrived anticipating a blue skies version of Grasmere with Vodka Martinis thrown in to enliven the dull bits. Somehow the culture scene had failed to deliver. Or perhaps it had simply rejected her.

When she had finished the glass of wine he had paid for he watched for a while to see what she would do. Eventually she took off the sunglasses to search the corners of her handbag for *pesetas*. It went on too long to be just an act. He understood the remark to the barman about friends now. She was apparently without cash. And her credit with the barman was no good either.

He ordered more wine. She began to tell him about her divorce. There were problems in getting the alimony through, her lawyer had produced fancy excuses. But he was in cahoots with the louse she had married. Probably they went to the same school together. All lawyers were bastards anyway. Very faintly he caught an echo of Sam Giordano.

Occasionally she glanced towards the point where the path he had followed joined the beach. He had the impression she was expecting another companion, albeit without much hope. At such moments he was able to study her features. They were as good as Evelyn's, almost identical except for the cheekbones which were higher. They gave her a faintly feral expression, a dangerous sort of beauty.

So far, all had gone his way. He guessed that, with hardly any prompting, she would move on to talk about her family. But her speech was becoming slower and less distinct: before long she would stop making sense. As he hesitated over ordering her more wine, she seemed alerted to his misgivings and stood up, holding on to the bar to stop herself swaying. 'I have to go,' she said, 'Somebody coming . . . mustn't be late.' The words were an effort. 'You coming?' He sensed it was an appeal of sorts.

One of her sandals had fallen on to the verandah. She spent a while trying to put her foot in it without bending down. He stooped to help her; the toes were grimy and scratched. Finally they set off up the path. She began with a show of determination to make it unaided but when he took her arm she rested against him, her head pressed to his shoulder.

At the gate of her cottage she looked round uncertainly but whoever she had expected (if it had been more than a hope), was not there. By now however it didn't seem to matter too much. He was sure she would collapse on to her bed as soon as she got inside. As she fumbled in her bag for a key he said, 'I wonder if you'd care to have dinner with me.'

She didn't look up from her search of the bag. Inside it he could see a variety of pill containers.

'Tonight perhaps?'

She delayed answering until the key was found then grunted in triumph. 'Fine! Let's do that, Mark.' She said it defiantly to some unseen presence. He told her he'd pick her up at around seven thirty. 'It *is* Mark, isn't it?' she called out.

He walked back to the hotel. Seven thirty meant that she would have nearly seven hours to sleep off the wine, assuming her visitor didn't turn up after all and start her drinking again. Depending on her condition when he collected her, he would either give her one stand-up drink

141

in the hotel bar or steer her straight into the restaurant. The challenge then would be to keep her wanting and able to talk.

When evening came, the heat had become sultry. Although the cottage was less than five minutes' walk it seemed wise to take the car he had hired at Palma airport. Parking it alongside the Metro with the cracked window he saw with misgiving that no lights were visible in the house. She could hardly be still sleeping off the morning session; but she might easily have forgotten their date and gone out. The door yielded to his touch however. When he called into the darkness behind, she answered in reassuringly lucid tones.

He followed the voice through a darkened sitting room and french windows on to a small terrace that ran along the back of the cottage. The only light came from a small lamp. In its beam he could just make out Jacqueline's face and shoulders. She waved at him with a cigarette. '*Salud.*'

On the table by which she was seated were a practically full wine bottle and two glasses. He could make out little else in the gloom but she seemed to be wearing a long evening dress of silk or chiffon, the collar severely high at the front. When she reached forward to pour his wine he smelled her scent; it was sharp and metropolitan, the antithesis of the gardenias in the hotel grounds. She was hepped up but he had the feeling it was from pills not wine.

She seemed to want to stay and talk their way through the bottle. He began to worry about getting her moving. Not that it was disagreeable sitting in the relative cool of the terrace with the lamplight tracing the line of her cheek and neck, sometimes catching the richness in her hair. The garden beyond was drowned in darkness. He had a

142

pleasant sense of displacement, of the world gone away.

She talked unrancorously at first. She was knowledgeable about the flowers he could smell but not see and spoke about the herbs that grew wild on the hillside behind. But before long she was back to people, this time not the slobs in the cultural colony but the island's indigenous inhabitants. The greatest of the demons was her landlord, a Palma wide boy, a bimbo. Her cigarette end glowed and danced as she gestured bitterly. 'George Sand was damned right about this place. They're all bimbos.' She had turned her head to stare into the darkness and in the general direction of the village. She made no attempt to lower her voice. 'Bimbos.' She wanted everything to be bad. There was a taut fragility behind the sentences and sometimes when she paused he had the sensation that she had disconnected from her surroundings.

Somehow he got her away from current discontents. Before coming to Deya she had stayed for a while in a friend's villa in Sardinia. That seemed to have been a happier time. She might decide to settle there once the alimony had been sorted out properly and the louse was paying on time. Or then again, it might be Nice. Or Lugano. But not here. She was pretending she retained some sense of direction, a capability for choice. But really she was rudderless. Divorce hadn't simply removed the louse, it had taken from her the sense of a structure to her life. Intention had oozed away leaving only fantasy and whim.

He drained his glass and leaned forward as she reached for the bottle of wine again. 'Why don't we go and eat?'

She rose jerkily, touching her hair, then took his arm. They were at last on their way.

He decided in the car that they would go straight to the

hotel restaurant. She was high but making sense most of the time. With food inside her and careful control of any more bottles, all might be well.

Falling momentarily behind her as they crossed the reception hall of the hotel, his attention was suddenly riveted on her body. Illuminated by the lamp ahead, in the corridor to the restaurant, was an arresting fact: beneath the virtual transparency of her dress, she was wearing nothing at all. As the head waiter led them to a table, Egerton saw the heads at first lifting casually and then becoming very still as the eyes focused.

She was moving with a pretended confidence, her gaze straight ahead as she concentrated on remaining steady. The manner she had assumed at first made him think she had planned the display, either out of bravado or to make these fuddy-duddy tourists on middle-brow packages sit up and take notice. Yet when they were finally seated, he became aware of the bewilderment in her eyes, a flicker of unease at the corner of the mouth. His annoyance slowly gave way to resignation. He realized that she had no idea what they had been looking at, only sensed that the stares were hostile.

There was no point in telling her. At least no further peepshow would be offered until they left the table again; and since it was late, most of the others in the restaurant would then have departed. When he smiled reassuringly, she smiled back with an almost desperate gratitude. He felt guilt that a few moments before his only wish was to be able to disown her; reaching for the menu he began to read out the dishes.

He had almost relaxed when he saw the manager bearing down on their table with the air of an undertaker. Somebody had alerted him to the occurrence of scandal. Bending low over Egerton, he offered whispered observations. 'Certain rules . . . consideration for other guests . . . service in your room of course . . .'

Jacqueline had caught the drift halfway through the sermon. He saw her mood lurch through embarrassed realization into belligerence; the manager was going to receive the George Sand treatment, strength five. Retreat even at the cost of humiliation seemed the wisest course. 'Come on,' he said, and took her by the hand.

They left the restaurant in a silence appropriate to high theatrical tragedy. The manager brought up the rear, his eyes cast down, away from sin. Jacqueline led the way to his car, moving now with grim defiance, calling the manager names between her teeth as she passed the reception desk. When Egerton began suggesting another restaurant after a trip back to the cottage for further covering, she rejected the idea fiercely. They would eat there; in the refrigerator was chicken and she would toss a salad to have with it. It would be better than anything else in this dump. She was not to be argued out of it. The suspicion grew within him that she might not be *persona grata* in Deya's other restaurants.

Standing beside her in her kitchen while she sliced tomatoes viciously, he managed at last to direct her thoughts towards her family. She spoke neutrally and without naming them of Giordano and Evelyn, affectionately of Lauren. She didn't mention Rylance or Camilla at all. 'Do you ever see your sister?' he asked.

'She visited a couple of months back.'

'From London?'

'No, she's not there now.' He couldn't gauge if it was deliberate reticence that made her stop.

She worked with surprising deftness making the salad and dividing up the meagre amount of chicken that had come out of the refrigerator. It seemed she could function

145

well enough in short bursts. When they had carried the food and a fresh bottle of wine through to the sitting room, she looked down at the dress as though suddenly reminded.

'To hell with that bimbo,' she said. She sat down and reached across to touch his glass with her own. 'I like you Matt.'

'Mark,' he said. He looked about him. 'How much longer are you planning to stay here?'

'I don't know, maybe to the turn of the year. That's when the lease runs out.'

'It could be rather lonely. You ought to have your sister come to stay again.'

She shrugged.

'Does she look like you?'

'Not really. Would you like to see a photograph? She sent one the other day.' Her fondness for Lauren was obvious. Reaching behind her she opened a drawer in a small desk. From an envelope on top of a pile of straw place mats, she extracted a Polaroid snapshot and handed it to him. He saw a folded sheet of notepaper was still inside the envelope.

Lauren was seated on what looked like a sea wall. Evelyn Rylance had been right in telling him the old photograph she had provided was still a good likeness. In this latest snapshot, Lauren looked hardly changed, just a little more assured. The man seated beside her was presumably Fernandes. He was much as Egerton had imagined him, thickset with sombre eyes but handsome in a rough-cut way.

'Is that a friend with her or someone closer?'

'I'll guess they'll marry soon.'

'What does he do?'

She slipped the photograph back in the envelope and

146

closed the drawer. 'He's going into politics in Spain. He's a Basque.'

He pressed on, trying to make his voice sound casual. 'Is that where the picture was taken?'

'No, they haven't got there yet.' He sensed the constraint as she spoke the words. She was holding back and however drunk she became she was unlikely to be tempted to say more. He needed to get at the letter that was with the photograph.

The chicken had been barely enough for even one person of normal appetite. Nothing else seemed to be on offer after they had finished the salad. Hunger gnawed at him. He decided that the wine was the only way of quietening the pangs inside.

Half an hour later he was still sober but only just. Jacqueline seemed to have reached a plateau of muzzy contentment. Seated beside him she was making a pretence of reading his palm. Nothing much she said made sense. Her face was very close. He kissed the back of her neck and felt her fingers tighten about his wrist to hold it against her body. When he gently turned her head so that he could kiss her throat, the grip slackened and she sighed as though some final residue of tension had left her.

After a while she picked up her glass and left him. When she returned, she stood in the doorway, empty glass in her hand, gazing at him silently. Her hair had been combed out and she had applied fresh lipstick. She had drunk too much to be wholly desirable; but someone could well say the same about him. When he raised his eyebrows she said, 'Let's work something out to put in that article.'

He contrived to force himself awake three or four times during the night. Each time he was looking for enough light from the window to feel confident of reaching the desk in the sitting room without blundering into furniture. Not that there seemed a real danger that Jacqueline would hear him. After they had made love, she had reached for her handbag and taken another couple of pills. By the time he had finally crept out of bed, she was lying on her stomach, her breathing heavy, a little trickle from the corner of her mouth moistening the pillow. He fetched the Minox from his jacket pocket and went to the sitting room.

Taking the letter from the drawer he switched on the desk lamp. The writing was untidy and hurried but easy enough to read.

> Hotel Constantine
> Nice.
> Tuesday

Dearest Jake,

I have to give somebody my world exclusive . . .! We decided today it really is a Thing so – we plan to marry as soon as we get to Spain in December and L. has introduced me to his parents. You are positively the first and only person to be told.

Enclosed is picture taken by passing American tourist from La Jolla (where else?) of happy couple before eating 200-franc celebration lunch. Am God knows how many kilos heavier than when I left London but relying on L.'s assurance that Basques like their women *sturdy*!

We leave this hotel at the end of the week and move to an apartment L. has rented. I'm not telling you where, then if Evelyn turns up in Deya you really won't know. You can always contact me in an emergency through L. He and his friends use the Basque Club at 115, Rue de l'Hôtel des Postes for their meetings and he collects his mail from there most days.

I hope you're feeling happier. Also that Rat QC is now coming through with the alimony regularly. I worry about you, Jake. If things got very tight, I could have some funds transferred from my account in Geneva. Don't forget that.

Must now go and collect laundry. No more news except you

can tell David, I *think* he's won! In three more weeks we'll know. Keep him safe!

Love, darling,
Lauren

The desk lamp could have been brighter but he took three shots each of the letter and the photograph and hoped for the best. The final stage of his search for Lauren seemed intoxicatingly near. On the face of it, all that was left to do was go to Nice, pick up Luis when he emerged from one of his visits to the Basque Club and tail him home. He put the letter and the photograph away again and tried the other drawers of the desk. There was more correspondence but this was from friends and the solicitor in London. Before he switched off the desk light he glanced at the books beside it. Three volumes of poetry and a biography of Robert Graves lay next to a Harold Robbins paperback. The Robbins had a page corner turned down. When the air at the mountain top proves inhospitable, he thought, you have to join the caravans in the valley.

He returned to the bedroom and dressed. It was barely six thirty. The pangs of hunger he had felt the previous evening were back, sharpened by a sense of triumph. In the kitchen he located the remnants of a stale loaf and wolfed it with a layer of apricot preserve. There was nothing else whatever that was edible. When he took a glass of orange juice and placed it beside Jacqueline's head, she still hadn't stirred from the position in which he had left her. It seemed pointless to disturb her dreams. Alongside the orange juice he left a scribbled note, announcing that he was going back to the hotel to work on the article but would look in to say goodbye later in the morning. Before he left he opened her handbag in case it might yield another letter from Lauren but there was none. Apart from tablets and some cosmetics the bag was almost empty, the only money a few small coins. It was impossible to believe that everything she had was going on white wine and pills; her solicitor must surely be extracting enough from Rat QC to keep her from these straits. But if so it was being siphoned off.

Back at the hotel, he was the only person about, apart from cleaning women and the odd floor waiter. On his bedside telephone he ordered a double breakfast and lay back to think about Lauren's letter to Jacqueline. It had been nearly a fortnight old but it seemed certain that she and Fernandes would still be in Nice. He could hardly wait to get a plane out of Majorca. But he would need to get Antrim's chop on it first.

It was nearly eleven before the hotel exchange got his call through to the Bureau. Antrim was in a meeting. Baxter wanted to take a message.

'I think he'll wish to come out for this.'

He had to say it three different ways before Baxter gave in.

Antrim's voice was already expectant when he came on the line. 'You've found her?'

'Almost.' He told him the story. 'If you approve I'll leave here today. I've a provisional booking on a Madrid flight this afternoon. I ought to be in Nice by tomorrow.'

'Right.' It was the first occasion Egerton had heard geniality in Antrim's tones. 'Rylance will be very pleased. Keep at it.'

He was back in favour, for the time being anyway.

He returned to Jacqueline's cottage with a bunch of roses. Food for the kitchen might also have been a good idea but he decided she'd find that eccentric. A light motor cycle, almost new, stood near the open front door. He found her seated on the terrace; she was dressed in

150

shorts and a bikini top. In the chair beside her a dark, good-looking youth of nineteen or twenty sat smoking a cigarette. He was a local, presumably the owner of the motor cycle; possibly the mysterious David who kept cropping up, as well.

Jacqueline raised an arm. 'Hi.' She pushed a chair towards Egerton. 'How does the article look?'

'Pretty good.'

'Will I be in it?'

'Oh yes,' he said.

She gestured towards the youth. 'Meet Pepe.'

So it wasn't David. He shook the youth's hand.

'Pepe wants to go to Madrid and be an actor. I suppose you don't have any contacts there?'

'I'm afraid not.'

'He's driving his mama up the wall because he won't work any more as a waiter. He just keeps asking his family for money to get him to Madrid. He keeps asking *me*. You're a bastard, aren't you, Pepe?' her hand was stroking his thigh.

The youth stretched with languid grace. It seemed doubtful whether he had understood all the words but he seemed to have sensed the general line. His air was a curious mixture of nonchalance and watchfulness.

'Do you speak English?' Egerton asked.

'A little. Little, little.' The youth laughed as though he had been witty. He lacked any sort of charm but his looks were undoubtedly handsome. He wore an expensive wrist-watch. Perhaps this was where the alimony was going.

Egerton turned back to Jacqueline. She had accepted the roses with suitable noises but he noticed she wasn't offering him a drink from the bottle of wine she and the youth were sharing. 'My plane leaves this afternoon. Is

151

there anything I can do for you when I eventually get back to London?'

'You could shoot my lawyer.'

'I hope things work out.'

She shrugged and picked up her glass. He wasn't of interest any more.

When he went out of the garden gate, the small boy who had spoken to him the day before was back on his perch on the bridge. This time he was mending a bicycle inner tube.

Egerton nodded and the boy smiled at him in the same way. He looked as though he knew everything and perhaps he did. But all he said was 'Goodbye, *señor*.'

14

On the plane to Nice, he pictured the last round, the final stake-out. From the tall windows of his bedroom in a hotel, small but immensely comfortable, across the way from the Basque club, he would keep watch. Because he would have chosen a room only one floor up, there would be no problem about the dash to street level when Fernandes was sighted; or about trailing him back to the apartment where he and Lauren were holed up. When staying indoors became oppressive, he would find a table at a pavement café which would provide an equally convenient view.

Reality proved as unrelenting as ever. No hotel, commanding a view of the courtyard through which the club was approached, existed in the Rue de l'Hôtel des Postes. Even access to the apartment block immediately opposite, supposing that could have been arranged, would yield no joy. At the vital spot, the Rue de l'Hôtel des Postes opened out into the Place Wilson, with a garden and children's playground occupying the length of a block; the foliage of the trees in the garden would effectively conceal the courtyard entrance from even the highest apartment. To maintain any long-term coverage, short of brazenly sitting on the stones of the courtyard itself, he had no choice but to alternate his time between two cafés on the corner where the Rue Gubernatis stretched northwards from Place Wilson and a bench in the children's playground. In the late afternoon of his arrival, after taking the film from the Minox to be developed, he seated himself amongst the infant hordes. Gloomily reviewing his plans, he was suddenly aware of an ominous blotching on the bench beside him. Looking up at what, an hour before, had been a brilliant sky, he realized that he still hadn't allowed for the worst.

By dawn next day, a grey hissing downpour made mockery of the idea of taking up his vigil. When, during a brief respite, he ventured on to streaming pavements to collect the developed film and prints, he found tables and chairs at the cafés stacked away as though for winter, the gardens of the Place Wilson a desolation of dashed flowers.

Eating his evening meal in the hotel he had found in the next street, he pinned his hopes on *Nice Matin's* robust assurance that tomorrow the *orage* would have yielded to *cieux éclaircis*. He studied the prints of Lauren's letter to Jacqueline in case it had more to tell him. But there was nothing, just the curious riddle of the final paragraph. The David whom Lauren had mentioned enigmatically to Sally Kirkwood seemed to have turned up in Majorca although there had been no sign of him at Jacqueline's. Perhaps he was hiding up in some other part of the village. But if so, why? From what? After a while he decided it was an insoluble conundrum. And anyway, it didn't seem relevant to his search for Lauren.

The next morning he saw with relief that they had got it right, those confident French forecasters, so different from the havering each-wayers at home: the *cieux* could hardly be clearer and, opposite his window, the roofs were already drying in the sun. Half an hour later he had his first coffee of the watch at a specially unstacked table on the pavement beside the brighter of the two cafés. But, as the day wore on, he began to doubt the practicability of his task. It was not only that the combination of fatigue and boredom from constantly watching in the same direction was an increasing strain. His regular appearance in one of three places excited more interest than he had forseen; and while tips ensured that cordiality outweighed the curiosity of the café waiters, he feared it might not be long before someone in the children's playground fingered him to the police as a child molester waiting to pounce.

When darkness fell, without a glimpse of anyone who resembled the photograph of Fernandes, he decided another plan was needed. Boldness was going to be unavoidable. He would call at the club the following day and ask for help in identifying an unknown Basque who had lent him money in a nearby bar when his notecase was stolen. The Basque had said the money could be left for him at the club; but now he had forgotten the Basque's name. He would then describe Fernandes as he looked in the photograph. If the story produced an address or a statement of when he was next expected at the club, he was practically home and dry. If it didn't and his enquiry was reported to Fernandes that might be unfortunate. But some risk had to be taken.

The following day, reckoning that the club would not be in effective operation much before noon, he spent a while in the alleys of the Old Town, absorbing the odours of new bread and old refuse. Returning to the Place Wilson via the Rue Foncet, he was brought to an abrupt halt. Standing near the entrance to the courtyard was a group of four men. Two were middle-aged, wearing dark suits and berets set very squarely on their heads. The others were younger and more casually dressed. Hand-shaking was in progress, preparatory to a parting.

Given the location and those berets, it seemed at least possible that they had just emerged from the club. More-

155

over, although one of the younger men was nearly bald, the other had the right build for Fernandes and hair curling into his neck in the way that Victor Crispin had found so thrilling. He felt hope surge inside. It was difficult to accept that his luck had revived in so handsome a fashion; yet, as the man broke away from the others and wheeled, his profile showed him to be a more than reasonable fit for the figure in the snapshot.

The man walked to the end of the block and turned north into the Rue Gubernatis. His disappearance from sight galvanized Egerton. If he proved not to be Fernandes, following would have cost only a little wasted time and energy. He walked quickly to the end of the Place Wilson and saw that his quarry had changed to the left-hand pavement and was strolling almost aimlessly as though to kill time. Finally he halted at a restaurant and went inside. After a couple of minutes Egerton followed.

It was barely twelve thirty and few of the dozen or so tables were taken. The room had a pleasantly faded and unfashionable appearance; black and white photographs of Nice in quieter times lined the walls. The man sat alone on a red velvet banquette, beneath one of the photographs. Taking a seat at the table immediately alongside, Egerton watched while he sipped a cognac and talked with an air of polite melancholy to a waitress. He seemed to be waiting for someone.

Egerton ordered and opened the copy of *The Times* he had bought earlier. In a side column on the front page there was a new GOLIATH story but not about leakages this time. A march of peace organizations opposed to the purchase of GOLIATH had taken place in London. Something had gone amiss in the liaison between the march's organizers and the police, with the result that traffic had been immobilized in the West End for several hours.

There was a photograph alongside the story, taken somewhere in the Mall, of Rylance in the back of an official limousine, looking very put out.

The empty tables were filling. Most of the arrivals were elderly men and women; the greetings exchanged with the waitresses were at once formal and intimate. Some nodded in the direction of the next table. With each acknowledgement the man half-rose in his seat and bowed courteously. The unwelcome thought began to harden in Egerton's mind that here was an ordinary local business man, a Niçois who happened to look rather like Fernandes.

But suddenly the other was upright and for the first time smiling. Hurrying through the door of the restaurant to accept and return his kiss, without a shadow of doubt, was Lauren Giordano. She took her seat between them on the banquette. Although lacking the fine-boned features and auburn hair shared by Evelyn and Jacqueline, she was more attractive than the photographs had suggested. She looked about her. Catching Egerton's eye she smiled quickly before her gaze travelled on; it was the smile of someone who still believed the world could be a good place and wanted others to feel the same.

It was impossible to hear her conversation with Fernandes, their heads were too close together: no one could doubt they were in love. Egerton ate slowly, trying to avoid getting too far ahead of them but they seemed set on lingering over their meal. Almost an hour passed. Toying with his second portion of cheese, he gazed at the photograph on the wall in front of him. It would have been taken, he supposed, towards the end of the nineteenth century: women were scrubbing laundry on the stones beside the river that ran through the town. One of the women had the look of Gwen about her. He felt a twinge that he had not sent her a postcard. At this distance her contribution to his domestic existence gave off a rosier glow. He decided he must take her a gift.

Fingers rested lightly on his arm and pressed. Startled, he turned. Lauren had leaned towards him, smiling. 'Would you mind if I looked at your *Times*?'

She studied the front page and made some remark to Fernandes. 'You can keep it if you like,' Egerton said.

She thanked him. 'Are you from London?'

'Yes.'

'Did you get caught in the great snarl-up?' She was pointing to the item about the anti-GOLIATH march.

He explained that he'd flown in two days before it happened. Pointing to the photograph of Rylance he said, to see how she would respond, 'Portrait of a cross politician . . .' She smiled but said nothing, her eyes returning to the news story. For all her apparent openness, she was quite good at dissembling, he decided.

He supposed that would be the end of the exchange but she went on to ask him which part of London he lived in. Fernandes said nothing but his smile was indulgent. The opportunity to keep them talking was too good to let slip. As they finished eating, he invited them to take brandy. It was hardly consistent with Evelyn Rylance's instruction to have no contact with Lauren. But she had not allowed for circumstances in which Lauren might approach *him*; now that had happened, there seemed little point in holding back, provided she wasn't alerted to his role.

They exchanged names. Fernandes gave his in full, Lauren only her Christian name. She embarked on more questions about London, mostly light-hearted but with a touch of wistfulness. She might have been some exile encountered in a remote, forgotten place. Mundane facts about the strike on the Underground and the new programme at Covent Garden she greeted with relish. Once

158

or twice Fernandes added his own questions, but Egerton suspected they had been invented simply to please *her*. For the most part he sat quiet, admiring each tiny movement, each shifting plane of her features.

'What do you do?' Lauren asked. 'I mean – what's your work?'

He had forgotten that he might face that question. He picked up his glass of wine to give himself more time to think of an innocent-sounding answer. 'I'm in estate agency, my firm's planning to open an office here. I came to look into the possibilities.'

He sensed that some train of thought had started in her mind.

'Are you going back to London soon?'

'Tomorrow or the next day.'

Her eyes turned towards Fernandes spelling out a question. He remained silent but gently smiling. She said to him, 'Do you suppose he could perhaps deliver your letter? It would be a way round . . . the problem. Don't you think?'

Fernandes looked into his brandy. 'I don't want to inconvenience Mr Egerton.'

'A letter . . .?' Egerton asked.

Fernandes shrugged. 'It's for a friend in London. There is some family business on which I have written – very personal. Unfortunately letters to her can go astray. Someone in the apartment block, the porter perhaps, is unfriendly. I do not wish to risk the post. But it may be out of your way.'

'What address?'

'She lives in Crawford Street, Marylebone. It is near the High Street.'

'But I go quite close every day.' He wasn't even having

to tell a lie. 'It would be no trouble if you feel it would help.'

He waited for Fernandes to make up his mind, not wanting to seem more eager than courtesy demanded. If, as seemed likely, Fernandes hadn't got the letter in his pocket now, it would surely be natural to invite him back to their apartment for a drink. That would remove the hazard of having to tail them after this lunch. Moreover, Bellamy had spoken of Garcia Fernandes perhaps being back in England for a terrorist operation. Luis's letter might be intended for him. If so, it would amount to a useful extra bonus from his trip to Nice. One in the eye for the sarcastic Rivers too.

'If you are really quite sure . . .?' Fernandes said.

Lauren looked triumphant. She squeezed Fernandes' hand: she had solved a problem for him. Turning to Egerton she said, 'Why don't you come to dinner tonight? Then Luis can give you the letter. Are you free . . .?'

'Absolutely free,' he said.

The address they had provided was up the hill from the town, almost into Cimiez. Halfway along a cul-de-sac, Egerton's taxi driver pointed to a cement-faced block of flats, less grand than most of its neighbours. There were balconies looking out to sea, bright with pot plants and sunblinds. The board in the entrance hall said that 'Fernandes' was on the highest floor of all. He rode the elevator, big with expectation of a sunset view across the Baie des Anges.

But the apartment skulked at the back of the block. The balcony on to which Lauren led him gave on to a strip of scrubby hillside and the foundations of apartments higher up. A second-hand glory from the sun was reflected in the window panes above.

160

Rising from a basket chair beside which Fernandes stood, was an untidy, middle-aged man, his forehead crowned by a thicket of grey hair that looked as though it would see off the attack of any normal comb. He was dressed in voluminous shorts and sandals that revealed plump brown toes. 'Arthur Boyd, our neighbour,' Lauren said, indicating the balcony of the adjoining apartment. The man extended a hand. His eyes were very sharp.

Drinking cassis, they sat on the balcony while the orange glow deepened in the windows behind. A smell of flowers and cool foliage drifted into their nostrils. On the Boulevard de Cimiez a few hundred metres away the noise of traffic died to a murmur. The view might be a write-off but the place still had the edge on Prince of Wales Drive.

It appeared that Boyd was a writer which accounted perhaps for the ferociously unkempt appearance; every year he came to the adjoining apartment for a month or two to work on his books. At other times he lived in Epping with a wife who was a gynaecologist and their Shi Tsu dog. He showed a marked reluctance to talk about his writing; obviously for him, it was like stockbroking or the manufacture of condoms, not a trade to be worn as a badge. But on other subjects he was articulate. Resting one foot on the knee of the other leg and wriggling the plump toes he showed himself to be well-informed, whenever his views were sought.

Dinner was *bouillabaisse*. Lauren's campaign for the seal hadn't apparently widened to cover other forms of marine life. Dipping his bread vigorously, Boyd uttered knowledgeable praise. Lauren accepted it with an unforced pleasure that was engaging. There was nothing brittle or blasé about her; a capacity for simple pleasure had survived whatever childhood had been like with

161

Giordano and Evelyn. It softened a manner that would otherwise have been over-intense.

Fernandes talked very little, preferring to watch and listen. When Egerton asked him where in Spain he came from, he said with a dismissive gesture, 'You would not have heard of the place. It's in Vizcaya – a Basque province.'

'You're a Basque yourself . . .?'

'Yes.'

There seemed no reason not to press on boldly. 'Do you support the Basque nationalist movement?'

Fernandes smiled politely. 'Of course.'

'. . . To the extent of wanting independence from Spain?'

'Not full independence, no.' Fernandes hesitated. He was plainly wondering whether the occasion called for more than a superficial response. 'I should like to see a proper acknowledgement of our identity and culture by Madrid. I can remember when, in my village, if you were heard using even a few words of the Basque language you were taken away to the police station.'

'But that was under Franco,' Boyd said.

'Old attitudes die hard.'

'Even with your present government?'

Fernandes shrugged. 'Whatever government you have in Madrid it will always say it is worried about the integrity of the State. Ministers eventually become obsessed by what they see as threats to it. People in Madrid say "Give the Basques an inch and the Catalans will take a mile." Of course there is an element of truth in that. But what most Basques ask for is no more than the restoration of the rights we had as a separate people – our *fueros*. Restoration *in reality*, not just on paper.'

'You might then become a State within a State.'

'Perhaps.'

'But do you expect to achieve that?' Egerton asked.

'I *expect* nothing. God will decide.' He used the word casually as if he had been referring to someone living, albeit very senior. 'We must simply carry on the struggle.'

Lauren was watching Fernandes in a way that was both admiring and protective. Egerton said cautiously, 'But there seem to be fundamentally different views on the means.'

'One follows one's conscience,' Fernandes said. 'God speaks through that.' It was an evasion and intended as such.

Lauren said gently, 'But never through killing.' She had looked down at her plate. Fernandes waited until her eyes lifted again. He spread his hands wide in some message and smiled. She smiled back.

Lauren was in the kitchen making coffee when the telephone rang. The call was for Fernandes and he disappeared to answer it. 'Do you know anything about Basque politics?' Egerton asked Boyd.

'A little. I've met one of the nationalists who gave up the armed struggle when the present government took office in Madrid, a man named Barillo. He used to live in Nice until a year or two back. We got into conversation in a café one day.' Boyd loosened the belt straps on his antique shorts. 'Luis has also talked to me about his aims after he's had a few drinks. He's going into politics when he returns to Spain.'

'I was surprised to see there's a Basque club here. I thought the Spanish Basque emigrés were over on the west coast.'

'That's where the bombers hole up when the Spanish police flush them out. After Barillo decided that violence ought to be dropped and ETA should reach an accommodation with Madrid, he moved away from Bayonne where he was living and came here. It was a way of distancing himself from the terrorist wing of ETA. His supporters came with him and established the club. Luis is a great admirer of Barillo. The club was probably one of the things that drew him and Lauren to Nice. The organization Barillo set up here is still very active amongst Basques living abroad.'

'What exactly do the initials ETA stand for?'

'I can't remember the words but they mean Basque Homeland and Freedom.'

'Does Luis support ETA?'

'Not the military wing. He may have done once. But like Barillo he's now fundamentally opposed to violence. He genuinely believes in a Spanish entity. But it has to accommodate all the ways in which the Basques insist on being different.'

There was a chill in the air now. Lauren closed the balcony doors while they drank coffee. She played a tape of thirteenth-century *cantigas* Fernandes had bought that afternoon. Sometimes alone, sometimes accompanied by a harp, a woman sang. The sounds reached out to them like the call of distant bells: it was as though each syllable had been rinsed by the crisp air of the uplands before it descended to fill the silences far below.

They listened with their eyes closed or fixed on the ceiling. When Egerton glanced across at the others their appearance was relaxed. Yet in both Fernandes and Lauren he could sense a tension. About Fernandes there was always a look of vigilance, as though he was prepared for something to happen elsewhere. Lauren's manner was different: she was alert for any shift in Fernandes' mood, any threat to his wellbeing.

By the time he rose to leave, the letter was still

unmentioned. He wondered if some remark he had made or his questions to Fernandes about Basque affairs had caused misgivings about entrusting him with it. But in the hallway Fernandes took from his pocket an envelope and handed it over. 'Are you sure this will not inconvenience you?'

'Quite sure.'

It was addressed to Señora Castillo at 11d, Hoddershall Mansions, Crawford Street, London W1. In the top right-hand corner of the envelope, in polite reminder of Egerton's commitment, Fernandes had written 'For Personal Delivery Only.'

'If Señora Castillo is out when you call, would you please place the letter under the door of the apartment, not in the mail box? It is on the first floor of the block at the front. The entrance doors are open in daytime.'

'Of course.'

'One further request if you will be so kind: it is important for me to know that you have been able to deliver the letter safely. Would you telephone me when you have done that? Perhaps this will cover the cost . . .' He had begun taking a banknote from his wallet until Egerton made him stop. Lauren was copying down the telephone number for Egerton; she handed it to him and then stood, her head against Fernandes' shoulder, fingers linked with his. The chances of Evelyn Rylance or anyone else succeeding in breaking up their relationship seemed very slim.

The following morning he waited until he could be reasonably confident Antrim would be in his office before he called to give him the news. Antrim was making sounds close to enthusiasm as he took down the address and telephone number.

'Would you like me to fly back today?'

Antrim hesitated. 'No, stay where you are until I've spoken to Rylance. I don't suppose there's anything more for you to do but we'd better see. I'll get back to you, probably tomorrow morning. Enjoy yourself in the meantime.' He was being uncharacteristically expansive.

Outside the hotel, the day had the clarity of crystal. Coffee smells mingled with the perfume of passing women as he walked beneath the arcades of the Place Masséna. He was free as the air, at liberty to do whatever he wanted. Yet, now the euhporia of success was past, he found he had no appetite for pleasing himself. Meeting Lauren and Fernandes, observing their relationship, having their trust placed in him over the letter, had changed the character of the search from an abstract challenge to something tiresomely complicated by human feelings. He had wormed his way into their sanctuary simply to play them false, Lauren by betraying her whereabouts to the Rylances, Fernandes by letting him think the letter's contents would be seen by no one except Señora Castillo. Lauren could tell her mother to go to hell, of course, when she showed up in Nice. But the elaborate steps she had taken to avoid the confrontation were proof of how much she would hate it.

About Fernandes, there had been an authority, a moral tone, that made deceiving him seem just as squalid. Even if Boyd had read the signs wrongly and Fernandes retained an association with terrorism which went beyond remaining on close terms with his brother, he somehow deserved better than to have his hospitality abused. He was conscious of a vague resentment against Antrim for having given him this task; an illogical sense of having been exploited grew inside him.

Trying to shake off the mood, he embarked on a desultory exploration of the town, ate well, drank good wine, studied women; but nothing pleased. By the evening he was conscious only of a sour weariness. Entering a cinema he found himself watching pornography and realized that that was to be the flavour of the day, feeling exploited.

Relief came the next day before he had finished breakfast. It was announced by Baxter speaking with careful condescension. 'I believe you're waiting for instructions, Egerton.'

'Yes.'

'I'm to tell you that you can fly back as soon as you like. Or, rather, as soon as possible.'

'Right.'

'How does the *Côte* look?'

He gazed down from his bedroom window. Outside a lingerie boutique, a cat slept in a shaft of sunlight. It was going to be another fine day. His mood began to lift. 'Quite good. In fact, marvellous.' He enjoyed the thought of making Baxter envious.

He booked a seat on the afternoon plane to Heathrow, regretting, now that departure was no more than hours away, that he had made so little of the previous day. In pursuit of lost opportunity he visited galleries, walked in the Roman Arena, then took a taxi back to the beach and lay gazing at the sky in a last farewell to summer.

He arrived at the airport bare minutes before the final check-in time shown on his ticket; but hurrying through the entrance hall he saw from the indicator board that the plane from London on which he would be making the return trip had landed less than a quarter of an hour beforehand. Handing in his luggage he went to the airport shops in search of gifts for the women in his life, Gail and Gwen. When he emerged, the London passengers were beginning to appear from passport control. He stayed to watch, seized with the thought that he might glimpse Evelyn Rylance among them, on her way to browbeat Lauren.

The crocodile diminished to a trickle. She was hardly the sort of person who would be trailing in the rear but he lingered until a new surge of passengers appeared with an air of vivacity that ruled out an Anglo Saxon flight. It was just as well she hadn't been there, he reflected: she might have caught sight of him and embarked on an interrogation long enough to make him miss his own plane.

As he turned to make his way to the departure lounge, he glanced briefly through the airport doors to where cars were picking up passengers from the new flight arrival. A squat man carrying an overnight bag stood in profile for a second or two. He wore jacket and trousers of black leather with an open-necked white shirt; around a gorilla throat was a gold chain. An older man in a broad-brimmed hat and a cashmere top coat was greeting him. As they turned away from Egerton, a uniformed chauffeur held open the rear door of a limousine with smoked glass windows. They climbed inside. At this distance it was impossible to be sure. But the squat man with the gorilla throat had certainly had the look of Sam Giordano.

15

There was a note from his secretary when he opened his diary after reporting back to Antrim. Gail had telephoned the day before he left Nice and asked when he would return. She'd been told there was no news and had rung off without leaving a message. He wondered if her call had been an SOS. Half of him hoped it might have been. He reached for the telephone directory then remembered she had no phone of her own; there was probably one in the house but it would be in the name of the Gujerati landlord and he didn't know that.

Jamie was the only certain source of news. To his surprise he found that he was listed and rang the number but there was no reply. That could mean he was away on one of his trips. If he couldn't raise Jamie by the evening he would have to call at Gail's when he left the office for the day.

His door opened. Antonia Strachan was looking round the side of it with an expression of enquiry. He should have stopped by her room before now to give her his news.

'I hear you got your girl.'

'How did you know?'

'Baxter told me last night. Congratulations. What's she like?'

'I think she's rather nice. So was Fernandes for that matter. If Evelyn Rylance has turned up there I hope they show her the door. In fact I'm sure they will.'

She seated herself on the corner of his desk. 'I hear you're getting a week's leave as a sort of prize.'

He grimaced. 'I'm sorry, I thought I'd be back with you

today. When I said so, it was made clear that I was not expected to look a gift horse in the mouth. I'm to go off tonight after I've written up my notes.'

The look on her face was ironical. 'Our leader is bucked I imagine.'

'He did give that impression.'

'Onwards and upwards to his "K",' she said. 'That's what he's thinking.' She slid abruptly from the desk and pulled up a chair. 'You didn't hear me say that. So tell me how you found them.'

He told her. She had her head resting against the back of the chair as she talked. At the end she turned it towards him; soft black hair fell across her cheek as she nodded, 'So that's that . . .'

'Pretty well. I'm told Rylance wants to see me sometime, presumably to hear the details. But he's just off to a conference in Washington and won't be back for a week or so. Baxter's supposed to fix a date for when I return from leave.' He opened the folder in front of him. 'Before I forget . . . I was told to ask you to have Fernandes' letter to Señora Castillo fiddled open and, assuming it's about Basque business, a copy sent over to Rivers in Special Branch. Then somebody can push it under the Señora's door.'

'What explanation do I give to Rivers for our having intercepted it?'

'Antrim said you'd think of something.'

She compressed her lips. He watched her tapping the letter against the palm of her hand and wondered again about the *affaire* she was supposed to have had with Antrim. 'You *will* see it's delivered afterwards . . .' he said. When she raised her eyebrows at his tone, he went on, 'It's simply that meeting Fernandes, hearing him talk – ' He broke off. 'Well, I don't care to let him down

170

to the extent of not even delivering the bloody letter. I'd like to be able to ring him and say I've arranged it.'

He was being wet about both Lauren and Fernandes; he could imagine her pausing, as she wrote his next annual report, at the column headed Moisture Content or whatever the approved phrase was.

She gave no hint of what she was thinking. 'How are you going to spend your leave?'

He gazed out of the window so that he couldn't see her expression. 'There's something I must . . .'

She looked politely interested. He felt obliged to go on. 'I have a friend with a problem that needs sorting out.'

'What sort of problem?'

It was almost certainly unwise to have embarked on this. But he had to talk about Gail to somebody and she was the most level-headed person he knew. 'It's a girl who's been injecting heroin for rather a long time. If I could get her away from London for a while, I might talk her into having treatment. The trick is going to be to make her *want* to get off it. The last time it was tried, she walked out of the clinic.'

'How close are you?'

'Close?'

'I mean – are you in love with her?'

'I was when we were at university. Then she met someone else, an actor. They lived together when she came down from Oxford. Unfortunately he was also on heroin. I discovered the other day that he died about a year ago.'

'Sad,' she said.

He wondered what she really felt but she had turned so that he couldn't see her expression.

'I'd thought of having her to stay in my flat for a while but London's hopeless for anyone who's trying to stop, there are too many pressures. Somehow I must get her away.'

'Do you still love her?'

He knew that she was no longer looking away from him. It was the first time he had squarely faced it. 'I never really stopped I suppose. It was one of the reasons I had for going to America the year before I joined the Bureau. Yes, I do still love her. Very much.'

She was brooding. 'It's possible I can help. My mother's house in Shropshire is empty. Since my father died last winter she's been staying with her sister in New Mexico. I visit the house to keep an eye on things but I'm not going this weekend. You can have the key if you like. It's eight miles from the nearest real village and nobody is likely to call round offering heroin. As far as I know, incest is the only local diversion.'

'You wouldn't mind my taking her there for a week?'

'You'd be doing a favour by airing the place for me.'

Now the opportunity was there, he wondered if he would actually succeed in persuading Gail to go. At present he didn't even know where she was. But he didn't want to sound lukewarm. 'That's marvellous,' he said.

When she was leaving him, she hesitated by the door. 'You were both taking drugs at Oxford, were you?'

He felt a surge of relief that she had asked. 'Yes.'

'Heroin?'

'Yes.'

'But *you* stopped . . .'

'Eventually.'

'And never went back to it . . .' Her tone was matter of fact, perhaps too much so.

'Never.'

It was his opportunity to get it all out in the open. But before he could go on, she nodded briskly as though she had as much of the story as she wanted. 'Let me know if you want the key.'

He watched the door close behind her. He hadn't told her about the man in black leather at Nice airport who had looked like Giordano or of the questions it had raised in his mind. She would probably have said it wasn't his business, and she would have been right.

For an hour or two he argued himself into a mood of optimism about getting Gail to leave London for the week. If necessary he would pack her bag and simply bundle her into the car. Late afternoon brought news that killed the plan stone dead. He had finally got a response from Jamie's number. When he asked about Gail, Jamie sounded surprised. 'Haven't you heard?'

'Heard what? Is she all right?'

'I imagine so. She was when I saw her the night before she left.'

'Left for where?'

'Barbados.'

He stared at his blotter only half-listening to the explanation. Some sprig had come into a million from his family trust on reaching twenty-five. He had chartered an aircraft and flown a party to Barbados to celebrate. Gail had been invited along. The gossip columnists were making the usual meal of the affair. The sprig's name meant nothing. 'How did she meet him?' he asked.

'I introduced them – that night at Dido's.'

His heart had begun to sink. 'I gather she tried to get me at the office. Do you know why?'

'She told me she didn't want you to misunderstand her reason for going. It just seemed a marvellous chance of some sun.'

He wondered if Jamie had invented that to make him feel better. 'This is somebody you supply, I suppose.'

There was a pause at the other end. It had been an indiscreet thing to say on an open line but to apologize now could make it worse. 'Just a chap I know.' Jamie's voice was faintly aggrieved. It was the closest he ever came to sounding angry.

He went to look for Antonia and told her he wouldn't be borrowing the house. She didn't ask why. 'So you'll stay in London?'

'No, I'll probably visit my sister. Her son's my godchild. I haven't seen him for months. He's a fiend but I'm fond of him.'

She went back to the file she'd been reading. 'Don't forget to leave your number. Other fiends may need to contact you. We're still short on evidence for the Beynon prosecution.'

He inclined his head and left her. If it wasn't intended as a crack that he'd left the case only half-wrapped up, it came pretty close.

For nearly four days that world went away. Together with the evening sun it dropped behind the horizon as he stood at his bedroom window, suitcase still unpacked, and watched the fiend operating a ray gun against a cow that had strayed into the orchard. The next morning he cut the grass, fetched Joanna's provisions order from Cirencester, mended her steam iron and resumed the godfather role. It was less demanding than on previous occasions. In the months since his last encounter with Marcus, there had been a shift from mass destruction to conservation. Lauren Giordano might not have gone for the style however. The garden shed was now a combined laboratory, clinic and concentration camp. Tea chests, jam jars, matchboxes, each with its occupant, covered the floor and potting bench. The prisoners were paraded once or twice

174

a day, put through an exercise programme and returned to confinement with rations that were varied and experimental. Those who failed to respond vivaciously to the regime were released, the others were doomed to languish in custody. The prize inmate was a mouse of exceptional beauty.

Away from the shed Marcus's attentions were focused on the river inlet at the foot of the orchard. He had built a dam of mud and branches; twigs, felled by notional lumberjacks working further up the river, swirled into sight, to spin for a few aimless moments before drifting against the dam wall. Concentration on these events, at first reluctant, eventually became unforced, even absorbing. Once, lying full-length to catch the drama of six logs, roped together, hurtling into the pool, he turned his head and saw a buck rabbit watching with the same intentness. The Bureau ceased to have a reality. He thought now of Rylance and Lauren and Fernandes as figures in a show that had closed long ago.

But he was wrong. That evening, after he had left Marcus at last in bed with the mouse in its plastic box to see him through the night, he settled by the fire to read a newspaper while Joanna hunted hens in the long grass. At the bottom of the overseas news page was a story datelined Nice.

MORE 'DIRTY WAR' DEATHS?

The bodies of Luis Fernandes, whose brother Garcia is one of the most wanted members of ETA's extremist military wing, and Lauren Giordano, an American national who had been living with Fernandes, were discovered in a Nice apartment today. Both had been murdered.

Luis Fernandes is not believed to have been involved in terrorist activities during his stay in France although his past association with ETA is well known. The French police consider the killings are either the result of quarrels among factions within ETA or, more probably, in revenge for the recent murder of an Army colonel in Barcelona. They suspect the hand of the mysterious GAL (Anti-Terrorist Liberation Group) which is dedicated to eliminating prominent ETA figures in France.

The English author, Arthur Boyd, who lived in the next apartment heard the killings take place and was injured when he tried to intervene. He called the police on recovering consciousness by which time there was no trace of the killers.

This latest eruption of the so-called 'dirty war' (assuming police suspicions are correct) will provide additonal ammunition for the French Prime Minister on his official visit to Madrid next week. It is known that he already intended to protest to the Spanish government about both Basque incursions and activities of GAL in France. There have been allegations that GAL represents clandestine counter-terrorist activity by Spain's principal intelligence service, Cesid.

He sat staring at the wall opposite, shaken by the thought of them lying dead in the apartment where he had been their guest hardly a week ago. Only now was he conscious of how much they had engaged his sympathies. It was as though he had ceased to see them as quarry and joined them in spirit against those who had been their hunters.

After supper he decided he must find out more. 'Have you ever heard of a writer called Arthur Boyd?' he asked Joanna. She had switched on the television set and was clicking through the channels.

'Yes. He writes sexy thrillers.'

'Sexy thrillers!' He saw again that ungainly, vaguely academic figure in the outsize shorts and open sandals. It was impossible to credit. 'You must be thinking of someone else.'

'No, I'm not, I've read one. His wife's a gynaecologist. They live in Epping with a Shi Tsu.'

'How do you know all that?'

'I read about them in a Sunday colour magazine. His

wife does the sex bits. The books are very hot on technical detail.'

'The clinical approach,' he said. 'Do you suppose that really turns people on?'

She shrugged and gave him wool to hold while she balled it. 'Of course.'

He thought of Marcus upstairs with the mouse in the plastic box. She was right.

'Why are you interested in Arthur Boyd?' she asked.

'He knew two friends of mine who've just been killed. I'd like to ask him some questions.'

The next morning he left Marcus to do the logging on his own and drove to Cirencester. Research at the public library reproduced the telephone number of the Boyds' house in Epping. If the gynaecologist wife was at home, she could presumably tell him whether Boyd was fit enough to take calls in Nice and, if so, what the number there was. He went to a telephone box.

The answering voice was intimidatingly deep but also familiar. After a second or two he realized it belonged to Boyd himself. Apparently his injury hadn't immobilized him; he had flown back to England to consult his own doctor about it. If all proved well, he was returning to Nice at the weekend to get on with the book.

'I wonder if I might come and see you before then?' Egerton asked. 'I could drive over to Epping tomorrow if that suits.'

There was silence at the other end. He sensed Boyd's surprise. 'It's just that I'd very much like to hear what you think happened and why. The story in yesterday's paper struck me as a bit odd.'

Boyd grunted. 'That's one way of describing it.'

He agreed Egerton could visit him at noon. As he was

saying goodbye, he said, 'You're not really an estate agent are you?'

He couldn't very well keep that up now. 'No, I'll explain tomorrow.'

Apart from the bandage tied at a rakish angle round his head, Boyd looked well enough when he opened the door. The results of an X-ray ordered by his doctor had come through that morning and had been satisfactory. On the rest of his body he had suffered only bruises.

He led the way to a small conservatory at the back of the house and extracted bottles of German lager from a refrigerator in the corner. A gardener was staking asters in the herbaceous border outside. There was no sight or sound of the gynaecologist wife. Presumably she was on the job somewhere, getting the technology sorted out for the current work.

'Since you're not an estate agent,' Boyd said, 'what are you?'

'When we met I was being employed by Lauren's mother to locate her. I'd be grateful if you'd keep that to yourself.'

That seemed safe enough. The newspaper report hadn't connected Lauren with Rylance and from her caginess at their meeting, he felt sure she wouldn't have revealed the relationship to Boyd.

'Lauren's family didn't approve of Luis, so she'd run off with him, I take it,' Boyd said.

He nodded.

'I thought something like that had happened. So what are you after now?'

'Although the family haven't asked me to pursue this, I have the feeling there's something very strange about Lauren's death. As I told you on the telephone the story

178

in the newspaper seemed unlikely to me. For one thing it shrugs off too easily the fact that *she* wasn't a Basque. Do *you* believe they were murdered by this anti-terrorist organization, GAL, the Spanish government are supposed to be behind?'

Boyd made a gesture of disgust. 'Total balls.'

'You're sure . . .?'

'Absolutely. Luis was a Basque nationalist all right. But whatever might have happened in the past, he wasn't a terrorist when I knew him. As I think I told you, Barillo was the man he admired most and *his* objective was a negotiated settlement of all Basque claims. It makes *slightly* more sense to imagine the extremists killed Luis because he was about to come out in opposition to their methods.'

'But you don't sound as though you believe that either . . .'

'No.'

'Then why have the French police taken the line it was a political killing?'

Boyd shrugged. 'It suits them. Blaming Spanish in-fighting saves trouble – they don't have to look for other reasons. And blaming GAL is even better. After all GAL have been getting very active in France recently. The French want Madrid to rein it in.'

'So what do *you* think was the explanation for what happened?'

'I don't know exactly. I'll tell you what I told the police. You'll have to judge for yourself from that.'

Boyd poured himself another lager. Something had happened two days before the killings which he was convinced was connected. Going on to his balcony in the evening to water the plants, he had heard Lauren talking next door. She had two visitors, and he could tell from their voices that they were American. Unusually she had closed her own balcony doors so that he couldn't catch more than a few of the words spoken but it had been a quarrel, she was being threatened. Fernandes' voice was absent. He was often out, meeting his Basque friends in the early evening and Boyd guessed he hadn't been in the apartment.

The following day Boyd had met Lauren in the entrance hall to the apartment block. She seemed very quiet. She spoke of Luis deciding that after all it would be convenient if they went to Spain now instead of in November as had been their original intention. She said they'd probably be off at the end of the week.

The killings took place the following evening. Boyd had been working at his desk when he heard a commotion. The noise had come from the next apartment. Curiosity drove him to the balcony to listen. But all he heard now was a half-shout which could have been from Fernandes, then the noise of a chair or table overturning.

He hadn't been sure what he ought to do. Since he couldn't hear any more sound, it occurred to him that Fernandes had been drinking in the apartment alone – he knew he drank heavily on occasion – and had collapsed in a stupor. Finally he opened the door of his apartment, intending to go next door and knock. At that moment he was relieved to see Lauren coming down the corridor. She gave him a little wave with her latchkey and went into the apartment. Boyd withdrew, reckoning that if Fernandes *was* out cold on the floor, she'd be able to handle it.

His memory then was of events moving very fast. Almost at once there had been more noise, a scream from Lauren that seemed to be strangled in her throat and the low murmur of a man's voice that certainly wasn't Fernandes'. Boyd went and hammered on their door.

After a pause during which there was dead silence, the door was opened by a young man. Boyd noticed he was wearing gloves. When Boyd asked what was going on, he said he was a doctor who had been called to deal with a patient who had become violent. Boyd wouldn't buy that and began pushing the door open behind the man. He just had time to see Fernandes tied and gagged in a chair before Lauren seemed to materialize from nowhere, screaming to him for help. Behind her was another man with a gun which he brought down on Lauren's head to stop her reaching the door. Boyd rushed towards Lauren and that was the last thing he remembered before he was felled himself. When he recovered consciousness, he was still in the apartment. The place was in chaos – everything had been ripped apart in a systematic search. Fernandes had either been freed or had broken away from the chair because he was lying, still gagged, near the balcony doors. He'd been shot and was in a pool of his blood. Lauren was propped up in a corner. There were curious burn marks on her face. The cause of death, Boyd learned later from the police, was a brain haemorrhage which had occurred some time after the blow on the head.

Outside the conservatory, the gardener had turned to cutting down blackened lupins. Apart from the asters, no colour remained in the border. It was a world that was spent, over. Egerton stared into his glass, remembering the expression on Lauren's face as they told her the *bouillabaisse* was fine, perfect. 'It must have been a ghastly experience for you.'

'I've dreamed about it most nights since.'

'Do you know how the burns got on her face?'

Boyd pushed his fingers through the nest of grey hair that remained exposed by the bandage. 'This is only my idea . . . I believe Lauren was still alive after the blow on the head and recovered consciousness for a while. The burns looked as though they were made by a cigarette. I believe she was being tortured when she died.'

'But why?'

'They wanted something she had. *She*, mind you, not Luis. It was whatever they searched the apartment for. That's one reason why I don't believe what happened had anything to do with Spanish politics. Besides which, the men I saw weren't Basques, or any sort of Spaniard, they were *Niçois*, local thugs. I know the type from seeing them in the courts there when I was researching a book.'

'You told the police this . . .?'

'Of course. I even picked out from the mug book they showed me at police headquarters somebody I was pretty sure was one of the thugs. The chap who interviewed me said he belonged to a gang led by a big local crook named Raoul Baptiste. But by the next time they saw me they didn't want to know. Their line was, it could only be political. They got a bit uneasy when I persisted in talking about the visit of the Americans two days earlier. But they weren't going to be shifted from the story that suited them.'

Outside, the gardener had gathered together his tools and put them in a wheelbarrow; he was off to lunch. 'Did you happen to look out of your window when the Americans left and see the sort of car they had?'

Boyd shook his head. 'You forget, my apartment's at the back of the block.' He was watching Egerton curiously. 'What sort of car did you think it might be?'

'It doesn't make much sense at present,' he said. 'But I wondered if it was a limousine with smoked glass windows.'

16

Back at the Bureau, he found the going hard when he tried to interest Antonia in theories he had begun to form.

'You're not even sure it was Giordano you saw at Nice airport.'

'It looked like him.'

'But how did he know where Lauren was staying?'

'He may have telephoned Evelyn Rylance just after I passed the address back. She'd have had no reason to withhold it from him.'

'So he feels so keenly about her relationship with Fernandes that he goes to Nice and threatens her . . .'

'No,' he said patiently, 'He *may* have felt keenly about Fernandes but I suspect the reason he went was that when she visited him in the summer she acquired something he badly wanted to get back.'

'What sort of thing?'

'That I don't know.'

'So when she refuses to give it to him, he goes out and finds two thugs who agree to rough her up. That strikes me as pretty unlikely. Giordano may or may not have a line to the underworld where he comes from. But this was in Nice. He probably only knows the place from flying in on the way to film festivals in Cannes.'

'The man who met him off his plane seemed to be local. Not French but possibly an American living there.'

She was still looking unreceptive. 'Look,' he said, 'I accept that I can't be sure it was Giordano I saw. But I also can't forget what Sally Kirkwood said about something having happened during Lauren's trip to the States. Or my feeling that Giordano was holding back when I saw him at Claridges.'

'But are you suggesting she stole something from Giordano – papers perhaps that showed he was involved in criminal activity? That she was using them as blackmail? From all you've been told about her, from everything you *saw* of her, she doesn't sound like a person who'd go in for that.'

That of course was true. He could imagine Lauren Giordano being stubborn, even unbending when she was fighting for someone or something she cared passionately about. But she was too principled to be a thief. Nor was she the sort to get down in the gutter in order to pressure her own father. Or might she just bring herself to do it if it were for Fernandes' sake? He didn't know the answer to that. But, in any case, what could Fernandes need or fear from Giordano?

He gazed grimly at a photograph that stood on Antonia's desk. It was of a man with fair, wavy hair and a sunburned face; he seemed to be standing on an airfield. Presumably it was the husband who was said to have died in a flying accident. It occurred to him that perhaps she'd never been able to accept the fact of his death and this was the reason why she hadn't remarried. 'How much do you think I should mention of this to Rylance?'

She raised her eyebrows. 'You're still going to see him?'

'Apparently. I'd supposed he might have cancelled the appointment. But Baxter says I should assume it's still on. I'm going to Chester Square this evening.'

She pursed her lips. 'He's entitled to know what you've learned from Arthur Boyd.'

'Not more?'

'Anything else is really speculation. It's also very delicate ground. If he wants to pursue Boyd's story, it's up to him.'

'I don't think it ought to be dropped.'

'Perhaps not. But is it our business?'

He couldn't say it was. He felt she was being irritatingly casual about it, all the same. He picked up the photostat she had shown him earlier. It was a copy of the letter he had brought back from Fernandes for delivery to Señora Castillo. Apparently an inner envelope had been addressed simply 'Garcia.' Pinned at the back was the translation done in the Bureau.

The letter was a long and complicated affair with allusions that were often too cryptic to grasp to the attitude of different government ministers in Madrid and recent developments in the Basque territories. The thrust of it was plain however: Luis was pleading with Garcia to call off some imminent operation; he was also claiming to know that Madrid would do a deal over Garcia's past activities but that chance would be lost if the operation went ahead.

He handed it back to Antonia. 'It makes Luis Fernandes' position pretty clear. Rylance and his wife might get some satisfaction from knowing that the man Lauren went off with was not only not a terrorist, but he was trying to prevent some terrorist operation here. Can I tell him that?'

'I think you should.'

'What was Special Branch's reaction to the letter?'

'They were very pleased. They've been on tenterhooks for some Basque operation in London this autumn so they now know Garcia is holed up here for that.'

'Have they traced him?'

'Unfortunately not. The Castillo woman slipped surveillance the day they believe she delivered the letter. One of their surveillance team got caught in a lift.'

He remembered Rivers' voice on the telephone, that crack about how one should behave if one wanted to be thought professional. He could almost be sorry for him; but not quite.

Back in his room he found that most of the Beynon files had been deposited on his desk again. He turned a few pages without enthusiasm. He still felt sore at Antonia's lukewarm reaction to his suspicions about Giordano. After a while he knew he wasn't going to settle down before he had tested his theory. In the phone conversation he had listened to in the suite at Claridges, Giordano had talked of staying at the Excelsior Hotel in Rome after he left there. An hour later he found himself talking on a crackling line to someone announcing herself as Mary Jane Cord, Mr Giordano's Personal Assistant.

'Miss Cord, this is the British Department of Health,' he said.

She made a baffled noise. He went on, 'I expect you're aware from the press that the plane on which Mr Giordano flew from the United States to London a short while back carried a suspected smallpox case.'

She said she hadn't read it and wondered if she ought to tell him.

'No need just yet. But we're trying to keep track of passengers' movements and also their contacts. Did he travel directly to Rome from London?'

'Yes, he and Mrs Giordano.'

'Ah yes,' he said, 'that would be Joan Giordano.'

'Correct.'

'And have they both been living since then at the Excelsior Hotel?'

186

'Yes.'

'No trips outside Italy?'

He heard pages being turned. 'Only one, a visit to France for discussions about finance of the production he's working on. That was about ten days ago.'

'You went with him . . .?'

'No, Mrs Giordano and I stayed back here and did the shops. We had quite an orgy, I haven't recovered yet.' She laughed. She sounded better than Giordano deserved.

'Perhaps I'd better have details of the exact dates,' he said.

He knew before she read them out that they were going to match. It *had* been Giordano he'd seen at Nice airport; and he hadn't returned to Rome until the same day the killings had happened, albeit in the morning. His pulse was going quite fast. 'And the address where he stayed . . .?'

'I don't have that, only the telephone number.' She gave it to him. 'If you'd like me to ask Mr Giordano this evening – '

'That won't be necessary now, Miss Cord. You've been very helpful.'

Before he rang off, she said, 'I was on that plane to London. You've got a note of me, have you?'

He was into the spirit of it by now. 'M.J. Cord. That's right. You've saved me making a separate call.' She sounded very impressed as he said goodbye.

He got the supervisor on the Bureau exchange to check out the number he had been given. It proved to belong to a Frank Catini, living in a villa in Antibes. The case for further enquiries, he told himself, was unassailable. This was the moment to find out if Bellamy had been right in saying he'd made a friend in Chief Superintendent Clayton of the Serious Crimes Squad.

Contacting Clayton took most of the day. First he was said to be with the Commissioner, then out to lunch with a foreign liaison contact. The sergeant who answered the calls spoke of his movements in weary tones and declined all responsibility for arranging that Clayton should call back. It wasn't until the fourth attempt that Clayton came on the line. His voice had an impatient edge but warmed when he discovered who Egerton was. He asked if this meant more tit-bits from Chester Square.

'I'm afraid not. How's that going by the way?'

The photographer, it seemed, hadn't made any admissions but he still looked very interesting: one of his lenses could have produced a decent print of anything Rylance might have had on his desk before it was moved away from the window. He had become steadily more shifty as he maintained his story of not pointing the camera at anything except girls in spicy positions.

'What we need,' Clayton went on, 'is to establish a connection between him and someone on the *Globe*. Then I reckon he'd break. We're working on that. Anyway, thanks for the information.'

'Could I ask a favour in return? I have an interest in two men, both foreigners. The first is an American film producer from Beverly Hills named Sam Giordano. I haven't an exact address for him but he's quite well known. He was staying in Claridges a couple of weeks ago, and he's now moved on to the Excelsior in Rome. I'd like to know if you or the Americans have any sort of criminal record for him. I don't know the nationality of the other man but it's possible that he's American too. His name is Frank Catini and he has a villa in Antibes. Whether he lives – '

Clayton was interrupting him. 'Frank Catini – you're after Catini?'

'You know him?'

'Catini is Mafia. He was a big noise on the West Coast of America until a few years back. Then when it looked as though he was going to be nailed for tax fraud, he took off for Europe and settled in the south of France. He runs Catini Enterprises, a conglomerate he built on the Mafia money he managed to launder. But he also has drugs and gambling operations. He's got at least one going here.'

'What's the operation in England?'

'A club that opened last year, aimed at the high rollers. On the face of things it belongs to a twit who used to be in the Life Guards. In practice we know Catini's the real boss.'

'What would particularly interest me is if the American police are aware of some tie-up between Giordano and Catini.'

Clayton said, 'Pity you didn't get me this morning. I've been having lunch with Hal West, the FBI man at the Embassy. Anyway, leave it with me.'

He had half-feared Clayton would ask for something on paper, a formal request. Relieved, he said, 'It's a rather delicate case – I'd appreciate it if you'd pass the answer to me personally.'

Later in the afternoon, seeing Antonia talking to someone as he turned a corner in the Bureau, he beat a hasty retreat. At some stage she'd have to be told what he'd been doing. But it would be better to have Clayton's answers first.

This time it was a manservant in black coat and striped trousers who opened the door of the house in Chester Square. He looked faintly surprised to hear an appointment with Rylance being claimed. Leaving Egerton to sit on a velvet sofa he went away. After a while he returned and conducted him to what was obviously Rylance's study. He said that Rylance might spare him a few minutes shortly.

The room was next to the one in which Egerton had sat with Evelyn Rylance while she stoked up on negative ions. In front of what was plainly the vital window, were heavy velvet drapes. He went over and parted them. The net curtains were neatly in place behind. Clayton's visit had persuaded Evelyn that her sensibilities about rooms behind gauze had to yield to the demands of bumbledom, for the time being anyway. The desk was also well away from the window. Egerton looked up at the lights of the apartment block behind the house. Where windows were uncurtained, he could see clearly the detail of ornaments standing near them. The reverse view, with a downward angle would be even better.

The door opened behind him and Rylance appeared. He was halfway into evening dress, his tail coat over his arm. 'Egerton, I'm afraid that owing to various preoccupations, I overlooked that I'd arranged to see you. As it is, I'm now in rather a hurry. I have to call in at the House on my way to a dinner at the Guildhall. I'm sorry.' Slipping on the tail coat he went to a cabinet behind the door. 'However, that doesn't mean I want you to go without a drink.'

He handed Egerton the tonic water he asked for with only one eyebrow slightly raised, poured himself a large brandy and sat down. 'I asked to see you to express my appreciation for your efforts in tracing my stepdaughter. It was excellent work. The tragedy that happened afterwards doesn't diminish what you did.'

The words were rapidly spoken but he raised his glass

at the end. He was keen to do his stuff, even if the effect was rushed. He seemed a nicer man than had appeared in his room at the House of Commons.

'My wife will be sorry to have missed seeing you. She's in Nice until tomorrow, arranging for Lauren's body to be brought over.'

He wondered how hard the news had hit her. The only feeling towards Lauren she had displayed when they had talked had been exasperation. 'Was she able to speak to Lauren before it happened?'

'Yes, she telephoned her the night after we got your news. They had quite a long conversation. Although Lauren wouldn't agree to my wife visiting her in Nice, she eventually promised to come back here to spend a weekend. The next thing that happened was a call from the French police about the murder. Fortunately I took it, having just got back from a trip to Washington. My wife had gone to stay with friends in Ireland while I was away. The police found the number in Lauren's diary and rang in the hope of tracing next of kin.'

'Did your wife think Lauren sounded upset when they spoke on the telephone?'

'If she did, she didn't mention it. I believe Lauren expressed surprise she had the number and they then got into the usual argument about Fernandes.'

It seemed as good a moment as any to pass on what Fernandes' letter had established about his character. 'I have one piece of news that may be some consolation to your wife over Lauren's relationship with Fernandes. There's incontrovertible evidence now that he was opposed to all extremist activity. One of the last things he did before he died was to attempt to persuade his brother Garcia to abandon a terrorist operation he'd planned.'

191

'So I *was* misinformed about him . . .?' He was still sticking to his previous line.

'Yes.'

'Interesting.' But Egerton guessed he wasn't really interested; he wasn't concerned with what sort of a person Fernandes had been now that the relationship with Lauren no longer had a relevance for his political career, or amounted to an irritant in his marriage.

'There is something about the deaths I think you and your wife should know. Some information that doesn't fit with what's been published.'

Rylance raised his eyebrows.

'I believe the killings had nothing to do with Basque politics.'

'But the French police – '

'The story put out by the police can't be squared with the facts. I'm not sure *why* they gave it to the press – possibly because it's convenient for domestic political reasons. But it's phony.'

'Why do you say that?'

He described what Boyd had told him. Rylance listened with a frown; for the first time since they had met, he was wearing an expression that was not in some degree calculated. At the end he shook his head in bafflement. 'Are you saying it 'was Lauren and not Fernandes who was the real target?'

'Yes. But they didn't plan to kill her when they went to the apartment. Their purpose was to make her give up something. I believe Lauren's killing was an accident resulting from Boyd's intervention. After they discovered she was dead they decided to kill Fernandes as well because it was too dangerous to leave him alive. But they weren't interested in him.'

'I don't understand what Lauren could have had in her

possession that would have been of interest to French crooks.'

'Nothing. They were working for others. Boyd believed the answer to it all lay in the visit of the two Americans. They sent the thugs. I have no idea what was so important to them. But you'll remember that Sally Kirkwood told me she believed that something happened when Lauren visited the States in the summer that was linked with her decision to go away with Fernandes.'

Rylance went to replenish his glass. It was plain he still had difficulty grappling with Boyd's story. When he came back he said, 'Are you quite sure that Boyd isn't fantasizing? He's a thriller writer, you say. He probably lives in his imagination.'

'I learned some things this morning that persuade me he could be on the right track. I may be able to discover more in a day or two. What I'd like next is to find out what the French police *really* think happened. After all, Boyd identified one of the thugs for them.'

'Is it possible to get at that?'

'I'm not sure. But there's someone in the Sûreté in Paris who's been very helpful to me in the past and may have friends in police headquarters in Nice. I'd ask his assistance, off the record of course. But I'd need my Director's approval to approach him.'

He stopped short of saying that it would also call for a request from Rylance himself. Rylance was swirling the brandy in his glass. 'What does your Director think of Boyd's story?'

'I haven't told him yet. He's away in Scotland until Monday.'

'Do you want me to speak to him?'

'That would be helpful.'

Rylance looked at his wristwatch and stood up. 'All

right, I'm grateful for what you've told me. Of course I shall want to pursue this. If you get any more information from the enquiries you've already made before Monday, please telephone me. I shall need to know at once.' He was being Ministerial again.

On the way down to the hall, Egerton said, 'Did your wife happen to speak to Mr Giordano when you heard the news I'd found Lauren?'

Rylance paused, frowning. 'I don't – no, wait, I believe she may have done. He'd been in touch with her earlier about your call on him when he was staying at Claridges.' He opened the street door and gave a faint smile. 'You're not suggesting that Sam Giordano might have been one of Lauren's mysterious American visitors, I hope.' His arm was up, signalling to the driver of his official car.

It seemed for a moment he might have to admit he *was* suggesting it. But the manservant came hurrying across the hall with a message and Rylance turned away.

17

Afterwards he pinpointed the beginning of the sense of unease, the premonition that the ground was about to shift remorselessly beneath his feet, as coinciding with the arrival of the letter from Boyd. Postmarked Nice, it was written in a neat italic hand that seemed at odds with the ungainly figure who had greeted him in Fernandes' apartment and later at the house in Epping. He read it with his breakfast coffee.

Dear Egerton,

When you gave me your address in case I had further thoughts about the ghastly business next door, I didn't think I'd have occasion to use it. But within a day of arriving back here, I had a visit from a curious little party. Two were Basques, the third could have been French, perhaps local, although since he insisted on speaking English throughout, I wasn't sure.

They announced themselves as friends of Luis Fernandes and said they were enquiring into the circumstances of his death on behalf of his family. I told them the story I told you. They'd picked up quite a bit of it already – the non-Basque had some private line into police headquarters.

Their chief concern was to discover if I could amplify what I'd said about Lauren's American visitors; they seemed to have all they needed about the two thugs who were responsible for the killings. I said that I had no idea who the Americans were or what they'd been after, but I'd gained the impression that you might know more. They asked how they could contact you.

So this note is simply to say that they (or some London friends of theirs) may pay you a call. I don't imagine they'll give you any trouble – they were extremely courteous in a stolid sort of way. They just want to get to the bottom of what happened and why. In view of the refusal of the police to bother about the underlying facts, I can't say I blame them.

Sincerely,
Arthur Boyd

A perfectly civil letter; but the touch of malice didn't escape him. Boyd had enjoyed handing over his name and address and suggesting his visitors applied there for further information. Egerton's lack of frankness had got to Boyd more than he had shown. When he had spoken vaguely of being employed by Lauren's family Boyd had pretended a lack of any further interest. In reality he had been piqued at not being let in on Egerton's speculations about who the Americans might have been. Now he was relishing the thought of Fernandes' friends putting Egerton through what might be some awkward hoops.

It might have been the unease prompted by the letter that made him suspect he was once more being shadowed when he returned to Prince of Wales Drive from the Bureau in the evening. He spent time looking down from his window, without the light on, for anyone loitering outside. A car with two occupants parked a few yards further up towards Albert Bridge engaged his attention for several minutes before he identified it as belonging to people in the adjoining block.

The hospital call drove the thoughts from his mind. The voice was female and very business-like; she made him repeat his name before she opened up.

'Mr Egerton, we have a patient who has asked you should be told she's here. A Miss Gail Henderson.'

His mouth became as dry as parchment.

'You *are* a close friend . . .?'

'Yes. Has she been in an accident?'

The woman appeared not to hear him. 'She tells us she

has no near relatives.' She was waiting to see if he would contradict that.

'Is she very ill?'

'Not now. She's had a lucky escape. If she's – ' she paused fractionally ' – sensible from now on, she'll be all right. After treatment.'

'It was an overdose, was it?'

Once again she rode over the words as though oblivious to them. 'She should be well enough to be discharged for the weekend. We understand she has no regular doctor we can inform. She ought of course to attend an addiction clinic. I hope you'll be able to persuade her to do that. Meanwhile she must be in someone's care.'

'I'll accept the responsibility of course.'

'She will be given a small supply of tablets when she leaves. Taken regularly they should alleviate the addiction symptoms for a few days. But they are *not* a substitute for treatment.'

'I understand.'

The voice became a little warmer. 'Good. Perhaps you'd visit her tomorrow between two o'clock and four. I'd like you to call in at sister's office beforehand.'

'Can't I come sooner?'

'No, tomorrow will be best. We can then make arrangements with you for her discharge the following day.'

At the office next morning, he went in search of Antonia only to be told she was away until the afternoon. When she was still not back at two o'clock, he scribbled her a note and left for the hospital.

Now the suspicion that he once more had someone following him returned more solidly. Glancing from the upper deck of his bus as it pulled away down Baker Street, he glimpsed the face of a man he felt sure he had seen as he returned to Prince of Wales Drive the previous evening. The man had stepped forward from behind a queue waiting for another bus and hailed a taxi.

When he left the bus in the Fulham Road, he waited for a few seconds, watching to see if a taxi was slowing down. There was no sign of one. He walked back to where an oil tanker was blocking traffic. An empty taxi was beginning to manoeuvre round the tanker. If the man had been inside it, he had had time to slip into one of the nearby shops.

He bought chrysanthemums and made his way into the hospital. His mouth was dry again. But she looked better than he had feared. Sitting in an armchair at the end of the ward, wrapped in a hospital dressing gown, she gave her boxer's salute of triumph as he recognized her. Her hair had been freshly washed and there was colour in her cheeks; only their hollowness seemed sinister.

He sat down beside her. 'Sorry about this,' she said.

He took one of her hands in his. 'Why didn't you send me a message before?'

She shrugged apologetically.

'Do you know how you got here?'

'Jamie brought me.'

Somehow, it was the last answer he had expected.

'The Indian who owns the house found I'd flopped on the bathroom floor. He telephoned Jamie.'

It still didn't make much sense. 'He had Jamie's number?'

'Jamie had told him when he found me the room that he was to ring if I was ill or anything.'

Jamie, the Good Samaritan, he thought ironically: if you need hospitalizing, leave it to me to get you there, it's all part of the service.

'I still can't understand why one of you didn't tell *me*.'

'I made Jamie promise not to. I didn't want you to see me until I was better. At least until I wasn't quite such a mess.'

He glanced down at the hand he was holding. The finger nails seemed to have been bitten back more than ever. 'You *are* going to stop now, aren't you?'

She was chewing her lip.

'Yes, *yes*, YES!' he said.

'How?'

'We'll get you back to the place in Devon . . .'

'Maybe they won't take me again because I ducked out before.'

'They will, I'll talk to them.'

She was shaking her head. 'You have to stay at least six weeks. It would cost hundreds, thousands. I can't go to Ma or Leo for the money, after what happened last time.'

'You don't have to worry. I can find it.'

She gazed at him doubtfully but didn't ask how. That was fortunate since for the moment he had no idea.

'Why should you?'

'Because I want to.'

She said. 'I began to think about stopping while you were in Majorca, about managing it on my own. I had the idea of going to live somewhere in the country, a long way from London where I wouldn't know anybody. Plenty of people, after all, just take a decision to stop. Why shouldn't I? Then the chance of the trip to Barbados came up. I thought, well, afterwards.' She looked away. 'Stupid of course.'

'Forget about that. Think about the treatment. When it's over you'll come back to my flat. We'll keep each other in a state of grace.'

She smiled wanly. He could tell the concept remained unreal to her; but he had to get her started. 'Anyhow, we're going away for the weekend, so that we can talk it through properly.'

She was beginning to look tired; her nod was the

slightest of movements. He leaned closer. 'You tried to telephone me while I was away. What was it about?'

Her eyes were on his hands still holding one of hers; she placed her free hand over them. 'I wanted you to tell me not to go on the party. I knew what it would be like of course. I oughtn't to have gone. But you weren't there.'

He was afraid she was going to fall apart in front of him. He turned and held her by the shoulders until she looked into his eyes. 'I love you,' he said. 'You're going to kick the thing for your own sake. But you're also going to do it for me.' He was trapping himself he knew: there'd be no escape. But the idea of escape was absurd anyway, because he had never been able to stop loving her. Now there was no longer Julian between them, the thought of losing her again was unendurable.

Outside the hospital he told a cab to take him to Jamie's address. Occasionally he looked through the rear window to see if another cab was following but saw nothing.

Jamie's apartment was in a mansion block in Portland Place. A superior sort of concierge in a black coat sat in the entrance hall with a bowl of flowers and a telephone. His name had to be telephoned through to Jamie before he was allowed into the lift.

Jamie was buttoning on a shirt as he opened the door.

'Mark.' He showed absolutely no surprise at the call, just polite pleasure. 'Come and see this pad, it's really rather grand.'

They entered a vast room that had drapes for curtains, swagged and splendid; behind the drapes security grilles dense enough to dishearten flies had been fitted across the windows. The furniture was ornate and highly polished. Here and there, suspiciously pale-looking busts in the Roman style stared out from half-moon tables of florid marble. It was as though a dealer in fake antiques had supplied a job lot. But perhaps they were actually genuine. 'You own all this stuff?' he asked.

'Yes, I bought it from the Lebanese who sold me the flat. He was leaving the country rather quickly for reasons not disclosed and wanted to get rid of everything. So I took it.' He waved an arm casually. But he was quite proud in an amused way.

A bronze and porcelain clock had announced it was a quarter to five. If he was going to be back in the Bureau in time to catch Antonia, he needed to hurry. 'I've been to see Gail in hospital. I wish you'd called me.'

'I tried. There was no reply from your number the night I took her in. I remembered you'd said you were going abroad and I thought you might still be away. When I saw her the next day, she made me promise not to contact you. She said she wanted to do it herself. How is she?'

'They've decided to discharge her tomorrow. I'm taking her to the country for the weekend. She's more or less agreed to go back to the place in Devon for treatment.' He hesitated. 'Do you believe she O.D.'d deliberately?'

'I don't know.'

'I *have* to make her stop this time. If she ever contacts you for more stuff, you've got to say "no". Whatever she says or does, never supply any more.'

Jamie slightly changed the position of a cigarette box on the table between them. After a while he said, 'All right.'

'Jamie, if you supplied her just once more, I think I might kill you.'

He smiled. 'I said – All right.'

'I also need some help. The treatment is going to cost. You know she hasn't got the money. Neither have I. I want to borrow it from you. In the New Year I get an increase in pay – I'll start paying you back then. But I want a few hundred now and a lot more later.'

He had been prepared for hesitation, perhaps a polite enquiry about the amount of the pay increase. He watched Jamie go to a drawer and open it. When he came back he counted out five hundred in twenties.

'If you come back on Monday I can let you have more. But make it before one thirty because I'm due to take a plane trip in the afternoon.' He brushed aside thanks.

He walked Egerton down to the entrance in Portland Place and asked the black coat to find a cab. On the way out of the apartment Egerton had heard the noise of water running. Somebody in a room off the hall was taking a bath or a shower. He wondered if Jamie had been dressing, not just changing his shirt when he opened the door to admit him. He had walked past the room without giving a sign that he was conscious of the sounds. Like so many other things in his life, they remained unacknowledged. Behind that door could have been a girl, a piece of rough trade or even some innocent cousin from Glasgow, up on an Away-Day to goggle at the apartment and return with a tale of wonder. All seemed equally likely.

Back at the Bureau, he went to Antonia's room. He stopped to listen for a moment in case she had somebody with her. There was no sound. It crossed his mind that she might still be out but the door was unlocked when he tried the handle.

She sat smoking a cigarette and staring through the window at the darkness. None of the files on her desk was open. When she glanced over her shoulder, he wasn't sure she was recognizing him since the only light was from her desk lamp.

'Sorry, am I disturbing you?'

She stubbed the cigarette out and turned back abruptly from the window. 'No. I was just reflecting I ate far too much lunch. A man in the Canadian Embassy took me to the Savoy. We have a mutual friend in Alberta.'

He sat down. 'You know Canada . . .?'

'Not really. I went there on a case with Ludo Fender who used to be an Assistant Director here until he retired. The RCMP man who helped us resigned a while ago to run a farm. He's the mutual friend.'

She gazed at the heading on the file that was uppermost in her tray but he could see she wasn't reading it. 'Have you heard of the pika rabbit?'

'No.'

'When the sun shines in Alberta, the pika rabbit cuts all the grass he needs for winter and lays it out to dry. Then he goes away. You might think he'd forgotten it. But he's always back before the weather breaks to get the grass under cover. That's the extent of my knowledge about the pika rabbit.'

She sat back with an exaggeratedly relaxed gesture, saying, 'Well . . .' There was more to it than pika rabbits, he thought, but he was never likely to be told. 'By the way,' she said, 'I heard over at the Yard today that Clayton, the head of the Serious Crimes Squad, finds you quite acceptable, considering you're a member of this department. I didn't know you had dealings with the Great Spotted Clayton.'

He cleared his throat. 'I have a confession to offer.'

He told her about his calls to Giordano's personal assistant, Mary Jane Cord and to Clayton. At the end she looked less frosty than he had expected. 'How did you get

Clayton to agree to put questions to the FBI for you?'

'He owed me a favour. A lead in one of his cases that I picked up by accident and passed on through Baxter may turn out to provide the solution.'

She weighed up the new facts. 'So you know it was Giordano you saw at Nice airport and that he stayed with a local crook over the period when Lauren and Fernandes were killed.'

'Not just any old crook – a big fish who belonged to the Mafia in America and still has drugs and gambling operations running.'

She acknowledged herself imrpressed. 'What do you want to do?'

'If Antrim will agree when he gets back from Scotland on Monday, I want to ask Pasaquier of the Sûreté if *he* can help – off the record. He may have a friend in police headquarters in Nice, someone who will come up with what they really suspect, or know, about the murders.'

She looked at him with an amused expression. 'Don't you think you should be waiting for Rylance to ask for that?'

'He more or less has done. He's going to speak to Antrim.'

She nodded in a resigned way. Before she could pick up a file again, he said. 'I'm afraid I've also come to bore you with my private affairs again.'

He told her about his visit to Gail. 'I want to take her away for the weekend somewhere quiet. She has to decide – really commit herself this time – to go through with the treatment. I wondered if I could take up the offer of your mother's house? I guarantee to be back early on Monday morning.'

She made a knot in her handkerchief. 'I'll bring the keys tomorrow.' As he was going out of the door she said,

'You think she does *want* to give it up this time?'

'Yes.'

'I hope you win.'

'I have to.' She knew enough now, he thought, about the way he felt, for him not to have to explain that.

Buying provisions the following lunch time to take down to the house, he again had the feeling that he was being watched. Once he turned sharply to confront a woman, small and mousy, carrying a plastic shopping bag as her badge of innocence; but her expression of bemused alarm convinced him he had made a mistake. In the evening, on his way home to Battersea, with paranoia beginning to grip again, he spent time doubling back on his tracks and waiting at corners to see if he would recognize a face.

When he started out again with a weekend bag to collect Gail from hospital, Gwen had appeared in the lobby to bend over her array of plants. She had on her lurking look.

'Going away?'

'Just for the weekend.'

'Your sister again?'

'Not this time. Somewhere in Shropshire.'

'There are storms coming from the west according to the radio forecast. I hope they won't get as far as where I'm going.'

He registered that she was prompting a question from him; moreover he now realized she was dressed for something more special than bingo. 'Where's that?'

'Portugal. It's a five-day package. We're leaving tonight.'

The fireman again, he supposed: romance was gathering pace in her life. He tried to see if she was still wearing the wedding ring from the master mariner who had gone down with his ship off Land's End, but her watering can was in the way.

'Have a good time,' he told her. He had almost escaped when she said, 'You had an odd sort of visitor today.'

'How odd?'

'I heard a noise and opened the door. He was standing here in the lobby near to your flat. For a moment I thought he'd come out of it. He said he was calling on behalf of the First Church of the Holy Crucifixion. There were some pamphlets in his hand but he didn't try to give me one.'

He put down the bag. 'Do you think he was a thief?'

'I did feel rather suspicious. He went off in such a hurry.'

He went to look at the lock on his door. There was no sign of forcing. Inside, with Gwen twittering at his heels, he checked the places that mattered. Nothing seemed to have been disturbed. In the lobby again, he examined the door jamb. Now he could almost persuade himself there were scratches on the paint where a plastic card had been slipped in to tease back the catch.

There was no way of being certain. The man might after all have been genuinely hawking religious pamphlets. On the other hand it would have been natural for him to try Gwen first. 'You're sure he hadn't rung your bell or knocked on the door . . .'

'I'm positive.'

He looked at his watch. It was already twenty minutes past the time he had promised to be at the hospital. Before they could start the drive to Shropshire he had to take Gail to her own place to collect clothes. He picked up his bag again but as he did so he began to register that Gwen had been saying something important. 'You got what?'

'His number. When he left, I thought, well, just in case . . . so I watched from the window. He went to a yellow car across the road. I took down the registration number.'

There was no doubt, she would have made a marvellous concierge. 'Could I have it?'

She fetched the pools coupon envelope on which it had been scribbled. 'What was he like?' he asked as he slipped it into his notecase.

'Dark, medium height, ordinary sort of suit. He had a cockney accent. And bad breath.'

He shook his head. 'You've missed your vocation, Gwen. Why aren't you in the police? Or MI5?'

She smiled up at him, pink with delight. 'My late husband always said that.'

18

Waking and going to the window, he found a garden alight with gold. Either Gwen had misheard the forecast or the weather men had got it wrong again. An Indian summer had arrived. Bees moved lazily amongst the flowers beneath as though they had all the time in the world.

He and Gail had entered the house in darkness, stumbling about in search of switches and taps specified in Antonia's note. As they drank coffee beside an ancient electric fire, they had occasionally glanced at the night through the open curtains and wondered what it held. The house, creaking in its shadowed corners, had seemed like a third presence; they had found themselves talking in low voices as though they might disturb it. When Gail had fallen asleep, almost in the middle of a sentence, he had carried her to the room where they had earlier made up their bed. She had lain with her head pressed against his cheek, fingers gripping his and tightening when he moved, as if, even in sleep, she feared he or she would float away.

He made tea and toast only to discover they had forgotten to bring butter with them. When he took a tray to her, she was gazing drowsily at the ceiling. He sat on the bed. 'I'm driving to Ludlow to buy one or two things. Sorry there's only dry toast. Will you be all right?'

She nodded. There was no trace of tension, she seemed completely relaxed. Going downstairs again and seeing her handbag on the floor where she had left it beside the fire, he told himself he needn't look, then changed his mind.

Apart from make-up and the usual oddments, it yielded only the pills the hospital had given her. He had zipped it up and was returning it to the carpet when his fingers detected an unevenness in one corner. Fishing with her nail file at the gap behind the end of the zip, he located the package in the lining and knew he had been right to check. There was enough in the package for three, perhaps four, fixes. He flushed it down the lavatory in the lobby and went out of the house.

When he returned with butter, newspapers and a bottle of wine, she was dressed. Beside the chair in which she sat was a vase of dahlias she had gathered from the garden. The handbag hadn't been moved. He kissed her. 'How do you feel?'

'Super.'

'Honestly?'

'Honestly.' She seemed to mean it.

They were standing side by side in the kitchen, making a salad for lunch when she began to talk about the overdose. 'Did you wonder if I did it on purpose?'

'It crossed my mind.'

'I didn't. I was just being terribly careless.'

He felt like telling her that it could sometimes amount to the same thing. 'It occurred to me that something might have gone wrong in Barbados.'

'What sort of thing?'

He shrugged. 'Somebody you met . . . perhaps didn't match up. That sort of thing.'

She was smiling as she sliced the beetroot. 'You're mad. Why would I want anyone else to match up?'

They took lunch and the newspapers to the pear tree that grew outside the kitchen window; in the garage

Egerton had located canvas chairs, cobwebbed but sound. When they had eaten, she handed him *The Times* while she flipped through the *Globe*. Apart from a chain saw that whined occasionally in the distance there was absolute silence. When he reached forward to brush a wasp away from her, she took his hand and slowly kissed the palm.

Finally she tired of reading. Dropping the paper on the grass beside her, she yawned and lay back to study the fruit above their heads. 'Your rival for the blonde you were eyeing the other night seems to have made the big time. She'll never look at you now.'

She had to explain before he realized she was talking about Camilla's companion at Dido's, Simon Bowe, 'What's happened to him?'

'He's been appointed the *Globe's* gossip columnist. It's a plum job.'

'Isn't that a rather meteoric rise? You said he was just a writer on one of the give-away magazines.'

'So he was.'

He picked up the newspaper she had dropped. There was a box on the right-hand side of the front page in which the news was announced. Bowe was described as the man to whom all doors were open. He frowned then shook his head slowly. Suddenly he could see Camilla in a new light; himself too.

'What's wrong?' she asked.

'I think I know how one of the doors they mention happens to open.'

She grinned. She had guessed he was referring to Camilla, but not in the way he meant. If she knew how big a fool he'd made of himself, she might not think it was so funny.

The evening brought a telephone call from Antonia.

She asked how they were surviving. 'Fine,' he said.

London had been like an oven, she told him. She was off to the theatre and then to supper with a friend, sex undisclosed. He wished her a pleasant evening. 'Are you winning?' she asked.

From where he stood in the hall, he could see into the kitchen. Gail was unwrapping the pasta they had brought from London. If he was going to be strictly honest he would have to admit he wasn't sure yet. 'We're going to talk later.'

'Don't let her fudge it.' There was that familiar crispness in her tone; he sensed an implication she perhaps wondered whether he was just messing about. The message was that he wasn't there to enjoy himself.

Back in the kitchen, Gail asked him who had called. 'Antonia Strachan. She wondered how things were.'

'Is she your actual boss in the Bureau?'

'I work for her, yes.'

'Efficient?'

'Yes.'

'Attractive?'

'Very.'

She dropped the pasta into the boiling water. He stood beside her and watched it uncurl. One of her hands reached out to his. It was trembling a little. He wondered if she was beginning to get the shakes.

'Have you remembered to take those tablets?' he asked.

She nodded. 'What were you saying to her you thought would be all right?'

He decided he might as well be frank. 'She knows why we came. I said we were going to talk about the treatment this weekend.'

She was silent.

211

'Perhaps we don't need to,' he said. 'Shall we just ring the clinic in the morning and fix when you arrive?'

She was still looking at the pasta in the saucepan. 'I haven't changed my mind, if that's what you're asking. I mean to stop. For ever. Do you believe that?'

'Yes.'

'There's just something I have to know, beforehand. To stop me making a fool of myself. Are we together now? I mean, *really* together? If I do beat it, is that what *you* want?'

He knew and supposed she did too, that at the end of it all, the struggle might have changed her so much, their relationship would simply crumble whatever they might now say or want. But the chance had to be taken.

He said, 'You know I love you, that I've always loved you.'

She was trying not to weep. He shook his head at her until she smiled. 'So it's settled.'

But she went on, 'One more thing. I'd rather you didn't come to see me while I'm there. I've got to do it on my own. I want to feel I can reach you on the phone but not to have you visiting and then going away again. I want to wait for afterwards.'

When he tried to argue her out of it, she proved immovable. Finally he gave up. 'You don't have to worry,' she said.

Sunday dawned better than ever. They took their breakfast rolls and coffee into the garden and had pears plucked from above their heads as starters. Afterwards he telephoned the clinic and fixed her arrival for the Monday. She refused to let him drive her down so it was arranged that she would go by train from Paddington. Once the call was over she seemed totally relaxed again. There had been no return of the shakes he thought he had noticed the previous evening. As he watched her energy awaken, the thought that perhaps she had managed to hide some stuff on their arrival and had been using it in the bathroom briefly numbed his happiness. But he decided that he had watched her too closely for that to have happened.

They walked in the woods that stretched to the south of the garden. She made him tell her every detail of how he had felt in the clinic in New York. She was like an explorer about to embark on an expedition, determined to find out about the terrain from someone who had gone before.

They made love in a birch grove where old leaves rustled beneath them and this year's were still up there, dancing in the sunlight. Watching through the branches the occasional wisp of cloud, he was conscious that, impatiently as he awaited the coming days, he also wanted to hold them back.

When, after the drive to London through a cloudless dawn, he put her on the train at Paddington the tension was back in her features and she was sweating a little. Most of it could have been simple foreboding at what lay ahead but he wished he was going with her. They agreed that she would be the first to telephone. As the train began to move he said through the open window, 'Remember, it's Us now.'

He had half-resigned himself to driving straight from the station to Somerset Square and pleading for a space in the office garage. But it was barely ten to nine as he turned into the Bayswater Road. He decided that he had time to call at his flat, change into a clean shirt and pick up a bus.

He slotted the Mini into a space on the park side of Prince of Wales Drive. Reaching for his overnight bag, he saw a familiar figure step from a Rover parked at the entrance to his apartment block and lift an arm in greeting. After a few seconds he realized who it was: Newth, one of Mansell's people. It was to Newth he had been handed over on his first day in the Bureau, immediately after receiving Antrim's benediction. Newth had given him the Official Secrets form to sign and a card with security classifications printed on it which he was to stand on his desk. I'm your man, Newth had said, a little too breezily, if you have any problems: how to handle the press if they get through direct to you about a case, obtaining passes for other Departments, things like that; oh, and details of the squash club in the basement. I expect we'll meet a good deal. Then Newth had vanished, to be glimpsed again only in a cluster of others from Mansell's division at the bar or in the canteen. Personnel people move in packs to avoid being waylaid, older hands had told him. Best left alone. Never call them, let them call you.

'Hullo, Egerton,' Newth said. His greeting was still breezy but lacked the warmth of that first day. 'We thought you'd probably call back to dump the car.'

The shape of another person was dimly visible in the back of the Rover.

'Nice weekend?'

'Yes, thanks.'

'We'll give you a lift.'

He raised his eyebrows. 'Were you waiting for me?'

'Yes.'

'Something up?'

'A tiny crisis.'

'I see.' Egerton looked at his watch. 'If you'll give me five minutes, I'm going to change into a clean shirt.'

Newth was shaking his head jovially. 'Mansell would

rather you came straight away. A few problems to be sorted.'

Anxiety had started to seep into his stomach. 'What sort of problems?'

'I'd better leave it to Mansell to explain if you don't mind.' Newth reached out and took the overnight bag. 'Let me put this in the boot for you.'

Climbing into the Rover, Egerton recognized the figure in the back seat as another of Mansell's acolytes. They exchanged nods; then the other looked away, to study a perfectly ordinary privet hedge.

As they swung into the traffic approaching Chelsea Bridge, Newth nodded towards the east. There was the sun, an orange ball, riding up the river to zap the autumn mist; already the Thames had a glassy sheen.

'Look at that sun,' Newth said, 'It's going to be really hot today.'

It seemed the most ominous remark yet.

19

A cardboard box lay on Mansell's blotting pad. It contained what looked like the whole contents of the desk in Egerton's flat: letters, bills, old diaries, even some cufflinks he'd mislaid. He stared at Mansell; apprehension gave way to anger. 'Why has my flat been searched?'

Mansell said carefully, 'It was a decision of the Director's. He concluded that in view of the information he had received, there was no alternative.'

'Were the police involved?'

'No.'

'So there was no search warrant . . .'

'No.'

'I understand that's illegal.'

'Would you rather the police *had* been brought in?' Mansell raised his eyebrows; he seemed entirely confident of what, on reflection, Egerton's answer would be.

'I'd like an explanation.'

Mansell slid two fingers under a folder that lay on his desk alongside the box. They reappeared with a photograph, postcard size. 'On his return from Scotland on Saturday morning, the Director found that an envelope containing this photograph had been delivered for him at his flat by someone who left no name. It shows you standing at the entrance to a block of flats in Portland Place and talking to a man. On the back has been pasted a typewritten note, unsigned, which says that if the head of the Metropolitan Police Drugs Squad is consulted, he will provide interesting information about the identity of this man. The note also says that even more interesting information will be obtained if a thorough search of your flat is made.'

Mansell held the photograph in front of Egerton. It showed Jamie standing beside him, with his hand on his arm; it must have been taken the afternoon Egerton had gone to Portland Place from seeing Gail in hospital.

Mansell said, 'The Director telephoned me. I collected the photograph and saw Lancaster of the Drugs Squad at his home during the afternoon. He said that he recognized the man with you as James Hendry Buchanan, a known dealer in heroin since coming down from Oxford a few years back. The Drugs Squad have been anxious to move against him for some time. Apparently they've had problems in establishing his sources of supply.'

He put the photograph down and sat back. 'In the circumstances you don't presumably feel too much surprise at the Director's decision.'

'My going to see Buchanan had nothing to do with *getting* drugs.'

'Why *did* you go?'

'I'd been to visit a friend in hospital. She was recovering from a heroin overdose. Buchanan was her supplier. She'd decided to give it up. I went to Buchanan and told him that. Also, if she asked him for more, not to supply her. He agreed.'

'Why should he be concerned with your wishes?'

'We were friends at Oxford, I know him very well. If he gives a promise he keeps it.'

'And the friend in hospital – did you also know her at Oxford?'

'Yes.'

'May I know her name?'

'Gail Henderson.'

'A close friend?'

'I'm very fond of her.'

'She's visited you at your flat I suppose . . .?'

'Once or twice.'

'Did you use heroin there with her?'

'No.'

'You never touch it . . .?'

His throat felt very dry; but at least the facts were going to be out in the open at last. 'I took it at one time. But I stopped. That happened before I came to the Bureau. I've never taken it since.'

'Why didn't you tell us any of this when you joined?'

'I wasn't asked.'

'Don't you think you should have disclosed the fact before now?'

'Perhaps it would have been better in view of what's happened. But it was all in the past. As I said, I don't touch heroin or any other drugs now.'

Mansell was tapping two fingers on the photograph; he seemed to be thinking. Egerton said, 'If you doubt it, you can have me medically examined. I'm willing to – '

'An examination wouldn't necessarily show you weren't still using heroin – by inhaling for example.'

'If I were, why haven't you found traces in my flat? Why hasn't Newth found any in my overnight bag which he so considerately took charge of? If you're still not convinced, perhaps you'd like to have my clothing searched?'

He silently thanked his stars that he'd had the sense to flush away the heroin as soon as he'd found it in the lining of Gail's handbag. Yet suddenly a premonition was upon him that something ghastly lay ahead. Mansell's fingers had reached under the file again. When they reappeared, they were holding a plastic packet.

'Perhaps you could explain why this was on the top of the wall cabinet in your bathroom?'

He made himself take the packet from Mansell. He wet his finger and tasted the powder inside.

'You agree that is heroin?'

He nodded, sick in the pit of his stomach. There was only one explanation: Gail had left it the morning she and Jamie had stayed behind in the flat while he went to report to Antrim. Although he had asked Jamie not to let her fix there, he had let him down. They had both let him down. Presumably she had placed the packet on the cabinet while she did it and then forgotten. If she'd remembered the next day, he would already have been on his way to Majorca.

'How do you account for it?' Mansell asked.

'I've never seen that before.'

'You mean it isn't yours?'

'Yes.'

'Then who does it belong to – Miss Henderson?'

If he said it did, he couldn't be hurting her; and no doubt she'd back him up if Mansell wanted corroboration. But, something was making him pause. He stared at the packet, frowned and tasted the powder again.

Mansell said, 'Are you going to say it's not heroin after all?'

'No.'

'Then what?'

Nothing made any sense any more. 'I just don't have an explanation at present.'

Mansell sighed heavily. 'Well, if you don't wish to say more . . .' He scotchtaped the packet, placed it in a drawer of his desk, then locked the drawer. 'I have to tell you that the Director, after hearing the results of the search at your flat, decided to suspend you while a full report was prepared for him, incorporating any statement you wished to make. If you want to add to what you have said I advise you to let me have your submission in writing in the course of the next week. Meanwhile I suggest you go back to your flat and think things over. I shall arrange for these articles – ' he placed his hand on the cardboard box – ' to be returned very shortly.'

Mansell's voice had begun to sound remote. Egerton stood up. 'I want to repeat that the heroin isn't mine, that I haven't used drugs since I joined the Bureau and that I'm very opposed to anyone else using them. Miss Henderson will confirm that's my attitude. And if you want the address of the American clinic where I was treated and the name of the doctor who discharged me, you can have the details any time you like.'

Mansell said nothing, simply looked uncomfortable. It did, after all, sound pretty pathetic.

The secretary smiled at him charitably as he emerged from Mansell's office. His overnight bag was beside her desk, having presumably been parked there by Newth after his prying fingers had turned everything inside out. She handed the bag to him. The gesture had a symbolic flavour. There wasn't much doubt what would now happen: he was going to be sacked. On what they had, he could hardly blame them. The next few days would be spent assembling a formal case on which to justify the action in case, later on, he tried to make waves through an MP or a newspaper.

In the corridor he saw Antrim's driver waiting for the lift that went express to the Director's lair. The driver was carrying a brace of grouse, no doubt part of the dividend from Antrim's visit to Scotland. Until a short while ago, he had supposed that, about now, he would be taking that lift himself, en route to seek Antrim's agreement to his asking Pasquier for help in discovering what the police in Nice really believed about the killings of Lauren and Fernandes. Already the idea had become unreal.

He went in search of Antonia to tell her what had happened. Nobody knew where she was; her secretary thought she might have called in at the Yard on her way to the office. He waited about for a while, then gave up and handed the Beynon files back once more to the secretary. Mansell would presumably tell her soon enough that her establishment had gone down by one, this time permanently.

Walking out into the sunshine in Somerset Square, he crossed to the central gardens and sat on a bench hidden from any curious eyes that might be watching from the Bureau's windows. He was the only person in the gardens. Above him the sky was almost hidden by arches of gold and bronze formed from the foliage of chestnut trees. At about this time yesterday he had gazed upwards to find the sky through the dappled shade of a Shropshire wood. He had made love to Gail and begun to feel that life at last held meaning and the hope of joy. Now everything was about to fall apart. A terrible lassitude crept upon him. Somehow he had to fight it: if this was the finish for him in the Bureau, the sooner he started combing the Situations Vacant columns in *The Times* and the *Telegraph*, the better.

But something even more immediate demanded attention – the plastic packet Mansell had conjured from under his file. Perhaps it really *had* belonged to Gail. Yet he couldn't believe it. The taste and colour had been all wrong for pure heroin, the contents had been cut with coffee powder to provide a cheap sell on the streets. The idea of Jamie supplying Gail with that was nonsense. Nor would she have cut the stuff herself.

He looked at his watch. Jamie had asked him to call not later than one thirty to collect the rest of the cash he was borrowing. After that, he would have to pay it into his bank before he sent off the further cheque he had promised the clinic would be in the post that night. He went to catch a bus to Portland Place.

Jamie was dressed in a dark grey suit and his college tie; on a chair in the hall of the apartment was a Gucci bag already packed. Wherever he was going, a vaguely merchant banker look had been thought to match the occasion.

They were in the drawing room. It looked more than ever like a dubious antique dealer's set-up. Jamie took an envelope out of the desk. 'Two thousand in twenties. That all right?'

'It's going to be a while before I repay it.'

He was waving a hand. 'I'm not worried.' He watched Egerton put the envelope inside his breast pocket. 'Has she started the treatment?'

'This morning.'

'Did you drive her down?'

'No, she went by train.'

A politeness had descended upon them. Egerton gazed at a Roman bust. 'Tell me something. Has she ever to your knowledge used Chinese?'

Jamie looked surprised. 'I can't say what happened when Julian was alive. But she's never had Chinese from me.'

'The morning I left you both in my flat, did she fix?'

'No.'

'You're sure?'

'Pretty sure. Why do you ask?'

He shook his head. 'Something odd has occurred. I can't understand it at the moment.' He didn't feel like telling Jamie what had happened to him. He walked back into the hall. 'How long are you away for?'

'Difficult to say. The people I do business with are a bit unreliable about exact dates and times of appointments. Could be a week.'

At the far end of the hall, a middle-aged woman appeared briefly, passing from one room to another. 'Mother,' Jamie said, following Egerton's glance. 'Come to hold the fort while I'm away.' It could have meant anything from keeping an eye on the furnishings to handing over small packets in discreet corners of bars; but even Jamie would surely not have got Mother into dealing. If it *was* Mother.

He was almost through the door into the corridor outside when he knew he couldn't just leave without a word of warning. 'Perhaps you should stay away longer.'

Jamie raised his eyebrows. 'Really?'

He nodded.

'Would that be . . . advice?'

'I'm just saying . . . think about it.'

Jamie closed the door again. He smiled. 'Have you heard something?'

'No. But you can't go on with this for ever – they'll get you sooner or later. It could be sooner.'

'Ah,' he said. 'Well, I suppose so.' He was still smiling. 'But I take precautions you know. Someone does quite well out of making sure I don't have an unpleasant surprise early one morning. It's one of those tiresome business expenses.'

'Whoever it is could still let you down.'

'He could. But he won't. You have to trust people.' He was completely relaxed.

* * *

The phone was ringing as he put the key in the door of his own flat. It was Antonia. 'You've heard,' he said.

'I had a message from Newth. I've been trying to get you ever since. Where have you been?'

'I had things to tie up. I'm sorry I missed you this morning – you weren't around when I left.' Before she could speak again, he went on, 'I want you to know that I've not misled you on anything. Anything.'

She was silent.

'I suppose Newth told you about the heroin . . .'

'Yes.'

'It wasn't mine, I knew nothing about it. At first I assumed it must have been left by Gail. But it was Chinese heroin – it wasn't pure, it had been cut with something else. The person who was supplying Gail gave her only pure heroin. I checked that this morning.'

'But if *she* didn't leave it in your bathroom, who did?'

'It must have been planted. My neighbour found a man in the lobby outside our two flats on Friday. She thought he might have come out of mine. I'm convinced now there's a connection with my being followed again towards the end of last week.'

'Have you told Mansell this?'

'No, I wasn't certain until after I'd left him. But even if he believed me, I'm not sure it would make that much difference now. The fact I never volunteered that I was once on heroin is going to be treated as sufficient reason by itself for applying the chop.'

'You volunteered it to *me*. Didn't you tell Mansell that?'

'No.'

'Why not?'

He hesitated. 'I didn't want to drag you into it. Anyway

they might have taken a poor view of the fact that you hadn't passed it on.'

Her voice became decidedly cool. 'Just leave me to look after myself. I've been waiting to see Mansell to get all the facts but he's been tied up since I got back to the office. When I do, I shall tell him what you told me. Also that if you say the heroin isn't yours, I take your word for it.'

Before he could reply, she went on, 'We ought to talk about what you do next to get to the bottom of this. Come and have supper tonight.'

She was the one friend at court he had; but he still didn't want her going out on a limb for him. 'I'd rather not involve you if there's a risk – '

'Shut up,' she said, 'just shut up and say when you'll come.'

The apartment in Little Venice was one of three converted out of a mid-Victorian house that was not quite facing the canal. It seemed to have left no particular impression on him from his previous visit. Now, wandering about the living room while Antonia was in the kitchen, he decided that it fitted her to perfection. The room was cool and high-ceilinged, with white-painted, folding shutters to close out the night. Modern, mostly Italian furniture was grouped in pools of light. Elsewhere, the emptiness of the shadowed corners seemed a touch austere. But the arrangement of roses on a coffee table beside the fireplace was as vivid and crisply elegant as she always seemed to him.

When she came back he was gazing at a photograph of the same man as the one on her desk at the Bureau. 'Your husband?'

'Yes. He was a test pilot.'

'Do you ever think of remarrying?'

'Not lately.' She began putting mats and cutlery on a dining table.

'Why not?' He was conscious of being on the edge of discourtesy; but curiosity drove him on.

'I find things in myself now that probably wouldn't do much for a marriage.'

He persisted. 'You mean your career . . .?'

She shook her head and looked at him mockingly. 'Just things.'

She gave him a bottle of wine to open. She wasn't going to be drawn. Perhaps she had simply stopped liking men; but he didn't get that feeling.

During the meal she told him about her conversation with Mansell. 'He still likes you. If we could prove the heroin was planted I think he'd be on your side. Tell me more about the man your neighbour saw.'

'When she challenged him, he said he was calling on behalf of the First Church of the Holy Crucifixion. He had some pamphlets but she didn't find him very convincing. Because she was suspicious she took the registration number of the car he drove off in.' He extracted from his notecase the note Gwen had made. 'I wondered if you'd mind putting through a trace to find out the owner?'

'Did she describe him?'

'A cockney – medium height, dark, bad breath.'

She put the note away in her handbag. 'Does he sound like any of the people you saw following you?'

'Not much.'

She was frowning. 'You started being followed at almost the same time you began looking for Lauren Giordano. It could be coincidence – or not. Then you're mugged. Nothing's taken, but the passes that say who you are and where you work seem to have been looked at. When you come back from your leave in Gloucestershire you find you're being followed again. But of course it may never have stopped. You could simply have failed to notice it in the meantime.

'The people following you find out about Gail when you go to see her in hospital. From there you call on a man who deals in heroin. For anyone wanting to do you harm as quickly as possible, planting the heroin in your bathroom and then tipping off Antrim about it was an obvious next move. But who wants you out of the way so badly?'

He stared at the wall behind her head. 'There's something that doesn't fit in all that. I came to the conclusion that the mugging must have been the work of Garcia Fernandes or some friends of his who were here for the ETA operation Rivers was on tenterhooks about. When I was making enquiries to try to find Lauren I asked in the Basque restaurant in Camden Town for news of *either Luis or Garcia Fernandes. And* I left my name and telephone number. If it got to Garcia's ears that a stranger was sniffing about for him as he was about to set up some secret operation, he'd want to find out who was taking the interest. The man who followed me almost as far as the Bureau the morning of the day I was mugged *could* have been a Basque from his appearance.'

'So what isn't fitting?'

'The man behind me when I visited Gail in hospital wasn't any kind of Spaniard, I'm sure of that. Furthermore, I don't see a Basque terrorist successfully convincing Gwen that he's a cockney.'

'You're saying that two different sets of people have been interested in you . . .'

'It looks like it.'

She brooded, crumbling bread in her fingers. 'Would you agree to take the advice of somebody who could be a very good ally? He used to be an Assistant Director in the Bureau until he retired a few years ago. His name is Ludo Fender. He has the shrewdest brain of anybody I know.'

He tried to compose his features in a polite expression. Fender might be the Wizard of Oz but it was difficult to imagine what he would have to contribute. 'I appreciate – ' he began, but she cut him short. 'Believe me, with Ludo on your side, it's going to be a lot better.'

'How is he to be convinced he ought to *be* on my side?'

'I shall tell him. After all, you convinced me.' She made it sound very simple.

'I'm not sure how I did that.'

'Perhaps I just can't stand the thought of having to pick up the loose ends you left in the Beynon case.'

She didn't intend him to get the idea that she was over fond.

They spent the rest of the meal going over the day's events without any flashes of enlightenment breaking in. Towards the end he said, 'One of the not-so-minor things that bugs me is the thought of somebody else following up Boyd's story and discovering whether I was right about Giardano.'

'Perhaps it'll wait until your suspension's lifted and you're back in the office again.'

She was trying to buoy him up. He shook his head. 'I don't see Rylance allowing himself to be kept hanging about. He'll already have been on to Antrim asking what progress I've made. I wonder how my non-availability has been explained.'

She remained silent but looked sympathetic. He guessed she thought he wasn't getting his priorities right.

Before he left she asked about Gail. It reminded him that he'd forgotten to return the house keys; the weekend already seemed several years back. He placed them on the table and told her she was in the clinic by now.

'You think she's made the commitment?'

He pushed away the thought of the packet he'd found in the lining of the handbag. 'Yes.'

'Is the treatment rough?'

'Not as nasty as the propaganda makes out. You feel lousy for a fortnight but it passes. That's only withdrawal of course. Staying off is the real trick.'

'She has you now. That should give her the motivation she needs, if anything will.'

He nodded. He had to believe it.

'And you have her.' She was watching his face closely. 'It's what you truly want, isn't it?'

'It's what I want,' he said.

After this hideous day, it was the one thing left to feel confident about.

20

Egerton watched as the fingers with a final jerk reached their objective to grasp the glass of whisky on the bedside table. The operation had begun with a grunting lunge that threatened the seams of the pyjama jacket. Between two buttons a lozenge of dazzling white skin swelled and strained, then subsided. It had been like a mountain in movement, he thought, almost a geological event. 'I do most humbly apologize for receiving you like this,' Fender said, not for the first time.

In fact, he had greeted them, dressed in a blue towelling gown, at the door of his cottage. Hard-soled slippers had slapped against the uncarpeted floor of oak as, snuffling and wheezing, he had led them to a table where their supper awaited. He had told Antonia on the telephone that he hoped they would excuse the discourtesy of his remaining in bed; he had been laid low, it seemed, either by flu or an autumn cold of monstrous virulence. The Woman – an anonymous daily slave – would see they were admitted and shown the supper prepared for them.

Having opened the door, however, he showed no immediate sign of returning upstairs; nor was The Woman visible. He had lumbered about, indicating the whereabouts of supplementary supplies and possible refinements of their comfort, if they were so inclined. Towards Antonia his manner had been a shy but watchful concern to which she responded gently. Egerton he had greeted with an extravagant warmth as though anyone who accompanied her could not have too much of his esteem; but the eyes, brown and

230

sombre, studied him each time he spoke with a brooding kind of concentration. Finally he had withdrawn aloft, taking with him the notes he had asked Egerton to bring, describing his experiences of being followed and what Mansell had said at the interview.

The meal was cold chicken with a respectably prepared salad and a bottle of Sancerre. By the time they followed Fender to the bedroom, carrying coffee, the world had become a better place than it had seemed driving through London's southern entrails to this Sussex village at the height of the evening rush hour. The room was low-ceilinged, a crooked place of beam and plaster walls and waxed floorboards. On a beam opposite the bed was a crucifix. The only other adornment for the walls of the room was oddly out of keeping with everything else, a group of brightly coloured Indian miniatures in which martial and erotic events took turns.

In a double bed, supported by a triangular padded object and pillows, Fender lay waiting in flannelette pyjamas, ready to hold court. On one side was the table with his medicine, a bottle of Chivas Regal; on the other, down against the wall, a hillock of used tissues was not quite concealed by a chair. Now that Egerton could study him in the light of the bedside lamp, he looked younger than he had expected. The cheeks were smooth, even rosy; the short black hair, cut like a schoolboy's, had no trace of grey in it. Since leaving them to their supper, he had brushed the hair so that it gleamed smoothly. But the sheer size of him was what held the eye. Within and at the margins of the pyjamas, flesh swelled in a gently heaving mass. He was a hippopotamus of a man.

He welcomed them again as though they had just arrived. When they were seated, he smiled benignly at Egerton. 'So you've been addicted to heroin, Egerton.'

231

He said it baldly without changing his expression. 'I believe you're the first addict I've met. Knowingly that is.'

'I'm not an addict. I was once. But not now.'

'I understood that the latest medical view was that once established the condition was permanent. Have I got it wrong?'

'Some doctors – not all – take that view. I don't. I know I'm not an addict any more.'

Fender nodded politely. 'Where did you start?'

'At Oxford.'

'Tell me why. Were you led into it by others?'

He felt resentment growing inside him. He had not expected an interrogation about the past, at least not in such uncompromising terms. It was as if Fender were provoking him in order to study his reactions.

'I don't think I was led. It was simply that people I admired were already taking heroin. That made it a social thing. I suppose the element of risk appealed as well. Then, unfortunately, someone I knew – the person in the photograph that Mansell had – became a supplier. He was a very efficient one. It was even quite cheap through him.' He shrugged. 'I don't suggest any of those were good reasons. But that's how it happened.'

'You must surely have thought about the dangers at some time?'

'I suppose so. But I was quite sure *I* wasn't the type to get addicted. I saw myself as giving it up after I left university.'

'But you didn't. . .'

'When I came down from Oxford I took a job in a merchant bank. I discovered, or thought I had discovered, that I could function better if I took a little. After a while it became quite a lot, particularly in money terms. For that and other reasons, I decided to make a break from London. Some friends from Oxford who also took heroin were there and I thought that if I didn't see them, I'd find it easier to taper off. I went to stay with a cousin in New York which turned out to be not a very bright idea. Things got worse not better. Then I had a crisis one night that made me decide I had to get treated and I went into a clinic my cousin knew about. When I was cured I came back to England and answered an advertisement to join the Bureau.'

'One *can* be sure one is cured, can one?' Fender said. His tone was casual.

'You know whether you're really going to stop, or whether, deep down, you're keeping the door open. At least I did.'

'So you feel you have freed yourself from the past?'

'I feel it's behind me. I hope others will too.'

Fender said, 'Of course, some would say that is impossible. The past is always there a prison house on our backs.'

'Do *you* say that?'

'On the whole, yes.'

He had had enough. 'Well, that part of my past is *not* a prison house. It's gone. I *know* I won't take heroin again. I loathe everything about drugs. If you find my word so hard to accept, it seems pointless continuing with this meeting.'

Antonia was looking embarrassed. Fender gazed meekly into his whisky. 'You mustn't mind my exploring a little. I find the facts interesting. As to the reality of your word, if Mrs Strachan believes in it, as she tells me she does, I am not likely to take a different view.'

Fender was allowing his glass to nestle in the ledge of linen formed by the upper part of his belly. He lifted his gaze. There was no longer any sign of the snuffles and vague infirmity with which he had greeted them. 'So our problem is to discover who has taken advantage of this background to create the means to have you removed from the Bureau.'

Twenty-five minutes had passed since they had entered the bedroom and only now did he show signs of getting down to what mattered.

'Somebody wishes you ill.'

'Clearly.'

'Who are your enemies?'

'I don't know of anybody who would think it worth-while doing this to me.'

'Then we should perhaps look at the cases you have been recently handling in the Bureau. There can't be many since you've been there so short a time.'

Antonia said, 'There's been only one where an individual knows that he's about to be prosecuted largely as a consequence of the investigation Mark carried out. A man named Beynon was successful in corrupting several very senior people in the Property Services Agency. Mark interviewed him without disclosing he was an official and bluffed sufficient facts out of him to get the case on its feet. We know Beynon is extremely sore. But he must also know that geting Mark sacked can't change things now.'

'Revenge is still a consolation of sorts.'

Egerton shook his head. 'Beynon might pay somebody to beat me up. That flashed through my mind when I was being mugged outside my flat. But he wouldn't bother with subtleties like planting heroin in the bathroom.'

'What about the drugs world – does anyone there hold a grudge against you?'

'I don't believe so. I wasn't a part of it to the extent of

getting involved with the criminal side. The friend I had at university was the only person I ever obtained heroin from in this country.'

'He is . . . still a friend, is he?'

He hesitated. 'I find it difficult to think of him in any other way.'

There was a brief silence. 'Forgive me for saying this,' Fender said slowly, 'but since by your own account you loathe the whole world of drug addiction, how do you reconcile thinking of a man who deals in heroin as a friend? Shouldn't you be doing all you can to get him prosecuted?'

He gazed at the mound of tissues beneath the chair, searching for the words to explain what he felt about Jamie.

'First of all you have to know I owe it to Jamie – his name is Jamie Buchanan – that I'm still alive. In our first year at Oxford, we went river swimming together. Some maniac had dumped a lump of reinforced concrete in the water. Several of the metal rods were sticking upwards out of the river bed. I must have dived into one of them, the point went through my side. I couldn't pull myself away and lost consciousness. Jamie somehow got me free but I know he nearly passed out in the process.'

He moistened his lips. 'All right – now he's dealing in heroin, on quite a big scale probably. People become addicts because of what he supplies. I know as well as anybody that's a terrible thing. But they *are* doing it *to themselves* – as I knew I was all the time I was acquiring the habit. When I think of Jamie I remember not only that he saved my life, but how kind he was. You have to understand that about him too. He was the most *uncalculating* friend. If one went to him for help, he always gave it. I know he has hardly any moral sense. But he doesn't *push* drugs, or even talk much about them. He just gives people what they say they want. That's how he began at Oxford. He enjoyed the risks involved in getting hold of heroin and the status it gave him. He reckoned those he supplied should accept responsibility for their own actions – they knew what they were doing. If you condemn his attitude you also have to condemn the tobacco companies and everybody who supplies liquor.'

Fender said coldly, 'I regard that as sophistry.'

Egerton shrugged. 'You asked why I think of him as a friend. That's my explanation.'

'He's certainly no friend to society.' Fender was looking towards Antonia. Her face was impassive. Neither of them had been the smallest bit impressed.

Egerton drank the dregs of his coffee and put the cup down. 'My father once told me a story I often remember. At university he had a friend who shared his distaste for the Franco side in the Spanish Civil War which was on at the time. One day the friend said that if my father really wanted to give practical help to the Spanish government and all it was fighting for, he'd introduce him to somebody else at university whom he named. My father didn't take up the offer. Years later he heard the name again. The person concerned had died but was referred to in Parliament as having been a Communist spy. My father's friend who had become a fairly senior politician said in a television discussion my father watched the same evening that although he and the spy must have been contemporaries at university, he'd never actually known him.

'My father had to decide what he should do. One part of him said he should go to the security people and report what the politician had said years ago. Another part remembered the politician as the most admirable person he had known in those days. He had thought of him as his truest friend.'

'So what did your father do?' Fender asked.

'He did nothing.'

In the High Street outside, a truck thundered by, shaking the windows. Fender said heavily, 'We must all act as our conscience dictates.'

'I realize my father may have been wrong. But I understand how he felt.'

Silence took root now that the truck had gone. At last Fender said, 'Well . . .' as though he was turning a page. He wasn't going to reveal his judgement of the story. 'Perhaps we should move on.' He picked up Egerton's notes from where they lay on the counterpane. 'In describing the surveillance of which you've been aware you speak of an intervening trip overseas. What was this trip?'

'I was trying to locate someone whose family were anxious about her.'

'Were you doing this as a personal favour to the family or what?'

'I was instructed by the Director to look for her. It was the stepdaughter of a Minister.'

Fender raised his eyebrows and swivelled his gaze towards Antonia. 'The Bureau now undertakes searching for missing persons, does it? Antrim *is* spreading his wings.' The touch of sarcasm was unmistakable.

She shook her head. 'This was something exceptional. Mark can give you the facts if you think you should know about it.'

He adopted a spuriously tentative expression. 'Perhaps it would be *just* worthwhile.'

When Egerton had finished, he let his head fall back against the pillows. All traces of the cold or flu or

237

whatever he'd been suffering from had now entirely gone. He presented the appearance of someone who had enjoyed a very agreeable meal. 'Fascinating,' he said, 'Quite fascinating.'

He smiled at Antonia. She smiled back. Her smile seemed to Egerton to be a blend of affection and faint exasperation. Between them, he sensed a bond amounting to more than the relationship of people who had worked together. Not physical, surely, he thought, studying the gross figure humped beneath the sheets. Yet, in their glances, there was an intimacy that made him uncertain. During the time he had hovered about the supper table, Fender had touched her hair with the tips of his fingers, making some remark about the effect of the light upon it; then he had clasped his hands together and looked away quickly.

'I imagine Antrim will not have felt too displeased at having obliged Rylance so efficiently,' Fender said.

She remained silent.

'No doubt he makes himself very visible about White-hall these days.'

She shrugged. She wasn't rising to his fly. He went on enjoying his thoughts for another few moments then sighed as though regretting the necessity of returning to the problem in hand.

'So . . . from what you said on the telephone, the enquiry about the gentleman with the religious tracts has not been productive.'

'We established easily enough the registered owner of the car. His name's Frederick Agar. However when Mark went this afternoon to look at the address in Shoreditch he'd given when he licensed it, he found the building was demolished six months ago. People in the neighbourhood didn't remember much about him. They thought he worked as a bookmaker's clerk.'

'What about his description?'

'Agar's a cockney all right. The rest of the description *could* fit the man who was seen, but not too well.'

'Shoreditch,' Fender said. 'Edward IV's mistress, Jane Shore, is supposed to have died in a ditch there. Hence the name. Unfortunately, like most stories of that kind, it happens to be untrue. She was, however, a remarkable woman.'

His remarks, inconsequential and casually delivered, were clearly a form of interval music while his brain concentrated on something else. He addressed Antonia again.

'Does Seagram still grace the Metropolitan Police?'

'Yes, he's a Commander now.'

'*Is* he? That could be very convenient. An admirable police officer.' Fender launched into an account, apparently for Egerton's benefit, of his past relationship with Seagram, of one-time conflict giving way to something more profitable to both parties. At the end he said, 'This evidence of being followed – your notes imply it didn't continue during your overseas trip. Why?'

'I saw no signs of it.'

'But were you actually looking out for surveillance?'

He had to admit he wasn't.

'Were there empty seats on the plane to Majorca?'

'I seem to remember one or two.'

'So anyone following you to Heathrow, would not have had difficulty in catching the same plane . . .'

'I suppose not.'

'What about the occasion you went to the girl's apartment in Nice?'

'I went by taxi. But I do remember looking back when

it dropped me. The road was empty. I don't see how there could have been anybody on my tail that night.'

Fender lay back against the pillows and closed his eyes. They sat in silence. There was nothing to be done except hope he was thinking rather than dozing. Finally he sat up and smiled politely at them both. 'Well, I suppose you'll be wanting to get off back to London. Aided by your excellent notes, Egerton, I shall now give some thought to all this.' It seemed that the audience was over.

Fender put on the towelling robe and accompanied them to the street door. As he stood watching Egerton unlock the Mini, a cat arrived from out of the shadows to brush against his calves. He lowered himself gingerly to stroke it. 'This is General Tarragon. We are close neighbours. We have many chats. I hope he will join us when you next come.' He was looking towards Antonia as he spoke.

There was frost on the windscreen of the car. 'Shouldn't you be back in bed?' Egerton asked. 'The air's chilly.'

Fender shook his head. 'Don't worry about me.' His features were reporting noble self-sacrifice. 'I shall be in touch again through Mrs Strachan. If my old colleague, Antrim, issues an invitation to resign, whether or not accompanied by money, please consult me before agreeing. In the meantime, try not to get despondent. This is only the beginning.' He stood back to wave them away. General Tarragon was already waiting impatiently in the doorway of the cottage.

On the road north, Egerton said, 'He seems to be doing his best go do down with pneumonia.'

Antonia was lighting a cigarette. 'Ludo is as well or as ill as the occasion demands.'

'I hope he's going to be well in that case.'

'My guess is that he'll be *very* well.'

240

'I still don't altogether see what he can contribute. The main hope seemed to lie in finding Agar. That looks as though it could prove impossible. Apart from which, the description of Agar I got from neighbours doesn't match at all well with the man Gwen saw. So where does that leave us? He's not going to get anything from my notes.'

He was conscious that he sounded graceless. He owed her something better than that. 'Sorry, you really think he'll pull something out, do you?'

'If anyone can help, Ludo will. He'd have been Director of the Bureau if there hadn't been all sorts of manoeuvring against him.'

'Wasn't he popular?'

'Not really. I'm afraid his nicknames weren't very affectionate. Sideways Ludo was one. But mostly it was the Black Pope.'

'I can imagine him in a cassock.'

'When we were in Rome last year, I knew that was where he really belonged.' She smiled.

'I thought the case you had together was in Canada?'

She was gazing into the night, her hair hanging loose and wanton against the cheekbone. He could understand Fender being tempted to touch it. 'That was earlier. He came back to the Bureau to do a special investigation which involved going to Rome. He had a bone to pick with the Pope.' She was still smiling. 'I'll tell you about it one day.'

The feeling that there had been something special between her and Fender amounted now to a conviction. It was faintly repellent. Had she a taste for fat elderly men? In that case, why didn't she simply up sticks from Little Venice and go and live with Fender in his gingerbread cottage?

'How does he spend his time now he's retired?'

'He's a great reader. He's also a butterfly buff. And I imagine he keeps the correspondence columns of *The Tablet* well supplied. What's wrong with the Catholic Church is probably his favourite subject.'

'He's against it . . .?'

'No, he just feels he ought to be running it.'

They had reached a point on the A21 where the lights of Tonbridge glimmered like a thousand orange stars over to their right. The road ahead was empty of traffic. He opened the throttle of the Mini. There was nothing to do except hope she was right about Fender. Beside him she was stubbing out the cigarette. 'Anyway, with Ludo in action, at least you won't be bored,' she said. It seemed he might have to be content with that.

21

He woke early from a dreamless sleep. Something awaited, he thought, something to be done. When memory came slouching back, he realized the opposite was true. His only lead to the person who might have planted the heroin had run into the sand, or very nearly. He could in theory make a round of every bookmaker within a ten-mile radius of where Agar had had his address to ask if they had news; he could tackle people in shops and the local post office; he could drink with all the barmaids in Shoreditch in the hope that one knew him. But it was difficult to believe that any of that would have a practical result – certainly not in the time scale he must reckon with: the breathing space before suspension was turned into dismissal could scarcely amount to longer than a week. And all the time the melancholy suspicion hardened, that Gwen had misread the registration number of the yellow car and the man pretending to be from the First Church of the Holy Crucifixion had not been Agar at all.

That left, as his remaining hope, the unknown quantity of Fender, who had been induced to take an interest solely on account of some unimaginable past relationship with Antonia. Whether Fender's help would amount to more than a spot of intellectual dowsing, in between feuding with the Catholic Church and poring over his butterfly collection, remained to be seen. Only the mention of Seagram, the old acquaintance at Scotland Yard, raised hope that something more than cerebration was contemplated.

He lay inert contemplating the cracks in the ceiling above his bed until the telephone bell roused him. It was a little after eight o'clock. He put on his dressing gown and went to the hall. Judging by past form he would now be greeted by the insistent tones of Rylance's voice, once more engaged in stirring into activity those appointed to do his bidding. There would be a grim satisfaction in telling him that he was off the case, off every case for that matter; if Rylance would like some different answer, he could speak to Antrim about it. But when he picked up the phone, it was a wrong number.

His thoughts turned to Gail. He had no news since dropping her at Paddington station early on Monday morning. He couldn't even be sure she'd arrived at the clinic. He had promised not to call her first; but that, he told himself, didn't exclude asking the clinic for news.

He dialled the number. Somebody said in moderately reassuring tones that she was perfectly all right, just a bit rough for the moment, but that was to be expected. No, she wouldn't feel like coming to the phone. He asked for her to be given his love and the voice said, yes of course, and would he remember for the future the morning wasn't a convenient time for calls.

He had done nothing else, had not even shaved when Clayton rang from the Yard. 'Your office said they didn't know when you were going to be back. I hope you're not sick?'

'Just a few days off,' he said.

'I asked for your home number since you said that enquiry was urgent.'

He managed to summon interest into his voice.

'There's nothing against Giordano, the FBI says he's

got a clean record. In fact he's just been nominated for a Presidential Commission on Relations between Organized Crime and the Film Industry which must mean he's rated *respectable*. Catini, as I told you, is a different story but West didn't have a lot to add to what I mentioned.'

'Did he know of any relationship between Catini and Giordano?'

'If he does, he's not saying. He was a bit evasive on Catini. I don't know why. Anyway the general picture's clear enough – Catini runs a sizeable piece of the drugs action round Marseilles and Nice, working in with one of the local gangs. It's unusual for a foreigner to get big in that scene because the Frog competition doesn't like it. But he pays top prices for the stuff and has export arrangements they can't match so he's become accepted.'

'The name of the leader of the local gang – have you got that?'

He heard paper being turned over. 'Yes. He's a guy called Baptiste, Raoul Baptiste.'

The old envelope on which he had scribbled his notes after his talk with Boyd in Epping was still in his pocket and he fished it out. But he didn't really need to check, the name had stayed in his mind: it was Baptiste's gang the man identified by Boyd had belonged to.

The link between what had happened in the apartment and Sam Giordano could hardly be doubted now. Even if he was to be denied the chance of pinning it on Giordano, somebody else, briefed with the knowledgde he now had, would be able to do that. Meanwhile the Rylances needed to be told the facts, though they might not be pleasant for Evelyn to face.

Her voice answered almost at once when he dialled the private number; she must have been sitting at her desk.

'Mrs Rylance,' he said. 'This is Mark Egerton.'

There ws a pause before she answered. 'Yes.'

'I would like to see you or Mr Rylance about Lauren's death. I have some information – '

She cut in. 'Mr Egerton, should I be talking to you?'

'What?'

'I have been told you're off work.'

'I'm not working in my department at present but – '

'Your Director told my husband that he'd had to suspend you from duty. It's not my business what you've done but I guess it's pretty serious. Since you're no longer working for us, why are you calling me?'

'You should be aware there's a connection between the thugs who killed your daughter and somebody well known to you. If I could call on you – '

'Who is this somebody?'

'Your former husband.'

'*Sam*!?'

'Yes. I'm sorry, but – '

He heard a noise that hovered uncertainly between astonishment and annoyance. 'Mr Egerton, he and I may have had our differences but if you think that means I can be sold any crappy story – '

'It's not a story. As I told the Secretary of State when I last saw him – '

'What you told my husband didn't sound as though it was going to add up to sense. But we agreed it ought to be followed up and that you could do that. Then we heard that you were suspended so we decided to employ a private investigator who operates in Nice. Presumably he'll tell us if there's anything in what this screwy author and you have been saying.'

He swallowed back anger. 'If you won't listen to me at least let me give your new investigator the facts I've got.'

He could tell that behind impatience she was forcing

herself to think about it. Eventually she said, 'All right, if he isn't satisfied from his own enquiries that it's all moonshine, he'll talk to you. That is, if your Director OKs it.'

'Wouldn't it be better if – '

'I've given you my answer, Mr Egerton. I haven't anything more to say except I don't expect you to ring this number again. Is that clear?'

He stood listening to the dialling tone for perhaps half a minute after she had disconnected, torn between frustration and fury. She didn't give a damn what had happened to Lauren and why. All she cared about was that a potential embarrassment on the way to becoming the hostess at No 10 no longer existed.

Somehow the day passed. His mood was slipping into the despondency against which Fender had uttered his unctuous warning. The next morning despondency was still there but beneath his sloth a vein of energy began unexpectedly to throb. Before it faded, he went out in search of paint to obliterate the primrose emulsion with which his predecessor had covered the bathroom walls. This time nobody bothered to pick up his trail, either on his way to the shops or coming back. He was definitely not of interest any more.

The sun was full on the lake as he turned into Prince of Wales Drive again. He crossed to the park. A flotilla of ducks sailed up and down as though offering a performance. Seated on a bench he reviewed the events of recent weeks, hoping that, like the splash and glitter as one of the ducks took wing, a clue to why he had been framed would surface in his mind. But nothing came.

He washed down the bathroom walls then made himself a mushroom omelette before going back to try out the paint. His spirits lifted a little. Only once, gazing at the cabinet where the heroin had been planted did the black dogs come racing back.

The bathroom was finished and he had started on the kitchen when news of a sort arrived via a call from Antonia.

'Ludo's in town. He'd like to see you at his club tomorrow afternoon. Two fifteen. Ask for him at the porter's desk.' She sounded rather tense.

'Will you be there as well?'

'No, I'll already have seen him – he's staying overnight at my flat. Incidentally he'll have read the file on Beynon, also your reports on the interviews you had when you were looking for Lauren and on what happened subsequently. I expect he'll have some questions to ask.'

'You're showing him the office files?'

'Yes.'

He didn't attempt to keep the surprise out of his voice. 'That's . . . all right, is it? I mean – '

She interrupted him. 'He asked for them and I decided that he was only going to be in a position to help you properly if he knew everything you'd been doing lately.'

He could understand why she sounded tense. Fender might have been an Assistant Director in the Bureau once but that didn't entitle him to see current files. She would surely be in trouble if it became known she had taken them out of the office for him to read.

'Has he come up with any ideas?'

'He's found out something that might prove useful – we can't be sure yet. I expect he'll tell you about it, if he's feeling communicative.'

'You think he might *not* be?'

She laughed shortly. 'You don't know him very well yet. Incidentally he asked if you could find out the name of the club in London which Catini is supposed to own.'

248

'I'll ring Clayton. Anything else?'

'I don't think so. What are you doing with yourself?'

When he told her about his internal decoration programme, she said, 'The trouble with painting is it leaves
the mind free to chew the cud. You sound rather mouldy
to me. After you've spoken to Clayton, take yourself out
for a change of scene. There must be a film somewhere
you'd like to see.' She was being firm in a friendly way.

Before she rang off, she said, 'Don't be late for Ludo,
he gets scratchy if people aren't on time.' An echo came
back: she had spoken almost those words about her lunch
date when they had been talking in the Bureau on the day
he had had his appointment with Rylance at the House of
Commons. So one mystery was solved. Fender had been
the notional uncle pacing the hall of his club, impatient
no doubt for a chance to touch her hair with his finger tips
and imagine more.

He picked up the phone again and rang Clayton at the
Yard. His sergeant said he was out and wouldn't be
returning before close of play. He promised to get him to
call back the next morning. Returning to the kitchen and
staring at the expanse of unwashed wall that awaited
attention, he decided that Antonia had been right, absolutely right. He showered and changed and took himself
to a cinema. Afterwards he went to a restaurant and ate
well, on the basis that if he was really going to be out of a
job and broke, it might be no bad thing to notch up a
meal worth remembering.

It was nine o'clock and the wind blowing off the Thames
was turning chilly when he got back to Prince of Wales
Drive. He had closed the entrance door to the flat and taken
off his coat when he registered that the table lamp in the
sitting room was alight. He went in. Seated in the armchairs, their gaze lifted towards him with expressions of

249

solemn but watchful politeness, were two men, dark and thickset. He judged them to be in their middle thirties. One held in front of him a cigarette which he had apparently been about to light. They might have been sitting in their favourite bar, observing the arrival of a stranger.

The man holding the cigarette said, 'Mr Egerton, I hope you will forgive us coming inside to wait for your return. The heater in our car has broken and we did not know when you would come back. I assure you nothing has been disturbed.'

His English was heavily accented and he spoke slowly. While he was saying his piece the other man had risen and moved behind Egerton to close the door into the hall. When he had done so, he stayed there.

'Do you always break in when you're visiting people?'

'We did not have to break in, Mr Egerton.' The man held up some keys.

He stared at them. But it wasn't hard to work out. 'I suppose those are duplicates you took when you mugged me.'

The man looked apologetic. 'I regret very much that occurred. I was not responsible. At the time some friends were anxious for the safety of another friend. The enquiries they had been told you were making appeared to them a threat which they needed to investigate. That was done rather clumsily. I hope you will accept our apologies.' His manner was one of grave courtesy overlaying a relentless determination to control all aspects of the situation. He placed the keys on the coffee table beside him. 'Let me now surrender these and assure you that you will not experience any further annoyance.'

Egerton looked behind him. The other man remained beside the door. To get past him and out of the room before the first could lend him assistance was clearly impossible. He thought of shouting. But Gwen was still away. Whether his voice would be heard in any of the other flats seemed doubtful.

The man with the cigarette said, 'Some colleagues of ours in France have been talking with a Mr Boyd who writes books and has an apartment in Nice. Mr Boyd suggested you might have some information of interest to us.'

He waited.

'You were in Nice recently?'

'Yes.'

'You told Mr Boyd you had been sent to find the American woman, Lauren Giordano?'

'Yes, her parents were worried about her.'

'You also had an interest in Señor Garcia Fernandes' brother, Luis?'

'Only as her companion. I thought I might trace her through him.'

'And that is the reason why you were asking about both Garcia and Luis in London?'

'Yes.'

The man with the cigarette spoke to the other in what Egerton assumed was Basque. He was explaining something – perhaps what Egerton had been saying. The other man's replies were monosyllabic and grudging. Eventually he spread out his hands as though in resigned deference.

The first man looked down at the cigarette still unlit between his fingers. He lifted it in Egerton's direction, seeking leave before he snapped open a lighter. 'That explains something that was puzzling to us, particularly when we learned which department you belonged to.' He blew smoke in front of him, slowly and evenly. 'Mr Boyd believes you know the identity of the Americans who

251

visited Señor Luis Fernandes two days before he was murdered.'

'I have no certain knowledge, only a suspicion about the identity of one of them. Why should that interest *you*?'

'Anyone who may have been concerned in Señor Fernandes' murder is of interest.'

'To you personally?'

'Not to me, no. But his brother is naturally very anxious to know who was responsible for his death.'

So this wasn't Garcia himself. Not unless some elaborate deception was being practised.

'Then your colleagues in Nice should be looking for the men who did the actual killing. Boyd believed he recognized one in the police photographs he was shown.'

'Unfortunately that man as well as his companion have disappeared from Nice.'

'Why not ask the leader of the gang they belonged to? His name is Raoul Baptiste.'

The man smiled sardonically. 'Monsieur Baptiste does not make himself very available.' He rose and fetched an ashtray from the other side of the room. Within the limits he had set for the meeting his manners were faultless. 'If you would now tell us who you believe the Americans *might* have been, we can leave you in peace, Mr Egerton.'

He could refuse. Presumably, although perhaps not certainly, they would become rough. What he had to decide was whether there was any point in refusing. The information was of no use to himself. Nor was there cause to hold it as an exclusive titbit for the Rylances' French investigator, assuming he ever made contact. And Luis Fernandes' brother had more right than most to know who could have been behind the killings.

The man smoked and waited patiently as though aware

there must be considerations demanding attention, if only to meet the requirements of face. Egerton said, 'All I can tell you is that Miss Giordano's father, a film producer, was in Nice at the time. He was staying with another American named Catini who has a Mafia background and is close to Raoul Baptiste.'

'Why should he have wished to harm either his daughter or Señor Fernandes?'

'I doubt if he intended them physical harm. My guess is that what happened was unexpected. The men were trying to recover something she had taken from her father. The killings occurred because they were interrupted. Although they were employed by him, he can't have intended *that*.'

The man was too polite to appear openly sceptical. He simply rounded his lips for a moment before drawing on the cigarette again. 'Can you tell me where the father is now?'

'When I last heard, he was staying at the Excelsior Hotel in Rome.'

The other looked down at the carpet. He was thinking it through, taking all the time in the world. Then he stood up. 'Thank you, you've been very helpful.' He moved towards the door. 'I hope you will once more accept our apologies for having disturbed you.'

'Before you go, I'd like you to answer one or two questions of mine.'

The man stopped and inclined his head. 'Of course. How can I help you?'

'You were having me followed shortly before I was mugged outside this block . . .'

'Yes.'

'Were you doing it again last week?'

The man raised his eyebrows. 'Why should we follow

253

you once we had established who you were and decided you were not a threat?'

'You swear to that?'

'If you wish, I will swear.'

'The second question is – did you plant anything in my apartment?'

He had to explain what he meant. The man looked baffled, then laughed. 'For what reason?'

'To harm me – by then telling my department.'

'Why should we wish to harm you? You are only a government official dealing with matters that are not our concern. We have no quarrel with you or the British government.'

He could have been lying. But his manner, slightly condescending, carried conviction. As he went through the door on the heels of the other man, he turned to give a formal nod of farewell.

From the window Egerton watched to see if they had parked their car outside. But they were too professional for that. He just caught their movement in the street lights as they walked briskly towards Prince Albert Bridge.

22

He found Fender's club in a corner of St James's Square. A haunt of old India hands, Antonia had told him; if he ever invites you for a meal, ask for the curry. Curry lunches and recumbent afternoons in the days of the Raj had perhaps been Fender's downfall, he reflected, the explanation for that monstrous girth.

A porter took him to a room overlooking the square. Beside flasks of coffee, a regiment of cups stood in close order. Beyond was the predictable panorama of armchairs and oil paintings: in the chairs men slept or offered slivers of conversation across their newspapers.

The porter pointed towards the fireplace. Gently heaving, like a great ship at anchor, Fender dozed in one of the larger chairs. Today he wore a crumpled grey flannel suit and a check shirt, its collar points curving limply outwards from a stringy tie. On his lap was a newspaper folded at the lead story. The heading read NEW BISHOP HAD YOUTHFUL CONVICTION FOR IMPORTUNING: NO 10 KNEW. A SPECIAL GLOBE REPORT.

He seemed oblivious to the world about him, yet he could not have been completely asleep. Opening his eyes in the exact moment Egerton bent forward to whisper, Fender said with elaborate warmth, 'Egerton! How *very* nice to see you!' He struggled to his feet with an appearance of urgency; but it was only for the purpose of making a theatrical gesture towards a chair he wished Egerton to draw up beside his own. 'A glass of port? Coffee? No?'

He sank back, shaking his head at a waiter who was discreetly hovering. 'And *how* are you?'

'Fine.'

'What have you been doing with yourself?'

'I'm in the middle of decorating my flat – following your advice not to get despondent.'

'Splendid.' Fender accepted from him the newspaper that had fallen to the carpet during his eruption from the chair. Tapping the lead story with a plump finger he said, 'Have you read this stuff?'

'No.'

'I trust you never sink to becoming an investigative reporter.'

'You don't like journalists . . .'

'Devourers of living flesh,' he said grimly. He threw the newspaper on the table beside him. There seemed a strong likelihood they were about to ride off in a totally irrelevant direction.

'Antonia said you'd discovered something.'

'We have some way to go of course. But I am a little encouraged.' Fender took from the side pocket of his jacket a notebook and began to turn the pages. They were covered in writing that was surprisingly neat for a man who could appear so clumsy.

'I enjoyed reading the reports of your efforts in the Beynon affair and also over the unfortunate Miss Giordano. There are one or two small things that are not yet entirely clear to me. Perhaps you'll be so good as to answer a few questions.'

The light in the square outside had begun to fade before he put his head back against the chair with an air of moderate satisfaction. They had covered, or so it seemed to Egerton, not only every smallest action he had taken over Beynon and Lauren, but also the suspicions, hopes

256

and misgivings that had accompanied each. Fender's approach appeared to be omnivorous. By the end, it was difficult to believe that his mind retained a capacity to distinguish between what might be relevant and what certainly wasn't.

He was gazing at the ceiling. 'I take it there have been no new developments?'

'Just a couple of callers last night I wouldn't care to have as enemies.' He described the visit by the two Basques.

'So you are now satisfied that those who were following you last week and who can be assumed to have obtained the photograph of you with – ' Fender paused for a moment, pursing his lips over a choice of words ' – your friend, the dealer in heroin, were quite separate from these Basques – nothing to do with them in fact?'

'Yes.'

'Excellent.' He offered no explanation why he found the answer satisfying. His manner of speaking even allowed for the possibility that he disagreed with the conclusion.

'Did you by any chance manage to acquire the information I asked Mrs Strachan to mention to you?'

'The name of the club is the Medmenham. It's aimed at the very big gamblers and occupies a house on Chichester Hill in Mayfair. On paper the club's owned and run by a man who used to be in the Life Guards. Catini is the real power behind the scenes. He operates, according to Clayton, through a Maltese who acts as manager.'

'Does he indeed?' Fender resumed his study of the cornice above him as though it had struck him as having an unusually pleasing character. A waiter appeared at his side to announce there was a telephone call for him. He glowered at the interruption. 'From whom?'

'A lady.'

'A *lady*?'

'Yes, sir.'

He stared at the waiter as if suspecting him of deliberate fabrication, then struggled reluctantly to his feet. 'I suppose it could be The Woman wanting to know when I'll be back and what she's to do about the milkman or something equally trivial.'

When he returned, his mood had mellowed again. 'Tea, I think,' he said and ordered it, demanding anchovy paste with four rounds of buttered toast and attributing the volume of the requirement to Egerton without even a glance in his direction. As the waiter moved off, he said, 'Did that distinguished, erstwhile captain of industry, our Secretary of State for Defence, give you tea when you called on him at the House of Commons?'

'No, it was rather late for that.'

'And how did you find him?'

'I'm sorry . . .?'

'How do you rate him?'

'Since he's the first Minister I've ever met, I have no basis for comparison. He seemed fairly formidable.'

'And Mrs Rylance . . .?'

He shrugged. 'Attractive, ambitious, tough.'

'According to the press she intends to be a Prime Minister's wife.'

'I can imagine it.'

'American wives of politicians,' Fender murmured. 'Always *especially* energetic in my experience. The challenge to liven the old world up . . .' They seemed to be drifting off down another byway that had taken his fancy but he collected himself. 'Where were we?'

'I'd just told you about the Medmenham Club.'

'Yes, indeed. As I'd rather hoped, that fitted intriguingly with something I learned yesterday.' He took out his notebook again. 'Since your pursuit of Agar had run into the ground, I thought we might look from another angle at the visitor who was observed by your neighbour. I asked Seagram, whom I think I mentioned the other night is an old acquaintance, if there was any trace in the Yard's *modus operandi* records of a housebreaker who, when challenged, claimed to be canvassing for the First Church of the Holy Crucifixion or something similar. This produced a direct hit in the shape of James "Holy" Coleman, occupation listed as "general trader" – always an interesting description I find. Coleman's physical appearance as quoted by Seagram was remarkably near to that provided by your neighbour.'

'Does he own a yellow car?'

'It's not known that he does. However, I think we should regard the car as unimportant. Coleman may well be prudent enough not to use his own when out on serious business.'

'Did Seagram have Coleman's current address?'

'No, nor do the police in Shoreditch where, like Agar, he seems normally to have his being. But Seagram arranged for an enquiry to be put out in an effort to trace him.'

Egerton cursed under his breath. 'If it doesn't produce the answer we're stuck again.'

'Not quite. Seagram was good enough to read to me from what is now called a print-out – ' Fender's lip curled in profound distaste ' – the paragraph in which associates of the subject are listed. These included, as somebody for whom Coleman is suspected of performing occasional commissions, the name of Anthony Boffa. Does that mean anything to you?'

'No.'

259

Fender raised his eyebrows, like a schoolmaster seeking acknowledgement of dereliction. 'I fear you failed to press Chief Superintendent Clayton for all the useful information he had about the Medmenham club. Anthony Boffa, who is Maltese, also happens to be the club's manager.' It was delivered as a reproof. All the same, it was the first good news of the day.

The waiter had arrived with tea. Egerton waited impatiently while Fender groped in his trouser pockets for coins. As the waiter moved away, he said, 'So, if, as seems certain, Coleman planted the heroin, we have a direct line back to Catini?'

'Yes.'

'Which can only mean that Giordano asked Catini's help in getting me run out of my job in the Bureau. But what would have caused him to do that? He didn't know I suspected him of having anything to do with Lauren's death. At the time I was being followed and photographed I'd told nobody apart from Antonia.'

'You did however mention to Rylance Boyd's story of the two Americans he heard with Lauren Giordano. It would have been odd if he had not told his wife.'

'You're suggesting she would have passed it on to Giordano . . .'

'Since he was the girl's father, wouldn't that have been natural – some news about mysterious visitors threatening her shortly before she was murdered?'

He nodded slowly. 'It *would* fit.'

Fender took his third piece of toast. 'As you say, it fits. However, there is rather more to it.'

'More?'

'Does nothing else occur to you?'

'Not at present.'

'Ah.' Fender was savouring both the toast and the

260

opportunity to be maddening in more or less equal measure. 'Well, I do have some advantage over you. Let me explain. When it still seemed possible that you had been followed by only one set of people both before and after your trip abroad, I asked Mrs Strachan to have a check made on the passenger manifests of the plane that took you to Palma – you'll remember telling me it was only partly full – and also the plane on which you flew back to this country from Nice. It seemed worth discovering if there was someone who had stayed on your tail throughout, in which case his or her name would have shown up on both manifests. Mrs Strachan telephoned me with the answer a few minutes ago.'

'And *was* there anybody?'

'No. It was of course a long shot. However, Mrs Strachan has the invaluable quality of knowing when to interpret instructions flexibly. She decided, in addition, to check the manifests for flights from Nice to this country on the evening of the killings and also the following day. These produced no name of anyone who had travelled with you to Palma. But they did yield a most interesting passenger.'

Fender wiped his fingers on a fairly grey handkerchief. He was facing the fact that he must finally make an end of his game. Lifting his gaze reluctantly to Egerton's face, he said, 'The person in question was Evelyn Rylance.'

About them the armchairs had emptied of all except a few ancient sleepers, dreaming of the road to Katmandu. Fender said, 'Let us construct a theory and see if it stands up. We begin with the premise that the Americans threatening Lauren Giordano in that apartment were her father and Mrs Rylance. It's true that in his account of what he overheard Boyd didn't suggest one of the Americans could have been a woman. But you mentioned in

261

your notes that Mrs Rylance had an unusually deep voice for a woman. Given the fact that Boyd found almost everything that was said inaudible, I fancy he could easily have made a false assumption about the sex of the person with Giordano. We believe they were there not out of anxiety for their daughter because she had run off with a Spaniard with terrorist connections but because she had in her possession something of vital concern to them both, possibly taken from Giordano's house in Beverly Hills when Lauren was staying with him during the summer.

'After the private detective fails to find her, Evelyn Rylance presses her husband to use the official machine. No doubt she suffers from the usual misapprehensions about police computers chattering omnisciently to each other all over Europe. Rylance of course faced the problem of justifying a request to use official resources in what was essentially a private matter. Fortunately he discovered something about Fernandes' background which persuaded him that the public interest was involved and that he could approach your Director with perfect propriety.'

Egerton shook his head. 'I'm absolutely sure he made up the story that he'd been told Luis Fernandes was a terrorist.'

'Quite possibly,' Fender said evenly. 'One must accept that to a politician with a wife on his back it would have appeared a moderately white lie. What mattered was that your Director, on hearing the story, at once offered his help. As I would expect of him.' He allowed himself a brief, ambiguous smile and began to fill a pipe with tobacco.

'At any rate, you undertook the search for Lauren and succeeded where the detective had failed. The outcome of your efforts was obviously a great relief to Evelyn

262

Rylance. We can assume that when the news reached her, she telephoned Giordano in Rome to meet her in Nice the following day. While there Giordano stays with the Mafia man, Catini. Perhaps Mrs Rylance does also – we don't know that. Next day they call on Lauren but fail to persuade her into giving up what they want. So they turn to Catini for the services of some local thugs who will extract it from her by force if necessary.'

The smell of latakia mixture entered Egerton's nostrils as Fender lit the pipe. 'But things start going wrong.'

'Badly wrong. Boyd's well-meaning intervention leads to the deaths of both Lauren and Fernandes. The thugs are sent off into hiding for a while. The risk remains that a thorough investigation will eventually establish the involvement of Giordano and Evelyn Rylance. But the police for whatever reason – perhaps Catini has influence in that quarter – come out with the statement that the killings were political. Boyd's belief that he has identified one of the killers as a local crook is quietly ignored. Paris is no doubt obliged to the police for providing further ammunition for the French Prime Minister to use when he goes to Madrid to protest about the Spaniards allowing their internal political problems to litter French soil with bodies. Catini and his gangleader friend, Baptiste, are no doubt equally obliged. And Giordano and Evelyn Rylance breathe freely again.'

Egerton closed his eyes. A vision had come into his head of a pistol butt smashing down on Lauren's head as she tried to reach Boyd and the open door of the apartment. 'And Rylance – how much of all this did *he* know?'

Fender lifted the massive shoulders and let them fall with a sigh. 'Perhaps everything, perhaps nothing. Evelyn may have kept it all from him, including the true reasons why she was so anxious to have Lauren traced.'

'I wonder what they were.'

'It's irrelevant for present purposes. But suppose Lauren had taken possession of evidence of a discreditable episode in the lives of Giordano and Evelyn Rylance when they were married – something that she had always kept from Rylance himself.'

'Do you suppose the thugs got it back for her when they searched the apartment?'

'If they didn't, it was a terrible exercise in futility.'

They sat in silence except for the steady snoring of the man seated on the other side of the fireplace. 'It's bizarre,' Egerton said.

'But wholly feasible. When Evelyn returns from making arrangements for Lauren's body to be transported, Rylance mentions that you are full of a curious story of two Americans who were threatening Lauren in her apartment before she was murdered. He says you already have some enquiries under way and hope to be given authority to make more. Clearly this constitutes a threat. The only way of nipping danger in the bud is to remove you from where you will otherwise continue to make mischief. I think it likely that she then telephones Giordano who decides they had better ask Catini's assistance once more. Catini says he has just the man in London to take care of things. Enter Anthony Boffa, the manager of the Medmenham club, who is told he must either find or manufacture some dirt about you as quickly as possible. He has you followed and his watchers come back with news of your visit to Miss Henderson in hospital where she is recovering from a heroin overdose and a photograph that turns out to be of you on very friendly terms with a heroin dealer. By itself the meeting in the photograph may be capable of being shown by you as having an innocent explanation. So a small packet of heroin is planted in your bathroom and the anonymous communication which your Director couldn't possibly ignore is delivered to him on the back of the photograph.'

Fender put down his pipe. 'Do you agree?'

It seemed convincing enough. 'I think so. But how do we set about proving it?'

'How indeed?' He looked more solemn. 'We badly need Seagram to come up with Coleman's whereabouts so that we can question him.'

'He'd just refuse to talk, surely? As would Anthony Boffa if we went to the Medmenham club and tackled him head on. Why should either of them incriminate themselves?'

Fender sighed. He knew it was the truth but was reluctant to acknowledge it. 'What one would dearly like of course would be the opportunity to look through Mrs Rylance's personal effects – her desk, handbag and so on. I can't believe there wouldn't be some small scrap to establish a connection with either Catini or Boffa.'

'How would we use it, if we had it?'

'I'm not sure. You would at least have a story with sufficient backing to make your Director pause over dismissing you.' He shook his head. 'We are drifting into the realms of fantasy. Even if you had Coleman's talents as a housebreaker, you would be hard put to get inside the Rylance house unobserved, given the existence of servants and no doubt a permanent police guard outside.'

Fender's expression was becoming morose. A terrible flatness consumed Egerton. 'I can think of nothing – ' he began, and stopped abruptly.

Fender looked up. 'What is it?'

'There *is* a way in which I might get in.'

'Do you mean you could break in?'

'No, with the help of someone living in the house.'

'Why should anyone want to do that for you?'

He shrugged. 'She wouldn't *want* to. But I'm in a position to, as it were, lean on her. At least I think I am.' He paused to collect his thoughts. 'When I first visited the Rylances' house in Chester Square, the police were due to call in connection with an investigation into leakages in the *Globe* about GOLIATH, the new weapons system. Perhaps you read about them . . .'

'I noticed there had been a row in the House of Commons on the subject.'

'The police had decided, after drawing a blank in Rylance's department and elsewhere, that since Rylance had once worked at home on papers from which the leakages could have come, they ought to look at the security arrangements there. Rylance's daughter by his first marriage, Camilla, met me when I arrived and assumed I was a police officer who'd come about this. She told me she'd seen a man with binoculars in the apartment block behind the house and asked if it would be technically possible for someone in the block to take photographs of papers on the desk in Rylance's study. She said she hadn't put the possibility to Rylance or her stepmother because of embarrassment arising from the fact that they failed to make any use of curtains which Rylance's security people had specified.

'I told the police without saying where I'd got the information. They decided that photography *would* have been technically possible. They also discovered there was a likely candidate in the block behind. As far as I know, they're still investigating this chap, trying to establish some link with the *Globe*.'

Fender's fingers were working impatiently on the leather arm of his chair. 'I don't see quite – '

'I didn't think much more about the business until last weekend when I read that a man named Simon Bowe had landed the job of running the gossip column on the *Globe*. It's one of the highest-paid columnist posts in Fleet Street and represented a pretty spectacular jump from his previous one. It so happened that I'd seen Camilla in Bowe's company on two occasions and it was obvious that they were very close.'

'You believe the girl took notes of material she saw in her father's study and gave them to this man . . .'

'I can't be *sure* of it. But I think that when she bumped into me at the house she was in a panic about the police's decision to explore the possibility that the leakages had been through someone there. She hit on the idea of diverting attention by telling a perfectly true story about the man with the binoculars in the block behind and the net curtains not being used properly.'

'Have the leakages continued?'

'Not as far as I know. I imagine she's too scared to provide Bowe with any more material. In which case the editor of the *Globe* is going to be disappointed. I imagine that in giving Bowe his columnist job he was not uninfluenced by his apparent ability to contribute stories out of the Ministry of Defence for the news pages.'

'Have you told the police what you now suspect to be the true story?'

'Not yet. I'd forgotten about it until a few moments ago.'

'I see,' Fender said. He was staring into space and beginning to look more cheerful. 'A very reasonable oversight in the circumstances. Also, one of which it would be remiss not to take advantage.'

'I can't be one hundred per cent sure my suspicions are right.'

'No doubt a few well-judged words with the girl will put the question beyond doubt.'

'I ought to stop the police wasting their time on a false trail.'

'Your hold on the girl may be the only way of establishing facts to show you have been the victim of a cruel conspiracy.'

When Egerton remained silent, Fender said briskly, 'Moral dilemmas are invariably tiresome to resolve. However, as your adviser and one familiar with all that is at stake, I shall take the matter out of your hands. You will not tell the police. You will instead seek to use this knowledge for the purpose of getting the girl to act in your interests. All we now have to decide is how *best* to use her.'

He waved a pudgy hand at a waiter to take away the tea tray and sat forward. Some trick of the light as he moved gave him the appearance of actually growing in size. 'I think we may at last be in business.'

Egerton was soaking paint brushes when Antonia rang. 'How did you get on?' she asked.

'Well, for better or for worse, we have a plan. I hesitate to tell you what it is. I'm not sure you'd want to hear anyway.'

'He rang me before taking his train back to Sussex. He didn't say much but sounded pleased with things. I promised to pass on a couple of questions he failed to ask you. Did you note the licence plate of the car that met Giordano at Nice airport?'

'It didn't even occur to me to *try* to see it. I had no reason to then.'

'He thought there was a chance – it's the sort of thing he would have done.'

'But we know Giordano stayed with Catini anyway.'

She adopted a soothing tone. 'You have to understand that Ludo likes to have twice as many links in a chain of evidence as anybody else.'

He grunted. 'What was the other question?'

'Who was David?'

'What David?'

'The person mentioned in the letter from Lauren which you saw and photographed at Jacqueline's house in Deyá.'

He failed to swallow back his irritation. 'How does he expect me to know that? There didn't seem to be any David hanging about there. Does he think he has to know everything about *everything*?'

'Keep your wig on,' she said. 'And the answer is usually "yes".' He heard her laugh. 'Remember what I told you.'

'I'm sorry I sounded rude. What was it you told me?'

'That with Ludo in play, at least you wouldn't be bored. You're not bored, are you?'

'No,' he said meekly. 'I'm not bored. Baffled, but not bored.'

23

A maid answered when he called the Rylance house. He asked for Camilla to be told there was a serious development in the matter she had reported to him a week or two back.

A satisfactory note of anxiety sounded in her voice when it came on the line. 'That story you gave me,' he said. 'We have some fresh information which makes it look pretty funny. Not to say misleading.'

She didn't speak.

'Did you really believe it would do more than buy time?'

She was still silent. He was sure now he had been right. 'You'd better come and talk it over. I'm preparing a report. What goes into it depends on how cooperative you are over something I want. Are you going to be cooperative or do I have to make all this official?'

'Do you mean only you know so far?'

'So far.'

He let her mull over the implications of that before he went on. 'In the circumstances I'm prepared to talk about this with you away from the office. You can come to my flat if you like.'

He could tell she was trying to guess what was going to be the price – money or sex or a combination of both. 'You won't get another chance.'

'Where do you live?' she asked. He gave directions and then told her if she spoke to anyone else beforehand, he was going to know about it. She swore solemnly she wouldn't tell a soul.

She arrived inside thirty minutes, her eyes wide, the mouth ready to tremble. Although she must have moved fast she had taken trouble with her appearance before she left; under her velvet jacket a white silk blouse had its upper buttons invitingly out of action.

She started on her mitigation even before they were seated. 'I'm desperately sorry about the story I told you. It was terribly wrong of me I know. You see I was in a complete panic. I imagined everyone in the house was going to be asked questions and Slade the butler would remember seeing me come out of Pa's study one night when I was supposed to be changing in my room.'

'Did Bowe ask you to do it?'

'No.' She was twisting her hands in her lap. 'He was quite glad of course to have the stuff but it wasn't his idea in the first place. It began as a bit of a lark. And he was so keen to get taken on by a Fleet Street paper I thought it might give him the boost he needed.'

'You must have known you were committing a criminal offence.'

'It was only the one time.' She gazed at him pathetically. 'I never did it again, I swear.'

'The trouble is that you made it worse by trying to mislead us.'

She started to cry but not uncontrollably; she wasn't going to ruin her appearance in case the deal included him taking her to bed, and tears might put him off. He waited until she stopped. 'I'm prepared not to pass on this information to anyone else, in return for certain cooperation on your part. I can't guarantee somebody like Superintendent Clayton won't find out by other means in which

271

event what he does will be out of my hands. It's just that he won't hear of it from me. Is that clear?'

It was beginning to dawn on her that it wasn't going to be the sexual option after all. 'What do I have to do?'

After he had explained to her, at first it seemed he was not going to carry the day. She stared mutely, just shaking her head. She was hoping to convey it was all beyond her powers, bound to fail through some crass blunder on her part. When he refused to buy that, she fell back on the awfulness of engaging in such dishonesty. He smiled grimly. 'Copying your father's secret papers for your boyfriend to peddle to the press wasn't dishonest . . .?'

She looked sulky. 'That was different. I wasn't letting him do what he liked in the house.'

'I'm not interested in the house – just one room.'

When at last she accepted that he wasn't to be budged, she said, 'What will you be looking for?'

'Nothing that affects you or that you need to know about.'

'Is it something against my father?'

'No. At least not directly. I'm only interested in your stepmother.'

She grimaced. 'All right.'

Before she left he made her repeat back to him his instructions. She did so impatiently, anxious to get away. As soon as she had gone, he was attacked by misgivings. For the moment she was plainly too frightened to double-cross him. But once she had had time to think over the deal, would she resile? She could decide that the best course was to own up to Rylance about everything. She might reason that Pa would find it politically inconvenient if she was prosecuted and that he would surely have the clout to ensure that any proceedings against her were killed. Therefore all she would really have to weather would be his annoyance. It might be considerable but it wouldn't last forever.

Fender pooh-poohed his anxieties when he reported them later in the day. 'The incentive to keep you on her side is very strong. And I don't imagine her stepmother evokes protective feeling in her. In any case the risk has to be accepted, we have no choice. Relax and be patient. If good music interests you, there is an Elgar concert on the radio tonight which I recommend as therapy.'

Egerton gritted his teeth. 'Meanwhile, what shall I do about the Bureau? It's nearly a week since Mansell had me in. He said that if I wanted to make a submission – '

'Send him a note straight away, saying that you have important enquiries in train that you are confident will prove that the heroin was planted. You expect to report the outcome in a few days. Don't go into more detail.'

It sounded sense. He typed a letter out and took it round to Somerset Square himself to be sure it got there. The receptionist gave him a puzzled look as he handed it in but he didn't give her time to ask questions.

A weekend crawled by with a single bright moment when Gail's voice came through from Devon as he was beginning to think he'd never last the evening without a drink. He could hear conversation in the background; presumably she was ringing from a common room or the hall of the clinic.

She began so softly he could hardly catch the words. 'They told me about your calls.'

'How do you feel?' he asked.

'*Marvellous* . . . well, not exactly. But it seems marvellous by comparison with the last few days. They say I'm over the withdrawal bit. Apparently I've been quicker than most.'

'What do you do all day?'

'I've only been out of bed since yesterday so I'm not into the routine yet. There seems to be some sort of therapy going on most of the time. I'm also allowed out for walks.' He heard a ghost of the old laugh. 'I went into a coffee bar today and felt tremendously daring. It's rather like being back at school.'

'So now you've changed your mind.'

'About what?'

'About not wanting me to come to see you.'

She paused before replying but he guessed it was only a gesture towards her earlier mood. 'You *could* come next weekend – if you really want to.'

'Why not before?'

'What about your work?' She sounded puzzled. He would have to tell her some time what had happened, but now wasn't the moment. 'I can fix things for more or less any day,' he said grandly. It wasn't quite true bearing in mind the call he was awaiting from Camilla; that was something else he could hardly explain now.

They agreed finally that she would telephone him again on the Tuesday. He asked about the others in the clinic and she talked in the old jokey way, her voice growing stronger. But suddenly she said, 'I hated you for a while yesterday.'

'Why?'

'I looked in the lining of my handbag.'

'I see.'

'It *was* you who took the smack, wasn't it?'

'Yes.'

'At first I thought it must have been the staff here. Then I remembered I'd vaguely looked for it on the train coming here and couldn't feel it.'

He wanted to ask her *why* she looked. Instead he said, 'I'm sorry I didn't tell you. But why had you kept it?'

274

'I had a plan. I was going to wait for the really bad moment, the just-one-more-time moment. Then, I told myself, I'd get the packet out and watch myself flush it down the loo.'

'Was that what you were doing when you looked for it yesterday?'

'No. I just happened to notice when I was trying to mend my zip.'

When he didn't say anything, she went on, 'You believe me, don't you?'

'I have to,' he said. It sounded bad. His voice lifted. 'Darling, what I mean is – I trust you. So I have to believe you.'

He thought for a few moments that he had spoiled everything. But when she came back she told him she loved him.

Monday brought bills, a delivery of the builder's weapons for tackling the damp rot and a message from Mansell's secretary. The message was tantalizingly uninformative: he was invited to call on Mansell at three o'clock. Her voice remained carefully neutral throughout the exchange. No doubt it was part of her special talent, concealing from those she summoned any hint of the climate that awaited them.

He applied polish to his shoes and chose a decent shirt to wear before he set out – not for Mansell's benefit but his own. If he was going to find himself walking the plank, it would not be looking like a slob.

Mansell's welcome was ominously genial. He guided Egerton to the sofa in front of the bookcase and sat beside him. He spoke of the weather, announced that his daughter was also moving to a flat in Prince of Wales Drive, enquired about the best route from Twickenham when he and his spouse wished to visit their offspring. In the middle of it all, the secretary appeared to place a tray of coffee and digestive biscuits in front of them.

So he was definitely out. These preliminaries were all part of pentothal time, the happy hour before the knife was produced. His temporizing note hadn't worked. As Mansell paused to stir his coffee, Egerton said, 'If you don't mind, perhaps we could get to my position.'

'Yes!' said Mansell. He made the word sound as though he wanted nothing more than to be obliging. 'I've talked to the Director about the report which was prepared for him. I've also shown him the intriguing note you sent me. He was of course very interested that you believe you will be able at some time to prove the heroin in your bathroom was planted by someone anxious to get you dismissed.'

'Not just "at some time" – very soon. I now know the identity of a person with a criminal record who was seen by my neighbour near the door of my flat the afternoon when I believe the heroin was planted.'

'Who is this person?'

'His name is Coleman. He's known to the police as a housebreaker.'

'Have you located him?'

'He's disappeared from his address.'

'So he can't be interviewed . . .'

'Not at present. But I'm hoping soon to have evidence linking him with another person who's behind all this.'

'And the name of that person is – ?'

'If I tell you now you'd refuse to accept it. I need a little more time to get the proof.'

Mansell said, 'I see,' as though he absolutely understood and felt immeasurably sympathetic. 'Naturally I shall be very interested to hear that information in due course. However, I have to tell you that a more general point has weighed very heavily with the Director.' He cleared his throat, 'I'm sure you recognize how essential it is for employees of this department to be free from associations that create suspicion.'

'I've explained why I went to see Buchanan. Apart from – '

'It's not only Buchanan I'm thinking of. You also have as a close friend, Miss Gail Henderson, whom you acknowledge to be a drug addict.'

'She's stopped. In fact she's under treatment in a clinic now.'

'And it is your intention to live with her afterwards?'

'Yes, I want to marry her.'

'I'm sure that's all admirable. I hope things will work out as you want. But you must admit you face us with an unfortunate picture. It would certainly be better if you had never involved yourself with drugs, or others who take them, in the first place.'

'I accept that. But I'm no longer involved with drug-taking myself and I've told you I never will be again. Is something that came to an end by my own act before I joined the Bureau to be held permanently against me?'

'Elsewhere I'm sure no problem need arise. But you must face the fact that the Bureau is a very sensitive department. We cannot afford to take risks, the public would not approve if we did. I'm bound to tell you that in your own interest I think the time has come when you should consider the advantages of a mutually agreed resignation. That way I can arrange for the terms of your departure to be generous. There would be a substantial gratuity and naturally I would do all I could to help you to find other work. Perhaps a return to merchant banking – '

'I want to stay in the Bureau.'

He was surprised to hear the vehemence in his own

voice. He had been vaguely conscious, as the Beynon case progressed, and more especially after that three-hour interview with Beynon when he had got the disclosures Antonia and everyone else had never believed he would, that something about the work had begun to grip him. Working with Antonia had turned out to be his happiest time since leaving Oxford. To give it up had become unthinkable in the moment Mansell had proposed it.

Mansell was saying, 'As far as your work is concerned you can expect an excellent reference. A fresh start –'

'I still want to stay. I'd like to make my case to the Director personally.'

'I don't see –'

'I need only a little more time in which to establish how and why I was set up with that packet of heroin. I believe when all the circumstances are known, it'll be seen that nothing justifies asking for my resignation.'

'Do I draw the inference that someone in the Bureau set you up?'

'No.'

'Then who?'

'You'd tell me I was mad if I gave you the name. I won't do that until I've got the evidence. But that could come any day.'

Mansell stood up. He didn't look particularly sceptical or even unsympathetic, just tired. He went back to his desk and let his eyes fall on a file. It was obvious he wasn't reading, he had just decided he would be happier like that.

'I believe the Director can't refuse to see me.'

Mansell sighed. 'If you insist, of course I'll try to arrange something. He's extremely busy this week. You may have to wait a few days.'

'I accept that.' He might have added, the longer the better.

'Your suspension will remain in force meanwhile and of course you'll continue to receive pay. Afterwards . . .' Mansell was making clear how he saw afterwards.

Antonia's door was open. She beckoned him in. 'How did you get on?'

'They want me to resign. The note I sent didn't work. if I go quietly there'll be what Mansell calls a substantial gratuity and help in finding a new job. If I don't accept – well, that wasn't spelled out but I can guess.'

'What did *you* say?'

'I asked for an interview with Antrim and for more time in which to make enquiries. I said I believed I knew who was behind the planting but he'd have to wait for the name until I had the proof.'

'Is he going to arrange the interview?'

'Yes.'

She pondered. 'If we don't get the evidence before that and Antrim refuses to wait longer you ought to have a case against him in law. He'd be denying you natural justice.'

'Is that really a starter?'

'Probably. You can argue almost anything about dismissal is a denial of natural justice. Anyway Kendick as Legal Adviser is bound to get the willies and tell Antrim he'd better think again.'

He guessed she was engaged in an effort to keep his spirits up. He tried and failed to look convinced. With a touch of impatience she said, 'Don't assume the worst until it happens. While you're waiting for Camilla Rylance to say the coast's clear for action, there's something else you can be doing.'

279

He raised his eyebrows.

'This morning I looked through your reports of interviews with people who had known Lauren. There's one person you never got to although Lauren was actually living with her when she went off with Fernandes. Lisa Husak – she was away in Singapore. With any luck she's now back. Let's assume the worst and you fail to get proof of a link between Evelyn Rylance and Catini. The single key to your achieving control over the present situation may lie *in discovering what Evelyn and Giordano went to get from Lauren*. They failed. How do we know the thugs they employed and who killed her didn't also fail? And isn't it at least possible that Lauren dropped some hint to the person who seems to have been her closest friend that would lead you to it?'

'And then?'

'Your next move would depend on what it turned out to be.'

There was something in the idea but he didn't care to let her know how little he thought it was. 'I could try ringing her sometime.'

She pointed to the phone. 'Try now.' She watched, unsmiling, until he picked it up.

There was no reply from Lisa Husak's home number. He got through to Victor Crispin, sounding as delighted as ever to be distracted from work: Lisa *was* back, he confirmed, but off somewhere else soon; he read out her office number from his diary.

He just caught her. A distracted voice announced that it was on its way to Edinburgh in ten minutes and wouldn't be back before the end of the week. When he said he wanted to tell her, as Lauren's closest friend, something important about her death, her tone changed. 'Can't you tell me now?'

'No, it's too delicate for the phone.'

Slightly to his surprise, she was hooked at once. For a moment he had the impression she was even thinking of postponing the Edinburgh trip. Finally they agreed he would call at her flat for a drink on Saturday evening when she was due back.

He replaced the receiver and told Antonia. She grimaced at the delay but then shook her head. 'Still . . . it's worth doing.'

He rose. 'I'd better get back in case Camilla Rylance calls.' As he went out, he was conscious he must have appeared dreary and undeserving. The fact was his hope had begun to leak away. He was quite sure Camilla wasn't going to call anyway.

He was wrong. She came through as he was trying to decide whether frying eggs would be less trouble than scrambling them. She declared in sullen tones that the coast at Chester Square was clear for action. Rylance was in Aldershot for the night attending an Army function. Evelyn had left for dinner with friends; afterwards she was going to a charity film première. Hope began to trickle back. 'What is she wearing?' he asked.

'Wearing . . .?'

'Yes, has she gone in a formal evening dress?'

'Yes.'

'So she's carrying only a purse – a small bag, anyway . . .?'

Puzzlement was struggling through the sullenness. 'I expect so, I didn't notice. Why – ?'

'Never mind. Are you now the only person in the house?'

'Slade, the butler and his wife are in the basement flat. They're off duty and won't come up again. There's no one else here.'

Conditions sounded as good as they were ever likely to be. 'I'll be round in fifteen minutes,' he said.

She hadn't bothered with dressing to please him this time. The jeans did nothing for the puppy fat and her hair needed washing. He told her to go and watch TV and he'd let her know when he was leaving.

Evelyn's study-cum-dressing-room-cum-health-laboratory had presumably been tidied by her maid after she had left for the evening. A chair was still positioned where she would have taken her evening boost of negative ions but no clothing lay scattered about and the papers beside the typewriter on the desk were neatly piled and clipped.

He went first to the handbag on the dressing table but it proved a disappointment. He had hoped he would find inside her diary with an entry pointing to contact with Catini or at least Boffa or at least containing the Medmenham Club's telephone number. There was no diary. Presumably it was small enough to fit easily into her evening purse and she was one of those women who couldn't bear to be without it.

He transferred his attention to the papers on the desk. They were all innocuous, mostly concerned with do-gooding events she had attended or was invited for in the future. One clip contained political briefing sheets, another the minutes of a society for the parents of handicapped children of which she seemed to be a patron. There was also a booklet on local traditions and country dialect in Rylance's constituency. Evelyn wasn't going to fall short as a politician's wife through want of hard graft at the coal face.

He abandoned the desk top with a sinking heart and went to work on the drawers. This time he struck lucky; it wasn't pure gold but something approaching it. Hiding beneath a desk diary and a vitamin company's catalogue

282

was a plain envelope, containing several photographs. The star in every one was the same. He saw himself walking, standing, talking, even calling a taxi. They had been taken, he deduced, in the days leading up to the weekend with Gail in Shropshire. He was alone in only one, taken as he summoned a cab after his visit to Gail in hospital. The others showed him with another person – with Foxall, of the Bureau's Finance Division, as they entered a pub for a lunchtime sandwich, with Celia French, encountered on a corner of George Street having been last seen in a Tokyo swimming pool nine years ago, even with the unknown Arab who had buttonholed him with a request for guidance on how to get to Soho.

Hand-written notes on the backs of the photographs gave identifying details of the people he had been with. Foxall was correctly described, Celia had presumably been followed home since they noted both her name and her address in Regents Park and said what her husband did for a living. Only the Arab had defeated the watchers who had worked alongside the photographer; perhaps their attention had wavered while he was weaving his way through the peep shows.

The last photograph of all had obviously been the prize. It was a duplicate of the one Mansell had produced on the morning he had been suspended. The inscription said, 'The person Egerton is in conversation with is a member of the club and known to me. He deals in heroin. Also known to the police.'

It would have been nice to have had a signature under the inscription, or even just the initials 'A.B.'. But that was being greedy.

He pocketed the photographs and checked the other drawers, including a locked one which he had to fiddle open with his penknife; but there was nothing else of

283

interest. Downstairs he found Camilla slumped in front of a TV panel game and drinking brandy.

'I'm leaving now.'

She gazed up at him bleakly and without a word walked across the hall towards the street door.

He had half-turned away to pick up his top coat from a chair, when he heard the door open. It was not until he looked towards Camilla again that he discovered she was still a few feet away from it and that it had been opened from the outside with a key. Advancing into the hall, elegant as ever in a three-quarter mink coat, a flame silk dress sweeping the marble beneath her feet, was Evelyn Rylance.

Her gaze was momentarily cast down while she returned the key to her purse: she hadn't yet seen him. Ashen-faced Camilla was watching her as she passed. 'I thought you were going – '

Evelyn said brusquely, 'I decided to cut the première. There's a bomb scare at the cinema, God knows when they'll open the doors. Anyway I'm out riding early tomorrow.'

Her gaze finally lifted and she saw Egerton. She frowned in disbelief. 'What the hell are you doing here?'

There was nothing for it but to bluff his way out. 'I called hoping you'd spare me a few minutes.'

'I thought I made it clear I had nothing to say to you.'

'I felt you didn't quite understand – '

She had already turned to open the street door. 'Get out. Or do I have to tell the policeman outside to remove you?'

He was happy to oblige. Passing Camilla he shot her a last glance. She was still white with shock and had begun to say something to Evelyn about not realizing she

284

wouldn't want . . . Evelyn's eyes remained fixed on him. He wished them both goodnight.

Outside the policeman was stamping his feet against the cold. As Egerton passed him, he said, 'Air's treacherous tonight, sir.' And it was.

24

When he rang Fender to report, the voice at the other end was blurred and indistinct. Either he had been asleep or the Chivas Regal was doing active service. He quickly sharpened however when Egerton described the photographs. He asked about the handwriting in the notes.

'Looks like a man's. Nothing unusual.'

'Boffa's, do you suppose?'

'The mention of the club certainly suggests that.'

Words of satisfaction were coming from Fender when Egerton heard a crash; apparently he had dropped the receiver in his enthusiasm. When at last he was back on the line, he spoke as though victory was in the bag.

Egerton said, 'I feel uneasy.'

'Why?'

'Evelyn must have found my explanation for being in the house pretty odd. I suppose Camilla will back it up to protect herself. But if Evelyn really grills her, she'll get to the truth.'

'Let her. *We* have the photographs – that's all that matters. We can now show that at the very least she's been privy to the surveillance on you. What we need next is a specimen of Boffa's handwriting to compare with the writing on the back of the photographs. Then the linkage will be complete.'

'How do you suggest we get that?'

'Didn't you tell me the Medmenham is a gaming club?'

'Yes.'

'Then I fancy I know someone who should be in a

position to help, bearing in mind that Boffa is the manager. Unfortunately, I'm off tomorrow to Bristol to spend the night with a fellow lepidopterist but I shall telephone this person from there in order not to lose any time.'

'So when should we meet?'

'I suggest I come to your flat at eleven o'clock on Wednesday morning. If I get an early train from Bristol that should give me the opportunity to call on my friend beforehand. We can then discuss how you present this fascinating evidence to your Director. He should find it a bracing challenge, deciding how to handle the story in Whitehall.' He gave a satisfied grunt. When he took down directions for getting to Egerton's flat, he said, 'Prince of Wales Drive! How interesting! Has that become a good address these days?' He enjoyed a sly gibe, when elated.

Egerton's morale rose steadily throughout Tuesday. He even found affection for Fender beginning to take root. Antonia had been right: he was a redoubtable ally. If he now came up with a sample of Boffa's handwriting to clinch the source of the photographs, it was inconceivable that Antrim wouldn't accept he was in the clear. He told himself that after all he might be sitting behind prosecuting counsel, as the Bureau's representative, when Beynon stood trial at the Old Bailey.

Nine o'clock came. Gail had still not telephoned as she had promised. He was sure she wouldn't have forgotten and wondered if this meant a setback. But it seemed unlikely. He made himself supper, trying to decide how much longer to wait before calling the clinic. He felt a surge of relief when the bell finally rang. But the voice at the other end was unfamiliar.

'Egerton?'

'Yes.'

'I've got somebody here you know.' It was a man; the

tone was casual, almost jokey. 'She's going to say a few words, aren't you darling?'

There were muffled, unrecognizable noises. Then Gail spoke. 'Mark, is that you?'

'Yes, what the hell's happening?'

'I don't know. I thought you did.'

He still half-believed it was some stupid joke, high jinks amongst the others at the clinic perhaps. 'Where are you?'

She began, 'They won't tell me. I think – ' Then her voice faded, as though the headset had been removed.

The man was back again. 'Egerton, listen carefully because I shan't say this more than once. Your girlfriend is a guest of ours. She'll be all right as long as you do exactly as you're told. Have you got that much?'

'*Who are you*?'

'All you need to know is that we collected her while she was taking a little walk this afternoon. The reason is that you've been naughty, Egerton. You've been taking other people's property. That's *very* bad.'

Light had begun to dawn. He felt too sick to speak. The man said, 'I'm giving you a chance to put things right. You're going to bring those photographs to me. If you do that, my friend here *may* be persuaded to keep his works in their little box.'

'What works?'

'He thinks your girl hasn't been having too much fun in that clinic. So he's arranging to put things right. One word from me and she'll be back on the stuff in a really big way. You'll like that, won't you darling?'

His voice receded for a moment then returned. 'She's not too sure she wants it, Egerton. But she'll soon get used to the old buzz again. My friend thinks about half a gram would be right tonight. He'll get her up to a gram a day, maybe two, pretty soon. She's going to have a really

288

good time. He says that by the time he's finished with her, she won't have to bother with any more clinics.'

The man paused. 'On the other hand, I might ask him to leave her alone. It all depends on you. I get the photos, you get the girl – as she is. Is it a deal? Or does he make with the needle?'

He closed his eyes to shut it all out. But there was no escape that way.

'I'm not waiting any more,' the man said.

'All right. Just don't touch her.'

The voice became lighter, even encouraging. 'That's a good boy. Listen. There's a gate leading into Regents Park from the Outer Circle opposite Ulster Terrace. Be there tomorrow morning at nine o'clock with the photographs. And alone. Somebody will contact you.'

'I'm not handing them over unless you let her go at the same time. And I want to speak to her again.'

When he heard Gail's voice, he said, 'I have some photographs these people want. But they're going to free you if I hand them over tomorrow morning. There's no need to worry. Just don't let them give you any shots.'

The man cut in before she could answer. 'She's got that, Egerton. One more thing – we'll be checking the neighbourhood. If you thought of having the law about the place, forget it.' The receiver went dead.

Somehow the night passed. He dreaded the telephone ringing again in case it turned out to be Fender or Antonia calling him. He rated it good fortune of a sort that he couldn't ring either of them: Antonia he knew was in Dublin on a case until the morning while Fender was off with his butterfly friend. If they made contact with *him*, he would have to be frank about what he'd agreed. But there were no more calls.

At twenty to nine, he drove the Mini up Park Square

West and left it on the Outer Circle, a dozen yards from the gate the man had specified. At this end the park was mostly open ground given over to hockey pitches. A few people were walking dogs. The occasional jogger panted by. In a children's playground an Indian child was trying to persuade its *ayah* to sit on a swing and be pushed. Under a sky of shifting grey masses he tried to compose himself for waiting.

Nine o'clock arrived, then nine fifteen. Nothing happened. He studied cars parked nearby but none were occupied. Those that passed him seemed bound for innocent business elsewhere. He wondered if this might all be a cruel charade.

From the direction of the Marylebone Road, a boy of eleven or twelve was approaching on a BMX bike. He seemed solely intent on demonstrating what the bike could do to anyone who cared to watch. But by Egerton he reared it to a halt and looked up impassively. 'Mr Egerton?'

'Yes.'

The boy held his hand out. There was a note in it. 'Walk north until you're stopped,' it said.

'Who gave you this?'

The boy swung the handlebars and bounced the bike round. 'A chap,' he said. He returned the way he had come, his attention once more devoted to the ways of avoiding a natural progression.

Egerton entered the park and walked past the playground, past the hockey pitches, the dog strollers, three men raking leaves into piles for collection by a cage truck that hovered in the distance. Nobody showed the smallest disposition to stop him until he reached the gate leading out to Chester Road. Suddenly a balding man in a camel coat and blue-lensed spectacles was beside him. Like the boy he also held a hand out but this one was empty. 'Let's have them,' he said.

Egerton shook his head. 'First I see her.'

The man nodded over his shoulder. On the curve of the road, towards Queen Mary's Gardens, two figures, a man and a girl, stood beside a blue Granada; the man was holding the girl by the shoulders in what could have been an affectionate embrace. They were just near enough for Egerton to make out Gail's features.

'Get on with it,' said the man. 'We're not hanging about.'

When Egerton produced the photographs, he checked them carefully then stepped back and lifted an arm towards the Granada. The engine must have been running because it began to swing away from the kerb before the man with Gail had released her in order to climb in. It paused to give the camel-coated one a more dignified entry. Then it was away again.

Gail seemed rooted to the spot where she had been made to stand. As Egerton reached her, she began to sway, shivering. He held her until he felt her body steady, then pulled his head back to study her. She looked drained but unharmed. 'The car's about ten minutes' walk away,' he said, 'Can you make it?'

She nodded silently.

Halfway back to the Mini, she stopped him. Reaching up, she kissed his mouth but still didn't speak. The men were loading leaves into the truck now; one winked at Egerton.

'Did they touch you?'

'No.'

'Or give you any idea who they were?'

'None.'

He persisted. 'Did you hear them use names to each other?'

She shook her head. 'Once when we were driving to London, after they'd picked me up, the man in the camel coat ordered the driver to stop at a telephone box because he wanted to tell – ' she made a slurred sound ' – they'd got me. But I couldn't catch the word.'

'Might it have been Tony? Or Boffa?'

'I just don't know.'

He gritted his teeth. 'What about the house? Could you find it again?'

'Not really. It was somewhere in central London, I suppose, because it didn't take more than twenty minutes this morning to bring me here. They made me lie on the floor of the car all the way – the same yesterday evening when we reached the Cromwell Road. It was a house with an inside garage. I never saw the street.' She looked up, sensing his frustration. 'Sorry.'

He shook his head. 'It was just a slim hope.'

They had arrived at the gate where he had waited earlier. As they crossed to the Mini, she said, 'Was what happened connected with your work?'

'In a way.'

'So they were blackmailing you into giving back some evidence you'd collected . . .'

He nodded.

'Couldn't you have told the police so that they'd be waiting?'

'There were complications. It wasn't official evidence. it all had to do with *me*. Somebody has been trying to get me sacked from the Bureau. The photographs would have been helpful towards proving that – proving I'd been framed.'

There was a little colour in her cheeks now. 'But who

292

would *want* to get you sacked?'

'If you're sitting comfortably,' he said, 'I'll tell you.'

As he parked in Prince of Wales Drive, he saw Fender's mountainous shape impatiently shifting from side to side in the entrance to the apartment block. He was dressed in a belted overcoat and woollen muffler. On his head was a battered Homburg, presumably a relic of Whitehall days, brought out for forays into the metropolis.

Egerton guided Gail towards him. 'I'm sorry to have kept you waiting. Could I introduce Gail Henderson?'

Fender raised the Homburg and gave a little bow. 'Ludovic Fender. How very nice to meet you, Miss Henderson.' If he felt surprise that he was being confronted with someone he had been told was in a Devon clinic, he gave no hint of it. He turned to Egerton. 'Is Miss Henderson familiar with the matter in hand?'

'I've been telling her.'

'Then I suggest we go and consider our next move. I've collected from a good friend who works with the Gaming Board a form which Anthony Boffa completed in his own handwriting as manager of the Medmenham Club. I fancy we shall now be able to make an encouraging comparison.'

He smiled avuncularly at Gail, inviting her to share in the idea of a pleasure in store.

Egerton took out his key. If Fender was going to blow his top, as well he might, it had better be indoors. 'I'm afraid I have some disappointing news.'

25

Fender lifted a hand and fluttered it; a gold signet ring winked at Egerton in the light from the gas fire. As a gesture of reassurance, nothing could have been less convincing.

'Please don't think I'm concerned to reproach you. Given your anxiety for Miss Henderson's well-being, I perfectly understand you felt bound to cooperate.'

But of course he *didn't* understand. Wedged in the larger of the two armchairs, his fingernails picking morosely at loose threads of fabric, he gazed into the fire and contrived to convey that he had been personally robbed.

His post-mortem on the surrender of the photographs had gone on relentlessly from the moment they entered the flat. He hadn't after all blown his top, instead had moved from scarcely contained incredulity into an icy interrogation that was only now petering out in general gloom. Gail, attacked by dizziness, had gone to lie on Egerton's bed. Her place had been taken in the last twenty minutes by Antonia, summoned from her office desk almost as soon as she got in from Dublin by a telephone call from Fender. Her questions had been few and she had avoided comment. Egerton guessed she had decided the best way of moving to a more constructive phase was to let Fender work his irritation out.

They sat in uneasy silence. Antonia eventually rose and crossed to the window to gaze across Battersea Park. 'It was appalling luck Evelyn Rylance came back when she did.'

Fender said shortly, 'I accept that.'

She gave Egerton a brief smile. 'What do you think happened after you left the house?'

He guessed she was trying to move the focus away from himself. 'She must have decided Camilla was looking shifty and got the truth out of her. Then she searched her desk to see if anything was missing.'

'. . . And phoned Boffa for help.'

'Yes. I wonder why he didn't simply send some heavies round to take the photographs by force.'

'Perhaps after what happened in Nice, Evelyn said it had to be a different approach.' She turned to Fender. 'Isn't it quite likely that the man in the camel coat *was* Boffa? If we could get a photograph and both Mark and Gail can confirm it was, we should be able – '

'It wasn't Boffa. I saw a photograph of him this morning in the Gaming Board's file for the Medmenham Club. He bears no resemblance to their description. I wouldn't in any case have expected Boffa to risk his own neck in such an operation.'

'Even without that, surely Antrim will see – '

'When it comes to the important questions, at whose request, and why, the heroin was planted in Egerton's flat, we lack a vital link in the evidence. Given the status of our adversary and Egerton's unfortunate past, we need considerably more than we now have before doing battle.' Even to Antonia, he wasn't bothering to wrap up his responses with the usual flummery.

'So what do we do?'

He began the maddening ritual of filling his pipe. 'I confess I see this as a serious reverse.'

295

'Perhaps Seagram will come up with Coleman's whereabouts.'

'Unfortunately, that's unlikely. He spoke to me on Monday. According to informants in Shoreditch, Coleman has gone abroad. I fear we have to assume that he's taking a winter holiday at Mrs Rylance's expense at whichever foreign playground the British criminal fraternity now favours after the Costa del Sol.' He was taking pleasure in being negative.

'What about Giordano?' Egerton asked. When Fender raised his eyebrows, he went on, 'If he were suddenly confronted with our knowledge, not only that he was in Nice at the time of the killings but was actually staying with a man linked to the gang the killers belonged to, we might bluff something out of him we could use as a lever in dealing with Evelyn.'

'You're suggesting a visit to Rome?'

It had already begun to seem absurd. He shrugged.

Astonishingly Fender was playing with the thought. 'I suppose there's a small chance. I wonder . . .'

Antonia's expression became flinty. She took a cigarette out of her handbag. 'Even you, Ludo, wouldn't trick Giordano into saying anything remotely incriminating. You know that.'

He looked at her mildly. 'You think so?' Seeing the cigarette in her hand, he rose with a surprisingly swift movement to strike one of his matches for her, then hovered attentively until satisfied further ministrations were unnecessary. As he slotted himself back into the armchair, he said, 'Well, perhaps not. We need to take a little time for reflection. If we're to regain our advantage, we may have to change direction and go back to the mysterious something that took them both to Nice.'

They were almost the words Antonia had used two days

before. She said, 'That's the reason Mark is going to talk to Lisa Husak on Saturday.'

Fender frowned. Egerton realized they had forgotten to tell him. After hearing the details he expressed grudging approval. It was clearly irritating him that he had not had the idea first. 'No doubt you'll let me know the outcome,' he said stiffly. 'When you have a moment.'

Struggling to his feet, he looked about him in a helpless way until his eye lit upon his overcoat and hat. 'If you'll forgive me, I shall go away and brood.'

Egerton helped him into the coat. 'There's nothing else you think we should be doing?'

'No, what the situation now calls for is properly directed thought.' He paused at the door of the flat. 'It would be prudent, I suggest, if you took rather special care during the next few days. We don't want you run down by a car or removed from circulation by other means before we have decided our next move. The opposition may conclude that, after all, it would be safer with you out of the way. Mrs Rylance is a bold risk taker and Boffa obviously well able to organize strong-arm operations. Also I recommend that Miss Henderson does not return to the clinic just yet. She shouldn't stay here either. I would be delighted to have her as a guest in my cottage but I fear that might not be very attractive to her.'

'I can take her down to Gloucestershire to stay with my sister.'

'Very well.' He was perhaps a little disappointed his half-offer had not been taken up. 'Make sure you're not followed.'

When he returned from finding a taxi for Fender, Antonia was emerging from the bedroom, having said goodbye to Gail. 'I noticed you looked disapproving when

I spoke about the possibility of confronting Giordano. I realize it was a pretty desperate idea.'

She shook her head. 'It's just that we don't want Ludo pushing off to Rome. He'd love the excuse. If I believed in reincarnation, I'd say one of his lives was spent in the Vatican, probably working for the Inquisition.' She stubbed out her cigarette. 'I imagine Giordano would have to be a rack and thumbscrew job.'

He went down into Prince of Wales Drive again and flagged a taxi for her. 'Is he really going to come up with an answer now, do you suppose? Time's getting short.'

'Ludo doesn't accept defeat. Ever.' She squeezed his arm briefly as she climbed into the cab. 'Anyway, how do you know you're not going to dig something out of Lisa Husak?' She was still working on his morale.

Lisa was rather as he had imagined her, dark and shapeless and restless-eyed. She wore ethnic jewellery that chattered when she gestured which was often. He put her at about thirty-five, a moderate spare-ribber.

'Lauren never mentioned you,' she said.

'I met her for the first time when I went to Nice.'

She sat opposite him, sipping a large whisky thoughtfully. 'How did that happen?'

'We were in the same restaurant. She borrowed my copy of *The Times*. Then she and Fernandes asked me to have dinner with them.'

'So this was just before they were killed?'

'Less than a week. Afterwards I talked to a writer who had the apartment next door to theirs. He told me things that made nonsense of the police version of events.'

He gave her Boyd's story just as he had got it from him, but added nothing about Giordano or the Rylances. She was visibly shaken.

'And you believe the Americans he heard had some part in it all, that they employed the thugs?'

'I'm sure of it.'

'So it was criminal, not political?'

'Yes.'

She shook her head. 'But she was the last person to get caught up with criminals. I really can't imagine anyone wanting to harm her. She was terribly nice, terribly idealistic – everything I imagine her mother isn't.'

'Do you know her mother?'

'No, but Lauren talked about her. Her mother's obviously dead in any moral sense. What Lauren cared about meant nothing to her. She just believes in manipulating people for her own ends.'

'Were you and Lauren very close?'

She looked away from him. 'I suppose so. We cared about the same things. Like the peace movement.'

Several centuries had gone by since he had sat, dripping rain on to a schoolroom desk, and heard that from the pure-hearted Flora. He said, 'A girl she used to know at the school where she worked in Chelsea told me Lauren felt that to achieve something really big for peace would be the most satisfying thing in the world.'

'She was one of those people who are prepared to go out on a limb for it.'

'Do you mean by taking personal risks?'

'In a way.'

Something in her tone made him pursue it. 'Was Lauren doing something *dangerous* – something that could explain her murder?'

She laughed. 'No, no, not dangerous. What she was involved in could have been *embarrassing* if it became known. But it wasn't dangerous.' She laughed again and thrust her hand through her hair. A dozen or more charms, trinkets and other gewgaws caught the light.

'It would have been embarrassing because of who her stepfather was, I suppose.'

Her expression remained watchful. 'She told you, did she?'

It would be a very small lie. 'Yes. She explained it made life quite difficult for her at times.'

She was studying him closely but he could tell she was impressed he had been on those terms. She went to get herself a refill of whisky. 'She was usually cagey about it with others. She couldn't afford the risk of it reaching the press. I knew of course. But none of the other people in ANWA knew.'

When he frowned she said, 'Don't tell me *you've* never heard of ANWA?'

'Should I have done?'

She shook her head in resignation. 'I suppose it's not surprising, the papers and television give all the publicity to CND as though we didn't exist. ANWA is the Anti-Nuclear Weapons Alliance. Cross-party – no publicity-hunting politicians, no pop stars, no priests prancing about in cassocks, just serious people who work in areas where they can exercise influence. Quite a few are government officials. We even have a soldier or two. We intend to change things from the inside.

'I introduced Lauren to ANWA. She became a very enthusiastic supporter. One day after we'd been to a meeting at which opposition to GOLIATH was being discussed and one of the scientist members had described the effect of a single missile on a large town, she suddenly said she believed she could do something really big for ANWA. She believed her stepfather could be argued out of ratifying the proposal to buy GOLIATH.'

He shook his head, smiling.

'Don't smile. *I* didn't believe her at first. She wouldn't explain either. A few weeks later when I realized she was deadly serious, I asked her to tell me how. She explained that the key lay with someone called David who shared our views. David was going to convince her stepfather that he'd got things wrong. That whatever the military might say, GOLIATH wasn't necessary to an effective defence strategy over the next ten years and could actually make our situation more dangerous. She never gave me a hint as to who this mysterious David was but I came to the conclusion it must be some influential scientist in the Ministry who feels the way we do about nuclear weapons but has to play his cards very carefully not to get thrown out.'

'One man couldn't be confident of swinging the issue on a thing like that.'

'I was just as sceptical. But then it was announced, out of the blue, that Rylance had set up a special committee to report on possible alternatives to GOLIATH. I began to think there was something in what Lauren had said. Of course I looked to see if there was a "David" on the committee. But there isn't.'

'It's still very difficult to believe.'

'Whoever he is, she had great confidence in him. Whenever we read the leakages in the *Globe* and about the arguments going on in the Ministry, she used to say, "Don't worry, it's all irrelevant. He'll kill it in the end, you'll see".'

Somehow the mystery of David had to tie in with Evelyn's anxiety to trace Lauren. 'Did Lauren tell you she was leaving England? And why? It seems to me that if we knew the reasons, we might be closer to discovering what led to her murder.'

Lisa lit a cigarette; she drew the smoke in as though it

had to reach every corner of her being if it was to do its stuff. 'She told me nothing. I was shattered when it happened. She left no address, just a note saying I was not to worry, there were reasons why she and Luis had to take off and she'd write. There was a postcard from Geneva later, saying they were moving to Spain in the autumn and she'd let me know where at the time. Incidentally she added a postscript to that card: "Promise about GOLIATH still stands!" I went off to Singapore on a job not knowing what to think. The next thing was reading about her death in a newspaper on the plane that brought me back here.' She took in another lethal dose from the cigarette. 'Until you told me about the Americans, I'd supposed it was because she'd got caught up through Luis in some Basque feud.'

He watched her move to the window. She was trying not to let him see that she was blinking as she spoke. 'About those Americans – do you think it possible they were connected with the company that manufactures GOLIATH? That somehow they'd picked up a hint she was saying that she *knew* the deal was going to be dropped and were trying to find out what was behind it? These big companies stop at nothing.'

He guessed she would be hot on conspiracy theories to explain what went on in the armaments business. She was silent for a while, then swung round.

'Do you know the awful thought I sometimes had? I liked Lauren enormously, she was one of the most sincere and *good* persons I've ever known. But she was very intense, obsessive at times. She could become almost irrational when she cared about things deeply. When she talked about David and what he was going to do, I wondered once or twice whether she was fantasizing the whole thing because she so desperately wanted to *achieve*

302

something for ANWA. Did she perhaps know that her stepfather was likely to cancel the bloody thing for quite different reasons, like cost?'

'You thought that David perhaps didn't exist . . .'

'I don't like to say it but – yes.'

He shook his head. 'There's definitely a "David". Her sister, Jacqueline, knows him. I've no idea who he is but he exists all right.'

He thought she might ask when he'd talked to Jacqueline but she didn't. He went on, 'Anyway, we'll know Rylance's decision quite soon. Yesterday's *Times* said he'd made his mind up and was going to put it to the Cabinet soon. They seem to think the deal will go through.'

She came to sit down again. 'I saw that. I hope to God they're wrong.' She looked into her whisky. 'Of course even if they *are* wrong and it's dropped, in a few months' time there'll be talk of something equally ghastly. The military people won't rest until they've got the same toys as the Big Boys have.'

He smiled. 'If you're such a pessimist, why bother to belong to ANWA?'

'Because if there's a chance that people will listen and be influenced, you have to take it. I sometimes think it's about as unlikely as my premium bonds winning me more than peanuts. But just as I keep looking in the papers for my bond number, I have to stay with the anti-nuclear campaign. You've got to keep hoping.' She grimaced, then laughed. He decided that when she wasn't shaking her beads about, he quite liked her.

Before he left she said, 'If it wasn't a political killing or skulduggery by the manufacturers of GOLIATH what else could explain what happened? As I told you, she'd never

303

have been mixed up in anything criminal. So what was the reason?'

'Fear,' he said. 'She'd got some people very frightened. Of that I'm sure. But about what, I don't yet know.'

He was halfway back to his flat when he decided to turn north again in the hope of finding Antonia home. She opened the door wearing a skirt and jeans and nothing on her feet. Her hair was caught back in the neck with a rubber band. She looked younger and more vulnerable than the person he knew in the Bureau. 'Come in,' she said, 'you don't know just how welcome you are.'

He followed her into the living room. The smell of beeswax rose to his nostrils: he had interrupted a house-cleaning session. She waved him to a chair and sank down opposite. 'I was afraid there was never going to be an excuse to stop.' She looked about her grimly. 'I hate housework. But I inherited a guilt complex from my mother. The marks of the prison house on my back, Ludo would no doubt say.'

He smiled. It seemed a very long time since they had listened to Fender pontificate about never escaping from the past. 'I thought you'd like to hear what I learned from Lisa Husak. It was quite interesting, although I'm not sure it gets us anywhere.'

She listened impassively to his account. At the end she said, 'It gets us *this* far – we need to find David. Either directly or through Evelyn he seems to have a hold over Rylance. If we knew what that hold was, we might be able to start calling the tune.'

'You don't buy the theory that he's a Ministry of Defence scientist?'

She shook her head. 'Far more likely he has nothing to do with Whitehall. He knows something very damaging about the Rylances and Giordano and for reasons of his own he was allowing Lauren to use that knowledge as blackmail to turn Rylance round on GOLIATH. The Committee was a stalling device while Rylance tried to get off the hook.'

She was silent for a moment, then jumped to her feet. 'We'd better put this to Ludo. Have you heard from him?'

'Not a word.'

She swore with unexpected pungency. 'What *is* he up to? I tried to raise him yesterday.'

'Perhaps he slipped away to Rome after all.'

She groaned, went to the phone behind his chair and dialled. Her expression became grim again as she waited then suddenly changed. She said sharply, 'Ludo, where have you *been*? I've been trying to contact you for ages. Mark has some information from Lisa Husak you ought to hear.'

She held the headset away from her ear so that Egerton could catch Fender's responses. He was asking what the information was.

'We think the key to the whole thing could be David, the person Lauren referred to in her letter to Jacqueline. David has, or had, an armlock on the Rylances and presumably Giordano as well.'

He couldn't hear Fender's reply. Antonia was frowning. 'Somehow we have to locate him,' she said.

'Fortunately that's not necessary.'

'What?'

'I said it's not necessary.'

'Why not?'

This time Fender's voice came to him clearly. The tone was triumphant. 'David happens to be here.'

26

Although the sun was back to encourage Sunday joy-riders, the morning traffic south from London had been light. They arrived at Fender's cottage ahead of the time he had suggested. When they rang the bell, there was no reply.

'Church,' Antonia said. She shook her head as Egerton glanced enquiringly up at the spire opposite where he had parked the Mini. 'The other team play there. Ludo answers for his sins further on.' She was pointing along the High Street.

Trying to imagine Fender at confession was an interesting challenge. Would he even squeeze into the box? In the list of the week's misdemeanours, want of frankness would rate fairly high. About the mysterious David, after announcing the previous evening that he was actually present in the house, he had declined to say a word more, pretending to fears that the conversation would be picked up. He had instead summoned them to his presence.

They looked about them, irresolute, considering whether to kill time with exploration of the lanes that ran between the houses. Gazing up at lattice windows and tile-hung façades, Egerton said, 'Isn't this rather quiet for him? He can't spend all his days looking for butterflies and writing letters to the *Tablet*. I don't see him as a golfer somehow. Wouldn't you suppose he'd get very bored?'

'Ludo's never bored. He adjusts to the environment in which he finds himself. He imposes his imagination on it.'

He thought of Lisa Husak's misgivings about Lauren. 'Another fantasist?' he said. He was hoping to provoke her.

If she guessed his purpose, she wasn't letting it show. 'No, it's just that the essence of things is never commonplace for him. His mind can always discover something fresh. That's what makes him a marvellous companion when he's on form.'

Once more, he found himself wondering if there had been, perhaps still was, a physical bond. The picture it produced in his mind's eye was grotesque. Yet nothing he could associate with *her* deserved that description.

'The really sad thing about Ludo,' she said, 'is that he's so alone. To be able to share what he feels and sees – he needs that more than most people.'

'When did his wife die?'

'Nearly thirty years ago. They were living in India. He lost her and the baby she was having on the same day. It devastated him, locked him up.'

'He could have remarried.'

'I suppose so. But for a long time he's been convinced his appearance makes him some sort of a monster. Apart from which, he's maddening, of course. Most women would feel that taking him on was likely to be hell.' She smiled. 'And they'd be right.'

She lifted an arm suddenly. In the distance, on the other side of the High Street, Fender had become visible. He walked with a curious sideways gait, the trunk turned slightly towards the shop fronts as he passed them. On his head, instead of the battered Homburg, was a handsome fur hat.

When he recognized them, he quickened his pace. He was breathing hard as he reached where they were standing.

307

'My profound apologies.'

'We were early,' Egerton said.

'Ah . . .' his eyes searched Antonia's face. 'Are you sure you're not chilled?'

She shook her head. 'I like your hat.'

He touched it so that the angle became more rakish. 'A Christmas present from my sister-in-law. She has an unnatural passion for my ears and worries that frostbite will carry them off.' He was trying to make her smile.

Leading them into the cottage, he made small talk about the village while he brewed coffee. In the sitting room they looked at him expectantly. 'So . . .?' Antonia said.

He smiled inscrutably. 'Yes?'

'David . . . you said he was here last night.'

'Yes.'

'But no longer apparently.'

'Wrong,' he said. Moving to a table on which stood a video player that had not been visible on their previous visit, he picked up a cassette.

'This is David.'

He watched smugly as they stared. 'A codename, you see, not a person. It was Lauren's private joke. A codename to smite a codename, one might say. She believed, not without reason, it was going to stop GOLIATH.'

He turned the cassette over in his hands, as though it were some curious, faintly amusing artefact, for which he had just been informed of a use. 'Actually I fancy the name *wasn't* a joke. Lauren was, after all, a rather serious girl. She preferred her friend, Lisa Husak, to believe there really was a person named David who was going to argue Rylance out of buying GOLIATH. That presented a more respectable version of what she was doing. The reality was rather shaming: pure blackmail, albeit on an elevated level. She was saying that unless a decision against GOLIATH *was* taken, the cassette would find its way to – ' Fender paused. 'Well, I'm not sure exactly what she would have threatened.'

'To a newspaper?'

'That seems the most likely recipient. One of the guardians of our liberty.' He smiled sardonically.

'So the cassette contains something very damaging to the Rylances?' Egerton said.

'Very.'

'But where did *you* get it?'

'From the sister, Jacqueline, of course.'

'You've been to Deya since we saw you?'

'Two days ago. A very charming place I thought.' He paused again, enjoying the expressions on their faces.

'Does that mean Jacqueline was also part of the campaign against GOLIATH?' Antonia asked.

'No, Jacqueline doesn't appear to me to hold any views on whether or not the British should protect themselves with nuclear weapons. She doesn't intend to come back here anyway. She does, however, dislike her mother and stepfather very much and was quite happy to be a part of anything to discomfort them. Lauren had become anxious for the safety of the cassette after the burglary Crispin told Egerton about. She suspected that the break-in was an attempt to recover it and I fancy she was right. One of the reasons she told none of her friends where she had gone with Fernandes was her fear there'd be another attempt before the decision about GOLIATH had been taken. According to Jacqueline she had evidence that Evelyn had employed a private investigator. This prompted her to make the trip to Deya and ask Jacqueline to look after the cassette.'

Antonia had lit a cigarette. Egerton could see that she was trying to control a growing impatience. 'Ludo, if we're to make sense of this, don't you think you should explain what persuaded you to visit Jacqueline in the first place? You didn't even raise it as a possibility when we last saw you.'

Fender seemed mildly chastened. 'It occurred to me only on the train coming back here that day. I was reading a newspaper article about GOLIATH – what good value for money it was as a deterrent, how accurate, and so on – obviously planted by supporters anxious at the possibility of it not being bought. I started reflecting on how unfortunate it was to have given it a codename like GOLIATH. Everybody knows, after all, that GOLIATH was brought down by David with no more than a sling and a few stones. That reminded me of the other David who cropped up in Egerton's enquiries. Suddenly that odd sentence in Lauren's letter to Jacqueline became significant in the context of her interest in the peace movement. Quite a lot would begin to make sense if "David" was a thing and not a person and being used to shoot GOLIATH down, so to speak. It explained what had happened in Nice – the threats to Lauren, the ransacking of the apartment after she'd been killed. It also fitted in with the way the decision over buying GOLIATH had been postponed.'

'So you went to Deya on no more than a theory?'

'I found it seductive. If I was right, it might be used to turn events in our favour. And there was in any case nothing else to pursue.'

She shook her head, marvelling. Fender held out a plate of digestive biscuits. 'When I met Jacqueline, I confess I felt misgiving. Acting as sleeping partner with her sister in a campaign to influence the United Kingdom's weapons policy seemed an unlikely role for her. However, since I'd gone that far, I clearly had to press on.'

'You asked her *outright*?'

'No, I engaged in a trifling deception. I told her I had become associated with Lauren in the anti-nuclear weapons campaign, in fact that I occupied a rather senior position in the STOP GOLIATH movement. I showed her the newspaper article in favour of GOLIATH and said there were ominous signs that Rylance was again being argued round into buying it. Lauren had told me about "David" and said that if anything happened to her, I might have to visit Jacqueline to get "David" and revive the threat to use him. I believed the moment for that had arrived.'

He was trying, unsuccessfully, not to look pleased with himself. 'Most of the conversation took place over a meal in a restaurant some way up the coast from where she lives. The taxi was inordinately expensive but she'd insisted there were no satisfactory places to eat in Deya.' He compressed his lips briefly. 'Striking woman though she is, she would not be my first choice as dinner companion. We arrived back at her cottage in Deya around one in the morning by which time she was fairly drunk. She'd made no direct response to my enquiry for David. On the other hand her manner had convinced me I was on the right track.'

Fender sighed. Egerton tried to picture the scene but the images refused to oblige. Presumably she had remembered to put on her pants this time. Had she invited him to bed? How had he responded?

'What happened next?'

'She insisted on our sharing another bottle of wine and talked endlessly about the unspeakable behaviour of everyone in Deya. I came to the conclusion I was not

311

going to get anything out of her, that night anyway. But then things improved.' He took a digestive biscuit and looked sideways at a shaft of sunlight. It was almost as though he was inviting them to press him. He nibbled the biscuit reflectively. 'In the end she simply went to a drawer and brought out the cassette. I had it firmly in my head that "David" must be a file of papers filched from Giordano's house and disclosing crooked deals in which he and Rylance had been involved when Rylance was still running his computer business. However, I accepted the cassette with, I hope, suitable aplomb. She said I could have it if I would give my solemn assurance it would only be used in the campaign to stop GOLIATH and would then be destroyed. Of course I agreed.'

Reluctant admiration succeeded distaste in Egerton's thoughts. He was, after all, in no position to criticize. *He* had photographed Jacqueline's correspondence while she slept, after lying about his reasons for being in Deya. In worming into her confidence and securing the cassette with a fraudulent promise, Fender had behaved no worse.

As though he had been reading his thoughts, Fender said, 'A regrettable deceit, I fear. But I think you'll agree I had very little choice if I was to gain her confidence.' He spread his hands wide.

Antonia had risen to pick up the cassette. She said briskly, 'Well, it's done. Now you've whetted our appetites, perhaps we can see the thing.'

Fender examined his finger nails. 'You may prefer not to. That is, while I need Egerton to view it in order to tell me if the assumptions I have made about people's identities are correct, you could really spare yourself the trouble. You once asked me to show you round the village. I should be delighted – '

'But I *want* to see it. Is there any reason why I shouldn't?'

Fender was looking acutely uncomfortable. 'It's rather – distasteful. I would prefer – '

She was staring at him in amused disbelief. 'Are you saying, after I've driven fifty miles to find out who "David" is, *that he's not fit for my eyes?*'

'I simply feel you will find it distasteful,' he repeated stiffly. He rose to his feet and made an elaborate business of collecting the coffee cups. 'However, if you insist . . .' He gestured towards the video player. 'I imagine Egerton knows how to work this thing. I had to hire it from a shop along the street when I returned from Majorca yesterday. Meanwhile I shall make more coffee.'

He skulked in the kitchen throughout the playing of the cassette. After such a build-up, Egerton had expected a diet strong enough to turn the stomach. But it was relatively mild: he had been at parties at Oxford where people would have begun to jeer. There was no violence, no perversion, only the most conventional sort of titillation. In the centre of an extravagantly furnished room, two women and two men performed a series of sexual acts on what looked like a suede-covered mattress. The camera seemed to have been located at ceiling level or just below. Now and then it shifted from the couplings to probe the audience for reactions worthy of note. There were perhaps thirty people in all, mostly in evening dress. Moving behind those who were seated, and occasionally bending to whisper in a host-like fashion, was Sam Giordano. His paunch was hardly noticeable and there was plenty of hair on his head: the event must have taken place a few years back. Evelyn Rylance was on a sofa beside a small, grey-faced man in gold-rimmed spectacles. The man's arm was stretched along the back of the sofa, so that the fingers rested at the point of her bare shoulder. His manner towards the spectacle at their feet was largely phlegmatic but once the camera caught him making an exhortation towards the performers. Throwing back her head, Evelyn squeezed his thigh and laughed.

Towards the end the camera reached a tall figure standing a little apart from most of the audience. He was observing conscientiously but without apparent animation. It was Rylance, being British.

The picture faded. At exactly that moment, a church bell began to toll along the street outside. The incongruity of the sounds in relation to what had gone before offered a sudden comic relief. Egerton had avoided glancing at Antonia while the cassette was playing. He turned, smiling.

At some point she had lit a cigarette. She was frowning as though puzzled. Catching his smile, she returned it, then glanced towards the window. 'Do you suppose Ludo's ringing that bell as a sort of exorcism?'

Before he could reply Fender reappeared, bearing the fresh coffee. Perhaps he had been listening at the door to discover when it would be safe to return. He put down the tray. 'So you see,' he said unnecessarily.

'We imagined it was you ringing the bell,' she said. 'To dispel impure thoughts.'

He grunted.

'I'm sorry you thought I ought not to see it. Parts were quite pretty.' She was provoking him.

He gazed at her sombrely. 'Do you not find that sort of thing uncivilized?'

When she simply smiled, he went on, 'Quite soon we shall have a world in which nothing is left except sensation. Feeling, sentiment, will have been eliminated. They are after all tiresome, making demands that can seriously

314

interfere with the pursuit of money and power. Pure sensation will be as far as people care to go. Sensation is safe. Like electricity it can be switched on and off at will.'

She was studying his face as he spoke, her eyebrows raised slightly. 'You're exaggerating, Ludo. As you well know.'

He looked mournful but resigned. At some point in their acquaintance, it seemed, she had acquired the licence to tease him.

He seated himself and began speaking again in a more matter-of-fact voice. 'I don't know whether you share my impression but I conclude that was filmed at some party in Beverly Hills while Giordano and Evelyn Rylance were still married.' He glanced in Egerton's direction. 'You noted in one of your reports you'd been told Rylance stayed with them occasionally before he became a Minister.'

'Yes.'

'I take it the man strutting about in the background is Giordano.'

'Yes, he carries more weight these days but I imagine he would have looked like that ten years ago.'

'Rylance of course could be seen towards the end. Did you recognize anyone else, apart from Evelyn?'

'One or two of the faces were familiar from films. Otherwise, no.'

Antonia leaned back in her chair and looked at the ceiling. 'So now tell us the rest of the story, Ludo.'

'How do you mean?'

'I mean that while I accept the cassette could be a source of embarrassment to the Rylances if it found its way to a newspaper, it wouldn't be an absolute disaster. After all, they're not performing *themselves*. The idea of that, by itself, constituting a credible basis for blackmail to get GOLIATH stopped, simply won't wash. As to Giordano, what possible harm could come to him from it? Beverly Hills isn't Budleigh Salterton. Is he going to care at all if some columnist could prove he'd had a sex show at one of his parties?'

'You'll remember that according to the information Clayton supplied, he has just been nominated for a Presidential Commission on the Film Industry.'

She scoffed. 'And *that* would have got him thrown off it!?'

Fender was watching her face as she spoke. When she lowered her gaze until it was level with his eyes, he smiled in a placatory way. Reaching inside his jacket, he said, 'I confess there *is* a little more.' He drew from an envelope a sheet of paper with a press cutting attached.

'When you established that Evelyn had also been in Nice at the critical time, I thought it would be sensible to carry out some research into her background. Reference books are unhelpful on the subject. *Who's Who* confines itself to mentioning her previous married name, nothing about her parents and so on. I therefore telephoned an old friend from the New York Police Department who now runs an enquiry agency. This letter giving the results of his research was waiting for me when I got back from Deya.'

He put on his reading glasses. 'Evelyn's family tree is of considerable interest. She was born Evelyn Grace Brodsky, the daughter of a delicatessen proprietor, Peter Brodsky and his wife, Anna. They lived in Los Angeles until Evelyn was four when her father died in an automobile accident. Anna was ill at the time and no doubt things would have been pretty bleak had she not come from the sort of family which rallies round in such circumstances. It was a family of Italian stock. The name was Catini.'

He paused to look at them both over his spectacles. Antonia had turned her head to gaze out of the window while she listened; presumably she was signalling to him that she didn't intend to respond any more until he'd come completely clean.

'Anna Brodsky,' he went on, 'had a brother named Frank Catini who was becoming an important figure in organized crime on the West Coast. Frank set Anna and Evelyn up in a decent house in San Francisco and paid for Evelyn's schooling. She was his favourite niece and at one time she was going to marry the *capo* in his Mafia family but the man concerned got himself shot. After that she went off to be an air hostess and eventually married Giordano.'

Fender detached the press cutting from the letter. 'That's all my friend's report tells us. It doesn't say whether Evelyn and Frank Catini stayed in touch. But of course we know they did.'

He handed to Egerton the press cutting. It was an item about a political fund-raising dinner. A photograph at the head of the story showed a congressman giving a handsome smile to the camera. Next to him, modestly leaning back to leave the glory to the politician was a small bespectacled man. The caption said that Mr Frank Catini, President of Catini Enterprises, had acted as host at the dinner for Congressman Monciano. 'Do you recognize him?' Fender asked.

It was the grey-faced man who had been seated next to Evelyn on the video.

Antonia had turned to look over Egerton's shoulder. 'So *that's* what really mattered about the cassette – not the entertainment but the company.'

'Yes. If the press were put in a position to make that connection, Rylance's political career would of course be

317

finished. Even in today's climate a Cabinet Minister with a wife whose uncle is in the Mafia would not have total appeal.'

'And Giordano?'

'Suppose he was once involved in helping Catini to launder Mafia money through the medium of his film production companies, I could imagine that exposure of the relationship just when the Presidential Commission is about to sit would be very unwelcome.'

Egerton said, 'This explains a remark Clayton made which I didn't note down at the time. He commented that his FBI contact had seemed evasive when talking about Catini. That could have been because he knew of the family relationship with Evelyn.'

Fender shrugged. 'No doubt people in Washington sucked their teeth and then decided that United States' interests were best served by not mentioning the fact. After all the day might dawn when Washington would wish to apply a little moral pressure of its own on Rylance.'

A noise came from the window overlooking the garden. The cat Fender had introduced on the first occasion they had visited the cottage was standing erect on its hindlegs demanding admission. Its expression as it looked from Antonia to Egerton was one of astonished outrage at this evidence of intrusion.

'Rylance,' Fender said, rising to admit the cat, 'remains the one major enigma in all this. Did he *know* what was going on? It's tempting to assume he knew everything. But there's no evidence establishing it. That he was responding to pressure by hesitating over GOLIATH doesn't necessarily mean Lauren was threatening him with the cassette.'

When Egerton frowned he went on, 'Lauren may have

dealt throughout with her mother – made her threat solely to her. She knew her mother was capable of influencing Rylance if she needed to. The political writers frequently tell us he makes no major decision without consulting her first. While that may be exaggerated, I have no doubt there's a kernel of truth there.'

'Are you suggesting that Rylance doesn't even know about Catini and his relationship to Evelyn?'

'It's possible. One can't assume he did from the evidence of the cassette – the man on the sofa may never have been introduced to him. And when Evelyn married him she could well have decided it would benefit no one, least of all herself, to reveal she had an uncle who was an important Mafioso. Then out of the blue, years later, disaster threatens. Lauren tells her she's brought the video back from her trip to Sam Giordano's home in Beverly Hills and intends to let the press have it unless Evelyn persuades him to abandon the idea of GOLIATH. Evelyn has no choice but to go to work on Rylance, aiming to get him to prepare for a dignified U-turn by appointing a committee from which he can be sure of getting the sort of answer he wants. She also sets about enlisting help through Catini to have Lauren separated from the video as quickly as possible.

'The burglary of Lisa Husak's flat was an attempt that failed. Then Lauren, guessing what mother is up to, disappears with Fernandes. Evelyn becomes very worried indeed. She persuades Rylance to employ the private investigator, Ingalls, to find her and, when he doesn't succeed, to make use of the official machine. Things look up after *you* find Lauren but only for a while. The bungled operation by the thugs in Nice not only fails to recover the cassette but results in the deaths of Lauren and Fernandes with all the consequent risks of what a police investigation may uncover. In fact the local police, with or without some backstairs encouragement from Catini or his friend Baptiste, give no trouble. But *you* do: the hired hand starts asking awkward questions. From then on, Evelyn is engaged in damage limitation, trying to stop you getting to the bottom of it all.'

'For the theory to hold water that Rylance was ignorant of what Evelyn and Giordano were doing you have to assume he knew nothing of her trip to Nice.'

'But that *is* possible. If you remember, Rylance was on an official visit to Washington when she went. He told you that she'd been staying with friends in Ireland during his absence. He may not have learned the truth.'

Antonia said, 'It's an interesting theory, Ludo. But do we need to go into that ourselves? Our objective is to get Mark cleared and reinstated in his job.'

'I'm absolutely with you.' The tone was one of over-elaborate warmth: he was preparing for a sideways shift. 'I was simply facing the fact that how the evidence is handled is also important in a wider sense. If we hand over the cassette and other information to Antrim now, there is virtual certainty that we shall have condemned to obloquy or worse, a man who *may* be guilty of no more than paying undue attention to his wife's views on defence matters.'

'Good enough reasons for you, surely,' she said.

He shook his head. 'I do feel a moral obligation to discover the truth about Rylance's complicity or lack of it before Egerton reports these facts.'

She gazed grimly into the fireplace as though they had reached a situation all too familiar to her. 'What you're trying to say is that you're determined to confront Rylance first.'

He adopted a studiously bland expression. 'I think I must.'

'When?'

Fender glanced at his watch. 'In just over three and a half hours, I hope. That is, if you and Egerton will be so kind as to give me a lift to London.' He fingered the side of his chair. He was not oblivious to the frostiness of her expression. 'Last night I established that the Rylances were spending the weekend in their Chester Square house. After some difficulty I managed to get through on the telephone directly to Rylance. I explained that although my name would not be known to him, his stepdaughter, Lauren, had taken certain steps before her death which had resulted in my having been entrusted with a sealed video cassette. I had been given to understand that it was of great importance to him personally. I would like to see him and would of course bring the cassette along. Rylance expressed himself mystified. He said his wife was far more likely to know about the matter than he was. He asked me to hold on while he spoke to her.

'After a fairly long pause he came on the phone again. He said his wife knew all about the video, it was of great sentimental value.' Fender allowed himself a crooked smile. 'He asked when they could get it from me. I explained that I would be in London today and it would be convenient for me to meet him at the Connaught Hotel at four o'clock. He was rather put out that I insisted on seeing him personally and wouldn't leave the cassette at Chester Square. Eventually he agreed to come to the Connaught.'

'You don't surely envisage letting him have the cassette?'

He laughed, at ease now that he had shown his hand at

last. 'Certainly not. I shall use the occasion to get at the truth about his own involvement. If I conclude that Rylance was a party to all that went on, I shall tell him that he has no alternative but to telephone the PM in my hearing and announce his decision to resign from office. If I believe he wasn't, I shall say his only chance of avoiding public scandal is to make an immediate break with his unspeakably odious wife. At the same time he must inform Antrim of her responsibility for the wicked attempt to destroy Egerton's career and reputation.'

He sat back clasping his hands over his paunch. 'I now intend to take you both to lunch. Forgive me while I telephone for a table.'

When he had lumbered out into the hall, Egerton raised his eyebrows at Antonia. She had lost some of the sparkiness she had shown earlier. 'Is it really going to work?'

'Time for prayer,' she said.

27

Parked on the other side of Carlos Place from the Connaught, they watched uneasily as the light faded. On the way to London, Fender had yielded to their argument that while the confrontation with Rylance could hardly put him in danger inside the hotel, it would be sensible to have them at hand. Now nearly forty minutes had passed since they had dropped him and there was still no sign of Rylance arriving.

From the direction of Grosvenor Square came a small band of demonstrators, abandoning a vigil outside the United States Embassy. Their banners, still held aloft, denounced the evil of American weaponry on British soil. The largest read BRITAIN SAYS NO TO GOLIATH.

The demonstrators were weary yet still dogged in their determination to press the case on any natives they passed. A chauffeur, stretching his legs beside a Granada parked at the hotel's entrance, had a leaflet thrust into his hand. He glanced impassively at the text then balled it up and tossed it into the ragged column.

Antonia lit a cigarette. 'I meant to ask what news you had of Gail.'

'I phoned her last night. She sounded fine.'

'Is she staying on with your sister?'

'She may do. Joanna thinks it would be better than the clinic now. Joanna's very down to earth. She could be right.'

'Isn't it a risk?'

He shrugged. 'It so happens Joanna's GP has experience in drugs cases. And Gail's happy with her.'

'How do you feel about it yourself?'

'I think,' he said and paused. He hadn't wanted to face that. But suddenly he knew he felt differently now; his fingers weren't crossed any more. 'I think she's going to be all right.'

The chauffeur had begun polishing the Granada's paint-work. Beyond him, in the shop windows of Mount Street, perfections of ornament and furniture beckoned. Antonia said, 'Ludo will be fuming.'

Egerton glanced at his watch. 'Do you suppose Rylance decided it was a trap?'

'It's possible.'

He was gritting his teeth. 'I don't want to sound ungrateful but don't you find it annoying that he'd made the arrangement before we'd even arrived – and then didn't tell us for over an hour?'

'I warned you that he was infuriating. He's used to having his own way. Being frank and straightforward is very difficult for him. When he's like that, you have to remember his other side.'

Presumably she was on about Fender's sensibility again. It was useless to reply that he'd seen nothing of it. Whatever she'd discovered behind that devious, faintly menacing manner had disarmed her. She had been recruited to his camp and nothing was going to change that.

'Here he comes,' she said suddenly. He followed her gaze. Fender was emerging from the hotel entrance, buttoning his overcoat. Crossing to the Mini with a surprising burst of speed, he lowered himself into the passenger seat beside Egerton.

'As you will have seen, Rylance didn't appear. I have this minute telephoned his house. The call was answered by a police officer who was very persistent in trying to

324

extract my identity and would answer none of my questions. Something has happened. We'd better drive to Chester Square.'

Egerton swung the Mini round to head for Park Lane. His headlights, crossing the front of the Granada, fell on the occupants. The chauffeur had abandoned his polishing and was back behind the wheel. Beside him sat a burly figure who looked familiar.

At the South Audley Street lights, where he had stood watching Sally Kirkwood strike out unsteadily for St John's Wood, he made the connection. The man had been Gail's minder at the meeting in Regents Park.

The west side of Chester Square had been sealed off completely. White tape stretched across all the access roads. Behind the tape, quantities of police stood to prevent cars and pedestrians from entering. He finally found kerb space in Elizabeth Street. Abandoning the car, they returned to the square on foot.

At first the crowd of watchers proved too dense for them to be able to see anything. Fender, thrusting forward as relentlessly as a tank finally managed to get a view point. When Egerton joined him, his gaze was fixed on a gap between the trees where the Rylance house stood. Along the frontage were several police cars, a fire engine and a mobile crane. He glanced at Fender's face. His expression conveyed a curious mixture of recognition and disbelief. 'What is it?' Egerton asked.

Fender seemed for a moment or two not to have heard the question, his lips moving soundlessly. Then he pointed. A spotlight was being trained from the fire engine on to the façade of the house next to Rylance's. Abruptly brought into sharp relief where it lay across the portico was the twisted shell of a white Jaguar car. Along its side panels a frieze of small Union Jacks could be seen.

Another police car had driven up behind them and was waiting for a way to be cleared so that it could enter the square. As the car moved on, Egerton saw Antonia straighten. She had been talking to one of the car's occupants.

When she rejoined them, she said, 'That was Dick Moseley, the head of the Anti Terrorist Squad. Before he was appointed this year, he was on fraud cases. I used to see him a good deal.'

'Did you get any news?'

'He had only the bare facts. He'd just been summoned from a police seminar at Bramshill. The car is Evelyn Rylance's. It blew up as she tried to drive it away about an hour and a half ago. Rylance seems to have been standing by the car, talking to her, when it happened. She was killed instantly, Rylance himself is in hospital in a critical condition. There are two other casualties who haven't been identified.'

'Presumably his people on the spot have more details.'

'Moseley agreed I could hear their story. I had to twist his arm so I don't think he'd be amused if we all went. Why don't you and Mark wait in the car? I'll be back as soon as I can.'

Fender was grimacing. As when Egerton had told him the fate of the photographs, he had the appearance of being personally affronted by events. But he couldn't justify arguing with her. He managed a nod of acknowledgement, raised the battered Homburg, which had been substituted for the fur hat before setting out for London, and grimly led the way back to the Mini.

While she was gone, he talked hardly at all, answering remarks from Egerton with monosyllables. Most of the time he spent in a dirge-like humming from which melancholy snatches of Elgar surfaced. It suggested a spasmodic, weaving process of thought. But he was keeping the results to himself.

He sat up briskly when Antonia reappeared. 'So what have you to tell us?'

Her expression held a hint of triumph. 'I was in time to hear the Rylances' maid give her story to Moseley. Apparently she saw most of what happened.' She was looking at some notes she had scribbled on an envelope. 'Perhaps the most interesting thing was her description of one of the two unidentified casualties in a car parked immediately behind the Jaguar. A man in a camel coat and blue-lensed spectacles.'

Fender folded his arms. 'We are all attention.'

It seemed that the two men had arrived at the Rylance house in the middle of the afternoon. While one remained in the car, camel coat had rung the bell. Since Slade the butler was off duty, the maid answered it. He had obviously been expected since before she could ask his name Evelyn appeared in the hall. She had taken him away to the drawing room where Rylance was.

After about three quarters of an hour, during which camel coat had made a call from the telephone lobby at the back of the hall, they had all emerged. Rylance and Evelyn in the maid's opinion were very tense. Evelyn called for her coat. When the maid brought it, Rylance was expressing doubts about a decision against his accompanying her. Evelyn made some remark to the effect that since they agreed the whole thing might be a trap, it was better for him not to be involved.

They had gone out of the house, still talking, and crossed to Evelyn's car. Camel coat had joined his companion in the car parked behind. Leaving the door ajar for Rylance, the maid had then walked across the hall to

327

the staircase. At that moment an explosion had occurred which had thrown her to the floor.

Antonia replaced the envelope in her bag. 'That was all the maid could say. It was a car bomb of course. It could have been attached to the Jaguar several days before because Evelyn hadn't used it for about a week.'

'Did no one else drive it? Not even Rylance himself?'

'No, it was strictly for Evelyn's personal use.'

'Is there any more news about Rylance?'

'Moseley had a message as I was leaving. He'd just died on the operating table. The other two are not so badly injured and are expected to survive. They're still finding pieces of Evelyn on the front of the house.'

Fender's lips moved in what looked like a silent oath. Antonia glanced at him coolly. 'Moseley thinks this could be the first shot in an IRA pre-Christmas campaign. They know an active service unit is in London with orders to mount some spectaculars.'

'*He believes this is an IRA operation*!?' His eyebrows had lifted extravagantly.

'Subject to no surprises coming out of the forensic evidence, yes.'

'I hope he displayed greater penetration when he was dealing with frauds.'

'Why do you say that?'

He made a noise through his nose, intended to convey contempt. 'Could anyone of intelligence really suppose the IRA would set out to murder the *American-born* wife of a politician here? They really must be given *some* credit for political wisdom! Rylance would have been a very reasonable target. But the bomb wasn't aimed at him. It was meant to kill her.' He glanced at Egerton. 'I don't think there can be any serious doubt who *was* responsible for this.'

'Luis Fernandes' brother?'

'I would say so – or friends of his. After they had got Giordano's name from you, they no doubt paid him a visit and established Evelyn Rylance's part in organizing the operation in Nice. She has just paid the price for that. A simple matter of retribution in Garcia's eyes no doubt.'

'But what about Giordano? If you are right, once they had extracted the facts they would have killed *him* as they've now killed her. There's been nothing pointing to it in the press although to have had time to set up tonight's operation, they must have talked to him several days ago. How do you explain that?'

'A good point,' Fender said kindly. He was recovering from his earlier disappointment. 'Of course we may yet hear he *has* come to an unhappy end. If we don't, it can only mean he succeeded in convincing Garcia or his friends that he was not a party to the plot which led to the death of Luis.'

'Are you saying it wasn't Giordano Boyd heard threatening Lauren?'

'No, that *was* Giordano. But it has always seemed odd that, as you learned from his assistant on the telephone, he left Nice to return to Rome *before* the killings took place.'

'So what do you now believe?'

'That when he and Evelyn failed to move Lauren with their threats, he left Evelyn to decide with Catini what was to be done next.'

'And she asked Catini to drum up the two thugs . . .'

'That is my conclusion. In additon, contrary to our previous assumptions, I do not now think the killings were unintended. I believe that even if the thugs had recovered the cassette from Lauren, they would still have murdered her and Fernandes, *because that was what*

329

Evelyn asked for. She realized any lesser course would be too dangerous. Lauren *might* have given no further trouble, although she had shown herself to be very determined in her camapaign to stop GOLIATH. But Luis was much too formidable to leave alive. Once force had been used to recover the cassette he could certainly be expected to retaliate robustly.'

An ambulance passed them from the direction of Chester Square. Presumably it was carrying what remained of Evelyn. 'And Rylance?' Antonia said. 'Did he know everything?'

'Whether he was in on the whole thing from the beginning, we shall never know now. I would guess Evelyn left him in the dark until quite late in the affair. But by this afternoon he was aware of what was at stake. Otherwise he wouldn't have been taking part in the conference with Boffa's lieutenant. After my call this morning there was obviously a discussion between Rylance and Evelyn about the possibility of a trap – the maid's evidence points to that. I might have discovered the significance of the cassette and be planning to use it for blackmail as Lauren did. So Boffa was contacted. He sent round camel coat to discuss what should be done if all didn't go well at the Connaught. I imagine the call the maid reported being made from the lobby in the hall was a message summoning the other two heavies you identified outside the Connaught to go there and wait. If Evelyn's persuasion and or bribery had not succeeded in separating me from the cassette by the time I left the hotel, I conclude I should then have received other attentions.'

Fender glanced at his watch and sighed. 'There is obviously no point in remaining here. Perhaps we might adjourn to more comfortable surroundings to consider your next move.'

Egerton switched on the ignition. 'We could have a drink at my flat, then go round the corner to a restaurant I know.'

'Splendid.' Fender began to look cheerful at the prospect of refuelling and even hummed a few bars of Mozart. On the way down Sloane Street, he said, 'You will have a powerful story to tell Antrim. I wish very much that I could be there.'

'Is that impossible?'

'Unfortunately, yes. It would be very counter-productive to your cause for him to learn I had been advising you and giving a small amount of assistance. It would also reveal that Mrs Strachan had introduced you to me.' He smiled briefly. 'That would never do.'

'But how shall I account for the help you've given?'

'I shall provide you with the cassette, also the press cutting that identifies Catini. You can say that you obtained both during your enquiries, together with details of Mrs Rylance's travel back from Nice at the critical time. I suggest you say that the relationships between Catini, Boffa and the man who planted the heroin, Coleman, can all be confirmed by reference to police records. He can hardly fail to be impressed by your efforts.'

'He *could* be impressed without necessarily wanting to keep me in the Bureau.'

'Reflecting on what you know, he will certainly not want you *outside* it. If it came to notice in certain quarters of Whitehall that he had not only accepted a private commission from Rylance to search for his stepdaughter but had continued using official resources after learning Rylance had lied when offering his reason for the request, the consequences would be disagreeable. Of course you mustn't interpret what I say as a personal criticism of your Director.' He smiled wolfishly. 'I am simply stating a fact.'

'But none of that would come out unless I disclosed it.'

They were halted by the traffic lights at the junction with Pimlico Road. In the window of a television shop beside them, perhaps thirty sets offered their silent images to the night.

'These things have a curious way of becoming known,' Fender said. He turned his face towards the shop window. To fathom what was in his mind, to make out the thought that lay behind the words and then the inner thoughts beyond, was like trying to assimilate at one and the same time what each of the images was saying.

Leading the way up the stairs to his flat, Egerton was conscious of a stirring in his spirits. It was not that Fender had convinced him that Antrim would actually want him back. He had been living a nightmare that had begun to fade.

The phone rang as he was pouring their whiskies. It was the first call for days he had answered without any sense of foreboding. A woman spoke. 'Mr Egerton?'

'Yes.'

'Please forgive me for troubling you. We haven't met.' The voice was very quiet. He detected a Scots accent.

'My name is Janet Buchanan. I believe you're a friend of my son.'

He searched his mind. 'I am?'

'Yes. Jamie Buchanan.'

Suddenly the wind was up again, the dogs whimpering, the bats everywhere in the rafters. 'I see. How – '

'Jamie gave me your number. He said if I could speak to you, you would explain some things.'

'Where is Jamie?'

'He was arrested this morning. Apparently he and a business associate were met by the police when they landed at an airfield in Buckinghamshire. It was a private plane owned by the other man. They had been on a business trip, Jamie told me, when I was allowed to see him for a few minutes this afternoon. I believe it had to do with drugs.'

'They were carrying drugs?'

'So I understand.' Her voice wavered for a few seconds. She sounded drained. 'I hope I'm not disturbing you at an inconvenient time.'

So Jamie's arrangement with whoever was supposed to forewarn him hadn't worked. People could let you down, however well you paid them.

'I'm very sorry,' he said.

'Jamie wanted me to know that whatever the police might say he'd never encouraged anyone to take drugs. He just supplied them to people who asked for them. He thought that if I understood the difference I wouldn't think so badly of him. Of course he doesn't realize my feelings are regardless – ' Her voice broke. 'He's really a very kind boy,' she said.

'I know.'

'He told me you knew him as well as anybody did. If he's prosecuted, as does seem probable, I wondered if you'd be willing to speak for him. It would perhaps make a difference to the way he's treated by the court.'

'Did he say he wanted me to do that?'

'No. He only said *I* might feel happier if I talked to you. He thought you would help me to understand.'

After a few seconds he realized she had begun to weep.

When he returned to the sitting room, he saw that some part of the conversation had registered with them. Their expressions were polite but enquiring. He sat down and glanced at Fender. 'I remember you once spoke of one's past being a prison house from which one couldn't escape. It sounded excessively gloomy to me at the time. But you had a point.'

'What has happened?'

He explained.

'I've promised to go and see her now. She's in his flat in Portland Place, sounding very alone and bewildered. Perhaps you'll forgive me not joining you for a meal.'

His cheek was twitching. He smiled apologetically. 'I think this kills the idea of trying to stay in the Bureau. I hope you won't think me ungrateful for the efforts you've made if I just resign.'

'Why should you do that?' Fender asked.

'Even I accept it's no joke for the Bureau if one of its staff testifies on behalf of a drugs dealer. My own history would have to come out.'

'There is no obligation on you to testify.'

'I feel there is. I have to speak up for him.'

'Then you must put the facts squarely to Antrim. You feel you have a moral obligation to testify. I hope he would recognize he has no less of an obligation to stand by you as one of his employees.'

'In his shoes, would you go on employing me?'

Fender gazed at the ceiling, assembling careful words. 'It is only human to hope that one's integrity will be taken for granted by the world and never put to the test. I should not welcome the challenge. In my darker moments I might hope that you would come to me and say that after all you wished passionately to join the Forestry Commission and needed only a testimony of your compe-

334

tence. I confess too that some of your views and attitudes are alien to me. But, yes, I *would* go on employing you. To have fought and overcome drug addiction is no small thing. Others have weakness no less inimical to character but cloak them successfully. I would not want a Bureau staffed only by reformed sinners of course. But even less would I want one that contained only plaster saints and timid virgins.'

He lowered his gaze and settled into his chair more comfortably. 'Moreover, there is a reason additional to those I have already given you why your Director will no doubt prefer to avoid the consequences of discharging you. I conclude from certain observations made to Mrs Strachan by Mansell that enquiries into your associations at university which might well have militated against your recruitment to the Bureau were omitted. This resulted from Antrim's decision that he wanted no delay in acquiring your services. Very understandable, I'm sure. But investigation of this whole business would no doubt highlight a decision which would be rather difficult to defend.'

Fender's expression invited seemly satisfaction at this thought. When Egerton did not respond, he adopted an air of impatience that was only partly calculated. 'What is wrong with your generation? Is a post in which you serve the public interest not worth fighting for? Once, when I was young, it would have seemed a great prize. Imagine being doomed to one of those innumerable occupations which are either parasitical or absurd or both.' He fluttered his fingers contemptuously. 'Speculators, Parliamentary lobbyists, Euro-MPs!' For some reason he had let investigative journalists off this time.

He was conscious of Antonia watching him closely. 'I *will* think it over carefully of course.'

'So I would hope,' she said.

'Perhaps I could drop you both off at the restaurant on my way to Mrs Buchanan.'

She drained her glass and stood up, still looking sombre. He knew that if he didn't make a fight to stay in the Bureau, she would have no more time for him. Neither would Fender. But that would be easier to bear.

When they arrived at the restaurant, she said, 'Speak to me before you go to Antrim.' He hesitated and she went on fiercely, '*Mark*!'

'I promise,' he said. Her determination irked. Yet at the same time, he was warmed. He looked at each of them in turn. 'I haven't said how grateful I am to you for believing in me. Whatever happens, I'll never forget that.'

As he watched them cross the pavement, he saw Fender reach out as though to guide Antonia through the restaurant door, then withdraw his hand suddenly. The audacity of the gesture had overwhelmed him. She must somehow have been aware of the movement. She glanced up at his face with an expression that was at once ironical and tender. Then she put her own hand on his forearm and kept it there.

He wondered if they would go back to her flat later. Sunday night trains to Fender's part of East Sussex were no doubt few and far between. She would perhaps invite him to stay. And then? He guessed they had a prison house of their own that neither, in the final analysis, would choose to be without. An alliance almost impossible to believe in, he thought, pulling into the traffic and heading for Portland Place. But, there it was. They were a match.